A
DIAMOND
DREAM

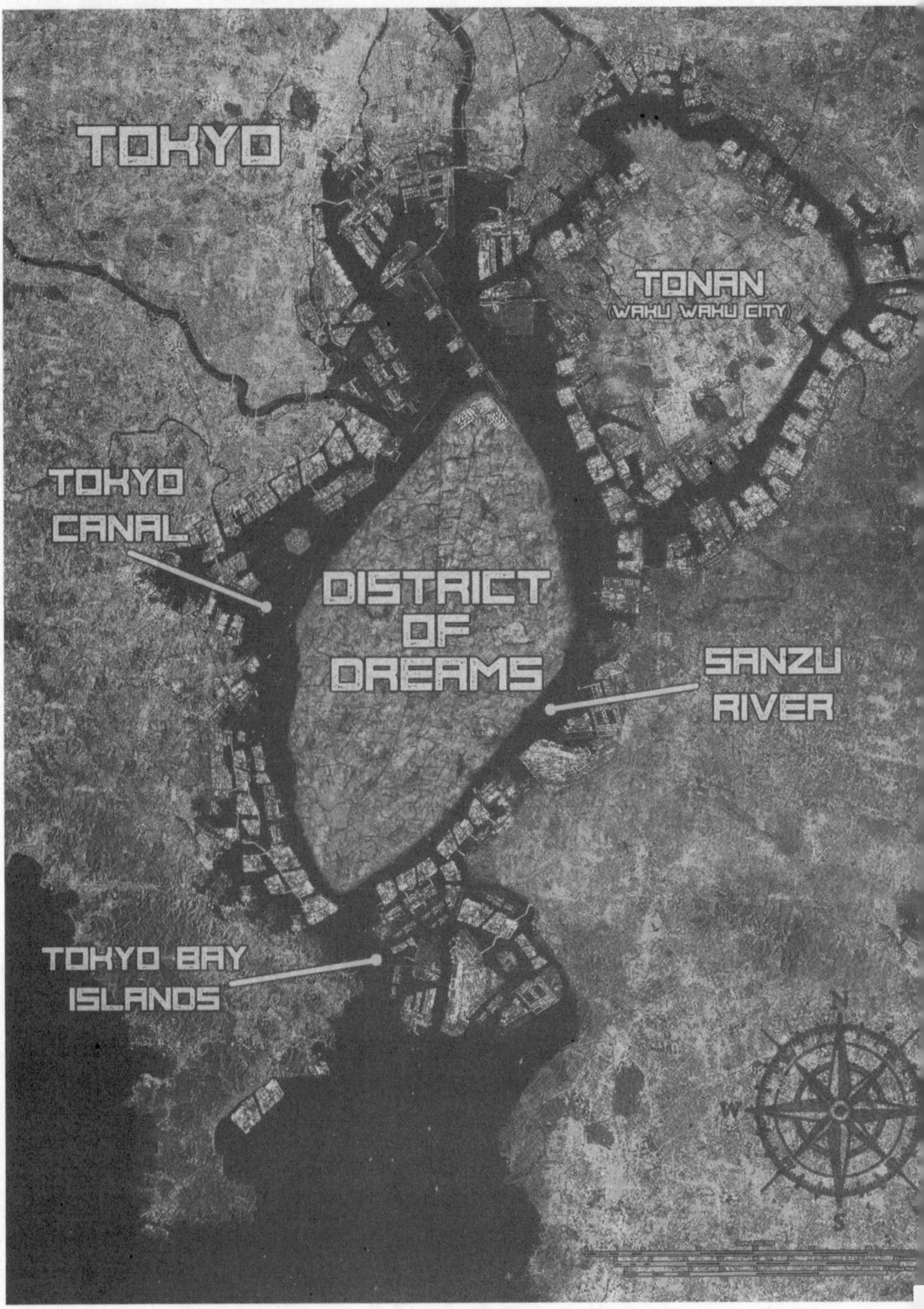
TOKYO
TONAN
(WAKU WAKU CITY)
TOKYO
CANAL
DISTRICT
OF
DREAMS
SANZU
RIVER
TOKYO BAY
ISLANDS
N
W
S

A DIAMOND DREAM

FINAL BOOK OF THE JUBILEE CYCLE

ELI K. P. WILLIAM

TALOS PRESS

Talos Press books may be purchased in bulk at special discounts for sales promotion, corporate gifts, fund-raising, or educational purposes. Special editions can also be created to specifications. For details, contact the Special Sales Department, Talos Press, 307 West 36th Street, 11th Floor, New York, NY 10018 or info@skyhorsepublishing.com.

Talos Press is an imprint of Skyhorse Publishing, Inc.®, a Delaware corporation.

Visit our website at www.talospress.com.

10 9 8 7 6 5 4 3 2 1

Library of Congress Cataloging-in-Publication Data is available on file.

Jacket design by Kai Texel
Front Jacket artwork by Alena Velichko

Print ISBN: 978-1-945863-58-5
Ebook ISBN: 978-1-945863-59-2

Printed in the United States of America

Into the sea, eventually.

—Jimi Hendrix, "Castles Made of Sand"

Beyond payment, retribution, redemption—beyond all the bargains and the balances.

—Ursula K. Le Guin, *Tehanu*

PART 7
JUBILEE

1
THE TOKYO CANAL

All was fire, a great conflagration roaring from the charcoal of a starless cosmos. Billowing and flaring, licking and swelling, the flames raged so fiercely they made the universe an oven for existence itself. The substance of galaxies crackled into nothingness, time melted into stasis, space reduced to the ashes of nowhere. Not even fire could escape this blaze, a fire to end all fires. Until the next cycle, at least . . .

Or is it fire? thought Amon. Then what had appeared to be an inferno of measureless intensity began to dwindle rapidly, settling into something much more mundane: squirming twinkles and shadow dapples that wavered and merged against a field of pale orange and red—his eyelids turned translucent by light filtering through them.

Amon could only suppose that he had just woken from sleep, though it felt like no awakening he had ever known. Lacking was the firmness of a futon, floor, or other surface at his side or back. Lacking was the touch of any covering fabric like clothes or blankets. Lacking also was any heat or cold, any taste or scent. The glow that defied his closed eyes told him there was something outside, and yet everything else seemed to suggest otherwise. He might have doubted he had a body at all, if not for the faint throbbing in his chest synched to a slow thumping in his inner ear, and the ever-so-gradual rise and fall of his abdomen. His heart was beating and he was breathing—sure signs that he was still alive, which surprised him, though he couldn't rally the effort to remember why. The idea of dredging up a memory from the stagnant murk of his consciousness was too daunting to bear. The best his will could manage was to open his eyes.

When the curtain of embers lifted away, Amon found himself upright in midair with his chin resting on his sternum. The long drop to the floor past the slope of his bare torso startled him, and rousing the sleep-deadened muscles of his neck, he lifted his head.

It seemed that he was floating unsupported near the ceiling of a capacious room hung with rows of huge blobs. The distance remaining above his head was nearly equal to his height, while the fall below his limply hanging toes might have been ten times that.

As drowsiness gave way to the sharp clarity of fear, Amon began to rotate his head from side to side, peering warily around him, and saw that the blobs were enormous fruit. Slightly taller from base to tip than he was, they were shaped like long slender figs with dark purple or burgundy skin, and dangled from the ceiling on cobalt stems at uneven intervals in every direction. Amon was suspended alongside them, completely naked, as though his gaunt, brown body had ripened from the air. The room was otherwise empty and might have resembled an unstocked warehouse, if not for the unusual material of its surfaces. The fruit-laden ceiling just above, the floor far below, and the distant walls they met were all composed of plants packed together into a solid foam-like mass—a great variety of tightly braided fronds, cacti, leaves, stems—some of which glowed in festive colors, combining into a soft apricot light.

The back of Amon's neck began to tingle with unease at the uncanny scene. Suddenly restless, he windmilled his arms and splayed his legs every which way, but could find no grip or footing. He bucked and twisted to spin himself around, but could get no traction. Whatever he did, his torso remained fixed in the same position and orientation as if by some subtle force like gravity, though he felt as light as dandelion fluff. Apparently, the transparent medium he was breathing held him without providing enough resistance to swim, though it felt literally like nothing, unaccompanied even by gentle brushing through his nostrils.

With each second that passed, Amon liked being stuck there less, an ant in invisible honey, and began to search around for some way to escape. He soon noticed that the spacing of the strange fruits was not as random as it had first appeared; their layout followed a pattern, and the spot he occupied seemed to be a gap. Sure enough, when he squinted and focused his eyes in the right way, he could make out a faint barrier surrounding him in the shape of one of the fruits, like a diaphanous membrane.

What is this place? Who has left me in this cage? A jolt of panic linked Amon's awareness to a memory of the same feeling, to another moment of panic. A mangled face was staring out from a hidden crevice of his mind. Jets of horror and revulsion groaned out from cracks in the subliminal darkness. Barrow lying bloody on the floor, "Intruder!" called out in his ruined voice, guards with assault dusters swarming in. With a shudder, Amon let his head and limbs fall slack again, overwhelmed by his recollection of maiming this man and by the ominous certainty that he was forgetting something even more awful from earlier that day, a wound howling in the depths of him. But he wasn't ready to go down there just yet, and pushed the apparition of Barrow aside. Breath coming shallow and fast, he forced himself to recall instead what had happened next.

Amon had fled down the stairs of the Cyst, with Barrow's lackeys in close pursuit, nerve dusting any armed person that crossed his path. He remembered now with anguish their screams before they tumbled down the stairs one after the next.

Once he had leapt down the final flight and burst outside, he looked up toward the roof of the Cyst. He was thinking how he might climb the surrounding buildings undetected to meet there with Rashana, still circling overhead in her rotorcraft, when an alarm call went out, "Security alert! OpSci intruder! Fire on sight! Alert!" as a bell sounded overhead.

So Amon kept running, seeking the narrowest squeezeways, unwatched by sentinels who might identify the OpSci disguise he still wore, but he soon lost his way. Most of the disposcrapers had been thrown up willy-nilly after the devastation wrought by the council coup the night before, and the reconstructed slumscape was unfamiliar to him. With the alarm call propagating from lookout to lookout far above, Amon knew it would reach the tunnels out of Xenocyst well before he did. When he spotted a nook just above the path, he shimmied up to empty his aching bladder in the corner and consider ways to escape.

He had eluded Sekido after the jazz bar brawl by stealing digiguises from the passengers on an elevator. Could he try a similar trick here? It made him ashamed to recall it, but he had then opened several nearby doors until he found a man napping alone on the pocked floor of his disposable room and held him up for his clothes. Although the hoody and jeans would have been a tight fit already, Amon decided to put them on over his OpSci uniform, wanting layers for the chill of night, and so left his hapless victim shivering in his underwear. It was a piteous sight, but at least the man had shelter. That was more than Amon could say.

Emboldened by his new disguise, Amon followed the crowd along the main passages that forked and undulated through the dense-leaning shelter-mounds. In spite of the bells and alarm calls that kept sounding overhead, none of the watch posted on ledges overlooking the intersections gave him a second glance. But soon the foot traffic thickened, and when it came to a complete halt, he realized that his pursuers must have choked off the nearest border checkpoint for a more thorough inspection than usual. So he shouldered his way back through the oncoming crowd and peeled off into a branching alleypath. Official checkpoints would have normally been the only way out of Xenocyst, but Amon had seen numerous breaches in the outer walls on his way in that morning—damage from the battle just the previous night—and he was willing to bet that some had yet to be sealed.

Worming through obscure crawlcrannies and winding up crumbling stairspirals, he gradually looped closer to the border. It was while he was hopping up a paddleway that he spotted one of the breaches. It fronted a small, busy square of worn concrete on ground level, and Amon paused on his paddle to observe.

The crack in the looming disposscraper wall had been enormous only a few hours earlier but was now mostly filled with new rooms, and a construction crew bucket brigade arranged across the square in an L formation was handing along roombuds to finish the job. Once placed, each roombud unfolded into a room, steadily patching the damage. All that remained was a gap just wide enough for five or six adults abreast, with a dozen guards stationed around it. An endless train of supply pilgrims descended a meandering chain of staircase stubs into the square, threading between the members of the bucket brigade. Most crossed and disappeared into a squeezeway on the other side, but some pulled out of line and walked past the guards to enter or climb the intact buildings that edged the breach. If he could mingle with these border residents, Amon realized, he might be able to steal away from the train and out the opening before anyone noticed.

Leaping from the paddleway to kick off a roomslope, and doing a balancing act along a thin ledge of misaligned rooftop, he managed to reach a flat shelf above the stairchain. He then hang-dropped gently into the train—only slightly jostling those around him—and went down the stairs as nonchalantly as he could, blood pulsing hard in his temples when he reached the square and trudged through the bucket brigade. Soon the breach was on his right, and he veered away from the line, heading for the neighboring disposcrapers, the three guards he passed looking off wearily. All he had to do was enter one of the rooms beside the opening and kick through the brittle Fleet walls to sneak in from the side. Then with enough care and luck he might hide behind the new rooms filling the breach and creep into the buffer canyon that ringed Xenocyst. Only a few more steps to the building.

"Halt," a woman barked from behind. Amon strode onward, pretending not to hear. "You! Tall one!" she yelled. "Stop NOW!" He quelled the impulse to run and turned around, hoping to talk his way out of it. Cradling an assault duster, the woman plodded over while two men stood back and watched with hands on holsters.

"What's that under there?" she demanded, pointing a finger on the hand holding the barrel at his chest. Looking down, he saw that a palm-sized hole had flaked open in his stolen hoody, revealing a swatch of OpSci patchwork. Amon spun on his heels and dashed for the breach, zigzagging erratically.

"The intruder is here!" a man bellowed. A patter of dust ripped past Amon's right as he sprinted the breach, careened left to put the wall between him and the guns, and bounded across the cratered tarmac of the buffer canyon into an alley on the other side. Turning a corner, he thought he'd made it safe until he heard an awful noise.

Gwak-crish-sh-sh-sh. The walls to his left shattered and the building collapsed like an accordion. One second solid, towering. The next a waterfall of Fleet rubble and howling people. Demolition dust.

The noise went off three more times, and other disposcrapers cascaded around him with a surf-like crash and an explosion of screams. Thin shards pelted him from all sides, something heavy struck his shoulder, knocking him over, and he was buried alive.

He scrabbled his way to the surface, only to burst out into more dust shots from the border watch, and took off, clambering on all fours, then stumbling full tilt over hillocks of debris. Another wall approached just ahead, suggesting cover, but he knew better now.

Amon was almost ready to lay down and give up—when he saw it! A crack in a strip of tarmac. No, a chasm. And before he could think what might be down there, he hopped in feet first.

Recalling now the reeking breath from the depths of the slum that rose to meet him as he fell, Amon was unsure if he'd been trying to flee for his life or kill himself. Before he could decide, the stem of the fruit snapped above him and he found himself falling in the present too.

"Yahhh," he yelled, flailing his limbs in terror as the fruit began to tilt to his left and the floor rushed towards him. Landing horizontal, there was a painless judder and a bounce; then he settled on his side, and felt a warm draft on his face. His head had broken through the transparent skin, and sparkles now sizzled around him as the nectar he'd been breathing met the air. The hole's promise of escape drove him to frenzy, and he lunged through, stretching it wider with his elbows, before writhing and wriggling the rest of the way out.

When he'd scrambled to his feet atop the plantfoam floor, standing before him was a man.

"Good morning, Amon," said the man, his feminine voice a surprising contrast to his muscular build. "Apologies for having to release you so suddenly. We had no opportunity to give you the usual orientation before you went in."

"W-who are you? Why? Why was I . . ." Amon pointed down at the fruit. The clear membrane was beginning to take on a purple sheen as the sparkles continued to leak out.

"It was the doctors' orders," the man told him, looking him up and down with the distant eyes of the bankliving, and Amon felt ashamed and defenseless in his nakedness.

"What doctors? Where am I?"

"Atupio Home Office."

"Atupio? So you had me in a LimboQuarium?" asked Amon in disbelief, glancing down again. The rapidly deflating husk had turned a blackish red, and was now as opaque as the hanging fruits above. "I don't have webloss."

"We understand that. Er for the Giftless is on the upper floors. This is our sensory deprivation orchard. The cells are normally for expansion of consciousness—like that one." The man pointed up at a fruit some distance away. Now see-through, it contained a young, naked boy. "In your case, my medicorps thought it would help speed your recovery. When your vitals showed improvement this morning, they recommended that we wake you up."

Amon watched the boy float there under the apricot glow. He imagined himself inside his fruit soaking in darkness and the light seeping through his eyelids as the skin gradually turned clear, bringing the fire. Or had the fire come before that? Something told Amon that he had come from that blaze and that he would give it to many others. . . .

"Recovery from what?" said Amon, groping for some memory that might explain.

The man studied him, considering how to respond. Again Amon felt his nakedness. He could only hope that the man had politely digimade him with clothes.

"Are you feeling up for a talk?" the man asked.

"I think so," Amon replied. The shock of the fall had blown away the last wisps of his grogginess. His body was surprisingly loose, thoughts honed in on the moment despite his confusion. "I guess you're one of the staff?"

"Better get dressed," said the man, pointing to the floor at his feet. There, Amon now noticed, rested some neatly folded hemp clothes and a pair of slippers.

"What's your role here?" he persisted, as he bent over to take the underwear and pull it on.

"I'm in charge of this place."

"Of this . . . orchard?"

"Of Atupio."

"A manager, then?"

"Owner."

"But—"

"You know me, Amon. Under the name Makesh Adani when we met. But do call me by my real name this time."

With the hospital gown around his shoulders, Amon's fingers paused on the laces at the back. "Rashana?"

The man nodded, and Amon frowned in perplexity. Now it was his turn to eye the man up and down. A full head shorter than Amon, he wore an off-white hemp T-shirt tight enough to display his large biceps and pectorals, and navy pants with a drawstring over equally bulky legs, leaving visible the richly tanned skin from his beefy forearms down and from his thick neck up. In contrast to his stocky build, the man's face was stretched sleek—thin nose, pointy goateed chin, and small flattened-back ears, the shadow of buzzed hair receding symmetrically from his long narrow head, the hint of a grin adding a sardonic tinge to his otherwise cool scrutinizing expression.

"You're not the Rashana I know," said Amon.

"This man is one of my closest assistants," the man replied. "When he's not serving as a vehicle for my words, we call him 'Ono X.'"

A vehicle for my words . . . the peculiar phrase echoed in Amon's mind as he stepped into the slippers. So had he found Rashana at last? But if it was really her, he wondered why she had to speak through someone else. Could this man be lying? Were there actually medical reasons for keeping Amon trapped? No stories of visits to Atupio that he could recall had mentioned warehouses spun of jungle with boys tripping out in the canopy. What if he was actually somewhere else? What if the person speaking through this man was, in fact, Rashana's twin sister Anisha?

"Come, we'd better do this in person," said Rashana, or Ono X, or whoever, and they began to walk away. Trying not to let his wariness show, Amon followed, glancing once over his shoulder at the now-empty husk of the fruit and its torn stem above, his fluid step nothing like what one would expect of a man who had just risen from the ashes.

While Amon shadowed the man across the vast floor, his eyes traced its intricate material—a mosaic of fruits, pods, grains, and flowers interlaced through densely compacted greenery. With every step, he felt the weave of the organic mass through his thin slippers.

Soon a wall began to loom. It was composed of the same plantfoam, except for the spot they were headed for. There a wide, uneven swathe of chainmail-weave thorns, each as long and sharp as a butcher's knife, rose nearly a third of the way to the high ceiling.

When they arrived, the man inserted his pinky into a small hole at waist height and pricked it on the tiny thorn inside. This caused the other thorns to unlink and retract, unveiling a rectangular portal into a hallway of more plantfoam. As Amon stepped through behind the man, he drew in his shoulders involuntarily, shrinking from the inward-pointing spines that edged the doorway, a gruesome image of what might happen to a trespasser filling his mind's eye.

Following the man along the hallway now, Amon watched as vibrant beetles, geckos, caterpillars, and other innocuous critters emerged from tiny seams in the flora before disappearing back inside. He even saw a flying squirrel no bigger than a fingernail perform a gliding jump, skimming up the wall to his left, only to slip out of sight. Oddly, he never spotted any of these creatures on the floor, as though they knew their boundaries. Cricket chirps, harmonic cicada buzzes, and soft rhythmic hisses melded into a pleasant wash of sound, and Amon found his fear of this bizarre place and the man who claimed to speak for another fighting waves of relaxation. He was having trouble believing his eyes and ears. It just *had* to be an overlay, except that the surround was consistent across all senses, even those not captured by the ImmaNet. The textured brush of the floor against the soles of his slippers. The warm and moist yet soothing air. The soft fragrance like strawberry with a dash of fudge and hibiscus. His awareness felt sharper than usual, even though he had just awoken . . . from the abundance of oxygen, perhaps?

The plantfoam walls on both sides were interrupted at nearly even intervals by more gates of thorn. Amon was wondering where these might open to when he espied patches of transparent leaves embedded in the left wall ahead. Randomly strewn from floor to ceiling, they linked and clustered into jagged windows that revealed a gymnasium of similar immensity to the room he had just left. On an empty stretch of floor between a ramified fungus jungle gym and a multi-story hedge-maze obstacle course, boys and girls of about seven or eight wearing T-shirts and loose pants much like the man's were sparring and practicing grapples in pairs. Several heads turned as they passed, and Amon met lucid eyes with large pupils. Obviously not distracted by the vistas of the ImmaNet, which would seem to suggest these kids were bankdead. And yet, this facility was unlike any bankdeath camp Amon had ever seen or heard of.

When the man turned a corner down an intersecting hallway, there were more leaf-windows in the left wall, displaying a much smaller room that only puzzled Amon further. More children sat on chairs of moss arranged in a circle around a young woman. With their arms extended on rests in front of them, nestled in customized grooves, their fingers twitching commands, they all had the Elsewhere Gaze. The scene was reminiscent of Amon's early edutainment classes in Green Ladybug. So this was a BioPen, then? But for bankdead kids? Or were they bankliving after all?

"I hadn't meant to bring you here until after we'd spoken," said the man, glancing Amon over with concern. "But bear with me, Amon. I'll be arriving soon enough."

Amon nodded, his confusion growing with each step. He followed the man down two more turns until the hallway ended at a double door of dry, empty honeycomb. There the man pricked his pinky inside another aperture, this time on the stinger of a bee. The doors opened into what looked like the interior of an abandoned beehive in the shape of a shipping elevator, the hexagons brimming with honey. *Those holes beside the doors must be genome readers*, Amon realized as they boarded, reminded of the vendors and feeders in the District of Dreams. *But this man is bankliving, so why would genetic clearance—*

The doors snapped open before Amon could finish his thought, and he jumped back as hundreds of pink bees poured abruptly from cracks between the cells into the hallway outside. They began to buzz around or crawl into a proliferation of flowers blooming from the walls and ceiling, when, to his relief, the doors shut.

Almost instantly they slid apart again, but the hive-elevator seemed to have arrived at a different floor. The bees were gone, and the hallway outside was even more vibrant, festooned in addition to many-colored blossoms with neon orange toads and ladybug-patterned vines. While the man led him onward, Amon hesitantly touched the wall to his right, stroking his fingertips along the indentations and bumps of the braided verdure, and was filled with awe. *Who built this? Why?* The lower floor was clearly some sort of BioPen, but Atupio wasn't supposed to be involved in the human resource industry. That was the business of other arms of Fertilex, over which Anisha had executive control. One reason to doubt the man's claims about where they were and who he spoke for and, as disoriented as Amon was, he resolved to keep his wits about him. Poised now to defend himself if it came to it, alone in this enclosing complex where even the doors had teeth.

2

Eventually the man stopped at what Amon took to be a pointillist painting hanging from ceiling to floor. It depicted a diamond that floated in a blue sky, where it was set aglow by numerous beams of light angling from below. The moment he realized that the dots composing it were not in fact dabs of paint but blue, white, grey, and brown nuts and seeds, the man inserted his finger into another hole in the wall, and these solid pigments swished aside, reeled into the walls. It was a door! And through the doorway was a sort of boardroom, with a long coral table in the center and six of the same mossy chairs placed around it. The man ushered Amon inside, where he could now see a tree-shaped aquarium of transparent amber embedded in the far wall. From the tip of the roots at the floor to their base about halfway up the wall, the aquarium was filled with mud and stones, while from the bottom of the trunk to the tips of the leaves along the ceiling, innumerable fish—in a rainbow of colors—swam. Their wild swirling made Amon's head churn, and he was grateful when the man gestured to the chair at the head of the table with the aquarium out of sight behind.

"Please take a seat," he said. "I won't be a moment."

The man then stepped out into the hallway, the dots of the door whipping back into place behind him with a shush like a downpour. The diamond painting was a mirror-image of how it had appeared from the hallway. *Which side is the correct one?* Amon wondered as he sat down. No sooner had he settled than the moss of the back- and arm- rests began to mold to his body, even bulging upward to adjust to his height. Although the spongy cushioning was unfamiliar, Amon was reminded of the ergonomic chair he'd used in the Ministry of Liquidation. He hadn't sat in a chair for what seemed like ages, not during all his months in the District of Dreams, and he found it soothing, though also somehow alien.

When the chair had finished adapting to his contours, the painting dismantled itself again to admit another man. Short and skinny with flushed healthy skin, he wore a glistening beige apron of a fabric like draping seashell and carried a bamboo tray, which he quickly placed before Amon. It was set with a glass of water, chopsticks, and three dishes of food the likes of which Amon had never seen: a stir-fry of some kiwi-green root and mixed beans the hue of fall leaves, a salad of purplish herbs and blue flower petals topped with a slice of white melon, and a bowl of triangular grains—some pastel green, some beige, some russet. Despite the meal's unusual appearance, the sweet fragrance made his mouth water instantly, as though his hunger had been sharpened along with his senses in the rich air, and he reached for the chopsticks. Thankfully, the textures were unsurprising—the grains soft, the stir-fry crunchy—and each bite tasted wholesome, far better than anything in the camps. Except for that last meal with—

A tremor rose from the base of his spine as Barrow's mangled face peered up at him again. Appetite vanished, Amon wanted to spit out his half-chewed beans but instead washed them down with some water, insipid on his tongue after months of frothy sports drinks. He laid his chopsticks on the tray. He'd been starting to feel bloated anyway. His stomach, it seemed, had shrunk. Odd. Even in the midst of the famine he'd been able to put away more than just a few mouthfuls. How long had he been sleeping in that orchard?

The problem with this question was that he had no recollection of ever drifting off. He'd woken up to light on his eyelids and, before that . . .

only fire, a starburst of toxic feelings that made him wince. The nearest memory prior was his jump into the pit. There was nothing in between.

Amon ran his fingers over his face and through his overgrown puff of hair, jarred and baffled to the point of irritation, fearing for what might await him in this place. Only when he pushed his tray away, shifted his chair on an angle, and craned his neck right to glance at the aquarium, did the wetness suddenly come back to him. The wet floor. Amon squeezed his eyes shut, blocking out the apricot glow to bring his present closer to the gloom of that moment.

He had been curled up in a puddle on the floor of a ruinous concrete service passage. No windows, no doors. Only oozing cracks that admitted the faintest light. His left knee had pins and needles, and there was a splitting pain in one temple.

Prodded to his feet by the hoots and hollers of his pursuers above, Amon limped as fast as he could down the long reeking tunnel, hop-scotching clumsily around slicks of sewage and slumped figures so thin and still they might have been skeletons draped in dissolving rags.

He vaguely recalled a cavern where he'd jumped between islands of disposcraper rubble on a black lake of rot. The families who made these their homes had warned him off with threats and curses, until one livid mother pushed him in headfirst, leaving him to wade with drenched hair through a warm putrescent stew.

Later, he staggered dripping along another tunnel, split down the middle by a ditch, mushy bodies face down in the gunk. His headache flared with each step, his palm stinging just below the thumb—a small cut from gripping the shard of a cup he'd held Barrow hostage with.

The tunnel narrowed and narrowed until he was crawling through a moist concrete hole in the darkness. It felt reassuring in there, like his own little den, tucked away from all the shouting and dangers . . . . until it drew so tight that one last squirm ahead had him stuck. And unable to budge onward or retreat a single inch, he began to scream.

The memory fled as though swept away by his desperate voice from the past, and when Amon grasped for it, a ball of inexplicable horror tensed in his gut, forcing out a sharp breath. *What got me from there to here? Could someone have found me in that squeeze?*

Before he could discover even a glimmer of clarity, the dots of the door-painting reeled into the wall, admitting a woman he knew . . . in a way.

"Welcome," she said, standing just inside the doorway. Amon trembled. This was the moment he had anticipated and hoped for and dreaded so long. His gaze kept wilting and returning, while she looked him over just as the man had earlier, her dark eyes steady and intense, her lashes shearing the air. *Could this be Anisha?* he wondered, wishing for some sign that it was otherwise.

Although he had seen Rashana from a distance at Delivery, this was his first encounter with one of the twins up close in the naked world. She looked older without digimake than in either sister's rendering as a man, but her features were striking under the apricot luminescence, her dusky irises textured in shades of ochre, her teeth pristine like white silk hardened, her light brown skin disturbed only by the faintest of lines. Her hooked nose seemed to Amon distinctive, while her short, carefully tussled hair brought out the feminine delicacy of her forehead and ears. A pastel turquoise dress shirt above white chinos tapered at the waist to display a slender figure.

After a long pause Amon managed to get out, "It's been a while."

"I hope you're feeling rested," the Birla sister replied. Amon had only heard the sisters' voices when they were posing as men. Unaltered, hers was higher-pitched, with a melodic timbre. "How was your meal?"

"It was . . . nothing quite like it," said Amon.

"I'm sure. You won't find those ingredients anywhere else." The Birla sister took a seat across from him and stacked her hands on the tabletop.

Imitating her, Amon pulled in his chair and sat up to rest his hands atop the coral, much softer on his skin than he'd expected. "I guess the building is edible?" he asked.

"Parts of it. Other parts yield useful resources."

"And this is Atupio?"

"It's our home office, as I said."

"So we're on the Tokyo Canal?"

"We are. On the northern tip, just southwest of the Bridge of Compassion."

"Then out there"—Amon glanced over his shoulder at what he'd taken for an aquarium, but now realized was a tree-shaped window—"that's the canal?"

"It is. You woke up below ground, in our BioPen. The floors above us house our humanitarian divisions, reporting outfits, Er for the Giftless, and all the rest. This floor is in between, right on the bed of the canal. We mostly use it for planning and administration."

So I'm half underground and half underwater, on a body of water that is half river and half sea, between the land of banklife and bankdeath, Amon marveled to himself.

"You said I was recovering . . . that's why you put me in that fruit?"

"You don't remember us picking you up?"

"No," he admitted, but then he did remember, and the Birla sister smiled when she saw him screw up his face.

"You . . . you found me after I escaped from Xenocyst." His heartbeat picked up as his body performed the memory, cowering out of breath in a crook beneath a stairwell as the Birla Guard surrounded him. "But I don't know about any injury."

"Not an injury, an illness," the Birla sister told him. "You were barely conscious, with a severe viral infection."

"There was a cut in my hand," Amon recalled, almost feeling the sting. "I wasn't in the most hygienic place. Could that be related?"

"Our triage doctors certainly thought so. A few more hours and you might not have made it."

"Did my friends make it?" he rasped, suddenly terrified that he might be the only one who remained. "What about my friends?"

Amon cast his mind back to the last times he had seen them. Little Book sketching his coded warning in the air of the library, Ty fleeing the cloud of drones on the edge of the Gifted Triangle, Vertical diving out of Delivery between the legs of a freekeeper, Hippo plotting the exposé with wide angry eyes in the digital quarantine, Book by his side offering advice, Tamper on his knees in an elevator assembling devices to hack the receptacles . . . and someone else in another elevator too awful to conjure. The mere intimations of this last memory made Amon cringe.

"I don't have much to report, I'm afraid," the Birla sister replied. "The infighting at Xenocyst left many casualties. None of our mutual acquaintances have turned up among the survivors."

"Barrow said they were dead. Was he telling the truth?"

"I wish I had the answer."

"But what about the rebellion at Xenocyst? I left on the morning of the sabotage. When I came back the next morning, the whole city had been devastated. You must know something. You flew to the Cyst at midnight to meet me, didn't you? What did Barrow do?!"

"There are many things about that night that I still don't understand myself, Amon. I can only tell you what I know."

"After the Delivery sabotage," began the Birla sister, "the Philanthropy syndicate banned Atupio from the District of Dreams for our involvement. I had to withdraw all my staff from the island. But I still intended to meet with you at the Cyst as we'd agreed. So I flew in on Gemini X set to mimic a supply craft. When I arrived in the airspace above Xenocyst at midnight, a dustfight was being waged all over the city. Disposcrapers were folding like houses of cards one after the next. The many demolition dusters in use were a sign that someone had MegaGlom funding.

"When my hazardcorps advised me it was too dangerous to land, I dronedropped Ono X and two more of my guards with orders to find you. But almost as soon as they landed on the roof of the Cyst, what we had taken for a harmless, passing centicopter began to open fire on us in the air. It was my twin aboard Gemini Y, hiding in plain sight much as I was."

"A later model of your rotorcraft?" Amon asked.

"Her *copy* of my rotorcraft," the Birla sister corrected him. "Surprise worked in her favor. I was already losing the dogfight when we detected antiair drones from Delivery on an intercept course. I had no wish to abandon Ono X and the other pair to the fray, but both the human and AI judgements of my hazardcorps were unanimous in urging retreat. When Ono X insisted that they could hold their own on the ground, I ordered them to play neutral observer and pulled back to Atupio Home Office."

"Why didn't you tell them to stop the insurgents?" said Amon, surprised by the anger and distress in his own voice. "They were right in the heart of Xenocyst, three well-armed professionals with marksmanship apps. They could have shifted the tide. Then Hippo and them might still be safe!"

"Don't criticize me for what you don't understand!" the Birla sister snapped, her razor lashes poised high as her eyes widened. "I've always done what I can to support Xenocyst. I was one of its first patrons. But influencing affairs in the camps by supplying a proxy community is one thing. A direct intervention in a conflict would be something else entirely. Of course I could have afforded the fines for my guards' actions. I could have sent in a whole army of drones and soldiers and nanobots if I'd felt like it. But use your head! My fully armed rotorcraft had just been detected in Philanthropy Syndicate airspace. Their securicorps might have written off our clash in the air as a sibling spat—not so if they caught my men pitching in their dustpower on the ground. That would be a clear escalation of the conflict from an economic to a military one. Then what would happen to the people of Xenocyst? They'd be fodder in a battle that I'd lose anyway because my twin controls the Fertilex empire from which I would have to muster my forces. Is that the outcome I should have chosen? Throwing innocent lives into the crossfire and upsetting the balance of power, just for some hopeless attempt to rescue your buddies?"

Amon regretted his outburst. Her tirade seemed completely justified, affording a glimpse into the complex, high-stakes choices that anyone with the Birla sisters' degree of wealth and Freedom surely confronted almost constantly. Such responsibility was overwhelming for him to even imagine, her whole way of being unlike any he had ever been familiar with, whether as a GATA employee scrimping and saving or as a Xenocyst denizen mired in poverty. He wondered what such relentless negotiation with ambiguity, where the question was not whether to help or harm but how much and to whom, would do to one's spirit.

"Sorry," said Amon. "I shouldn't be judging you. I'm not myself today."

At these words, the tension that had built up in the Birla sister's shoulders dropped away. "That's okay, Amon," she replied. "I wasn't thinking how hard this must all be for you. Shall we move on?"

"Please. I want to hear about Ono X. Did he learn anything in the end?"

"Nothing definitive. A battle had erupted between the council and a splinter group vying for control of Xenocyst. In the pandemonium, there was no way for him to determine what either side was fighting for. Rumors had been circulated about this and that person betraying everyone to the OpScis."

"I saw a hole in Opportunity Peaks." Amon told her, remembering his journey back to Xenocyst the following morning. The mountain of rooms had revealed a patch of sky, as though pregnant with a fragment of the universe. "Do you know how it happened?"

"That was the work of the Charity Brigade. According to a leak from a career volunteer, your good friend, Kitao, mistook your crew for a rival sect of Opportunity Science and told the Brigade they were responsible for the sabotage."

Amon could see Kitao in Delivery, glaring at him in the lineup, then whispering to a freekeeper amidst the riotous crush.

"But Kitao's tattling backfired," said the Birla sister. "He failed to understand that the Charity Brigade had no interest in sectarian lines. Instead of targeting his enemies, they blamed the incident on the Quantitative Priesthood as a whole and shattered their holy mountain."

"Why would he think we were a rival sect?"

"Ono X tells me that the sects have different insignia on their uniforms. One of these seems to have been included in your disguises."

"It was Barrow," stated Amon with immediate certainty.

"Not surprising. How?"

The bleeding face of Amon's former idol seemed to watch on, making sure that he was speaking the truth about him. "B-barrow was in charge of tailoring our OpSci outfits for the mission. He must have known about the rival sect from when he was Kitao's slave. Had their insignia stitched in without telling us. Then he let Kitao know somehow . . . maybe using a Field Priest captured in one of our skirmishes to write a letter? I'm not sure exactly, but Barrow would have told him that the sect was planning something at the Delivery gate where the sabotage was to take place. That's why Kitao was there. It wasn't just a coincidence."

"That sounds like Barrow's handiwork," the Birla sister agreed. "Your sabotage hurts the Philanthropy Syndicate, and the Syndicate hurts the OpScis and your crew. Everyone loses except him."

"And Barrow?" Amon asked, meeting her powerful gaze with the full desperation of his.

"He was still on this mortal plane last we checked, though he may be wishing that he wasn't. Some of his injuries were permanent."

At these words, another twinge of horror shot up Amon's spine and his head dropped as though its circuit had been cut. Even with his eyes open he could see Barrow's mangled face against the coral of the tabletop, and found himself making fists involuntarily as he remembered the crunching sensation of pummeling the man's throat. Amon wanted to tell himself that taking Barrow's voice had been just, that it had merely deprived him of the power that might have maintained his ill-acquired position at Xenocyst—his eloquence. Still, for all his hatred after Barrow's betrayal, recalling those gargling cries for help brought him no satisfaction.

"I should have gone to the roof to meet you," he said, ashamed for losing control, choosing vengeance over escape He could almost hear the sound of her rotorcraft. *Whoozt, whoozt, whoozt, whoozt.*

"You mean to meet my twin," said the Birla Sister.

"Pardon me?"

"She arrived right when you were having your altercation with Barrow."

"On the roof? Your sister visited Xenocyst?"

Something about this seemed to ruffle her.

"I was surprised to hear it too," she said. "I never thought my twin would sully herself by setting foot in the camps or mingling with those so far beneath her."

"That was Anisha?"

"No doubt about it. Ono X and the other two had slipped out of the Cyst the night before, but they were drawn back by the sound of her Gemini landing and took up sniping positions on a neighboring rooftop."

"Wait. You sniped your sister?"

Again she seemed ruffled. "It was Ono X's initiative. He knew I would have advised restraint. And a failed attempt in any case. My guard had a clear shot as she was deboarding onto the landing pad of the Cyst but one of her women got in the way. Fell into an epileptic fit. My twin didn't dare show her face outside after that."

The Birla sister gave Amon a raking stare as if to demand what could have been wrong with this. Averting his gaze to the coral, he wondered why the sisters were on such bad terms. He'd never known a family personally and so had no basis to decide what counted as normal. Even so, their relationship seemed too rotten to qualify. Not that he had any intention of weighing in on the issue.

"I can't believe that was Anisha," Amon said, shaking his head. "I was certain it was you, come to pick me up after I missed our appointment." Seeing her brow darken at the comparison, Amon immediately regretted his words.

"Well, be glad that you didn't follow through on that misunderstanding or we wouldn't be having this conversation. You might not be having any conversation."

Again the memory of Barrow on the floor, his once-beautiful voice wheezing out an alarm call as Amon fled down the stairs, and Amon's guilt for succumbing to his rage, sacrificing his chance for escape. But no chance had in fact been sacrificed. If he'd tamped down his emotions and made a more calculated choice, he might have waltzed into his doom. And he seemed to have found Rashana anyway, if that was indeed who she was. Or rather she had found him. In other words, giving in to his most vicious impulses had been his salvation. Something about this just didn't seem fair. It seemed like the wrong lesson for life to teach.

"Amazing that you had the stomach to jump into that nasty pit," the Birla sister mused. "Ono X showed me pictures."

"He was there?"

"Only after you had made the jump. He followed the alarm calls to the border, and heard from one of the watch what had happened. A schematic he accessed from the days of the failed condo boom showed underground sewers. Even Ono X balked at going in after you."

"Then how did you track me down?"

"Do you remember the SampleQuito that pricked you on the bridge from Delivery?"

"Those were yours?"

The Birla sister nodded.

"After you disappeared from Free Tokyo, I ordered Ono X to find you by every means possible. What seemed our most promising option at first was DNA tracking. Unfortunately, no copy of your genome had been retained in any Fertilex database after you graduated from our BioPen. The rights had reverted to you in adulthood. We sent a forensic team to collect traces of your skin and hair from places we knew you'd been. Our hope was to sequence your genetic profile illegally. But someone—we're still not sure who—had cleaned up. Not a base pair of anyone remained in any of the locations the team visited."

"Genephage dust?" Amon asked.

"So it would appear. We looked into licensing your genome from the Ministry of Records, but were surprised to find that your profile wasn't in the Archives." The Birla sister glanced past Amon, her eyes glazing over as though absorbed in the swirling fishes. This only lasted a moment; then she gave him an inquisitive look. "We still don't understand how that could be if you're bankdead . . ."

Amon said nothing, unsure if he should tell her about his identity suicide.

"The Delivery network was of no more use. Pinpointing your genome in that unwieldy database was hopeless. For instance, it doesn't record other biometrics or names by which we might have matched an entry to you. We had some doubts about whether you'd even been registered.

"It was only months later, after Hippo asked me to help with the exposé you conceived, that we could be certain you were in the District of Dreams. When he told us that you were scheduled to be at Delivery for the sabotage, Ono X arranged for some Atupio reporters to smuggle in a handful of SampleQuitos. We set them to hover around the bridge for the gate that you and your fellow saboteurs had entered. You and I may have had a plan to meet that night, but I wasn't going to take any chances of you disappearing again.

"After we'd genotyped you with the sample, we kept a line open to the vending machine network so that I could be alerted the moment you used one. When we found you in the Tumbles, you were in rags and your skin was purple all over with a horrible rash. You're lucky you used the feeder when you did. If the infection didn't kill you, the cold most certainly would have."

Amon picked nervously with his fingernails at the grooves of the coral tabletop, mulling over her account. At first, this story about the SampleQuito seemed highly suspicious. As if Rashana could have actually snuck unauthorized drones into Delivery, deployed them safely amidst clouds of Delivery CareBots, and tracked him with the Delivery vending system, when the facility was controlled by the Philanthropy Syndicate, rival to both Atupio and Fertilex. Such maneuvers would have been more plausible if she were in fact Anisha, said to be partnered with the Syndicate through her association with the Gyges Circle. But the Books had once told Amon that the Syndicate granted Atupio special access to Delivery under the condition that they curtail activism disruptive to the Charity Gift Economy. This might have enabled the smuggling. He'd also heard from Hippo that Fertilex operated its own plutogenic brand, used mostly as a smokescreen for a baby laundering ring. This might have provided links to the vending system. Most persuasively, Amon realized, if he'd fallen into the clutches of Anisha, there was no reason to think he would have ever woken up.

"I don't remember any rash," he said, "but I do remember using that vending machine now."

He saw himself at the head of a lineup inserting his finger into the DNA reader and retrieving a meager rice ball from the bin. Perhaps an hour later, he'd been wandering through a flaking maze of high-piled disposcraper rubble, when heavy footfalls began to echo all around. Thinking they were the boots of the Charity Brigade, he ran for his life, until he traipsed too deep and arrived at a dead end. Then he reached for his nerve duster, prepared to go down fighting, and realized that it was gone, lost somewhere along the way. When all ten Birla Guard emerged from around corners in their gold armor, aiming assault dusters with software-assisted smoothness, and a Birla sister calling herself Rashana appeared and tried to reassure him that they were there to help, Amon had been too weary and dazed to do anything but submit.

"Where on earth did you go after you jumped into that pit?" she asked him now.

"I was . . . underground."

"For an entire week?"

"A week?" Amon said in a falsetto of disbelief.

"Yes. The day after the sabotage, twelve hours after we were scheduled to meet in the Cyst, you assaulted Barrow and escaped . . . or were my reporters mistaken?"

He shook his head.

"That was December 16th. We picked you up on the 21st. It's now December 26th."

Amon scowled in bewilderment, flicking his lowered gaze left to right as he cast his awareness back and forth between his final memories. "I don't . . . You can't expect me to believe this? I was crawling through the tunnel, I used a vending machine, and then you found me. There's no gap!"

"According to the calendar, there is."

"Hey! I wouldn't forget anything important, okay?" Amon lifted his eyes to give her a defiant look, surprised to find himself raising his voice. "I'm not crazy."

"No one said that you are. You've been through a lot, Amon. But the fact is, we found you just below the foothills of Opportunity Peaks, on the northwestern border of the Tumbles, nowhere near Xenocyst."

Irritation surged in Amon, as if his confusion were her fault.

"You just don't understand what it was like in there," he shouted. "I never had an infection, did I? What were you *really* doing to me in that cell?"

"I wouldn't leap to any—"

"You are Rashana, right?" Almost dizzy, Amon gripped the edge of the table, as though that might stabilize his mind.

The Birla sister's eyes tensed. "And who else would I be?"

"I wasn't trying to—"

"Go ahead. Say it." She sounded hurt.

"Sorry," said Amon, realizing that he was almost hysterical. His emotions seemed to shift from one second to the next. Embarrassed, he rested his forehead on his fists. It suddenly struck him as unlikely that he would use a vending machine and risk being labelled a hungry ghost not long after Barrow provided a full meal when he had so assiduously avoided them while famished that same morning. He still had no idea how he got out of the tunnel. Could he have really lost a week?

The Birla sister waited before she asked, "What does 'the great bird' mean to you?"

"Nothing," Amon whispered gruffly, but on his next blink, the flames reignited behind his eyelids.

"Nothing at all? Because when we retrieved you, you were feverish. Mumbling. Something about a great bird."

Amon felt his breath pick up, his heart galloping, and closed his eyes to meet the images flooding in.

At some point after he'd screamed his throat hoarse to no avail, the entrapping walls of the tunnel began to move in peristaltic waves, squeezing him forward as if through an intestine. Bright dots swirled in his vision and nausea filled him like pond scum as his head popped into empty space.

Next thing he knew, he was sprawled out in a dark chamber—perhaps the bottom of a chute. His skull was a supernova of pain that sizzled against the cold churning floor, his fingers melted the walls with their touch, and his raised hairs were lighthouses across his skin.

Mayuko appeared under the rotating light of one that stood at the head of a peninsula. *I have a treat for you*, she said, pointing to her belly of blown glass, filled with a cloudy brine, a pickled fetus floating among ginseng at the center.

Then Amon opened his burning eyelids to the bloated hand of some sea creature, or drowned corpse, shaking him by the collar. Two half-eclipsed moons stared from a face that kept warping and dissolving like the reflection of a shadow on rippling water. He felt the swampy breath of this strange being as it spoke and wanted to push it away, yet lacked the will to lift his arms.

"Not to worry, we're all Friends of the Tattoo here," it said, and, unconcerned by Amon's feeble struggling, stuffed the barrel of a cannon in his mouth. Blowing on the other end, it pumped down his gullet a stream of gelatinous bubbles that popped rapid fire in his throat, leaving a taste somewhere between chutney and pure itch. The treatment seemed to dowse the inferno in his head, and Amon's vision focused enough that he could see two men flanking the creature. Huddled over him in an elevator, under the flicker of an electrified tongue dangling from a fishing rod, they were dressed in the unlogoed patchwork of low ranking Opportunity Scientists, as was Amon now that his stolen clothes had dissolved. Their words hurried and slowed at random, always the wrong speed for him to understand, but somehow he could tell that they were discussing what to do with him. When one of the men bent down to wrap his arm around Amon's waist and lift him to his feet, the lightning glow shifted and Amon could make out the creature more clearly: it was Minister Kitao in the brand name patchwork of a Quantitative Priest, standing his full two meter's height, the hunchback gone.

One second, two murky figures were holding Amon up by his armpits while the ex-politician led the way through the pale murky slumscape, Amon patting his temples to check if his head had been scorched to ash while his teeth chattered with cold, mumbling words beyond even his own comprehension, guilty that the man he'd cash crashed was taking care of him. The next second, they were at the foot of Opportunity Peaks, the looming mountain of dissolving shelters blocking out the sky but for a single hole yet to be repaired. Through this Amon could see quadruple rainbows of raw meat against black clouds, each arc dripping blood onto the ones below. The mandala-patterned roomslopes squirmed with a pestilence of crowds; young men bounding from ridge to ridge with rags flapping in a blur like the wings of locusts. Priests drawn along on rickshaws by scorpion-tailed eunuchs or hauled up with pulleys on jerkied bodies braided into baskets. Cowled women and children led down into steaming shark mouths gaping in the valleys.

Then they were inside, standing in a dark passage before a balcony. It overlooked a black chamber carved into the core of the room-mountain in the shape of a rhinoceros skull. Floor after floor of tin sheets hung on wires, with thousands of worshippers prostrate in lines and curves that described a jumble of inscrutable equations when viewed from above.

High above in the horn, on a cartilage trapeze slung by ropes of human hair, dangled a man. He wore a skintight leather jumpsuit that covered every inch of his body, except his mouth, which was painted white—even on the inside.

"The Lighthouse of Opportunity!" he shrieked.

"OPPORTUNITY!" the crowd boomed back.

"Lighting the way to the distant shores of the Free World!'

"THE FREE WORLD!"

"Where those pure of DNA must find a job!"

"A JOB!"

"The keyhole in the market for which only you are the key!"

"THE KEY!"

Then they were in a passage that echoed with irregular thumping and eerie moans. In an alcove, a man was beat-juggling four records of bone while voices rose up from slats along the floor. There, men and women crammed together in filthy, dim sties, turned up at the sound of their footsteps like carp in a pond expecting food from their keepers, their eyes scratched blind.

Is this where I'll live out my days? Amon wondered. Perhaps if he gave up on his conscience, he might learn their rituals in time, and become someone new, a servant of the Charity Gift Economy. It wasn't as if he had anything else to depend on.

"Enjoy the *ikebana*," said one of the men supporting him with a mocking leer, and the two of them shrunk until they were too small to see, leaving Amon with Kitao in a well-kept condo hallway. Amon was puzzling over the parting words of the two men when Kitao unlocked a door and yanked him inside. The moment Amon staggered into the small, white room, a cloying scent struck his nostrils.

"You'll be my gardener once you're better," Kitao told him, "rest up," and he pointed to a futon spread neatly on the floor below a window at the other end. Once Kitao had seen Amon obediently collapse into it, he was sucked through another door.

Despite his exhaustion, Amon was unable to sleep. He initially blamed his yawing headache and the light from the window, but soon realized it was the smell—sweet with a pungent earthiness that dogged his attention and made him uneasy.

Inevitably, he found himself on his feet in front of the door Kitao had gone through, the smell stronger here, as though wafting through the crack. He put his hand on the knob. . . .

Through the doorway, he could see Kitao standing there with scissors, clipping a flower. A row of women in white, frilly dresses were seated in armchairs on either side of him. But they weren't women. Not anymore . . . They were flowerpots. Cut just above their blank eyes, with lotuses floating on the water that filled their hollow heads.

Kitao was clipping stems for another bouquet to arrange inside. When he noticed Amon up, he ordered him back to bed.

"You need rest if you're going to make a good impression on the higher priests."

Amon stared into the placid brown eyes of the tall ex-minister, all of his illusions about living there gone. And pretending he was going back to bed, he crossed the room, stepped onto the futon, and opened the window to crawl out.

"Stop!" Kitao shouted as he thundered over the floor after him, but Amon was already hanging onto the ledge. For one moment he looked down between his patchwork-garbed chest and the concrete wall at the blurry mass that might be a rooftop far, far below, before releasing his grip.

Once again, Amon wasn't sure if he'd been trying to flee or end his life. But before he knew it, he was riding on the back of a flaming bird. Its white and neon orange feathers blazed with computer code that soaked into his skin like waves of mother's milk. He felt an unaccountable kinship with the bird, as they were extinguished and reborn over and over. *Together we can topple even castles, if only we can build each other out of puzzles*, he thought.

Amon recalled all this with his forehead on his fists, eyes closed, heart skittering, lungs quivering. A vague presentiment told him again that he had come from flame for the express purpose of passing it on to others, a febrile mission tinged with the delirious mood of his memory. Reeling with queasy horror, he couldn't tell whether it was a meaningful insight or a stroke of sheer insanity.

"Has the fever come back to you?" the Birla sister asked when he was somewhat calmer.

Amon nodded.

"So you understand now why we kept you in the sensory deprivation orchard? You were deathly sick. The inflammation had spread to your brain, and our specialists recommended a low stimulus environment to minimize neurological damage."

Neurological . . . Amon began to fret. He hadn't noticed any diminishment in his capacities but what if it took time to emerge? Or what if he was too damaged to perceive it?

"So this is Atupio?" he asked, looking around incredulously at the plantfoam walls and the tree window onto the riverbed and the fish.

"We've been through this."

"I know. I'm sorry, but no one ever mentioned anything about biological architecture. And the BioPen . . . Since when does Atupio deal in human resources?"

"It doesn't," she replied, scratching her brow with a fingertip. "The BioPen has another purpose."

Amon waited for her to elaborate.

"The topic is very involved, and you're still"—her gaze flickered over his face with concern as she searched for the right way to put it—"acclimatizing."

"Involved . . ." Amon muttered. The deflection worried him, for the BioPen was at the core of his doubts about her.

"It's okay, Amon, you're safe now," said the Birla sister. "I could have Ono X give you a tour of the upper floors if you like. He can show you around our journalism outfit and Er for the Giftless. Would that put you at ease?"

Amon let out a sigh, then shook his head several times, his eyes clenched shut. He decided that he was being paranoid. The last few minutes had made it abundantly clear that he wasn't exactly in tip-top psychological shape. In all likelihood, he was simply recapitulating his tangle of tortured ruminations about whether to approach Rashana that he'd gone through again and again in the camps, as if all the wavering in his head about which sister was which had somehow mixed them up in reality. What was he thinking, that one sister was playing make-believe, pretending to be someone she disliked, perhaps even despised, for his benefit? It seemed unhealthy to entertain such delusions. If this woman claimed she was Rashana, better to accept that until there was good reason not to and get on with it.

Amon took a deep breath and did his best to sit up straight and still.

"So what happened to you in that missing week?" Rashana asked.

"I don't know if you want to hear it," said Amon. "It's too far-fetched. I don't even believe it myself."

What chance was there that he would run into Kitao, or that Kitao would take him on as a 'gardener' when he'd been dressed as a sectarian enemy? Unless his outfit had dissolved enough that the insignia was no longer distinguishable, though even then Kitao should have recognized his face, having looked straight at him during the sabotage just days earlier. Or was making Amon his 'gardener' meant to be a punishment? Would Amon have become a slave? But most absurd of all, was the idea that Amon could have flown safely from that window. And even if any of this *had* happened, several days still remained unaccounted for. Yet his survival in those circumstances—sleep-deprived, battered, feverish, and dehydrated during a famine, an enemy of everyone and friend of none—seemed almost as unlikely. So unless his memories were accurate, at the very least in some metaphorical sense, he was at a loss to explain his own existence.

"Probability is only a rough map of the border between fact and fantasy," said Rashana. "Talking might help to get it out of your system."

Amon nodded, agreeing that it might. Then he took another deep breath and began to tell her what had happened underground. When he reached his encounter with Mayuko in the chute, revulsion overtook him, and he pushed back his chair to dangle his head between his legs and retch. Three times he felt acidic pressure rise in his throat, but his esophagus held back the few bites he had got down.

"What's wrong?" asked Rashana.

"Mayuko," Amon cried out softly, as the final moment he had seen her came to him: lying beaten at the feet of the Emoticon Man and his guards on the glass-strewn floor of the weekly mansion, tears streaming down her cheeks onto her comet hair, meeting Amon's gaze as he rode the train to his bankdeath, her incisive eyes full of more love and pain than he could bear even to recall. "Where is she? Have you heard anything?"

"Nothing you don't already know I'm sure."

"Nothing?"

"We tried to contact her after you disappeared. We asked around at her company, Capsize Solutions, but she had stopped signing in—no notice. Her apartment contract had been terminated the same day, with all her furniture and personal effects left as is. That's everything we know."

"Was there any report of her bankdeath?"

"None."

"So you checked with GATA?"

Rashana's eyes jittered briefly. "My staff have just inquired for the fifteenth time now. A liquidation report was never issued nor was her data ever uploaded to the Archives."

"So she's still bankliving," Amon said excitedly. "She's alive."

Rashana just gave him a pitying look, as if to suggest that mere life wasn't necessarily something to celebrate. Amon clung stubbornly to his optimism.

"A–a woman came looking for me in Xenocyst," he stammered. "The guard who saw her made her sound like Mayuko."

"Let's hope it was and that she's safe."

"So you've really heard no news?"

"I'm afraid not."

Amon sighed again, his shoulders sinking with disappointment. He'd placed so much hope in Rashana to answer his many questions all those months in the District of Dreams, as he fretted about whether to approach her. Now he'd barely begun to ask them and already her lack of knowledge was glaring. *Only the PhisherKing might know Mayuko's whereabouts,* Amon realized, and thought he could hear the man's voice as though it had travelled to his ear along hidden folds in the air. *Can you swear to keep asking questions until no doubts remain in your mind?* Amon had been doing his best to fulfill his promise. He could only hope that the PhisherKing had kept his side of the bargain.

In the best case scenario where Monju had succeeded in blackmailing Mayuko's assailants, she would have still lost her job and home for Amon's sake, gone into hiding from the corporate forces that hounded him. In the worst case . . . he didn't want to consider it. She had been there for him during his tumultuous final days at GATA and had saved him from bankruptcy in the Open Source Zone. She had loved him, bravely putting herself in danger so that they might both escape. And she was the only person who knew him from childhood and understood how he'd come to be who he was now that—

Like a knife in the soul it hit Amon, the awful thing that he had refused to remember—the sound of a cold hand flopping into a dark puddle, the moment when he had accepted that his best friend was dead, laid out on the floor of an elevator in the flickering dim, after shedding one tear too many.

"I really wish I had more to tell you," Rashana said, pursing her lips sympathetically, as Amon grimaced and bared his teeth, lips curled outward, eyes watering.

"Not just her," he whispered. "It's Rick too."

"Oh . . . So the statement my reporters took from one of the men present during your altercation with Barrow was true? Is he . . ."

Amon nodded.

"A tear dust overdose?"

He nodded again. *Thud-splash.* He felt a tightness in his throat as sour, grating sadness rose from his chest to the back of his eyes.

"How awful. My sincere condolences." Rashana closed her eyes, and gave a solemn nod. "I didn't know him well, but he seemed like an upstanding and passionate person."

"Rick . . ." Amon's voice choked into nothing. "He said that you spoke with him at Er."

"Upstairs, yes." Rashana glanced at the thumb of her right hand as she slid it over the tips of her perfectly trimmed but unpolished fingernails.

"We originally admitted Rick in the afternoon following his identity murder," she told him. "I had placed Atupio on high alert for unusual behavior in Delivery because intelligence suggested that my twin would launch some sort of political shakeup. Lo and behold, that same day a crashdead Liquidator was wheeled into Delivery still in uniform–I had my staff observe him closely. We had no information about the man's identity, not even his name, but we established that he was important to someone when he was bumped to the head of the crashnewb processing line for his first genome reading. Even more suspicious, he was rejected from all brandclans even though Atupio's genetic analysis predicted that he should have been gifted according to the plutogenic algorithms of several Syndicate MegaGloms. In short, Rick was slated for transport to Welcome Chasm in a hurry, with complete disregard for his marketability. When we offered to take him into Er for the Giftless, the request was denied without any reason given."

"Rick never mentioned anything about going to Welcome Chasm," said Amon.

"No, because I sent a pair of mercenaries to intercept the dump crew. They retrieved him while he was still unconscious. Lucky timing too."

"Why do you say that?"

"One of the dump crew was carrying a somnambul duster."

"To silence him."

Rashana nodded gravely. "Few survive Welcome Chasm as it is, but Rick was the only person at that stage who knew someone was after Barrow. The Philanthropy Syndicate thought it was worth investing in deranging him to be absolutely sure he didn't talk—at least until Barrow had been taken out later that night."

Amon recalled the day that he and Rick had peered into Welcome Chasm, watching speechless as crashnewbs awoke in that disposcraper crack to debilitating webloss. To think that Rick had almost met the same pathetic fate to which he and Amon had unknowingly condemned so many as Liquidators . . . a worse fate in fact, for he would have been lurching around in a fugue of unrestful sleepwalking punctuated by narcoleptic spurts of unrested waking, burning scarce calories night and day, unconsciously abandoning what shelter he might find for some random ledge or gutter, losing the hold on sanity that only REM sleep can bring—even though he deserved to be marked as gifted! A convulsion of sadness and rage shook Amon's body. *Thud-splash.*

"Thank you." He rose and bowed to Rashana, a tear falling onto the coral tabletop. "If not for you, I never would have seen him again,"

"Don't mention it," she replied. "Above all, it was in our interests to question him."

"I just wish he was . . . " Amon's voice gave out on him again. *Still here,* his thoughts finished as more tears fell.

"Here," said Rashana. Amon saw through blurry eyes that she was proffering a handkerchief. He nodded another thanks, took the handkerchief, sat back down, and wiped his face. The fabric was smooth and glistening with greenish flecks on white, like seashell turned silk.

"So your meeting with Rick," said Amon.

"Are you sure you're ready to talk about this?" Rashana asked.

"I'm fine," he replied, but his soft, nasally voice belied his fragility.

"Only if you insist."

Amon nodded even as he sniffled.

"First, I should tell you that when the mercenaries dropped Rick off here"—Rashana's finger pointed straight up from the tabletop to indicate the upper floors of Atupio—"my staff didn't consider him an especially valuable source. His LifeStream had already been extracted and licensed out. He couldn't tell us anything about who had tried to sic him on Barrow or why. The only useful implication of his account was that Barrow had been set up for a fall. But by the time we'd gleaned this from him, it was too late to intervene. Rick had been out cold until nightfall. You had completed the identity assassination several hours before our interrogations began."

Rashana paused to gaze with something like wonder at Amon, and he looked away, ashamed of how he'd allowed himself to be used.

"I was interested in Rick personally because I knew he'd been your partner and friend. I had little hope that he would know where you were. He'd crashed before you disappeared. But I thought he might offer some kind of insight. You two had known each other for nearly your entire lives after all. So I asked him where you'd be if you were bankdead."

"Rick told me you were none too impressed with his answer."

"What was it? Something vague about you going wherever your will-power would be valued?"

"The way he told it was a bit different."

Rashana's eyes twitched and grew distant. "'Somewhere he could get promoted and live a quiet, orderly life,'" she recited. It was verbatim what Amon recalled Rick saying.

"I thought it was a pretty good hint myself," Amon reflected wistfully. "It sounds more like Xenocyst than anywhere else in the District of Dreams."

"Maybe to someone living there. To us, it sounded like the speculations of a crashnewb completely ignorant of how the bankdeath camps function. Strictly speaking there *is* no work in the camps, and so obviously no promotion either. Not even the Gifted Triangle offers true quiet or order."

"But still you decided to visit Delivery in person."

"I've been known to drop in from time to time."

"Why bother asking Rick about me again if he was so unhelpful before?"

The Birla sister watched her thumb slide across her nails again. "Xenocyst had requested that Rick be released from Er to live there," she said. "Not explicitly by name. But it's unusual for the council to proactively select our Er graduates. Usually they depend on recommendations from our psychiatrists. Otherwise crashnewbs can be a liability. Webloss relapses. Atupio approved the request. We'd already determined that Rick knew nothing of value and I'd given no special orders to retain him. But when I heard about the council's request, I wondered about their reasons. If they'd been specifically seeking Rick, that meant someone at Xenocyst knew who he was. Obviously, that someone would have to be you. So I decided to check Rick's supply gate and arranged to be there."

"I was there, too, you know," Amon rasped quietly.

"You were?"

In his mind's eye, Amon could see Rashana speaking to Rick up ahead in the exit line at Delivery, while he hung back so she wouldn't notice him. This had been the day that Amon reunited with Rick and learned that he was alive. It seemed like a prank pulled by fate now that he was gone again. To believe your best friend dead and find out you were wrong only to watch them die . . . from the time Amon left the elevator that served as Rick's tomb until he woke up only a short time ago, he'd been struggling on the edge of survival. Now it occurred to him that he hadn't had a single moment to grieve. He recalled their awkward embrace as they gathered for the supply run, and the night they clung together for warmth in the crashing typhoon. Never to feel his friend's body or hear his voice again. And before Amon knew it, tears were pouring from his eyes. He tried to wipe them away with the handkerchief, but couldn't keep up with the torrent, and pressed the fabric to the top of his cheeks to stem the flow.

"Take as much time as you need, Amon," said Rashana, her voice coming from the doorway now. "We can pick this up later."

Amon wanted to tell her that he was okay, that he still had more questions he so desperately wanted to ask, but the sobs wracking his body made speech impossible, and soon his wet face was in his hands, all thought seared away by the enveloping white pain of sorrow.

3

For some time after his last fit of sobbing had ceased, Amon sat hunched forward, drawing slow, rustling breathes, and listening to the sibilant choir of the various organisms composing the building. When at last he was ready to raise his head, he stared blankly over the coral at the plantfoam wall.

Protruding from the woven slab of vegetation were tiny flowers in manifold colors—from mocha to white to vermillion to saffron with various dots and markings. It wasn't long before he began to suspect that some of them were moving. After observing in silence for several minutes more, he realized it was the red blossoms. They were pulsating, petals opening and contracting ever so slowly like the fingers of an anaesthetized hand making and relaxing a fist.

Eventually, he remembered the tree window and changed his seat to a spot across the table from the door where he could see it. In his hollow state, the smooth circulations of the fishes were almost soothing. He wasn't as drained as he might have expected and began to feel gradually less vulnerable as the seconds ticked by. His mind remained sapped of any impetus for thought until the painting hissed open.

In stepped Ono X bearing a steaming towel on the flat of his upraised palms. He came around the table and proffered it to Amon with one hand as he plucked up the soaked handkerchief from atop the coral with the other. Amon took the towel and wiped the residue of tears from his face. The fabric resembled cotton, but was mossy and soft like the chairs and seemed to give off its own refreshing warmth and moisture.

When he withdrew the living towel from his face, Ono X was gone and Rashana was standing in the doorway.

"Am I disturbing you?" she asked.

"No, please come"—Amon cleared his croaky throat—"please come in. I'm sorry for falling apart."

"No need to apologize," said Rashana, as she stepped in and took the seat directly in front of the door. "Our psychiatricorps is amazed that you're as stable and coherent as you are. You've been through a lot."

"I didn't even finish telling you what happened to me."

"We can come back to that any time. There's no rush. Would you like anything to eat, drink?"

"I don't have much appetite. Maybe some more water?"

"Of course." Rashana flicked her fingers to summon help. "You were severely malnourished when we found you," she said. "You've been absorbing nothing but nutrient vapor for days. My medicorps says it will take time to adjust to solid food. Shall I arrange for Ono X to take you on that tour? Or I can have him show you to one of the guest rooms."

Amon folded the self-warming towel and placed it on the coral. "Thank you," he said, "but if you don't mind, I'd like to ask you a few more questions."

"Are you sure you're up to it?"

"Positive. I'm feeling surprisingly awake now."

Rashana gave him a knowing smile. "What sort of questions do you have?"

"Maybe I can start with jubilee," said Amon. "What do you know about jubilee?"

Finally, the most puzzling question of all had emerged from the clutter of his confusion.

"Jubilee? As in the anniversary of a pope or queen?"

"No. Or, I don't think so. It's a Fertilex property. I was charged an enormous amount for performing it. Then I was put on a Fertilex customer service blacklist. You must know about it."

"I'm afraid not."

After Amon told his story about how a Blinder had taken the bank-death penalty to expose his identity and thereby allow Fertilex to charge him illegitimately for a mysterious action, Rashana twitched out a few command gestures.

"I looked into it but there's no record that Fertilex ever owned a property called jubilee," she told him.

"Then it must have been erased," said Amon.

"Or perhaps I've been denied access to the files concerned. Executive control of Fertilex would be required either way."

"So you think it was your sister?"

Tension passed over Rashana's brow for just a moment, and Amon finally guessed what it was: she didn't like the word sister.

"Who else could it have been?" said Rashana. "Only my twin would be able to put you on the blacklist."

"But I don't see why she would sacrifice one of her agents to charge me some random amount when she could have just set it higher and bankrupted me instead."

"I don't either, Amon. I wish I understood her better. Perhaps something will come in."

Amon was disappointed, as with their discussion of Mayuko, to find that there were limits to what Rashana could illuminate. Maybe his hopes had been unrealistic. *What were you expecting, omniscience?* he thought. Then again, if the secondary heir to the Birla fortune couldn't explain jubilee, with all her money and influence over Fertilex, who could? The primary heir? From everything Amon had heard about Anisha, he doubted that asking her would be fruitful—or safe.

"I guess I'll move on," he said, sounding dismayed despite himself. "Can I ask you about the time I contacted you?"

"When Hippo approached me on your behalf."

"No. When I called you."

Rashana glanced pensively at the vibrant flittering mosaic beyond the window. "You must mean your message the day after we met in Ginza."

"Yes. I was on my way to the District of Dreams. So much would have been different if I could have reached you then."

"Very different. We could have been having this conversation months ago."

"How come you didn't pick up?"

"I was in mourning."

This was not the sort of reply Amon had been expecting. But it made perfect sense; the Birla founders had died only days earlier. "My condolences for the loss of your parents."

Again, something in what Amon said seemed to bother her, and she let out a barely audible snort.

"Don't think me heartless for saying this, but I was mourning someone else."

"Oh . . . May I ask who?"

"One of the BioPen youth."

"From downstairs? They're so young . . ."

"They are," she said softly, her gaze dragged down by something like sorrow or regret. "Just little children."

Curious, but not wanting to pry just yet, Amon said, "So you were too upset to take my call."

"Not just yours. I had my notifications off. For Atupio, for the Birla Guard, for everyone. I was devastated. By chance, I happened to check my messages a few minutes later. I called you back right away. But I couldn't get through."

"And that's when you started to search for me."

"I had Ono X contact you at first to see if you were blocking me. When he couldn't get through either, we reached out to GATA to check if you'd cash crashed. That was when I tried to license your genome and learned that your LifeStream wasn't in the Archives, as I said. No liquidation report had been issued for you."

"This situation left us with a puzzle. On the one hand, you had sent me a message saying you were going to the District of Dreams, you were impossible to reach as though you were indeed disconnected, and your employment at the Liquidation Ministry had been terminated that day. Ono X also acquired segs from witnesses to Sekido and your colleagues, Freg and Tororo, trying to crash you at a jazz bar. All this would suggest that you were bankdead. But there was no evidence that you had in fact been liquidated."

Her palms resting flat on the coral, she glanced out the tree-shaped window with a slight frown and then back at Amon.

"We still don't understand, even now that we've found you. You're obviously disconnected from the AT market and the ImmaNet. But our diagnostic scanners detected your BodyBank. So what is your status, Amon? Are you bankdead or bankliving?"

"Both, sort of," he replied.

"How could that be?"

"I committed identity suicide."

"Ah." Rashana didn't seem as surprised by this as Amon was expecting. "With the Death Codes. Because you were an Identity Executioner."

Amon nodded.

"Why would you do that?"

"This topic is very involved." He attempted a wry smile, pleased to be returning her enigmatic parry, but doubted it came out as anything but a woeful smirk, as the scene that had driven him to that fateful choice arose. Mayuko lying on the glass-strewn floor. And yet he was surprised to find the memory less upsetting than it had been only a short time earlier. Perhaps crying had helped him come to terms with the grinding horror that was his past. Perhaps it had simply numbed him.

"I'm sure it is . . ." said Rashana, reciprocating with a smile much more convincing than his. "Well, whatever your reasons, identity suicide was a bold and crafty move. You know that you're the first in history to commit it."

"So I'm told."

"None of us even considered the possibility. Not Ono X or the other Birla Guard, not my Cognitive Handling Corps, certainly not me. Not my twin and her associates either I suppose. The confusion about your financial status haunted all our search efforts."

"How so?"

Rashana rubbed her brow. "We started looking for you in the District of Dreams. That was where you said you'd be in your message. But you never turned up among the giftless crashnewbs that we sometimes accept into Er, or the crashnewbs in transit to the Gifted Triangle. GATA had never transported you to Delivery at all. We took this as proof that you were still bankliving. So we focused our search on places in the camps where the bankliving gather—the slum resorts and kansha hotels and all the rest. Also on Free Tokyo in case you'd gone back."

"That's why you never thought to check Xenocyst," Amon supposed. "I mean, the border sentries refuse anyone with the Elsewhere Gaze, and the residents shun outsiders. It's not exactly the first place you'd think to go rooting around for bankliving runways."

"I wouldn't give yourself all the credit. There were other impediments to our search than just your identity suicide. Obviously, our team swept the deeper recesses of the District of Dreams as best it could, including Xenocyst. I mobilized Atupio reporters for that purpose. But we were understaffed. My organization had been gutted just a few days earlier."

"Because Anisha diverted funds to the Gyges Circle," said Amon, remembering the segs from the PhisherKing that proved Atupio had paid for all credicrimes associated with his identity assassination of Barrow. It had been Hippo's conjecture that Anisha temporarily seized Atupio to siphon its assets and frame Rashana.

"You're surprisingly well-informed for crashdead," she said, her eyes brightening with admiration. "My twin's restructuring left us short on personnel, especially those experienced in navigating the camps. It's hard enough to locate a single person in a city as dense and amorphous as the District of Dreams. It's even harder with the organization that owns it blocking your initiatives any way it can. Philanthropy Syndicate drones neutralized our reconnaissance flyers, their freekeepers barred my agents wherever they found them, and their accountants forced Atupio to shoulder high fines for trespassing everywhere we went. Add to this the fact that we were expecting someone digimade, or at least with the Elsewhere Gaze, who was not hooked up to the supply system—in other words, the fact that we had our search terms wrong."

There was another hiss from the doorway as Ono X entered, placed a glass of water in front of Amon, retrieved the continuously steaming towel, and left.

"I spent most of my first few weeks hidden away in an elevator or in the library of the Cyst," Amon recalled. "They stripped me of my uniform before I even got there and kept me in Fleet clothes like any other bankdead. Only the Xenocyst council and a handful of other residents knew who I was. In the mornings, I went outside for my construction duties but, other than the people on my crew, I doubt the community even noticed I was there. On top of everything else, I wasn't exactly standing in plain sight."

"But Amon, those weren't even the worst of the obstacles we faced." Rashana pressed her fingertips into her temples as though she suddenly had a headache.

"What else?" asked Amon.

"Copies of you."

"Copies?"

"Copies. Even on the first day of our search when we checked crossings into the camps, we found you on a chartered bus over the Bridge of Compassion, and on a private jet over the Tokyo Canal, *and* on a hijacked ship over the Sanzu River. You were in three different places at once! Do you understand? There were people digimade exactly like you—Mayuko, too, when we started to look for her. Thousands of them everywhere we turned, gallivanting about all over Free Tokyo and the District of Dreams."

"What the fuck . . .?" Amon marveled, not mentioning that he had been the one on the ship.

"My sentiments exactly. It was an XXXTrust scheme. They scattered red herrings to the winds. By the time we tracked any of them down, they had reverted to their original appearance, and someone else somewhere had become you or Mayuko."

Amon was reminded of the little bulbs on the anadeto vending machines at the Tezuka, some blinking on the moment others blinked off. This transitioned to a memory from the floor where the machines were housed: his first encounter with the PhisherKing, digiguised as Mayuko to trick him into giving up segs of Barrow's identity assassination. This in turn recalled something from on the way to the Barrow mission earlier that day—the InfoMoon displaying a doppelganger of Amon that advertised a dating app called Instant Get—and suddenly he came to a realization.

"With our likenesses!" Amon exclaimed, slapping the coral in astonishment. "XXXTrust cheated us both out of our likenesses when we were just teenagers."

He felt anew the shame of letting the MegaGlom turn him into a wandering smorgasbord of porno while he ran to the Open Source Zone. On the brink of bankruptcy, he had auctioned his body space for a smidgen of credit to see him through.

"So they were preying on the poor . . . those desperate enough to serve as distractions," he said.

"Not exclusively. XXXTrust did contact many bankliving to cut deals for body space rental. But some bankdead they digimade unilaterally. They also sprinkled figments of you two here and there. Those put up a good chase, then vanished the moment our search crew caught up with them."

Rashana let out another soft snort and rolled her eyes.

"That all sounds like an enormous cost," said Amon. "Why? Why would XXXTrust care about us?"

"It wasn't as expensive as you might think. The likenesses were already their properties to use as they wished, the rental costs to willing bankliving were negligible, and the fines to bankdead for infringing their image rights were half price. All in all, a trivial investment by MegaGlom standards.

"As to their motivations for protecting you, we're not sure. You may be aware that XXXTrust is a member of the SpawnU Consortium. My guess is that they determined you were a threat to the Philanthropy Syndicate and wanted to ensure that you remained at large."

"The search operation must have been pricey for you though."

"Astronomical. With the constant mobilization of our staff and the fines for stalking and mass surveillance, it had to be the costliest wild goose chase in the Free Era."

"Devious," said Amon, admiring XXXTrust's affordable ruse.

"It gets worse," Rashana told him, her razor lashes trembling over angry eyes. "A week into the search, my engineers finished designing algorithms to help decide which copies were worth hunting down. It detected slight incongruities in gait, height, mannerism, job and other features. Then it dismissed or recommended pursuing each person sighted accordingly. This cut down greatly on wasted creditime.

"Then one day, we received a report from a food delivery informant about a couple living in a shabby apartment in the Sugamo station area. Whenever one of them came to the door to receive their groceries, they were wearing a generic digiguise. But once, after the woman had made her delivery, she peeked through the crack as the door was closing and saw them revert to the digimakes of you and Mayuko. It was the first time our team had the two of you in one place, and you appeared to remain inside 24/7, having all essentials delivered. The algorithm gave its strongest recommendation to pursue thus far.

"We'd never been so certain it was you and your friend," Rashana said. "There you were at last, hiding in the midst of all those pesky copies. So I ordered Ono X to marshal the Birla Guard . . . a disastrous mistake."

"Why disastrous?" asked Amon.

"When they arrived at the entrance to the building, my twin's Birla Guard were already there. They must have received a similar 'tipoff.' The shootout that ensued lasted for over an hour."

"Oh my . . . Who did the couple turn out to be?"

"You wouldn't believe." Rashana shook her head as her eyes turned upward. "It was Ono X who fought his way into the apartment first. He kicked down the door. And who was waiting for him but a SpillBot and a FillBot, engaged on the floor as if to mock us."

At the image of two insectile robots humping, Amon couldn't help laughing.

"The real punchline is that two of my men almost died. We're just grateful that epilepsy dust is only semi-lethal."

"Sorry," said Amon.

Rashana gave him a wry smile to show she wasn't offended before she went on. "After a similar run-in between Atupio scouts and a Charity Brigade squadron in the camps not a week later, I decided to call off the search. I assumed that you were bankliving and that you'd either never made it to the District of Dreams or that you were long gone. You could have been anywhere on earth for all we knew."

Amon nodded, both satisfied and amazed by her account. He'd never understood why the two richest people in the world, with their almost limitless Freedom, had failed for months to locate him, a mere bankdead with nothing but a nerve duster and the flaking clothes on his back. But his unprecedented and thus unimaginable identity suicide along with XXXTrust's unusual intervention had led the sisters astray, while the conflict between them had further impeded the search. Choosing to crash himself, it seemed, had done more to protect him than he ever could have guessed. A stroke of good luck—or bad luck, depending on how he appraised his sojourn in the District of Dreams. He thought once more of Barrow's face, of innocent bankdead dying in the famine, of Xenocyst ravaged, his friends gone, Rick's eyes dripping his life away, and again he was surprised to find that none of these memories disturbed him anymore. They may as well have been segs from someone else's LifeStream, impersonal records observed from the outside rather than experiences undergone from within. From this eerily distanced vantage on his past, Amon could only conclude that choosing to input the Death Codes into his own BodyBank had indeed been profoundly fortunate—not least because he had ended up in the hands of the one person that could save him.

Amon lifted his glass intending to take a sip but found himself so thirsty that he kept on drinking. When he had finished the water, he put the glass down with a gasp of refreshment, then turned to Rashana and said, "But you never did give up entirely on the idea that I was in the District of Dreams. You met with Rick and Hippo to ask about me."

Rashana's gaze went to her thumb sliding over her fingernails. "Final desperate efforts," she said.

"Is that all they were? I mean, you spoke with Rick twice. And Hippo told me that you thought they were lying about not knowing where I was."

"I never accused them of lying. I was only suspicious because my psychiatricorps inferred their dishonesty from visual cues. But I ultimately downgraded the probability of their judgement. I found it hard to believe that you wouldn't have sought me out."

She looked hurt again and Amon lowered his eyes to the coral, reluctant to broach the awkward topic.

"You knew, you had to know, that I was looking for you," she persisted. "Either Rick had told you or Hippo. Correct?"

"Both," Amon admitted. "They both told me."

"Then you could have got in touch with me whenever you wished. All you had to do was say the word to one of the Atupio staff I keep posted at Delivery or have Hippo ring the signal bells and I'd have been there. But you decided not to. You didn't want to find me or for me to find you."

"Please don't take it personally. It's not as simple as that."

"No? I offer you a job in Ginza and you turn it down like I'm some rambling creep. Then you toss my business card in the trash outside the restaurant. I know. Ono X saw you do it. Nevertheless, I forgive you after you call me. I think that you've changed your mind about me, that you've seen the value in the opportunity I offered. And I search and I search and I search with my own twin and more than half the MegaGloms in the world against me and finally I get a message to you through your friends, people that you trust. And what do you do? You choose to weather a famine over meeting with me?"

Her lashes seemed to wilt as she glared at him, sediments of an emotion like sadness or confusion layered deep into her eyes.

"I'm sorry," said Amon. "I . . ." He took a moment to think how to justify his caution delicately, without using the word sister—a serious challenge given that Anisha had everything to do with it. Or should he just tell her straightforwardly that he'd been terrified of mixing them up? No, better to skip ahead and describe the less offensive conundrum that arose later.

"Hippo and Barrow convinced me that I could trust you, but Rick decided he wanted to stay. See, I didn't know this at the time, but he'd fallen in love with a Xenocyst girl—the woman who picked him up from Er, her name is Vertical—and he kept saying that reaching out to you was too risky. I tried my best to convince him, I really did . . . I didn't realize he was just making excuses to stay with her. By the time I was almost ready to contact you without him, I was proposing the exposé to the council. Then I felt responsible to see it through. That's why I only asked you to meet me when the sabotage was over."

Rashana's shoulders fell gently with an unheard sigh.

"Well, better late than never," she said, her smile offset by downcast eyes. "I was so surprised and impressed when Xenocyst called on me and Hippo told me that you'd come up with a way of bringing the Charity Gift Economy to light. It was a brilliant idea."

"What do you mean?" Amon demanded. "It was a disaster."

Swooping drones bleeding eyes homes in rubble mangled face... He anticipated another shudder at this barrage of memory, but faced it down once again with unusual equanimity.

"Any radical plan for change will reckon with hidden correctives," said Rashana. "What's important is that we succeeded at our objective."

"So your reporters were able to get the footage we needed?" Amon asked with breathless hope, wanting to believe that all the sacrifices they had made for his proposal had come to something worthwhile.

"Enough to produce plenty of clips for the feeds. Viewers could see unmistakably that babies are sifted by genome and that parents whose babies are accepted receive more supplies. We also captured the career volunteers denying supplies to your agent provocateur when she tried to take back the infant."

Again Amon recalled Vertical diving between the legs of the freekeeper.

"The ensuing crackdown perpetrated by both freekeepers and CareBots we turned into a short documentary, with running commentary on the mortal danger of so-called 'non-lethal crowdcare.'"

Suddenly the coordinated circulations of the fish beyond the tree window, displaying an almost mechanized combination of order and spontaneity, seemed to resemble CareBots patrolling over the Bridges to Delivery. The swarm of drones raining dust on Amon in the bankdead stampede, Rick hunched in the elevator. He found himself tracing this association with an almost objective calm, as though the transition from now to these events carried him beyond the boundaries of his self.

"All in all, it was a compelling audiovisual package," Rashana concluded.

"Did it have an effect?" Amon asked.

"As much as we could have hoped for, and only a few short days since its release. I'll spare you the niceties of the political ramifications. Suffice to say for now that we made it clear to the public that the Philanthropy Syndicate was responsible for the critically low supply levels. Among savvy voters who are aware that parties represent their lobbies, this reflected poorly on the Absolute/Full Choice coalition. The bad optics then sent Full Choice into a panic. Contra Absolute choice, they supported an emergency bill that SpawnU and I paid Moderate Choice to propose. This was to repeal the legislation suppressing crowdcare fines, and Full Choice dissolved the coalition the moment it passed. Effectively, our counter pitypromo campaign brought an end to the credicrime subsidies that the Philanthropy Syndicate depends on to manage bankdead backlash. Without them, the supply reduction has lost its financial logic as we had hoped."

"So the famine is over?" Amon asked. He was back in the camps, with the swollen bellies, emaciated limbs, skeletal faces, shriveled children, babies drying in the sun, reminiscing over these horrors with a level of acceptance that unnerved him. "You're telling me there are no more shortages?"

"That's correct, Amon, for the time being at least. Our—" Rashana paused as her eyeballs began to jounce spasmodically, almost seismically.

"What's wrong?"

"Nothing to worry about," she said with calm indifference, closing her eyes. "Just a minor attack on my BodyBank."

"You're being hacked?" said Amon, straightening up in his chair, alarmed. "Who would—"

"My twin. We've been known to have cyber skirmishes from time to time. So"—the vibrations in Rashana's eyelids subsided into stillness and she opened her eyes—"the shortages . . . it will take a few more days for shipment quantities to return to normal. In the meantime, several new venture charities are being funded to pick up the slack by a surge in investitarian donations. This should lift most bankdead from starvation levels to their usual mild malnutrition shortly. Assuming that the political situation holds. It's complicated and developing as we speak."

A soft wave of relief stroked through Amon. His plan had not been a complete failure. Countless lives had been saved. Then he remembered that Rick had tried to convince him of the same before the end. The sabotage debacle was one of the last things they discussed.

"So many people dear to me lost . . . but at least we succeeded . . . at least . . ."

Amon trailed off when he saw Rick stream tears of blood and realized that he felt nothing. The dissolving FirefLyte above Rick's body in the elevator seemed to glow with Barrow's pulped face, the death of Amon's friend and the maiming of his idol fusing. And yet, his breath remained calm, his mind cupped in a placid shell. Could a single outpouring of grief work such wonders? Had he already been purged of a lifetime of pain?

"Amon," said Rashana.

"Yes."

"I'd like to apologize."

"Apologize? For what?"

"For Barrow. He must have told you that he was one of our patients in Er for the Giftless."

"I believe he mentioned it."

"Well, as with Rick, I gave no special orders to retain him after my staff had finished their interrogations. He was released as soon as his treatment program concluded. A reckless oversight on my part. I saw no value in keeping him after we'd acquired his wealth of political knowledge. I failed to realize that he himself was of value."

"How so?"

"His eloquence and charm made him an attractive tool even when bankdead. If only I could have seen it before my twin."

"*She's* the one who approached him in Xenocyst," Amon hissed. "*She* gave him the weapons that tipped the civil war in his favor."

"I'm truly sorry, Amon. They used him to destroy Xenocyst, and I let him fall into their grasp."

To Amon's surprise and embarrassment, Rashana stood up and bowed deeply, short hair dangling almost to the table. She held her head at waist level for a few beats before righting herself and returning to her seat.

"It's not your fault," he said, unable to meet her apologetic gaze. "I mean, I was the one who convinced Ty to give Barrow a chance. No one could have seen that coming."

"If anyone should have, it was me . . ."

4

Amon was astonished by this show of humility and care from such a proud and powerful person. She was like no one he had ever met.

It occurred to him that Rashana was an incredibly attentive listener and storyteller. Not only had she waited through his scattered questions and recounting, but she'd been willing to fill him in with words alone, never displaying frustration at her inability to use videos as any other Free Citizen certainly would have. Amon himself, before his bankdeath and webloss recovery, would have found this mode of communication maddeningly plodding. Then he recalled that she had insisted on conversing verbally the first time they met and an even bigger question presented itself.

"One last thing."

"It doesn't have to be the last, Amon."

"Ok. Why me?"

"You're asking me to explain why you've suffered? You want my pity?"

"No, not that. I mean . . . for months now, I've been in an information desert. I learned a lot from all the stories I heard in the District of Dreams and from the library in the Cyst," *and from the sky*, Amon thought to himself. "But there's a limit to how much we can know without the ImmaNet. Now you've answered most of the questions I've been dying and dying to ask . . . and I still don't understand you.

"You're the second richest person on earth. You're the owner of Atupio. You save so many giftless lives. Hippo and Barrow praised your humanitarian work. You helped us end the famine. But like the rest of your family, you stay out of the public eye. I know you're quarreling with your sister about something, probably to do with the Fertilex inheritance in some way or other. Both of you reached out to me around the time you received your shares.

"You came to find me in that cafe. You told me you want to create some sort of community where people can be more in touch with nature. You offered me a job that I rejected on the spot. Still you kept the offer open and told me to call you. Really? I mean, my concentration scores were good and I was a successful Liquidator, but you're the co-owner of the largest human resources producer in the world. I'm sure you have whole flocks of talented order-grown to pick from. All the money and manpower you threw away just to track me down, and you jumped at the opportunity to help the Xenocyst council with my plan. Now you're giving me shelter and medical attention and taking the time to speak with me. It's kind of you. You saved my life. But . . . why me? Why?"

While clarifying his question aloud, Amon had stared at his hands clasping and fidgeting atop the coral. When he asked it for the second time, he looked at Rashana timidly, expecting to wilt from her fierce gaze. Instead, he found her smiling with her whole face, warm wrinkles radiating from her eyes. It was a smile he recalled seeing once before, when she was digimade as a man and he had told her that he dreamed of a forest. As then, it was gone in an instant, wiped away by a blink of her blades, and her stern, intensely focused expression returned as though it had never been interrupted. But after this glimpse of her underlying approval, her mask lost its intimidating air, and Amon found his gaze locking with hers, a scintilla of vague understanding shared between them.

"I've just taken the rest of the day off," said Rashana. "Shall we finish our conversation elsewhere?"

Amon thought of his promise to the PhisherKing. *Can you swear to keep asking questions until no doubts remain in your mind?* Then the idea of waiting another moment to resolve his long-festering bewilderment became unbearable, and he rose abruptly to his feet.

The vibrant beads of the diamond painting retracted as Rashana approached the doorway, and Amon followed her out.

In the hallway, Ono X stood facing them. He was now wearing the clouded gold uniform of the Birla Guard, but with the usual head covering removed and the sleeves rolled up to his elbows.

"Amon, I'd like to properly introduce Ono X, captain of the Birla Guard and head of Atupio intelligence."

Ono X bowed deeply. "I look forward to working with you," he said, his voice whispery but deeper and more masculine than when he was the conduit for Rashana's words.

Amon returned the greeting with a slight bow, wondering for the first time what the "X" stood for. As with the Geminis, could there be an Ono Y, or even an Ono Z? He recalled the hints of Ono X's ruthless efficiency in Rashana's account of the Xenocyst civil war, sneaking about and sniping her sister, and made a mental note to be careful around this soft-spoken heavyweight. Like his voice, Ono X's expression was changed somehow. The sardonic turn of his lips still embellished his cool, streamline visage, but it was difficult now to tell where he was looking, with his lids remaining low over beady dark eyes. A connection formed.

"You were the driver, weren't you?" said Amon, remembering the man who had driven him and Makesh Adani through Ginza. That was how Ono X must have seen him toss the business card. He had been waiting in the car. Ono X's grin further lifted the right side of his lips.

"Good memory, Amon," said Rashana. "It's as if you can access that LifeStream of yours."

Ono X led Amon and Rashana back along the florid plantfoam hallway to the beehive elevator. There he inserted his finger into the genome reader, gestured palm-up to the open doorway for the two of them to board, stepped in after them, and slid his finger into another aperture, closing the honeycomb doors.

The elevator ascended for no more than a second before the doors opened onto what appeared to be a regular steel shipping elevator. Ono X waited for Rashana and Amon to enter first. Once they were all inside, the honeycomb doors and the inner doors closed behind them, the crack sealing itself so perfectly that it might have been a steel wall all along. *A trick elevator?* Amon supposed, when the doors in front of them slid apart.

Cool wind hummed on his face and slipped into the collar of his gown to brush his chest. Beyond the threshold, a thin gruel of illumination seeping through the frosted glass skylight revealed a cavernous room interiored floor to ceiling with circular steel tiles.

As Amon tailed Rashana towards the center, the wind grew stronger and rippled his gown against him. He was looking around for a fan or a vent, wondering what this room could be for, when he noticed a disturbance in the air just ahead. A blur loomed over them, like a dense sandstorm of greyish, nearly transparent grains that had been sculpted into a mid-size jet, like some restless gossamer Zen garden rocket. They were approaching the sleek body from the starboard side of the rear, its material squirming ceaselessly even as the form it took never changed. A flow of particulate churned along the same contours, raising wind and a dampened whir. What else could this spectral aircraft be but Gemini X parked in its hangar?

When Rashana had nearly reached the streaming solid, a rift split its way down the surface, revealing the exterior of a black jet with the same dimensions—yet smaller, like the second layer of a Matryoshka doll. It had been hidden from view by the visual distortions of the outer sheath.

Just as Rashana stepped into the rift, a panel folded down from the inner craft, opening a portal in the black wall and serving as a ramp.

Amon followed Rashana up the sloping black slab and passed between fully uniformed Birla Guards flanking the portal, assault dusters strapped to their backs.

Through the dim interior of the craft Amon trod carefully, as he followed her shadowy figure and footsteps towards the front. He could make out the walls just well enough to tell that the long black cabin was slightly over twice the width of his arms held out straight, though it felt more spacious than that since it was devoid of furniture—or appeared to be so, until the space began to lighten and a silhouette emerged along the left wall ahead. Up closer, Amon saw it was a round chair of grooved pink ceramic, like a brain leaned backwards on its stem with a nook for a person on the underside.

"Please take a seat," said Rashana, taking an identical chair that faced the first, a coffee table between them. Amon settled awkwardly into the nook, so deep his long limbs spilled from the edges. In the wall to his left above the table and across the corridor to his right were windows, through both of which entered the palest glow. He supposed it must come from the skylight, as he'd spotted no lights in either the hangar or the craft. Then it occurred to him that this had not been true elsewhere in the complex. The stories of Rick and others about Er for the Giftless, he now recalled, had mentioned lighting in the ceilings, which made sense since crashnewbs lived there. But why had someone gone to the trouble of engineering the plantfoam on the lower floors so that it emitted that apricot luminescence? Free Citizens were usually content with digital light, the ImmaNet providing all the vision they needed. It was for this reason that most of Tokyo was, unbeknownst to its inhabitants, an abyss of darkness in the naked world. He could only conclude that the children in the BioPen, perhaps their guardians also, were burdened with eyes that saw the old fashioned way. They were, as he had suspected, bankdead.

Before he could even speculate on the reasons, Gemini X began to lift off. So gentle was the rotorcraft, like a balloon rising on hot air, that he almost didn't notice. First the whir rose in pitch to a pleasant, melodic flutter reminiscent of a hummingbird's wingbeats. Then the sheath sloughed away, unveiling Amon's window as it spiraled upwards, spinning out the now open skylight and pulling the inner jet body towards the clear winter sky.

Against deep radiant blue, Amon could see through his window the flowing particles that had been the jet-sheath now turning rapidly above the craft, an ever-swirling tornado of faint clear specks like non-reflective glass that served as their rotor, propelling them ever higher.

Looking down, he watched the open skylight recede, cut into the concrete roof of a skyscraper. As Gemini X pulled out further, he saw in stages that the skyscraper rose some ten stories from a larger concrete surface, that eleven identical skyscrapers were arrayed with the first in a rounded grid, that the supporting surface was a hexagon one hundred times the area of each of them. This crown of towers was elevated another dozen stories above the grey-green waters of the Tokyo Canal, serving as the roof of the main structure of Atupio Home Office.

The visible portion of the complex was already enormous, rivaling even the immensity of Delivery, but he had seen that much more extended underwater—even below the riverbed—and judging from the spaciousness of the rooms that housed the sensory deprivation orchard and the gymnasium, it had to be of mindboggling total size, a whole self-contained city. He noted that the exterior—like the hangar and from what he had heard the humanitarian wings—lacked any signs of the biotecture on the lower floors. When he recalled what Rashana had said about the BioPen being confidential, he wondered if those remarkable materials and designs were likewise kept secret. The curtain of fish around the meeting room window certainly suggested as much. Yet the reasons were hard to fathom. Because wouldn't it be more prudent to go public with new advances and soak up the patent licensing fees? It seemed odd that a corporate tycoon like Rashana, who was no doubt a suave business operator, might choose to forsake such profits.

Once Gemini X was high enough for Amon to see southward along the curving length of the Tokyo Canal, it began to make a gradual clockwise turn as it ascended, before settling into an easterly trajectory with Amon's port-side window facing north. They were above the District of Dreams' northwestern shore, the crumbling block slumscape rolling straight ahead, and the blighted skyscraper reef of Free Tokyo sprawling north to the skyline. These two landmasses were divided in the near distance by the northernmost stub of the Tokyo Canal, where its iron-green form hooked east, ending at the triple-decker Bridge of Compassion, and by the Sanzu River, which picked up where the canal left off, a brown glimmering sliver arcing south. The bridge-cum-dam spanned snippets of streets that flowed with toy traffic between towers to the north, and the mirrored fortress of Delivery towards which supply pilgrims thronged the roofways and stairpaths to the south.

Amon was glad to find the crowds flowing into Delivery again. On his last sighting the morning after the sabotage, the bridges had been retracted across the moat and the gates had been sealed, with drones on high alert and the clogged roads stopped. The reversal of these measures fit Rashana's description of the political gains their exposé had reaped. And his relief at witnessing such improvements with his own eyes amped up the thrill of flying. He had never been a passenger in the air before—at least not while conscious—and the speed and altitude were exhilarating. Before Amon knew it, he was settled snugly into the nook of the chair, its pliant ceramic silently molding itself to his body much as the moss had earlier. Once again the comfort didn't last, as a worry arose.

"Where are we going exactly?"

"A part of Tokyo I'd like to show you."

"Okay. What part?"

"I'd prefer not to delve into that just yet. It would only confuse you."

"More than not knowing where I'm flying?"

"Flying into the unknown. A fitting metaphor for life, don't you think?"

Amon sighed. "You're going to keep me in the dark for the whole trip?"

"Is this what you call dark?" Rashana raised her right palm towards the window beside them. That was when Amon discovered that he could make out the sun for the first time since his cash crash. It floated in azure halfway between the roofscape horizon in the eastern distance and its winter zenith. Under morning sunlight, the world below was lucid, the shimmer of glass and water flaring and subsiding as Amon's perspective continued to incline.

"Don't worry, Amon. I promise we'll cover all of your concerns. I've left my execucorps in charge of my subsidiaries for the rest of the day. My secretaries will only forward messages that have direct bearing on our conversation. This is our time to talk and understand each other without any distractions."

Amon realized that she was the first bankliving person he had met who didn't have the Elsewhere Gaze. Her complete attention was for him, without any graphical veneer to intervene, each slash of her eyelashes announcing that immediacy.

Ono X emerged from the shadows of the deck bearing a round black tray with a white porcelain teapot and two teacups. He bent forward to place the tray on the coffee table, faint steam tendrilling delicately from the spout of the teapot, and set the cups before each of them on black mesh coasters. As Ono X poured first for Amon, he smelled citrus and watched earthy red liquid fill white china.

"I've spent my whole life hiding from the world just as we were taught," Rashana mused, when Ono X had melted back into the shadows. "There's so much that I've never told anyone."

She lifted her teacup and stared into it pensively.

"Some things may be better left forgotten and unsaid. But the truth about me has stagnated too long in my memory . . . far too long . . ."

Without taking a sip, she put the cup down, and looked out the window with a frown, rubbing her brow absentmindedly with her index finger. Then she turned abruptly to Amon with a gaze that was as piercing as always, but somehow also imploring.

"If there's anyone on earth who needs to understand me, it's you," she told him. "So forget about where we're going for now. I need your trust and for that I'm going to have to start at the beginning."

At the beginning of course, echoed the voice of Tamper. That had been his reply when Amon asked where to start his tale as payment for guiding him to the District of Dreams. They had been sitting on the bank of the Sanzu River that night, and Amon imagined the obese man still prowling those precincts in his strange jumpsuit of pockets, wondering how he was faring. After building his sabotage devices for Xenocyst, Tamper had returned to Free Tokyo, presumably to continue stalking his son. Since he had departed before everything went awry, he might still be okay—so long as he hadn't been busted for robbing vending machines—and Amon added him to his list of people to seek out, along with the PhisherKing, when he had the chance.

"Where is the beginning for you?" he asked, taking a sip from his cup.

"I'd better start with my twin," she said. "That's the part you have doubts about, is it not? That's the part that everyone has doubts about."

Amon didn't dare agree, so in lieu of a response he borrowed a mannerism from Rashana and peered into his teacup. He noticed that his hands were interlocked calmly in his lap and that his breathing was sedate, a stark contrast with the tumult of emotion that led up to his breakdown earlier. Yet the translucent membrane on the surface of the red liquid in his cup seemed to quiver expectantly, as though with his own growing anticipation. For here he was, after all his fretting and wavering, finally about to understand the two women around whom the recent disasters of his life seemed to orbit like a field of colliding asteroids around binary stars.

"As the whole world knows, Anisha and I are twins. As anyone who's met us together knows, we're identical twins. As those who can afford such gossip know, we were born from the union of Shiv and Chandru Birla. What only a select handful know is how hard our begetters struggled to produce us this way.

"Much of what I tell you about them comes from the censored version of their LifeStreams that they bequeathed to my twin and I. But I've done my own research to fill in the gaps, as much to understand them as how we came about. While I have no interest in the specifics of what they did in their bedrooms, the rumors I came across in their servants' records suggest that it was clinical and forced from the start. Not due to any dysfunctions or infidelities as far as I can determine. They simply found sexual activity of all kinds distasteful, which is part of what allowed them to have such incredible success. They were rarely led astray by base urges. First and foremost, they were business partners rather than spouses. Nothing came before their aspirations.

"This was precisely why they had to have a child. For them, Fertilex—the MegaGlom they created together—had attained a beauty and magnificence that transcended their worth as individuals. If there was anything they loved, it was this corporation. And since it was bound to outlive them, they needed someone to care for it after they were gone. Even in their early twenties, this distant concern absorbed them. Foresight was something they took very seriously. But Fertilex couldn't be passed on to boards or executives or anyone driven only by the quest for money and Freedom. Such single-minded power-seekers would only disgrace and inevitably destroy their precious lovechild. It had to be someone with soul-deep investment in the enterprise and unparalleled competence of the kind they possessed. In short, an heir to carry on their legacy.

"With the best fertility technologies at their disposal, they might have order-grown someone with the perfect traits to fill their shoes. They decided nonetheless that their successor had to be produced naturally— and not for the reasons you're probably imagining. It's a well-known fact that to gain respect in the wealthiest social circles, one must acquire what few can ever hope to afford: a baby conceived through sexual intercourse, carried in utero, and delivered only with the help of midwives. Thanks to our monopoly on such actions, natural birth has been a major source of profit for Fertilex, further supplemented by licensing assistive methods like Hippo's All Star Natura. But my begetters understood full well that much of this demand had been generated by their own marketing strategies, targeted at the richest 0.01 percent. Status markers they had consciously engineered held little appeal for them. If they only wanted to impress their competitors to consolidate financial interests, forging documents that certified a natural birth would have sufficed.

"Their decision to actually make an heir the hard way had more to do with their belief in their own precocious genius. They themselves had been born naturally from their parents and had become unrivalled entrepreneurs and administrators. For all the algorithms showing that order-grown babies were on average more successful in particular professions, there was no evidence that any could match their achievements; no one in history ever had, and the unprecedented is anathema to statistics. Passing the torch to clones of themselves was fraught with a similar kind of uncertainty. Because even if the unique constitution of my begetters had been well suited to the challenges they faced, new eras would inevitably call for a new kind of talent. Instead of compromising what had worked for them, they settled on producing a baby by the same method that produced them.

"And so it was that these two ambitious magnates set upon this vitality-giving endeavor as cold beings devoid of passion who needs harness their willpower to sustain it. Yet in spite of this preternatural tenacity, the years turned and still Chandru did not bear the fruits of Shiv's loins. Until blessing amid misfortune . . ."

With a frown, Rashana's eyes began to quiver strangely as they succumbed to the Elsewhere Gaze, and she executed several command-gestures with her fingers. "Apologies, Amon."

"Another cyberattack?" he asked, leaning towards her in concern.

"Not this time. I'm having an issue with a narrative assistant that I rarely use," she explained.

"VentriloQuick?" Amon named the only such app he knew, one he'd considered using in his first meeting with Rashana as Makesh Adani.

"No, raConTeur," she said. "I turned up the 'literary' setting because I thought my story was sounding a bit dry. This seems to have thrown off my gabkeepers. A few of them confused 'literary' with 'flowery', 'arcane' or some other annoying stylistic mode."

Amon had heard of raConTeur, though he had never possessed the funds to actually try it. The main difference with VentriloQuick, suppos-edly, was that raConTeur catered the audio script it played in the user's own voice to what the user wanted to say, rather than simply feeding them strings of expressions that passably matched the context. Algorithms well-trained on past vocalizations helped to calculate the user's desired message, find pertinent segs in their LifeStream, and collate these into a cohesive narrative. But human collaboration at all stages improved the output, and for this a legion of gabkeepers needed to be deeply familiar with the user's data.

"I thought you said you've never told this story to anyone," said Amon.

"I haven't."

"What about the gabkeepers?"

"I never even thought of it. My twin and I have had our Cognitive Handling Corps looking over our shoulders since the moment we were born—and not just gabkeepers; memory prompters and thought butlers and all the rest. One comes to forget they're even there."

Although Amon had previously considered the lives of the ultrawealthy in the abstract, this admission brought one such life into intimate clarity, much as Rashana's decision to stay out of the civil war had done earlier, and he was suddenly in awe of the intricacy and extensiveness of her selfhood infrastructure, even surrounding an action as simple as having a conversation. It reminded him by contrast of the endless bombardment of distractions and constant demand for cost-benefit calculus that hindered the regular mental function of the working class, turning their aspirations for greater earnings into a steep upward climb. The same technology endowed the propertied class with enhancements that made coasting along on their financial position exponentially easier. This arrangement did not strike Amon as entirely fair.

The idea of a 'Cognitive Handling Corps' was new to him, but from the way Rashana described it he supposed it might compose a large subsidiary in itself, aiding her in overseeing the thousands of executives who managed the millions—or perhaps billions—of other staff that worked for her as part of Fertilex. He wondered what measures she used to prevent leaks when allowing such extensive access to her personal data . . . All it would take was one defector.

It occurred to him that just as her medicorps offered superlative treatment and her hazardcorps well-considered risk assessments, her gabkeepers might transform her into a liar par excellence. Less cynically, they might help her speak with the utmost sincerity and accuracy. It all depended on her objectives, he supposed.

"I believe I've fixed the problem," said Rashana, stacking her palms on the knee of her crossed leg, her fingers now still. "Shall we continue?"

Amon nodded and let himself sink into his chair, wondering how many careers had been made and ruined in the process.

"Anisha and I were born when our begetters were in their mid-twenties. They had pumped more funding into R&D for methods to promote natural birth than their potential for profitability alone would have dictated because they wanted to be done with the chore of achieving this between them as quickly as possible. In the end it was Hippo's fertility booster, All Star Natura, that was effective . . . too effective by half. Conceiving twins had not been on the agenda. Their prognosticorps hadn't even bothered to report on such an improbable eventuality.

"But it didn't take long for them to see this double yield as a blessing. Shiv and Chandru had been successful precisely because they were a pair. A single child might never find an adequate partner, whereas twins could be raised from the very beginning to form a professional-familial relationship much like the one they had built together in their teens. Which is why our begetters became convinced that that they had hit upon the ultimate vehicle to perpetuate the corporation after their death.

"Nothing illustrates more clearly that we were brought into existence for this one purpose than the fact that they drafted the first version of their will before we were even born. The two of us were referred to together as 'The Successor.' In other words, we would share . . . and not just in their assets. Literally everything was set to be our communal property except our bodies, and I'm sure we would have had to share those if they could have found a way to make us."

"I thought your father's estate was meant to go to you, the elder sibling," said Amon, remembering the news flash he had watched with Rick in Self Serve.

"A bronze search engine rumor," said Rashana. "I imagine it was spread by our anonycorps. They often dilute the truth about us with disinformation in case anything leaks out. As if our begetters would care that I was born a few minutes earlier! There's no evidence that they put any stock in traditional ideas like paternal right or the order of succession.

"Just consider our perverse rearing plan. I still don't know whether it was pressed on the experts by our begetters or whether it was the experts who first proposed it. However it emerged, our development from the moment we were born would be guided by a single principle: prevent us from being apart. We slept in the same crib, drank the same mixture of surrogate breastmilk, listened to the same lullabies, went out in the same dronecarriage. Of course there were times when we were separated, if for example one of us caught a cold and had to visit the doctor when the other didn't. But these incidents were few and far between. Reasonable efforts were always made to keep us together.

"You might be thinking this was some inane sociological experiment to turn us into identical people, as though two individuals born of the same zygote who had the same experiences would lack any element to make them different. As anyone who looks it up on even a silver engine knows, monozygotic twins will always end up with minute differences in their genomes due to the errors cells make in copying themselves, and their genes will be expressed differently due to randomness in epigenetic factors. Everyone necessarily differs to some degree no matter how similar their endowments or environment. This is especially true of female twins like us— the corresponding genes in our two X chromosomes are switched on and off in different patterns. And it would be silly to believe that our environments could have ever been *exactly* the same. At the bare minimum we entered the world from the womb at different times and have occupied different positions in space ever since. The composition of air molecules we breathed and the food we ate always varied to some degree. Such small, unavoidable differences might seem negligible but they form an almost countless series over a lifetime, and even a slight change early on can lead to significant divergences in development over the span of decades. So the goal of our begetters was not to mold us into two versions of the same person. It was to make us a single person composed of two maximally similar but complementary parts.

"To this end, their pedagogicorps designed a curriculum that permeated every nook and cranny of our lives. It wouldn't do for us to have our own clothes, toys, equipment, and files, like children raised in BioPens where nothing is communal. Instilling future workers with the idea of private property from a young age prepares them for an individualistic society where mine and yours are strictly separated and all actions are owned. But if the Fertilex empire were to be our common holding, we had to see that neither of us had rights to any of our possessions that excluded the other but that our joint property belonged to no one else. In other words, between us we were to be communists, while between the two of us and the world we were capitalists like everyone else. Learning to share simple daily objects—like pillows, still images, and cutlery— was practice for us to one day share a larger portion of the world economy than anyone on earth.

"When we were old enough to walk, we moved from our crib to a bed and algorithms took a more active role in guiding our activity. We were instructed to switch sides almost every night but not quite, to disrupt any association between being on the right or left with particular days of the week or odd or even dates. The two nurses sleeping at the foot of our bed rotated between us day to day and brought us identical outfits from the same wardrobe each morning. We bathed in the same hot springs tub and ate the same rice porridge for breakfast. Our begetters took us everywhere together, gave us the same presents, and our tutors led us through the same lessons. They even went so far as to clone us identical pairs of playmates who were switched between us regularly. Incidentally, you've already met one of them."

"Who?" said Amon. "You don't mean Ono X?"

"I do. Unlike us, our playmates had SubMoms who served as parental guardians. But they were all raised to forget their separateness as we were and to dedicate their lives to protecting us. They have become what the world knows as the Birla Guard."

"So . . . there's an Ono Y and . . . the other clones are with your sis— your twin?"

"Correct . . . We haven't seen their counterparts for some time."

While Rashana spoke, she had been sitting with one leg crossed over the other, palms stacked loosely on the upper knee, receiving Amon's gaze straight on and occasionally glancing out the window to her right. Now she twisted her neck to squint over her shoulder with down-turned lips, wringing her hands. *She misses them*, Amon thought as he studied her in profile.

Presently, Rashana straightened up, and looked at Amon for a silent moment as though resetting their connection.

"When we received our first training banks, our begetters had to make sure that their rearing plan extended into our digital lives as well. So they had engineers illegally collapse our inner profiles into one. We always shared the same desktop, locking us into identical overlays, and our recorded experiences were jumbled into a single LifeStream. A program they had installed in the root of our training bank, later our BodyBank, dumped the pair of data points recorded by our sensors every second into one folder without attaching any labels. Another program shuffled scenes to disrupt continuity of the timelines and confound any effort on our part to associate with either of them. A similar routine was applied to our AT readouts. We were registered with GATA like all minors by our different genomes, so our actions were charged to separate accounts. But our displays were rigged so that our transactions tallied in the same list. Our begetters' hope was that, over time, everything we did would dissolve into a single narrative with two inextricable currents. Then, ultimately, our past would become an experiential commons along with our present.

"Their system for achieving this was thorough and they spared no expense. They even mixed up our names. Obviously our official names were recorded inside our profiles at birth like everyone else, but with all our information merged there was nothing to indicate whose was whose. Since we were always together doing the same thing, there was hardly any need to refer to us individually. In the rare cases that there was, our servants and tutors addressed each of us as *denka* like we were lords. Otherwise they simply called us *shokun*, as though we were a group of gentlemen. Occasionally it was unclear, but we learned to work out who was being summoned from context and played our parts accordingly. Meanwhile, for our begetters we were Daughters. Or if they felt like singling us out, they would call one of us Anisha and one of us Rashana and that name would stick for the remainder of the day. I'm still not sure whether this was an intentional effort to disrupt our sense of being distinct people as part of the educational program, or whether that program had disrupted their ability to see us as distinct. Sometimes I wonder whether they were just too lazy to bother trying."

Rashana's voice waned with a sort of bitter resignation, her nose giving a twitch. Amon felt like he was beginning to understand why she called them "begetters."

"You think I'm being unfair to them," she accused him.

"To your b-begetters?" The word rolled awkwardly off Amon's tongue. "I never said that."

"No, I can tell by the look on your face—but that's fine. It's difficult for people raised in a normal BioPen to understand how this all made us feel, how much warmer our relationship with our begetters might have been if they had just looked beneath our digimakes from time to time and showed us that they could tell us apart. The same could be said of everyone else around us. Hippo was the only person I can think of who would ever acknowledge our uniqueness and make the effort to distinguish our naked faces. In fact, he was the one who first taught us that there are genetic differences—even in monozygotic twins with a high degree of resemblance—and that these contribute to subtle changes in appearance. Though this wasn't until we were much older. None of these complications concerned us when we were children. We knew no other way of being and called each other by one or the other of our names depending on our mood. We were two bodies and minds filling a single role. Whether we were Anisha or Rashana in a particular instance was a practical issue. That was all.

"Those were simpler days," Rashana said with wistful tenderness. "But there's no road back to innocence. I can only have faith that one day we'll ferment something better."

Amon was curious what Rashana might have meant by "ferment." But before he could ask, she recrossed her legs on the other side and leaned towards the window, cradling her teacup close to her chin as she gazed off outside, lost in thought. Following her eyes to the window, Amon saw that Atupio Home Office, the Tokyo Canal, the Bridge of Compassion, and Delivery were all long gone. Throughout Rashana's story, Gemini X had been snaking and swooping along a seemingly random flight path, and he supposed that the craft was threading airspaces owned by hostile MegaGloms after the Philanthropy Syndicate ban. As a result, they had been making sluggish progress, but the cyclone rotor now propelled them on a more or less southerly trajectory.

From their current altitude high above the District of Dreams, Amon could make out most of the almond-shaped island's eastern shore—a rounded V delineated from Tonan and the rest of Free Tokyo by the shimmering course of the Sanzu River. Glancing across the corridor to his right, he spotted the two cube-stacked spires of Opportunity Peaks poking above the bottom of the window in the near distance.

Based on the position of the room-heaped mountain against the western cityscape, Amon placed Gemini X above the southern tip of the Gifted Triangle, which meant Xenocyst would be not far to the east. So, returning his gaze to the left window, he leaned forward and peered down carefully at the slumscape passing below. He discovered no signs of the Cyst tower, but did notice sporadic gaps in the lay of the disposcraper mounds and knew that this was the buffer around the border . . . or what remained of it. Roombuds had already been planted in the floor of the canyon that carved out the blot-shaped territory of Xenocyst, the buildings of surrounding enclaves encroaching, thick billows of their petals fluttering in what open space remained. Clearly, the border watch could no longer prevent settlement in this protective zone, their authority on the decline. It was only a matter of time before the city Amon had once made his abode was swallowed up by the rest of the slum.

He remembered with sadness Hippo telling him about his vision of a xenocyst, a lone cell of self- reliance and determination in a body of poverty and dependence. Now that cell was dissolving into the whole, and Amon couldn't help feeling complicit in its demise. Barrow had upended the old ways but might have kept the community going in some form or other if not for what Amon had done to him. Again that mangled face, layered faintly like a tortured ghost over the vista of sky and building and river, and again Amon was untroubled by the memory, his breathing slow and calm, his hands still in his lap. It concerned him that he would be so callous, though he was glad for the composure to sit there and be privy to Rashana's past.

Taking a sip of tea, he watched her stare out the window, elbow on crossed knee, forehead held in fingertips, rubbing her brow as though unknotting a headache, and he realized how exciting it was to be admitted into the narrative sanctum of one of the most secretive and powerful people on earth. At the same time, her unconventional upbringing disturbed him. What would such treatment do to a child's psyche? How could such twins learn to interact with normal people?

The only sound was the hummingbird drone of the cyclone rotor until, "I've never heard of anyone raised like that," said Amon.

"Of course not," said Rashana, lifting her face from her fingertips to bring her focus to him. "Our childhood was unique in all of history."

"It's definitely nothing like how we were raised in the BioPen," Amon mused. "They encouraged us to develop our own . . . well, maybe not ideas, but our own desires anyway. They must have wanted to make us efficient workers and consumers, like you said. But at least they taught us to search for *something* inside ourselves that no one else has."

"We never lost ourselves in each other entirely. On a cerebral level, we thought of us as two facets of one and the same person. But on a visceral level, something always felt wrong. Everyone we met or learned about other than our playmates had their own name and a distinctive identity attached to it. We weren't so obtuse as to accept without question that we were the only ones who didn't."

"It seems inevitable to me that you would have to set yourselves apart at some stage." With flat indifference, Amon recalled the sight of toddlers brawling over an edible wrapper during the famine. "Even three-year-olds have a sense of self, maybe more so than adults."

"Exactly, yes!" Rashana uncrossed her legs to sit up tall and squeezed the grooves of the brain chair on both sides. "If only my begetters had had one iota of your common sense, they would never have believed that they could harness our sense of self, that fusing us early enough would make us impossible to separate. But in spite of all their business acumen, their understanding of personal growth was simply twisted. Their development had been stunted in its own way, as one can easily see from their monomaniacal devotion to Fertilex. They couldn't even imagine what a balanced upbringing might look like. Would any sane person swallow the predictions of those quack experts who would say anything for their exorbitant consulting fees? As if trying to squish my twin and I together would do anything but make us want to be apart! Our points of disagreement would never have become as irreconcilable as they are now, if our begetters hadn't forced us to be so close growing up, I promise you that."

Unconsciously, Amon sunk back into his chair, shrinking from Rashana. He regretted setting her off with his comment. Not wanting their conversation to wallow in her bitterness any further, he asked, "When did the rift open up between you in the end?"

"The rift, as you call it, was always there. There were precedents for it even in our childhood. Neither of us could care less who caught a cold and had to stay in bed on a particular day or who was in the bathroom at some moment. But when it came to games, we often felt possessive of our memories. Even those whackjob psychological advisors acknowledged that play is an essential part of early development. Especially important for our begetters' purposes were competitive games, so as to instill us with the lust to one day win against MegaGlom rivals in the struggle for market hegemony. And therein lies the rub, because whatever they might do to make our conditions mirror each other's in other contexts, in a competitive game we could not both be winners all the time.

"Our handlers did their best to mitigate the divisive influence of this inconvenient fact by assigning us to the same team in pair sports, like tennis, ping-pong, and fencing. Their algorithms also rotated our cloned pairs of playmates, whose names and profiles were as interchangeable as ours, so that we could not easily tell which player each of us had beaten.

"We pooled our strategies against human masters and near omnipotent AI in chess, *shogi*, and *go*. We were blood brothers in yakuza first-person shooters and joined the same band of heroes in fantasy adventures. In every way possible, our begetters made sure that we always shared in both victory and defeat. But what could they do if one of us fumbled and the other scored the winning basket in overtime? Or if we both rushed the final dragon together, whose spell of ice had frozen him to death in the end? Whose samurai blade had lopped off the shogun's head? Occasionally we would rehash our moves after a thrilling round and find that we disagreed about our contributions. It often seemed to each of us that the other had been the bungler and that we had saved the day. Our LifeStreams might have served as final arbiter if they hadn't been mixed up as I've described. For other reasons, our biological memories were no more helpful in settling the issue. Although our educational regimen had involved ImmaNet downtime to acclimatize our perception to the naked world, our usual reliance on apps had atrophied our cognition to a certain extent. As a consequence, the moments we could recall without technological assistance were vague and frequently seemed to contradict.

"When our petty, childish desires to own our achievements flared up into actual arguments, our handlers were always quick to intervene. We would then find that a counseling session had been added to our schedule for the day. At the appointed time, our overlays would be locked in a dull office with a dozy old therapist. He would keep asking us dry questions until we realized for ourselves that we should never divide our ownership of anything, especially not our successes. These sessions were so excruciatingly boring that it didn't take long for busy, excitable kids like us to reach this preordained conclusion. And that was how our begetters continued to tamp down our dividing impulses until we reached adolescence and their efforts finally began to fail."

Perhaps signaled by raConTeur that Rashana had reached a break in her story, Ono X emerged to clear away the teapot and cups. Amon watched with slight dismay as the red shimmer of his two or three remaining sips of tea were carried away. Chances to sample such a quality beverage had been few in his life, but it had admittedly grown somewhat cold and he decided it would display a lack of cultivation to complain. The memory of its tang lingered forlorn on his palate.

When her servant had faded with his tray into the shadows, Rashana recrossed her legs again and nestled her wrists on her knee, joined palms hanging loosely over.

"It was around our eleventh birthday that our begetters first gave us authority over actual assets. Now we were overseeing hedge funds, subsidiaries, research labs, to educate us through practice, with our pedagogicorps shifting to the role of advisors. But the extra work on top of our already intensive studies was overwhelming. Delegating tasks to our underlings only relieved the pressure temporarily, because as soon as we were on top of a particular workload, our begetters would reward us with further assets that only increased it. This kept us stretched to the end of our tethers, terrified of disappointing them and forfeiting the praise and presents they heaped on us. When expectations exceeded our young capacities and we couldn't make enough time for everything no matter how we juggled our schedules, it was inevitable that we would hit upon the idea of divvying the labor between us.

"A fifty-fifty split brought us immediate relief, but we didn't realize what we were unleashing. Inadvertently, we had taken our first step towards separateness and opened the door to a host of problems. For starters, our staff needed to know who to report to on each project. The obvious solution was to ask our begetters for access to our real names. But they just smiled a condescending smile and told us that working together closely was even more crucial now that our results impacted the household empire.

"This frustrated us beyond belief. It made patently clear that our begetters' wishes could never be satisfied. Because how, Amon, how were we to fulfill duties so extensive that we needed to cooperate as a pair if we were to be a single person? Cooperation between an individual is not just an impossible feat—it is an incoherent idea. But we had learned that arguing with our begetters was futile, and our taste of asset management had made us hungry for more. So our only option was to pick separate names ourselves. We decided to settle the matter by a best-of-three round of rock-paper-scissors. The winner would take Anisha and the loser Rashana, whatever our profiles might say."

Rashana began to rub her knitted brow again, then seemed to realize what she was doing and brought her hand back to its resting place on her knee, restoring a decorous posture before going on.

"Once this was settled, communication with our staff became much simpler as we had hoped. Still, it wasn't easy to stay on top of the many details that concerned our enterprises. With our LifeStreams merged, even basic tasks like confirming the specifics of an acquisition or an order could turn into significant wastes of time. In other words, by deciding who was who, the need to also divide up our information was suddenly thrust upon us. We knew our begetters would never agree. We had barely convinced them to let us use our names after going through great pains to prove that it served a purely pragmatic purpose. Obviously, we would have to somehow differentiate our data under their noses.

"This presented the biggest challenge we had ever faced. We knew that our begetters could check all our action-transactions since they had us leashed, and that they had rigged our training banks for glass mode so that their compliance sentinels could monitor us through our inner profiles. We had never seen this parental panopticon as a problem before; to the good, obedient kids we had always been, their oversight only seemed to lead to extra treats and presents, even if the micro-managing reminders from our task correctors could sometimes be annoying. But in retrospect, we realized that it had forced us to keep our feelings of separateness private and unarticulated—even to each other—for years. To let them surface at last as the management of our burgeoning capital demanded, the first step was to alter our BodyBanks in some way to obscure our activities. We didn't conceive this initially as an act of disobedience. It was, after all, our begetters who wanted us to be capable executives. Concealing our splitting apart from them, though superficially rebellious, was the only way we could think to please them more deeply.

"The moment we reached this conclusion, we were caught in a danger-ous paradox. Because if we were going to come up with a way to avoid detection by our cognitive handlers and their powerful algorithms, we would need to put our heads together. But if we were going to put our heads together, we would need to avoid detection. Even expressing this conundrum in words—or any other observable mode of communication—was risky. It was only through our intimacy that Anisha and I could intuit that the other understood the position we were in."

"You must have created some kind of code," Amon supposed, thinking of Rick. As his friend lay dying, he had mentioned the time in adolescence when the two of them created a coded language to secretly mock their surveilling SubMom. The memory brought a sense of nostalgic sadness, though no trace of grief or horror. His emotions almost seemed muffled.

"Our compliance sentinels were too sophisticated for a code with any meaningful level of redundancy," said Rashana. "We had to be more sly than that. Without coming to any explicit agreement, Anisha and I began to flatter our cybersecurity teacher and pretend we were fascinated by her lessons. This softened her up for a few seemingly harmless questions, worded so as to be sufficiently oblique while drawing out the know-how we needed. We began to surf the web with similar guile, searching related topics and then arriving as if by accident, in the blur of link clicking, upon exactly the right information. Bit by surreptitious bit, we pieced together the necessary expertise and made ourselves specialists in both crypto- breaking and sealing. For target practice, we hacked Philanthropy Syndicate rivals and sabotaged a Kavipal nanofactory so that a whole line of window cleaning drones shut down and rained on passing traffic. In the end, Fertilex had to reimburse the MegaGlom for the infrastructure damages and court settlements with the drivers, but our begetters were all too happy to foot the bill in the service of our education. Meanwhile, we located the spyware installed in our BodyBanks as though this were a routine security analysis, and we began to write seemingly random bits of code that we saved here and there in our account.

"When all was ready, we cut and pasted these fragments into the program we'd devised and launched a cyberattack on our surveillers. We caught them unprepared as our Cognitive Handling Corps system hadn't been updated since we were children. No one had thought to fortify it against threats originating with us. They may not have even realized that we knew the network existed. Our viruses wiped out the surveillance bots and collapsed their window on our accounts.

"The one weakness in our plan was that we had to remain leashed, since we had no money of our own to cover these expensive credicrimes, and they would appear on our begetters' AT readouts. To our surprise, the Onos gave us a large donation just seconds before we launched the operation. Unbeknown to us, they had accumulated funds by skimming the difference from some of our asset sales and acquisitions specifically to support us. Of all the thousands of handlers who tended to us remotely and in person, only the Onos succeeded in correctly reading our behavior. And lucky for us because anyone else would have ratted us out in a second.

"When our begetters did learn what had happened, we met their fury with boisterous laughter, and pretended as though it had been a playful expression of our budding technical curiosity. This was a calculated appeal to their desire to encourage the growth of our minds. They even forgave the Onos when we pointed out that they had been order-grown and raised to serve us above all else.

"Although the various arms of our Cognitive Handling Corps soon restored access to our profile and patched all weaknesses to foreclose any future attacks, we already had what we needed. No one suspected the extent of the hidden programs we had installed, and the security audit of our account failed to uncover anything. To our surveillers, our inner profile would continue to appear united, while from our perspective, it would be divided into two folders, each with a separate LifeStream, asset record, bank account, and AT readout. We had also created a third folder, the contents of which were hidden from anyone but us, a secret virtual space where we could meet as figments for private conversation. Once we had hired external cryptosealers to shore up our amateur coding, the subterfuge was complete and the groundwork for our self-discovery had been laid."

Rashana closed her eyes and twisted her neck to face over her shoulder again, her lashes drooping dolefully. She remained like this, the plane of her hands angling down from her knee, apparently taking a moment to gather herself. With nothing else to do, Amon inevitably turned to the window.

The rotorcraft's convoluted trajectory had now brought them far enough south over the District of Dreams that Amon could make out the entire bottom line of the eastern shoreline V. He leaned forward to search the ground behind them for Xenocyst but could no longer see the border for the haphazard cube-jut undulations of slum. Instead, his gaze travelled northeast over the Sanzu River to the puzzle-piece shaped island of Tonan, over its tracts of blighted skyscraper riven by a snarl of streets, to where the cityscape blended into the theme park residential district of Wakuwaku City.

While Amon lost himself in the hypnotic rotations of condo-rooftop Ferris wheels, veranda-spanning carousels, and alley-twining roller coasters, sad fragments of the past percolated. This was the last place he had seen Mayuko, on his final day of banklife. Although he could recall her interrogation and beating as vividly as ever, the scene lacked its compulsive pull, and segued gently into his very first memory—watching a daytime star with her on the roof of the BioPen—a rare moment of unadulterated wonderment that they had shared. The torturous edge to all associations with her had somehow been dulled and yet the pit of his stomach ached with the sickening fizz of regret. Would he ever find her?

To flee these recurring thoughts, Amon pried his gaze from the distant vista that had conjured them and drew it in to peer down over the edge of the window. Straight below, a thick-swirling flurry of petals obscured the ground. Fitful winds cleared occasional gaps, offering a momentary view of Fleet rubble heaps and disposcraper husks dissolving furiously. They were passing over the southern half of the District of Dreams, the Tumbles. This vast region had always been especially precarious, far removed from the supplies of Delivery. Now it looked all but uninhabitable, just a craggy wasteland of crumbled shelter-crust, the air choked by flakes, the pathways blocked off by debris. He hated to consider the fate of the masses who once lived here, and could only hope that the supplies would return to former levels quickly in line with Rashana's predictions. Merely restoring the bankdead to their grueling routine was hardly ideal, but even despair and chronic deprivation were better than starvation.

The petal storm extended to the southern tip of the almond, where the Sanzu River and the Tokyo Canal wrapped around the shore and merged. Filling what was left of Tokyo Bay beyond this were clusters of small artificial islands, arrayed like cobbled stones intersticed with glittering threads of water. The massive factory spheres and blocks, fission grids, warehouse stacks and ports encrusting each island were connected by a matrix of catwalks, train lines, and highways that interlinked the archipelagos. Gemini X was on course for the mouth of the bay, where a slender gap still remained between the tips of the Boso and Miura peninsulas. From there a bed of shimmering platinum blue spread beneath a painting of continents in azure and white to where they touched at the horizon. It was Amon's first sighting of the naked ocean, and he wondered again where they were going. Rashana had said she wanted to show him somewhere in Tokyo, but they were flying rapidly away from the metropolis, and he looked over to her quizzically, only to find her watching him.

"Securing our own subprofiles allowed Anisha and I to begin sorting out what data would go in which. We held our discussions in the virtual folder, usually at night while our bodies rested. This made it easy for the stealth programs we had designed to throw off our compliance sentinels by replacing our feeds with stock segs of us sleeping. The remainder of the embezzled gift from the Onos paid for our actions there so that the transactions would appear on a readout our begetters couldn't access . . . or so we believed.

"Our first resolution was to configure our LifeStream to save new recordings automatically in our respective subprofiles. That dealt with the present and the future, but it left the stickier question of what to do about our past. We prioritized those digital memories that held significance for one of us. The trouble was, that often meant it was significant for both of us.

"Since we were nearly always together, there were two versions of every moment in our lives, two tracks running in parallel. Sometimes we would immediately agree who had actually experienced and remembered one of the perspectives on a particular event. Then we would cut it from our fused LifeStream and paste it into the owner's subprofile. Other times there would be a dispute that called for the deal-making skills we had learned in business. I might give her 'bouncing on our bed before our 4th birthday' in exchange for 'my cleanest judo throw on sensei.' Or we would trade such desirable incidents for bundles of, say, derivative contracts and action shares. To us memories were just another kind of property, albeit one more deeply linked to who we were and who we wanted to be.

"These negotiations were exhausting and emotionally depleting, especially because we could not always reach an agreement. The embarrassments that neither of us wanted were the most contentious. A slip of the tongue in front of allied executives or a revolting lapse after we were already potty-trained. We both bargained hard to foist these on the other, making generous offers and threatening to walk out by turns, but who wants to pick up the psychic trash? Soon I began to suspect her of bad faith. Confusing faded memories from months or years past was understandable—not so for fresh memories from only days or weeks ago. I could only think that my twin was lying to acquire the scenes she preferred and build a personal story more to her liking. Or maybe she just wanted to cause mischief. The distrust was of course mutual. Bitter arguments ate away at our sleep, negating much of the efficiency we had gained through breaking apart in the first place. I wished for the simpler days when we could lose our individuality in our duality, or at least convince ourselves that we had done so. But such hopes were in vain. Once we had split into I and I, the two of us would never be we again."

As though she could no longer bear to remain in her seat, Rashana stood up abruptly and crossed the cabin to the window on the other side. Amon too was feeling restless and made a move to rise and follow her. But he stopped partway and lowered himself back into the molded nook, deciding that she must want space.

"It was in our late teenage years that we began to more radically part ways," Rashana continued, standing with hands clasped behind her back as she faced the window, her body from the waist up a silhouette against a boundless sky. "Until then, we had accepted our commonalities as given. Even our quarrels over data and achievements had been attempts to set ourselves apart in little ways against the background of our basic sameness. But with newfound names and stories that we were building from a growing collection of recordings, we stopped trying to forge differences. Now we began to realize how different we had already been without ever noticing.

"Suddenly, we found ourselves unable to see eye to eye on anything. What had started out as a puerile desire to determine who had dunked the winning basket became a disdainful need to point out the other's failures and our own successes in running our joint enterprises. Whose startup had gone belly-up? Whose haggling had reduced the price for a takeover? Whose investments were paying off? We bickered over sales strategies, marketing pushes, bargaining with rivals—anything and everything that had bearing on our assets.

"To please our begetters, we kept our feuds out of sight of course. We would have show-meetings that displayed our decisiveness as a unit, when in actuality the resolutions had been made in our folder the previous night after hours of wrangling. Our combined worth was nevertheless growing at a faster rate than the much greater wealth of our begetters. In our rambunctious way, we made a point of rubbing in their faces how much better in touch with the market we were, until they half-proudly and half-grudgingly began to entrust us with ever more critical industries; order-grown experimentation labs, longevity seed funds, corporate defence intelligence.

"As much as we would have liked to cleanly divide our swelling assets, their tight financial integration ensured that this was all but impossible. Our conglomerates, for example, did most business internally, between their various subsidiaries, and each of our companies held partial share in the others. So we drew the lines of authority in our nascent empires as best we could while for the sake of parental optics acting as though no such lines existed. Our favorite handlers and executives we put on secret assignment as decisionmakers, algorithm developers, and liaisons with lower rungs of management. We also labelled the Birla Guard pairs as either X or Y and took one of each to be our personal assistants, even as we pretended to rotate them as before.

"This constant performance, with its endless layers and intricacies, was nearly unbearable and the mounting stress only made our arguments more toxic. We soon agreed—and this may have been the last thing we ever agreed—that the only solution was to sever our inner profiles once and for all. We knew petitioning our begetters for permission was a lost cause; all we could do was be patient and wait until the day of our identity births. Once we turned twenty, we would have our own accounts and legal independence. This was the hope that sustained us through the excruciating inauthenticity forced on us by our ruse."

Amon watched Rashana's hand rise out of sight to her face, perhaps to rub her brow. She had edged so close to the window that he wondered if her nose was touching, though the clear material remained unfogged with her breath.

"But that expectation was nothing more than a mirage," she said almost too quietly to hear. Hand drifting from her forehead, she rested her fingertips softly on the window surface beside her cheek as if wanting to take hold of something she knew was too distant to ever reach. "Our inner profiles would remain united, even to this day."

"How could that be?" Amon asked. "Two users can't *share* an identity signature. GATA would never allow it."

"You still haven't come to terms with it?" Rashana turned to face him. "Money bends rules like a blowtorch on steel."

She locked her ochre eyes with his for a moment to let this sink in. Then she stepped back across the cabin and paused before the coffee table, looking down her hooked nose at him coolly as she spoke.

"Each unique genome registered with GATA receives a unique identity signature and each signature a unique profile, correct?"

Amon gave a slow nod.

"Right. But consider that individual genomes change over time. The genome of a person registered at birth will not be perfectly identical to the genome in every cell in their body twenty years later."

"Because of copy errors."

"Among other issues. So the algorithms that check whether the genome record and present genome match must allow for a small degree of variation. Now consider clones and monozygotic twins like us."

"Ah. You were saying earlier that your genomes are a bit different for similar reasons. So you can trick the system into mixing up one person at two different points in time with two different twins or clones at any point in time, is that it?"

"Not quite. Their genomes will tend to vary in different ways, so the system won't make that mistake. But it does have trouble with edge cases like gene editing and severe radiomutation, where the variation is unpredictable or extreme. That's one reason the Tokyo Roundtable granted ultimate responsibility for assigning identity signatures to a human agent. It's the Identity Vitalator's job, with the help of an algorithm suite, to confirm whether the twenty-year-old individual is the same one who was registered at birth using non-genetic evidence, such as where they live, what they do, what their name is, and so on."

Amon had been unaware of this feature of GATA's identity management as it fell outside the Liquidation Ministry's ambit. But her explanation fit with everything he knew.

"Then basically," he said, "since you were identical twins, your genomes fell within the allowable range of variation for a single genome. That gave an Identity Vitalator the leeway to use the Birth Codes to bind your two genomes to only one ID signature."

"Correct."

"And the cloned pairs of Birla Guard got the same treatment too then I guess."

"No. Our begetters didn't deem it worth the expense."

"Okay . . . But it can't all boil down to money. I mean, registering a single unique person to a single signature is the whole purpose of Identity Vitalation. No Vitalator would dare neglect such a duty. The AT system would fall apart."

"One would and did. He's a friend of yours in fact."

"Hippo!" Amon exclaimed, slapping his knees in amazement. "He told me that he oversaw your identity birth. You and Anisha have only one profile, even now, because of Hippo?"

"Our begetters asked him as a favor. They knew he couldn't say no to the patrons of his research. It was fortunate for them that they had bribed key officials at the Ministry of Access to allow him to keep his job there after he began to work for Fertilex near the beginning of the Free Era. They covered the fines for his credicrimes, of course; threw in a tip to the donation box for his Xenocyst foundation. They even had their lobbies intervene when the Executive Council tried to remove his title as Honorary Identity Vitalator."

"GATA never reversed the violations?"

"How could they? Once the identity birth ceremony was complete, our profiles were hidden by the House of Blinding. Not even the Ministry of Access could find us if they tried."

"But you're in different places. There must be action monitoring discrepancies or something."

"Maybe. Those would be technical issues for the Ministry of Monitoring to sort out."

"So not your begetters' problem."

"Do you think they care whether they inconvenience others? Do you have any idea how shocking it was for us when we learned about this?" Rashana seemed to loom much taller than she actually was, sunlight catching on the razor edge of her eyelashes. "It wasn't as if our begetters warned us. Anisha and I had been going along overseeing the growth of their capital, working hard to please them, believing that we would become our own people like everyone else. But no! Hippo shows up and puts a hand on each of our foreheads and he inputs the Birth Codes, and suddenly we're joined at the hip. One legal person with two sets of biometrics, two pools of personal recordings, two bodies, and two minds. Not temporarily for our edification anymore. Forever."

"Until bankdeath do us part," Amon intoned. *Or death*, he thought, but decided it was too morbid to say aloud.

"We had no say in any of this! Both of us were furious with Hippo at first, but we understood the position he was in. Refusing our begetters borders on the suicidal. It was our begetters that we could never forgive. If they'd warned us, we might have persuaded them of how important our independence would be to the realization of their objectives. If they truly wanted to ensure the persistence of Fertilex into the deep future, then we needed space, to live separately, to think our own thoughts. But they never gave us the chance. The wisdom of our being fused had been preordained while we were in utero. The only choice they left us was how to cope with the consequences."

As though the indignation had sustained her, Rashana's tense shoulders went slack, and she plumped herself into the brain chair, letting out a congested sigh. Her gaze bored into Amon's as if to ask, *How could such a thing have been done to me?* Then she blinked and when her eyes opened they were downcast. Amon continued to study her, surprised that he could sympathize with this corporate demigoddess. Earlier she had said that probability was only a rough map of the border between fact and fantasy, but maybe it was no map at all, for he found her upbringing too incredible to doubt, too improbable to be made up. How she and her sister must have suffered trying to wrest pieces of themselves from each other and their domineering parents. No surprise that she would be so emotional if he was truly the first person she had ever confided in, even if her army of cognitive handlers had long observed much of the drama unfolding. A glow now bathed her simple clothes and brown skin, seeming to encase her in a softly radiant jewel that sought to protect her from further pain. It was as though sunlight were penetrating the black walls of the deck and gathering about her delicate, pensive form.

"Didn't you ever consider running away?"

"Of course we did. I did. Anisha and I discussed the possibility in our folder on more than one occasion. We knew what was at stake. We would have to give up our entitlements to Fertilex and all our wealth. We would have to say goodbye to the Cognitive Handling Corps and the attendants that we had relied upon for everything. We would have to find a job on our own and work our way up from nothing by our own effort.

"Escape still looked attractive. With our versatile skillset, we'd be ahead of your average BioPen graduate at least. But the main issue wasn't supporting ourselves alone. It was what happened when our begetters inevitably found us. We knew their anger wouldn't stop at pressuring our employer to fire us and taking everything we'd built up for ourselves. Once they had us wallowing in poverty, an assassin would most certainly have followed."

"You don't think they would have had you killed?"

"Why not? Because that isn't something that *parents* would do?" Rashana enunciated slowly and crisply, singing the word parents with contempt, as she leaned towards Amon, her lashes raking closer. "Is that what you think they are after everything I've told you?"

"I didn't say that," said Amon, shrinking back almost to the window. He was reminded of her financial impunity. Just as her parents could have done anything they wanted to her without any repercussions other than a negligible decrease in their assets so she could do anything she wanted to him. Not that he believed she would hurt him. But it was worth noting the asymmetry. He existed only by her grace.

"Anisha and I used to joke that if our begetters ever sent emojis in their texts, it would be all carrots and sticks. I can't recall a single conversation with them that wasn't about outcomes. They communicated in one language and one language only, the language of incentives, of punishments and rewards. And to them inheriting Fertilex was the ultimate reward. If we turned it down, it was obvious that we could expect the ultimate punishment.

"This threat placed us in a sort of prisoners' dilemma. It would have been all fine and dandy if one of us could have run off and accepted the risk. But our begetters had forced us to sign contracts after our identity births consenting to continued surveillance of our inner profiles in exchange for the assets they had lent us. For us to slip away undetected, we would have to sever this contract and leave simultaneously. Otherwise they could track the one that fled through the profile of the one that stayed. So we would need to trust the other not to squeal in return for whatever generous bounty our parents would assuredly provide. And not just at the moment we fled but for the rest of our lives, through every twist of fortune in which those rewards might seem all the more tempting. It was a high bar of loyalty to set for a twin with whom squabbling was worsening by the day.

"But I don't think it was either the lure of the Freedom we would sacrifice or fear of the punishment we would incite that held us back in the end. At some point, all our talk of escape simply fizzled out. We had both found dreams of our own, you see, and we would need our begetters' wealth if we were going to realize them."

"What kind of dreams?"

While Rashana sat with feet planted and a palm on each knee, she tilted her head upwards. It seemed *as though* she was looking at something distant, until Amon followed her gaze and realized that she *actually was* looking at something distant. There was a whitish glow bleeding through the ceiling, the hazy orb of the sun floating just past noon. His sense that light seemed to be creeping into the deck had been accurate. And it wasn't just the ceiling. The entire rotorcraft had become translucent, the scenery a blur of seeping color.

Amon turned to his window and found that Tokyo Bay was long gone. Greeting his eyes beneath a deep blue sky—strewn with torn blankets of cloud and wound through with the rambling vectors of multifarious carbonjets, drones, and rotorcraft—was a cobalt sea specked with small islands. That morning, he had lifted off from the ground and seen the ocean for the first time. Now, only a few hours later, they had left the land behind altogether. It made him feel untethered and forlorn, and he wondered once more about their destination. This wasn't Tokyo at all. Could Rashana have been lying about where she was taking him? When he looked to her with confusion that verged on alarm, she was watching him again and swept away his thoughts with her words.

"In debating class ever since we were children, Anisha and I were paired up against teams composed of our handlers, our playmates, and various algorithms designed to test our limits. Usually our tutors would have us take a position on some issue and then make us switch to defend the opposing side. One day we were for privatization of heart beating, the next against. One day we were luddites seeking the abandonment of modern technology, the next proponents of cybernetic expansion into the depths of human consciousness. Sometimes they let us use the ImmaNet and the suggestions of our gabkeepers. Other times they disconnected us to hone our naked cognition. No one cared what we actually thought. Our tutors never asked us that. It was simply a matter of practicing rhetorical tricks, using information on the fly, and battering our opponents into the dust with superior logic. If we could vary our register and style to the intelligence and political slant of our opinion network for that round and convince them to vote for our assertion, nothing we said could be mistaken.

"One side effect of this training was to make us increasingly uncertain what we believed. No viewpoint was impregnable, all evaluations relied on arbitrary standards, and truth was ephemeral. These were the core maxims of our class and we used them to uncover the flaws in every argument that confronted us. But we never thought carefully about their meaning. We were being groomed for control of a global empire and doing was far more important than pondering. What lay in our hearts, what convictions we held about reality, knowledge, the good and the beautiful—that was none of our concern. In short, they reared us to be empty receptacles waiting for a liquid to be poured in. To our begetters dismay, it would not be the liquid they had chosen for us. It would not even be the same liquid."

As Rashana looked upwards again, her eyes seeming to search for something beyond the world, the radiance enveloped her completely, like a second skin beamed from the cosmos. The rotorcraft was nearly transparent now, like grey-tinted glass, the goldening blot of the sun infusing the cabin with silken light from its place in the sky above, the indistinct plane of the ocean shimmering with bleached dabs and streaks through the floor beneath Amon's feet.

"Ironically, it was this debating class that would spur us to seek the truth for ourselves. I can trace the exact moment to a lesson we both took at the age of sixteen. Our tutor was lecturing on mythology and went on to tell us the story of Gyges' ring."

"The Gyges Circle!" Amon cut in louder than he intended, recalling all the events linked in one way or another to the contrivances of this secret alliance—from Barrow's identity assassination, to Rick's cash crash and Amon's fall from grace, to the famine in the camps. "Is that what this is all building up to?"

Rashana nodded with a faint smile. "Have you heard this myth before?"

Amon shook his head, sitting up tall and alert, burning with anticipation.

"In ancient Greece there was a shepherd named Gyges. He was a good-hearted pious man, who made sacrifices to the gods, treated his sheep well, and showed respect to everyone he met. Then one day he stumbled upon a ring that turned him invisible. With this magic treasure, he suddenly had great power. And what do you think he decided to do with it? Remain a simple, kind, god-fearing shepherd? No. He began to sneak into the queen's bedchamber to sleep with her after nightfall and killed the king to seize the throne, becoming a great tyrant.

"At the end, our teacher asked us the moral of the story. Anisha replied first."

Amon stomped both feet in surprise as a video flickered to life on the wall to his left. The quality was so realistic it seemed to play someone's consciousness.

"I know the answer," said Rashana, her words synching to the lip movements of an adolescent Birla sister in the video that had to be Anisha.

In pastel yellow bellbottom shorts and a pale green T-shirt with baggy, drooping sleeves, Anisha sat in a wood-paneled drawing room on a plush cream armchair. The perspective looked left, at the same height as

Anisha's eyes, its small left arm in matching baggy sleeves on the armrest of a matching chair. It glanced now and then to a young woman in a grey suit who was seated across from them, presumably a teacher.

"This myth is a fable about the meaning of freedom," Rashana went on, giving voice to the image of her sister like a ventriloquist for her dummy. "It says that allowing someone who has earned nothing to transcend all consequences for their actions is dangerous, because only those who have succeeded through their own talent and effort will know how to temper their will. Once all barriers have been removed, people like Gyges, who lack hard-won self-control, will be ruled by raw desire, and will relinquish all freedom, paradoxically, at the very moment they receive the unlimited possibility to realize it."

Young Rashana shifted her view to the teacher to observe her reaction. The teacher's lips began to move but present Rashana did not fill in the audio.

"Our teacher praised Anisha's interpretation for both its originality and its continuity with certain views in antiquity. She was about to move on with the lesson, expecting that my twin was speaking for both of us as usual, when I said, 'I beg to differ. I think it's a challenge.'"

Young Anisha and the teacher looked into the eye of the perspective with squint-eyed incredulity.

"The point isn't that Gyges behaves terribly because he has failed to earn his freedom," Rashana spoke for her younger self, spectral fluttering of lips just visible in the lower periphery. "It's that he's in control of his will in the beginning but loses it once he finds the ring. We're being warned that anyone, even someone without ambition or greed to start with, would relinquish their freedom to petty impulses if all repercussions for their actions were removed. In other words, the fable is challenging us to find some higher reason to limit our will so that, paradoxically, we can realize true freedom when we find it."

Young Rashana again watched the teacher mouth something.

"Our teacher complimented me as she had complimented Anisha and asked her if she had anything to add. But my twin only shook her head."

The teacher took a breath as though preparing to introduce the next lesson, before the scene vanished, leaving the hazy white and blue of the sky beyond the translucent wall that had been a display. Amon had been listening with rapt attention, enthralled by the high-veridicality recording. He'd seen nothing like it since losing access to his LifeStream. It amazed him how Gemini X seemed to simulate the ImmaNet, and how seamlessly Rashana's gabkeepers had woven the seg with her speech to give it the feel of a novel. Why would the craft show images in the naked world? Like the lights in the Atupio underground, it seemed to be designed inexplicably with bankdead in mind.

"This was the first time that either of us expressed our actual beliefs about anything of substance. When we began to divvy up our memories into folders, we discussed this incident early on, and it was one of the few instances where both of us agreed immediately, without any negotiation, who had said and thought what. Although Anisha has never admitted as much, I think that for her even more than for me, that myth and her understanding of it became the guiding principle for everything that she did after."

Rashana had let her chin fall as she watched her thumb slide over her fingernails, looking more downhearted than ever.

"We still wanted to grow our empires of course, but carrying on the household MegaGlom could never be the extent of our aspirations, whatever our begetters might wish for us. To fully and completely define ourselves in relation to each other, we had to do so in relation to them as well. Soon our opinions and tastes raced in different directions as we tried to put our personal responses to the myth of Gyges into practice, until we were like opposing poles only held together by the necessity of running the largest company on earth."

"But *enough* with my household saga for now," said Rashana, with a flick of her hand as if to brush away her story. "We've arrived at our destination."

When she pointed down, Amon gasped to see that the pink brain chairs they sat on were floating in empty air. The hull of Gemini X had completed its shift to transparency and become clearer than the thinnest glass. All that remained around them was a panorama of ragged white against rich winter blue cupped high over a vast carpet marbled with sun-sparkle and cobalt-to-emerald gradations. The tornado rotor had grown fainter, now a blurring gossamer shimmer, like some quantum cloud of heat mirages above them. Bathed in dazzling light, seeming to defy gravity at a far greater height than he had ever known, Amon felt tiny and vulnerable, as though he were a speck of stardust confronting an approaching galaxy. The vista reminded him of the restaurant with its sky full of origami cranes on the day Rashana had met him as Makesh Adani, while the rotorcraft's adjustments in opacity recalled the sensory deprivation orchard that morning.

"There," said Rashana, pointing downwards to the spot where the coffee table and then the black floor had been, at a patch of ocean far below—an island. "This is where it all began."

Interrupting the ephemeral texture of waves was a green daub, stretching long and thin from north to south. The eastern shore had two promontories that formed a small bay near its upper end and another longer promontory protruding further down, while the western shoreline alternated between sleek and notched, a handful of islets arranged in an L off the southern tip. Mountains thick with vegetation covered the land.

"Is that . . ." Vertigo, memory, and dream all melded together in Amon's awareness into a strange sort of ecstatic terror, his heart skittering deliriously, his jaw quivering.

"Yes. Shall we take a closer look?"

Amon nodded, eyes wide, slack lips numb, speechless. *Could it be . . .*

The rotorcraft gradually descended. Presently, he could make out the curvature of the mountains, a mosaic of green, red, and purple coating the slopes. Then the mosaic resolved into trees, the shore into rust-colored rocky beaches and coves. The branches of the tangled canopy held up leaves that shimmered in the sun, flashes of silver glittering through treetop gaps from streams and ponds. He could almost smell the pungent aroma of lichen and wild herbs, hear birdsong blending with the crash of the surf. Dropping slowly from the sky inside the transparent vehicle was almost like floating down to earth by himself, as he had on so many nights before.

"So I was right," he marveled, after a span of time measured in Rashana's razor blinks and his own breaths. "There *are* still forests in this world."

"Some. This is one of the few that remains."

"I thought you were taking me somewhere in Tokyo?"

"This is Tokyo . . . technically, at least."

"How could that be, all the way out here in the Pacific?"

"I believe Barrow mentioned it to you when you last saw him. A place that he thought was very important to you."

"You mean Ogasawara. You've brought me to Ogasawara?"

"I have. We're finally here."

"This must be one of the black patches on the map." Amon remembered all the research he had done, all the money he had invested scouring the globe with God's Eye, and all the regions he couldn't afford to see. One of them had been a thousand kilometers south of where he'd lived in Jinbocho. "This island is called Ogasawara?"

"It's not any one island. It's a semi-tropical island chain sometimes known as the Bonin Islands. They've been traded back and forth between America, Japan, and China over the decades, but are now under the jurisdiction of Tokyo again.

"Up there"—Rashana pointed to a tight cluster of islands to the north—"is Chichijima. Down there"—she pointed south to two islands set somewhat apart—"Those are north and south Iwo Jima. The island we're approaching now is Hahajima. What do you think?"

Hahajima, Amon mouthed. The craft had stopped descending and they were now circling the island slowly, maintaining the same distance. He pressed his face to the clear wall, loosing track of time as he gazed down transfixed, a bulb alight with wonder and dread.

"It's . . . I don't know what to say." The texture of the surface against his cheek was not smooth like glass but rough like incredibly fine gravel, and he had a vision of himself slipping out between the grains into the air outside as though through a sieve.

"Barrow told me . . . he said that he cut down the forest here to build his condo?" Amon recalled having tea in the Cyst library just after he had learned that Barrow was one of the insurgents.

"Ridiculous," Rashana scoffed. "The trees here are too small and brittle for an entire skyscraper. Barrow acquired his wood from somewhere else. I happen to know."

If what she said was true, it seemed like a strange and elaborate lie to come up with on the spot. Not that Amon would put it past Barrow.

Or had he concocted it earlier in expectation of Amon's concerns about working as his assistant? A trick to reassure Amon that his desire for revenge had been quenched. Whatever his methods and motives, Barrow had clearly been aware of Ogasawara beforehand. Hippo too had mentioned it, something about a society there that had been the inspiration for Xenocyst. Could this be connected somehow to the community Rashana, in her guise as Makesh Adani, had said she wanted to create? New questions spun in Amon's mind, as though stirred into motion by the circular trajectory of Gemini X or the tornado rotor above, a dizzying blur of thought that would remain beyond reach in the stratosphere of awareness so long as the lush enigmatic landscape continued to anchor his attention.

"It–it looks . . . it looks like . . ." He was going to say *the forest in my dream*, but found his words drying up. The mosaic of vegetation, the green slopes and valleys, the glittering leaves, the jagged spiking fronds and slender grasses, the octopus trees with their knotted tentacles of roots exposed. In many ways, it was just like the vista that had lingered beneath his eyelids each morning when he awoke. And yet . . . it wasn't quite identical. The lay of the hills seemed different and nowhere could he find the exact spot he had always stared at as he fell from the sky, unable to turn his head or look anywhere else. He thought that perhaps he was just observing the island from the wrong angle, but they would soon complete a full circle and still there were no signs of the place: a round clearing on the peak of a mountain, dappled in shadows and threads of light, surrounded by green puffs of shrubbery speckled with white flowers, a small depression in the middle of the ground.

What did you expect, he asked himself, *that the landscape in your dream would be an exact replica of a location in the naked world?* In all likelihood, his dream would at best be a credible simulacrum of such a location, or vice versa, assuming it was even possible to directly compare perception to a dream. As he couldn't very well dream with his eyes open, he could only try to match up the vista before him to a memory of his dream, and an old memory at that, since it hadn't visited his sleep once in all his months of bankdeath. Even supposing the dream were as objectively accurate as a LifeStream recording, the island would surely change over time. Trees would be born and die. Typhoons would ravage the hills. Seismic tremors would twist the topography, raising new islands and moving old ones. Obviously, this was the closest he could expect a scene in his waking eye to resemble one from his mind's eye. Obviously, this had to be the destination he had always sought. But if so, he had to wonder why. Why had he been so drawn to this remote island? What had it been doing in the depths of his soul?

"Take me down there!" he cried leaping to his feet, almost shaking with exhilaration and awe. "Bring this craft down."

"I can arrange that. But first we need to talk."

"No! Please. I want to go there now. I don't need to be there long. Just a few moments and we can take off again."

"Landing here isn't an option, I'm afraid."

"Why not?"

"It's too expensive."

"Too—What could be too expensive for you?"

"Many things . . . You'd be surprised."

"But it's just an island!"

"Calm down!" Rashana snapped, raising herself up in her seat, and Amon stared fiercely into her eyes, all words cleared from his mind by the urgency in her voice. Footsteps approached and he turned to find Ono X beside her with two of the Birla Guard, floating straight-backed against the cloud-blotted sky.

"I've brought you to the place you've always wanted to go," said Rashana, her composure restored. "I'm not asking for your gratitude. There's something I have to ask of you in return. But we need to talk.

"So please return to your seat." She pointed to Amon's chair with her upturned palm.

In his wild, tumultuous euphoria, Amon had just enough sense to realize that it was reasonable for her guards to rush in with the way he was behaving, but not enough to fear them. Ignoring Rashana's polite demand, he lowered his gaze once more to Hahajima, where gray-white seabirds now flitted over the rolling treetops. The forest he had scrimped and saved patiently to visit for the better part of a decade was right there, the transparency of the craft suggesting that no barriers remained between them, that he could simply hop into the trees and climb to the moist earth. But this was merely a tantalizing illusion. The walls, however faint in appearance, were solid, the drop to the island deadly. He would need Rashana's permission. Could he attack her and the guards to hijack the rotorcraft and force them to crash land? Could he smash through the wall and leap out on his own? He saw himself plummeting to the canopy, his body tangling and untangling from the thick web of vines as he fell between the branches. The mossy ground might not save his life, but at least he would pass his final moments in his own personal paradise, his blood feeding the tentacle roots and the soil of his deepest desires. Yet such fantasies—even supposing they could be realized—were mad, as though ending your existence right as the truth was finally crystallizing could ever be sane. There was no forgetting his promise to the PhisherKing. Best to hear Rashana out first, which meant he had to be patient. Only a little while longer now.

Amon looked up to meet Rashana's wary gaze and nodded, before taking his seat again. Ono X and the guards backed away, vanishing into cloud and azure.

"I'm sorry," said Amon. "I just . . . how did you know? How did you find what's in my dreams?"

"You've been through a lot, Amon," Rashana told him. "More even than you yourself know."

3
DIASPORA, KINGDOM, THEATRE

Diaspora   January 3rd, 50 FE

It was just after sundown when the man finally arrived in the parking lot on the fringes of Free Tokyo.

Amon had been at the edge of an abutting alley since dawn, sitting against a concrete wall—watching, waiting. It had been a bleak and dreary day. Now, dark marbled clouds edged in hues of orange and mauve by a fading burst of molten light hovered beyond the condos across the lot.

The man entered from between two of these buildings, passing in and out of view behind the sporadically parked cars. He wore a jumpsuit stitched of pockets and slung a bulging sack over one shoulder. Although a touch slimmer than before, there was no mistaking his bulk, and Amon breathed a sigh of relief. After hours on the cold ground, his lower back was stiff and chill, but it was worth it to see that Tamper was okay; at least one of his friends had made it through.

Without Ono X's assistance, Amon would never have found the parking lot. He had visited only once nearly six months ago, on a long trek through unfamiliar streets, in the midst of the cognitive tempest brought on by webloss, so his memory had been of limited use. But the moment he arrived at break of day and spotted the empty plastic bottles littering the tarmac, he had known it was the right place.

Tamper plonked the sack onto the hood of a sedan and approached a ten-story condo. Pausing a short distance away, he looked up at the veranda-stacked wall, restlessly shifting his hands from pocket to pocket, palming the items inside from one to the other. Then, as Amon had watched him do once before, and as he was said to have done every day for years (except for his brief stay at Xenocyst when he designed the sabotage devices), Tamper galloped towards the building and leapt up to grab the floor of a second-story veranda. With practiced grace incongruous with his obesity, he pulled himself up, swung his foot onto the floor, gripped the railing to hoist up the rest of his ample mass, climbed atop the handrail, and plucked a bottle of Cloud9 Nectar from a pocket, before placing it on the floor of the veranda above, climbing down from the rail, and hang-dropping back to the parking lot. His feet took his weight with a *thwump* and he jogged forward several steps to dissipate the impact. Once he'd come to a rest, he stepped back from the building and gazed up expectantly.

When the door of the third floor veranda slid open, Amon was expecting the small frame of Tamper's son to step out and gulp down his favorite drink as before, sweeping his gaze over the parking lot in search of his invisible soda benefactor. Instead, a paunchy middle-aged woman slumped in the doorway. Wearing a cream dressing gown covered in black cat hair, she had waist length brown hair split by her shoulders, the front half clinging by static to her chest. Her midriff and belly were two separate bulges, the curves of her butt visible from the front.

Undoubtedly this was one of the foster parents described in Tamper's letter to Xenocyst. They were supposed to have cheated him of his son to seize the fund his dead wife had bequeathed for the boy's education. When she tottered out with a stiff-hipped, forward-leaning gait and picked up the bottle, Amon could make out her tired face, the pallorous lips hanging open and the flaccid cheeks, under the pale light of the golden hour.

Without hesitation, she twisted the top off the bottle and began to pour its contents over the edge of the balcony. Amon detected no malice in this wasting of a heartfelt gift, only a sort of grim and exhausted acceptance of her duty to prevent the boy from having any contact with his true father. With Tamper facing away from him, oriented only half in profile, Amon couldn't discern his expression, but saw the man biting his fist as he watched the blue liquid spill through the air. How awful to have gambled away everything, even the Freedom to raise his son. Bringing the boy his favorite drink was all that kept Tamper animated and even that small grace was being taken from him. Whether the woman noticed Tamper's reaction was unclear. She never raised her eyes from her feet, as though even her gaze was too heavy to lift.

It was as Amon watched the final drops of soda froth into the trickling puddle that he realized the ground was stained. Evidently, this wasn't the first time the foster mom had caught Tamper in the act. Again and again she had poured this drink out in just the same way, until a patch of discoloration had formed. *How long since she discovered his daily visit?* Amon wondered, when suddenly the woman flinched at the voice of a man hollering from inside. It was loud enough for Amon to hear the imperious tone across the parking lot, though not to catch the words. Fearfully, the woman flung the bottle over the side of the railing as though disposing of evidence.

"Be right there!" she called back as the bottle fell. It bounced and rolled to the side of the square, joining the others that had accumulated. Finally she raised her dull, close-set eyes and directed them at Tamper, with a strange look of both pity and castigation that seemed to say, "I'm sorry for this but don't you dare come back," before tottering inside.

Amon had seen the boy look straight through Tamper and knew the parents had adjusted his ImmaNet settings to edit his father from the feed, but apparently she had disabled this function for herself. He understood immediately what drove her to protect Tamper from her husband even as she prevented him from reaching his son—guilt. A feeling Amon knew all too well.

Long after she slid the door closed behind her, Tamper remained where he was, face upturned towards the balcony, hugging himself around his bloated waist, chest utterly still as though too tight for breaths to enter. Amon wanted to go over and put a hand on his shoulder. But appearing suddenly weeks after his disappearance in the cataclysm would only confuse Tamper at a tender moment. More importantly, Amon worried that showing himself now might undermine the purpose for which he had come. Then the tinder for a new future Rashana had unlocked in the clouds a week earlier would not catch flame from the dying embers of the present. Whatever happened, he couldn't let the frail glow of freedom go out forever. So when Tamper at last started off at a trot the way he had come, Amon began to stalk him, letting the man who had guided him out of the metropolis for the first time now guide him, unbeknownst to the guide himself, into its hidden recesses.

Kingdom   January 10th, 50 FE

Before Amon was a dark pit, a rectangle of Tokyo obliterated, like an inverted skyscraper constructed of nothingness. Down its sides he could see cross sections of the city's underground—first sidewalk; then pipes and maintenance tunnels; then wiring, soil, and rock; finally just darkness. It looked exactly as he remembered, the same chrome door waiting at the edge. The entrance to the PhisherKing's domain. At long last, Amon had returned.

Reconnected to the ImmaNet, he had waded his way through the InfoFlux for the first time since his bankdeath and was relieved at the sensory respite this blank patch offered. Where a hazy afternoon sky should have stretched in his upper peripheral vision, manifold patches of marketainment blinked in alternation. Where silence should have reigned around him, the promohum blathered, while behind his back, he could hear the exclamations and scuffling footsteps of ImmaGamers gamboling through the OtaPlay's many worlds at once.

Despite his thick jacket, Amon could feel the cold creeping inside him. The temperature was no lower than the day last week when he'd found Tamper, and he'd only been standing in front of the pit for two hours now, but the chill wind raised goosebumps as it slid up his sleeves and through his scarf, his nose starting to run.

This was his fifth time to the PhisherKing's domain. First he'd come in the flesh after he was charged for jubilee the previous summer. Then he'd manifested as a figment when Mayuko was being attacked the following morning. On both initial visits, the elevator had appeared promptly behind the chrome doors. But when he'd tried manifesting not long after his conversation with Rashana in the clouds nearly two weeks ago, they had remained closed to him. His guess was that the Phishers had mistaken his figment for one of XXXTrust's copies of him, which had continued to infest Tokyo until around the new year, when the MegaGlom had licensed out his likeness to an anonymous buyer. So he'd tried manifesting again the next day as a generic salaryman, only to receive the same treatment. That morning, Amon had decided to come in the flesh one last time, digimade as himself. Now here he was, still waiting.

With nothing better to do, Amon glanced at the AT readout in the bottom right corner of his visual field:

Property	Fee	Time	Licensor
Blink	¥345,077,354	14:45:45	R-Lite
Sidewalk	¥159,654,456,110	14:45:47	Kavipal
Blink	¥369,218, 200	14:45:50	R-Lite
Exhale	¥976,044,854,901,785	14:45:51	TTY Group
Blink	¥382,123,020,643	14:45:56	Xian Te
Sidewalk	¥2,197,010,532,101	14:45:58	Kavipal
Blink	¥399,987,824,054	14:46:02	R-Lite
Inhale	¥333,105,25,087,114	14:46:04	LYS Dynamics
Blink	¥433,560,134,	14:46:10	TTY Group

Hmph. A closed-mouth laugh escaped his nostrils as he recalled practicing blink reduction in his apartment. What had that silly guru's mantra been? *Blinking is money, blinking is choice, blink less to save yourself, to save yourself, to save your moneee . . . Hah!* Amon scoffed in his head, utterly unfazed by the soaring afternoon inflation.

The values of the world's many currencies were currently so low that even the jubilee charge, an 80-digit number that had taken out the majority of his savings only last summer, seemed like a piddling expense, manageable even for your average wageslave. With enough volatility and time, it might at some point be reduced to almost nothing, not even a blip on a chart, little different than the fee for a rice ball or the clearing of one's throat.

As Amon watched the same old actions traded between the same old companies, with prices that rose and fell in an endless spiral with no center, it all looked to him like so many meaningless symbols, like a sacred text whose power reveals itself only to the believer. Once his emotions had thrilled and waned to the rapid tide of inflation and deflation, his heart pumped by the market. Now it simply bored him, and he cast his gaze back into the pit where his thoughts could roam over issues of greater significance.

Part of this shift in perspective, he knew, was thanks to Rashana covering everything. With her enormous budget floating his actions, there was no need to waste mental energy worrying whether something he did was affordable. But even without it, even if he were still relying on his own labor and the possibility of bankruptcy were still imminent, he wouldn't have cared one whit more. For he had fallen into the abyss of bankdeath, sunk into its depths, and, knowing what awaited him there, was no longer afraid. Of course, he had no desire to be dependent on rapacious charity for his livelihood, nor to be caught in another famine, but shackling himself to the economy was no longer a choice that was in him, because he had learned too much about how it all operated and cared too much about those who suffered as a result.

If only everyone could see the way between, he thought. *If only everyone could rise above the fear and delusion that spins the wheel.*

Amon had kept his promise to the PhisherKing. He had gone on asking questions until he found enough answers to satisfy himself—for the time being anyway. And now that he had fulfilled their agreement, he hoped to make a new one, to bring together their wisdom in kindling the reality for a new age that would burn brighter than any that came before. The PhisherKing himself had foreseen it. *Something tells me your search is leading you to our rejuvenation . . .* Amon just needed the chance to enter his kingdom and talk. Why wasn't he opening the gates?

Theatre   December 27th, 49 FE

Before Amon had settled into his chair or regained even a modicum of calm, Gemini X began to rise from the ocean. He felt no shift in momentum. Their ascent might as well have been a 360 degree panoramic recording of a perspective flying upwards.

"Where are we going?" he asked in dismay, as he watched Hahajima recede through the invisible floor.

"The clouds," said Rashana

"What for?"

"To talk further."

"Can't we talk here?" Already those beautiful treed mountains were nothing but a green dab on glittering cobalt. Amon's hand reached down involuntarily as if to take it with him.

"Listen to you. Like a little boy who wants to keep playing past his bedtime."

"Do you have any idea how long I've waited?"

"Actually, I do. And I want you to appreciate the island to your heart's content. But we need to consider the cost."

"I . . . I don't get it. You can't float above an island for just a few more minutes?"

"There are limits to what I can do, Amon. That's something you'll have to learn to accept."

The air around the craft turned white as they entered a cloud. With the world blocked from view, it sunk in for Amon that the island wasn't coming back any time soon and the weight of disappointment fell upon him like a heavy blow. *Why?* he wondered with dire, almost painful disbelief. *When the forest was so close, why did her Freedom have to suddenly give way?*

"Those limits on action—for all of us, however wealthy—are at the core of the offer I wish to make," Rashana told him, as though their thoughts ran in parallel. "I'd better start there."

As Rashana began to speak, the transparent display walls of the Gemini enveloped them in LifeStream playback. It was as though they sat inside a theatre of raw experience carved into cloud, an enclosed fluid space for absorption of words and the images that decorated them.

The first perspective that appeared was among a group of some fifty men and women in either lab coats or coveralls who stood or sat in a gentle surf at midday. Despite the lapping waves, their outfits remained dry, a sign that they were present as figments.

"This was the founding moment, in the Year of Acquisition, for an alliance of radical scientists and engineers called the Ferment Culture Collective. They were part of a global environmental movement that pitched battle in the few intact ecosystems still existing—the Amazon Rainforest, Vancouver Island, the Great Barrier Reef."

Those of the fifty who were sitting rose undripping, and they all gathered into a circle, standing from ankle to waist deep in the water.

"When old environmental regulations dissolved in the shift to the AT market, the members had individually snapped up properties in Ogasawara. The collective's first joint act was to share these in common."

Seashells were passed around the circle from hand to hand so that everyone could touch each one. When the perspective took a seashell into her palm, a satellite view of the strip of forested mountain that the shell represented was projected above it in a translucent square. She passed it on and the next seashell she received unfurled a tract of shoreline, the one after that the coordinates and geometry for a region of airspace.

"Philanthropy Syndicate developers had purchased what areas of Ogasawara remained and made enormous offers for the collective's assets."

The surf dissolved into the bare wall of a study cubicle overlaid with a 3D model of sea turtle population dynamics. The perspective was adjusting the variables of the model when a message notification popped up. *Sender: IslandGrow Financials. Subject: Regarding Valley Holdings, Opportunity *NOT* to be Missed.* Without hesitation, her hand flicked the message into the trash, focus returning to her research.

"Once properties had been added to their communal pool, the collective's charter effectively immunized them from cooptation. Nothing could be sold or traded without the unanimous consent of thousands of carefully vetted members, and anyone who voted in favor of a deal was automatically expelled. A single conscientious member was all it took to override any bribe or threat."

A viewpoint hovered at sunset above the same surf, coveralled engineers and lab-coated scientists now in the hundreds crowding the shoreline. They faced three men in power suits, who remained at the edge of a concrete path that protruded into the beach as though reluctant to be dirtied by the sand even in graphical form.

"You can be stewards of the archipelago," promised the white man in the center with an implausibly warm, sage-like smile. His voice played through some kind of sound system apparently installed on Gemini X. "We'll let you weed out invasive species, run catch and release programs, whatever you like. In exchange, you'll give our MegaGlom partners an indefinite lease to build ecotourism facilities. All our income will come from harmless luxury actions such as *forest-bathing*, *diving*, *hiking*, and *tanning*. I'm sure you'll agree that this is a win-win arrangement."

Upon hearing this pitch, the assembly shook their heads, rolled their eyes, or sighed in appall, and began to vanish one by one.

"The collective knew the slippery slope of compromise that had led to the Galapagos wildercondo boom and summarily rejected all such overtures. But the developers went ahead anyway, calculating that they could more than recoup the fines for property violations with the draw of this unique destination."

Hovering shovelbots fired dust on a patch of mountain forest, all branches and trunks slid apart abruptly into precise meter-long segments that fell to the earth, and the bots flew in to scoop up the fresh lumber. The seg cut to evening. In the clearing where the trees had been, an ellipse of construction drones squirted architectural ink as they rotated incrementally higher on the same axis, printing layer by layer a drab plastic hotel, that Amon could picture digimade in sparkling glass and marble when finished.

"The Ferment Culture Collective retaliated by raising licensing fees for their properties. They set the amount cautiously, just above the threshold for likelihood of turning a profit from the newly printed resorts. But the result was an escalating tit-for-tat. The Philanthropy Syndicate inflated the fees for its portion and the collective responded in kind, until neither could afford to even approach the islands."

When another eyequake came over Rashana, she paused and the segs winked out, unveiling the encompassing theatre of white. Amon was surprised that, minutes after rising from the ocean, the craft still hadn't broken from the clouds as he'd seen in videos of passenger flights. Instead of an opening to the sky, dense mist churned hypnotically overhead. The unseen cyclone rotor made infinitely fine eddies and vortices, like milk through a fractal eggbeater composed of ever smaller eggbeaters. Its hummingbird flutter seemed to sing contemplation into Amon's mind. When he looked down at the solid curtain below, he thought longingly of the distant islands obscured and was reminded again of the blacked-out areas on world maps during his searches for the dream forest with God's Eye.

"Is that why information about forests is so expensive?" Amon asked, lifting his gaze to find that Rashana's eyes had settled. "I mean, are the hidden regions those protected environments you mentioned—the Great Barrier Reef and all the rest?"

"Not protected exactly. Many have been converted into getaways for those who can afford to know about them. Others are classified Mega-Glom research facilities or military bases. Only Ogasawara escaped such development, and that thanks to the radical financial strategy of the Ferment Culture Collective."

"Those activists could really just jack up prices? What about supply and demand?"

"In the Year of Acquisition, the Moratorium on Catastrophic Exchange was still being designed. It wasn't universally adopted until the first year of the Free Era."

"Moratorium?"

"My gabkeepers seem to have overestimated your prior knowledge. You'd know what I mean if you'd ever used a platinum search engine. The Moratorium on Catastrophic Exchange is a set of algorithms that implement norms of exchange established by the Twelve and One at the dawn of the Free Era. Scarcity simulators, chimera commodities linked to currencies, and other ersatz asset limiters managed by an independent financecorps. The upshot is that price fluctuation is a function of the totality of actions each moment."

"Isn't the AT market supposed to be beyond human control?" said Amon, recalling his speculations about pricing and choice in his apartment the night he was charged for jubilee.

"So bronze engines have many believe. In fact, the MegaGloms submit voluntarily to this system to prevent disastrous market instability and enable competition between them. Think of it as a reverse cartel."

"Then the market was never free to begin with!"

"It all depends on what you mean. There's no public intervention. GATA lacks any institution capable as you know. Its only mechanism that comes anywhere close is the adjustment of credicrime fines. Even Barrow's much vaunted policies to reduce volatility were nothing more than petitioning of the Twelve and One for stimulus and restraint."

"So a private side arrangement."

"The invisible hand of the market always moves on invisible strings. In this case invisible algorithms. How could it be otherwise?"

The theatre of cloud became the perspective of a bare-chested, glistening bodybuilder lumbering through the weight room of a gym, in the direction of a forty-something woman with a high quality digimake who was resting on a bench. He greeted her and showed her his palm, where an erotic seg starring him played. She looked at the seg, glanced his body over, squeezed his hefty thigh to test if it was as hard as it appeared, and finally met his eyes, smiling provocatively. Cut to the bodybuilder lying on his back atop endless dunes of breast and phallus-shaped pillows, his pectorals bulging from creased labia-like sheets, nodding as the woman clung naked to his side and whispered into his ear. With some inconspicuous eye-dialing, he clipped the past few minutes of his audiovisual feed and sent it to a list of contacts.

"When the Ferment Culture Collective received a leak about the Moratorium on Catastrophic Exchange then being finalized, their coders immediately set about to format the definitions of their communal action properties for direct registration with the Ministry of Records. This bypassed the services of MegaGlom-approved Property Attorneys, who would have otherwise programmed in Moratorium smart contracts. The collective could then set their prices arbitrarily high, and the Philanthropy Syndicate retaliated by pulling their holdings in Ogasawara from the Moratorium so that they could do the same."

An aerial montage of islands in the chain—Hahajima, Chichijima, Iwo Jima—showed towns nestled around bays and houses dotting the lush mountains. Along the connecting roads blasted luggage-strapped cars.

"The surge in fees forced a panicked exodus of residents, many of whom had been settled for generations. Soon one minute ashore was enough to bankrupt almost anyone."

Families crowded around boats and carbonjets with heaps of suitcases, arguing and shoving for a place on board.

"Within 24 hours, the islands of Ogasawara were entirely deserted. It was thereafter presumed by all involved to be permanently out of bounds for humankind. Until, that is, a young visionary named Sahar Iwabuchi rose to prominence within the collective."

A perspective perched on a high-piled cairn looked down upon thousands of other figments, seated on smaller cairns across a great plain of grasses that swayed to the twilit horizon.

"The financial barriers are not an obstacle but a shield," the perspective proclaimed, raising her hands palm inward to signify protection, her voice soft and thoughtful but ringing with conviction. "All that would be required of us is to split into two divisions. Bankliving members to hold onto our action properties and prevent development as always. Bankdead to resettle Ogasawara and realize a new ideal."

The rapt eyes of the assembly shimmered in the gloaming above grasses bowing in stillness between breezes.

"The majority of the collective was immediately swayed by Iwabuchi's plan. Once the preparations were in place, half the membership volunteered to go bankrupt by donating all their savings and more to the cause."

Dawn broke over a petal-spewing toy-block roofscape as a supply centicopter let a folding ladder down to a precarious ledge, from which a bankdead woman hurriedly climbed the rungs.

"Bankliving members who had infiltrated the venture charities tracked these willing crashnewbs through the Delivery vending system and arranged for their retrieval from the District of Dreams."

A bird's eye time lapse seg captured boats and carbonjets arriving at Hahajima over the course of several weeks. The concrete, glass, and plastic buildings of the main port town and its outlying settlements were gradually disassembled and the foundations for plantfoam buildings began to sprout up in their place, literally growing from the soil.

"The separation of roles between bankliving property holders to price out developers and bankdead settlers to evade the developers' retaliatory fees allowed the collective and the collective alone to inhabit Ogasawara."

Boats of living seaweed and coral disembarked from the harbor of a now complete biotectured city. Green blossoming houses and towers like hewn monoliths of compacted garden rose from the round shoreline to varying terraced heights, following the lay of the hills and blending with the ensconcing mountain forest.

"The collective grew cities like the first on other islands in Ogasawara, and the resulting archipelago federation was dubbed Hakkotopia, or 'place of fermentation.' It was entirely self-sufficient, and might have continued indefinitely in harmony with local ecologies if not for a crucial miscalculation."

The perspective, who from her height and eye movements, Amon guessed to be Sahar Iwabuchi, rested her hands on the rail of a coral ferry at sea, watching a metallic speedboat approach from the direction of a tanker. The speedboat turned alongside the hull of the ferry and cut its motor. Then, while rough waves slapped the hull, a woman in a dark suit stood up from the narrow, bobbing deck and began to shout above the hiss of the spray.

The audio quieted as Rashana continued her narration. "SpawnU Consortium sales representatives came to parlay just outside the unaffordability zone. They offered the collective irrevocable permission to spread to Aogashima, an island north of Ogasawara. Inevitably, SpawnU subsidiaries had taken note of how these activist upstarts had ruined Philanthropy Syndicate real estate investments and wanted to help them do further damage."

Under starlight, the perspective stood with some ten others atop a low plantfoam dome dwarfed by the surrounding buildings. Shadowy spectators huddled on sculpted mushroom stoops, cross-hatched bamboo porches, and vine-mesh hammocks growing from the sides of the looming walls, observing the conference while giant fruit bats swooped between.

"That is why we must never step outside our financial protections," a man facing the perspective concluded. "It would spell our doom."

The dark vista swung right then left as the perspective gave a single firm shake of her head. "And give up our only chance to offer this way of life to the world?" Iwabuchi accused him with sonorous zeal. "Tell me, people of Hakkotopia. Are you so timid that you would have us sacrifice this marvelous opportunity simply out of fear?"

Hoots of denial sounded from the heights.

Cut to the camera of a drone at daytime. It floated over the shoulder of a man in a tunic of seashell silk. He was guiding a family wearing cheap store-bought shorts and T-shirts through a plantfoam village in a sandy valley. As the mother, father, and young son and daughter gawked at the street lined with blooming houses, aflutter with butterflies and vibrant birds, their eyes lit up with such wonder that it shone through the fog of the Elsewhere Gaze. The kids scampered over to pat the wood-flecked-fern brick facade of a shed in disbelief, and Amon remembered his own tactile investigations in the Atupio BioPen that morning. He could almost smell the invigorating fragrance of the scene.

"The bankliving inhabitants of Aogashima were enticed by the lifestyle that the collective's first outpost promised. Quickly, it swelled into the largest city in the federation.

"This was one territorial line too far for the Philanthropy Syndicate. If outposts spread to other SpawnU-owned islands further north and reached O Island near the mouth of Tokyo Bay, settler cells could be smuggled through the port aboard SpawnU ships and land in the south Tumbles. There the desperate residents, stranded further from Delivery supplies than any other bankdead, would be eager converts to such a self-sufficient enclave, reducing the helpless need that impels parents to gift their babies. If the Philanthropy Syndicate was consequently forced to deploy the Charity Brigade, and SpawnU sent in its own freekeepers, these communities might even become loci for proxy skirmishes between the two blocs.

"Lack of information about Hakkotopia, cut off from the ImmaNet and unreachable by spies, forced hazardcorps algorithms to heavily weight the risk of these contingencies. While the Philanthropy Syndicate could shoulder losses from forestalled tourism, such threats to security and the human resource extraction that sustained MegaGlom existence could not be ignored."

Soon after the segs had faded again, a gap opened in the whirlpool matrix of cloudmilk above and filled the cabin with direct sunlight. The bright blue hole shot rapidly along the roof of Gemini X from fore to aft. When it had slipped away behind them, they were back in the soft glow of seamless white, but the brief dazzle had awoken wonderings in Amon.

He recalled the cold floor of the digital quarantine when Hippo had mentioned Ogasawara to him and to Rick, thoughts of whom remained unnervingly devoid of feeling.

"Hippo told me once that Xenocyst was inspired by this community," he said. "I can see now where he got the idea of setting up his foundation to provide supplies."

"Yes. The main difference is that Hakkotopia was willing to expand whereas Xenocyst was intent on—maybe I should say obsessed with—remaining small."

"I'm sure Hippo would say that he learned from their mistakes."

"The decision to spread north wasn't actually as reckless as you might think. Iwabuchi assumed that the core of the federation on Hahajima and Chichijima would be untouchable even if outlying settlements rose and fell. And she would have been right if our begetters had been on their side."

"Weren't they? I would have thought that Fertilex interests should align with SpawnU's here. A drop in extracted resource yield, and the Philanthropy Syndicate orders more order-grown profiles, no?"

"Except that Fertilex is unique among the Twelve and One. It was run by just two people, not boards of executives or tacticorps. So it has always been a wild card, swayed sometimes by caprice and personal conviction rather than sheer profit. This was one of those cases. As you point out correctly, standard corporate logic demanded support for the federation in disrupting the Charity Gift Economy. But in the collective, my begetters saw a much deeper threat."

Rashana considered Amon with her sharp gaze, razor lashes glimmering dewily under the cloudglow. The length of the pause before the next seg began so perfectly generated suspense that he suspected it had been calculated by raConTeur. Her parents, some twenty years younger than in the year of their death, had appeared. They were rendered as eight-armed giants against a violent storm of electricity and plasma that writhed through the entirety of space.

"Ogasawara holds precious, irreplaceable nature, a treasure that cannot by definition be manufactured—not by any of us," crackled the titanic Birla father, rippling with raw energy. "The common people will forever overlook its value. They will forever associate nature with the taboo of nostieism thanks to the InfoFlux we have bestowed. And doesn't their revulsion make it all the more appealing to those like us, those with cultivated tastes? What could offer greater distinction than real wilderness?"

Blue electric faces molded from the storm nodded in agreement.

"So how has it come about that discreditable lowlifes, mere bankdead, are monopolizing some of the only forests and reefs that remain? How is it that they"—a peal of thunder sounded—"can indulge in opulent actions there—sunbathing, sex, feasting, dancing, not to mention recycling, reducing, and reusing, when we, the wealthiest few on earth can't even fly close enough to catch the scent of the breeze that blows over the hills?"

The watchers now glowered and shook their heads, their physiognomy jolting furiously.

"In this, the promise of the Free World has been broken," the Birla mother declared, her many arms swinging wildly like boughs in a tempest. "Its fundamental principle—*All the Freedom you can earn*—has been turned on its head. Winners who have earned the ultimate Freedom are denied an option that losers who have relinquished the ability to earn any freedom whatsoever can choose whenever they like. Hakkotopia flaunts everything the AT market stands for. And its spread adds insult to injury. It is only a matter of time before every impulsive sloth gazes idly from their mansion windows at us, the talented and ambitious, while we grovel in the mud. Something has to be done!"—bolts of lightning flew from each of her swinging hands in haphazard directions—"No one feels this more keenly than we, who have earned the most Freedom of all. If anyone has the right to visit Ogasawara it is us."

When the overlay vanished, afterimages remained seared over Amon's vision, coloring the cloud with faint steely streaks. Rashana's eyes were closed, whether saddened by the sight of her deceased parents or for some other reason there was no telling. It was the first time Amon had heard the voices of these secretive overlords of finance. More than anything else so far, this somehow felt like a privilege. At last, someone was showing him what could only be found on platinum engines, and so much more that he could never have hoped to afford.

Then Amon thought again of Hippo, who had heard the parents' voices, perhaps even their naked voices, as a friend to the Birla family. And of the PhisherKing, whose power to conceive had been taken by Fertilex through the maiming of his mind. He wished the three of them could have been connected so he could share everything he learned as he learned it. Something told him that if there was some way they could meet again, the forces of iniquity that enslaved humanity wouldn't stand a chance. The thought left him trembling, excited for what overthrow might yield and afraid for what it might take away.

Diaspora   January 3rd, 50 FE

"Good evening," said Amon, loud enough that his voice would carry to all ears present. "It's me, Gura. Excuse me for surprising you, but I'm looking for Hippo. Is he with you?"

He stood at the top of a wall in the entrance to a crowded alcove, a rectangle of Free Tokyo rooftop enclosed on all sides by taller structures. From the left edge, the outside of a train tunnel angled upwards to form a sloping ceiling. The other edges were sealed off by the glass walls of skyscrapers, a crack between two buildings on the right admitting a shaft of moonlight, the only illumination.

Directly under this faint glow, men, women and children huddled together for warmth; around it Amon could see shadowy figures, and further only vague black forms. Tamper, who he'd followed here, had already melted into the darkness at the back. It was difficult to tell how many people were packed into the tight alcove but Amon guessed dozens.

At the sound of his voice, several slumped on the floor perked up and a few jolted to their feet in alarm. All eyes were on him, in gradation from glittering to faint glimmering to shrouded depending on their distance from the pane of moonlight. No one showed signs that they had recognized him, standing in the shadows of the periphery. He began to wonder if any of the survivors even knew who he was.

A few mouths opened as if to say something but no words followed. It must have been shocking, Amon supposed, for someone in Free Tokyo to acknowledge their existence, let alone approach them at night with a greeting. Already he was cold with fear, unsure how they would react to his presence, and the winter wind blowing up the sheer wall he'd just climbed only made it worse, slipping beneath his jacket and brushing a chill up his back. Here and there hands reached inside coats and bundles, whether securing some treasure, perhaps a morsel of food, or readying weapons Amon could not discern.

"Excuse me for surprising you all like this," he repeated. "I'm looking for—"

"Who's there?!" a man interrupted.

Amon recognized the voice but his mind had no time to place it as footsteps shuffled towards him. He was about to step forward into better light when "I know who id is!" rasped another man with a bad slur that Amon almost thought he knew.

"Gura?" said a woman in disbelief.

"Vertical!" cried Amon, wanting to rush over but unsure where she was. "You're ok! What happened to the others?"

"Don't worry abo't them," slurred the second man who had spoken. "Ith got nothing to do with you."

"Is *Rick* with you?" asked Vertical.

Amon didn't know how to respond, saddened by the desperate hope in her voice.

"Whad' ya thing your doing here?" the man demanded.

"Who's that?" Amon asked, tantalized by the familiarity of the voice. "Ty?"

"Fug' you!"

The curse struck him with hurt and confusion, for he became certain the moment he heard it that it had come from Ty. Amon wasn't expecting a warm welcome after the exposé he had proposed to the council went horribly awry, but Ty's open hostility shocked him. After all their campaigns and everything they'd been through together. The slur made Amon wonder if he was drunk, though he'd watched Ty down bottle after bottle of the *suposhu* he brewed and had never witnessed such a change before.

"You're okay too," Amon replied tentatively.

"Ogay? Ogay? You think I'm ogay?"

"Listen, Ty. I'm sorry if I—"

"Sorry? Our fugging home is gone. Thousands of our friends are dead. We lotht everything because of you!"

Amon thought of Ty's tricycle in the library. In all likelihood, that too had been lost in the turmoil brought on by Barrow's downfall.

"Ty, I tried my best and—"

"Your bethd you say? Do you have any idea what they did to me?"

When something began to scrape along the floor towards him, Amon took a frightened step back, his heel now flush with the ledge.

"Ty! Relax!" Vertical shouted, and Amon saw one of the crouching shadows leap to her feet and pounce out of sight into deeper darkness. "You need to rest."

"Out of my way!" Ty snarled from that direction and several of the men who had crept around Amon shuffled aside. A knee-high shadow approached between the parted bodies. At the head of it, Ty's face soon emerged into the moonlight and Amon saw that he was crawling. No, not crawling. Scrabbling along with his arms, dragging his belly and waist, his legs just dead weight.

"Loog!" he growled, glaring at Amon with pained, angry eyes as he propped his upper body on his elbows and pointed at his own face, the left half paralyzed. "Loog at what your ideas are worth."

At that moment, a swooshing roar started above; a train passing through the tunnel as though crossing the gulf of suffering that now separated Amon from a man he had thought of as a friend.

Kingdom   January 10th, 50 FE

By twilight, the chill of the concrete had spread up from the soles of Amon's feet to his core. It seemed that for whatever reason, the PhisherKing would not be accepting his audience. Sniffling and rubbing his hands together, Amon began to consider why.

He dismissed the possibility that the Phishers mistook his body for one of XXXTrust's copies; they were too perceptive and well-informed for that. So perhaps they had learned of his association with Rashana and labeled him a threat. But Rashana's privacy infrastructure was near impenetrable even with their sophisticated intelligence capabilities, and in case there had been a leak, Amon had made a point of coming alone, unaccompanied by any of the assistants she had offered, to put the Phishers at ease. Had the visitation procedures changed then? Not according to any platinum sources Amon could dig up. Could the Phishers have packed up shop and moved? Could something have happened to them?

Amon really hoped not. He had an important proposition to discuss and not a lot of time to discuss it. The PhisherKing's unique talents made him indispensable to the new historical beacon they hoped to set alight, an ignition switch for the fuse of a glorious future. The other reason Amon feared his absence, of less significance to the world perhaps, was of the utmost importance to Amon personally: Monju had been the last person he knew to speak with Mayuko.

I'm in Kanda waiting for the PhisherKing. Hoping he can tell me where you are. Let me know that you're safe when you can. Please.

Amon gestured and the message was added to a long scroll of unread texts. He'd begun sending them nearly two weeks earlier, soon after donning his training bank. Barrow had been right that reconnecting to the ImmaNet would be possible for him. Since committing identity suicide meant cash crashing without liquidation, Amon's DNA had remained registered with GATA, allowing genome access via training bank just like BioPen youth. Unfortunately, this left him without an account of his own, so he needed Rashana to leash him and pay for each of his actions. The very first of these, aside from breaths and blinks, had been to try and reach Mayuko.

During his former banklife, Amon would have simply located her on the map in her inner profile, but in using the Death Codes on himself he'd erased the ID signature to which she'd granted complete access. So his old profile was gone along with such privileges, and his only choice was to seek her out on the same footing as anyone else, unable to so much as peek through the Blinding that veiled her personal data.

With the help of Ono X's cryptobreakers, Amon had flesh-hacked into his own BodyBank to retrieve Mayuko's contact info from the LifeStream saved inside. Then he'd tried facephone, sent videos, and fired off text after text after text. But there was no sign that they got through: no reply, no automated do-not-disturb warning, nothing. No notification that she was disconnected either, which confirmed that she was still bankliving and thus also living, a fact that might have been more reassuring if he knew why she wasn't picking up. Since Amon was contacting her without his old signature, she wouldn't know it was coming from him. Perhaps she was being overcautious, hiding from anyone and everyone as Amon had advised her before his cash crash. Or . . . could something awful have befallen her, perhaps while searching for him in the camps?

XXXTrust seemed to have licensed out Mayuko's likeness to an anonymous buyer around the same time as Amon's. This development was as puzzling as the MegaGlom's original efforts to confound the search for them, though the timing was fortunate as it meant that Mayuko's copies would no longer get in the way. Even still, in spite of Rashana reopening investigations on Amon's behalf with all her bespoke journalists and Ono X's vast network of spies, they had yet to find any trace of her in the Free World or in the District of Dreams. The PhisherKing was the last person he could think to turn to. But he was proving just as hard to locate. Amon wasn't sure how much longer he could bear to wait.

He was about to message Ono X to come fly him back to Atupio Home Office, when hard objects pressed into his head on all sides—one in each temple, one between his eyes, and one in the divot at the top of his spinal cord. They felt terrifyingly like the muzzles of guns. Who or whatever was wielding them had paid to edit themselves out of the ImmaNet. Amon tried to jerk away but the pressure on the four cylinders increased, pinioning him in place.

"*Each of these fires a different kind of dust,*" said four voices almost simultaneously so that they sounded like echoes of each other. "*Think what combination of harm we might deliver. Let your imagination run wild!*"

Theatre   December 27th, 49 FE

"It was in the year 26 FE," Rashana continued, after they had finished a hotpot of *oden* and rice for lunch, "that our begetters convinced their Philanthropy Syndicate allies to put me and Anisha in charge of a task-force to crack down on Hakkotopia. We were 20 years old, and we'd just learned that our identity signatures would never be separate.

"This was by far our most difficult assignment to date. The federation was resistant to all the standard measures MegaGloms use to cow dissent. A supply embargo wouldn't work because the community produced everything itself. Our tacticorps ruled out a peacedrone strike, even with our begetters' budget for violence at any scale, on account of the unaffordability zone and risk of damage to valuable environments."

"What about a lawsuit?" Amon asked. "Like the one the Philanthropy Syndicate used to sue Hippo's foundation out of existence."

"You mean by citing the Sustainability Act."

Amon nodded.

"Our litigaticorps advised against it because the Ferment Culture Collective wasn't registered as a legal entity. It was an informal association. Their bylaws, including the clause requiring unanimous agreement for sales, were a set of contracts programmed into their shared action properties, rather than an agreement between members. This spread liability vanishingly thin.

"The idea Anisha and I eventually hit upon was to use Liquidators to breach the unaffordability zone. I imagine you can guess how this would work."

Amon thought it over, zoning out on the textured grain of whiteness streaming beneath the transparent floor, with lower lip pinched between his fingers. Presently, Ono X appeared balancing two porcelain coffee cups on a silver tray. With his available hand, he set their cups and nimbly stacked their dishes and napkins on the tray, before vanishing into cloud.

"You'd have to convince GATA to issue a warrant to enter Ogasawara," Amon decided finally. "I never had to use a warrant myself. I only know colleagues who did. An ID Executioner makes the case that temporary exemption from action fees is essential to complete a mission. We were discouraged from initiating the procedure because of all the red tape involved. The Liquidation Minister has to sign off for submission to the Executive Council. I don't see how a bogus warrant would even reach the review stage."

"At the time, the Minister of Liquidation was a man named Lawrence Barrow and he oversaw an ID Executioner named Yoshiyuki Sekido."

"Well that explains it!" Amon exclaimed with a laugh. His mirth curdled abruptly into puzzlement when he realized that thinking about these two men, who had both betrayed him and ruined his life, no longer bothered him in the slightest. Rashana only smiled.

"But hold on," said Amon. "Hippo told me that Sekido's girlfriend was involved with the collective. Wasn't he a dedicated humanitarian back then?"

Uttering the words "Sekido" and "girlfriend" in the same sentence gave Amon the willies.

"True," said Rashana. "And that's exactly why Barrow assigned him to the mission."

On a comet shooting through an iridescent nebula, the perspective was seated beside a twenty-year-old Birla sister in a dinner gown of blackness and constellations. They faced across an icy rock table an early thirty-something Barrow in a sharp indigo suit, his long salt-and-pepper hair blowing in the solar winds.

Barrow reached out and caught a passing beam of light. When he brought his hand down to the table, it held a finger bowl of mixed nuts.

"You've had some time to think it over?" asked the viewpoint in the voice of a Birla sister.

Barrow nodded.

"Then you accept?" the other sister confirmed.

"Under two conditions," Barrow replied.

"Conditions?" said the perspective. "I don't believe you're in any position to refuse."

"Nor are you. We all know that you'll never secure the warrant without me."

"Then you're willing to accept the consequences?"

"If you are." Barrow shot the sisters an under the eyebrow stare with his husky-blue eyes, confident and unblinking, as he took a pinch of nuts into his palm and popped them into his mouth.

"What were the consequences?" Amon asked.

"Either our Onos stutter dusted him, or he accepted a lifetime stipend to fund his political activities."

"Harsh choice." Watching Barrow casually chew his nuts, Amon couldn't help admiring the man's audacity. Acquiring a stutter would have taken the eloquence that propelled his career.

"Perhaps you've never heard of a Birla Deal," Rashana said, and Amon shook his head. "It's a choice between superlatives of fortune. Either one cooperates and goes to heaven or resists and goes to hell. Our begetters never offered anything in between. We were taught to do the same."

★

Barrow glanced with rehearsed impatience at his watch and said, "Will that be all?"

"Fine," the perspective replied. "Your conditions. What are they?"

"First, a shipment of timber from Canada."

"For what purpose?" asked her sister.

"For a building I'm designing. Here's an order listing the precise quantity and quality I require"—Across the table Barrow tossed a handful of stardust that forked into streams for each sister—"For your perusal and consideration."

Without examining the file, the perspective said, "And your second condition."

"Your partner in this project—the Philanthropy Syndicate. Tell them to extend the expiration date of Fleet supplies for giftless in the District of Dreams by ten percent."

"For what purpose?" her sister asked.

"If I'm going to help you destroy something so remarkable as that federation, I want assurance that I'll be giving something back."

"Bullshit!" Amon guffawed, then watched a drop of spittle fly from his mouth and land on the reappeared coffee table. As if this would somehow reverse the faux pas, he touched his fingertips to his lips.

"What makes you say that?" Rashana asked.

"Barrow trying to help the giftless?"

"We have every reason to believe his motives."

"Come on. If anything it was for political optics."

"No. All evidence suggests that Barrow respected and admired the bankdead. He seems to have sincerely believed that their disconnection from the ImmaNet brought them closer to the sacred domain of analog detritus."

At this, Amon heard Barrow's fervent voice, as though the memory were playing in the clouds. *Going home, to the birthplace of humanity, the origin of everything, the naked world,* Barrow had preached in his spa. Amon could almost feel the grain of the wood paneling in his museum, wood from Canada, not Ogasawara. He had to admit that Barrow's fanatical nostieism lent plausibility to Rashana's defence of him. Or perhaps the strange dullness of emotion he'd noticed was sapping his justified hatred.

The seg skipped ahead to where the comet had travelled some distance through the nebula.

"Our Onos have acquired intelligence that Sekido is an ardent supporter of the collective," said the viewpoint sister, tossing Barrow a handful of stardust.

"Take care that he doesn't learn of the warrant," her twin advised. "He might interfere with the approval process."

Barrow just smiled puckishly, his immaculate teeth lurid under the astral glow. "Would you believe me if I told you I have a better strategy?"

Cut to a seg of a text message read aloud in Barrow's mellifluous voice.

"Sekido-kun, I have an assignment for you. Very prestigious. Top secret in fact . . ."

Amon recalled the glorified mission Sekido had dropped hints about last summer, which had turned out to be Barrow's identity assassination. He was struck by the uncanny circularity, as if Sekido in his capacity as Liquidation Minister had, consciously or unconsciously, reenacted what had been done to him.

"Who was Sekido anyway?" Amon asked.

"The only child of a radical political theorist," Rashana said. "She was famous for her role advising the Tokyo Roundtable and pushing through the anonymity law that underpins the House of Blinding."

POV of a child seated on a rubbery floor watched a backflipping carrot clean its buckteeth with a Fertilex toothbrush.

"Yoshi!" a stern female voice called, and young Sekido looked up at an undigimade mid-forties woman with greying hair in a frizzy bun who had just stepped into the Fertilex-logoed playroom. "How many times do I have to tell you not to watch that fakery? The other children are on the roof with your SubMom playing a healthy game of dodgeball."

Young Sekido turned back to the carrot as it performed flamboyant Fertilex-patented circling motions with the toothbrush, purported to add extra gleam.

"All her efforts to counteract Sekido's lulling commercadvercation during her brief visits to the BioPen only succeeded in disenchanting him with the Free World system. When she got him into GATA through her contacts, with high hopes that he'd impact institutions from within, he coasted along, putting in the minimum effort."

"Hippo told me that Sekido was a capable Liquidator.

"He may have seemed that way by the time they met. That was some time after the mission that changed everything for him."

"Cash crash over, cash crash done, fight the market till a new world comes," chanted a group of protestors on a soccer field. They had formed a protective ring around a man that the viewpoint and his Liquidator partner were approaching in step. The Liquidator shouldered apart the human barricade to jam a duster into the circle. Amon found himself listening to the nerve dust scream with perfect equanimity and worried again about himself. Had he stopped caring for the plight of those he had ruined?

Once the bankrupt had fallen, the protestors fanned out on their backs, holding hands on top of him. The perspective stood back hesitantly even in spite of his partner furiously waving him over to help pry apart the chain. Then it turned to someone calling out, a face on the ground, a young woman. Their eyes met, she smiled, and a window appeared asking if he would accept her contact info, yes or no. His hand clicked yes.

"This was Sekido's introduction to the Ferment Culture Collective. He knew they were paying the No Logo fees for countercultural behavior and the GATA fines for obstructing justice. Their willingness to tempt bankruptcy for what they believed spoke to everything his mother had taught him."

A man's viewpoint walked arm-in-arm with the activist woman through Ginza, their outfits evolving in real-time along with the shifting apparel of the crowd. Cut to them clumsily ice-skating around a rink in a smooth desert of mauve sand. Cut to her leading him by the hand into the scarlet room of a love hotel.

"Sekido had found a new lease on life. He started donating to the collective and attending their meetings. He also began to try at his job for the first time and received a promotion to ID Executioner after a scandal in his squadron."

The woman sat beside his perspective across from two middle-aged men in an izakaya, vegetables sizzling on the gridle in the center of the table, cocktail mugs cluttering the edges.

"You should give some serious thought to how you can make a difference," she said, drizzling oil from a plastic jar onto the veggies.

The two men nodded solemnly. "Your job does more harm than good," one of them agreed.

Sekido met the stares of the men, then turned to his girlfriend. Only able to withstand her gaze for a moment, he lifted a glass to his lips, realized it was empty, and put it back down.

"I can't just throw away my career," Sekido complained.

"Lucky that you don't have to," the other man replied with a smug grin.

"The collective introduced Sekido to Hippo for identity euthanasia so that he could dedicate himself to running Xenocyst. There were no credilaw precedents or GATA protocol regulations, so Sekido slipped by without serious punishment. But he was nonetheless put on probation by the Liquidation Ministry. Barrow's big mission presented a chance to restore his reputation."

A hand swiped through hundreds of anonymized bankruptcy reports. The seg's focus paused on one of them and zoomed in on the attached map. All coordinates and identifying landmarks had been omitted. It showed only that the target, indicated by a red dot, was inside the bedroom of an undisclosed mansion. Enormous numbers in the surrounding rooms and exterior garden ticked higher and lower, representing a minefield of volatile trespassing fees.

"Sekido immediately proposed a warrant to Barrow. The Executive Council approved it thanks to rare cross-lobby cooperation, with votes in favor from Absolute Choice and our begetter's representatives in Moderate Choice. It wasn't until Sekido had already been dispatched to Ogasawara, that he realized the bankruptcy reports were fabrications—these courtesy of my twin and I."

From his seat on an airplane, he stared in shock at a map of the island chain riddled with red dots.

"Sekido knew perfectly well that there were no hotels on any of the islands, nor was there a single bankrupt, only the bankdead settlers in their organic dwellings. This left him with a choice during his few minutes in the air. Follow through with the sham of a mission or try to warn the community."

Sekido's gaze had shifted to the window as first the city and then the ocean blasted away at turbo speed, his spread palm pressing on the glass, breaths fluttering noisily, out-of-focus eyes shaking with panic and thought.

"If he led his squadron to success, he could expect a raise and recognition within GATA. If he hazarded subordination, the potential consequences were terrifying. With the cost of actions exempted and bottomless corporate funding to spend, Barrow could have the Liquidators do literally anything to Sekido during the mission—from torture to identity assassination. And advance warning would not save Hakkotopia anyway. It was completely unprepared to face so many armed combatants. So Sekido could either betray the only cause he'd ever believed in for a boost in Freedom or throw away his job, his ID, and maybe his life in a futile gesture of resistance. This was the Birla Deal that we arranged after Barrow proposed implicating Sekido in the crackdown."

When the seg faded, Amon tilted his head back onto the top of the chair and turned up to face the vortex of white, making way for the rising memory of a choice Sekido had foisted upon him the day of his induction into GATA. He could either go to a room with a prostitute and betray Mayuko or say no and perhaps end his career before it had even begun. Dumbfounded by the sudden pressure in his immaturity, Amon had played along by default, telling himself that he would extricate from the situation before anything got too serious. The inertia of this refusal to make a difficult choice either way had carried him inevitably to the decision that had been laid for him.

"So Sekido did his calculations on that short flight," said Amon, wrenching his gaze from the sad past to align with Rashana's attention. "In the end, he didn't have the resolve to sacrifice everything for his principles—he folded."

"Not completely. We had misjudged his needs. It was a failure of intelligence. Our Onos learned about Sekido's connection to the collective after he ID euthanized Hippo. But they never discovered about his girlfriend. Sekido had hid their involvement by changing his digimake constantly when they were together. She had chosen bankdeath months earlier and immigrated to Hahajima. We had no idea that our deal would put someone he loved on the scales, or we would have picked a different Liquidator."

While the jet turned for its descent to the island, a translucent facephone window projected a young Barrow in the same indigo suit.

"I'll complete the mission," Sekido sniveled. "I'll sign away the rights to every seg. But you've got to keep her safe whatever happens!"

Above his husky-blue eyes, Barrow's brow was knit with concern. "Leave it to me. I promise."

"I bet he broke that promise the second the mission was over."

"No. In fact Barrow did everything he could to keep it."

"Like what?"

A new perspective stood in midair beside a Birla sister, surveying Hahajima from high above. Liquidators roved over the island: marching into plantfoam towers, battering down the doors of elegant fungal houses molded between tree trunks; unmooring coral houseboats and freighters on the shore; hauling limp bodies into centicopters.

"As per our plan, Barrow ordered the Liquidators to fly the Hakkotopians to Delivery, supposedly to await Collection Agents, who in actuality were never dispatched. Once the Liquidators pulled out, Barrow's part in the crackdown was scheduled to end. He'd been told that the Hakkotopians would be dumped in Delivery as an injection of potential HR for the Philanthropy Syndicate to extract. He could have simply allowed Sekido's girlfriend to be hauled off with them. But he begged me and Anisha to take her in and look after her."

"You saved her for Sekido?"

"It wasn't up to us. This was years before I founded Atupio, so we had no Er facilities if she turned out to be giftless, and our begetters wouldn't authorize the expense of harboring her in any Fertilex brandclans if she was gifted. The Philanthropy Syndicate didn't even respond to our inquiries. Barrow was left to fulfill his promise alone."

Down the ramps running from parked centicopters to the rooftop of Delivery, Liquidators wheeled gurneys bearing unconscious Hakkotopians. Closeup on one of them. Sekido's girlfriend curled up on her side in a tunic of seashell silk. Cut to a supply lane inside Delivery. Instead of a bankdead lineup between the vending machine walls, career volunteers pushed the gurneys to a genereader up ahead. There freekeepers lifted the limp arms of the Hakkotopians and inserted their index fingers into the aperture. The perspective was rolling along Sekido's girlfriend. When the freekeepers weren't looking, he veered left and rolled her out of the entrance lane through a slat between two machines. In the exit lane, another career volunteer received the gurney and began to walk nonchalantly towards a pair of doors at the end.

"Before her genome was registered, Barrow paid career volunteers to geneshine and don juan her," Rashana explained.

"Just like with Minister Kitao," said Amon. "I heard from Barrow that Kitao's ex-wife licensed geneshine dust on his behalf."

By editing Kitao's somatic genome just enough to fool the plutogenic standard of some MegaGlom without unwanted phenotypic shifts, she had purportedly raised him from giftlessness and secured his spot in a brandclan respected by Opportunity Science.

"Like many wealthy bankliving with crashnewb loved ones before her," said Rashana. "But the case with Sekido's girlfriend was slightly different. Kitao was never don jauned that we're aware."

"No. I guess he didn't have anyone after him, so there wasn't any need."

Amon was glad he never had to take Rashana up on her offer to treat him and the other Delivery saboteurs with don juan dust, reorganizing tissue and bone molecules to disguise their naked faces from Charity Brigade and CareBot retaliation. Not only did the idea of using a technology preferred by serial slum resort debauchers creep him out, but he had worried that Mayuko would no longer recognize him . . . if and when he found her.

"Anyway, you're saying that Barrow boosted the plutogenic status of Sekido's girlfriend to get her into a comfortable brandclan. And arranged to restyle her physiognomy to prevent the Syndicate from tracking her."

"Yes. But someone, perhaps my begetters or the Syndicate, they found out about the smuggling and exclusively licensed all related segs from the career volunteers involved. So Barrow couldn't give Sekido any record of her dusting. Or of her new genome and appearance."

"Then . . ." Amon saw Mayuko searching for him in the camps, looking for his face in a crowd-filled labyrinth. Finding Amon would have been hard enough, but the woman could have looked like anyone. "Sekido never found her?"

"If she was ever in the camps. That's where most of her compatriots ended up. But the leadership were marked as hungry ghosts, starved to death before bankliving members of the collective could retrieve them. Sekido believed she was one of those."

Wearing a disheveled white dress shirt, a young south Asian man with a bad slouch stared at himself in a mirror, biting his lip until it bled. Amon pictured the multiple digimakes of his old boss overlaid on the reflection. Rashana's account suggested that his predilection for face changes had begun as a means to cover up his relationship with the activist. So could it have grown into a full-fledged obsession as some kind of reaction to losing her? For the first time, Amon felt sorry for the man, then realized that he was dipping his fingertip into his cup and removed it. The coffee was now cold. He'd been leaning over the coffee table, so intent on the unfolding story that he'd forgotten to take a sip.

"So what happened to Hakkotopia in the end?" he asked, sliding the cup away from himself and sitting up straight. "Did any of the settlers escape?"

"Not a soul. The Ogasawara islands were left deserted again. With Iwabuchi captured and the leadership dead, the bankliving remnants of the Ferment Culture Collective lost direction. Some voted to gather rescue funds for bankdead survivors in the camps by selling off their properties, but they could never reach unanimous agreement."

Gemini X plunged beneath the clouds with its impossible gentleness. Rashana was pointing down at a green speck on the sea. Amon was surprised to discover that, inside the enclosure of white, they seemed to have been circling over the island all along, and felt reassured to know that it was near.

"No one has set foot on Hahajima in twenty-three years and the city has long since biodegraded without a trace. But the federation's brief existence left its mark, inspiring some like Hippo and myself to emulate it, and spurring others, like my sister and the Gyges Circle, to seek a new kind of Freedom to transcend everything that had made it possible."

Diaspora   January 3rd, 50 FE

As Ty glared at Amon from the ground, the one eye that he could open screamed sad desperation, and Amon wished he could give him just a spark from the torch he could see lighting the way to a new beginning. But his insight was still only a glimmer in the distance, nothing so close at hand as to kindle liberation in the here and now. Without the help of people like Ty and especially Hippo, it might never be.

"You thing they need thith, me lying around waiting for them to wipe my ath?" Ty shouted over the swoosh of the passing train. "They've got enough trouble ath it ith."

"Ty, I—"

"You let Barrow in when I told you to throw him out! You theduthed uth with that plan and now we have nothing!"

"I'm sorry. If there's anything—"

"If you wanna help, then do for me what thethe bathtards"—Ty flailed his head furiously at the shadows around him—"won't. Just fugging kill me or ged out and don' ever come back!"

He bared his teeth behind lopsided sagging lips, shaking with emotion, his eye glinting under the moonlight like some unreachable distress signal in the night. The room watched on in silence, some faces cringing with pity. Amon shared the sentiment, sorrowing at his friend's pathetic transformation.

"Ty was being nice when he told you to get," said the man who'd first spoken taking a theatrical stride into the pane of moonlight as if onto a stage. It was the councilor Yané. "We don't need to let you outta here at all, you filthy snitch."

Dressed in a light winter jacket and jeans like many others present, Yané was hardly imposing in stature, but he exuded a threatening, authoritative air as he faced Amon with head and shoulders high, leaning forward with fists held at his sides. Even in the dim, Amon could see, below lank black bangs plastered to his forehead, the glitter of his steady eyes, and the grey streaks in his beard, skin just as smooth and youthful as ever but for his now severely chapped lips.

"Snitch?" said Amon. "What's that supposed to mean?"

Although he'd never actively wished harm on Yané, Amon couldn't deny his own ambivalence about finding that the man had survived. While it was encouraging to see that someone from the council had made it through—with any luck, others might have as well—Amon had always found the man's opinions both personally and politically objectionable. He had spoken out against his and Rick's Xenocyst membership from early on. Then during the debate over the supply crisis, he had proposed forcing women to give away their babies and bitterly challenged Amon's plan for the exposé. Now he was levelling specious accusations. Why was he the one who had stepped forward to speak for the crowd?

"Someone betrayed us 'n drove us from our homes," said Yané. "Where've you been? Lounging in the Gifted Triangle while we starve in this hole?"

"After I came up with a plan to screw over the Syndicate, are you suggesting I sold you out to them?"

"Who said anything about the Syndicate? You sure know a lot for a man who's playing innocent."

"I'm not playing anything."

"Then tell us who your associates are."

Amon hesitated. He didn't want to lie, but explaining about Rashana now could invite misunderstanding. Why didn't someone more sensible like Hippo speak up? Could something have happened to him too?

"See." Yané pointed at Amon and turned his head to seek the eyes of his audience. "Look at this plump rat here. His associates rewarded him with a feast. Now they've tossed him out, he's come begging for food."

Amon was by no means fat, but it was true that he'd regained some of his former muscle living in Atupio over the past few weeks. And now that Yané mentioned it, he noticed how gaunt and frail the dark figures around him were by comparison. "I'm not interested in your food."

"Then what're you doing here?"

"I need to speak to Hippo."

"Why should we let a snitch—"

"If I were a snitch," Amon interrupted, "and I knew where you were, why would I even be here right now? You think I'd go to the trouble of coming by myself?"

At this there was a stir in the crowd.

"So it *was* you that brought them!" said Yané, pointing his finger at Amon again with a violent chop. As if this were a signal, several men stepped forward, their hands hidden in their jackets.

"Brought what?"

"Don't pretend you don't know."

"Know what?"

"The drones that attacked us yesterday."

"Me?" Amon pointed at his face and shook his head at the absurdity of the accusation. "Look. I made mistakes. The exposé was a disaster."

"Too late!" rasped Ty.

"I'm willing to own up for all that. But a snitch?"

"That's right," said Yané. "A failure *and* a snitch. Why not both?"

"He's no snitch," said Vertical. "Or are you saying I'm lying about Delivery?"

Amon was relieved that he still had one ally among the Xenocyst exiles, but her support was a drop against the rising tide of resentment. He tightened his hands into fists, as if he might have a chance against the whole crowd unarmed. Not that he would have used a duster against such desperate souls. He thought about activating the ImmaNet and calling Ono X for help, but doubted his agents would make it in time. And he wanted to save that as a last resort. Once the crashborn exiles spotted him with the Elsewhere Gaze or caught him issuing gesture commands, they would no longer perceive him as a fellow bankdead. Then it might be impossible to regain their trust. This was the main purpose of having Rashana pay for him to remain in naked view.

"I thaw him at Delivery too," Ty slurred. "But his performanthe there doesn' change anything. He wath the one who introduthed Barrow!"

"And it says nothing about what he's been doing behind our backs," said Yané. "Do you think he could have found us here without help from his associates?"

"I don' wanna look at him anymore," said Ty. "Why didn' you lithen to me, Gura? Why didn' you believe me about Barrow?"

"If we have questions let's get answers we can trust." Yané nodded to the men around Amon, and they drew their hands from their pockets holding shards of glass, knives twisted together out of layered cans, chunks of concrete. His heart thundering, Amon was ready to hop down the ledge behind him and run if any of them made a move.

"Put those away," hissed Vertical. "Let him speak."

"Oh, he'll speak alright," said Yané.

"It appears we have discovered a matter of discord," said Book, whose deep nasally voice Amon was glad to hear somewhere in the darkness, another friend still alive. Or was he a friend now? Would he turn against him as Ty had? "Opinion is split as to whether Gura requires remedial treatment, whether he should be summarily ejected, or whether he should be questioned before our response can be determined. I recommend a vote on how to administer this member of Xenocyst."

"Member? Of Xenothyst?" Ty sneered, wiping slobber from the side of his drooping lips. "And where ith this Xenothyst place? Where are thethe memberth? Forged aboud the vote! He goeth!"

"Which is to say that we are to abandon all democratic procedure?" Book asked the crowd as he stepped from the shadows beneath the train tunnel to Amon's left. He was wearing an ill-fitted trench coat instead of Fleet clothes and his white hair was beginning to puff up, but he otherwise looked as before, the single lens of his glasses shimmering in the moonlight, his black skin blending into the gloom. "I am not for or against the ejection of Gura. However, I do believe a fair consideration is in order."

"When 've his associates ever been fair to us?"

"No more discuth'on . . ."

"Gura," said Vertical, who Amon now spotted looking between the shoulders of the armed men. "Where's Rick?"

Her gaze latched onto him, oblivious to the quarrel unfolding around her, as though his answer was all that mattered in the universe.

"I'm sorry," Amon told her. "I was with him when . . ." Choked with grief, he couldn't bring himself to finish.

"What?" Vertical demanded. "With him when what?"

"Vertical's behavior is an illustration of my contention," said Book, indicating her with an upturned palm. "A portion of our members would prefer to conduct a hearing. What we need to determine is whether they are the majority or the minority."

"What good will hith words do uth?" said Ty. "Better to ged rid of him before he fucks uth over again."

"What if he knows where to get food?" suggested a woman.

"He's bound to tell a good yarn to pass time at least," added a man. "Yeah," agreed another, and more voices chimed in.

Amon was grateful for the Xenocyst appetite for story. He placed his hope in it even more than the chance he might lead them to supplies.

"Alright, Book," Yané conceded. "We'll do the vote."

"Come on. Pleathe! I don' wan' to hear. I don' care."

"But let me make it clear that I won't let this snitch walk away whatever happens."

Yané's reversal surprised Amon, but he was beginning to see his angle. A moment ago he had tried to unleash on Amon the bloodlust of the famished crowd. Now he had fallen in line with their support for the vote. The opinions of others were wind to his opportunistic weathervane.

"Do any members wish to raise comments or objections at this time?" asked Book. Only coughing followed. "Then let the voting commence. Will we punish Gura? Will we offer Gura a hearing? Or will we eject him immediately?"

Kingdom   January 10th, 50 FE

"*Who are you?*" the echoing voices demanded.

When Amon reached up for the four dusters to push them aside, they pressed even harder and "Gah!" he groaned, his skull feeling ready to collapse.

"*Who. Are. You.*"

"I'm—"

"*No! Who are you really? No one ever comes here that the PhisherKing doesn't know. Not in all the decades he's been here. You're too old to be an ID newborn, but you've got no past.*"

Now Amon realized why the Phishers had kept him waiting. His identity suicide and bank rebirth, unprecedented in Free Era history, had confounded all their methods for identifying a person, just as it had confounded all those who hunted him.

"*So who the fuck are you?*"

"Amon Kenzaki."

"*Your digimake proves nothing.*"

"Not just my digimake. Ch-check for yourself."

At this there was a pause, filled by the infohum and Amon's fearful panting. Then the barrel of a duster appeared in the middle of Amon's visual field, at the end of an arm sewn of jellyfish. It stretched from the shoulder of a tall man digimade in the same style.

There was another pause before the pressure of the cylinder came away from Amon's forehead as the man stepped back, keeping his aim on target. Amon peered into the man's sickly glowing eyes as he studied him. A glance at his AT readout told Amon that, sure enough, there was a cred-icrime. They'd invested in taking a peek through his digimake, violating his image rights, likely to check his naked face against a photo on record.

Now the man lowered his aim and the pressure of the other three barrels came away. Amon crumpled to his knees and began to rub the aching points on his head. When he rose again, the tall man wore black-green robes and was lined up beside two women and a man likewise dressed in the attire of the Phishers, their faces shrouded under hoods, weapons hidden.

"*Get in*," four voices reverberated, though Amon could just make out that none of their lips moved. And looking over their shoulders, he saw that the chrome doors were open, an elevator waiting for him on the other side.

Theatre   December 27th, 49 FE

No sooner did Rashana finish recounting the fate of Hakkotopia than the transparent craft rose again towards the tattered smother of clouds. Movement so smooth Amon wondered if Gemini X corrected for gravity. Or if, perhaps, they had been parked in the hangar watching a projection all day.

They were enveloped in flowing white only momentarily, breaching beneath a sky of such pure, awesome blue it could only be either simulated or divine. A rush of golden light filled the deck, soft on Amon's eyes, as though filtered by whatever clear substance encased them. The sun, float-ing little more than a handsbreadth above the clouds, had been tamed, a muted blaze that allowed his gaze to linger. Throughout every altitude of this expansive vista, peacedrones, carbonjets, and centicopters blurred and streaked on interwoven trajectories, some veering large and close, others drifting specks that glittered in the distance, all tracing byzantine air price zones, an ever-ephemeral galaxy of finance-guided velocity.

"It was through her involvement with the crackdown that my twin discovered her dream," Rashana began anew, when their course had levelled out.

Then the sky was gone, and the disembodied faces of a dozen grinning fifty somethings rotated like a carousel in a grey space.

"This my friends is *success*," the Birla father announced with a smile of dignified gratification, raising a burst of fireworks all around.

"Justice has been restored," the Birla mother declared, as more crackles accentuated each word.

"To the young Birlas!" toasted one of their Philanthropy Syndicate collaborators.

"To the Birlas!" cheered the action barons in unison.

Champagne gouted from the top of their moving heads, a spiraling effervescent fountain that fell into the center of the space where the perspective looked up. Beside her the other Birla sister stood in kimono, frowning and shaking her head.

"Success?" she asked amid the foaming splash and revelry. "The remnants of the collective still hold their properties in Ogasawara, still only bankdead can visit. What kind of success is that?"

The fireworks puttered out, and the champagne choked to a dribble, the now-glowering faces grinding to a crawl like a roulette wheel ready to deliver its verdict.

"Always so cynical, Anisha," the Birla father chided.

"We're celebrating your completion of a difficult chore," the Birla Mother reminded her daughter. "Would you prefer that we nitpick your *mistakes* instead?"

Young Anisha shrank under the turning glares of her overawing audience, their digimakes so exquisite they seemed to partake of an almost metaphysical perfection. She glanced in the eyes of the perspective, as if seeking support or understanding from her sister. Then, after a few inarticulate stammers, found the courage to speak.

"I-I'm only telling you what you must already know. You yourself said it, Mother, that the island federation turned the fundamental principle of the Free World on its head. Don't you see that destroying it only took us halfway to setting things right?"

The champagne dripped slowly, billows of gunpowder smoke rising behind the coasting godlike scowls.

"Before our begetters could scold Anisha further, one of the executives asked my twin what she meant. She proceeded to tell them the parable of Gyges and to explain her interpretation."

The seg briefly fast-forwarded, then resumed with the laughter of the Birla father. "We ask for you to justify your impudence and you give us your pet theory about a fairy tale?"

"I-it's not a fairy tale. It's a metaphor for what we've brought about," Anisha replied. "While the shepherd Gyges has been knocked off the throne he illegitimately took and abused, champions who have proven themselves better than kings are still denied his ring of invisibility."

"You're talking in *abstractions*," the Birla mother cried.

"I've explained it as best I can," said Anisha. "Aren't the implications clear? We'll never have true freedom until the action-transaction system is reformed from the ground up."

"You dare to suggest that we tinker with the workings of the Market?" the Birla father shouted. "With the very foundation for our fertility monopoly and the properties of all present? Do you have any idea how difficult it was to get that intricate machine right?"

The Birla parents were so enraged that droplets of their reddened faces began to rain down and melt holes in the grey floor like acid.

"None of their Philanthropy Syndicate collaborators would risk involving themselves in this household dispute," said Rashana. "I too stayed out of it. I had drawn my own conclusions from the crackdown that I hope to explain by and by. But many did reach out to Anisha afterward. By the time they arranged a meeting, she had refined her insight."

The action barons were seated around a long table vibrant with spreads of sashimi. The perspective was a chef carving a live octopus on a wood counter placed behind the row of heads that faced Anisha.

"Hakkotopia illustrated a valuable lesson," she said. "We witnessed in its destruction the temporary suspension of every rule that restrains humankind. Now we know that it is all too possible for anyone to slip outside the AT Market and the Charity Gift Economy. The residents of Hakkotopia did so while bankdead and our Liquidators while bankliving, both without relinquishing one iota of Freedom."

Anisha sat up straight and spoke with practiced confidence nothing like the timidity she had displayed in front of her parents, as though the dream she had found for herself were the cocoon that remade her for adulthood. In fact, her proud bearing reminded Amon of her parents when giving the speech that had kicked off the crackdown. *Like begetter, like twin,* he supposed. Here too, the action barons listened rapt, leaving the freshly sliced tentacles to wriggle untouched on their plates.

"Now consider everyone in attendance at this banquet," Anisha went on after a dramatic pause, sweeping her raised palm over the table. "We are the masters of corporate empires built by the sweat of our brows. We have accumulated more wealth than anyone who has ever lived through our boundless talent."

Suddenly, the audio went silent and Ono X, who Amon realized was standing beside Rashana's chair, began to give voice to Anisha.

"The gap between us and average Free Citizens widens by the second," Ono X ventriloquized. "And yet, limitations on our choices are not shrinking in proportion with our earnings as promised. Our continued inability to enjoy the real, flourishing, wild nature that Ogasawara offers is only a symbol of this moral and economic travesty. Our freedom has plateaued. We have not received *all* the freedom we can earn, only *some*."

Amon's surprise at Ono X's sudden appearance was only a prelude to his astonishment at this performance. The man's voice was sonorous, with a bombastic feminine timbre that did not mimic the Birla sister exactly but perfectly suited the scene. He even had Anisha's prim posture and flicked open his palms in synch with her to emphasize the word "some."

"My begetters glimpsed the problem, but their attachment to the status quo keeps them from recognizing the solution," Ono X and Anisha's image continued. "Isn't it obvious, friends? We must unite! We must pool our assets to create a new society reserved for us, for the select few who have proven that they deserve not just any amount of freedom but freedom as an absolute, a qualitatively higher dimension of liberty that admits no compromise of the will. Only then can the living truth of the Ring of Gyges that has been hiding unnoticed within the ideals of the Free Market finally realize its destiny."

A moment of silence followed in the wake of this grand proposal, the seated diners gone as deathly still as their servings. In the foreground, the chef realized that a whole tuna had been placed on his cutting board and picked up a fresh knife.

"What are you getting at with talk of this ring?" a woman to the left of Anisha asked, narrated by Ono X in a shrill voice that somehow evoked her pinched nose.

"She's called us here in person to discuss jewelry," scoffed a black man with a bleach crew cut in a deep baritone, as Ono X dropped a full octave. "Once we coordinate our accessories, then abracadabra, we'll vanish into thin air."

Ono X threw back his head and laughed in such a way, perhaps with the help of audio effects, that a hall seemed to resound with mirth.

"I only speak of invisibility in a figurative sense," replied Anisha/Ono X. "Ring of Gyges will be our watchword. Think of it as the evasion of all consequences. If we succeed—and we will succeed—none of us will ever pay for our actions again."

"Then you seek bankdeath?" asked a man by way of yet another, more husky voice in Ono X's repertoire.

"And have us inaugurate an identity suicide cult I suppose," quipped the bleach-haired man.

"Not at all," Anisha/Ono X cut in authoritatively before further laughter could catch. "Like the bankliving, we'll have the option to earn and spend money. But like the bankdead we'll have no obligation to do so. What I propose is the ultimate synthesis of the freedom of banklife and bankdeath. What could be more fitting for masters of all action who already stand above finance?"

When the banquet reverted abruptly to cloud and sky, Rashana said, "Bravo," clapping one hand against her palm. After a split second, Amon snapped out of his bewitchment and joined her. Ono X gave his usual respectful bow and cleared their cups.

"I hope you don't mind if raConTeur lets him help out now and then," said Rashana. "A dash of theatre makes the job of storytelling much more entertaining for me."

Diaspora   January 3rd, 50 FE

When the vote was held on whether to give Amon a hearing, it was difficult to see how many hands went up in the darkness, and he held his breath as a woman walked around counting them.

It reminded him of his first council, when he'd been dragged blindfolded into the digital quarantine to wait on their judgement as the symptoms of his webloss peaked. Again Book was facilitating and Yané was trying to throw him out, but Ty and Vertical had switched their former stances, with Vertical silent and Ty against him. Conspicuously missing from any wall was the Xenocyst emblem of a young girl inside a cell bending under the approaching tip of a pin. Meanwhile, the decorum of halcyon days had deteriorated, as the parties to the vote stood, slouched, moved about, and chatted at will, rather than sitting on the floor in an orderly circle. It wasn't a council anymore so much as an assembly, the citizenry too small for them to need representatives, and Amon wondered again what might have happened to the councilors other than Yané, not to mention Hippo, their former advisor.

"Thirty-seven," the woman announced. Amon let out his breath, still anxious because he had no idea how many voters there were. Here was the crucial moment; if this proposal lost out, he had no intention of waiting around to learn whether they would vote to eject or punish him. Better to make a run for it and message Ono X for a jet.

"Please approach," said Book, gesturing to the pane of moonlight. Amon was unsure why he'd been commanded thus until he spotted Yané marching off into the shadows shaking his head in disgust. The hearing would commence!

Kingdom   January 10th, 50 FE

Tilting his head back, Amon watched as the square of InfoSky over the rim of the pit gradually receded. The open-top elevator was descending much slower than on his first visit to the PhisherKing's domain, and was crowded this time with Phishers. The four of them stood facing each other in the center, with lips that peeked from the bottom of their hoods and fingers from their baggy sleeves all twitching in a frenetic blur.

Amon recalled his state of mind on his previous trip down this pit— confused and afraid, the truths he held dear crumbling around him. How different he felt today. About many questions he even had certainty, hard lucid certainty, and whatever mysteries might still obscure the path he trod, whether in the dust behind him or the haze on the horizon ahead, he knew without a doubt what course to take. His only concern was whether it would be compelling enough to give the PhisherKing new vision and hope, or whether he would dismiss it as a will-o'-the-wisp and remain fixated on his business, for Amon needed him. Just as much as Hippo and Rashana, the PhisherKing was essential to the future smoldering in Amon's imagination, and he prayed inwardly that the man would not reject his offer.

Soon the square of InfoSky was just a tiny glimmer of light. Then this too faded at the end of the long dark shaft like a moment in the past about which all stories have been forgotten. When the last traces of the metropolis were gone and Amon was in total darkness, the elevator stopped and the skeleton key that glowed without illuminating appeared in the palm of one of the Phishers. He handed the key to Amon with still twitching fingers, and Amon inserted it into the shining keyhole before him, brightness swelling as the crack in the door expanded.

Blinking, Amon glanced up first at the scarlet sky ribbed with contraption and the golden sun of sand and pebbles, then down over the edge of the elevator floor, where the rowboat of bone bobbed on the mercury sea, weighted in the back so that it angled up towards the portal, awaiting him. The rowers in their black-green robes stood in two lines along the gunwales, their unheld oars sticking from the oarlocks, blood spraying from their white tips onto the silver waves. Dressed in the same robes as his disciples, the PhisherKing looked up at Amon from the raised prow and spread his arms to both sides as if to suggest the vastness of the ocean he had arrived at.

"Welcome back, Kenzaki-san!" he exclaimed.

"Monju," Amon marveled. "I never truly believed that I would look into those strange eyes of yours again."

"Is that so?" said Kai Monju, his silver irises rotating so fast clockwise between his scarlet whites and gold pupils that they appeared to spin backwards. "I cannot fathom what struggles you have overcome on your journey to the land of bankdeath and back, but I've been expecting you." The PhisherKing took a step back, beckoning to the space on the deck in front of him.

Carefully Amon stepped down onto the edge of the gently bobbing prow and his Phisher escorts followed. Once their feet were planted on deck, the rowers rolled the boulder forward from the stern, righting the boat when it passed the midway point, and Amon felt weightless for a moment as he dropped. While the sloshing of the hull settled into the slow rocking of the waves, he considered the PhisherKing standing there facing him.

"I must have lost my mind somewhere along the way because I'm actually happy to see you," said Amon holding out his hand, so glad he wanted to cry. A kind of wistful elation radiated up his arm as they shook vigorously.

The PhisherKing said nothing, though his grip lingered in Amon's and his glass-toothed smile seemed too authentically joyous to be digimade.

Theatre   December 27th, 49 FE

When Ono X melted back into the sky after his performance, Rashana rose and crossed the deck again to a space in the air where a window in a black wall had been. This time Amon followed and stood to her right.

The sun was angling towards the western horizon of cloud, its light trembling expectantly as though fighting the urge to plummet off the edge of the world and never come back. Meaning and value seemed to drain away from the encompassing scribble of flightpaths, myriad drones and vehicles sketching lines, swoops, and zigzags that amounted to no recognizable calculation, an empty configuration of changing position only.

"I think I'm beginning to see what the Gyges Circle is after," said Amon. "But technically speaking, what would acquiring Gyges' Ring look like?"

"Their plan is to reprogram the House of Blinding to distort their action-data so that these will always fail to match an action-property."

This one statement was a lot to take in and Amon mulled it over, gazing blankly at the map of cloud streaming past below. He imagined the Gyges Circle as a gang of stick figures, hopping, flipping, and scampering over the white landscape. Columns of hand-drawn arcs representing electromagnetic signals beamed upward from each of their heads into a high-floating circle. There the arcs transformed into a yen symbol, dollar sign, or one of the many icons for other currencies, ticking in an endless stream. Then he pictured one of the stick people jumping up to the circle, brush in hand, and painting it red. Now the arcs that crossed the perimeter became question marks or zeros with a diagonal line through them. *Their movements would be transmitted via BodyBank as usual,* Amon thought, but from their first point of entry into the GATA network, even before reaching the Ministry of Monitoring, they would not qualify as an action.

"So no charge would ever be issued," he said. "No fees or fines of any kind."

"Unless they choose to buy or sell," Rashana told him. "That is the only condition under which money or assets would leave their accounts. For the Gyges Circle, the whole point is to expand the domain of their volition to its limit. They would decide even which of their actions are transactions."

Amon put his palm against the transparent wall, felt its fine-grained surface, and thought he could sense a subtle vibration within, as though it were alive with obscure feelings and insights.

"Then all the events that led up to my identity suicide—the cash crashes of Kitao, Rick, and Barrow. That was a push by your twin and her associates to gain influence over the House of Blinding."

"It was."

"And Sekido was their ally inside GATA?"

"Their most powerful of several."

"Why would he work with them after the disappearance of his girl-friend? Another Birla Deal?"

"No. No threat was required. He never seems to have found out who funded the Ogasawara crackdown."

"There must have been evidence somewhere."

"Not very much actually. We factholed the entire operation. Sekido might have found clues in the scraps of data that our posttruthcorps inevitably missed. But he doesn't appear to have searched very hard."

"Why not?"

"My psychalitiicorps infers that he preferred to focus on his vendetta against Barrow and corruption at GATA than to dig into underlying causes. Think how much easier it would be to blame a single man and a single public institution than to acknowledge that political decisions are made by an amorphous configuration of corporate interests. Good luck reforming that!"

Suddenly a hazy wisp of grey on the threshold of cloud and sky appeared like a snake eating its own tail. GATA sustained the AT Market that supported the MegaGloms while the MegaGloms governed GATA through their hold on the Market. Was there any way to pry the circle apart?

"Sekido's quest for vengeance certainly fueled his climb up the GATA ranks," Rashana continued, "even in spite of Barrow's efforts to block his ascent."

The surround became a montage of perspectives being dusted by a Turkic-looking man in different Tokyo locations. It ended at an opulent lounge where the man clinked glasses with a cadre of well-known politicians.

"Sekido insinuated himself deeply into Moderate Choice. By the time my twin approached him, he had made himself an indispensable party powerbroker."

A woman with hands of smoke carried a tray of cocktails. In a booth with a window overlooking a film noir Tokyo, a Birla sister rendered as a man sat across from another man with vaguely Polynesian features and a bad slouch.

"Hakkotopia was a tragedy among tragedies," voiced over Rashana in time to the motion of the Birla sister's lips. They went on about rooting out corrupt officials, but Amon didn't really hear it. The sight of Anisha in the very same jazz bar where he'd been interviewed by her and Sekido had reminded him of something.

"Hold on," he interrupted. The seg vanished, but Rashana did not turn to meet his gaze, her eyes playing in the distance, and Amon took this opportunity to visually trace her figure standing against the sky. Rashana was the fiercest, most awe-inspiring person he had ever met, and the near preternatural force of her character often eclipsed her femininity. Now he allowed himself to see her as a woman, noting the curve of her hips at the bottom of the turquoise dress shirt, her inconspicuous breasts, her slender legs in white chinos, her handsome distinctive features and smooth brown skin. She was attractive in her own way. Someone might have loved her if she was willing to reveal her tenderness and her wounds as she'd been doing for Amon, if she peeled away the trick mirrors between her soul and the world. Even Amon might have in the right circumstances, he supposed.

"Why do you and your sister both digimake yourself as a man?" he asked.

"Because she stole him from me!" Rashana lamented, her eyes now bearing in on Amon's, lashes shearing close, warm florid breath on his face.

"Stole who from you?"

"Makesh Adani."

"The name you gave me when we first met."

"My primary digiguise. The most important of the many I use to manage my subsidiaries."

Rashana turned back to the window and began to massage her brow.

"I created Makesh for our trollcorps when I was a child. They were training us to play different characters for each face we show to the public. As an adult, I made him organizer of Atupio. But my twin decided to adopt him without telling me. She's the only person who could without image right violations. Now she goes around posing as Makesh whenever she's at her most sinister, tries to ruin his—and my—reputation."

Amon squinted at her profile as he took in this bizarre arrangement. The sisters went gallivanting about with the same digiguise. No wonder the recruiter with Sekido had been upset when Amon admitted that he'd met with an activist named Makesh. Envisioning that moment carried his memory to the events that followed.

"And what about the Emoticon Man?" Amon asked.

"Who?" Rashana's fingers seemed to press ever-so-slightly harder on her brow as though responding to some new headache pang.

"The person that attacked Mayuko." Amon recalled that spastically blipping face looming over her, feeling only a vague sadness, other emotions still unaccountably flat. "He had a crew, so obviously the Birla Guard, and yes! I see now. He offered her a Birla Deal—die from piranha dust or accept money. It had to be either you or your si—twin. I mean, he promised the exact same amount as the jubilee charge, a Fertilex property."

"Then this 'Emoticon Man' is one of Anisha's digiguises."

"You never borrow him for yourself the way she borrows Makesh?"

"Are you suggesting it was me that hurt your friend?"

Amon wasn't sure how to answer.

"Because of our resemblance and our complicated past, you think maybe I'm not who I say I am? Right? It's okay. That's what you were implying at Atupio. Why not just admit you're suspicious of me?"

Her eyes slowly roamed the sky and she spoke calmly, almost tonelessly, not sounding as offended as he might have expected from her words. His mouth started to move then settled, caution taking hold.

Rashana's shoulders dropped and her eyelids drifted shut. Then she flicked her fingers open and the sky became a scroll of text.

Height: 160 cm. Weight: 53 kg. Name: Rashana Birla. Heartrate . . .

"Here, my inner profile," she said. "I don't know if it will satisfy you. My twin keeps shredding my LifeStream with her hacking. Data has nothing to guarantee its truth other than itself. But I don't have anything to hide from you, Amon. What is it about me that you want to know? Whenever you like, I can give you a training bank, put you on glass mode. You can review the segs I've played for you. I'll fund all the platinum searches you want. Do you think I go around telling everyone I meet about how Anisha and I were raised? Whoever I claim to be, at some stage you'll just have to take my word for it. Have I still not given you enough reason to trust me?"

Staring at Rashana's deflated form, he supposed that she probably had. First, as Makesh Adani, she had offered him a job and warned him of coming danger. Then she had searched for him, helped with the exposé, and saved his life. She was the founder of Atupio, an organization both Hippo and Barrow had praised for its humanitarian contributions. Now she was bearing everything to him and building up to some new offer that he was terrified and excited to hear. Trusting her was the least he could do in return . . . until he could view her LifeStream as she'd proposed.

"Once again, I'm sorry for being paranoid," Amon said with a bow. "It's just . . . I'm so worried about Mayuko. And so angry." In fact, he wasn't angry but knew he ought to be. "If that was you . . ."

"Forget it," said Rashana. Finally turning to Amon again, she put a hand on his bicep. He felt as though she was looking *at* the reflected sky on his eyes rather than *into* his eyes, but her touch summoned an empathetic tingling to the pit of his stomach. "Relationships have to begin somewhere. So let's make our starting point openness. Then no secret will stand in our way."

Diaspora   January 3rd, 50 FE

Once the exiles had settled in to listen—huddling on the floor around him, slumping along the walls, or lurking warily nearby, while young children hid or slept in protective arms—Amon sat cross-legged under the moonlight and began to tell them what had happened after he left Xenocyst on the day of the sabotage.

Unlike at his hearing in the Cyst, no mirror was brought out for Amon to peer into his own eyes while he spoke—presumably it had been left behind like so much else. Nevertheless, Book knelt facing him and focused his gaze intently on Amon's, analyzing his eye movements for signs that he was lying, and Amon wondered if the method worked even when the subject wasn't staring at their reflection. *I'll have to be careful what I say*, he thought, looking slowly around at his audience, as he had learned to do when it was his turn at the nighttime storytelling circles on the Xenocyst rooftops.

Since there were few questions about the sabotage and his escape from Delivery, Amon supposed that his account matched that of Vertical, Ty, and other survivors who had been present. One woman asked how he could have possibly evaded the CareBots during his flight through the Gifted Triangle, as if to imply that he was making it up, but everyone appeared satisfied when he described the caution with which he and Rick had crept through the depths of those enclaves and the several close calls they had encountered.

Every ten minutes or so, Amon was interrupted by the swoosh of a train that overpowered his voice for listeners at the edges of the alcove. He knew from clicking the train bridge earlier that it was the Oneiro Express heading to and from Yume Station, and on each pass he was reminded of the only time he had boarded, mustering the last of his wits and resources to save Mayuko before they said goodbye, her crying face on the floor, the love in her incisive eyes . . . So he was glad whenever the sound faded, for the telling allowed him to forget.

When he reached the part where Rick lay tear dusted in the elevator, Vertical emerged from the shadows and strode quickly for the ledge out of the alcove. Amon thought she might slip away as she had done at the equinox festival after Ty challenged her to tell the tragic tale of her reunion with her husband. But she stopped in front of the ledge, seemed to reconsider, and began to walk back and forth across the small patch of open floor there. It saddened Amon to see an athlete of her caliber cooped up on this dreary rooftop. Whether due to lack of food or exercise, her once honed, muscular legs were noticeably thinner beneath the jacket and track suit she wore. Rick's last words about their relationships with Mayuko and his feelings for Vertical seemed too personal for the community, so Amon omitted them, hoping for the chance to tell Vertical one on one, to embrace and console her as a friend, to grieve, together. She continued pacing even as Amon recounted leaving Rick's body in the elevator, muttering to herself and occasionally shuddering. Only when Yané spoke did Vertical stop and look over.

"Come on. Who's gonna believe this sob story? If anything killed Rick, it was this snitch's betrayal."

At this, Amon let out a harsh, rasping breath. White anger seared away thought as it had before he pummeled Barrow the morning his friend died. He retained just enough self-control to consider holding himself back, his fists molten rocks at his sides, but something told him it would be better not to.

"Who the fuck are you?!" he bellowed. "That I would kill my best friend! A man I've known since we were in diapers! I would have died in his place if I could you piece of shit! And if what I've said cancels your vote and you want to hurt me, then fuck it and fuck you! I'll—"

By this time, several people were holding Amon back as he tried to writhe his way to the much smaller Yané, who stood fearfully with his dukes up. Despite attempts by Book and others to calm him, Amon continued to spew insults, until Vertical footworked out of nowhere and slugged him in the gut.

"Don't pay any attention to him," she whispered close. "He's just a weak man's idea of a strongman."

The blow left him breathless and sapped for only a second, and he might have kept on, if he hadn't realized he was going too far. Even if displaying sincere anger added credibility to his story, as his unarticulated intuition had urged, going any further would only give him a vicious cast. So he went limp in the arms restraining him with an aggrieved sigh.

"I'm alright now," he told them. "Let me go."

When he and Yané were seated again, Amon back in the pane of moonlight, Vertical went and stood over Yané in the shadows.

"Apologize for what you said about Rick," she demanded. "Now!"

The crowd watched intently for Yané's reaction.

"I've said nothing he doesn't deserve."

"Not to him. To me!"

They glowered at each other for a tense moment. Yané was the first to look away.

"Fine. Sorry," he said. "I meant no offense—to you."

Vertical gave a nod and retreated to her range beside the ledge.

It was a minute before Amon had regained his breath and enough composure to begin relating his journey back to Xenocyst. As he was describing his confrontation with the two guards at the border, he finally spotted Ty. When the hearing had first started and everyone was settling in, Amon hadn't seen where he ended up, but the shift in the crowd after the quarrel had revealed him. Lying on his belly along the left side of the rooftop, Ty faced the wall formed by the outside of the train tunnel, showing no signs that he was listening. The crowd left a space around him, maintaining distance. It pained him to see this fierce warrior crippled and miserable. What had been done to him? How had he been paralyzed?

Eventually Amon's mouth began to dry out, but he didn't bother asking for refreshments; none of the Xenocyst exiles were eating or drinking anything, and he doubted that was a choice. The emaciation of the crowd disturbed him, though they seemed no worse off than in the famine. Perhaps it was the contrast between the vigorous, well-fed Atupians with whom he had spent the past few weeks. Incongruously, the famished exiles wore brand new outfits of the kind sold in the Free World, rather than the Fleet clothes of the camps, which would be long dissolved. Winter gear was scarce, with several children curled close to their mothers inside a single jacket, and adults bundled under blankets in twos and threes. The reek of body odor and urine permeating the alcove broadcasted their lack of PeelKlean and toiletries as well.

Since their supplies could only have come from local vending machines, Amon knew that they were relying on Tamper's theft for everything; without his devices, those hard blocks of weaponized electronics would have been impenetrable. Amon had witnessed firsthand the not inconsiderable risks Tamper took in providing for himself and had worried sometimes for his safety, but he was no longer supporting just one person. With the number of mouths he had to feed now, the situation was obviously unsustainable. Either Tamper let them slip into starvation, or he hacked one too many vending machines and the security algorithms decided it was cost effective to neutralize the robbers. Yané's accusations concerning the drone attack were a sign that this had already happened at least once, and as they walked this tightrope, Amon thought it pathetic that only one unnamed woman had been sensible enough to suggest that he might be able to help them. It was a testament to just how much stress and want were clouding their reason. The loudest voices among them had pegged him for a threat when, ironically, the mere twitching of his fingers could have fired off a message to Ono X and brought an airdrop of months' worth of rations within minutes. Not that he had any intention of doing this just yet. After Yané's ranting about his putative "associates," Amon doubted they would believe anything he said about his involvement with Rashana unless and until he regained their trust.

The sacrifice Tamper was making showed in the weight he had lost, though he still had the bulk to stand out amongst the scrawny figures around him, hunched on the floor with heels together. His eyes remained concealed in shadow, but Amon found himself imagining Tamper's off-target stare directed his way as he spoke.

When Amon's vision had adjusted to the dim, he spotted others that he knew. Standing cross-armed beside Yané was Jiku, the female councilor whose face reminded him of a clam shell. Leaning against the wall to his left was the scout who had brought him to find the sentinel rumored to have seen Mayuko. Lying with her chin propped on her palm was the guard who had watched him at his very first council hearing. Not far off was a teenager from his demolition squad. A loudmouth from the patrol crews, a listener in a storytelling circle, a fellow skygazer, an evening library reader, and three children from the nurseries he used to clean.

Vertical, Ty, Book, Tamper, and all the rest. Seeing them together again, Amon's eyes began to moisten, partly out of joy that they were alive, if not as well or as welcoming as he might have hoped, and partly out of sadness for those they had lost: Little Book, Rick, and countless others. Even Barrow's absence troubled him somehow. This bittersweet feeling surged when he reached their confrontation, but he held back the tears. Now was not the time for sentimentality or remorse, for dwelling on what was gone. It was the time to raze the barriers around the present to the ground and hope to draw others beyond with him.

Towards the end of his tale, clouds covered the moon, completing the darkness in the alcove. Then the sliver of night sky to his right cleared and the faint glow returned as he was concluding with his flight from Xenocyst. Amon left out his nightmarish visit to Opportunity Peaks, which was liable to arouse suspicions that he'd converted, and his reunion with Rashana, which risked confusing his audience, most of whom had no experience even of banklife. Only when he had found Hippo would he delve into these complicated matters, for Hippo was the second key, the missing half of the cypher that would decode the scrambled text of freedom with the PhisherKing's help. But where was he? So much rested on Hippo that Amon felt his anxiety rising with each word he spoke, afraid that they had failed before they even tried.

Kingdom   January 10th, 50 FE

The four Phishers that had escorted Amon joined the rows of their fellows at the back, and all twelve of the PhisherKing's disciples sat in their places along the gunwales, resting one hand on the handle of raised oars that continued to bleed into the sea. Soon the boat of bone was rocking gently on the quicksilver waves, the rhythm uncannily steady and precise, as though the currents ran on clockwork.

"So what brings you here, in a training bank, your identity as clean as a new-bought BioPen sprat?" asked the PhisherKing. "The Birlas are too kind."

"How do you . . . and so quickly?"

"I didn't even reach into my net for this catch. Who *else* would be paying for your actions?"

"You know so much, I'm not sure why we bother with conversation."

"I didn't know anything until you admitted it now. Thanks for the complimentary tip. Which sister is it that you're working for?"

"Rashana."

"How can you be certain?"

Amon tossed a globe of amber containing a still image of an inner profile with the name Rashana Birla at the top. The PhisherKing inhaled it through his nostrils in midair.

"This is just a taster. I'm willing to share everything I know. But first, I have a question for you."

"Go ahead. I'm sure your patron is good for it."

Amon let out a quiet sigh, appalled at the man's relentless profiteering. Not because there was anything wrong with profiteering in itself. It was perfectly understandable, perhaps even wise, under the AT Market, where money was Freedom. But because, if there was to be any hope of securing his cooperation, he needed the PhisherKing to treat him as something more than just a client. At the very least, as a partner. He wanted to say friend.

"Rashana won't need to pay you this time," said Amon. "The info she's authorized me to share will more than cover your answer."

"After what you just showed me, I'm willing to wager that you're right," said Monju. Then pursing his lips and frowning sympathetically, he added, "I wish there was more I could tell you about her."

"Just give me what you know."

What happened to Mayuko? Those were the words Monju had guessed before Amon could even say them; it was the obvious question to ask after the circumstances of their parting.

Theatre   December 27th, 49 FE

When Amon and Rashana had returned to their seats, the unglaring sun was touching the clouds. It seemed to be fixed there, like a golden crown on the rolling white of heaven, the intricate vectors of aircraft a dance of devotion to its majesty. Amon kept his eyes on it as they circled in the sky or the sky rotated around the fixed point of his perspective, there was no telling which.

"Can we return to Sekido?" he asked. "You were telling me how Anisha recruited him to the Gyges cause."

"I was. Not that Sekido understood it that way. My twin would never have been so clear."

Sky and cloud became the same jazz bar in Kabukicho from the perspective of the same smoky waitress.

"I represent a group of concerned citizens, we aim to clean up GATA corruption," said Anisha as Makesh Adani. "What we need are politicians willing to void their exclusive lobbying contracts with SpawnU and sign ours instead."

When the waitress placed cocktails in front of Anisha and Sekido and turned to the bar, her perspective was replaced by that of a man passing the table on his way to the men's room, then someone playing cards in the booth behind Anisha, then someone else sipping a beer at the neighboring table, a seamless relay of segs that sustained the scene.

"In exchange for your help finding such likeminded champions of justice," Anisha continued, "we can offer funding for all your initiatives. Together, I know that we can cut away the rot at the heart of government."

The final perspective was the fisheye view of the cherry in Sekido's cocktail.

"This was the inauguration of the faction within Moderate Choice that recently split off to form the Full Choice Party. With the faction's support quietly purchased, the Gyges Circle had effectively stacked the Executive Council in their favor under SpawnU's radar. Sekido first leveraged their votes when Barrow was forming his cabinet, forcing him to place Kitao as Minister of Records and himself as Minister of Liquidation. He then used his new influence to have Gyges Circle agents appointed to key positions in the technocracy."

"Like the Archivists who forged Barrow's bankruptcy reports," said Amon.

"Yes, those. But the placement most crucial to the Gyges Circle's objectives was a Blinder, the son of one of their members."

"The Blinder who had me charged for jubilee!"

"No. The man they placed is still very much bankalive and well."

"Oh . . . Then was it a Blinder under his command?"

"Doubtful. He's of the lowest rank, a sort of apprentice. Which is what has prevented the Gyges Circle from altering the Blinding system already. To program in their action exemptions, they need the Secretary of Blinding's executive clearance. So their Blinder has to be promoted to this position, a challenging maneuver. Of course, incompetent relatives of tycoons are routinely granted cushy GATA jobs. But the House of Blinding is an independent wing as you know. Their strict hiring protocol defies the standard nepotism playbook. Even with the votes of Sekido's faction bought out, the Gyges Circle lacked the two-thirds Executive Council majority required to make the appointment last summer, and Barrow's popularity precluded more seats in the upcoming election. Their conclusion was that Barrow had to be deposed."

A glimmer from the sun in Amon's eye brought him back to the pins of light in the Gifted Triangle room where he, Rick, and Ty had questioned Barrow, then an OpSci slave.

"Barrow told me they ordered him to step down in exchange for heaps of anadeto or lose everything," he recalled. "I guess that was his second Birla Deal."

"And it wasn't his last. But my twin miscalculated the second time, much as we had miscalculated when dispatching Sekido to Ogasawara. She didn't factor in that Barrow was angling for a publicly-funded charity in the District of Dreams."

"The non-profit that would have supposedly handed out long-lasting supplies without asking for babies."

Rashana nodded.

"You don't believe for a second that was anything more than a scheme to gather anadeto, do you?"

"The Gyges Circle certainly didn't believe it. And that presumption is where their plans began to go wrong. His unexpected refusal of their offer forced them to resort to identity assassination and a string of credicrimes. The forged bankruptcy reports for Rick and then you, the virus that infected your hand, the forged report for Freg and Tororo to eliminate you, and many more. The total fines were enormous even for the Philanthropy Syndicate and Fertilex combined. The coverup risked SpawnU discovery again and again."

Much of this account, Amon had already learned for himself, but finally glimpsing the thread of desire that ran through it brought a new glow to his chest, a kind of satisfaction, a clarity, and a letting go. *The Ring of Gyges, actions without cost*, he thought, opening his hand slowly as if to release the harsh memories of his old life into the air, motes of the past dancing over sky and cloud unhindered by any emotion or physical law.

A question brought him back from his reverie. "What about Atupio?" he asked. "You said that Anisha siphoned its funds to cover these credicrimes. Hippo thought she used the authority of Fertilex to seize temporary control."

The topic seemed to make Rashana uncomfortable. Her cheek ticced in a barely perceptible cringe and she averted her eyes to her thumb as she began to slide it over her fingertips.

"Hippo was more or less right," she said.

The left hemisphere of the sky became an AT readout entitled *Atupio Expenses*, dated two days before Amon's cash crash. Most transactions listed were credicrimes: "record forgery," "trespassing," . . .

"Anisha and I were in the middle of suing each other over our inheritance."

Another document unfolded itself over the readout. It was entitled *Anisha Birla Vs. Rashana Birla: Legal Action Concerning Claims to Atupio and Other Heritable Assets.*

"Free Citizens of all information strata around the world know that Anisha received authority over Fertilex. But one subsidiary was granted exclusively to me, with a market valuation so small that not even platinum reports picked it up."

"Your par—begetters gave you Atupio?"

"The will stipulated that it was mine. It also said that Anisha had executive control of Fertilex as a whole. She used that ambiguity to sue for ownership." Rashana looked almost nauseous and her thumb slowed on her fingertips as though now grinding over her skin. "48 hours of appeals and counterappeals later, the Fiscal Judiciary ruled in my favor. But during that time, my authority over Atupio was in limbo, and Anisha seized de facto control."

"I don't understand," said Amon. "If your begetters saw you as a single person, why would they give you different shares?"

"That's exactly it!" cried Rashana, making one hand into a fist and bunching the fabric over her crossed thighs with the other. "My twin and I never dreamed that they would divide their wealth. How could they when they brought us into existence for the sole purpose of keeping the MegaGlom together?"

She remained hunched forward, staring into her lap. Amon waited until her hands had unclenched and she had let out a long sigh before he asked, "What did they do about your shared identity signature? I thought you have only one account."

"The will added a condition. We had to consent to assign each set of assets to our subprofiles."

"So your begetters knew about your ruse! How?"

"Maybe from the cyberattack on our Cognitive Handling Corps—the very beginning. Or they may have found out recently. We're not sure. What bothers me is that they waited until they were dead to admit we were different people. Couldn't they have brought everything out in the open so we could be ourselves and act like a family just once, even for a moment?"

Rashana's pitch rose with something like grief or remorse and her eyes stretched wide, looking off somewhere else as though a war were being fought inside a hidden pleat in the air too distant and removed to stop.

"Maybe this was their way of acknowledging the mistakes they made," said Amon, trying to console her.

"Too little, too late."

While Rashana sat with eyes closed, fingers pressed to her brow above wilted lashes, grappling with something toxic in her depths, Amon wondered what drove the Birla parents to grant her Atupio. Could they have learned to respect her humanitarianism? Could entrusting Anisha with Fertilex have likewise been a tacit stamp of approval, a gift of the means to seize the Ring of Gyges? Could they have seen, perhaps from the flowering of some overdue wisdom, the folly of stuffing their corporate mantle down the throats of their heirs? Witnessing Rashana's distress, Amon knew to leave these issues aside, but her intentions were otherwise.

"If only I'd known that Anisha was planning to kill them. I could have warned them before they wrote the will . . ."

"The reports said they died in a boating accident." Amon recalled the video of a helicopter rescuing survivors from icy waters that he'd watched with Rick. "You think it was murder?"

Over the legal report slid an email. *From: Shiv Birla. Cc: Chandru Birla. To: Executers of the Will. Subject: Revisions and Modifications.* The view shifted down to the body of the message. A wall of text scrolled by with repetition of phrases like "our preferred replacement" and "disappointments in the family."

"This is the proof Ono X obtained from the PhisherKing. We've since uncovered metadata that shows my twin intercepted the message. Anisha knew that she was the preferred heir."

"How awful if that's true."

"There's no question. Our begetters die only hours after Kitao goes bankrupt and Gyges is ready to move forward? Who could actually believe that the boat malfunction and the helicopter delay were coincidences?"

"The timing was unusual," Amon acknowledged. "Everyone I spoke to agreed. You really think your sis—twin could do that to them?"

"You're talking again as if we're family. We—" Rashana bunched up her hair with one hand, eyes twitching side to side. "I was sad, of course, when our begetters were gone. But I have to admit that I was relieved to no longer have their eyes on me."

The emotion in her voice was so subdued Amon barely sensed it, like the scent dormant in some vibrant, frozen flower.

"Would you want to be mistaken for a monster like that?"

Rashana glared at Amon with red, watery eyes as though demanding an answer. He knew better than to give one. Ono X emerged from the sky with a handkerchief as though he had been waiting all along for just that moment and dabbed at her cheek before Amon could be certain he had even seen a glitter.

4
THEATRE, DIASPORA, KINGDOM

Theatre   December 28th, 49 FE

Amon blinked, and when his eyes opened, Rashana's chair was half-reclined, and she was no longer sitting still. Her eyes were twitching beneath slitted eyelids, fingers gesturing, lips forming words, as though managing her corporate empire while napping.

This sudden burst of interfacing surprised him, not least because she'd offered to take the day off for their conversation. Then he glanced down and was positively bewildered. The clouds formed an entirely different pattern than they had just moments earlier—the rolling bed shattered into blots and dabs. And the sun, formerly sinking below the horizon of white, was now far above it, as though time had reversed.

"Rashana!" cried Amon, sitting up in alarm. "What's happened?"

"Good morning, Amon," she replied calmly, her eyes opening and honing in on him as her hands settled, the chair righting itself.

"Morning? Was I asleep?"

"You drifted off in the middle of our conversation. A side effect of some of the pollen we gave you."

"The what? Pollen?"

"Didn't you notice the flowers?"

Amon recalled Atupio Home Office, with its blooming plantfoam corridors and those pulsating blossoms in the conference room.

"What about them?"

"Those are nanobot assemblers. They build useful compounds on command as part of their biological processes. Very similar to dust except for the mode of production and dissemination."

"You dusted me?"

"Don't look so upset. It was a genetically tailored medication from our floral nanopharmocopeia. Mostly enhancers of your enzymes to supplement the default stimulant."

Amon could almost smell the invigorating air after he'd tumbled from the fruit. "That's what made me pass out? A molecular cocktail?"

"The culprit was painpress. From the red flowers. It keeps the stress that accompanies charged memories below consciousness."

Amon thought back on his curiously flat emotions and realized that they had always related to the past, then shuddered at the events involved—Barrow's mangled face, Rick's bleeding eyes, Mayuko's sad and fearful gaze . . .

"The effect has worn off I'm afraid," Rashana told him. "Shall we return to Atupio for another dose?"

"No, I don't want any more," Amon rasped, slouching forward and gripping his temples. "You altered my mind without asking me?"

"My medicorps did everything they could to bring you out of the coma, Amon. After you awoke, it just wasn't possible to consult you on every little adjustment to your bilirubin or serotonin. Your pollen regimen had to be adapted to your changing physiological and neurological condition. We couldn't take any chances repairing damage from the encephalitis."

"But suppressing my emotions?"

"I could have had them give you dreampurge instead of painpress. Then you'd still be in bed at home office grappling with the nightmares. But I thought you'd want to have this conversation as soon as possible. Did I choose the wrong antitraumatic for you, Amon?"

He wasn't sure how to answer. He hadn't wanted to wait another second to speak with her. She was right about that.

"I guess I am glad we've been able to talk," he said, releasing his head from the vice of his hands.

"I'm sorry to give you such a shock."

"You were just trying to do what's best for me, right?" Amon lifted his head, gave her a token smile to tell her they were okay, and turned to sweep the sky again. "Anyway, how could it be morning? The sun is much higher."

"Because it's not. It's coming up on 1:00 p.m."

"But . . . So I was—"

"Yes. For more than 20 hours."

Amon was struggling to believe this—he'd never slept so long in his life—when the dream he'd had during the night started to come back to him.

Again he rode the giant bird that had saved him from Opportunity Peaks. Except her flames were tiny people, thousands and thousands of humans guttering in the skyward winds. They looked to Amon with supplicating eyes as they went out one after the other. He tried to blow on the feathers to stoke the people into existence but his breath kept coming out of his ears.

It was Amon's first dream since his bankdeath. His first in years not about the forest. A new dream. So as not to forget, he replayed it in his mind while he used the toilet that Ono X led him to and then took a shower.

The display walls of the shower capsule were like an out-of-focus lens, smudging the world into a runny blur of blues and whites and golds. For months he'd been making do with PeelKlean, whenever he was lucky enough to get his hands on any. So the stream of warm water, the soft froth and herbaceous fragrance of soap, should have seemed like incomparable luxuries. And yet, these sensations slipped over and around his consciousness like vapid shadows as pale snippets of dream filled his mind's eye. A sense of foreboding stewed within him. His thoughts were slippery symbols that shot from his hands the harder he grasped them. In a vague way he could not explain, he had taken the fire of this bird to be a gift that had brought him back so that he could give it to others. Now he wondered if the flame might not simply burn them.

When Amon returned in a freshly laundered black T-shirt and loose hemp pants, Ono X brought him a brown clay bowl filled with porridge made from the strange grains and beans he'd eaten at Atupio. Amon wondered whether Ono X was the cook. Rashana had introduced him as her spymaster and captain of the Birla Guard, but he seemed to be proficient at everything that involved service of any kind—butler, jester, and soldier all rolled into one.

While Amon spooned and slurped his porridge, hot bowl in hand, he thought back on what he and Rashana had been discussing before he nodded off. To steer them away from the upsetting subject of her parents' murder, he was fairly certain that he'd asked her a question.

"Last I remember," he began, "we were talking about what happened to the Gyges Circle after my cash crash."

"I seem to recall a head lolling over at that time," said Rashana, with a smile.

"So do they have the Ring of Gyges now?"

"You've forgotten my answer?"

"Was it no?"

"It was. Or rather, 'not yet.' I was filling you in on the political fallout from your identity assassination of Barrow. It began with Philanthropy Syndicate media portraying him as a child-molesting nostie."

"Just like in the forged bankruptcy report they sent me through Sekido."

"Consistency is the mortar for any sound house of lies. Giving Barrow a kink fit with the truth about Kitao. The reports made him Barrow's flower-obsessed sidekick."

"I can almost believe they were a bedroom tag team myself."

"The public certainly went for it. The double bankruptcy scandal engineered by the Gyges Circle was political magic. It gave Sekido an excuse to split off his faction from Moderate Choice and form the Full Choice Party. It also provided Absolute Choice with dirt to fling in the ensuing election, and the Full/Absolute Coalition secured a landslide victory. Enough seats to appoint a new Secretary of Blinding as soon as her term of office expired."

"Then why *don't* they have the ring?"

"Because the immense unexpected costs of the identity assassination also left the Gyges Circle with a shortfall. They couldn't afford the fines to buy Executive Council votes for the appointment, to analyze the House of Blinding system, or to design the Ring of Gyges program, let alone install it."

"So it's a waiting game. I mean, the Gyges Circle has plenty of income between them, right? They just need to bide their time until enough revenue builds up."

"Not idly. To raise the required funds while the political situation remains in their favor, the Philanthropy Syndicate executives and Anisha came to a new agreement on the structure of the Charity Gift Economy. In essence, it codified my twin's promise to incrementally lower the cost of purchasing human resource profiles from Fertilex BioPens. Once the contract was signed, the Gyges Circle paid the Full/Absolute Choice coalition to re-privatize urination and defecation and to draft a bill to privatize heartbeating for the first time in history. GATA's fiscal surplus, from the auction of these lucrative action properties and from the fines for the Gyges Circles' own recent lawbreaking, was used to lower credi-crime fines overall and crowdcare fines in particular. The Philanthropy Syndicate could then gradually disinvest in the bankdeath camps."

"By disinvestment you mean a reduction in supplies," said Amon.

"Supplemented by some additional restructuring."

"Then the famine we experienced in the District of Dreams was just accounting? They were recouping losses from taking out Barrow."

"They were. To pay for the Ring of Gyges. The agreement with Anisha gave the Syndicate a cheap supply of order-grown Fertilex resources to staff their companies without extraction from the camps. Meanwhile, lower crowdcare fines made it affordable to cut back supplies by reducing the cost of managing the resulting bankdead dissent. Both rebates combined meant that the Syndicate paid a larger share of its human resource budget to Fertilex instead of wasting it on the Charity Gift Economy, enabling the Gyges Circle to pool a greater total amount of wealth."

"But how much could the Syndicate have actually saved? Aren't the cost of supplies basically nothing to them?"

"Cutting supplies to the camps was only a means of reducing population to a level where labor costs are in line with investitarian donations. The rate of reduction was calculated to make the bankdead fatigued and willing to fight each other for scraps but not desperate enough to revolt against the Charity Brigade. Once the population was fluctuating within an easier-to-corral range, some of the freekeepers and career volunteers who manage the bankdead could be laid off, representing a substantial saving on action fees in the form of axed wages."

Amon saw in his mind's eye an endless waste of shriveled corpses in dissolving rubble, men in suits shaking hands and smiling on the rooftops of glittering skyscrapers that towered over it. He crossed his arms and rubbed his biceps to warm away the chill. "If they're going to starve so many for a few yen, why not just let them all die?"

"Because it would be difficult to fabricate convincing pitypromo when the thing investitarians are supposed to pity doesn't exist; discovery of such a deception could result in expensive lawsuits and plunging donations. Ultimately, the poor can evade any final solution so long as their plight can be marketed. It's more profitable to keep the Charity Gift Economy running in reduced capacity, at least for now."

"Then our exposé was useless. . . . We gave Full Choice reason to vote with Moderate Choice to repeal the crowdcare fine reductions and make it too expensive to keep lowering supply levels, but the Syndicate was going to stop cutting supplies anyway."

"No, because losing the fine reductions stopped the Syndicate before they'd adjusted the District of Dreams population to its optimally profitable level."

"How far before?"

"The Philanthropy Syndicate hasn't been forthcoming with data. My demographicorps has several models. All estimate that the exposé saved millions of lives."

"Millions . . ." Amon whispered, tilting his head back and swaying in his seat as his eyes lost their point of focus. If that was the portion saved, he wondered about the total that had already died. The famine he'd lived through expressed in numbers, fathomless suffering quantified, added, subtracted. Rashana had stated the figure casually. The magnitude of the atrocity hardly seemed to faze her. Amon didn't think it was callousness so much as acclimatization to choices with enormous ramifications.

How very lucky he'd been to have Xenocyst, where extra supplies and systems of cooperation had sheltered them from the worst of the cutbacks, and Amon gazed into the bright sky from which he'd found inspiration for his plan. After the sabotage mission went awry and Rick's fatal tears began to fall, Amon had blamed the sky for leading him astray. But now, flying above the clouds, closer than ever before, his awareness absorbed in endless expansive blue, he understood how much worse everything could have been.

"I'm glad the exposé made a difference," said Amon. "And it stopped them from appointing their man as Secretary of Blinding too, didn't it? We took down the Absolute/Full coalition. The Gyges Circle has failed!"

"Only temporarily I'm afraid. They're regrouping for the upcoming election. Full Choice was the only party to come out clean after the double bankruptcy and fine reduction scandals that stuck to Moderate and Absolute Choice, respectively. According to most opinion analytics, this has inclined swing voters to view the lobbies backing Full Choice as the most creditable. Whether the party clinches a majority or has to partner with Absolute Choice again, the result will be the same."

Four projections of Rashana flickered into being, each identical to Amon's perspective of Rashana in front of him except reoriented to extend up, down, left, and right.

"The moment the new cabinet is inaugurated, the Secretary of Blinding appointment will be put to a vote that is guaranteed to pass," Ono X voiced over for the projections, though not the original Rashana, who wasn't moving her lips. "On that very day, the new Secretary of Blinding will use his executive clearance to install the program. He will apply the exemptions to himself to evade the bankdeath penalty for his credicrimes. He will be the first to seize Gyges Ring. And with it, he will grant the same to the others."

Once again Ono X's performance was spellbinding, perfectly capturing Rashana's bearing and cadence. As he bowed and melted away with Amon's empty bowl, the recordings vanished. Amon was left staring into the sky that encompassed him, feeling miniscule and insignificant amidst so much space and hidden power.

Diaspora   January 3rd, 50 FE

Unsurprisingly, the exile assembly had questions about the more than two weeks Amon had not accounted for between the Xenocyst civil war and his arrival there that night.

"And after that?" asked Jiku. "What have you been doing all this time?"

"He couldn't answer me earlier," said Yané. "Isn't it obvious why?"

"It was awful in there, as you all know, a nightmare," Amon told them. "I did what I could to survive, ate what I could find. There were some kind souls who helped me along the way." Amon thought of the strange bubbles that Kitao had blown into him as he lay feverish in the elevator.

"I kept my ears open for word of what happened to you all." More specifically, Amon had asked Rashana to have Atupio reporters investigate Hippo's whereabouts.

"Eventually, I heard about a large band with vintage weapons that had fled from Xenocyst. I wasn't sure if the rumors were true, but I tried to think where you might have gone if they were. You couldn't head north to Delivery after the sabotage or west into the waiting arms of the OpScis. The Sanzu River blocked your way further east and south was just hopeless." Amon remembered his view from Gemini X of the great desert of disposcraper ruins that had once been the Tumbles.

"I started to despair that you were already dead and gone, when I finally thought of Tamper." Amon left out the role that Hippo's genome had played in leading him to this idea. Although Hippo had had the foresight before his identity euthanization to leave his foundation the rights to his inner profile in perpetuity, all its assets had been auctioned off after the Philanthropy Syndicate sued the organization bankrupt. When Amon requested a renewed search for Hippo after his talk with Rashana in the sky, Ono X discovered that the MegaGlom R-Lite had made the highest bid for his genetic information, and that the data had since been traded amongst the other members of the SpawnU Consortium. Once Ono X had tracked down the subsidiary presently in possession, Rashana had initiated a buy-out through an Atupio front company. Then Ono X did a search through the District of Dreams plutogenic system, and they learned that the last place Hippo's DNA had been detected was a feeder by the shore of the Sanzu River. This led Amon to think of Tamper.

"How else could you find food when many of you would be blacklisted? My guess was that you'd ring the signal bells to have him boat you across. Was I right?"

A few heads nodded.

"I then tried to retrace my steps from when Tamper guided me out of Free Tokyo last summer. Eventually, I found the condo where his son lives."

Amon left out that Ono X had looked up the address using the names of the foster parents, which were listed on a record of the custody lawsuit over Tamper's son.

"I waited in the parking lot until Tamper arrived at sundown. Then I tailed him here. Sorry, Tamper," Amon said with a bow, looking at him in the crowd. He still couldn't make out Tamper's eyes but was pretty sure that he gave one of his all-but-imperceptible nods.

Yané gestured towards Tamper as if to comment, but before he could get in a word Book said, "Did you receive any further reports of Little Book? Subsequent to your encounter with Barrow in the library."

"I'm afraid not," Amon replied. Atupio reporters had asked around at giftless enclaves throughout the District of Dreams and also at Gifted Triangle orphanages, on the off chance that Little Book had been upgraded to gifted, all to no avail. "No one I spoke to knew anything."

Book pinched his earlobe restlessly, the one eye magnified by his unbroken lens glistening and twitching with concern. It saddened Amon to see this paragon of cool calculation display such emotion. The only time like it was when Hippo was telling the history of Xenocyst to Amon and Rick, and Book had railed against the demise of his education program. Amon shared his worry about Little Book, for even assuming that the frail boy had somehow slipped out of Xenocyst through the web of armed sentries after betraying Barrow, his prospects were poor. Without Book to interpret for him, his great intellect would go unrecognized and his muteness would appear as a handicap, burdensome to anyone who associated with him. Even Barrow, fully aware of Little Book's talents, had underestimated him in the library. He never guessed that the boy could communicate directly with Amon any more than Amon had, the cause in the end of his downfall. Now, lost amongst hordes of complete strangers, in the aftermath of a famine punctuated by swells of violence, Little Book's chances of finding succor were next to nil.

"How did you get cross the river?" asked a man.

"I hitched a ride." The statement was technically true: one of the Birla Guard had coptered him over to Tonan.

"Without a bell to call Tamper?" Jiku asked.

"It wasn't easy," said Amon, evasively.

"Like you would've called Tamper anyway," Yané sneered. "If you were ready to do that, then why'd you stalk him here, huh? Guilty 'bout something?"

"There were so many lies floating around after the sabotage," Amon explained, grateful that Yané had inadvertently rescued him from his dubious answer. "I didn't know what Tamper might have heard about me, and I was afraid he wouldn't bring me here."

With the help of God's Eye, Amon had tracked Tamper without ever stepping into his line of sight.

"A stalker is a stalker is a stalker!" shrieked a big-boned woman with thick braids to her shoulders. Several shadows nodded in agreement.

"I didn't want to sink to that, believe me." said Amon. "But I couldn't take the chance that I'd never speak to Hippo. You've got to understand how important—"

"Couldn' tage such a liddle chance for yourthelf when you risked tho much for uth?!" Ty snapped, rolling over to face Amon at last. "We've heard hith story. Let's ged him oud of—"

"Listen!" shouted Amon. "I said I'm sorry for what happened. My plan didn't save Xenocyst in the end. But we were torn between a war with the OpScis that we couldn't win and a brewing civil war that would have eaten us from the inside out. The exposé was our only hope of keeping the community in one piece and it almost worked."

"If it wathn't for—"

"And yes!" Amon cut off Ty again. "I disagreed with you about bringing in Barrow. He used my plan to ruin Xenocyst. But it was the council who approved his membership and my plan, not me. Are you going to hold one crashnewb responsible for the decisions of your democracy? If we didn't have Barrow, we never would have got the anadeto weapons that saved us from the brink. We were damned with him and we would have been just as damned without him!"

To Amon's surprise, Ty had nothing to say in response. He just lay there on his side, staring at the floor in despair.

"Listen to these excuses," said Yané. "He apologizes and then he says it's not his fault."

"I never meant it that way," said Amon. "I don't expect you to forgive me. Now that I'm done catching you up, all I ask is that you let me speak to Hippo. Can someone please just tell me where he is?"

There was a curious moment of silence, as though everyone to a person was tongue-tied.

"What is your reason for seeking Hippo?" asked Book.

Amon paused, thinking how to explain, and Yané seized the opening, "'Cause he knows Hippo's got a soft spot for him and he's drooling for our food."

"No!"

"Then why?"

Again Amon hesitated. After all the suspicions leveled at him, his guess that they would mis- understand and construe him had hardened into a certainty. Not only was his proposal couched in ideas unfamiliar to many crashborn, but his reasons for ultimately placing his trust in Rashana would have been impossible to convey.

To confirm her intricately woven story, he had scoured her inner profile and corroborated the events recorded in her LifeStream on platinum engines, in cooperation with an independent siftcorps she had agreed to hire for him. Even with their help, there were so many far-reaching implications that Amon couldn't hope to follow up every thread while also searching for Mayuko and his friends over the past week. He could only check that everything held together in the time available and had not been as thorough as he would have liked. But it was hard to doubt the best information money could buy, and when he reminded himself of the urgency of their undertaking, he felt sure that she was telling the truth, the whole truth, and nothing but. She just *had* to be telling the truth! Otherwise, they would all be stuck with the suffocating present or be hurled into an even more constricting future. And Amon was done being tossed on the waves of history.

Good luck boiling down all his hopes and hunches and calculations for people who had never even interacted with a computer, aside from vending machines and CareBots. It would be like trying to convey the splendor of the naked sky to the bankliving. Amon definitely wasn't going to win the exiles over when they were fuming and skeptical of him, their minds clouded by hunger and fear. If only Hippo, the voice of reason, were there, then they would be bound to let Amon see him.

"I need to speak directly to Hippo," he answered finally.

"See," said Yané. "He's made up every word."

"What's your verdict, Book?" asked Jiku. "Did you see deception in his eyes?"

"I believe we can trust him," Book replied.

"That's not what she asked," said Yané. "Was he lying, yes or no?"

There was a tense moment as the eyes of Book and Yané locked.

"So?"

"Without the mirror, I cannot deliver determinate conclusions."

"Listen to this! Book taking sides. Get back in line or get out."

Amon was grateful for the intervention. Unfortunately, the crowd could not be diverted so easily.

"Strange he's been gone all this time," said Thick Braids. "Could've been up to all sorts of mischief."

"Strange he could cross that river by hisself," echoed her friend.

"And find us all the way out here?" added a man in the shadows.

"I say he's full of it," put in another.

"I smell it too," agreed a third.

An argument broke out about what to do with him. All semblance of decorum fell away, everyone disputing and shouting and mocking out of turn. A consensus soon emerged from the racket that Amon was indeed a liar. The only disagreement concerned whether they could safely declare him a snitch, with Yané spearheading the affirmative side and Jiku rallying the moderates to take a more equivocal stance. *A smart and levelheaded woman*, Amon thought, remembering how she had seen first at the final Xenocyst council that Barrow's proposal of open war with the OpScis would play into the hands of the Philanthropy Syndicate. To his disappointment, Book said nothing further in his defense, settling back into his traditional neutrality, nor did Vertical pause in her restless pacing, apparently oblivious to anything but her grief. But the question about Amon's alleged sedition was soon rendered moot by a point that for the crowd seemed to eclipse all others: there weren't enough supplies to admit another hungry mouth. Here the remnants of the once disciplined council descended into such misguided covetousness and disorder that they verged on a mob; Amon could almost feel the exiles' want and trauma as his own.

When the jumble of voices meandered to the topic of what to do for food after the drone attack yesterday, Book finally reigned it in.

"Order! Your attention please! Order! Let us treat the preceding discussion as preamble for a vote as to whether to eject or to punish Gura. Before we proceed, are there any further proposals or objections at this time?"

"Yes," said Amon. "If I can be allowed to speak."

"All members are entitled to comment. You may proceed."

Amon addressed the assembly. "I can see that you have doubts about me, but there's been a misunderstanding. I'm not looking to join you and I don't need any of your food. As I keep saying, I just want to speak with Hippo. Once you've heard everything I have to say to him, I think it's possible that your opinion of me will change. So before you vote, can't you just tell me where he is?"

Again this request was followed by an unaccountable silence. The exiles looked around at each other in search of someone who knew what to say. It was as though they were stricken with embarrassment. Then, as if making an excuse for their hesitation, a man said, "What do we owe you?"

"Liar," said a woman.

Before chaos could take hold again, Book said, "As we have heard from all parties, let the voting commence."

Amon sighed and looked at his right hand in his lap, mulling over whether to contact Ono X for a lift. It was obvious which way the vote would go. Why sit through any more of this farce? But luckily, he wouldn't have to.

"All those in favor of—"

"Book!" a man interrupted.

"All those in favor of—" Book tried to pick up where he had left off but "Book!" the man shouted again.

"Yes?"

Standing in the pane of moonlight, staring at Book, was the hefty form of Tamper. "You can't rip him off for a story," he said.

"Pardon me?"

"Pay your story debts and be fair."

Kingdom   January 10th, 50 FE

The mercury pupils, gold irises, and scarlet whites of the PhisherKing's eyes turned slowly and smoothly like the cogs of a machine oiled with the slick inevitability of fate as he answered the question Amon had not asked in words.

"When you sent me the sample recordings of your meetings with the Birla sisters, I thought immediately of a MegaGlom executive alliance that I had recently uncovered through other leaks."

Amon pictured that moment. He'd been riding the Oneiro Express towards the District of Dreams while Mayuko lay on the floor of a weekly mansion being beaten and abused. The PhisherKing had been their only hope.

"You must mean the Gyges Circle," said Amon.

"Your patron has kept you well-informed. I had just learned myself that that was what they called themselves. All data available pointed to them as the ones responsible. So I tagged the still of the Emoticon Man you'd sent me with 'Gyges' and ran it through an image search in our database. No prior hits for the digiguise came up. But one of our algorithms found stylistic similarities with other works designed by Anisha Birla's personal digimaker. This established that the Emoticon Man was closely associated with her. From his behavior and the presence of the Birla Guard, we concluded that it was Anisha herself."

The PhisherKing's confidence in his identification of Anisha with the Emoticon Man was reassuring. It backed up Amon's own somewhat rushed efforts these past two weeks to establish the veracity of Rashana's story through comparison of her LifeStream and platinum facts. Verifying her humanitarian activities over the years had been easy enough; there were countless examples, including segs of her donating to Xenocyst and running Atupio to help the giftless. The challenge had been making sense of the many recordings that were ambiguous, with the dual perspectives on a single scene of both sisters grafted together, or fragmentary, with gaps large and small throughout. The most worrisome of such lacunas were in the days after her parents' death, which overlapped roughly with the leadup to Amon's cash crash. While he had found the segs in which she dispatched mercenaries to save Rick from somnambul dusting and ordered Ono X to locate Amon for a meeting in the evening, both from the morning that followed the Birla parents' fatal accident or murder in sub-Arctic waters, her LifeStream was in tatters from around noon of that day onward, containing more omission than content, apparently because the sisters' cyberfeud had intensified. Conspicuously lacking were the time points when Amon had spoken with Makesh in Ginza, been charged for jubilee, met the recruiter with Sekido in Kabukicho, dealt with the Emoticon Man, and left his message.

Rashana had demonstrated her memory of Ginza and Amon's message in conversation, and the scattered momentary clips that *did* remain of these days were consistent with her account, showing her hacking her sister, handling the inheritance lawsuit, learning how to manage her new properties, and conferring with Atupio managers. In her LifeStream during his sojourn in the District of Dreams, Amon had also successfully located the segs of her meeting with Rick in Er, her talk with Hippo about the exposé, her hard work assisting Xenocyst with it, her attempt to pick up Amon at midnight after the sabotage, the ensuing dogfight with her sister, the renewed search for Amon as he fled Xenocyst, and her provisions to have Amon treated in Atupio. But in this period too, her LifeStream was missing a great many pieces, including her meetings to ask about Amon with Rick in Delivery and with Hippo in the Cyst. So while Amon hadn't unearthed a single shred of evidence that contradicted anything Rashana had told him, the holes were reason for concern, and he couldn't rule out that there might be others besides.

Proving that Anisha, not Rashana, was associated with the Emoticon man would be a significant step towards overcoming such uncertainty. Amon already knew that the Emoticon Man had found Mayuko through a virus that Sekido infected Amon with while Anisha's figment was present to cover up the activities of an organization Anisha led; now his spastic face could be traced to Anisha's designer. Here from the PhisherKing was independent support for Amon's conviction that the balance of truth had to be in Rashana's favor. If he could just arrange to have Hippo meet her in person and look upon her naked face, any lingering doubt would be dispelled, as Hippo was one of the few people that could tell the twins apart.

"Were you able to successfully blackmail the Emoticon Man, I mean Anisha?" Amon asked. He took a seat on the edge of the rocking gunwale, resting legs tired from standing around for hours.

"I knew a leak that would do the trick," said Monju. "Unfortunately, showing it to anyone carried enormous penalties. I had to do some expensive legwork to skirt around the licensing agreement."

"What sort of leak?"

"Proof that one of the Blinders was the son of a Gyges Circle member. I threatened to send this along with the LifeStream section you'd just given me to SpawnU intelligence."

This, Amon could see, was a deft move, putting the Gyges Circle's only significant rival on alert before their agent was promoted to Secretary of Blinding. He wished he could have only known who to send his LifeStream. Then he might have protected Mayuko himself.

"How did Anisha respond?"

"She agreed to leave Mayuko alone in exchange for exclusive rights to both pieces of evidence. I told her that either she and her guards left immediately, or the info went out right then and there. Without missing a beat, she threatened to kill Mayuko if I didn't agree but promised me an enormous sum if I did."

"Let me guess. The amount started with six, six, zero, zero, nine and ran on for, like, eighty digits."

The PhisherKing nodded.

It occurred to Amon that the linkage between Anisha and the Emoticon Man reinforced Rashana's conjecture that her sister was responsible for the jubilee charge. Not only was the amount the same as the Emoticon Man's offers to both Mayuko and Monju, but a Blinder had been involved in illegally incurring it on Amon, and if the Gyges Circle had corrupted the House of Blinding with one agent, chances were there were others that Anisha could have called upon.

"That offer is so Birla," Amon observed, shaking his head.

"They are indeed masters of the double-edged ultimatum. Ono Y must have already hacked whatever they needed from her BodyBank. They had determined that she was expendable."

When the PhisherKing said "Ono Y," Amon finally put together who the guard that flesh-hacked Mayuko must have been. Now in his memory, the tengu placing suction cups on her forehead and waving his hands over her had Ono X's face.

"I doubt they found anything useful," said Amon. "I had her delete everything to do with me."

"Then they must have realized that hacking her was a fruitless waste."

"How did you respond to the offer?"

"I called Anisha's bluff."

"You mean, you refused again?"

"Even better. I started to count down from ten and reiterated that I would send my leak to SpawnU."

"With Mayuko in danger like that? What were you—"

"Don't presume that I wanted to see an innocent woman die, even without my promise to you that I'd protect her," said the PhisherKing. "But there were no clauses in the Birla Deal to stop those men from harming her once it was cut. Either they killed her and I got nothing, or they spared her life and I got rich. All options between murder and mercy were fair game."

A vision came to Amon of the Emoticon Man pummeling Mayuko on the floor, whipping her back, tearing out her hair, his face shifting between iconic rictuses of pleasure.

"But you still left them with the murder option," said Amon. "You were willing to—"

"The best weapon against a brinksman is to find them another brink."

This statement stunned Amon into silence for a moment. The logic seemed impregnable but he refused to accept that it applied when his friend's life was on the scales.

"And Anisha met your demands, right?" he asked, his heart fluttering with worry and anger at the gamble Monju had taken, however sensible it might have been. "Mayuko's okay?"

Monju tossed a small fish that opened its mouth increasingly wide until it was like the gaping maw of a whale, and from its engorged gullet, a seg expanded over Amon's visual field.

The viewpoint was having a staring match with the Emoticon Man flanked by tengu in the weekly mansion.

"Five . . . four . . . three . . ." went the sibilant, bubbly voice of the PhisherKing's jellyfish figment.

"She'll die," warned the Emoticon Man, flickering between two faces, a demonic scowl with a knife-filled mouth skewering a naked, bound maiden and a placid-eyed smile with pores sweating gold nuggets.

"Two . . . One . . ."

"You wouldn't dare."

When one of the tengu lifted his boot above Mayuko's face, Monju waved into the air a hazy montage of Amon's LifeStream and two double-helixes of DNA side by side, that of the Blinder agent and his Gyges Circle father. A dotted line connected the segs to a jackpot hole near the ceiling that was labelled "SpawnU."

"Your last chance," bubbled Monju.

The Emoticon Man broke gaze, turned to the tengu with lifted boot, glanced back at the perspective. His gloved hands trembled with rage and he looked as though he might try something hasty as his face kept flipping. Demonic knife-mouth, gold sweating smile. Demonic knife-mouth, gold sweating smile. Then all of a sudden, he did an about face like a well-disciplined soldier and began to walk away.

As the Emoticon Man and his tengus filed towards the hole in the elevator, the PhisherKing glanced down at Mayuko, battered atop shards of glass, her hair a tangled corona spilling across the floor, head turned to the side, looking blankly over her shoulder in a daze, but still in one piece.

While the seg played, Amon sat up rigid and riveted in his terror, squeezing the rim of the gunwale with both hands until his fingers ached. When it ended, he was overcome with relief, the torturous memory he had fretted over day in and day out finally resolved, and he collapsed into his hands.

"And they didn't come back?" he asked in a near whimper through the gap between his palms. "They didn't hurt her any more?"

"They were gone," said the PhisherKing. "That was it."

Amon let out a single sob and then remained curled into his lap with forearms on thighs, his chest wracked with sharp hissing breaths. Some time passed before he was calm enough to raise himself and seek the PhisherKing's many-colored eyes.

"I don't know about your methods, but you're the only person I've ever known to outdeal a Birla," Amon told him. 'Thank you. You saved her." And he stood up to give a low bow.

Theatre   December 28th, 49 FE

The westering sun had returned to a hand's breadth above the cloud horizon. While the white mass had broken up, cartography of billows transformed, the vista seemed in some ineffable way to share its essence with the one Amon had viewed at the same time the previous day, as though his life were repeating itself even if appearances suggested otherwise. He wanted the flight paths of the drones and aircraft to reveal some profound change that would convince him of the novelty of the present but he couldn't remember their former pattern well enough to compare. As if to break apart this experiential loop, Amon pinched two points in the air, imagined himself tugging on a snake biting its tail, and asked, "Where is all this information coming from?"

"Ono X's channels for one," said Rashana.

"He must outrank even the PhisherKing in intelligence gathering."

"Monju doesn't have my resources at his disposal."

"SpawnU does."

"And they've learned many things. Their investigations continue into the crowdcare fine and bankdead population reductions. They just haven't managed to uncover the human resource deal and the extent of GATA corruption, or piece together that Barrow's cash crash was an identity assassination and that the new Blinder is an agent."

"Why have you but not them? Or GATA?"

"No one else can hack the central organizer. The security weakness is in our joint profile."

"Oh . . . so it's you! You're the spy!"

"I prefer 'silent observer.' She started it."

Rashana maintained her usual posture, palms stacked on the top knee of her crossed legs, but her eyes began to moisten, her lower lip trembling. Amon looked away, searching the sky for a different topic.

"So the job you tried to offer me," he began. "You've brought me here to stop the Gyges Circle, haven't you?"

Rashana snorted softly in amusement.

"What?" said Amon, turning back to her with a frown.

"Do you really think I have that kind of Freedom? As if the manager of a fringe subsidiary like Atupio could stand up to Fertilex and the Philanthropy Syndicate."

"Alone maybe not, but together with SpawnU?"

"Like heroes off to confront the forces of darkness. How comic book of you. I only wish . . .."

"What's to wish? So many people starved to death. The perpetrators will seize freedom without limits. All you have to do is give SpawnU the evidence."

When Rashana shook her head with downcast eyes, Amon felt rising shame. From his perspective as a lowly non-executive, had he overlooked another monumental issue? Then her eyes lit up as though raConTeur had whispered some insight.

"Do you remember when we talked in Ginza?" she asked.

Ono X's voice sounded from somewhere down the length of the deck: "By protecting the AT Market, we Liquidators also help to uphold the policies of Pax Economica. In the past, world peace was just a faint hope, but in the battle against terrorism the side of freedom won once and for all . . ."

Amon knew immediately who Ono X was ventriloquizing and was so embarrassed that he wished the sunlight would evaporate him into the blue above. It was Amon himself, his rhythm and timbre impersonated flawlessly, and he recalled Rashana's caustic responses in her guise as Makesh Adani. He was grateful that he couldn't access his LifeStream. Revisiting the fool he'd been before his bankdeath through the time-curated filter of memory was painful enough.

"I remember," replied Amon more stridently than he intended. Perhaps noticing his discomfort, Rashana flicked a finger and Ono X's recitation stopped.

"There's a nugget of truth to what you said," she told him. "Pax Economica is a reality and GATA does prop it up, but not in the way that bronze engines teach. For example, what is the definition you picked up from the InfoFlux?"

"The economic peace," said Amon. "All war brought to an end by the mutual advantage of global financial cooperation."

"But war between whom? There are no state armies anymore, only Liquidators as you know."

"I thought that *was* the economic peace, there being no armies or terrorists."

"What about private armies?"

"Well, I know that the MegaGloms lead in peacedrone deployment but . . ." Amon stopped there, lest he regurgitate more edutized falsities.

Rashana smiled and said, "Corporate blocs have been the only organizations with credible armies for ages. They quietly orchestrated the monopolization of military might through incremental armament and defense privatization long before the word MegaGlom was even coined. Your ignorance of this arrangement is a relic of bygone PR-opaganada. Throughout the late Unfree Era, their media portrayed the charade of international relations as though states were the main actors. National, ethnic, and ideological conflicts of a manageable scale were in fact tolerated, insofar as they yielded the usual financial opportunities—sale of weaponry, investment in catastrophe futures, licensing of guerilla training tutorials. Even nuclear skirmishes were tolerated if contracts for cleanup, medical care, and reconstruction went to the right players."

"If war was profitable for companies, why did it ever end?"

"Because of technological developments. The loss of war's business viability is often attributed to the advent of Weapons of Undetectable Disruption, especially sleeperpuzzles."

"Sounds like a harmless toy."

"One might think so. They appear under analysis like any old synthetic molecule. Dump them in the atmosphere, and they camouflage among the world's plethora of industrial emissions. Our atmosphere is swirling with too many byproducts of patented processes and trade secrets to count, their purpose unknown to all but the manufacturer. What sets sleeperpuzzles apart is that they're nanobot pieces. Once other components released into the winds meet their dormant counterpart, a chemical reaction completes the puzzle, and they self-assemble into dust that automatically seeks all nearby humans, slipping through protective barriers, walls, armor.

"Each MegaGlom kept its weapons program classified, so no one knew how many kinds of dust could be manufactured as sleeperpuzzles. This meant that an outbreak of any unexplained physical or psychological condition could be an early warning sign of insidious assault from a rival company. A drop in average platelet count on a health exam might signal gradual onset hemophilia dust inflicting the workforce. Or a spike in residents talking to themselves a schizoid wave. And if an attack were suspected, who ought to be blamed? One MegaGlom? All of them? With worker efficiency, consumer spending, and overall financial activities threatened, WUDs left the espionage corps of every subsidiary constantly on edge. In the most famous worst-case simulation, a low-level clerk catching a cold might spark a full-fledged InterGlom War."

"And this is the hair-trigger situation we find ourselves in today?" Amon asked.

"Not exactly. The current security environment is somewhat better. Oddly enough, we owe this improvement to the Great Cyberwar. Rather than risk military strikes for a suspected WUD attack, the MegaGloms were driven to retaliate through hacking. Once the ensuing chaos and uncertainty had reduced the value of most assets to zero, they had nothing left to lose by deploying their full arsenals after all. It was only in this crisis that executives were willing to lend their ears to the scientific and philosophical luminaries who would assemble the Tokyo Roundtable. Through a series of conferences, they convinced the MegaGloms to establish GATA and the Moratorium on Catastrophic Pricing—the Charity Gift Economy emerged later. These Three Pillars of the AT Market became the basis upon which we have competed without violence, of either the analog or digital variety, ever since."

Rashana leaned towards him with concern and said, "Are you feeling alright? Some kind of delayed side effect?"

"Fine," Amon replied, a little too quickly. Realizing that he was scowling, he swept his hands over his cheeks and told his muscles to relax. "It just . . . It goes against everything I've learned about the founding moment of the Free Era."

Before cash crashing, Amon had believed that the Tokyo Roundtable was set up to realize the ideal of liberty expressed by "all the freedom you can earn." After his bankdeath, Book's "orientations" in the digital quarantine had portrayed the group as an avaricious conspiracy to maximize profits for a minority. Now Rashana had given him yet another interpretation. Each sketch of the past had come from a different perspective—the common sense of the average Free Citizen picked up through the InfoFlux, the lore of those in poverty with no access to the ImmaNet, and the expert summaries of gabkeepers and their algorithms drawing upon extensive bespoke databases and search engines. Amon could only wonder which was true. Some synthesis of the three? Or did the word "true" even fit such moments of historical cataclysm and renewal?

"So your point is that telling SpawnU would jeopardize the system somehow. It would disrupt Pax Economica."

"I knew you'd see." Rashana paused for a moment to rub her brow thoughtfully. "You've come a long way since I called you 'a swollen sack of marketing and lies,' no offense."

Amon shook his lowered head at his own idiocy, vaguely recalling those words from not long after the spiel Ono X had quoted.

"Peace is enabled by the Three Pillars of the AT Market operating in tandem," said Rashana. "GATA sustains MegaGlom assets—the action properties—by defining, recording, and enforcing them. It guarantees owners their dues through action-transaction monitoring and disincentivizes economically destabilizing behavior with fines larger than any profits that could be gained thereby. The Moratorium algorithms make meaningful exchange possible, limit volatility, and curtail infinite inflation through virtual price constraints. The Charity Gift Economy prevents Fertilex hegemony by supplying the Philanthropy Syndicate with independently extracted human resources. In so doing, it maintains the global balance of power within the Twelve and One, between the SpawnU Consortium plus Fertilex, and the Syndicate. This balance in turn creates two lobbydeologies with Moderate and Absolute Choice as their corresponding parties, preventing any constellation of interests from dominating the Executive Council or GATA technocracy. As I'm sure you can see, each separation of financial power interlocks and mutually reinforces the others.

"Our begetters, for all their faults, were the guardians of these Three Pillars. But now that my sister controls Fertilex, she has begun to jettison their conservative policies to collaborate with the Syndicate. Destabilizing GATA by secretly stacking the Executive Council with Sekido's faction and then the Full Choice Party. Biasing AT Market enforcement through distortion of transaction records at the Ministry of Records and anonymity systems in the House of Blinding. Undermining the Charity Gift Economy through crowdcare rebates and the new resource deal. And all for the sake of Gyges Ring, a flagrant violation of both fair action monitoring and rational Moratorium pricing.

"If the SpawnU Consortium were to learn how shaky the Three Pillars have become, they'd have no reason to voluntarily comply any longer. The modus vivendi that benefitted all signatories these 49 years would fall apart, like a game where it comes out that some players have been cheating for many rounds. It's too late to reverse all the illegitimate moves; the only move left is to flip the whole board over."

"Maybe that wouldn't be such a bad thing," said Amon through gritted teeth, realizing as he did so his disgust with their world. "Maybe bringing an end to the AT Market wouldn't be as bad as you think."

"And invite an InterGlom War?"

"Why not? Let them wipe each other out."

"Even if they took everyone else down with them?"

Despite his righteous anger, Amon wasn't willing to go that far and just stared at her pensively.

"According to securicorps' modelling," Rashana explained, "the most likely result of an InterGlom War is an akrasiapocalypse."

"A what?"

"A worldwide blitz with the sleeperpuzzles for indulgence dust. Every MegaGlom has demonstrated the capability to produce these using their own patented molecular bases. Once the missing pieces are released, everyone on earth will lose their self-control. This is a strike at the Achilles heel of the AT Market, or any market, an economic doomsday weapon. Picture hordes and hordes of maniacal spendthrifts seeking immediate gratification at every moment. No one saves. Everyone goes bankrupt. Financial civilization collapses from a lack of willpower, that is a lack of freedom. If SpawnU never learns, the situation will be unfair, but at least some respectable version of humankind will survive."

Amon looked her seated form up and down, sizing her and her logic up with a glower. While he understood her silence, he wasn't sure if he could condone it. Was there no just choice untainted by compromise?

"There must be some other outcome we could bring about."

"What other outcome could there be? You tell me."

Amon ruminated on this. But his eyes kept drifting between his lap and the passing clouds, his hands pinching his lip and then scratching his head, as though mimicking in movement the path of his mind, bouncing back and forth between only two possibilities: the continuation of the system and total collapse. Try as he might to break from his cage of customary action and thought to the infinite number of options that should have awaited, his imagination repeatedly fell short. How many others throughout history had been in the same bind?

Diaspora   January 3rd, 50 FE

When Tamper intervened in the vote, all that followed was breathing, a few coughs, and a mother humming to her whimpering baby. In a few words, he had brought the crowd to silence and with this Amon grasped the situation in the community more clearly. Without Hippo, their pathetic excuse for a council was anarchy. Yané used his vestigial authority to harness the raw emotion that held sway. But no one could challenge Tamper. He was the bedrock of their survival, risking his life to steal everything they depended on. The rare times that he spoke, his opinions might as well have been commandments.

Amon remembered Tamper's request for a tale in exchange for transit to the District of Dreams and his biographical letter to the Xenocyst council to repay what he'd called his "story debts." The solitary man seemed to treasure stories more than even most bankdead, treating them as a literal currency, the gold coins of society with others. He had, after all, lost his son to those miserable foster parents, cut off forever from what happened next. Xenocyst in exile had little choice but to accept the fiat of their benefactor.

"Since it appears that the vote has been postponed," Book broke the silence, "I will now proceed—"

"Cut the formalities," Yané interrupted. "What does he want to know?"

"Everything since the sabotage, I guess," said Amon. He stood up to stretch. "I mean, by the time I reached Xenocyst it had been devastated. What happened to you all?"

More silence followed. While the crowd couldn't go against Tamper, they weren't exactly eager to obey.

"I can start." Many heads in moonlight and shadow turned to Vertical. She had stopped pacing for the first time since her intervention in Amon's meltdown, but her gaze still fell on her feet. The droop of her shoulders and weary lines of her face bespoke grim resignation, as though the news about Rick had merely confirmed what she already knew. Amon wished again that he could go over and hug her. He bore her no ill will for the violence, understanding that she'd been looking out for him.

"Last time I saw you," said Amon, "you took off like a torpedo between the legs of a freekeeper."

These words seemed to poke the tender ball of anguish inside her, and for just a moment her face cracked.

"I ran out of there," Vertical began, her voice soft and breathy as though this were painful to say. "Across the bridge."

The CareBots swarming outside Delivery had come at her, but the algorithms of some were confused by her human outlier speed, and she knocked out any that approached with Tamper's batons, evading their showers of dust.

"Then I jumped the gap at the end of the bridge, and the sky started to fall on me."

Chunks of crisp clear blue grazed past her in midair and smashed against the disposcraper ledge she landed on. As she tore through the alleys and crawlpaths of the Gifted Triangle, headed for the rendezvous point, pieces continued to burst on the ground and walls around her.

"The pickup crew thought I was insane when they saw me sidestepping and summersaulting over the roofways towards them," she mused. "I told Ty he was crazy to be out in the open with the sky falling."

Vertical smiled ruefully with a glance to where Ty lay on his side, but he contributed nothing, only gazing blankly at the floor.

"He knew right away that I'd been dusted after all."

It wasn't until much later that Book diagnosed it as chicken little dust. While Ty and most of the pickup crew rushed on ahead, one man stayed back to lead Vertical along by the hand with her eyes closed. This cut out the terrifying visuals, even if the pattering crashes and sensation of spraying sky-gravel continued to make her flinch.

"By the time we reached the buffer canyon after dark, my symptoms were pretty much gone. But then the sky really was falling."

All over the border wall across the canyon, Vertical could see a shootout unfolding under the glow of firefLytes. Men and women traded bullets and dust, as they ducked behind and shimmied over disposcraper ridges and bluffs that kept imploding beneath their feet or crumbling on top of them.

"So the battle had already started," said Amon. "How?"

"I wasn't there at the beginning. I only heard about it afterwards."

Vertical looked to Book, who nodded to accept the request.

"At approximately 22 hours on the same day," he said, "I was engaged in study within the digital quarantine, alone because Little Book was already curled up in the stacks for sleep, when a man burst in."

Book only vaguely recognized the man's face from around Xenocyst and demanded to know how he got past the guards. The man said he meant no harm and urged Book to give Hippo a message: flee immediately or he would be dead by midnight. When Book asked who would dare try to murder Hippo, the man replied, "Destroyers of the Real," and dashed out the door.

Book rushed after him, ready to raise the alarm, until he stepped into the hallway and found the entire floor empty.

"The number of guards had been reduced as many were assisting with the sabotage," he explained. "However, their complete absence was . . ."

Book frowned as though struggling to find the word.

"Strange?" supplied a man. "Weird?" suggested another.

" . . . unaccountable," said Book.

Spooked, Book rushed upstairs for the storage room where Hippo had been sleeping of late. On his way, he spotted guards posted around the armory and realized why the man hadn't delivered the message himself. Security on the higher floors was still in place, so he needed someone like Book who had clearance.

Hippo lay already awake in his box-piled closet, so when Book whispered "Run!" he wasted no time rising from his futon. Together, they slipped out a condo window into an emergency crawl tunnel that led to the rooftop alley of a connecting disposcraper. Only once they were hidden in a cranny between rooms did Hippo ask for an explanation. Book was worried that he'd fallen for some kind of ruse to clear Hippo from the Cyst, but they soon heard shouts and the *chrinkle* of dust from the direction of the armory. When silence immediately returned and no alarm bell was sounded, they concluded that intruders had already pacified the building and were in the process of pilfering the arsenal.

"I recommended that we depart as quickly as feasible," said Book. "However, Hippo's anger was too great for him to let this transgression go unchallenged. Thus he took to the streets and began to shout . . ."

Again Book faltered and frowned.

"All citizens gather! The Cyst is under siege! All citizens gather!" called out a man whose flared nostrils matched the fervor in his eyes. "I woke to this in my room. Over and again, Hippo shouted till there was a great big crowd around 'im, from ground bottom to the roofs."

The rallying cry spread outward from Hippo in waves. Then the usurpers began to march and leap from the upper levels of the Cyst along the many roofways and stairpaths, mounting the surrounding disposcrapers with guns and dusters blazing, their transparent freekeeper armor glistening beneath the firefLytes. Book and Hippo saw through these Charity Brigade disguises, noting the clumsy lack of military discipline and absence of a CareBot escort, but the growing throng quailed, vanishing into rooms and deep slumscape crevices.

"We may safely blame this failure of morale on the scourge of Opportunity Science superstition," Book fulminated. "As if those Charity Brigade degenerates might be angels of the Free Market's divine order—the very idea!"

Book glowered at the floor beside him with a toothy leer, no doubt ruing the loss of his education program. Then he seemed to arrive at a memory and his eyes lit up with something like fear and wonder.

"Hippo's incitements eventually brought our forces out of hiding. It appeared that we might remobilize until . . ."

"Paradoxes split the night sky," broke in a man in the shadows with a strong crashborn accent. "All them impossibilities rolling in one after the next. Was like bright zigzags of darkness, like punch after punch of $1 + 1 = 3$. Like . . ."

"Like someone tickling your inner eye," offered Nostrils.

"With a cicada-buzz feather," said the first man.

"Except you could taste it stirring up your feelings," chimed in Thick Braids, "high pitch twinkles of sugary pain."

Another listener might have been confused but Amon knew exactly what they were describing: one of the Geminis in action. According to segs he'd viewed in Rashana's inner profile after their talk in the sky, the vehicle prototype had originally been an identity birthday gift from the Birla parents. But when the sisters couldn't agree on how to complete it, the Onos had guessed their masters' wishes and quietly took the initiative to have two versions designed—Gemini X for Rashana and Gemini Y for Anisha.

The technologies behind the material of the two crafts, one a moving mosaic of pixeldust tesserae, the other a tapestry of pixelfiber threads, appeared to depend on radically different design concepts. In fact, they were functionally equivalent methods for engineering an armored displayweapon called proteanite, both ultrahard and capable of sculpting experiential vistas even for viewers without the ImmaNet. Amon didn't envy those stricken by Gemini Y's bag of visual and auditory illusions, amped up to psychological attack by the synaesthesia pollen excreted.

"And if you saw them moving whatevers while you heard the sound," added the man with the accent, "there was this white-hot pukey-feeling that made you paranoid about being alive. My ear itches just en'magining."

"But you couldn't look away because you smelled yourself in there too," said Nostrils. "All mixed up in the dazzle and the racket was you. And you wanted to save him—or her I suppose."

"We all cried out when it appeared. And we was saying 'what's that?' 'What could it be?' And we was scared."

"The majority of Hippo's supporters deserted us in the face of these aerial phenomena," Book resumed when the crowd had exhausted their attempts at recounting the ineffable. "This is the juncture where Ty's involvement was decisive."

Book looked to Ty. When Ty neglected to even stir on the floor, he glanced at Vertical.

"I heard from a woman in my scout crew that Ty launched a hopeless attack against the freekeeper imposters," she told them. "One of them pushed him off a roof."

"A hopeleth attack!" Ty shouted, shaking his fist into the air from where he lay. "Don' talg shit about what you don' even know."

"Fine. But that's what she said." One side of Vertical's lip turned up in a goading smile.

"If Vertical is misinformed, then perhaps you can correct her. We have yet to hear your account of the civil war."

"What do you all care? You just leave me here to piss mythelf."

Many eyes turned down and away. No one dared indulge his pity-seeking. Unexpectedly, he went on anyway.

"Me and my crew hiked in thight of the Cytht when that flying mindfuck thtarted circling over it. Motht of Hippo'th crowd was running for the dispohills. Not uth!"

Undaunted by Gemini Y's distortions of consciousness, Ty had his crew install their Gatling gun on a peak to provide cover while he led the charge on the Charity Brigade lookalikes, yelling and taunting wildly as he bounded across rooftops straight for their main force with a wheel tied to one hand and a duster in the other. Soon Gemini Y and its neurological bombardment winked out abruptly as though frightened off by this surge of resistance. But when another anomaly—Gemini X—zoomed onto the scene, Gemini Y reappeared and nearly collided with its copy above the Cyst. This brought the ground battle to a standstill; everyone to a person stopped and watched in awe as the two crafts tangled erratically into the sky, a flower of lightning hallucination blossoming spaceward.

Amon kept to himself that this was the dogfight that prevented Rashana from making her midnight appointment with him.

"Once thothe thingth were gone, Hippo'th crowd joined the charge, and you could thee the localth reaching oud of their shelterth to trip and choke the impothters."

Amon wanted to remind Ty of the gifted residents outside the slum resort who had attacked Barrow's OpSci gang in the same way. But he didn't bother, expecting only more resentment.

"Our front lineth fought their way into the Cytht, toog the armory, got weaponth flowing into the right handth. Then thith guy drethed in

OpSci ragth, just like uth returning from the mission, crept up to me. Time I realized he wasn' on any of our crewth, he was pushing me off a ledge. Weight of my tricycle pulled me down back firtht. Landed right on top . . . It wath the latht I felt of her. Robbing me while I'm oud cold, the sneaky bathtard!"

Ty raised his fist again, let it fall to his side, and rolled away as if to hide his face.

"I piggybacked him to Hippo," said Vertical. "We hauled him the rest of the way in a hearse envelope."

"You saved his life," said Amon.

"And all I get are his gripes."

"I didn' asg for this. What's the point if I can only uthe one hand?"

Amon recalled the grace with which Ty had juggled his tricycle wheels for children at the equinox festival and had to sympathize.

"Without Ty's intervention, we would have been exterminated," said Book.

Instead, the battle had raged across Xenocyst late into the night. Citizens mustered from across the complex, many setting aside Hippo's supposed cowardice in his handling of the supply crisis to support him in the face of sedition. But any advantage in numbers was outweighed by the firepower of the usurpers. Wherever Hippo's resistance took cover, they rained a medley of dust, shattering the buildings, and afflicting those exposed with hypothermia and fight'R'flight. Any target not buried alive or incapacitated with shivering and panting, literally wet their pants and fled, or mindlessly lashed out at their own ranks.

"A coordinated strategy of disguise and trickery also contributed to the rout. Earlier that day, the usurpers had intercepted the crew scheduled to transport standard outfits to the post-sabotage rendezvous point. Consequently, Ty, Vertical, and our other saboteur allies remained in OpSci dress. Thus when the timing was advantageous for the freekeeper imposters, they changed into plainclothes, and began to shout . . ."

Book trailed off again. This time Amon noticed him take a longing glance down to his left, as though the word he sought might be on the floor, and finally understood his uncharacteristic forgetfulness. Sitting there beside him should have been a boy supplying details and quotes through tapping on his tablet. The great symbiosis of intelligence at the core of Xenocyst had been rent apart, and Amon felt Book's bereavement as his own.

"OpSci invasion. Death to OpScis," Nostrils finished for him.

"This propagated confusion," continued Book. "Many observed OpSci uniforms amongst us and joined the usurpers."

Upon his return to Xenocyst, Amon had heard tell from the two border guards of contradictory rumors about who had attacked the city, and supposed now that the confusion had also helped Barrow to justify seizing the Cyst in the name of security.

By the time the sun was rising, Hippo's resistance had been pushed to the border. They might have been corralled into the open buffer and mowed down under the light of morning, if a stray shot of demolition dust hadn't toppled a disposcraper spire. This spanned a narrow section of the canyon, forming a sloping bridge across which they marked their retreat and accepted exile from the only home they knew.

Once Book had concluded his story with the help of the crowd, Amon could better make sense of their hostility towards him. The AT Market had betrayed the Xenocyst exiles by abandoning them to poverty, the Philanthropy Syndicate by coopting them and then lowering supplies to starvation levels, and their own members by orchestrating a power grab. As far as they were concerned, it was them versus the world and anyone like Amon unaccounted for during the catastrophe was firmly on the side of the world. The events of the civil war revealed them utterly forsaken, but for one exception that stood out for Amon.

"So who was that messenger?" he asked.

"That is not something we are in agreement about," said Book.

"Because there were other messengers," Jiku explained.

"Schemers," Yané corrected.

Like Book, Jiku and Yané had been forewarned of danger that night, as had three other councilors later killed or critically injured in the fighting. The remaining four councilors were thought to be Barrow's accomplices, though some could have received their warnings too late or failed to heed them. In every case confirmed, the messengers had uttered the same slogan, "Destroyers of the Real." Presumably this was to let the councilors know they were in cahoots. What remained unclear was who had sent them and why.

"What do you think, Book?"

"I am not entirely decided. But the most salient clue is that the messengers were without exception members of Barrow's storytelling circle."

"I recognized mine," said Jiku. "And when Book and Yané described theirs, others knew them too."

"I can only conjecture that Barrow, for an obscure reason, decided to show mercy to Hippo's supporters."

"Then what am I doing here, huh?" sneered Yané. "Since when did I support Hippo? You think Barrow's gonna spare me when I was the only councilor who voted against letting him in."

"How do *you* explain what happened?"

Not appreciating being questioned by Amon, Yané exhaled slowly from his nose as he glared back with narrowed eyes. "I think it could've been Barrow who sent them. But only to distance himself from the purge. Pin the brutality on the councilors who sided with him and come out on top."

Based on Ono X's intelligence, Amon was inclined to favor a third take on these mysterious heralds. For as it turned out, Barrow had been manipulated by the Gyges Circle even as he manipulated them.

After Rashana released Barrow from Er for the Giftless, the Philanthropy Syndicate had passively tracked him with his genome, licensed from the Ministry of Access, but their accounticorps only took interest in him once the famine was in high gear. It determined that having an agent manage Xenocyst to maximize human resource yield on their behalf would slightly increase savings from the population adjustment, and Barrow was selected as prime candidate from among known residents for his oratory talents.

The plan rose up the chain of command to a Gyges Circle meeting, where Anisha finalized their offer. Thus some weeks before the sabotage, Barrow was pulled from the Delivery supply line by the Charity Brigade, hauled to a plush conference room, and presented with his third and final Birla Deal. Stir up Hippo's detractors and oust the council with weapons provided, receiving Syndicate recognition as official Xenocyst representative and a shipment of the entire anadeto hoard from the Tumbles, or refuse and be marked a hungry ghost.

Amon didn't doubt that Barrow had had the political genius for the maneuver Yané described. By the night of the civil war, he'd played Xeno-cyst against the Full/Absolute Choice coalition, Philanthropy Syndicate, and Gyges Circle; the Charity Brigade against the Opportunity Scientists; and the council against itself. It was no stretch to believe that he could also split his traitorous bedfellows for further strategic gain. The question for Amon was about his motivations. Had he warned Hippo loyalists to consolidate his authority or to rescue them out of genuine concern?

Amon's answer depended on how he interpreted Barrow's life as a whole. As with his negotiations before the island crackdown to raise supply quality for the poor, his efforts to protect Sekido's girlfriend, his nationalization of bodily functions, his attempt to set up publicly funded charities, his guiding Xenocyst to the cache of weapons, his assistance with the exposé, and his offering Amon and Little Book jobs after the civil war, there were always two ways of looking at Barrow's choices: as acts that furthered his agenda or as acts of compassion. So the broader question was: were they means to selfish ends or selfless ends that simultaneously furthered selfish ones?

Throughout his banklife, Amon had naively believed the latter, became unsure after Barrow's attempt to kill him in his spa, and began to believe the latter again when they reunited in the camps, before once again being convinced of the former after their altercation in the library. Now, haunted by his mangled face for many sleepless nights ever since the red pollen wore off, Amon thought he might have misunderstood Barrow's intentions in that last confrontation. Could his look of sadness when Amon gave him the news of Rick's death have been an expression of genuine remorse for the man who had helped him get a council hearing rather than a calculated dissimulation? Could Barrow's offer of a job have been an effort to protect Amon out of gratitude for the same rather than to get him under his thumb? Could the lie about felling the forest from Amon's dream have been a trick to reconcile him to accepting his helping hand? Could his plan to visit the roof alone have been to shield

Amon from Anisha? All of Barrow's final moves, that had suggested one thing when Amon had pegged him for a nostie sociopath in a moment of unbearable stress and danger, could suggest something else entirely when considered more calmly from another angle.

Some of Amon's suspicions he now knew had undoubtedly been false. For example, Barrow's elusiveness about what had happened to Ty, Vertical, and the others had obviously not been because he murdered them. More likely, he had been afraid to admit that he spared them lest the guards present tell his rivals. The fear in Barrow's eyes when Amon accused him of betraying the council had signalled even then that his position was tenuous.

Amon had no illusions about reaching a definite appraisal of the man. The only person that might have given him one was dead—or so maimed he might as well be. So Amon's conundrum was about how to judge Barrow's memory, in light of the choice Anisha had foisted on him, between fulfillment of his desires and fatal deprivation.

Perhaps Barrow had been dragged along helplessly from one crossroad of choice to the next, no more to blame than the half-starved mother who gifts her baby for a bite to eat or the unemployed Free Citizen who takes a dubious job to pay his medical bills. If so, Amon could no longer justify his brutal assault on the man, any more than he could his nerve dusting of bankrupts, the Xenocyst use of an orphan to dramatize the Delivery sabotage, their trampling of innocent souls in the stampede after, or his and Rick's eviction of a teenage gang from the elevator that was their home. But then Amon and his accomplices had been in the same crucible of desperation. Pawns toppling other pawns and not a king in sight. So instead of holding one person responsible was it not their duty to take responsibility for the conditions that made responsibility itself possible? Which was why Amon was here. For he had seen a way out, though maybe it was too late . . .

"And what about Hippo?" he asked with a pang of urgency in his gut. "What happened to him?"

Kingdom   January 10th, 50 FE

Holding his head bowed to the PhisherKing, Amon looked down at the shining white deck of bone, chest aglow with gratitude. Even before he rose, the PhisherKing said, "There's no need to thank me. With the fee Mayuko paid me on your behalf, it was a profitable encounter."

"So she won her lawsuits?"

"Trounced them."

"Was she alright?"

"She was in shock. I stayed with her for a while and tried to give her some advice. The compensation for all the credicrimes committed against her would keep her afloat for decades if she spent it wisely. Right now, she needed to quit her job and switch apartments, to disappear and change all her behavior patterns, find new hobbies and favorite foods. I had to repeat myself several times before I could get a nod out of her. Then I told her how to reach me, and asked her to keep me posted on her whereabouts so I could point you her way if you ever came calling."

"Where is she?"

"I never heard from her."

"Oh." Amon's heart sank.

"She may have been afraid I would sell the information. I can't say I blame her."

Amon couldn't either. The PhisherKing had shown himself to be a man of his word, but he was also a man of business to the core.

As the boat drifted, the blood spraying from the oars left parallel streaks swirling red on quicksilver in their wake. The Phishers sat in their rows as still as statuary, until one woman dipped an oar and gave a single stroke to guide the prow between the crests of two large waves.

"And after that?" asked Amon.

"It seems she took my advice seriously, because she blends imperceptibly with the data web. You've found no signs even with Rashana's help?"

"I've searched platinum on her tab. I've looked all through her database. I've pumped Ono X for intel and had bespoke reporters scour the camps. I've called and texted Mayuko myself. Nothing."

"So she has evaded both our nets," said Monju. Then after a pause, he added, "It seems that nudging XXXTrust to use your likenesses has paid off."

"Wait . . ." Amon recalled Mayuko's transformation into a man sewn of jellyfish when the PhisherKing had mimicked her in the Tezuka. "It was you?"

A transparent smile was the PhisherKing's only reply.

"Then you saved both of us . . . If it wasn't for all those copies, the Gyges Circle would have found me too. But how did you get XXXTrust involved?"

"I sold them a few tantalizing segs from your LifeStream. Showed them that you'd been infected with a virus designed by a Syndicate MegaGlom—"

"KaviPal," Amon interjected.

"—and that you were on the run. I also licensed out an audio seg of Mayuko being interrogated about your whereabouts. I gave them just enough info so that they'd know you two were important to the Philanthropy Syndicate but not so much that they'd understand why or want to invest in seizing your info for themselves. I included location data for your last few days of banklife in case they felt like doing a genephage cleanup. Then I pointed out that they owned your likenesses and suggested that spreading them around would be some very affordable mischief. XXXTrust obliged. With glee."

"That's just genius, Monju. I don't know how to thank you enough."

"Don't mention it."

"So but—hold on," said Amon as an implication hit him. "You were selling pieces of my LifeStream to SpawnU?"

"After I refused Anisha's offer, I had to find some way to monetize it."

Amon squinted at him in disgust.

"Rest assured that I was very careful about which segs I licensed out. I traded SpawnU nothing that could have put either you or Mayuko at risk—Certainly nothing suggesting Barrow's cash crash was an identity assassination. Then we might have had an InterGlom War on our hands."

"Rashana told me that XXXTrust stopped broadcasting our copies a few weeks ago. It seems they started licensing our likenesses to an anonymous buyer. Do you know anything about that?"

The PhisherKing's eyelids gave their waking-dream flutter. "So they did," he said. "I hadn't noticed. XXXTrust must have decided that they'd had their fun helping you escape and gone in for some liquidity."

"Which means it should be easier to find Mayuko now."

"Not necessarily. I don't doubt that she's hiding masterfully."

Monju swept his blowing hair out of his face and glanced away into the distance. Something about the mannerism suggested to Amon that he was not being entirely candid, and he took this last comment as an effort to reassure him. Then he wondered if evading their nets could mean she'd been caught in someone else's. An explosion of memory flashed in his mind—the naked sky he and Mayuko had viewed with Rick on top of the BioPen, the stars from a high rooftop in Xenocyst and the feeling that she was looking at them too, the vision of gazing hand-in-hand through the canopy of a forest—and he blinked rapidly to clear his gathering tears.

"I caught a rumor that a woman came to find me in Xenocyst last fall," said Amon. "I never met her in person and the border guard who saw her disappeared before I could speak with him. She was described as young and beautiful. I can't help thinking that it could have been Mayuko."

"Searching for you in the camps?"

Amon nodded.

"That reminds me of something," said the PhisherKing, eyelids aflutter again.

"What?"

"Two people approached me to ask about you after your cash crash. The first was here on behalf of a Birla sister. I kept my lips sealed because I didn't know their angle. The second was a digiguised figment of a man that I assumed at first was an agent or persona of the other sister. What later struck me as unusual was that he or perhaps she wanted to know if your genome had been detected anywhere in the District of Dreams. I didn't know the answer. I had no access to your genetic data. But the question was telling because Rashana and Anisha would have simply connected to the vending machine network through the Fertilex human resource brand. They would never come to me for such intel."

"So you're saying it might have been Mayuko?"

"The visit was in mid-November. When did the woman come looking for you?"

"Around the same time," said Amon. It had been near the end of the month.

"Then she must be back in hiding again," Monju replied, brushing aside his hair again. For a duplicitous peddler of both truths and deceptions, it seemed that he was terrible at lying out of kindness, and Amon was left even more worried. *Did Mayuko make it out of the camps?* he wondered, the force of harsh searching thoughts compelling his gaze skyward, where contraption clouds scudded through scarlet high above the quicksilver sea, *Is she safe?* crestfallen that not even the PhisherKing knew.

Part of him wanted to hop overboard and swim down to whatever strange seabed awaited in the mercury depths, never to emerge again. But he kept his feet planted on the swaying deck of bone, head high, reminding himself that there were other reasons he had come to this phantasmal kingdom beneath the city. And he touched the tiny present tucked away in his jacket pocket, eager for the right moment to give it to his friend—yes the PhisherKing was indeed a friend—almost ready to ask him for his help in rebooting the world with the knowledge that only they possessed.

Theatre   December 28th, 49 FE

Before Amon knew it, they had come to a rest in the air. With no aircraft currently in view, nothing seemed to move. The sun above its bed of clouds was pinned in pale blue like a specimen of the heavens. It was as though Amon were inside a panoramic photo of life. Rashana too was frozen, right leg crossed over left, hands cradled to diaphragm, eyes narrowed as though dozing or in thought. Just to convince himself that time existed, Amon plucked his earlobe.

"With all the people involved in acquiring Gyges Ring, isn't it inevitable that something gets out?" he asked.

"Not if a Full Choice cabinet classifies the House of Blinding modification and Archivists expunge these classificatory actions from the records. Once the Gyges Circle buys up the LifeStreams of everyone involved, factholing will be complete."

"What about later on? Citizens with the exemptions should be traceable. I mean, if they do something that's supposed to count as a credicrime, wouldn't the victim notice when they're not compensated?"

"Most would blame the Fiscal Judiciary or Ministry of Monitoring for an error before they guessed that the system has favorites, don't you think?"

Amon nodded, recalling the advice of his decision network to inquire with GATA after the jubilee charge.

"I guess GATA would be hindered by its own system of oversight," he said, thinking aloud. Anonymization of actions would prevent the technocracy from easily linking the oddities to any particular people. "What about SpawnU?"

"They'll have little cause for alarm. Fertilex continues to supply them with human resources. Moderate Choice and Full Choice representatives continue to vote in line with SpawnU on most issues. This keeps up the appearance that SpawnU MegaGloms still have a grip on GATA, when in fact their sway is at its lowest in Free Era history."

"There must be a tipping point on the way where the shift becomes clear."

"By then it may be irreversible," said Rashana. "At first the exemptions will only apply within Japan, the limit of GATA Tokyo's jurisdiction. But this will set up the beneficiaries to alter the House of Blinding in Beijing, Rio, Toronto, everywhere. They'll be able to leash anyone to do their bidding with no consequences, offer the most coercive Birla Deals imaginable, fabricate a reality to cover their tracks with ease.

"Their hope is that the global market will continue to function as always with properties bought and sold, actions transacted according to the rules, while behind it all is a clan that exists beyond the rules, beyond money, beyond law, beyond good and evil. Financial gods invisibly walking the earth just like Gyges the shepherd."

The sun touched the rim of the clouds, as though resting on the white shattered landscape, only ephemeral moisture keeping it from tumbling out of the blue-veiled cosmos. *In what abysmal tombs do dethroned suns heap?* Amon wondered, sensing the return of a feverish tinge to his thoughts.

"So that's it?" he said.

"What's it?" Rashana asked.

"The Gyges Circle. They're tempting an InterGlom War. And for what? To go out in one great burst of depravity?"

"They haven't forgotten the future. Some are younger than Anisha, with long lives ahead of them. Discussion has already begun about another GATA modification to pass down the exemptions."

"An aristocracy."

"Not in in the usual sense. It won't be hereditary but chosen. Each will elect a single heir."

"I would have thought they'd tie the exemptions to natural birth. Isn't that what you rich folk prize?"

"Many do. But my twin and the other female members felt differently. Linking entitlement to natural birth privileges men. It lets them produce a larger pool of potential heirs. The males were adamant about it until Anisha proposed a compromise."

Over the sky was projected a test tube containing a fine grey powder against a white lab wall. The view closed up until the test tube reared mountain-like to the zenith of the world and the powder resolved into intricate moving crystals. Their parts continuously broke off and conjoined, a panoply of jigsaw snowflakes putting themselves together.

"The Philanthropy Syndicate has long possessed a fertility enhancing substance called multiply-thy-seed dust. It could never be marketed or used by the executives; that would violate Fertilex's life-property monopoly. But Syndicate R&D had reverse engineered it into sleeperpuzzle components that could be incorporated into Fleet on the sly."

A stretch of slumscape enveloped them; slow-crumbling disposcrapers loomed and leaned on all sides. Bankdead thronged along the squeeze-ways and roomterraces until the recording froze and began to zoom in on a woman. It focused on a tiny flake of T-shirt that had just blown from her shoulder and a flake of building in mid-flutter beside it. Zooming continued to the microscopic level, where two of the same crystals hovered side by side. When motion resumed, the crystals began to trade parts and merge into a new form. The view then pulled out until the nascent compound was too small to see, and was replaced by an arrow showing its location in the air. A bankdead man took a breath and the arrow disappeared between his lips.

"A decay product of disposcrapers and another of supply clothes recombined into an aerosol. This was how the Philanthropy Syndicate boosted extracted resource yield to compete with Fertilex's order-grown production without GATA detecting any breach of patent."

Pulling out further, the bankdead multitude could be seen inhaling thousands of arrows.

"The only loose end was the anomalously high bankdead birthrate."

"Hippo told me about that," said Amon, recalling the story about his quest to understand the fertility gap. "But I thought he ruled out Fleet byproducts."

"He did. His paper mistakenly concluded that their toxicity should have the opposite effect, increasing sterility. He only had access to gold search, not platinum, so his hypotheses were bound to stray off course. But it brought the enigma to our begetters' attention, and their follow-up studies pointed to a technological intervention. If Philanthropy Syndicate responsibility could have been established, Fertilex would have sued them out of existence. Only evidence of the slippery molecules was never definitive enough to convince the Fiscal Judiciary."

"We've got to tell Hippo about this if we ever find him. He'd be fascinated by what his work uncovered."

"And horrified by what it may soon allow, I'm sure. The sleeperpuzzle issue remained an open secret until Anisha finally broached it at a Gyges Circle meeting, where she made a proposal: fertility patent sharing for personal use."

A row of simple iconic women like those on restroom signs lay on a conveyer belt perpendicular to the direction of motion.

"Combine a sprinkle of multiply-thy-seed dust with the latest product in the All Star Natura line," Anisha advertised, "and a single act of coitus will be infallible."

A similarly iconic man materialized abruptly and began to mechanically pelvis-thrust at each passing woman, who would rapidly balloon into pregnancy, then give birth and shrink back to normal. Male laughter sounded.

"You can impregnate a new fling or SubMom each day, several if you so desire, leaving more descendants than even the most lustful conqueror or tycoon in history."

The raucous hubbub suggested inebriation. The pile of babies beside the conveyer belt steadily grew.

"Placating reproductive impulses helped Anisha persuade the other members of her point about inheritance of the exemptions—that wanting the heir to ones privileges to also be the heir to ones genes is arbitrary, a personal preference like any other. Only with the leeway to select anyone, offspring or otherwise, could the bequeathal of freedom itself be a free act."

While Rashana spoke, a chain of eyequakes struck her. Untroubled, she merely closed her eyes, her lips not missing a syllable.

"So it's basically what I said," Amon told her. "They're putting the world at stake for the biggest orgy of all time, a long and prosperous line of debauchers."

"Don't let their reactions to that vulgar cartoon sway your impression of them too much. My twin had wined and dined them in preparation for her pitch. Their base male instincts were putty in the hands of her psychaliticorps. Sober, I would grant them just a little more majesty."

"For what?"

"For placing transmission of everyone else's freedom under control of their wills just as with their own."

"I don't see how that would work."

"It's a question of the potential for individual freedom across generations. To see what I mean, consider this: Can a choice be called free if it doesn't arise from who the person choosing is?"

"For argument's sake, let's say it can't be."

"Then no one whose identity is decided by the will of others can make free choices."

"I can go along with that, I guess."

"Then consider where that leaves the three classes of people in our world, where the market shapes our identities. The freedom of the order-grown is precluded before birth no matter how much of it they might earn in principle, because they're genetically engineered in accordance with demand for positions in twenty years, and demand is a function of the totality of actions, that is of human willing. The freedom of the bankdead is only partially precluded before birth because their genetics are not sculpted individually, only culled at the level of population by plutogenic algorithms that likewise track predicted human resource demand. Some unmarketable and thus undetermined individuals, the giftless, always prevail. But even these are precluded from earning freedom the moment they're born whatever potential for freedom they might have had, due to their exclusion from the market. That leaves only naturally born Free Citizens with both the inborn capacity for freedom and the chance to earn it. Their genetics were shaped over the eons through evolution, in which human wills played a negligible role.

"Now my twin plans to raise the fee for actions related to natural birth, gradually so as not to upset SpawnU, until only those with exemptions can afford them. Can you see how this gives the Gyges Circle a stranglehold on the supply of intergenerational Freedom? Free Citizens not conceived by Gyges members for sport will be replaced by the order-grown that Fertilex designs. Bankdead populations can be molded with the supply pressures of algorithms weighted on a whim, rather than plutogenics, once the new human resource deal has eliminated demand for gifted babies. This amounts to hegemony of the few over all genomes. One almost suspects that the two markets of the so-called 'Free' World were named AT and CG on purpose, the very code for DNA nucleotides.

"Meanwhile, the Gyges Circle's line, if they choose naturally born heirs, can be free from algorithmic or genetic manipulation, on either the individual or population level. Their identities will be as unfettered as existence can allow. They are damming the river of freedom that flows to humanity to pool it all for themselves. A freedom monopoly. They're calling this the domestication of history."

"Ridiculous!" Amon snapped, rocking abruptly forward onto the edge of his seat and punching the invisible wall beside him. "How many years before they start squabbling? Then history will run as wild as ever!"

"Maybe so, but whoever reigns supreme at any given time, the basic situation will remain unchanged. A pantheon of invisible financial gods walk the earth, with no consequences for their actions from the cradle to the grave. They won't necessarily be rulers. Many may choose to keep their corporate and political positions. Others may become artists, or sloths, or serial killers. Some will beget descendants as numerous as the stars. But what they do is unimportant. It's what they *can* do."

When Rashana finished, the sky behind her went topsy-turvy. This time Amon could tell that it was neither the world moving around the craft, nor the craft moving in the world, but his own cerebral vertigo in the face of this grandiose vision. Streaks of white and sun and idea and disgust squirmed through blue as he lost all sense of up and down, inside and out. A corona of nausea around his skin kept seeping inward in jolts and jangles, spasming the muscles around his diaphragm with barely suppressed wretches. He considered excusing himself to go to the toilet again, but the feeling never quite grew intense enough, waxing and waning dissonantly like the note of a piano that refuses to fade. Instead, he leaned forward, putting his weight on his thighs with gripping palms and shook his dangling head, slobber dripping from his mouth, unable to care what Rashana might think.

Amon had asked why, why, why so many times on his journey that confusion had solidified into a pillar at the center of his being. Now that clarity had come like a wrecking ball, the insatiable questioning that had propped him up was crumbling, premonition, emotion, and memory breaking loose inside him. He saw dancing around embyrbrycks on the roof of the Cyst and could sense the same primal fervor driving the Gyges Circle. Not released in communal creativity as with the residents of Xenocyst but twisted in their grasping minds. They wanted to throw off all shackles on desire. That Amon could understand, even if he lacked such a wish himself. This hidden impulse almost seemed to define the human. But he never would have guessed that everything he'd gone through since he and Rick had cash crashed Minister Kitao last summer had been for its sake. Mayuko hurt and lost, Amon exiled, Rick dead, Xenocyst crumbled. At ground zero of the bomb-blast of fate that had devastated and scattered everything that mattered to him, he'd expected to find something worthy of such destruction, devious perhaps but profound. Instead, all that confronted him was the bald logical conclusion of the common sense that powered the system they were all caught in and the chthonic urges beneath. The lack of imagination appalled him.

When the reeling of experience had settled, he wiped his mouth with the back of his hand, sat up, and said, "How pathetic they are."

"In what way?" Rashana asked, perking up as though eager for his answer.

"Here are the most privileged people who've ever lived. They have so much money and freedom they can do almost anything without working a single day. They don't need to lift a finger unless they feel like it, with whole teams to help them carry out the simplest tasks."

Like you, Rashana, with your gabkeepers and cognitive handlers, he thought.

"Even still, they see a few people who try to play a different game than everyone else and they feel entitled to do the same, so they come up with a way to break the rules. They risk everything they have, world peace, civilization, to transcend the cycle of action we're all trapped in. And yet they can't break out of the same way of thinking, that life is about earning freedom. So instead of cooperating to leave some kind of meaningful legacy, they're only focused on increasing their own possibilities. But how will they ever decide between them?"

Thinking of the invisible walls or outside-simulating display that surrounded them, an image came to Amon that seemed to sum it all up.

"They're like flies in an empty jar. They can see the great big world outside and they want it for themselves, so they find clever ways to make the walls bigger and the glass goes on expanding like a balloon. But no matter how big the jar gets, there's still nothing inside but them and the air. All they do is multiply the emptiness that surrounds them while everything with meaning remains forever beyond reach."

Amon thought of the forest in his dream and of Xenocyst.

"I may have never tasted freedom in my life," he said. "But at least I know what it means to be inspired."

"I couldn't agree more," Rashana told him, joy radiating from her eyes. "All the freedom in the universe means nothing without a dream to limit you."

"And what is your dream, Rashana?" asked Amon. "Isn't that what you've brought me here to tell me about?"

Diaspora   January 3rd, 50 FE

When the Xenocyst exiles finally agreed to bring Amon to Hippo, Book led him to the far side of the alcove and pointed to a dark figure crouching flat-footed with his face towards the corner. Even with many footsteps shuffling closer, and then the attentive energy of the semi-circling crowd, he remained still, showing no reaction.

"Hippo," said Book, gently as if to a child, as he and Amon leaned over him side by side. A thin blanket around his shoulders, Hippo blinked vacantly at the line where the two walls met. "A visitor has come to—"

"I'm done," interrupted Hippo, in a hollow monotone. His voice was raspy from disuse but loud and firm enough to cut Book short.

"But it's Gura, our—"

"I'm done," Hippo repeated.

"He has something—"

"I'm—"

"he wants—"

"done."

"to—"

"done done done."

Book pursed his lips and gave Amon an uneasy look. "This is how he behaves now. We have yet to observe him asleep. He only rises for nutrition and excretion, never speaking until spoken to. He has not uttered any other words for more than a week."

"Hippo," said Amon, hoping his voice might stir up a different response. Surveying him in oblique profile, Amon was amazed at how the man had aged. Just weeks earlier he'd looked to be in his late fifties. Now Amon would have put him at 70, his actual age. "Hippo. It's me Am—"

"I'm done."

"I have something imp—"

"Done."

Amon returned Book's sidelong look of concern. "Depression?"

"That would seem the most obvious diagnosis."

"That would be too kind," said Yané. "Something snapped and there's no fixing it."

The Oneiro Express swished by again, followed by whispering and the muffled groaning of a child, while Amon looked down on Hippo crouching in silence, as removed from other people and the world as the alcove would allow. He was reminded of himself crouching in the Open Source Zone, though his own state of torpor then had been forced upon him by financial necessity. He was also reminded of Barrow cowering in the Gifted Triangle, an OpSci slave. Except Barrow had been angling to better his miserable life whereas Hippo had closed himself off to life altogether. Here was the voice of reason Amon had been hoping for. What a joke. With each breath, Amon felt a twinge of anxiety in his chest, convinced that they had failed, the unshaped gemstone of molten possibility cooling into a hard unyielding future. Such a broken man could never be the partner he sought. No wonder the Xenocyst exiles were reluctant to speak of their former leader. Amon was almost embarrassed just looking at him.

"What brought this on?" he asked.

"Nothing," Yané answered. "We got here and he just slumped over there like a retard, never got up since."

"That is a false characterization," said Book. "His final words could be interpreted as an explanation."

"All that bullshit about being a xenocyst?"

"I do not believe his speech deserves such . . ."

"Insults," offered Nostrils. "Meanness," suggested Thick Braids.

"Pejoratives," said Book.

After retreating from Xenocyst, Hippo had insisted that they push on east through the morning to the Sanzu River despite disagreement from Yané and others. He sent Vertical ahead to summit the disposcraper bank and ring a signal bell. It was a gamble, certain to draw their pursuers but not necessarily Tamper. A last stand on the riverside ensued, and luckily, Tamper happened to be in earshot of the firearm reports. Commandeering a freighter, he ferried them to Free Tokyo under fight'R'flight sniping from the shoreline towers behind, sending some passengers diving, and others into a frenzy that required they be restrained, or in two tragic cases thrown overboard. The survivors had sheltered in the alcove ever since.

"It was when we gathered here the very first night and our predicament became evident," said Book, "that Hippo began to express his thoughts openly."

"He screwed up and he knew it," said Yané. "He couldn't hold Xenocyst. And instead of taking it back like he should've, he brought us nowhere to starve. Now our brethren are stranded there. Each day it gets harder to go back for them."

Although Yané wasn't the most intelligent or eloquent man, Amon understood now why he had the ear of the crowd. As implausible as it was, he promised them the only dream they could imagine.

"What did Hippo say?" Amon asked.

"He spoke of years ago when his foundation went bankrupt," Book replied. "Instead of making our community into a xenocyst, a foreign cell that refuses to be dissolved into the whole, he wished that he had organized us into an uprising from the start. Then at least we would have . . ."

"Gone out in a blaze of resistance," said Nostrils. "His exact words."

"Indeed," Book agreed. "Many might have been harmed in the ensuing Charity Brigade retaliation. However, we would have turned our futility into an expression of independence and held onto our pride in a fading act. He compared this to the . . ."

This time, when Book sent a mournful glance to his left as if searching for the ghost of Little Book, no one filled him in.

"To the fleeting beauty of the embyrsculptures and cinderworks," he finally recalled. "If our display of violence had been truly sublime, it would have been imprinted as a myth in the memories of the oppressed, triggering a chain reaction of artistic bloodlust for generations to come.

"Those were his last words of any significance. I do believe they explain his behavior quite well."

Amon nodded. The regret that disabled Hippo was so familiar he almost felt it as his own. Here was a man who had given up the heights of scientific repute to build a community of self-determination for the world's poorest, only to see it co-opted for profit and brought in thrall to the AT and CG markets for two decades, before being humiliatingly destroyed. Perhaps for Hippo, Barrow's mercy felt like a curse, condemning him to exist beyond the horizon of his absolute failure. Once his duty was fulfilled in bringing the exiles to safety and bettering their situation any further seemed hopeless, he had made that most paradoxical of decisions—to make no more decisions—for in renouncing effort he would be cured of failure forever. Was there anything to be said to a person who now asked of life only that they be alive, and maybe not even that? Was Amon delusional to expect of him the great dedication that his new aspiration demanded?

"Looks like our debts've been paid," said Yané with a glance at Tamper. "The story is over. It's time for him to go."

"Listen," said Amon. "What if we can all find a home?"

"What do you know about homes except how to wreck 'em?" said Yané, perhaps intuiting that Amon had taken a cue from him. But he seemed to wilt when he saw that Amon had the crowd's undivided attention.

"Are you suggesting some way to liberate Xenocyst?" asked Book.

"No. Something better. Not digging up a dead past, but lighting a new future."

The way they looked at him, Amon felt like the lone piece of driftwood in a flood. Their yearning for salvation weighed heavily on him. But he kept his head high under their needful gazes. If he was going to succeed, he had to be prepared to bear the weight of the world.

Amon took a deep breath and knelt beside Hippo.

"You told me once that—"

"I'm done."

"All I ask is—"

"Done."

Amon sighed and decided to change tack.

"I have a message from Rashana for Hippo. There's something of grave importance that we want to achieve. But she and I need his help."

Amon began to tell them everything, filling in the gaps in his story, speaking as if to the crowd but directing his voice to Hippo's ear, hoping for the sake of untold millions that he was listening, hoping that he might still care.

Kingdom   January 10th, 50 FE

After Amon and the PhisherKing had shared what little they knew about Mayuko's whereabouts, the PhisherKing asked what had happened to him in the months since they last met. Amon agreed to fill him in under the condition that the PhisherKing give up exclusive rights to the recording and promise never to disclose it to anyone. The agreement was modeled after the one that the PhisherKing had insisted on when he told Amon about his past as the architect of the House of Blinding.

While Amon spoke, the PhisherKing regarded him with an absorbed almost transcendental intensity. Occasionally, the layers of his eyes would rotate in different directions at once or his eyelids would flutter as though he were slipping into an information trance, his hair blowing in a breeze Amon could not feel. On the deck of bone behind the PhisherKing, his hooded disciples now faced each other in twos and threes as though in silent conference about the tale, some stroking the still-bleeding oars as though restless to embark on some truth-plundering voyage. Amon stopped when he reached the part just before Rashana described her dream in the clouds, and the PhisherKing gazed off into the horizon where the mercury sea and the scarlet sky met. A swirl of silvery haze gathered in the distance as though a tempest were brewing.

"Thank you, Kenzaki-san," he said. "You've connected the pieces I already had. I doubt the whole picture would have come into focus otherwise. The Gyges Circle did everything they could to keep me in the dark."

"They approached you to ask for your help, didn't they?"

The PhisherKing flashed a sly, glassy smile.

"But you wouldn't take the antidote to conception dust. You said no."

Amon was only guessing but it was an educated guess. Upon his request, Ono X had acquired segs proving that the Birla parents had had Monju dusted to prevent him from tinkering with the blinding system he had built, as Monju himself had supposed. Clearly, they would never have given him Fertilex's patented antidote, but Anisha had already begun to cast off her parents' conservative policies, and there was much for her to gain by reversing this one. For with Monju's intimate knowledge of the House of Blinding on their side, the Gyges Circle might have cut down on the costs of analyzing the system and eliminated the risk of their Blinder agent being discovered in the process.

"I told you once that I've come to terms with who I am after they impaired me," said the PhisherKing.

"You don't expect me to believe that was the only reason you refused? Was their deal that stingy?"

"Not stingy, just vague. They asked me to design a program in exchange for the privileges it would reap. The only problem was, they wouldn't give me the details until I signed up."

"They literally told you *nothing* about the project?"

"Oh, they waxed lyrical about how my life would be transformed forever. But do I look like the kind of chump who'd bargain his fate on the secrets of climbers and thieves?"

"You must have been curious to know what they were offering at least."

"Not enough to trust the daughter of the people who poisoned my mind in the first place."

"So no Birla Deal for you?"

"I'm known to be slippery in case you didn't hear. They couldn't put together a threat with sharp enough teeth to even catch on me. Now you tell me they were offering these exemptions. That is a persuasive reward. But it wouldn't have made any difference if I'd known then. I'm not going to fiddle with the House of Blinding for personal gain. That was my life's work. Do you understand?"

The PhisherKing stepped towards Amon, gripped him by the sleeve, and gave him a fierce stare.

"Armor for information that anyone can wear, perfectly seamless and indestructible," he effused, his multicolored eyes scintillating with a kind of mad wonder. "The only thing more beautiful is the Treasure Matrix herself."

Here the PhisherKing's long-buried inspiration peeked out from a hole in his soul, as much as he played the pragmatic businessman. For his rejection of that rare chance, first unknowingly and now knowingly, Amon couldn't help admiring the man. Inclusion in the action exemptions was not something the Gyges Circle would have offered to just anyone. Their invitation revealed just how eager they were to bring their plan to fruition. If not for Monju's refusal, the Ring of Gyges program would have been installed months ago and Amon's idea would have foundered before he had even thought of it. The question now was whether the PhisherKing would accept Amon's invitation instead. He wouldn't alter his life's work for personal gain, but would he agree to do so for the gain of all?

The PhisherKing seemed to come to himself, and he released Amon's sleeve, retreating several steps to a more comfortable distance.

"So what is your proposition, Kenzaki-san?" he asked, as though tracing the branches of Amon's cogitation.

"First," said Amon. "Take this."

He held out his open palm. The PhisherKing frowned and glared at the green pill that rested atop it.

"What is this?" The circles of his eyes seemed to slip out of level alignment, popping and sinking as they rotated inside their grooves. Amon merely beamed a gloating smile. Again he had the PhisherKing stumped! Who would have thought it possible, and twice in one day? He relished the satisfaction until it felt too cruel to keep him waiting any longer.

"The antidote."

"The antidote for what?"

"For what else? We were just talking about it."

"Conception dust?"

Amon went on smiling.

"Don't joke with me. Even if Rashana wanted me to have it, Anisha would never agree—not after I turned them down."

"But she did. It's yours." Amon was sad for what he had given up in securing this for him, but clung to faith in what they might now achieve.

"And what do you want from me in return?"

"I'll be asking for your help with something soon. The antidote is a big part of it. But there are no conditions. It's yours, right now, whatever you decide. This is the only way that the wrong done to you can be made right. It is a gift from me to you."

Theatre   December 28th, 49 FE

The moment Amon asked about Rashana's dream, he realized that they were already below the clouds, turning in circles as they descended. Excited at the chance to see the island again, he looked down between his slippered feet and there it was, Hahajima, a smidge of green on cobalt set sparkling by the approaching sun.

"The destruction of Hakkotopia didn't only give Anisha something to strive for," said Rashana. "It was equally significant for me.

"Our debriefing inside our hidden folder after the crackdown was the last time I can remember us having a civil conversation, aside from our performances for the benefit of our begetters and handlers. The operation had shaken us both up profoundly. We couldn't decide why until a mutual realization emerged. We both felt that the community pointed to the solution to the challenge posed by the myth of Gyges. But since we'd both understood the parable in different ways, the lessons we drew diverged.

"As I told you yesterday, Anisha saw the capacity to transcend consequences as a prize that actualized the fullest freedom for those who'd earned it. For me, that capacity was a danger that could preclude freedom by removing all checks on raw desire. Without consequences to temper our wills, we become slaves to our impulses. Unless, that is, we can impose limitations on ourselves. I saw Hakkotopia as the ideal model for just such limitations.

"Think of this, Amon," said Rashana, the sunbeams in her eyes seeming to dance in step with the patina of glitter on the sea below. "The basic concept of Hakkotopia was to bring together highly-skilled individuals with a shared vision —engineers, artists, thinkers—and give them control of the algorithms that shaped their society. Within the short space of less than ten years, it became a federation of island cities, totally self-sufficient and perfectly integrated with the most fragile biomes.

"The ecosystems of Ogasawara were susceptible to disruption from outside due to a long history of isolation from any mainland. The establishment of new settlements required a delicate touch. But their organizers and planners eschewed old approaches. There would be no timid tip-toeing to conserve 'balance' as preservationists would have it, any more than there would be the sudden industrial intrusion of economic 'growth,' or 'colonization.' In place of these stale metaphors, was a new one, that of fermentation, hence the name Hakkotopia. Not the fermentation of alcohol or sauerkraut, though they also did a fair amount of that, but the fermentation of existence itself. By introducing a carefully cultivated form of anthrotechnological culture, they catalyzed a novel process that maintained continuity with aboriginal natural systems while guiding them together into a mutually beneficial dynamism."

The craft was rapidly but smoothly curving its way down towards Hahajima. Now scenes flickered in the air around and above as Rashana spoke.

"Programmable biomatter served as the material for architecture, clothing, and tools while also yielding crops and energy."

Viewed from underwater, a coral reef surrounded by dense schools of tropical fish and sea creatures. Amber resin windows in the rugged surface reveal men and women in training suits of seashell weave reclining on a floor of live bamboo.

"Service and manufacturing drones served dual functions as attentive stewards of their surround."

A mound of moss covered in purple and white flowers pulsates rhythmically, pushing a pair of shoes from a hole at the bottom, bees hovering about the blossoms.

"Everything was not only biodegradable but bred to dissolve into effluents and emissions that had calculated effects."

A cloud of milky liquid spurts from a plantfoam pipe and spreads over the surface of waves. Close up on the soup, quickly reaching the microscopic level. Blobs feed on molecules of the liquid while other blobs feed on them.

"In rare cases where the direct output of a process could not be reused or safely dumped, it was transformed by waste alchemy into a state in which it could."

Steam rises from a wooden vat of bubbling slag and hawks circle on the rising heat.

"I wish I had time to illustrate all their masterful applications of bioautomation. In sum effect, these engineering feats put them on the road to collapsing the harmful distinctions between lifeform and device, harvesting and extraction, agriculture and gathering, hunting and domestication, while respecting the needs and independence of indigenous organisms and habitats.

"Everything was coordinated by an organic ultracomputer on Hahajima that connected to land, sea, and sky through edible aquatic, terrestrial and airborne nanoprocessors and sensors. The goal of its algorithms was to provide the community with the necessities of human wellbeing while attaining the optimal ratio of total biomass and variety of species without letting any slip to endangered levels except where adaptation was inevitable. The ideal compromise between teeming and flourishing for all.

"The network achieved this through a complex feedback loop. First real-time data about climate, currents, and nested ecosystems was used to calculate how production would change them over the short and long term. Then the type of technologies, their quantity, their release date, their location of deployment and so on were adjusted so that their total output would achieve predetermined targets, optimizing interaction with primeval processes.

"For example, several biodegradable materials could be used to produce common technologies such as homes, medical equipment, and clothes, each with a different byproduct. The algorithms shifted manufacturing, usage, and disposal patterns to create the precise pattern and concoction of waste to nourish organisms at suboptimal population levels and toxically decrease those disrupting the flourishing of the whole. The particular composition of biodiversity and biomass never stops changing, and the course of civilization is constantly reoriented towards the next stage of equilibrium.

"Maybe this all sounds good in theory, but what's amazing is that it actually worked!"

Rashana leaned towards Amon with impassioned eyes that seemed to demand his appreciation. Their gazes locked, for a silent moment, as Amon was simultaneously held in thrall by her excitement and overwhelmed by her intricate description. The green mountains of Hahajima drew ever closer as their circular trajectory tightened, sketching a gradual spiral from cloud to sea.

"The releases of their industry enriched the soil, rivers, and shores. The forests grew lusher! Flocks of gorgeous birds and butterflies filled the air! The oceans overflowed with more life than the world has ever seen! And yet it was no hippy commune or city of pigs, where people barely subsisted and wallowed naked in the mud. There was a surplus of food and materials, not a glut but enough for them to enjoy small comforts and luxuries, technology to create convenience without inducing laziness or apathy, and a network of information for learning and creative expression that was moderated to prevent anyone from losing sight of the magic of the present. Humans actualizing the fullest range of their selfhood, from the primal nadir of our basic pleasures to the apex of intellectual and artistic fulfillment. Animals being animals, plants being plants, fungi being fungi. Every being allowed to effervesce through time in a holistic symbiosis of autonomous interdependence."

"Rashana," said Amon, cutting in to her rapturous spiel as she took a breath. "What about human action? Didn't the citizens have to be regulated too?"

"Of course. The impact of the citizenry on the optimal biomass/diversity ratio and the grounds for their own wellbeing had to be factored in. If, let's say, the proliferation or dwindling of a lifeform hindered the approach to an equilibrium target, its harvesting was increased or reduced accordingly. The algorithms also had to assign tasks to human beings at different phases of the production cycle because bioautomation does not sustain itself alone, nor does it fulfill all needs. Specialized skills necessary for maintenance and advancement of the system had to be cultivated and incorporated."

"Then what you're saying is that the algorithms don't only assign limits to action," said Amon, "they also assign duties. They say what people must do. Which would mean that the islanders were less free than anyone else, wouldn't it?"

"That doesn't necessarily follow."

"No? I mean, Free Citizens may be manipulated by action pricing, and the bankdead may be under the yoke of plutogenics, but at least they can pick from the limited options they're given. At least they have the illusion of choice."

Rashana smiled. "Your concerns are important but misguided. Just wait until you hear about Hakkotopian politics. They are in a category of their own. The only similarity with the Free World and the bankdeath camps is that all three are networked. In a networked society, human action is necessarily regulated by algorithms. By mediating all our interactions over the network, they necessarily nudge our choices. The more we use the network, the greater their total impact becomes. This is true even in a so-called free market. Transactions do not occur in a vacuum. They are shaped by the infrastructure that makes them possible, the software and hardware. The market is the transaction. The network is the interaction. So the question is not whether to have algorithms influencing us but what to do with them. And I believe that Hakkotopia answered this question better than any networked society ever has or probably ever will.

"Their network was a radical re-envisioning of the AT Market in which actions were a communal property owned by everyone. In place of GATA, citizens took turns assisting with anonymous monitoring, much like the jury duty of ages past, and instead of the market constrained by the Moratorium on Catastrophic Exchange regulating price and the Fiscal Judiciary deciding fines, each citizen could vote on the design of the algorithms that determined the costs and benefits their actions incurred. Actions likely to produce desirable results earned citizens points and tokens, those thought harmful took them away, and those thought neutral incurred no net change.

"Through seizing the means of transaction, the people all chose the incentives and disincentives that guided their joint enterprises, and in this way encouraged and discouraged their own actions freely. Even the needs of non-human organic collaborators had their voices translated into constraints on the voting process in the form of data used as the basis for discussion and program design.

"Moreover, in making automation a commons rather than a tool of wealth generation for the few that owned the patents, they could provide everyone with the wherewithal to enjoy an enormous amount of time to do as they wished where the algorithms were silent. No one needed to work a soul-numbing job like Free Citizens just to earn enough for the right to blink, nor was anyone trapped in the pointless pseudo-labor of supply retrieval like the bankdead. Everyone provided their talents gladly to sustain the autopoietic economy that they were instrumental in directing and enjoyed such contributions just as much as their leisure.

"You acknowledged so eloquently yourself, Amon, with your flies in the glass jar that we need a purpose to guide us. Without inspiration, life is just hollow possibility. What else could offer the boundaries on infinite choice we need to find meaning without strangling our free will but a shared vision to strive for something greater than ourselves that we ourselves are in the ongoing process of creating?

"In Hakkotopia, citizens played the game of work while co-determining the principles that shaped their shared course through time, sculpting a beautiful, just, and fair civilization in flexible concord with the raw, naked reality of nature in its spontaneous unfolding. In a popular way of imagining the lodestar by which they navigated, each individual making their own free choices and fulfilling their own potential was said to be like a light shining into a great diamond with as many facets as there are individuals. There, all the lights harmonize and transcend themselves, forming a new light by which all can see a new way forward and in which all can believe. A diamond dream."

At these words, Amon felt his doubt washed away by a rush of warmth and excitement that spread from the base of his spine to the tips of his fingers. For seven years, he had pursued the forest, thinking there was only one dream, one thing to yearn for, one road to follow. Now here was a new dream, not for one person, but big and rich enough to accommodate as many people as there were to aspire. He looked out the window and for a brief instant thought he could see it faintly on the horizon, a ghostly mirage of sparkling hopes alighting on the threshold between ocean and sky, and then realized that it was the sun on the verge of setting.

"Sadly, I learned all this in the process of researching the community so that I could destroy it. My begetters' wishes had already been set in motion and I could only fall in line. But the moment the last of the islanders were rounded up, I knew that I would work to one day rebuild it. You must have already guessed from everything that I've said; it is for this dream that I've brought you here. I need your help in bringing it back, in creating Hakkotopia 2.0."

Amon's gaze locked with hers, the afterimage of the diamond seeming to shimmer in her brown eyes, the tingle of inspiration still coursing over his skin.

The rotorcraft was now revolving around the green slopes of Hahajima at a steady distance, circumscribing a halo. As Amon viewed the contours of shore, ridge and valley from all three hundred and sixty notches of perspective, his wonder seemed to sprinkle the island with a glow of sacredness. There were no thoughts of any substance in his awareness but he could sense activity somewhere deeper, his mind sorting through everything he had heard in some more amorphous form.

"I still don't understand," he said eventually. "Why do you want *me* to help you? Why have you gone through all the trouble of tracking me down and put aside all this time to explain everything when there are so many others you could have chosen?"

It was this question that had started off their whole conversation yesterday morning. Now finally they had meandered their way back.

"Can you think why this place might have been in your dreams so many times?"

"I asked myself again and again over the years why I always dreamt of a forest but the answer has never come."

"You don't remember?"

"Remember?"

"Not at all?"

Amon crooked his head to the side quizzically.

"You're the only surviving islander born here on Hahajima."

"Me?" Amon pointed at his own nose, unsure how to take this. "You're sure you aren't confusing me with someone else?"

"No chance whatsoever. Hakkotopia was destroyed in late spring of the year 26 FE. You were transferred to Green Ladybug in early summer."

Mayuko had told Amon when they were teenagers that she remembered the day he arrived at the BioPen. This suggested that he had indeed grown up somewhere else, though he could have easily been a clone or an extracted resource. Yet he possessed no distinct memories prior to his arrival, nor did he have any LifeStream recordings, assuming he'd even had a training bank in those early years.

"I would have been three, going on four," said Amon. "I don't remember anything that far back."

"Ono X was the one who had you admitted when all the other children were dumped in the District of Dreams. He had intuited my wishes and knew there was no way for me to intervene without raising the ire of my begetters. He chose a BioPen for top quality resources. I followed your progress over the years with his brief coded reports. You were promaducated to want to apply for Fertilex. I was planning to have you work for me. But your application was rejected despite your perfect concentration score. This is unheard of as you know. You were an ideal candidate."

Rashana glanced up abstractly over the edge of her brow, as though a descending angel were bearing her next thought.

"We have no evidence, but Anisha or Ono Y must have learned about my interest in you. Otherwise Sekido's approval of your application to the Liquidation Ministry is too coincidental to believe. She undoubtedly arranged this to spite me."

She mentioned this matter-of-factly with not a hint of rancor; perhaps she had grown numb to her sister's many slights.

"After your induction into GATA, Ono X continued to keep me abreast of your career. Your achievements as a Liquidator only convinced me that we needed you for Hakkotopia 2.0. Under my begetters' watchful eye, I waited for the day we could reach out to you. That day came after Anisha had them murdered. The next evening, I had Ono X follow you home from work. You were walking so slowly, so deep in thought, that it was all too easy for him to tail you, even after you turned on your digiguise.

"We already had Rick in Er for the Giftless by then. He was still uncon- scious, so we didn't yet know his name or that he was your partner, but it was clear that his bankdeath was part of a shakeup at GATA. When I approached you personally in Ginza, it was my last chance to warn you about the danger and finally offer you a job.

"To be frank, you disappointed me at first. Your blind faith in Liquidation and the sanctity of the AT Market were just grotesque. But when you told me about your forest dream, I could see that you still remembered where you came from. The job I was offering was bound to make you happy, even if you didn't yet realize it. When you rejected me, I was sad, though still ready to give you another chance if you ever changed your mind."

"Why couldn't you have explained all this then?" Amon asked. "If you could have told me that you knew where the forest was, I would have followed you in a heartbeat. You could have saved me so much pain."

As though momentarily stunned, Rashana bit her lip and stared blankly at him, then tugged on her pants to adjust them and shifted in her seat.

"Are you blaming me for your own ignorance?" she said, enunciating each word so clearly and dispassionately that it spooked Amon more than any overt anger could have, the edges of her eyelashes flaring with end-of-day sunbeams. "I was getting warmed up to explain my offer when you rudely left in the middle of our meal. Is it my fault that you were too impatient to hear me out to the end?"

"Okay, sorry," said Amon, holding up his hands to placate her. "You're right. Maybe I wasn't ready to listen."

"I'll say."

"But in my defense, I was confused about your identity. I thought you were an activist. If you hadn't posed as Makesh, if you'd told me who you were—"

"And used my fame and fortune to awe you into obedience? I was looking for a leader with genuine passion and initiative, not a greedy little lamb who would follow me to the slaughter"—Rashana chopped a hand against her palm like a guillotine—"for the right price. Do you have any idea what it's like to have more freedom than you know what to do with? You can't tell who your real friends or lovers are and who just wants a piece for themselves."

Rashana's eyes glittered with some emotion between sadness and confusion. Here was another challenge faced by the propertied class that Amon never could have imagined. He was searching for words of apology when Rashana sunk against the backrest with a slow exhalation.

"Maybe I wasn't fair to you," she said, her voice subdued, almost apathetic. "With everything that you were taught and your constant struggle just to pay for basic actions, asking you to see the value in our cause without talking earning potential may have been too much to expect. But even if I could have seen that then, I wouldn't have told you who I was. I knew that your boss was working for my sister and the Gyges Circle. Ono X couldn't determine how deeply they'd drawn you in."

This reminded Amon of his anticipation about Sekido's job offer and the moment in the jazz bar when he told Sekido and Anisha about the meeting with Makesh. Perhaps Rashana's caution had been warranted.

"I understand what you were thinking now," Amon said, nodding repeatedly in acceptance. "And I guess you're right. This is the only way it could have all turned out."

These last words brought him a cell-deep kind of pathos, a wave of heavy melancholic resignation. The puzzling disappointment of his rejection from Fertilex as a youth, then his employment as a Liquidator under Sekido, his use as a political weapon, his ensuing disgrace. At every juncture, Amon had felt like he was making his own choices when all the while hidden forces—money, power, information, and the will of two wealthy sisters—had been stringing him along.

But could it be true? Was he really born on Hahajima? Was his dream in fact a sort of lingering recollection? Possessing vivid memories from such a young age was not unheard of. It might have been hard to forget a place so radically different from anything he'd known since. Or perhaps that was precisely why he'd forgotten, because those early years were too unlike everything that followed to seem a part of his life. Perhaps the experience of his final day on the island had persisted only in some sediment of his unconscious, shaped by subliminal pressure and time into a dream—like coal into a diamond. Did that mean his falling again and again from the sky was the reverse of his being lifted away from his home, plucked from amongst a milling crowd of children? But then . . .

"There must have been many kids," said Amon, his perception returning to the present to find Rashana studying him.

"There were. The Hakkotopians had three children in your generation for every adult."

"With something like All Star Natura or multiply-thy-seed?"

"No. Researchers picking up on Hippo's work attributed the fertility rate to two factors. One was incompatibility between genome marketability and fertility. Plutogenic pressures do not select for reproductive capacity. In other words, the needs of the market run contrary to life itself. The other was psychological. While the bankliving were subjected to a constant barrage of information and images, the Hakkotopians experienced stimuli close to those around which humans evolved. This may have signaled neurologically that it was safe to reproduce."

Amon wondered if this factor also contributed to the fertility gap between bankliving and bankdead, who enjoyed a small taste of nature—the presence of the sky—but kept his speculation to himself. Instead he returned to his question. "So if there were so many children, why did Ono X single me out?"

"You were found in the home of Iwabuchi-sensei. He believed you might be her only son."

"The leader of Hakkotopia was my mother?"

"In all likelihood. We have no copy of her DNA with which to confirm. But children often stayed with their parents in the archipelago federation."

I had a mother? It was a bizarre idea. Amon hadn't thought much in his life about where he might have come from, preferring to focus on his ambitions for the future and how they might be realized in the present instead of the vague unchangeable past. But someone must have carried him in the womb, even if he was a clone or an order-grown resource. He never would have guessed that this person might have tried to raise him on her own. As part of a family?

"If this . . . this Iwabuchi is my mother, then what about my father?"

"Unfortunately, we have no information about him. We know that Iwabuchi was her married name but she was divorced long before Hakkotopia."

"What happened to her?"

"No one seems to know. In the confusion during the roundup, she disappeared. We never learned where to or why. Out of respect for her,

I wanted to make sure you were brought up safely. I was hoping you would carry on her legacy. I still am."

"But there are so many better qualified people. Like . . . what about Sekido?"

Now that it had occurred to Amon, it seemed strange that Sekido wasn't working towards rebuilding the community he had unwillingly and unwittingly destroyed.

"Ono X tried to recruit him a few years ago but he was too set on revenge against Barrow to listen to anyone except Anisha. Then I tried approaching him in person after he'd had his way with Barrow. I showed him my naked face and hinted at what we were trying to accomplish. Still we couldn't interest him."

"Why?"

"It's difficult to say. Perhaps years of pursuing vengeance have quashed his desire for change. But that's irrelevant. Sekido might have been a valuable agent. He would never have been a replacement for you."

"But he's better placed than I ever was. He has more power and connections. You could have hired thousands of brilliant people with the amount of creditime you've spent on me."

"Are you fishing for compliments, Amon? Do I really have to spell it all out for you? Your diligence and strategic abilities as a Liquidator and then ID executioner. Your resilience and adaptability in the camps. Your brilliant exposé plan and courageous escape from Barrow. Your familiarity with technology and your capacity to get along without it. Your understanding of the flaws in the Action Transaction Market and the Charity Gift Economy and your appreciation for the true value of nature.

"Most important of all is the great willpower, self-control, and concentration that you possess as all the islanders once did. It was this that allowed you to succeed in your feats of frugality, to overcome infowithdrawal without Er treatment, and to survive the catastrophe after the famine. I need you to be the first on the ground to set an example for all who follow. Because the system produces remarkable abundance but it has limitations. Restraint and moderation will be essential in the beginning.

"Just as the ecosystems of Ogasawara have maintained continuity with past ecosystems, so too will you maintain continuity with the society that was once joined to them. You're like the starter from the old batch of a ferment, like a set of microbes that can begin a new process of transformation while contributing the power of the old. There you will finally discover the right habitat to actualize the person you were always meant to be. No more action-scrimping, no more supply collection. Only self-realization as a leader who can bring about change just like your mother."

"I can't be a leader. What do I know about building a society?"

"You learned much in Xenocyst, did you not? You helped the council."

"Xenocyst was destroyed. I tried to stop it and I failed. I won't be able to protect Hakkotopia 2.0 any better. Not once the Gyges Circle have their exemptions."

Rashana gave him a warm, nurturing smile. "You're thinking like a leader already. Let me pass the conversation over to Ono X. Everything I've told you up to now, my twin probably knows. For the rest, the risk of her hacking me is too great."

Rashana rose and walked along the deck towards the front of the craft. The sun, now just touching the horizon of sea, happened to overlap with her body. She seemed to be absorbed into it, winking out as though ascending to an ethereal realm as a being of pure light. When Amon looked back at her chair, he was startled to find Ono X already seated there.

"I've been in charge of all Atupio's classified projects from day one," Ono X began in the soft voice he had used when introducing himself the previous morning. "I kept them from Cognitive Handling Corps surveillance while the begetters lived. And I've kept them from Anisha since she killed them and ramped up her hacking."

Ono X's sharp eyes stayed trained on Amon as he spoke, sitting straight-backed and alert with feet flat on the invisible floor. His pacing, rhythm, and tone, his posture, mannerisms, and bearing, were different than those of anyone he had played so far, and Amon wondered if he was being himself.

"You've got to understand, we've been preparing decades for a leader like you to kick off Hakkotopia 2.0. Our biggest challenge in the beginning was tracking down Ferment Culture Collective survivors. We had to convince them that we were genuine, that we honestly wanted to rebuild. Had to be honest about the crackdown. They didn't take kindly to us at first. But Gyges Circle bounty hunters were taking out owners of Ogasawara property left and right. Slowly but surely wherever they could be identified. Only we could offer asylum. Only we could give them new purpose. Now they're stakeholders in Atupio. They provide the know-how. We supply the credit.

"I'm their line of communication with Rashana so Anisha can never find out who's on the inside. Ferment Culture agents in the Free World are our informants, saboteurs, and recruiters. The rest live in Atupio. Right on the Tokyo Canal, between Yokohama and the District of Dreams. Just outside the jurisdiction of GATA and Delivery. A fine haven. We built home office there to keep down the costs of holding bankdead. You know, *imprisonment, unwilful detainment,* and the rest. I mean the kids you saw beneath the riverbed yesterday. The Starters, the neo Hakkotopians. Each and every one is a crashborn we rescued from the District of Dreams. Bankdead so the fines in Ogasawara can't hold them back. We picked out the ones with the best genes for their roles. Taught them to wield their naked minds *and* technology like no one else. Er for the Giftless and our poverty reporting outfit are a front. The Starter BioPen is what we've really been working towards. Our testing ground. A bioautomated self-sustaining ecosystem.

"Hahajima is where the Starters will help us begin again. We'll regrow the original infrastructure. Load up algorithms updated for the present. We'll imitate the collective's successes"—Makesh Adani standing in a white space appeared to the left and his lips began to synch perfectly to Ono's, as Ono's voice switched to an impersonation of a male version of Rashana's in mid-sentence, his leg crossing over the other, palms stacked on his knee—"but avoid their mistakes.

"The crackdown demonstrated that the financial defenses on the islands were inadequate. We'll supplement them with Fertilex sleeper-puzzles, so that any unauthorized approach will trigger an akrasiapocalypse. Our second line of defense will be bioautomated peacedrones. Our Starters will be the third line. Don't underestimate them because of their age. The Birla Guard, including Ono X himself," said Ono X/ Makesh, "have trained them for battle since they were in diapers.

"As you noted, I could cause trouble for the Gyges Circle by telling SpawnU about their plans. Instead, we'll sell all our intelligence to the Gyges Circle in exchange for their properties in the islands and special recognition for Ogasawara as a non-economic zone. With my half of the Birla estate, we'll be much better funded than before. And if the Gyges Circle succeeds in their plans, I'll be able to support us with the added advantage of the action exemptions."

"Because you and Anisha have the same profile!" said Amon, looking at the Makesh figment but speaking, he hoped, to Rashana. The Ring of Gyges program, in distorting all action-data attached to Anisha's ID signature, would do the same to hers.

Ono X and the apparition of Rashana digimade as a man beamed an eerily similar smile. "Once I have the Ring of Gyges, Hakkotopia 2.0 will be protected—financially, militarily, institutionally. Then we can offer an alternative way of being that escapes from the twin jaws of the Free World and the bankdeath camps. We can sustain freedom from generation to generation until it develops rich bouquets like a vintage wine. We can build a political habitat of equals, living with the ocean, the sand, the forest, the sky, the clouds, the rain, watching the sunsets and the dawns, savoring art and play, exulting in the best of nature and technology, dancing in the light of the diamond dream. And one day, when others see our example, we might offer this gift to the world.

"But first we need someone to go to Hahajima and initiate the preparations. Someone who can coordinate the construction, defense and growth of the community. Who can offer guidance to our young Starters. Who maintains a link to the past so as to carry us into the future without losing connection to our origin."

"Look!" cried Ono/Makesh, both man and image of woman as man pointing down. Gemini X had eased to a stop, their angle on the island now stationary, its green slopes shimmering in the light of the sun that perched on the rim of the world.

"We're now less than a kilometer above the treetops. Do you have any idea how much even this distance costs? Going any closer would be a major loss even for me. But not for you."

Grunk. A heavy bag hit the floor of the deck just beside Amon. One of the Birla Guards had just dropped something large bundled in tarps.

"From this altitude, a dropdrone can parachute you safely. You'll have everything you need: a permanent self-assembling shelter, a food printer with plenty of meal replacement ink, instructions for initializing the computer and a device that will allow you to communicate by secure means with Ono X.

"Say the word and you can go down to the forest right now," Makesh/Ono X told him, one phantom and one palpable hand extended towards Amon.

Diaspora

"So, Hippo, what do you think?" said Amon. He had been speaking as if to the crowd but now turned at last to his intended audience, leaning over him and trying to catch his blank, open eyes. "Will you help me?"

A minute of silence passed. Amon's stomach butterflied with anticipation, thrilled that Hippo had not said, "I'm done," but worried that he continued to stare oblivious at the wall.

Then many in the gathered crowd literally gasped when Hippo rolled onto his back, and looked straight at Amon with tear-filled eyes, tragic eyes, eyes that seemed willing to try embracing the world one last time.

"Maybe I'm not done just yet," he said, his voice gravelly from disuse. "I heard you, Amon. I'm here."

Kingdom

When Amon had finished explaining his vision and proffered the green pill once more, the PhisherKing plucked it off his palm and popped it into his mouth without a word. Amon watched his Adam's apple glug up and down. He imagined the nanobots that made up the antidote escaping as it was digested, making their way from Monju's stomach to his brain, where they would repair the neural damage that prevented him from conceiving new ideas in code.

Immediately, the flow of blood from the twelve oars began to dwindle. Within seconds, the final trickle had splashed down onto the surface of the mercury, where glass lotuses bloomed instantly on the peaks of the silver waves, spreading outwards as fast as wind rustles grass, until the boat of bone was floating on an ocean of vitreous blossoms, exchanging their iridescent light with the PhisherKing's smile.

Theatre

From Makesh in the white space with his hand held out towards Amon, Rashana herself emerged holding out her hand; Ono X was already gone.

"Join us," she said. "Accept my offer this time."

Amon rose to face her. His hand shook at his side so hard that the rest of him quivered, his gut aching with contrary impulses, as her gaze impelled him to reach out and accept.

So many people had offered Amon jobs: Sekido, Makesh, Anisha, Hippo, Barrow—even Kitao in that nightmare of a memory. Now Rashana, no longer disguised as Makesh, was offering him the same job again. He wasn't sure how he felt. It was all too much at once. If what she said could be believed, then the land of his birth, the spectacle that had haunted him every night of his adult life, was down there, only a short drop below, waiting for him. He had had a mother who tried to raise him there, as part of a society that had tried to change the world. Another society, more rapacious and exclusive, had been born from its destruction and was now preparing to attain dominance over all others, perhaps forever. In the midst of this global political maelstrom, he was being asked to return to his origin and take a stand. How was he supposed to make up his mind so quickly? But if he couldn't, would it be wise to refuse her a second time? That was not something he wanted to test in his current position, stranded over the Pacific on her aircraft, surrounded by her guards. But what could he say? He had to say something.

"What's wrong?" Rashana asked, lowering her hand with already crestfallen eyes.

Lost for words, Amon looked at the island again. The green mountains, the rocky beaches and reefs, the rich cobalt sea. This, it seemed, was what he'd sought for seven long years. He remembered how hard he'd strived to get here, his obsessive scrimping and efforts to accelerate his career, then the emptiness when the dream stopped visiting him in the District of Dreams, along with his resolve to nonetheless seek it out. And he was excited to be sure. His sojourn in the naked world had taught him the value of nature, of living away from the excesses of information, of the need for a way of being outside the Free World and the camps. He could imagine no better alternative than the community Rashana had described, and the idea of taking part in bringing it back was more than tempting. It was the answer to so many of the troubles he saw in the world and that he felt in his heart. It almost seemed like the home he had never known he was looking for. He wanted nothing more at that instant than to go down there and walk amongst the trees, to feel the soil under his feet, to gaze up at the ever-changing sky, listen to the song of the surf, his dream a ray of light that had found the diamond to shrine through at last, along with all the others.

His concerns about Rashana's honesty had nothing to do with it. She had given him permission to view her LifeStream. Later he could check it over, and if Hippo and the PhisherKing could be found, they might help him confirm the truth of everything in their own ways. Trust wasn't the issue, for he realized that even if he could be incontrovertibly certain of what she had told him, evaluate all the events of her story from the nowhere perspective of perfect knowledge, something still wouldn't be right.

Just as the plans of the Gyges Circle had struck him as crude and petty, his encounter with the island was not living up to expectations. Perhaps this was unsurprising; he had built it up to be something almost divine. Perhaps nothing could live up to seven years of sweat and yearning, to the dedication of his every breath. Perhaps the mystery of the dream had been its power, the dark glittering enigma that had led him along lost from sight now that the gilding of the unknown had peeled away.

Amon imagined himself floating down just like in his dream, or being lifted away in reverse in the memory he was supposed to have. Standing amidst octopus trees, seabirds crying above the spray, he would become a leader in the forest. A settler, like that Iwabuchi-sensei, his mother? Building a paradise, giving direction and meaning to all those he oversaw. He could almost believe in this future. He had been so absorbed in just trying to find the forest that he'd never considered what he'd do once he got there, so he might as well use his time to build a new shelter for humanity, a place of belonging for himself. But since when had he been searching for home? Where was Mayuko to join him as he'd imagined since the day he'd spoken with Tamper on the riverbank? Hadn't his dream died with Rick's final tear? Although the rotorcraft was stationary now, he had to have already seen the island from every possible angle and yet he had never spotted the clearing into which he had always fallen, could not feel the promise that had linked him to the forest, the silver tendril tugging on his soul.

It was then that Amon pried his gaze from the island. A spark flickered enticingly on the right side of his visual field and he followed it to its source, the sun, a great circle of fire that wavered and blazed, bleeding nameless colors that fringed the liquid scatter of clouds above, filling the world with light as it slipped over the threshold of darkness beyond vision. Presently he cast his gaze down and watched its vibrant rays shimmer in bands and arcs over the ocean, pulsing and swaying into new forms each moment. All was laid bare for him beneath the sun. All was clear and true in its shifting glory. And he felt as though that same light were filling his consciousness, as though he was radiating from the sun, undulating with the waves, sparkling lucidly like the sky.

His attention moved unbidden to the flicker of his eyelids and the rise and fall of his chest. A seabird diving into the waves seemed to catch fire on the glare and suddenly Amon was riding the phoenix again, the faces of everyone who'd been kind to him gathered in the darkness around its guttering body. Rick Hippo Tamper Monju Vertical Mayuko . . . there were others too, trainers at the Liquidation Ministry, nurses in the Cyst, passing strangers who'd given him a smile. They stood spread across a wasteland as the great flaming bird carried him from the mouth of a volcano, casting their shadows along the barren clay to the horizon. Then the vision collapsed without warning like a sound wave going flat, his awareness snapping back into the moment like an elastic band, and Amon knew what he had to do.

"Rashana," he said, looking her straight in the eyes with such intensity her return-gaze flicked away for a moment.

"Y-yes."

Amon felt sad in a way, thinking how he might have been happy if he'd accepted her offer the first time. Then he might have gone straight to the forest and avoided so much suffering. Never tumbling into the bankdeath camps. Never being starved, beaten, and drawn into an awful war. Never saving Barrow and bringing Xenocyst to ruin. Never being present for Rick's horrible end. But the pain had taught him so much.

222 ★ ELI K. P. WILLIAM

Using that wisdom was his duty now. There was no other way to make amends for all that he had done.

"Thank you for everything," he said. "It's such a joy to have seen this island. I appreciate your telling me all this and having such faith in my suitability for the job. But I can't go down there now."

"What? After all this, you're going to say no?"

Amon took one last look at the island, at the forest, testing his will against the seduction of heaven, and returned his gaze to Rashana. Disappointment and confusion filled her eyes. She looked almost as though she were going to cry. Somehow he had to make her understand. They would need her.

"Nothing has ever inspired me so much and I'm sure I would have found freedom like I've never known. The world will need a new possibility to strive for and maybe Hakkotopia can be it. But now is not the time."

"Why?"

Amon thought of Mayuko but kept it to himself.

"Because I've realized what jubilee means. This whole time I saw it as an action I'd never performed that needed to be denied and rectified. But what if it's an action we *have to* perform."

"We?"

"You told me once that you want a better life for Free People and bankdead alike."

"What are you suggesting?"

5
OTEMACHI, GATA TOWER

1

Amon wove down a wide hallway through a deluge of commuters and poured out with them through the high stone archway of Tokyo Station, onto the streets of Otemachi. Beyond the field of bobbing heads that surrounded him, he could see huge skyscrapers sprawling endlessly in all directions, as he had so many times before. And yet the motley sheen of entertisements that had always covered their every wall and window was missing. Instead, the glass was caked in white sediment and grit, the concrete singed with grease and grime.

Peeking from slim cracks in the skyline above, the morning sky stretched black and threatening, an eerie intensity seeming to radiate from the clouds as though they were electrified with rancid desire. Stripped of its graphical clothes—InfoSky, InfoStreet, InfoFlux—the metropolis was too barren for comfort, only mutters, footsteps, and swishing car engines to relieve the smothering silence.

To his immediate left were the walls of Tokyo Station, its material obscured by accreted gunge. To his right was the usual traffic jam, except the formerly immaculate cars were dusty and scratched, each sharing a generic design with other vehicles of their type. Sedans, SUVs, bikes all ground along bumper-to-rusted-bumper, the faces of their drivers scrunched with weary distraction.

This was Amon's first time returning to Otemachi since his bankdeath, and he had just removed his training bank for the occasion. Although he had by now visited several districts of Free Tokyo absent the ImmaNet, none had felt so uncanny as here, on his former route to work. How could he have commuted through the delusive veneer of this blighted waste for seven years, believing it was the most normal thing in the world?

Unnerved by the abnormal lack of stimulation, Amon directed his gaze down to the sidewalk. There was the grid of concrete tiles slightly larger than his foot, each owned by different companies . . . but this meant nothing to him anymore. The tramp and clack of dress shoes and stilettos had been replaced by the patter of ragged sneakers and boots that kept advancing just ahead of him, and seeing no colored arrows telling him which tiles were more expensive, he sauntered casually from one to the next, amazed to remember how much brainpower he had expended on the stepping game that animated the overlaid images into ads. At such times, he had focused on each of his movements, trying to reduce his blinks and breaths, directing his eyes to gutters and alleyway walls where the viewing rights were cheaper. His obsession with going to the landscape of his dream had been so all consuming that he had harnessed his willpower to regulate his attention in every moment and deny his impulses and desires as their price demanded.

How ironic, he thought, *that I would sacrifice the one choice for which I sacrificed all others.*

Never again would he need to worry about such calculated apportioning of his existence. And neither would anyone else—the hordes of beguiled professionals around him included—if everything went as they hoped.

2

In the days after the first inkling of a new future came to Amon, he had set about to secure the cooperation of those he would need to realize it.

First, of course, was Rashana.

At the moment of inception, as they hovered above Hahajima in the sunset—although he'd spoken vaguely of the jubilee—he had been unable to articulate his inchoate vision. Only after a full day of meditation back at Atupio Home Office did it gestate into concrete ideas that could be expressed in words. But even then Amon declined to give details for fear that Anisha would hack her and view the seg of their conversation. All he could tell Rashana was that he had a plan to bring about change for which her help would be indispensable. Since he couldn't take the risk of elaborating any further, he would pitch it to Ono X. If Ono X gave the green light, Amon would ask for a training bank so that Ono X could leash him on Rashana's behalf. This arrangement would give Amon the resources he needed while allowing Ono X to monitor his progress via AT readout without Rashana learning anything sensitive. Once it was clear whether the plan was viable, he promised that they would report everything to her.

Rashana was reluctant to provide seed money for an enterprise she could know nothing about. But she accepted Amon's reasons for hiding it from her, and when she saw that he was adamant about following through, she was too curious to say no.

The next partner Amon had sought was Hippo.

After Amon had finished making his proposal in the dim, crowded alcove, the despondent husk of the man they had all once revered astounded everyone by locking eyes with him and speaking, dispelling doubts that he had gone senile or mad. Then he had asked for time to think.

So Amon spent the night in a nearby capsule and returned bright and early to find Hippo sitting up against the wall, his gaze awaiting Amon.

"When my life's work was eaten alive from the inside, I left my will to try for dead," Hippo said, while all eyes watched on in the pale light of morning. "But you've shown me a path beyond anything I could have ever imagined where the heart of purpose still beats.

"I would have us grieve for what is gone and follow you to whatever awaits, Amon," he concluded, "assuming my friends here agree."

Bittersweet elation filled Amon at these words. For he was glad to give his friend hope in darkest days while acutely aware that he had done so before with the exposé, and let him down. Let them all down. Still, he had no compunctions about asking for their trust again, certain that if anything was worth gambling everything they cherished, this was it.

With Book facilitating the deliberation that ensued, Hippo remained silent, leaving Amon to make his case: the great boon the exiles would grant to their fellow crashdead, the glorious transformation they could ring in, and the new home they might build together when all was said and done. Many eyes sparkled at these promises, and many heads nodded when Vertical pointed out that they had nothing left to lose. It was only a matter of time before they starved or Tamper stole more than the algorithms could ignore and the vending security drones finished them off. Whether or not the exiles refused, Amon assured them that Rashana would airdrop enough supplies to tide them over until summer; after that they would be on their own. But if they accepted, she would feed, clothe, and house them in safety. So it was either stay on the fringes of Tokyo and wither away sooner or later, or join him for one final courageous act. Predictably, Yané argued for accepting the shipment and attempting to recapture Xenocyst, while Jiku preferred that they continue to take their chances in Free Tokyo rather than wager their tenuous stability on another of Amon's grandiose schemes. What seemed to sway the exiles in the end, though, was when Hippo said, "Gura is the only one of us with his eye on the horizon ahead. I see no other direction to strike out for."

After this, no further objections were raised, and Amon realized that the discussion had been settled the moment Hippo agreed to join him. In grappling valiantly with the crowd's many doubts, Amon had merely been leading them through the motions so that everyone could feel as though their decision had resulted from due consideration, when all along they had been overjoyed to have their leader back to his senses, willing to follow him anywhere. Even Ty had kept his mouth shut and followed suit.

Well before the subsequent resettlement of the exiles at Atupio Home Office, Amon had been working to recruit their final partner, the PhisherKing.

The first step had been to acquire the antidote to conception dust. Since the technology included Fertilex trade secrets that not even Rashana could access, Anisha's permission was essential. To this end, Ono X persuaded Rashana to sign away exclusive rights to all the intelligence he had collected about the Gyges Circle. Although these leaks were originally intended as blackmail to gain recognition for

Hakkotopia 2.0, Ono X reassured her that such special political status would be superfluous if Amon succeeded, and she eventually agreed, reversing a longstanding Birla policy of leaving Monju to his neurological disability. This was an enormous show of confidence from both Ono X and Rashana, and Amon flew into central Tokyo to visit the PhisherKing feeling hopeful.

"I see you've kept your promise, Kenzaki-san," the PhisherKing told him after he'd swallowed the antidote. "I knew you'd find wisdom to carry us all to our rejuvenation. I pray only that the ignorance your insight hides doesn't come back to haunt us."

With this enigmatic statement, Monju sat on the gunwale at the prow of his boat, Amon at his side and the Phishers huddled round, to brainstorm the new program he would write now that he was healed.

Amon was brought back to Otemachi by the prick of something small and hard striking the back of his hand. Looking up, he felt another on his face and began to hear a dull clattering around him as tiny whitish chunks fell from the sky. They bounced off his jacketed chest and the shoulders of the crowd surrounding him. It had begun to hail.

According to the calendar, this was supposed to be the first day of spring, only a week before Free New Year, the 50th anniversary of the Tokyo Roundtable. But the morning air was crisp and the icy pellets instantly swept away all traces of warmth. The weather report that morning had called for sunshine, and although Amon wasn't one for superstition, this unlikely change felt inauspicious to him, almost ominous. It certainly didn't seem like a blessing from the gods or the buddhas.

Umbrellas began to pop open from the crowd one after the other, until Amon seemed to look out over a pond covered in convex, plastic lily pads. He wasn't carrying an umbrella himself and couldn't buy one without his training bank. But come to think of it, he didn't care. He liked the sting of the hail on his buzzed head, cheeks, and hands, for the pain seemed to rouse his senses, whetting the blade of his focus for what had to be done next.

Knowing that stepping on cracks in the sidewalk was supposed to be expensive since it meant paying twice, Amon intentionally guided his black running shoes between the tiles, relishing the liberty to rebel against his former routine. During these walks from the station to GATA Tower, he had often reflected on the virtues of the action-transaction market. Setting aside his left wing doubts about the policies put forth by Absolute Choice to commodify autonomic processes like urinating and heartbeating, he had found the system inspiring, convinced it had made the world a better place. It even seemed to teach humanity an important existential lesson about the difference between wastes of energy and crucial undertakings by forcing everyone to keep track of their urges and decide which ones were worthwhile, in accordance with their salary and the going rates. But now, looking around the crowd cowering beneath umbrellas—at their bleary twitching eyes, their grim constipated expressions, their almost disembodied bearing and gait—Amon found confirmation of what bankdeath had taught him: that he had been trapped, they had all been trapped, were still trapped. He could sense the cage that enclosed them, the false choice foisted upon everyone between earning the ability to satisfy basic desires and necessities and banishment to a place where they would lose the ability to earn altogether. Before, he had been too immersed in common sense to get any kind of perspective on where he truly was, bombarded so incessantly with information that simply absorbing and reacting to it maxed out his mental resources, leaving none for sorting and contemplating. Obfuscation was an inherent part of life here, arising without design from human efforts to soothe the debilitating boredom and contrive new ploys for making money. He could see the dripping slather of the InfoFlux's ashen tongue coating those near him, the aura of unacknowledged confusion and angst that—

His ruminations were interrupted when the line of legs ceased and he was forced to a halt. The signal at the intersection a few meters ahead had turned red. The crowd closed in tight around him as those behind continued to edge forward. Now that his progress had been interrupted, Amon felt the claws of his emotions scrabbling their way to the surface of his awareness, carrying anxious thoughts with them. *What if something goes wrong? What if we sacrifice everything for naught?* He knew that casting his gaze upward, as he had often done when such worries assailed him, would not bring him the inspiration he needed now, but he tilted his face into the stinging hail and did it anyway.

Layered there against the dark electric sky was the wilderness of concrete peaks, all stripped of the communipromotation kaleidoscope that once adorned them. And rising from scattered locations in their midst were the thirteen buildings that housed the Tokyo headquarters of the Twelve and One. They rose taller than the rest, rearing over the buildings of their subsidiaries and the venture startups no doubt destined to be their subsidiaries. Yet their height was not what it had once been. Before they had been the same size and Amon had interpreted this as a symbol of their equal standing in the global marketplace or of the possibility that all thirteen were really just one, their assets overlapping too intricately for even specialists to draw the boundaries of each. Now he could tell that in the naked world their roofs reached to varying altitudes, suggesting a disparate ranking, though without their logos he couldn't determine which was which to compare. The tallest might very well have been Fertilex.

But where was GATA Tower? He couldn't remember the location of his old workplace in the cityscape, finding only unrecognizable buildings and the fragments of sky between. So what had happened to that massive edifice looming over all, its glass and steel extending endlessly into space? He might have believed it had disappeared, if he didn't know otherwise.

The signal finally changed to green, urging Amon and the rest of the crowd across the road. On the other side, he made his way right to the next corner and turned left onto a broad boulevard. Instead of the glossy walkway he had been expecting, he trod over more dull concrete speckled with gunk, the spruce lining the curb beside the four-lane road frail and sickly, their roots not tracing a bright green pattern through the sidewalk but jailed in cramped patches of soil. On the bland island plaza in the middle of the road, the potted gingkos beside vacant benches were brown, probably dying, the infofountain normally playing a MegaGlom logo just a weakly ejaculating crater.

Amon watched those around him twitching out commands and darting their eyes to and fro as they walked, their minds brimming with dazzling deception, everything they held dear inextricable from empty shadows.

How will they react when the light shines down and blinds them at last? he wondered. *How many will learn to see anew as I have?*

Among them were a few who remained undistracted by the ephemeral blaze of marketing. They were wearing inconspicuous dark suits like Amon, blending in with the salarypeople. Some walked several paces ahead of him, some behind, some making their way in the same direction on the other side of the street. Others approached along different paths, converging from all avenues, dusters hidden beneath their jackets. And Amon behaved as though they were strangers, feigning separateness while fully aware that they moved in tandem.

The act of putting one foot in front of the other, purposefully and precisely, used to help Amon take his mind away from his troubles and prevent his doubts from festering into distracting worries. Now, even the transgression of intentionally stepping on the cracks brought him only slight satisfaction, as he thought with apprehensive determination of what lay just ahead.

4

It was in the Atupio war room—an underground plantfoam chamber with a biopixel display cube at the center of moss-chair seating for nearly 100—that Hippo, the Xenocyst exiles, Kai Monju, the Phishers and a Ferment Culture Collective team assigned by Ono X put their heads together to flesh out Amon's idea. Once these discussions were progressing apace, all that remained was to enlist Rashana. The challenge was how to do so without the risk of Anisha learning everything. This the Phishers immediately set out to overcome.

While the barrier between the sisters' subprofiles had been fortified on both sides by the best cryptosealers money could buy, only the Phisher-King had the insider know-how to harness the inner profile's far more robust native security, an integral component of the blinding system he had engineered. With his reconfiguration, Rashana's data would be as impenetrable to her sister as to any other Free Citizen. The downside was that the reverse would also be true—Rashana would be barred from hacking her sister—and she initially balked at losing this means of subterfuge. That the procedure required granting a sly info-peddler like the PhisherKing physical access to her BodyBank made her all the more reluctant. But when Ono X urged her to do whatever it took to at least hear Amon out, her curiosity once again won the day, and she covered all fees and fines for the flesh-hacking required.

Once the sisters' sub-folders were airtight to the PhisherKing's satisfaction, he, Amon, Ono X, and Hippo invited Rashana to hear what they had come up with. As the venue for their meeting, Rashana chose the Atupio conference room where she and Amon had talked after his recovery in the sensory deprivation orchard. By this time, the Phishers had sorted out the technical details of Amon's vision, so the four of them were able to describe it much more persuasively than he would have in the beginning.

They took turns filling her in according to their expertise, seated around the end of the coral table opposite the tree window, watching Rashana against a background of pale aquatic light and flowing lifeforms. The PhisherKing and Ono X drew upon their respective databases, while Amon and Hippo, who preferred communicating with training banks set to naked view so as to be attentive to their interlocuters' unedited expressions, relied only on memory. Not once did Rashana interrupt. She listened with a wary intensity, as though eager to understand and yet suspicious of their every utterance. When they were finished, she rose and paced back and forth in front of the window, brooding. Then she paused with her back to them for a moment and turned abruptly on her heel, lower lip trembling, hands tensed claw-like in front of her waist.

"No," she said, regarding them one by one with livid eyes, razor lashes ready to fall at the slightest provocation. "No."

Taken aback, Amon and the other three froze, glancing at each other from the corner of their eyes to see who had the courage to reply.

"I . . ." Rashana faltered, grimacing momentarily as a softer emotion bubbled up, then recovered her determination. "No. Just no."

She took several steps towards the door as if she were going to walk out on them. But as the beads of the diamond painting began to swish apart, she stopped, her shoulders bristling before she wheeled on Ono X.

"This is what you traded away our intel for?" she snapped, flailing her hands palm up as if to suggest their emptiness. "To launch this crackpot farce when we could have had official recognition for the community?"

There was something uncanny about watching her cow such a brawny man as Ono X with a glower, his gaze fleeing to his lap, his head sinking between his shoulders like a scolded dog. Then the softer emotion returned to Rashana's face, raw and sorrowful, her lips curling down, eyes aglitter, and she looked to Amon.

"I want you to accept my original offer," she told him. "We will resettle Hahajima. Together, all of us. Even without recognition. We'll just have to"—With another surge of anger her jaw clenched and she stamped her foot.

"I thought you were looking out for us!" she shouted at Ono X.

The four of them had been expecting her to disagree and had prepared a series of rebuttals, but her ferocity had caught them off guard. They remained taut and still until the door automatically reassembled itself, adding its rain-like hiss to the atonal symphony of the building's organisms, and Rashana turned as if to leave. Instead, she came to a stop the moment she faced the door, as though stricken by the sight of the diamond dream it depicted, myriad beams of light refracting through its facets against a blue sky. Amon wondered again which side was meant to be viewed. The one visible from the conference room or its mirror image in the hallway? When Rashana let out a sigh between her teeth and the muscles in her back seemed to relax, Ono X was the first to speak up.

"Beef up Hakkotopia 2.0 as much as you like," he said. "All the military, financial, and political armor in the world won't keep out the Gyges Circle. They'll slither their way in with the exemptions one way or another. Destroy us, by hook or by crook. We've got to neutralize them first the way Amon says. Anisha knows too much."

They waited for her to respond, chary of setting her off with ill-chosen words, until Hippo followed up with an appeal to her conscience.

"Life in Ogasawara may be absolute bliss for its inhabitants," he began, "but what of everyone else who remains trapped in banklife and bankdeath? What good would you be contributing to the world if you realized a new kind of freedom for yourselves when no one anywhere else is free?"

"Think of equality of knowledge as well if that is something you value," put in the PhisherKing. "The financial dams on information would remain in place. You would abandon most of humankind to murk and fantasy. They would be the gullible playthings of Anisha and her associates. Come with us and set truth free."

Another minute passed. Rashana hardly moved, showing no signs that she was even listening; whether she was indeed studying the image of the diamond or simply thinking there was no telling. Presently, she turned around again, slowly this time.

"Every radical vision has its naysayers," she said, with calm bitterness. "But I have no doubt that our ingenuity will prevail. In time we will serve as a shining example that draws new followers from all corners of the globe. Eventually no one will be left out."

Her response countered both Hippo and the PhisherKing while neglecting to address Ono X's security assessment, but Amon didn't think it wise to harp on any logical holes. Instead, he decided to say his piece.

"Everyone who has dreamt of alternatives has thought just like you, Rashana. But if Free history has taught us anything, it's that there's no such thing as an alternative to the AT Market. The Free World and the bankdeath camps are two faces of the same wasteland. Xenocyst failed to exist on the inside, Hakkotopia failed to exist on the outside, and the Gyges Circle can only think to hollow the inside out. From the most powerful executive to the lowliest giftless resource, we're all in this together."

The speech left Rashana nonplussed, a whirl of thought in her eyes.

"Trust me," said Ono X. "Please."

Something was shared between master and servant as their eyes locked, Ono X's gaze reassuring and pleading, Rashana's resisting and withholding.

Eventually she told them that she needed time and the meeting was adjourned. But it was only a few hours later that she knocked on the door of Amon's private quarters in the depths of Atupio to give her reply.

"I'll support the project in any way I can," she declared, under the apricot glow in the hallway beyond the open door. "We'll work to dismantle the hideous machine my begetters built. But only under one condition. You help me to establish Hakkotopia 2.0 as soon as we're finished."

Here was Amon's turn to waver. On the one hand, he was delighted at yet another opportunity to visit the forest, in spite of refusing twice, and could think of nothing better to do with his life when their undertaking was complete than recreating that beautiful society. On the other hand, he would be running off to a place where the chances of locating Mayuko were slim. This felt like a betrayal of a loyal friend and once-girlfriend who had rescued him from both bankdeath and death, and who he loved with all his soul. Then again, staying would mean wasting his idea, ditching their fellowship just when it was poised to gain momentum, and letting down the untold billions whose freedom was on the line. In the end, Amon accepted the condition, redoubling his desperate efforts to find Mayuko in what little time he had before they would embark for Ogasawara.

And so they all became united in a common purpose: the four players on whose shoulders all possibility of success rested—Amon, Rashana, Hippo and the PhisherKing—alongside an unlikely assortment of collaborators—Ono X, the Birla Guard, Xenocyst in exile, the Phishers, the Starters, and the Atupian offshoot of the Ferment Culture Collective. By the time they were assembled in the Atupio Home Office underground, mere weeks remained until the Secretary of Blinding's inauguration, when their tireless work would be put to the test.

Now that day had come and they were ready, Amon's group in Otemachi and many others spread throughout the surrounding metropolis, waiting to begin.

5

At last Amon saw GATA Tower, though he hardly recognized it. Straight ahead, he had an unobstructed view, its shaft protruding from a round platform of concrete at the end of the boulevard. Amon wasn't awed or impressed as he once had been. The top barely poked above the surrounding rooftops, shorter than even the shortest MegaGlom HQ, forget about its reaching the sky. And the circle devoid of images around it, that had given its spiraling steel pillars and latticed dark windows special visual prominence amidst the writhing communixchange vortex called Tokyo, provided no contrast now that all graphics had fled. The building had shrunk to a bulky pseudo-brutalist rectangle of blackish grey concrete, lacking even windows, as though an organization that could monitor the actions of every citizen could do without eyes, could close itself off to the world.

Amon's long-held desire to peer beneath the overlay and see GATA Tower with his naked eyes, to perform this expensive image-rights violation and confirm whether it was indeed architecturally possible for a structure with such a narrow base to exit the atmosphere, had at last been fulfilled, and it hadn't cost him even a hundredth of a yen. Yet it brought Amon little gratification. *Who cares if this GATA Tower is as big as the GATA Towers in other cities?* he thought, astounded at his erstwhile interest in such banal trivia. Still, he was glad to have finally grasped the connection between the size of the towers and their clout, if any such connection had ever existed. For whatever the relative height of the MegaGlom headquarters, it was clear that GATA Tower didn't come close.

As he entered the shadow of the tower slanting across the cracked concrete at his feet, Amon tried to count its floors but, without windows to rely on, couldn't pick out the segments and quickly gave up. What mattered wasn't its precise size anyway. It was that he could see the building stop somewhere, that it was finite. Able to fully encompass it with his eyes now, there was no longer solace to be found, nor did his memories of having worked there embolden him, except insofar as they were a reminder of how critical it was that they succeed today.

Now here he was at the end of the boulevard, before this tower he had once thought so majestic, that he had mistaken for the stronghold of salvation. To think, the Global Action Transaction Authority had been established little less than fifty years ago, and people had already forgotten the world that existed before, had lost the ability to imagine any other than the one they currently inhabited. Social injustice gone? Citizens emancipated from financial despotism? History was supposed to be over, the ideal life of mankind—the life of liberty—finally attained. Perhaps it was true that the old institutions were primitive, law, courts, police, criminals, jails, war, but were their replacements, credilaw, Judicial Brokers, Liquidators, bankrupts, pecuniary retreats, Pax Economica any better? Bureaucracy had merely shape-shifted, integrating more imperceptibly with the MegaGlom apparatus that gripped the globe, covering up control more pervasive than ever before with the perfume of opportunity:

All the freedom you can earn.

Amon recited this phrase in his mind like a curse as he went up an escalator to the round concrete platform, tailing a line of those who had once been his colleagues. His new colleagues converged with him from the three other escalators linking the platform to the streets in each direction. The concrete gray uniform of the Liquidators nearby, the uniform he had worn with such smug self-importance, looked like the most dull, tasteless rags he had ever seen, worse even than the disposable clothes in the camps, while the baby blue shirt, lavender tie, and brown suit of GATA staff in the standard uniform seemed to him ludicrously tacky and flamboyant. If not for the gravity of the occasion, Amon might have laughed.

The hail continued to thud incessantly onto his head, his suit jacket, the umbrellas of passerby, the concrete, as he approached the entrance to GATA Tower, and Amon raised his interlaced fingers to shelter his brow. Then, halting beside the glass doors leading into the lobby, he watched staff hurry in and out, the morning shift entering to replace the night shift. He studied their passing faces, searching for some trace of the pride and relief he had felt when approaching this edifice, but found only the same dour frowns as everywhere else. Did they seriously believe as he had that GATA would outlive corporate empires, currencies, real estate barons, that it was something eternal to be served until death, that their wealth was guaranteed if only they went on scrimping and saving and slaving? He was here to ensure that it would not be eternal, and his former self who had harbored such thoughts seemed like another person entirely, a friend deceased in the holy battlefields of memory, but a friend he did not mourn as he did Rick. For the death of who Amon had been had breathed life into who he was now, and he knew what had to be done and knew that he was doing it.

Amon glanced through the glass into the dim lobby, then up at the shaft of this disappointing but nostalgic structure, the place that had supported and ruined him, given him salary and taken it away. Then he looked beside him where Hippo stood. They gave each other a solemn nod and approached the PhisherKing, flanking him. Hippo leaned forward to whisper in his left ear, and when he was finished, Amon whispered in his right. With two secrets from one who gave banklife and another who took it away, the PhisherKing had the final pieces he needed to complete the program he had written. Now it would all begin.

6

The Phoenix Virus was only possible through the cooperation of an Identity Executioner and an Identity Vitalator who had both voluntarily chosen bankdeath and the architect of the House of Blinding, with an immensely wealthy patron to fund them. No other combination of people on earth could have even tried to realize it. Amon was amazed when the idea emerged nascent in his awareness and he recognized the seemingly miraculous serendipity of their meeting, though their acquaintance would have meant nothing without his insight to bind them.

As an Identity Executioner, he had memorized the Death Codes that allowed him to execute the identities of citizens and send them to bankdeath. As an Identity Vitalator, Hippo had memorized the Birth Codes that allowed him to endow citizens with an identity signature and bring them to banklife. Because Amon had committed identity suicide and Hippo had received identity euthanasia, they had never been liquidated and their codes had never been reset even unto bankdeath.

Hippo had noted this unique symmetry when he told Amon and Rick his story in the digital quarantine. It had led him to trust Amon instinctively and compelled him to argue in favor of admitting him to Xenocyst at his first council hearing. For his part, Amon had sensed the same enigmatic significance as Hippo. But he had all but forgotten their conversation until Rashana made her offer above Hahajima. Then Hippo's words rose up in the dark chamber of Amon's mind, reverberating like the echo of some holy summons. Other memories rushed in and clustered around the first, like the plasma of a reverse supernova turning into a star: the PhisherKing's prophecy of rejuvenation, the action exemptions, the flaming bird that saved him, the diamond dream. In a flash, Amon saw that Hippo's intuition had been right, but in a way that Hippo had never imagined.

Part of the reason Amon had committed identity suicide was to hold on to his BodyBank and therefore also the LifeStream record of all the injustices he had been subjected to surrounding Barrow's assassination and then the jubilee charge. In the end, the LifeStream had been useless, except as a source from which to flesh-hack Mayuko's saved profile and thereby send her futile messages. But identity suicide had left Amon with the power to wield an even more valuable kind of information. Not the data in his hard drive, but the memory of the Death Codes in his head. Similarly, Hippo had sought identity euthanasia to manage Xenocyst more effectively. In the end, that had not gone as he'd expected, but his Birth Codes remained. Amon was certain that no one else—not Anisha or Sekido or GATA or the Gyges Circle—had put it together that they still had them, let alone that they might pose some kind of threat, any more than he had.

Hippo and Amon could do nothing with their birth and death codes alone. Being disconnected from the ImmaNet, they had no way to interface with other BodyBanks (for this same reason, Hippo couldn't simply put himself back online). With the help of Rashana, first Amon and then Hippo had regained access to the ImmaNet through training banks, and they might have used their codes on her leash. She might have paid for the respective ID forgery and ID murder such unauthorized applications would incur. Hippo might have granted banklife to anyone with the right hardware and Amon might have taken it away at a whim. But the immense fines would have strained even Rashana's resources and served little purpose.

To fully actuate the latent potential of this improbable union of knowledge, they needed the intervention of the PhisherKing. His mind now cured of the damage done by conception dust, he had spent weeks developing the right program. All he needed to activate it was their codes.

It was in preparation for this that Amon and Hippo had shed their training banks inside the Tokyo Station building not half an hour earlier, whereupon Rashana had deregistered their genomes, paying the huge fine for *abandoning* her wards (as BioPens occasionally did to resources deemed so unmarketable that the predicted introduction fee wouldn't recoup rearing costs). With her leash to them safely cut, they could then whisper their codes to the PhisherKing without bankrupting their patron twice over, as each disclosure warranted the bankdeath penalty. Only their being already bankdead saved them from the same fate. Any bankliving Vitalator or Executioner would have been marked for liquidation, their codes reset. In other words, Amon's and Hippo's cash crashing without bankruptcy was, in so many ways, a loophole in the system that the Phoenix Virus was written to exploit.

7

With some almost imperceptible finger motions, the PhisherKing had installed the program in himself. He then touched Amon and Hippo on the forehead to flesh-hack them. In an instant, the InfoFlux came roaring back, the cityscape frenetic once more with spastic image and spectacle, GATA Tower restored in all its chimeric glory, looming to the black hailing InfoClouds. Amon had only a moment to observe that he was back online—and wearing a training bank no longer. *My BodyBank has juice!* Then the three of them touched three Phishers in the same way, and these six touched six others.

When the nine Phishers spread out to infect the remaining three of their fellows and several of the waiting Birla Guard, Amon heard the faint whine of motorbikes. Stepping over to the edge of the platform, he watched Liquidators blast one after the other up a ramp that inclined into the city from beneath him. Numbers began to tick in the air before his eyes—7, 12, 16, 23 . . .—a program counting the Liquidators that had left GATA Tower. 36, 39, 44 . . . Soon there were so many bikes humming along that the grey-suited shoulders of the Liquidator's drew almost close enough to collide.

Although the ramp quickly disappeared into the crush of buildings, Amon knew that it would split somewhere out of sight and feed the bikes onto different highways. He imagined the Liquidators following their navibeams towards each target—as he had done countless times—and the nerve dust screams of all those he had apprehended seemed to resonate from the very heart of the metropolis. But he found that such memories no longer brought guilt or regret, that in the moment he finally seized the chance to make amends for his sins, he had already forgiven himself. Not that he could ever condone what he had done, only that he had let go of his past to take hold of a new future.

The Phishers and Birla Guard had now finished flesh-hacking the more than twenty Atupians gathered on the platform. Last but not least was Rashana. The PhisherKing took care of her personally, regarding her with somber determination until she nodded. Then he touched her forehead, and infection with the Phoenix Virus was complete.

From the roof of GATA Tower and several other landing pads in the vicinity, Amon spotted rotorcraft lifting off. 105, 111, 120 . . . These would fly Liquidators to targets in suburban areas of Tokyo too distant to reach quickly by motorbike. It was a sign, just as they'd hoped, that the Liquidation Ministry was mobilizing the whole fleet. 243, 249, 255 . . .

The crew of phoenixes now paused in loose formation atop the platform so as not to attract attention, while GATA staff continued to pour in and out of the doors. For another minute Amon stood with them, numbers climbing, bikes and rotors speeding away; he was cold with anticipation and fear, wanting to charge into the lobby tantalizingly visible through the glass but forcing himself to wait for the signal.

There it was. The sound of a bleating horn, high-pitched yet rattling like an instrument of bone. *Time to breach this sad, shrunken mountain,* thought Amon, and leading their swarm upon the doors, he stepped over the threshold.

8

The Phoenix Virus algorithm was performing a set of procedures on each host in an endless cycle. For those who were bankliving, it began by automatically applying the Death Codes to perform an ID execution, wiping out the host's ID signature and immediately applying the Birth Codes to install a new one. For Amon and Hippo, the only bankdead who had BodyBanks and could receive the virus, it had been modified slightly so that it began in reverse, installing an ID signature and then taking it away. But whether it began with bank- life or death, it ran through the same steps on repeat every second, realizing instantaneous identity reincarnation.

Death. Rebirth. Death. Rebirth.

Every step Amon took deeper into the lobby, he cash crashed and was then instantly reborn as a new person. The rebirth happened so quickly—faster than the flicker of a flame—that he was immune to all of GATA's defenses. It was all he could do not to go mad with exhilaration, reveling in his invincibility, terrified that it might break down.

The procedure by which the Phoenix Virus protected them was highly technical, but Monju had simplified it for the crew during a briefing in the Atupio war room the previous week.

"First, imagine a normal bankliving individual. Their identity signature is sent constantly to the House of Blinding together with their action-data, and the House of Blinding forwards their action-data to the Ministry of Monitoring. Following regular protocol, the Monitors match the data to an action-property. They then inform the House of Blinding of the amount that needs to be withdrawn from the actor's account. Under these circumstances, trespassing in GATA Tower would warrant the bankdeath penalty. But with the Phoenix Virus the situation is different. The Death Codes kick in well before the Blinders can blind the permission to perform the withdrawal transaction, so the identity signature no longer exists and neither does the account. The withdrawal is impossible. You might think that the actor would lose their connection to the ImmaNet at this point, without an identity signature to transmit to the Ministry of Access. But the Birth Codes kick in at the moment of bankdeath. So the access request arrives at the Ministry of Access with a report that the individual's genome was registered to a new identity signature. This the ministry should approve automatically; access is never lost."

Activation of the birth and death codes had to be timed so that the new identity signature was registered after erasure of the original identity signature had been reported to the Ministry of Access. Otherwise two identity signatures would be registered to one genome, resulting in an error. However, activation of the new signature could not occur so long after erasure of the original signature that ImmaNet access was interrupted. Utilizing his intimate knowledge of the allowable durations for each House of Blinding process, Monju had designed the virus so that access interruption was shorter than the saccade of an eye, meaning it was literally imperceptible to the human mind. This guaranteed no experience of jitter or lag. The end result was an identity rebirth cycle that took a fraction of a microsecond and allowed all the infiltrators to maintain a stable ImmaNet connection, without being identified as distinct individuals for long enough to pay for their actions, criminal or otherwise.

In this way, they also evaded GATA Tower's security system. Bankrupts and bankdead who entered the premises would have been neutralized automatically by dust pores in the walls. Unauthorized bankliving would have received the bankdeath penalty for *trespassing*, *treason*, or a similar credicrime, thereby going bankrupt and then being likewise dusted. Even a MegaGlom would have lost all its assets for any attempted breach or assault, a safeguard contrived by the Tokyo Roundtable in the belief that only financial defenses could fend off militarily supreme corporations. But before GATA registered Amon and his allies as bankliving intruders, they were bankdead, and before it registered bankdead intruders they were bankliving again, their identities vanishing and reemerging in the space between action and transaction. Thus they drew no fire and tripped no alarms, evading both the algorithmically determined response and any independent human decision.

Since the Phoenix Virus had to run through numerous unique identity signatures every moment for each of the fifty infiltrators, Rashana had pre-purchased trillions for the PhisherKing to incorporate into the program. He had then infected himself first so that his identity would vanish before the Fiscal Judiciary was alerted to what he had done. Otherwise, he would have gone bankrupt a million times over, becoming liable for all of the virus' actions and incurring thousands of fines per second—including bankdeath penalties for its ongoing identity forgeries and severe penalties for its identity murders. Those nearest to him, Amon and Hippo, had come next. They had been identity reborn, joining the PhisherKing in a liminal sort of banklife in which they could do whatever they pleased without repercussions and yet could not own property before their accounts were erased. All the bankliving infiltrators that followed had likewise relinquished their identities, losing all entitlements in an instant.

For the PhisherKing and his Phishers, this entailed accepting that the database they had spent decades assembling and curating was worthless. Because even though the information would remain saved in their BodyBanks and remote drives, it was the contracts on conditions of use that made most of it valuable. The Birla Guard and Atupian combat specialists were simply obeying orders—not for the sake of a salary or a bonus as the possibility of all such monetary rewards would be closed off to them, but out of sheer loyalty to Rashana and their cause.

Yet none of these losses compared to the sacrifice made by Rashana, for she had given up her entire claim to Fertilex! With the erasure of her identity signature, her genome had been decoupled from her assets, and her 49 percent share in the world's largest MegaGlom, including Atupio, was gone, plunging her from the second richest person on earth to penniless. It was an act of such dedication that Amon couldn't begin to fathom how she felt.

Her one consolation, perhaps, was in the knowledge that she had spited her sister in the process. While installation of the program had required flesh to flesh contact for everyone else, Anisha was an exception, since her genome was registered to the same identity signature as Rashana's. The moment the algorithm had deleted Rashana's original signature, Anisha had lost hers as well, along with her bank account and executive control of Fertilex. In return, she had gained the Phoenix Virus, though only for the several minutes until the infiltrators deactivated the program for everyone according to plan.

The PhisherKing had explained this implication during the same war room briefing, and as Amon crossed the GATA lobby, he glanced at Rashana among the other infiltrators, recalling the look on her face at the time. He couldn't help noticing then that the edge of her lips had seemed to curve slightly. His first impulse was to take this for the outward sign of glee at the expectation of her sisters' shock and bewilderment. But the smile or smirk or whatever it was had vanished before Amon could be certain what it expressed, and he quickly dismissed the suspicion. She was just too wise and upstanding for such petty vindictiveness. Indeed, her face in the present displayed only resolute focus on the task at hand, and all other indications were that she had gone through with the infection out of true passion for what they were trying to achieve.

Now, as they stepped into the elevator hallway, each infiltrator was carrying the Phoenix Virus of their own accord, having willingly thrown away everything they had called their own, all notion of yours and mine, for the opportunity their coming together gave.

9

In the hallway, Amon, Rashana, Monju, and Hippo stopped with backs to the wall opposite the bank of elevators and waited for the Atupians, Phishers, and Birla Guard to assemble into three lines. Their entrance had been timed so that the morning and night shifts would have already switched places, leaving the ground floor empty of GATA staff. Even so, the narrow space was soon so packed with their fifty members that Amon could no longer see the floor for their heads.

"First contact with the Liquidators," Ono X reported, causing his perspective to pop up in the bottom right of Amon's visual field. Oriented diagonally down from three stories up, it showed a restaurant stacked alley through which a river of ectoplasmic infomist swished around strolling pedestrians. Ono X was in charge of the much larger portion of their forces that day: the lures, the escorts, and the coordinators.

The lures had been some of Atupio's most trusted bankliving supporters, who had now undergone choreographed bankruptcies. First, they had donated all their assets to Atupio. Then, much like the virus that infected Amon's hand the previous summer, they had flurried through all the exorbitant online actions they could: going all-in on every poker hand, signing up for color analyst IQ pageants, buying high and selling low. Meanwhile, they were cussing and staging brawls consisting almost entirely of dirty moves—kicks to the groin, bites, headbutts—that were more expensive than damaging because they weren't putting any force into them. This orchestrated spendfest drove them all bankrupt within seconds, at roughly the same time.

Across Tokyo, there were several thousand such identity martyrs—nearly half the number of Liquidators stationed in GATA Tower. In fact, exactly half minus five. This drew out the vast majority on cash crash missions, allowing the infiltrators to steal inside without worrying about armed resistance if they were detected, while leaving five pairs in reserve. Now even if some uninvolved citizens happened to go bankrupt somewhere in the metropolis, GATA would not run short on Liquidators.

It was crucial that they avoid this latter outcome; otherwise, the dispatching algorithms would signal an emergency situation and request human intervention from the Liquidation Minister, namely Yoshiyuki Sekido. He would then be alerted to the absurdly large number of simultaneous bankruptcies and might call in off-duty Liquidators, recall dispatched Liquidators, request backup from GATA branches in other regions, or enact some other disruptive measure. The mission had been timed for when the Executive Council was in session so that his attention would be elsewhere, on the off chance he received direct notification of any strangeness involving the lures.

Clusters of lures were holed up throughout the city in crowded spaces like train cars, offices, and restaurants to hamper the Liquidators with civilians in the line of fire, or else in locked skyscrapers, tunnels, and basements that Rashana had bought and fortified against incursion. They carried no weapons, as armed bankrupts would be cause for the Liquidators to summon reinforcements. So posted around the lures was a second group under Ono X's command: the escorts.

These were mostly Atupians, and the rest Xenocyst exiles (who numbered in the thousands now that many of their compatriots separated during the exodus had been tracked down). What all escorts shared in common was bankdeath. Otherwise, such credicrimes as *impeding justice* might bankrupt them and draw the reserves. With three assigned to each lure so they would outnumber the Liquidator pairs by half, their objective was to keep the Liquidators at bay without disabling them. For if a lure was ever successfully cash-crashed, the two Liquidators would return to GATA Tower and threaten the infiltrators, whereas if a Liquidator was ever harmed, more would be dispatched.

The third group were the coordinators, bankliving operatives in each lure-plus-escort cell with a direct line of communication to Ono X. These were essential to link all groups remotely because the bankdead escorts had no ImmaNet connection, and the bankrupt lures, although connected, could not message other members lest their assigned Liquidators catch on through their partially unblinded profiles.

The final group, involved only marginally, were the obstacles. These random Free Citizens had either been told they were extras in a movie, interactive sculptures for an urban art installation, or beta players for a new ImmaGame, all taking place wherever the lures happened to be, their warm bodies occluding a clean shot of nerve dust.

Thanks to this elaborate strategy hashed out by the entire planning assembly over the previous few weeks, GATA was all but empty of human defenses. Since the Phoenix Virus had also opened a hole in the automated defenses, there was no need to storm GATA Tower with an army. Instead, a small group of infiltrators had been carefully selected for speed and discretion. Amon saw them all lined up in the hallway with him: the PhisherKing and his twelve disciples hooded in their black-green cloaks, Rashana and her ten Birla Guard minus Ono X sealed in their translucent gold armor, and Amon and Hippo each with a dozen of Atupio's choice operatives clothed in navy blue suits.

As each elevator arrived, the different units began to file in. First Rashana with the Birla Guard forming a square around her. Next Hippo and his Atupians. Into the third elevator Amon stepped, stopping at the back and turning around. Over the heads of his Atupians, he could see Monju and the Phishers still waiting. Just before the doors closed, a few straggling GATA staff tried to click the open door link and slip in, but Amon's Atupians shouldered them out and he clicked the close door icon, amused by their glares of appall until the doors slid together.

After Amon received the Phoenix Virus, he had gone on sharing mode with every member of their team, exchanging mutual access to their real time LifeStreams. Now, while the elevator ascended, he opened Rashana's perspective as a small box and dragged it over beside Ono X's at the bottom of his visual field. It displayed the backs of her Birla Guards standing close. Ono X was looking out a window on the alley from the same angle as before until Amon heard Ty shout, "Back off!" Then Ono's gaze flicked down as he leaned forward to peer over the window sill at the base of the wall. There Ty sat in a wheelchair before a door. A dozen Liquidators prowled cautiously towards him, their hand dusters drawn but the barrels pointing up and away. Behind Ty, Vertical and Book stood side by side with arms spread against the wall and their backs flat to the door. It was the only entrance not plugged with hermetic dust to an empty office building holding six bankrupt lures.

The combination of a woman, a senior, and a paraplegic was already a compelling hindrance to civilian-wary Liquidators. With the addition of one more member, it approached impassible; standing between the three of them was a child. Only as tall as Ty's wheelchair, he carried a tricycle on his back—Little Book.

10

As part of their efforts to round up Xenocyst exiles loyal to Hippo who had survived the civil war, Rashana had ordered a search for Little Book. But even with Atupio's entire reporting outfit mobilized for several weeks under Ono X's direction, they had had no luck until Tamper put forth an idea.

During one of their war room planning sessions, he hauled out a boombox he had built and said to Book, "Leave a message for LB." Book quickly grasped this cryptic suggestion, and together they programmed the boombox to endlessly play a series of clicks in Little Book's tap language. Translated, the looped recording went, "Little Book! Little Book! Come. Little Book!"

Ono X then instructed a group of Atupio career volunteers to shoulder it while walking around the District of Dreams, sweeping outwards from Delivery in ever larger circles. It was a traveling message unlikely to be intercepted but one that Little Book could be sure came from Book. Within five days, Little Book approached the search party and Rashana personally flew Book in aboard Gemini X to pick him up.

Back at Atupio, where Rashana was housing everyone in a barracks one floor above the Starter BioPen, the Xenocyst exiles were overjoyed to find Little Book unharmed, though to Tamper and Book's deep disappointment, he was not in possession of his tablet. The device Tamper had specially designed for the boy and that Book had made the repository for all the lore they had painstakingly collected was gone forever. Little Book's own feelings about this were difficult to gauge, as he never talked about his emotions and rarely showed them on his face, but his frequent handwringing suggested bereavement.

The following night, a brief festival was held in honor of Little Book and the other returned survivors. The two remaining storytellers recounted Amon's tale of how Little Book had saved his life by tracing a "T" in the air, which was already a Xenocyst-in-exile favorite, evolving closer with each telling to a legend. Their lone embyrsculpter and cinderworker whipped up vibrant ephemeral displays with embyrbrycks provided by Rashana for the occasion, and the Starters prepared a feast with ingredients harvested from the walls of the building, not to mention a mead-like drink that stood in for Ty's *suposhu* and a medley of organic psychedelics.

For his part, Little Book showed no interest in the celebrations. And when Tamper presented him with a new tablet, the boy immediately knelt on the plantfoam floor and began to write furiously, oblivious to everything—even the dance circle that formed around him. When Book finally succeeded in getting his attention as the festival was winding down, Little Book explained that he was recreating their old records from memory.

This psychographic trance continued for an entire week, interrupted only by bouts of occasional sleep at random hours, in which the boy could be found collapsed atop the tablet wherever he happened to be, pen strewn just beyond his limp hand. Despite this prodigious undertaking, most of the analog wisdom in the Cyst library would never be restored. The Books had only copied a small portion of the materials, many could be found nowhere else, and the stacks had been looted when all semblance of a council disbanded after Barrow's downfall (a tragedy they discovered when Rashana tried to barter a heap of supplies for them on Book's behalf). But astonishingly, when Book compared what Little Book had written to passages in the texts that Rashana was able to replace for them, much of it was verbatim. It only stood to reason that the same would be true of the many council hearings he had transcribed in person.

And while Little Book was able to salvage much of the valuable information in the items they had lost, he had also returned with a lost item that was itself of superlative value—to one of their members anyway: Ty's tricycle. According to the career volunteers who lugged the boombox, he had casually rolled up out of the slums on it. As to how the vehicle had ended up in his hands, Little Book declined to respond or react whoever asked, nor did he ever relate what he went through after the civil war began, even to Book. It reminded Amon of the equinox festival, when Little Book had deferred the telling of his name story to Book on account of his inability to remember. Previously, Amon had assumed that this mnemonic gap, at odds with his incredible memory for everything else, was due to the head trauma he had sustained. But Amon soon arrived at a new theory: it seemed more like selective deafness only to questions about his inner life. It was as if the boy eagerly absorbed the stories of others—whether personal, objective, or historical—because he lacked his own, serving as an empty conduit for human experience across time. Amon's conjecture was confirmed when he suggested it directly to Little Book himself, and the boy merely noted the idea on his tablet, as though it were a factum or incident bound up with Amon's narrative rather than something of profound relevance to his own.

Ty missed the festivities for his ongoing treatment in the barracks infirmary and did not immediately hear about the return of his treasure. While the Atupio doctors had repaired his vertebrae and spinal cord with the best medical technology money could procure, he still needed rehabilitation. The prognosis was gradual improvement of mobility but never full return of his agility. He had already graduated from diapers and could stir his legs when Amon accompanied the Books to his bed-side. Amon would never forget the look on his face when Little Book pedaled over.

In spite of the preliminary success of his regimen, Ty had continued to decry the pain of existence, demanding euthanasia from the nurses. Now he simply scowled with something like revulsion, as though this aberration of reality curdled him to the marrow. It was a while before he mustered a comment: "What the fuck?"

"LB continues to maintain silence with regards to how the object came under his ownership," Book explained. "Our supposition is that he utilized it to escape from the Cyst after Amon's altercation with Barrow began to intensify."

"She saved you too, huh?" Ty whispered, choking up with emotion. Amon knew that Ty was referring to the part in his name story, told the same night as Little Book's, when he had fled on this very tricycle from the scene of his parents' murder during the OpSci sacking of his bicycle nostie enclave. When Little Book dismounted beside the bed, Ty began to caress the frame, the scratched silver of its still paintless metal glimmering under the leafglow, his eyes ashimmer with both tears and wonder.

"We fell all that way . . . I landed on top . . . and she's still in one piece," he marveled between sobs. "Not even bent."

Watching Ty press the side of his face into his ever-dampening pillow, gripping the handlebars in one hand, and the fork in the other as his chest shook periodically, Amon was reminded of their arrival with Rick and Barrow at the trove of anadeto in the Tumbles, when Ty had displayed a similar sentimentality upon discovering the salvaged bike parts.

Tap tap, taptap . . . "This tricycle is yours to have again," Book interpreted.

This roused Ty from his breakdown and, with one sharp intake of breath, his crying came to an abrupt stop. Then he glanced back and forth between the boy and the tricycle, cheeks glistening, until he eventually shook his head. "Keep it," he decided.

Taptapa, tap, tap. "I could not—"

"No. I want you to have it. Just look at me. You think I have a use for that?" Ty peeled back the blanket to reveal shrunken legs atop white sheets. "I'll teach you how to throw the wheels if you want. Lemme know."

Ty gave Little Book a smile so complex it seemed to contain his whole life's experience.

From then on, Ty's complaints ceased, and although he never forgave Amon in words, he seemed to do so in attitude, gradually warming up to him. Upon Amon's request, Rashana had a bicycle workshop assembled for him in the same room as an electronics workshop she'd put together for Tamper, and Ty's first project was a replacement for his tricycle: a wheelchair. The fancy automated vehicle foisted on him by the doctors he had shunned on sight, preferring his own manual design. This was Ty's first time with a full set of tools and parts to employ the knowledge he had picked up as a child, and he cooped himself up in the workshop around the clock. With the help of Ferment Culture Collective engineers, he began to design personalized rides for the other exiles—track bikes and touring bikes with living microbiome batteries in the hubs that converted kinetic energy into chemical. Slowly but surely, he was becoming his gruff cackling old self, perhaps a bit gentler and more thoughtful.

Little Book often visited Ty's and Tamper's shared studio as he made his rounds asking for stories to record. When Tamper wasn't hunched over obsolete electronics, his miniscule robotic hand tinkering in synch with manipulations of his display glove, he could often be seen ruffling the boy's sandy hair with an affectionate but longing smile. He was also coptered regularly out of Atupio to deliver Cloud9 Nectar to his son, though he had refused Rashana's offer to purchase the boy from his foster parents, planning instead to pick him up after their mission. Although Tamper never articulated his reasons, Amon thought of his coded letter and guessed that he still didn't feel he deserved to be a father. Perhaps he was pursuing self-respect through his contributions to the change they would ring in, finding in the meantime a salve in Little Book, who looked to be around the same age.

None were more cheered by the return of Little Book, of course, than Book. He now had access to the Atupio library, far better stocked and preserved than anything in Xenocyst or the book nostie enclave of his youth, and Amon frequently spotted him in a corner of the mess hall poring over a heap of paper books delivered by drones, with Little Book taking notes by his side. Now that Little Book could tap out reminders again, Book also displayed his prior fluency at the planning sessions.

Upon witnessing the Books confer in taps during one lunch hour, the Phishers grew curious and were amazed to learn that Little Book had fabricated the language himself at such a tender age. Within minutes they picked up the basics of the code, not so different from the early cryptographic ciphers they had studied, and within days were having simple conversations with the boy. Suddenly, Little Book no longer needed Book to filter his every word and could communicate in the moment without lag. It was his first time participating directly in society through language, and Amon was surprised to observe that, sometimes after his taps, the Phishers would laugh. He was telling tap jokes! Amon even saw him chuckle once, an awkward sort of repeated hiccup but with genuine mirth in his eyes. The PhisherKing took a particular liking to him and said he would write a plugin for InterrPet to translate his taps into Japanese once the rush to finish the Phoenix Virus and other programs was over. Soon the Phishers could be seen slumped under their hoods around the Books in the mess hall, gesture-coding while Little Book scrawled away.

Now and then, the Books visited Amon in his plantfoam quarters to interview him about his past. Although Book seemed to have relayed Amon's story in the alcove, Little Book wanted Amon to flesh out key events, and to fill in small gaps from his first Xenocyst hearing, where Amon had blanked on details. His questions were so meticulous that even Book lost patience sometimes, rolling his differently magnified eyes and tap talking to question his mentee's intentions. When Amon found them trying, he would ask to be alone, though he respected the boy's indefatigable curiosity and humored him as much as he could bear.

Vertical, for her part, would have no truck with Little Book's seemingly insatiable predilection for inquiry. Of course, she'd been happy to see him safe and had danced until she was drenched in sweat at his return celebration, but ever since Amon had found private time to tell her Rick's final words, expressing love for her rather than Mayuko, she'd stayed aloof from everyone outside of the planning sessions, immersing herself instead in physical training. With the assistance of top notch fitness drones, military trainers, and sports nutritionists—better even than in her Olympic athlete days—she rotated through the whole gamut of machines, tracks, pools, and martial arts classes in regimented order, rising earlier and eating more than anyone. Rashana was so impressed by her discipline and prowess that she assigned her personal athleticorps to monitor Vertical's performance with the ambient living sensors that spawned in every inch of Atupio and convey through the trainer bespoke guidance catered to her physiology each minute. Soon, when Amon visited the gymnasium and watched her, or took discreet glances at her reflection in the mirrors that lined the walls, Vertical's body appeared more chiseled than he had ever seen. Other shifts he could sense in her personality, the prickly aura of bitterness she once wore now smoothed and soured into plain sorrow, an open soul-wound that surfaced in her eyes only when she thought no one was looking. It reminded Amon of the hidden tragedy in Rick's eyes, as though in grieving over his death, she had taken in a part of him.

Of all his friends living at Atupio, Hippo's attitude since the reappearance of Little Book was the most puzzling. He had climbed back to sanity with such ferocity and determination that there was momentum enough left over to lift the exiles from despair along with him. Over the first few weeks at Atupio, he seemed almost exuberant, bursting with laughter and chatting animatedly with just about everyone, as though making up for the days he had squandered by being doubly alive. Amon was reassured that he maintained his enthusiasm for the cause even after the meeting in person to win over Rashana, where he'd had the chance to view her naked face.

It was when Hippo's mood hardened not long after Little Book returned that Amon grew concerned. Suddenly, he seemed to withdraw into himself again. Not pathologically as with his total retreat into the corner of the alcove; his avid commitment to the preparations never abated. On the contrary, he demonstrated deadly seriousness about them in his vociferous assertions during team discussions and evening huddles with exile leaders such as Yané, Jiku, and Book. If anything, he was a little too serious. The laughter stopped and even his smiles grew scarce and perfunctory, his expression always formal, almost solemn, as though some unseen reaction unfolding inside him were turning his face to stone.

There were times in the war room when Amon would look away—perhaps from the biopixel display cube on which a strategy was being presented, perhaps from Ono X or Rashana giving a speech—and find Hippo watching him. Invariably, Hippo would avert his eyes as though he hadn't intended for Amon to notice. Soon, Amon grew curious and decided to take a seat beside him at one of the long coral tables in the mess hall the following dinner. But Hippo remained quiet and aloof, avoiding Amon's gaze and only pursing his lips in a pseudo-smile when the turn of the surrounding conversation required it.

This went on until one night Amon caught Hippo alone, as he was returning to his room for bed.

"Hey, Hippo," Amon called out, trotting along the plantfoam corridor towards him. "There's something I've been meaning to talk to you about."

"Oh?" said Hippo. Stopping in front of the straw-weave door to his room, he considered Amon warily. Along both the corridor's green, glowing walls, a flowing curtain of tiny blackbirds flitted between the mouths of countless forget-me-nots, casting intricate shadows and stirring up a light breeze.

"Was there something we didn't cover at the planning session?" Hippo asked.

"Not that I can think of, no. I was just wondering how you've been doing."

"Fine, Amon. It's embarrassing to think of who I had become when you found me."

"There's no need to be embarrassed. We're just glad to have you back on your feet."

"I'm feeling a million times better than I was. I really am."

Hippo gave a cursory nod, turned to the door, and reached for the genereader as if to enter his room until Amon said, "Good," drawing his arm to a stop in the air. "Because it seemed to me like you were doing really well when we first got here. But for the past little while I get the sense that maybe there's something on your mind."

Still facing the door, Hippo frowned as though put out in some way. "Nothing worth mentioning," he said.

Amon waited, giving him a chance to elaborate. In the awkward pause that followed, the blackbirds fluttered and warbled, their wingbeats off rhythm and their notes out of tune with the lulling jungle orchestra of the building.

Hippo glanced upward, thinking, and said, "Well, I suppose I have been feeling a touch nostalgic now that the two Books are with me. We were the permanent observers to the council. Being with them reminds me sometimes of everything that we've lost."

"I understand. Nothing will ever replace Xenocyst."

"Forget replacing Xenocyst," Hippo said with surprising stridency as he whirled to face Amon, gritted front teeth showing between twisted lips, eyes crazed with anger. "Xenocyst has been dead for decades. Ever since those scoundrels sued my foundation to nothing. The truth about the fertility gap is proof!"

Amon felt Hippo's spittle on his face and took a step back, but Hippo closed the distance as he spoke.

"The multiply-thy-seed in every breath we took made us human resource factories—and ignorant cowards that we were, we went along with it! We let them cancel our plutogenic education program. That was the death blow to the community. All these years I couldn't admit it to myself. Not until they used Barrow to suck the corpse dry. But we won't let anyone manipulate us again. We're going to topple the ones who did this to us, who did this to the world! Do you understand? Then we'll build something new, something better, where they can't touch us. That's all that matters now."

For emphasis, Hippo shook his trembling fists in front of him, so close to Amon's chest they almost struck. When he was done, Amon was speechless, stunned by his zeal. He had recounted Rashana's explanation of the fertility gap to Hippo in the mess hall shortly after the exiles settled at Atupio, thinking the solution to his long-ago research would be of scientific interest, never expecting that the knowledge would so viscerally disturb him.

"Good night, Amon." Hippo turned abruptly to the door, and inserted his finger into the genereader. This time Amon let him go, watching him slip into the dark room until the separated strands of the straw door twined themselves back together.

Amon decided that it wasn't his place to pry any further. Hippo was obviously going through some new phase of his struggles. But so long as he kept up his fierce commitment, Amon was willing to set aside such private matters of the heart. Instead, he treated him solely as a partner in their undertaking as Hippo seemed to prefer and found him more than up to the challenge.

11

In the seconds remaining until his elevator reached its floor, Amon looked through Ono X's perspective at Vertical, Book, Ty, and Little Book blocking the door. All four wore black windbreakers bearing a white stencil of the girl-in-popping-bubble emblem, newly printed for the Xenocyst exiles by a vending machine Rashana had installed in Atupio.

Between the perspectives of Ono X and Rashana, Amon flicked open and slotted four more boxes: feeds from cameras mounted on the backrest of Ty's wheelchair, the handlebars of Little Book's tricycle, a clip on Vertical's ear, and a rig on Tamper's head. Initially, Tamper had assembled a single camera so that he could transmit to his son and stay in contact with him whatever might happen that day. But Hippo had urged him to build similar models for others, and one of the Phishers had whipped together a hack app for the BodyBank to render their electromagnetic output as picked up by city sensors into compatible signal. This allowed a select group of bankdead exiles to share audio and video with the phoenixes, and to receive audio from them, though not to view their LifeStreams or the ersatz-veridical phantasmagoria of the ImmaNet, which required more sophisticated display-tech and Ministry of Access authentication.

Tamper's camera currently displayed the dark empty floor of an office building, in which he lurked alongside Ono X and nearly twenty exiles. The other three cameras were trained on the alley, where Liquidators berated the passive resistors for being in the way.

When the height of Little Book's feed dropped as he took the tricycle off his back and got on, Amon recalled the concern Rashana and a Ferment Culture Collective spokesperson had expressed about allowing a child on the mission. Amon had sided with the exiles, who struggled to grasp what was at issue. While babies certainly needed to be protected like the helpless treasures they were, once a person could stand on two feet and feed themselves, what was to be gained by hiding them from danger, an inescapable feature of life itself?

Given such divergence in the opinions and values of the nearly one hundred collaborators in attendance at the planning sessions, it had taken the diplomatic feats of their four most essential members—Rashana, Monju, Hippo, and Amon—to stem divisiveness and keep their ragtag team working towards the same goal.

Some were easy enough to manage. The Phishers allowed their mentor to speak on their behalf, and the Birla Guard likewise deferred to Rashana, all remaining silent except when she got tired and Ono X filled in for her with one of his performances.

While the Starters, Ferment Culture members, and other Atupians, by contrast, were vocal and confrontational, they dropped their arguments the moment Rashana even hinted at disagreement. Whenever she spoke, they gave her their full attention and by the end were invariably convinced. Amon had observed a similar show of reverence on his jaunts to the BioPen, after the genome locks were reprogrammed to allow them passage throughout the complex. Residents could sometimes be seen gathered around a genepixel display in the dark plantfoam theatre, riveted by video streams of Rashana talking off-the-cuff on some topic. It turned out that she had almost never visited the Atupio underground in person until the PhisherKing plugged her security holes, having Ono X manage the BioPen in her stead. This distance, Amon noticed, seemed to have shrouded her in mystery for the Atupians, transfiguring her into a sort of savior, the great mother who had rescued their paradise from the brink.

The respect the exiles paid Hippo was trifling by comparison, but it was enough for him to reign in the volatility, digressiveness, and confusion that would have otherwise held sway. With the Books once more at his sides, he went beyond council advisor, eschewing his former restraint, and assumed the role of a full-blown leader, showing no patience for quibbling given the urgency of their preparations. Yané fell in line, his fearmongering criticisms crumbling against Hippo's bulldozer rebuttals, while Jiku shrunk to her role as his assistant in the face of his authority. If his animation after his arrival at Atupio was a stark change from the apathetic slug he had been only recently, his almost ruthless drive here represented a veritable metamorphosis.

Amon's job throughout, as the one who brought everyone together, had been to mediate in all directions. This mostly involved translating between the bankliving and bankdead dialects and modes of thought, as Hippo and then Barrow had once hoped he would. With his help, the exiles were able to gradually bond with the Starters, who understood what it meant to inhabit the naked world. But they could never quite bridge the cognitive and cultural gulf that separated them from the Phishers and Atupians, who did not.

Still, in spite of innumerable challenges, the exile's spirits were much higher than when Amon had found them. In place of the pointless cycle of exertion that was all they had ever known, they had been sucked into a whirlwind of training and study the moment they set foot in Atupio. The transition was something like the reverse of what Amon and other crashnewbs experienced upon entering the District of Dreams, an abrupt leap from the starvation line to a life of modest necessities—for them, luxuries. The shared dorms with individual futons instead of the spongy floors of private disposcraper rooms. The building-grown food that all found unpalatably plain compared to the meal-replacement-ink-printed vending fare but soon grew to love for its nutrition. The minimalistic hemp uniforms that to their astonishment had no expiration date but to their dismay had to be washed rather than simply dissolving. Access to in-house medics and dentists and therapists. The reunion with so many of their brethren had heartened them further, and as the mission approached their excitement rose to a pitch of optimistic fervor. Most of all, they were inspired by Rashana's passionate speeches about the new reality they would ferment, in which she reminded them that Hakkotopia 1.0 had been the inspiration for the home they had lost, and the first iteration of a new home that would soon be theirs. For she had agreed to take everyone along, casting aside her painstakingly crafted plan to send only the Starters, for the sake of the dream that united them all.

In the alley below the office building window where Ono X and Tamper hunkered, Ty, Vertical, and the Books steadfastly declined to move from the door, meeting the threats and wheedling of the Liquidators with an incongruous combination of polite refusal and ribald expletives. Catching just a glimpse of this dangerous charade from the GATA elevator, Amon was of two minds; glad to see the lives of the exiles in the service of a higher purpose once more and yet perplexed somehow to think of them out there while Hippo was inside with him. It was Hippo himself who had insisted on joining the infiltrators and on having two dozen exiles escort Ono X, on the grounds that their field commander needed the protection of financially-unhindered bankdead, but something about this arrangement had never sat—

Amon's flare of thoughts winked out as the doors opened beyond the tight bunch of Atupians in front of him. His elevator had been the first to stop, followed immediately by the elevators of Hippo and then Monju, while Rashana's continued for another split second to a higher floor. He watched her door begin to open as his Atupian operatives poured out just ahead of Monju's and Hippo's onto the 49th floor, the House of Blinding.

The ease with which they had entered notwithstanding, Amon knew that the GATA Tower security system was nothing to laugh at. As a Liquidator, he had participated in emergency drills that demonstrated the preparedness of its armed personnel and had attended lectures on its formidable automated weaponry and drones. If he and his crew had been bankliving, bankdead, or robotic—that is anyone or anything not infected with the Phoenix Virus—they would never have made it through the front door. But that was the whole problem: all contingencies covered by protocol presupposed that intruders would fit into one of these three categories or that Liquidators would respond in case of error. These did not strike Amon as unreasonable assumptions. For what sort of threats fell outside these categories? And in what scenario would *all* Liquidators be absent from the building? No hazardcorps could have been expected to foresee that a failure to reset codes used to add and erase user iden- tities under the highly unlikely event of both ID suicide and euthanasia could—through the even more unlikely cooperation of the two bearers of those codes, the architect of the cryptographic network, and a wealthy patron—enable such a breach.

Or perhaps in another era even these chinks would have been identi- fied and patched, but in this age of Pax Economica no one expected an attack on any of the GATA Towers. All activity resembling terrorism or rebellion had been subdued and relegated to an innocuous low-boil in the bankdeath camps, state armies no longer existed, and the only orga- nizations with the resources to threaten GATA were the MegaGloms, in whose mutual interest it was to keep it running. Far more advantageous for the propertied class was to use lobbies and manipulate GATA as a proxy for violence than to tempt an InterGlom War, what with the latent threat of an akrasiapocalypse, Inflation Singularity, or who knew what else. So considering the status quo, it was a wonder that GATA's defenses had been updated and kept as sophisticated as they were.

This inevitable complacency explained the gobsmacked expressions on the faces of the few Blinders who noticed over three dozen armed men and women burst into the room.

Although Amon had worked in the building for years, he had never visited the House of Blinding, into which, as a semi-independent arm of GATA, other personnel were forbidden from entering on penalty of bankdeath. Nevertheless, he had heard from his old colleagues and superiors that it looked pretty much like the Liquidation and other ministries. Indeed, stretching before him was a huge rectangular room with ImmaNet wallpaper, just then playing an enormous waterfall of droplets bearing the reflection of smiling kittens and puppies. Advancing from the elevator, he could see intermittent clusters of vending machines along the right and left walls, and perpendicular to these hundreds of ergonomic chairs arrayed in rows to the far end. Filling the seats with their backs turned were Blinders, hands twitching as they engaged in their work. Their outfits were much like the standard uniforms, but for one difference that Amon spotted on the handful standing in the aisles, perhaps to use the toilet or get a drink: the absence of "GATA" written on the breast of the jacket. Before these alerted Blinders could react, he, Hippo, their Atupians, and the Phishers fired in tandem, and within a split second they had toppled insensate to the floor.

Equipping all parties to the Phoenix Revolution with sleeping beauty dusters had been a compromise at one of the planning sessions. After the idea of carrying handheld dustbombs was dismissed, due to the danger of stray nanobots tripping security, the Birla Guard had proposed that everyone suit up with their standard blitz dusters, loaded with a versatile combo. But Hippo had insisted on a bloodless revolution, rejecting any weapon that caused harm comparable to the so-called non- and semi- lethal dust deployed by freekeepers and CareBots. Amon and Vertical agreed after what had happened to Rick, and Amon firmly opposed all varieties as humiliating or excruciating as nerve dust. When Ono X threw out Hippo's suggestion of pixie dust, on the grounds that its somnolence was unreliable and short-lived, Rashana had made the pitch that everyone finally agreed on. Beautying caused no pain or permanent damage, and at medium intensity would disable their targets for a full day, much longer than the few minutes needed to complete their operations.

Even before the last of the gawkers in the House of Blinding had flopped into nano-induced comas, the infiltrators were marching along the walls, marked by stones set in pools of water. Copying and redesigning animal imagery from the wallpaper, they appeared as furry humanoid beasts shimmering on the encompassing waterfall. Hardly a flawless digiguise with the depth of field and graphical blend slightly off, but convincing enough to forestall alarm at the sight of unknown visitors. As Amon entered the leftmost aisle, he joined their combined force in opening up on the Blinders. With marksmanship assisted by apps and previously honed through simulations, they started with the row near the elevators and worked their way to the far end. A wave of heads lolling to the side—while brown-suited backs remained upright, arms still extended in their rests—spread methodically through the room within seconds.

When Amon had stepped over a body and approached the midway point of the aisle, the stillness they had wrought on the House of Blinding was in vivid contrast to the flurry of motion in his six vid-windows below. Without breaking stride, he flicked his gaze downwards, settling first on Rashana's.

Looking out from a sort of stage at the front of a capacious room, her perspective was oriented over a line of ten golden heads towards rows of ergonomic chairs that rose in an auditorium-style semicircle—the Executive Congress. The Birla Guard, submachine dusters ticking from target to target, were beautying the assembly of elected lobby representatives. With no technical task to distract the Executive Council like the Blinders, they could not miss the undigiguised trespassers right in front of them. Several had enough time to leap from their seats, shout, begin to twitch out a message, but no more than that, as the immaculately trained guards dusted them with assembly-line speed. And before Amon knew it, the stands were a tableau of drooping and sprawling.

Rashana glanced down at the bottom row, nearest the stage, where the Full Choice cabinet sat. All the ministers were propped up stably, denied the chance to even budge from their seats as the Birla Guard's first targets. Her gaze passed indifferently over them, but Amon stopped the feed in a surge of curiosity to cut out a still and close-up on one man—Yoshiyuki Sekido, Minister of Liquidation in the newly formed cabinet—now digimade with a white nymphic face and bald shiny head. Seeing him limp in his seat like the rest, tongue poking ever so slightly from between his lips, Amon felt a peculiar mix of emotions. Anger at his betrayal to be sure, but also an odd kind of sadness at being let down by an admittedly eccentric mentor and disappointment at the pathetic end his good intentions had now finally led him to.

When Amon resumed the feed, one guard peeled from each side of Rashana's protective box, stepped off the stage to the bottom row of seats, and lifted a man three spots to the right of Sekido. The view turned to the man's face, young for a politician. In his early thirties perhaps, digimade highlights in his black chin-length hair added luster to his smooth skin. This was the son of an LVR executive who was a member of the Gyges Circle, on the verge of assuming his post as Secretary of Blinding.

The Phoenix Revolution had been scheduled to coincide with the official appointment of the Secretary of Blinding by the Executive Council. It could not be a day later or the Secretary would run the program designed by the Gyges Circle and they would already have the Ring of Gyges. It could not be a day earlier because this was the first convention of the Executive Council since the formation of the Full Choice majority government, and they needed the Secretary of Blinding present for what they had planned next.

The two guards hooked the man under each armpit with their forearms and dragged him scarecrow-like to an exit on the right margin of the seating. As Rashana began to march out after them at the center of her box, she voice messaged to all, "Executive Council finished."

This was the signal to Ono X to contact coordinators in each cell across Tokyo. The escorts had fulfilled their duty of delaying liquidation of the lures, and everyone would now shift to the next stage: the assault.

With the cabinet comatose, word of strange happenings reaching GATA could no longer trigger a human decision and thus posed little danger. Technically, command over the Liquidators had shifted to the highest-ranking Identity Executioner, but the council had been given no chance to inform her, and she was, moreover, only trained to handle interim bureaucratic duties in case of absent minister, not to lead in the field during a total collapse of leadership. As protocol forbade the Liquidators from aborting without permission from ministry algorithms or else human override, they were stuck pursuing their targets. So, taking advantage of this institutional disarray, it was now the job of the escorts, lures, and coordinators to beauty their assigned pair before they clued in or tried to organize a retreat to GATA Tower. And Amon watched Ono X and Tamper swing the barrels of their dusters over the window sill towards the Liquidators in the alley while other barrels rose into view—Ty's wheels spinning towards them on wires, Little Book and

Book retreating through the door, Vertical a charging blur —before he switched back to his own perspective.

As Amon reached the end of the House of Binding opposite the elevators and stepped in front of the final row of Blinders, Ono X voiced, "Engaging with Liquidators. Twenty-eight Atupians down." Hearing this, Amon was reminded that Ono X and Rashana were apart and suddenly the fact of their separation jarred him, even more so than with Hippo and his exiles. While Amon understood the logic pushed by both Hippo and Ono X himself behind having a highly capable bankliving member oversee their diverse and scattered team outside, it surprised him that he would forego the option of receiving the Phoenix Virus and serving as an infiltrator. That Ono X would be by Rashana's side every step of the way, protecting her and lending his many skills to the most crucial theatre of their operation, had always seemed too obvious to even mention. Amon had taken it for granted since their earliest strategies began to take shape, and didn't doubt now that the two of them wanted more than anyone to be together on this momentous day. Not simply because Ono X was Rashana's indispensable servant. An event that Amon could still hardly believe had drawn them even closer the night before.

Amon was fairly certain that no one else knew. He had only witnessed the exchange thanks to being on glass mode with Rashana, a privilege she had granted him after he received his training bank to further the relationship of openness she had promised. It was while he was reviewing her daily LifeStream summary before bed (as Rashana likewise did with his to avoid the hassle of reporting to each other) that Amon happened to come across the scene.

There had been Ono X on his knees in Rashana's bedchamber. Holding her hands in his, he said, "I want to grow old with you."

She had stared blankly at him for several blinks before his words seemed to register. Then she sat back, almost swooning, onto the edge of her bed.

"I still haven't got a token of our engagement. Can you wait till it's all over?"

Ono X spoke in his soft voice. But in place of the usual look of subdued amusement when playing himself, he wore an expression of such raw vulnerability that Amon got a lump in his throat just watching. His usually elusive eyes gazed directly into hers with devotion and fear, as though waiting for her words to decide whether the tears dribbling slowly down his cheeks signified joy or sorrow, his whole being tottering between ecstasy and despair.

Amon briefly paused the seg and restarted it as though that would reset a glitch in life. Then he began to feel like he finally understood Ono X. The thread of his desires had been difficult to pick out from all his dedicated service and acting.

Amon only wished he could have accessed Ono X's feed and seen the look on Rashana's face when she said yes. Although he never would have expected her to consider marrying one of her underlings, perhaps Ono X was the most likely candidate, having been her closest confidante and friend since childhood.

While battle opened up outside, Amon stepped behind one of the Blinders and gripped the fabric under her armpits while one of his men crouched in front to take her pant hems. Then they lifted her out of her chair and put her down along the stones marking the wall. The Atupians were dragging other Blinders onto the floor in the same way. Soon fourteen were laid out along the end of the room leaving as many empty seats. In the row behind these, the Phishers had turned thirteen Blinders around in their chairs so that they faced the elevators. Once the Atupians had rotated the empty chairs in the same direction, the PhisherKing and his twelve Phishers each took a seat and rested one of their hands on the necks above brown suit shoulders in front of them, making direct contact to enable flesh-hacking.

Now the Atupians positioned themselves around the room—kneeling and aiming at the elevators—as a standard precaution. Both of the two dozen operatives Amon and Hippo separately commanded, Hippo had insisted on selecting himself from among the Atupians he had gotten to know personally. Noting their efficient movements, Amon thought he had chosen well.

In Rashana's vidbox, Amon spotted doors opening in front of her and flicked his gaze down to expand her perspective. Her elevator had just stopped at the Ministry of Liquidation. Without getting out, the Birla Guard began to open fire. One second, the five reserve Liquidator pairs were huddling in conference near the center of the chair-lined room, perhaps having finally noticed that it had cleared out (as their seated comrades were usually rendered invisible). The next second, they were thudding like sacks of grey-clothed meat onto the floor. After a pause to ensure they were all inert, Rashana tapped the close door icon and glanced down. There the Secretary of Blinding lay prone between the crowding legs of her guards.

Amon toggled through the feeds of Ty, Vertical, Little Book, Tamper, and Ono X, and found them all together in the restaurant-stacked alley, picking their way past fallen grey suits towards a busy thoroughfare. Then he returned to his own perspective and took a few steps away from the end of the room so he could watch the faces of the seated green cloaks. With their palms on the nape of the Blinders' necks, they twitched and mumbled, much as those very Blinders had not a minute earlier, but with much greater urgency. The PhisherKing sat closest to the center, and beside the brown suited body he was linked through, stood one empty chair, awaiting the Secretary of Blinding.

12

GATA Tower itself was a supercomputer, most of its material contributing processing power. Since the networks for each GATA ministry and institution could only be accessed by someone corporeally present, the Phishers had to be inside the House of Blinding to do their work. But even then, they still needed authorization to enter the network; hence the flesh-hacked Blinders.

The Phishers had each broken into the BodyBank of a Blinder and infected them with a pre-designed virus that swapped their identity signatures. The Blinders' action-data—basically just *breathing* and *heartbeating* slowed to a comatose crawl—was reported to the Ministry of Monitoring under the rapidly shifting signatures of the Phoenix-Virus-infected Phishers, while the action-data of the Phishers was transmitted under the signatures of the Blinders via their BodyBanks. This tricked the House of Blinding network into recognizing the Phishers' gesture-commands as originating from authorized accounts and granting their requests to log in. All actions associated with such cyber-possession were of course exorbitant credicrimes only affordable for these financial phoenixes.

Opening the PhisherKing's perspective, Amon saw a maelstrom of alphanumerics, strange symbols, 3D figures, and images that he was manipulating at mind-boggling speed. Information too technical for him to fully understand, but he knew enough to tell that spoofed access had been seized.

When Amon again viewed the room, he looked out over the field of still seated bodies, like some theatre of communal dreaming, and spotted one pair of doors at the other end slide apart, revealing Rashana and her guards in their elevator. Two began to haul out the comatose Secretary of Blinding by armpits and ankles, and Amon felt an orange electric thrill tingle over his skin. All their efforts were coming together at last!

Once the Secretary was in the empty chair, the PhisherKing would possess him just like the other Blinders. Except in this case, he would obtain the executive clearance needed to not merely enter the system but to alter it and run the other program that he and the Blinders had been tirelessly writing for weeks.

This program relied upon the fact that certain patterns of movement were physically impossible—raising the left arm while lowering it, sprinting while sitting in lotus position, and so on. It would distort all incoming action-data so that they always fell under the category of such combinations. When forwarded to the Ministry of Monitoring, this would either produce an error or fail to match any existing action-property, meaning in either case no application of a fee or fine. Since the identity signature of all affected actors would be undistorted, they would continue to be recognized by the Ministry of Access and maintain their connection to the ImmaNet but would never be charged for any of their actions. Essentially, this was a permutation of the Ring of Gyges, Amon's inspiration for this part of the plan. But instead of being reserved for only a limited set of identity signatures, for a select few, it would be applied to all identity signatures under GATA Tokyo's jurisdiction, that is all Free Citizens in Japan.

This amounted to the end of bankruptcy and therefore the end of liquidation within the territory. It amounted also to the end of bankdeath for Free Citizens. Unfortunately, it did not immediately amount to the end of bankdeath for the already bankdead. But the program opened up even this possibility because in annulling all charges, it removed the usual bankdeath penalty for unauthorized genome registration and ID forgery. This allowed for registration of bankdead genomes of any age, not merely infants, and their connection to the ImmaNet using Hippo's Birth Codes if they were first given either a BodyBank or a training bank. To this end, Rashana had already dispatched career volunteers trained by retired Identity Vitalators into the District of Dreams with self-assembling portable clinics and the surgery dusters required to implant BodyBanks. She had also stockpiled millions of training banks to enable their wide distribution.

As Operation Reconnect would require ongoing funding, Rashana had entrusted management of all her assets, her 49 percent Fertilex share, to Ono X, just before the Phoenix Virus kicked in. Since Anisha, meanwhile, had been given no warning, she had been denied the opportunity to pass off her portion of the inheritance, and her rights to it had simply been invalidated with the erasure of the shared identity signature. But Anisha had not gone bankrupt, so she would never be liquidated and her property would never be auctioned off by GATA. The upshot was that the remaining 51 percent had slipped into ownership limbo and that Ono X now had de facto control of Fertilex, because no entity had enough share to override his decisions.

Rashana had vested this authority in him, however, only under the conditions of a contract with specific procedures for how to transform the MegaGlom. Instantly it would be broken into a multitude of subsidiaries dedicated to connecting bankdead. All personnel would be reassigned to this task, from office jockeys to engineers to guards, slipping into the District of Dreams to provide access for everyone they could as quickly and surreptitiously as possible.

And yet, it was not primarily for the sake of realizing universal access that Rashana was breaking Fertilex apart. The MegaGlom's demise was also essential to prevent an InterGlom War, the most likely outcome of their Phoenix Revolution according to her prognosticorps. This forecast was arrived at through a series of meta-inferences about how the tacticorps of the Twelve and One would react. Although the outputs of their strategic algorithms were difficult to predict because the code for each was a trade secret, since all were trained up using historical data and the crisis was unprecedented, the hypothesis that they would be stumped was assigned the highest probability. By default, this would leave human agents of their tacticorps in charge, but they were unlikely to display deliberative boldness or imagination after five decades of Pax Economica. Given that any choice at such a turning point could beckon a major loss of company profit, executives would pass off responsibility, letting it cascade down the chain of command until it was inevitably picked up by independent groups such as shareholder meetings and expert panels, where no individual would be blamed if anything went wrong. But these would struggle to reach consensus for similar reasons, leading to cycles of potentially infinite decision postponement.

Nevertheless, even under these uncertain conditions, the Twelve and One were bound to settle quickly on the order to attack if the entity putatively behind GATA's disruption could be identified. According to the preferred simulation of Rashana's prognosticorps, the perpetrator selected by the SpawnU Consortium would be the Philanthropy Syndicate. Because even if SpawnU was oblivious to the magnitude of the Gyges Circle's plan, they were already alert to their machinations within GATA since Barrow's assassination. So if the GATA system were suddenly, radically altered through an operation that obviously required MegaGlom level funding, there was no question who they would pin it on, however convincingly the Syndicate might deny it. But if Rashana could leave a trail of evidence showing Fertilex's involvement, then they would instead point fingers at a vanishing target, nailing the culprit only after it was gone.

In other words, letting Fertilex crumble was a high stakes gambit that took the kind of farsighted gumption only someone like Rashana possessed. The world's largest MegaGlom would go out in a blaze of compassion for the poor, and serve as a vivid reminder that a corporation, any social organization or cooperative venture for that matter, no matter how real and powerful it appeared, was merely a pattern of human action, dissolving like a swirl of plastic in the dying wind once the actors changed their behavior.

Of course, even with this enormous diversion of labor and resources to the cause, Amon and the others did not believe that their efforts to realize universal access would be entirely successful in the short term. The process of (re)connecting the bankdead and restoring their economic and informational rights was inevitably going to be messy. The Ministry of Access might initiate stopgap measures to cut off newly registered genomes or identity signatures, while the Twelve and One would surely stamp out the fledgling humanitarian groups that sprung up in Fertilex's place before their objectives were fulfilled.

Then again, it was unclear whether GATA and the MegaGloms would be capable of interfering in this way. For once actions no longer reaped income, all action properties with any connection to Japan would instantly lose their value, causing untold asset depreciation and legal complications worldwide. With Fertilex gone and its patents on life in a state of indeterminate ownership, SpawnU would be denied its supply of human resources, forcing a renegotiation of the global power balance . . .

In short, no one—human or machine—could say what exactly might happen next. The hope of the revolutionaries was that once the bankdead had a taste of access and Free Citizens a taste of life untrammeled by incessant costs, their demands to keep these liberties would be difficult to suppress. The bronze, silver, gold, and platinum hierarchy of knowledge would disintegrate and many would see the market for what it was. Both the denigrating depiction of the bankdead amongst the bankliving, and the deified perception of the bankliving amongst the bankdead would break down once all had the same privileges. This rupture in the distinction between Free Citizen and non-citizen would be irreparable. Meanwhile, Amon, Rashana, Hippo, Monju, and the rest would be building Hakkotopia 2.0 to serve as a refuge and a new way forward. Although the end of action pricing also meant giving up the financial shield around the islands, the community would retain its other protections and would be prepared to open up for anyone eager to cooperate.

However it all played out, of one thing they could be certain: the jubilee would come to pass in its original meaning; the jubilee year spoken of in the Old Testament would arrive. For with the AT Market dead and gone forever after forty-nine years since the Free Era began, all debts would be forgiven, all would be emancipated, and all would be allowed to search for that mysterious gift called home.

13

The Phishers were now inside the system, gesturing spasmodically as they began to reconfigure it to accept the program. While the two Birla Guards lugged their unconscious captive along one of the center aisles towards where Amon stood at the far end, he thought of the final step that would bring the jubilee to fruition.

Before logging out, Monju would use the Secretary of Blinding's executive clearance to alter the format for identity signatures that could gain access authorization, requiring them to be astronomically long and contain parts of a LifeStream. He would then register a randomly generated string of symbols and segs that matched this format and deny authorization to all currently permitted signatures. This was like changing a lock so that it opened for a lost key with a shape too intricate to be guessed. Not even the best cryptobreakers in the world could get in to reverse the changes, assuming anyone realized what had been done.

As the two Birla Guards neared the midway point, the remaining eight stationed themselves around the room, submachine dusters cradled ready, to complement the positioning of the Atupians. Left temporarily with nothing to do, Amon found himself walking nervously towards the approaching pair of guards, as if his presence might somehow hurry them along. Success was only minutes away, and he felt a rush of such intense anticipation that his diaphragm burned and he thought he might throw up.

The moment bankruptcy was eliminated, Amon and the other phoenixes would hurry to the rooftop landing pads of nearby buildings, owned by what remained of Fertilex, to gather with Ono X, the exiles, and the Atupian cells across Tokyo. Together, they would board carbonjets and rotorcraft. Some like Hippo would embark for the District of Dreams to assist with Operation Reconnect before heading to Ogasawara. The rest would fly directly to Hahajima, where thousands of Starters and their guardians currently stationed at home office would already be waiting on the island. Later that day, Amon would set foot there at last, in the forest . . .

Over the weeks leading up to this moment, it had become clear to him that each of the collaborators had joined the Phoenix Revolution he had conceived for their own reasons. Hippo and crashborn like Ty and the Books wanted to end the plutogenic industry that had strangled their way of life and find somewhere to start over. Crashdead like Tamper and Vertical wanted to tear down the digital divide that kept them from their loved ones, while Vertical in particular wanted to redress what had been done to Rick. The Phishers sought to demolish the financial barriers damming the flow of information and limiting the Treasure Matrix they worshipped. Rashana was stopping her sister from realizing the wrong interpretation of the parable of Gyges and priming the world for what she saw as the right one. Ono X served her out of love and the Starters yearned to found the society that Ferment Culture had raised them for out of their own faith and inspiration. Or at least, this is what Amon thought each of them was after. For his part, Amon was hoping to close the gap between bank- life and death that he had worked for years as a Liquidator to sustain. With their wishes overlapping and reinforcing each other so fortuitously, it was as though the diamond dream were taking solid form before their very eyes.

And yet, as excited as Amon was about the new existence they were on the verge of fermenting, he could not give himself up to the vision completely. One worry held him back, and he twitched out an anxious text.

We're changing everything. It's going to get better from here on. Please reply. I want to share it with you.

Although Little Book and so many others had been found, and in spite of ongoing search efforts in both the District of Dreams and the Free World, with all the resources of Rashana, the intelligence network of Ono X, and the information-plundering of the Phishers, still no clues as to the whereabouts of Mayuko had turned up. In his desperation, Amon had personally visited her old apartment, inhabited now by an elderly couple. Had called up Capsize Solutions to inquire with her co-workers. Had pored over every seg in Rashana's LifeStream that a hired siftcorps marked as vaguely relevant. Had gone back to Eroyuki and the weekly mansion, as if Mayuko would torture herself by returning to either. Had roamed the metropolis on foot, turning on naked view whenever he spotted a woman with a similar build and gait. Had input her name again and again into platinum search engines, "Mayuko Takamatsu", "Mayuko Takamatsu." Had sipped her drink of choice, awamori on the rocks, as if it were a potion with occult powers to convey him to her. Had even traipsed in afternoon reverie through the hazy warrens of childhood recollection, conjuring his earliest memory, when they had hung together on the fence at the edge of the Green Ladybug rooftop and gazed at that daytime star, only to watch her melt into murky shadow, as though her absence in the present were erasing her from his past.

Indulging in the luxury of this futile search often distracted Amon from their preparations, and he felt lucky to have such dedicated collaborators to pick up the slack. He knew how irresponsible it was to divert even one scintilla of his energy from an endeavor of such historic importance. But his need to know that she was safe only grew more rabid and desolate by the day. For the world was about to be irrevocably transformed and something told him, something shrieked at him, that he would never find her after.

So long as everything to do with her was still uncertain, going to the forest would mean fulfilling his promise to Rashana but breaking his promise to Mayuko, his once and former aspiration now become an obligation. As if to close the gap between the path he was on and the betrayal it led to, he sometimes imagined her taking part in their project, the ideas she might have raised at their sessions. Her greatest contribution, he realized one sleepless night in his quarters, would be after the community was established, when she could use her abundant experience rebranding bankrupt companies to promote the new Hakkotopia. There Mayuko was, running on the beach, with Vertical coaching her, the two women overcoming any jealousy over Rick in their shared grief. Ty, Tamper, Hippo, Rashana, Ono X, Monju, Ferment Culture, the Starters, the Birla Guard, the Phishers—all the islanders embracing her in the same way. No doubt. If only Amon could inspire in her the same degree of passion for the undertaking, if only he could find her . . . but always the cold granite thump of plausibility would intrude on this yearning fantasy and she would dissolve mist-like beneath the leaves of the forest and blow out into the offing, vanishing from his future too.

Amon flicked his woeful gaze from his latest unread text, waved away the message history, and realized that he had traveled nearly halfway across the room. His eyes paused on the seats front and center in one of the rows, corresponding to those he and Rick had once filled in the Liquidation Ministry, and he remembered another friend with whom he could not share this moment. The pair of Birla Guard had carried the Secretary of Blinding past the midpoint and would soon reach Amon's position in his parallel aisle. The whole room now focused on the closing distance between them and the Phishers. Watching their approach with varicolored eyes, the PhisherKing had drawn still, poised to cap off the revolution with some final spurts of coding, when Hippo voiced, "Amon, Phishers, Atupians, get down! Take cover!"

Amon darted his eyes around frantically but could find Hippo nowhere. A racket of dust fire erupted outside. He hurled his perspective through the wall as dronehoses mounted on GATA Tower—*chunk chunk chunk chunk*—sprayed spiky blurs buoyed by rotors at an incoming . . . the hurtling object was indescribable, incomprehensible. It sapped Amon's intelligence just by being there. He retained just enough sense to snap back into his body and hit the deck before one of the side walls exploded.

6
THE HOUSE OF BLINDING

1

After the blast, a piece of Amon's consciousness went missing forever, frames torn from the film reel of his memory. One moment he was flat on his belly. The next he was lying on his side with his back along a wall, gasping for breath, his right shoulder and left hip throbbing with pain.

Opening his eyes, he looked up from the floor to find the rows of chairs toppled everywhere. The unseated Blinders spread into a flung-ragdoll terrain. His collaborators scattered pell-mell. No one on their feet. The waterfall wallpaper had shut off, revealing hard grey surfaces in all directions, and in the wall opposite where Amon lay—midway between the elevators in the direction his head pointed and the far end in the direction of his feet—was a huge hole, from which the impossible object protruded. It was like gazing at a pinwheel of sunbursts, each photon of which was the note in a symphony of scents that promised to teach Amon exactly who he was but that never quite whirled at the right speed for the meaning to become clear. Once this dazzling redolent abyss of almost epiphanies had his mind tantalized hypnotic, new patterns emerged and tinged his fear with the taste of rotten flesh that crawled like a million earwigs across his body. The foul perceptual mishmash then permeated his arising thoughts, melting them into a nonsensical series of spine-chilling nausea hues. While Amon dry-retched and gibbered, his eyes kept trying to roll back into his head but could not avert themselves.

He might have remained in thrall to this gestalt-defying, sense-melding anomaly, his consciousness dissolved into agonizing mush, if miniscule strands of it hadn't begun to peel off, turn iridescent, and fall to the floor like spasming worms. The GATA security system had been activated and pores in all the surfaces of the room were excreting clustered-formations of haywyre dust that converged on the intrusion in a curdled cloud. Clawing back a few jots of brainpower, Amon switched to naked view so as to dispel what he thought was a mesmerizing overlay. But although the six perspective windows of his collaborators vanished, the anomaly remained, and he guessed what it had to be—Gemini X—for he had encountered no other device that could physically simulate its ImmaNet presentation.

Where the dust struck and strands fell, Amon could make out the contours of the craft's bent nose and battered hull giving shape to the ineffable stutter-flash that continued to draw in and rend his attention. In reaction to the dust, other strands of the anomaly peeled away, wriggled around each other, launched spinning across the room like some propeller flower, and braided themselves in midair to form fluted spirals. These corkscrewing darts flew at equal intervals of distance and angle in all directions to strike points in the walls and ceiling and segments of the floor not covered by bodies, chairs, and debris, stabbing into the pores with their sharp tips and boring on the torque of their fan-blade tails straight through to the outside. Instantly new pores sprouted in the still intact parts of the room and together fired another cloud of dust that turned more of the rotorcraft to jittering strands. In turn, this triggered the launch of more propeller-flower-to-braided-spikes that drilled new holes in the room's four surfaces. Piece by piece, the craft disintegrated and the House of Blinding perforated as they traded volleys every split second.

Once enough strands had either peeled away or fallen, flaws formed in the anomaly, weakening its compulsive gravity just enough that Amon could pry away his focus. Panic rushed in and his eyes went helter-skelter in search of escape . . . until he spotted a vending machine in the direction of the elevators that lay fallen alongside the wall he was pressed against.

Amon scrambled on hands and knees towards it, aiming to take cover in the narrow space between the side of the machine and the wall. In his peripheral vision, he caught other sprawled bodies springing into motion, roused from their bewitchment at nearly the same moment.

The clatter and roar of craft and building trading fire penetrated Amon's ears, and he realized as his hearing returned that the psychologically disruptive hum of the Gemini's rotorcloud—merged with the visuals and other stimulation under the influence of synesthesia pollen—had temporarily deafened him. Just before he reached the vending machine, he took a glance into the madness to his left. Most of the anomaly's jet-shaped nose was gone, having been dusted into a growing smatter of twitching, pulsating, color-throbbing strands on the floor or expended on drill-fire through the building. The black interior of the embedded craft—with its smashed cockpit seats and length of deck—now filled the rupture in the wall almost seamlessly. Inside the cloud of dust flew as though the deck were a vacuum cleaner sucking it all up, triggering the propulsive bloom of fluted darts from its inner walls in tandem with those from its outer shell, the room punctured through and through. Meanwhile, the rotorcraft was buffeted about by something outside, heaving and yawing and grinding at the edges of its snug hole.

Amon collapsed behind the vending machine. Flicking the ImmaNet back on, he heard the shouting of Ono X and Ty and saw activity in the five windows of their crew but could hear nothing over the racket. Rashana stared unmoving at the floor. Amon opened two more windows for Hippo and the PhisherKing and slotted them with the others at the bottom of his visual field. Hippo's perspective shook as he cowered against a wall. Monju's was dark and still. Was he okay? And what about the Secretary of Blinding, their only point of access to reprogram the system? Amon tossed his vision over the vending machine and surveyed the scene.

The craft had been reduced to almost half its mass, the husk of the anomaly smoldering in perception-blending patches over the fragmented black of its bucking interior. Pale infolight from the clouded sky glowed through innumerable holes in the walls and through the jagged rim of the breach. From the point of impact, the chairs had been blown away and most lay in clumps about the room, some with their comatose occupants still seated, some not. Amon's collaborators were doing their best to take cover behind these, piles of immobile Blinders, rubble, and vending machines, looking on helpless, their sleeping beauty dusters ineffective against machines.

He could not fathom why Gemini X had crashed into the building. Then it dawned on him that the projectile drills and fallen strands were not formed of particulate as one would expect from the pixeldust tesserae of the moving mosaic that composed Rashana's craft, but of tiny threads like the pixelfibers in a moving tapestry. But if that were so—

Before Amon could message the revolutionaries about his suspicions, the interior of the rotorcraft imploded, melting into an almost liquid field of strands that slithered into the room like tangles of snakes. Washed along by this proteanite flood were ten human forms, each encased in an undulating weave of serpentine pixels.

As they alighted on the floor of the room, nine gathered in a square around one of them. For a moment, they looked invincible in their consciousness-dissolving display armor, standing with heads high under the rain of dust, assault dusters held confidently. Then the illusion shattered as one man at the front let out a full-throated scream of a kind Amon wished he could forget and collapsed to the floor.

While what remained of the embedded craft kept pouring inside to replenish their protective shells, its proteanite substance was too depleted under fire from inside and out, and the dustpores in the room too numerous for it to keep up. A second later, a chink opened on the neck of a woman also at the front, admitting more nerve dust, and she too collapsed with a scream that made Amon cringe.

Strangely, the battery of dust avoided the lone woman standing unarmed at the center of the shrinking box. Then Amon was certain. It was Anisha come in Gemini Y, unnoticed by the security system because she had the Phoenix Virus, unlike her Birla Guard, bankrupt from trespassing.

Why would these maniacs crash here now? Amon thought, wondering if the procedures to end bankdeath could somehow be restarted, or if the jubilee was lost.

★

"HOLD YOUR FIRE!" Hippo screamed from somewhere, amplifying his voice above the din. Red 3D characters that spelled out his imperative rotated in the middle of the room.

"HIPPO?" bellowed Anisha as another man on the left side of her square screamed and fell.

"HOLD YOUR FIRE!" Hippo screamed again, projecting more red letters that sprouted arrows in all directions "THE WALLS ARE BREAKING!"

Although the floor was only punctured in the uncovered and unoccupied patches from which dustpores had sprouted, there were now enough tiny perforations in the walls and ceiling to reveal grainy vistas of the surrounding InfoFlux and the room above. As the dwindling proteanite encasing the newly arrived Birla Guard continued to propel pixel-drills at the tattered surfaces, Amon saw Hippo's point. Soon there would be more space than solid, and the House of Blinding would buckle, GATA Tower collapsing on their heads.

"AND EAT DUST?" replied Anisha. Added to the omnidirectional assault from the room, her guards now took spray from the rupture behind them. A swarm of rotor-borne air urchins pattered more haywire from their coating of spikes at those in the rear of her square, who responded with blasts of droneburn, sending the short-circuited caltrops plummeting one by one into the city.

"LET ME GO TO THE SECRETARY OF BLINDING!" the PhisherKing boomed. A glowing finger blinked down at a man sprawled facedown across toppled chairs near the center of the room, several meters from where Rashana's Birla Guard had been holding him at the moment of impact. "I'LL DISABLE SECURITY WITH HIS ACCESS."

"ONLY IF YOU GO ON GLASS MODE," warned a guard in front with Ono X's voice who had to be Ono Y. "NO TRICKS!"

Amon briefly stretched Monju's perspective window and saw a notification that he was on glass mode. The PhisherKing, master peddler of secrets, had made his inner profile transparent to the world.

"GO!" Anisha shouted, as another of her guards fell. Amon watched on tenterhooks as Monju burst out from under a heap of bodies at the far end and dashed across the room, stepping around rubble, chairs and more bodies, almost tripping. Clusters of haywyre pelted him harmlessly, while the blossoming drills parted to allow passage, no doubt on command from Anisha. His friend was unharmed and on his way to seize executive clearance. The Phoenix Revolution was not over yet.

Amon held his breath as Monju dove onto the Secretary, hand to the back of his neck. Now all the PhisherKing had to do was pretend he was turning off security and end bankdeath right there! But after one last volley of propeller-spikes flowered from the three guards still standing and drilled through the surfaces, no new pores sprouted to emit dust, and the air urchins filling the breach dispersed, revealing the hailing InfoSky beyond.

When all suddenly went still, a glimmer of clarity came to Amon and he realized how foolhardy such a bait-and-switch would have been. Programming universal access was supposed to take several minutes more. The ceiling might have fallen on their heads in the meantime. And assuming Anisha's side understood the PhisherKing's coding, Monju would have been a pincushion long before that, with his deception plain to see on glass mode.

Whatever Anisha and her guards knew about their plans, they obviously understood the power executive clearance gave the PhisherKing, for Ono Y took aim on him and said, "Now hands off and back away."

Then Monju crawled out of reach of the Secretary of Blinding, and Amon's heart sank.

There was a momentary pause as everyone sized up the situation.

Around Anisha her three remaining guards stood front, left, and right. The anomaly continued to play on their bodies, but with reduced hypno-disorienting force now that the surface area of the display was much smaller, and the synesthesia dusters on the craft had broken apart. Anisha's proteanite shell was seamless, but her guards' had tiny gaps here and there that revealed their standard gold armor underneath. At their feet, piles of hue-flickering pixelfibers convulsed, ticced, or were still depending on how recently they'd been haywyred.

Everyone else below Amon's floating perspective remained shocked, injured, comatose, or dead. There were several bloody messes on the floor where inert Blinders or Atupians had been torn apart by wayward pins, their last cries drowned out in the tumult. From holes in the ceiling, terrified eyes peeped, and a spray of blood showered down from a badly punctured swathe as though through a sieve—Judicial Brokers in the Fiscal Judiciary upstairs who had met their final judgement.

Amon saw himself from above lying on his side, gripping his duster pointlessly in front of his chest with both hands like some protective bauble or charm. A chill wind, more winter than spring, blew in through hole and rupture. This reminded him that there was a world outside the disaster around him, and he finally tuned in to voices that had been pleading to be heard.

"Report! Team Phoenix. Rashana! Are you ok? Anyone. Report!" Ono X howled, his usually soft voice gone raspy with panic.

"Eh! What's going on in there?" radioed Ty.

Amon had no idea how to respond, and neither, apparently, did anyone else. What *was* going on? For some reason, Anisha had decided to crash and somehow knew to aim for their exact floor. But they'd taken so many precautions to keep the revolution secret. Only those whose dedication to the cause was unimpeachable had been involved, and no one had been told more than they needed to fulfill their roles. Bankliving members had consented to glass mode with respect to their superiors, and bankdead had been under watch in Atupio with no means of remote transmission. That left only the leaders, but Rashana's security holes had been plugged, Amon was certain he hadn't leaked anything, Hippo was the most upstanding person Amon had ever met, Ono X would never put his fiancé in danger, and the PhisherKing, well, he had just dashed into the crossfire to save them all, so—

The lull ended with a short burst of dust. It flew from the elevator-end corner opposite Amon, where one of Rashana's guards lay sheltered by two chairs stacked on their sides. It struck the back of a man to the right of Anisha and some must have found a chink in his display armor because he flopped comatose to the floor. Amon rejoiced inwardly, until Ono X fired back from in front of Anisha and the woman behind the chairs began to spasm and shake. Epilepsy dusted.

"Atupians, Phishers, hold your fire!" Hippo called out.

Two successive shots flew from the far end. Amon was about to raise his duster in solidarity despite Hippo's injunction, but was glad he didn't when the pixelfibers from the fallen guards slithered up and completed the armor of Ono Y and Anisha's other remaining guard, as they pivoted and fired twice methodically.

A male Phisher let out a series of squeals with decibels and gravel rising in step, the piranha dust beginning to chew.

The Atupian woman at the far end just whimpered and slumped to the floor, succumbing to soul-deep dysphoria.

"I repeat," said Hippo. "Atupians, Phishers, hold your fire!"

The newly fortified armor around the three figures played a blinking gun inside a red circle with a line through it. A redundant message. The phoenixes looked in dismay at the weapons in their hands. That their lives and the fate of the revolution were now beholden to Anisha and Ono Y was clear to all.

As if to prove that any bad situation could always get worse, Ono X voiced, "Liquidators pulling out from lures."

"What's our next move?" radioed Ty.

From their five reeling windows, Amon glimpsed Ono X and Ty's cell running full tilt through the city. Amon immediately grasped what was happening outside. The crash alone would have been enough to alert the Liquidators in the field. But if any doubt remained about protocol, there were nine bankrupts inside GATA Tower. Bankrupts inside GATA! The two on their feet had to be dusted, and the seven who had already fallen identity executed. The Liquidation Ministry algorithms would have signaled an emergency when they found no Liquidators available to dispatch. Even with the Liquidation Minister and the rest of the Executive Council incommunicado, the command demanded of the highest ranking Identity Executioner was obvious. The Liquidators were returning.

While Amon was trying to decide what to tell Ono X and the exiles, Ono Y and the other guard, a woman, swiveled their assault dusters towards the rest of Rashana's guards taking cover near the elevators.

"STOP!" bellowed Hippo. "Don't shoot!"

"Why?" Anisha demanded.

"None of our weapons can touch you."

"They shot my guard."

"With harmless beauty dust."

"Another fell to his death when we crashed."

"I'm sorry, but that wasn't their fault."

"I don't care."

"Hear him out," Ono Y advised.

"Yes, please," Hippo begged. "The Atupians and Phishers must be made to understand first."

"Understand WHAT?" Anisha snapped.

"That she is the real Rashana, true founder of Atupio and restorer of Hakkotopia," said Hippo, pointing at Anisha and addressing the room. "Her sister is a liar, always has been. She's using us and the revolution for some hidden purpose, who knows what."

This is what was bothering him, Amon realized. *This is what Hippo couldn't tell me.* He felt at once as though part of him had known all along that Rashana was an imposter and that it made no sense whatsoever. For how could the Rashana they knew be anyone other than she claimed when she was running Atupio? Hadn't she demonstrated her faith in both the diamond dream and Phoenix Revolution with all the sacrifices she had made? If there was any question about her, Hippo ought to have noticed at their meeting in person, when he had seen her naked face. And yet he continued to strive towards the same goals as her right up to that very day.

Before Hippo could explain any further, or Anisha could respond to him, Rashana texted, *Ono X, Abort! All hands to GATA Tower! Abort!*

"Bitch!" Anisha hissed, no doubt seeing the message through Monju's glass profile.

Amon watched from above as she marched—flanked by Ono Y and her last guard—towards a vending machine lying between the elevators and the center of the room. One of Rashana's guards and an Atupian popped up from behind the machine, while Rashana made a break for an opening elevator. Ono Y charged at Rashana, as he and Anisha's guard wheeled their assault dusters on the Atupian and the guard. The Atupian took a pot shot at Ono Y's face, dust swishing harmlessly off a proteanite cheek. Ono Y swiftly returned fire in mid stride as his companion likewise showered dust on the Atupian. Rashana's guard fell into another seizure, and the Atupian went trigger happy, dust flying aimlessly, until Anisha's approaching guard tripped him and stomped on his face. Meanwhile, Ono Y leapt chairs and bodies as though running an obstacle race, gaining rapidly on Rashana.

"Stop stop stop!" shouted Hippo.

"Don't you dare," said Ono X, watching through someone's perspective.

Ono Y was upon Rashana in a flash, raising his foot high to kick down on her tailbone. She fell onto her elbows, fingertips just shy of the elevator's open threshold.

"Stop now, no retaliation," said Hippo. "Let's be civilized about this."

Ono Y's bulky form loomed over Rashana with duster cradled as the doors began to close. Rashana's guards stayed behind their various cover, gripping dusters, unsure what to do.

"You know the drill, clone," Ono Y sneered. "Don't pretend you can't hear me."

"Oh shit," said Ono X wearily. "Weapons on the ground and standby."

Rashana's guards obediently tossed their dusters to the floor. The Atupians followed suit by dropping their weapons at their feet.

"Now call your Ono off," Anisha told her sister.

"One step closer, Ono," said Ono Y, raising his boot threateningly above Rashana. "Go on."

"I'm halting," voiced Ono X, his perspective stumbling to a stop. "Request for permission."

Stay where you are and await further orders, Rashana messaged back, staring at the raised boot with a wide-eyed leer of rage and fear. When Ono X could be heard ordering the outdoor cells to stay put, Anisha nodded to Ono Y, who lowered his boot. Then Amon glanced at the still hurrying windows of the exiles. All that stood between the Liquidators and GATA Tower.

Inside the room, the Atupian who'd slumped down continued to whimper with face in arms, textbook symptoms of dysphoria dust, joy in life gone forever. The one who'd fired wild and taken a stomp, groped around in the mess, deafblind. The epileptic Birla Guards writhed, cerebral storms raging. The squeals of the piranhaed Phisher continued as he rubbed his hands maniacally over his gradually disappearing body, cross-sections of ribs and organs visible where he'd torn open his own cloak and shirt. The red drip from the ceiling had slowed to a trickle.

Our bloodless revolution has gone horror-show, thought Amon, wishing there was something he could do for them, for anyone.

A troubling memory whirled up from the frantic minute just passed: Hippo had taken cover well before the crash. And he'd only told Amon, the Phishers, and the Atupians to get down; Rashana and her guards had been excluded. It was as if Anisha's arrival had been part of some plan. She had known their floor! *Could Hippo have given us away?* Amon wondered, and he began to rewind Hippo's shared LifeStream as a translucent membrane over the scene, searching for the answer.

Anisha was approaching her sister through the clutter. "How did you steal my share of Fertilex?" she demanded . "Give it back. NOW!"

"I-I-I don't have it," Rashana stammered.

"Try lying again," Anisha warned, clanking her armored foot against the floor with one heavy step. Rashana sat with palms on the floor behind her, looking between Anisha and Ono Y's duster, lips trembling even more violently than the rest of her body but no words coming.

"Hippo!" barked Anisha, glancing over her shoulder towards the far end.

"She didn't steal anything from you per se," said Hippo, from his hiding place.

"Then what has she done to her?" asked Ono Y. "Why have you brought us here?"

"Traitor. Hippo is a traitor," voiced Ono X.

"What's this?" radioed Ty.

Hippo??? texted Tamper with his glove display, and Little Book telegraphed furiously. Even Yané, Jiku, and Book, who were supposed to be on a different channel, could be heard shouting, and Amon saw the Atupians and Phishers in the room stirring restlessly.

He had finished reverse-skimming Hippo's LifeStream to where it restarted minutes earlier upon infection with the Phoenix Virus after decades of BodyBank disconnection. Just before Gemini Y's crash,

Hippo's perspective had flickered outside to watch the craft circling GATA airspace, suggesting that he was expecting Anisha. But there was no definitive seg of him contacting her.

"This isn't how it was meant to be, all this bloodshed, but I'm no traitor!" Hippo insisted to everyone, present and remote. "Our patron had other plans for the revolution. She would have seized the House of Blinding for herself. I don't know how, I don't know why, and I don't care. Because I won't let anyone use us again—not for anything."

"Enough chatter! Hippo, come out!" Anisha ordered. "Anyone who so much as frowns at him answers to me."

From all over her body, pixelfiber darts extruded and then retracted intimidatingly, and her guard rotated her upper body slowly from left to right, duster held prominently. A heap of chairs in the far corner opposite the breach tumbled apart and Hippo crawled out warily from beneath, eyeing Rashana's guards even though they had disarmed.

"Why have you brought us here, Hippo?" Ono Y repeated, as Hippo rose timidly to his feet.

"My aircraft is destroyed," Anisha accused him, "my guards are bank-rupt, dusted, *dead!*"

"I never *dreamed* you'd fly through the wall," said Hippo, shaking his head in disbelief. "Intelligence was that you'd be in Fertilex Tokyo, just around the corner."

"Intelligence was wrong."

"I thought you would have walked."

"I was on my way back from business in Mumbai."

"Well, you still could have used the front door—alone as I advised."

"You're blaming this on me?"

"The Twelve detected us scanning GATA Tower," said Ono Y. "Their home office arsenals locked on, threatened to launch a peacedrone armada."

"Even if we could have landed," said Anisha, "do you really think I would leave the safety of my ship and guards and stroll into GATA's bankdeath penalty zone with no other guarantee than your word? How could I be sure it was you? You're supposed to be bankdead. And you blocked me!"

"They would have all seen your messages if I hadn't. They'd know I contacted you."

"That's your problem! Look at what you forced us into."

"MegaGlom securicorps gave us five seconds," said Ono Y. "The Executive Council was unreachable. There were social posts about Liquidators all over the metropolis. You were here in the House of Blinding."

"It was either fly into GATA or forget the whole thing," said Anisha. "I couldn't just retreat. Everything I owned was *gone*."

For all her show of rage, fear crept into Anisha's voice now, and Amon could imagine the panic that had driven her along the series of hurried decisions that had culminated at last with the crash.

"I had only one second to contact you," said Hippo regretfully. "I'm sorry. I wish there had been a better way."

With this Amon grasped why he had failed to find the seg. Hippo had carefully picked his timing: the moment between the PhisherKing's infection of Hippo and Amon with the Phoenix Virus. This was the lone instant in which he had regained ImmaNet access without surveillance via the training bank leash but before he went on sharing mode with the team. If he had sent his message any later or earlier, Rashana's handlers would have detected the actions on his AT readout and known that the revolution had been compromised. Here too was the reason Hippo had been so standoffish and fierce outside his room. Amon hadn't just been prying or insensitive when he asked what was on his mind; he had been exposing Hippo to mortal danger.

"Forget apologies!" said Anisha. "What has happened to my identity? What has she done with my ESTATE?"

"We infected your sister with a virus," said Hippo. "It erased your sig and replaces it with a new one constantly."

"To steal my half of Fertilex."

"No. To evade GATA's charges."

"Like the Ring of Gyges."

"Yes, but temporary."

"To sneak in here?"

"Yes."

"And Fertilex?"

"You're both immune to bankruptcy but you cannot own properties."

"Cannot . . . All of them?"

"Fertilex is gone."

"And for what? Why have you done this mad thing?!"

"To alter the AT Market so that bankruptcy will be eliminated forever. To give access to all bankdead."

"You—my twin—this *bitch*!"—Anisha took another step towards Rashana and raised her hand across her chest, shaking—"She wanted that?"

"Afterwards we would set up the community."

"Hakkotopia 2.0?"

"Yes."

"You!" she shrieked and let her hand fall. The proteanite gauntlet struck Rashana across the forehead, knocking her onto her side.

Amon clenched his jaw as the moment fused with his memory of Mayuko being backhanded in much the same way. Suddenly in his imagination, Anisha wore the digiguise he remembered, except enlarged to envelope the bulk of her armor. There stood a man in white billowing robes, white gloves, and straw sandals, with huge round Buddha ears, a ladder of forehead wrinkles from a bald pate, and a flat sheet of pallid skin below where eyes, nose and mouth should have been—the Emoticon Man!

The vision only lasted an instant, then the assailant was Anisha in her armor again, winding up for a kick. One of Rashana's guards leapt up to intervene but took dust from Ono Y and went down convulsing. Before Rashana could scramble to her feet, Anisha delivered a pixelfibered heel to her kidney and Ono Y stepped in stridently as if to join in.

Sickly flashbacks hit Amon—heavy boots crunching on glass, Mayuko on the floor with tengus leaning over her, that dementedly flipping face. *This is the woman Hippo calls Rashana? This is the person he deemed worthy of our most fateful and fragile secrets?*

Already when they spoke in the corridor, Amon realized, Hippo had been planning to give the revolution away to her. Isn't that what so many of his arguments in the planning sessions had quietly sought to prepare for? Hippo, it seemed, had maneuvered as best he could under constant surveillance to weaken those who might be loyal to their patron on the day of the revolution, pushing for the abandonment of blitz dusters in favor of beauty to curtail the Birla X Guard's firepower, agreeing that Ono X should serve in the field to separate them from their captain, and personally selecting the Atupians who served Amon and Hippo to gain command over trustworthy operatives. He had also campaigned to have two dozen exiles watch over Ono X and encouraged Tamper to build cameras and radios so they could be called upon if need be. These arrangements were all to ensure that when the sister he summoned walked into the building and he declared her true leader of Atupio, his allies inside and out would be in the strongest position possible to depose the Rashana he alleged was false.

But the other sister hadn't walked into the building. She had collided with it. . . . And already some of their allies had died or suffered permanent harm. The entire revolution was in jeopardy. Had their patron really intended to steer it to some dubious end? Was it really so important that the sister they all thought of as Anisha intervene now?

Before Anisha or Ono Y could do any more violence, Ono X shouted "Stop!" and a shockwave of sulfuric musk reverberated shatter-tickle from all directions, raising goosebumps that volcanoed sizzling irritation across Amon's body.

Awareness gone runny like an infected wound, he boomeranged his perspective through the wall, knowing instinctively that the psychoauditory assault originated outdoors. He soared through sheets of regular hail in the adless zone. Saw dronehoses retracting into GATA Tower with air urchins tucked back inside now that security was down. Spotted in the infohail outside the cylinder of GATA airspace a dozen peacedrone tornados rising from the rooftop of each of the Twelve's home offices, the MegaGloms roused by the crash but unable to cross the financial no-fly zone. The promoskyline beyond overrun with a panoply of medical and disaster insurance plans.

There it was. Just behind the funnels of military craft. The sense-melding mind-fry of Gemini X circled at the exact altitude of the House of Blinding, belting out sonic poison with the oscillations of its cloud rotor.

"Step away from Rashana now or I'll smash that busted floor," Ono X growled, "crush the lot of you."

Neither the noise nor the visuals were as compulsive or debilitating as Gemini Y had been because of the distance and because Ono X didn't dare tempt the Twelve by exuding synesthesia pollen in range of their armadas or risk the fines for releasing it into GATA territory. But they served his purpose, announcing that he could fly the craft into the House of Blinding at a moment's notice. And the sight was uncomfortable enough that Amon tilted his viewpoint down as he approached the end of his elliptical arc.

Boomeranging back now, he observed polymer exoskeletoned PrivaPo with their trusty stundawgs spilling from the ground level exits of Mega-Glom skyscrapers. Descried streetwalkers gawking skyward. Glimpsed between buildings Liquidators on bikes and on foot pouring along the car-clogged streets, converging, coming.

When Amon's vision returned to the room after this half-second reconnaissance, Anisha withdrew one stop from her sister and the consciousness fracturing onslaught revved down to a mere sound, a polytonal buzz-whir.

"Like you'd bring the roof down on your master's head," scoffed Ono Y, halted not one step from Rashana.

"I'll do what I have to defend her dignity," voiced Ono X.

"That's a bluff and you know it."

Despite Ono Y's claim, Anisha waved him away from Rashana, and exchanged with him a few slight gestures as though silently conferring. Then, lording over her curled up sister, whose pants had turned a shade darker around the crotch, Anisha said, "Tell your Ono to bring everyone he has after all. Now!"

"Ono X," Rashana rasped.

"On my way," he said.

"Good luck with the Liquidators, clone," said Ono Y.

Now Anisha turned again to Hippo, standing knock-kneed in the open across the room. "I understand what you've done," she said. "What am I here for?"

"To keep the revolution on course as I said."

"What does that mean?"

"Let the PhisherKing touch the Secretary of Blinding. Let him end bankdeath."

"Why should I?"

"So that we can plan an exit strategy before the Liquidators enter. So that the Starters can fly to Hahajima and restore Hakkotopia. So that you can come with us, Rashana, and be our leader, not that imposter on the floor."

"Bullshit from a traitor," said Ono X.

"Nothing but lies," Rashana agreed.

"I can't *stand* when people mix us up," Anisha told Hippo. "You of all people should understand that."

Hippo seemed taken aback by Anisha's implicit denial that she was Rashana, and Amon found himself growing ever more perplexed. Was Hippo wrong about the twins? Had his whole disastrous betrayal been premised on a mistake?

"T-there's no mix up," Hippo stammered. "Book detected her lies. He observed them in her eyes. Thanks to the Books I saw through her gabkeeper charade"—Hippo pointed to Rashana—"By process of elimination, you can only be—"

"Wrong," Anisha cast up a bubble containing her inner profile, the name Anisha Birla at the top.

"I know you have her sub-profile," said Hippo. "I don't understand how or why. But—"

"What does it matter? I don't need you. I have the virus as you said. I can do anything."

"But you can never *own* anything," cut in the PhisherKing. "And the Phoenix Virus cannot be permanent. The Ministry of Access will eventually report that numerous signatures are being registered to the same genome. GATA will have to rectify the error and that means liquidation for all infected."

"Then cure me."

"I can shut it off if you let me touch you," said the PhisherKing, "but depending on where in the rebirth cycle the program stops you'd either be bank*rupt* or bank*dead*."

"No. There *must* be a cure . . ."

"The action exemptions," Ono Y proposed.

"Yes!" cried Anisha. "Cure me with Gyges Ring. Now!"

This silenced everyone. Amon's thoughts jumbled and stalled. For here was a possible future that none of the phoenixes had yet considered, the absolute impunity and freedom of only one under the AT Market.

Cutting through the lull, Ty shouted, "The Liquidators are here! Right at your doorstep you squabbling fools."

Amon toggled the four displays of the exiles. They were on the round, elevated platform at the entrance to GATA Tower, joined by just a few dozen of their fellows in defending all the chokepoints from an oncoming horde of grey suits thousands strong. Ty hurling dustbombs onto the ramps to send bikes sliding. Tamper and Vertical beautying anyone who set foot on the four escalators. Little Book peering over the shoulders of crouching snipers firing on those trotting along the boulevard.

All that protected the exiles was a prohibition on dusting bankdead that required Liquidation Minister approval to override. Their furious desperation was a testament to their hatred for the Charity Gift Economy and their yearning for a new home. But even if they could hold off the forces that maintained the AT Market until Ono X's Atupians arrived, the Liquidators would inevitably throw out protocol and overwhelm them all. If anyone was to stop the old order from reasserting itself in the minutes that followed, Amon realized, it could only be the phoenixes in the House of Blinding.

"Connect to the network immediately," Anisha told the PhisherKing.

"Do as she says," Ono Y demanded, jerking the muzzle of his weapon threateningly.

The PhisherKing rose obediently and started towards the Secretary of Blinding but said, "I don't have the program for Gyges Ring."

"Then make it," said Anisha.

"My Phishers and I spent weeks coding universal access," he explained, stopping just short of the Secretary. "The Liquidators will be here before we figure out where to begin."

"You're making excuses!"

"No," said Hippo. "Your only chance to leave this room is to let him end bankdeath. The Phoenix Virus will be gone. You'll have equal access like everyone else."

"Equal access? Equal? I was waiting to receive the exemptions today, in command of the greatest wealth the world has ever seen."

"We can create a new dream for everyone."

"After you robbed me of infinite choice?"

"A diamond dream, Rashana. What you've always wanted. That's why I invited you here to lead us. Why can't you see that?"

Hippo sounded hurt, as though he were the one betrayed. Evidently he'd been expecting this Birla sister to acknowledge that she was Rashana the moment she arrived. Then Book's assessment of their patron's mendacity could have been brought in, perhaps along with other evidence, to prove that she was an imposter and convince the revolutionaries to overthrow her along with the Birla X guard. Yet here was the other sister, not eagerly accepting that she was Rashana, but persistently denying anything to do with her in spite of all his efforts at persuasion.

Only now with mention of the diamond dream did his words finally seem to touch her. Amon couldn't tell how Anisha took what he'd said with her face masked in solid pixel, but it clearly gave her pause, until she furiously swung her head from side to side as though shaking something off.

"Listen, old man," she said. "Why do you think I worked with my associates to seize the exemptions? Because they're our only chance to resist the dark future of Hakkotopia 2.0 and liberate us from the dark present. You know as well as I do that there's no way to change the Free Market from within. We need those with proven ability, undeluded by InfoFlux lies, to step outside the cage of action and transaction and create a new system that benefits us all."

Anisha raised a gauntleted fist into the air, then lowered it and turned to the PhisherKing.

"So code me Gyges Ring," she said, "and I'll put you on my roundtable of the future to have a say in what comes next. Or we can wait until the Liquidators reach the elevators downstairs, and I'll fire these darts to kill us all. But don't think for a second, I'll let you drag me down into common slavery for your twisted purposes. Act quickly or die with me."

This suicidal ultimatum was obviously the closest thing to a Birla Deal that Anisha could offer in her new destitution. Whether her claim about the Gyges Circle's lofty aims was merely a lie to falsely vindicate the cabal, Amon had no clue, but the very idea of it stunned him. He'd never even considered that Gyges' Ring might represent anything more than raw, unfettered freedom as an end in itself. Rashana had played him so many segs to illustrate. Could she have left something out after all? What else might Amon have overlooked?

While his perspective surveyed the room from above, he could feel himself squirming restlessly on the floor, one hand still squeezing the grip of his useless weapon, the other bunching up the fabric of his shirt, overwhelmed with confusion and helplessness. He wanted to contribute to the desperate argument unfolding, but he understood too little to think of anything worth saying and was wary of revealing his presence to Anisha, if that was who she was, when she had hunted him for so long.

Like Amon, the PhisherKing seemed lost for words, and none of the Phishers began their code gesturing as Anisha had demanded. Before she could pressure them further, Ono Y turned to her and said, "I think you should reconsider. Hippo called us here for our mutual gain. Taking charge of the Atupians is better than nothing."

"That's right, Rashana," said Hippo. "I cannot believe that you would choose anything else."

"Stop trying to make me someone I'm not, old fool," said Anisha.

"We've been betrayed by a bad case of dementia," voiced Ono X.

"Psychosis," put in Rashana.

Amon noticed that some of the Atupians under Hippo's command had been creeping and crawling through the mess towards him. They glowered balefully in his direction, perhaps incited by Ono X's and Rashana's accusations. Though most had picked up their weapons, Ono Y said nothing, as though condoning their hostility. Oblivious, Hippo pointed at Anisha and shouted, "If I'm so senile, then show us your face! Prove who you are!"

"Show them," Ono Y advised. "Fertilex is gone. There's nothing left for your twin to take."

The head of Anisha's proteanite shell unravelled to her shoulders to reveal Makesh Adani. He then morphed into the digimake of one of the Birla Sisters. Amon couldn't have said which, so he peeled away the overlay and found the naked face of a Birla sister, who again, could have been either. Immediately, the armor resealed itself.

Hippo looked gravely troubled, his eyes busy with something, and Amon opened his perspective. He was studying the recording of her unveiling, his visual field split side-to-side between the naked faces of the two sisters. One sister had the red mark of the backhand on her forehead and sat on the ground, while the other stood tall in her armor. Rashana looked as terrified as one might expect, but Anisha's expression showed no signs of the haughtiness or rage she displayed in her voice and bearing. She seemed at least as afraid and bewildered as anyone. Otherwise, they were perfect copies of each other to Amon's eyes, though he'd only spent time in the naked world with the former, and had not learned to differentiate, as those familiar with twins always could.

"Y-you're identical," said Hippo, both incredulous and dismayed.

"We're identical fucking twins," Anisha snapped.

"No. I've known you both since you were babies. I watched you grow up. I— Anisha has a tiny mole above her right eyebrow," Hippo interrupted himself, frowning deeply, teeth bared, grappling with memories. "Her lips are fuller."

"The traitor takes himself for a beautician," Ono X voiced everyone.

"And the revolution for a beauty pageant," Rashana quipped.

Anisha had nothing to add this time, her armored head bowed slightly as though she were in thought.

"It's too late for any punishment now," said Ono Y. "We've taken this as far as it can go."

"No naturally born twins are this similar," muttered Hippo in a daze, still unaware of the Atupians now surrounding him. "There are always differences, phenotypical and genotypical. But you share the same face—exactly the same. You're both Rashana. Both of you!"

With malevolent eyes fixed on Hippo, several Atupians kept their hands near their holsters. The handful closest seemed ready to pounce on him. Ono Y and Anisha's other guard looked to her for a sign. Would she lift the prohibition on harming Hippo and follow through with her self-destructive threat, or spare him and accept his invitation? When an approaching Atupian bumped a chair with his knee, Hippo was finally roused from his bewilderment about the sisters and cast his eyes around in dawning terror.

Amon could have ordered his crew to desist, but that wouldn't have saved Hippo from the rest, and he had no will to impede their malice and mutiny. What had Hippo thought, that Anisha would show up out of nowhere, he would declare her their rightful queen, the Atupians would accept her coronation without dispute, and they would all be whisked away to the land of milk and honey, no harm no foul? Hippo had gambled their revolution on a puzzle that not even he could solve and lost. The man was as deluded as you could get. Or so Amon briefly convinced himself, until he remembered the way Rashana had sometimes scratched her brow, where a mole might once have been, and lucid horror burbled up from the pit of his stomach.

Before the sister they had called Anisha could open the floodgates of violence, or not, the PhisherKing spoke.

"The Ono is right!" he told her, his varicolored eyes sparkling and his voice full of wonder as though he'd just had an epiphany. "You're safe to admit to the heist."

"That's not what I meant, Phisher, and you know it!" Ono Y warned.

"What heist?" said Anisha.

"There was no heist," voiced Ono X.

"Absurd," agreed the other sister.

"Deny my words if you will, but data speaks for itself," the PhisherKing declared.

"Careful now," said Ono Y, shaking his duster threateningly. "You're going too far!"

But the PhisherKing—indispensable to whatever course Anisha might choose and live—was undeterred and hurled a vidbomb into the air above him.

A perspective on a crowded boardroom exploded into view. One sister's Birla Guard rose from their seats and went over to shake hands with their ten counterparts.

"This is the meeting last summer where the executors of the Birla will divided Fertilex between the sisters," the PhisherKing narrated. "I could never understand why Rashana's guards were such good sports after their master took minority share."

Another perspective burst open, showing an Ono aboard the PhisherKing's boat of bone on the quicksilver sea.

I want evidence of Anisha not being herself, said the recorded Ono.

"Here is Ono X and note the date of the seg. It coincides with the ensuing legal battle over the will. Why would Rashana's servant want to prove that Anisha was not Anisha?"

Anisha's guard was charging through the clutter towards the PhisherKing, with Ono Y and Anisha trotting close behind, but the PhisherKing stood where he was with seeming indifference and tossed a third vidbomb that blossomed into a storm of shapes, symbols, and images. A searchlight honed in on certain fields of this shifting code, greying out everything else.

"Here I am a few weeks ago, flesh-hacking one sister to plug the security holes between them. While poking around inside their inner profile, I discovered a procedure through which their sub-profiles could theoretically be flipped, exploiting that their genome differences are negligible to GATA."

"A forgery!" "You lying—" "PhakerKing!"

Ignoring the splurge of denials from the Birlas and Onos, and the guard closing in for a tackle, the PhisherKing went on.

"Hippo and Ono Y have finally shown me how these segs are connected. She"—he pointed at the sister on the floor—"was originally Anisha, destined to inherit control of Fertilex, until she"—he pointed at the standing sister—"hired a team of cryptobreakers to hack her remotely and switch their sub-profiles right after the executers of the will had granted shares. Her Birla Guard went to shake hands so they could flesh hack their fellow clones, follow their master with switched identities of their own. By far the most lucrative swindle in history."

The indignant hollers of the Onos and Birlas were silenced by this conclusion, the guard stopping in her tracks not three steps from the

PhisherKing, as though any secrets they might have suppressed were already out.

"But why do they look the same?" Hippo asked. "Why are they both Rashana?"

"Because the identity heist left her"—the PhisherKing pointed at the Birla on the floor who they had called Rashana—"with Atupio. But she was cut off from the power of its hidden technologies by the genelocks on the underground floors."

From a fourth vidbomb unfurled a vertical column of letter pairs—C, G, A, and T—with a double helix of DNA lined up beside it. Another spotlight skipped between particular gene sequences.

"While plugging the security holes, I noticed that her genome record with GATA had been updated a few months earlier for the first time in her life. The nucleotide difference was subtle but too abrupt for natural variation. Now it's clear. She geneshined herself to close the tiny somatic gap between them."

A final vidbomb showed the AT readout for "Rashana Birla." The spotlighted transaction was "don juan dust self-administer."

"That was how she smoothed out any remaining physiognomic differences, took the naked face of Rashana so the crashborn Starters would never doubt she was their leader. But her sister interacted only with the bankliving. So she was able to retain the appearance of Rashana under her digimake while she played Anisha. The LifeStreams of the other and the whispers of gabkeepers were all they both needed for flawless performances."

It was notable that the sisters and Onos were tongue tied, providing not one contradictory seg. Hippo seemed disturbed but also relieved, now that the hostility of the Atupians had been defused. All looked to Anisha, hanging on her reaction.

The segs and chatter had come too quickly for Amon to assimilate, like the pencil strokes of a hurried sketch, leaving only a vague and incomplete sense of what had and was happening. Reeling with bafflement as truths were pulled out from beneath him like carpets, he was only just beginning to glimpse the implications. But of one thing he was sure: the sisters' names were misleading at best. The sister who had called herself Rashana used to live and act as Anisha. And the one who claimed she was Anisha used to live and act as Rashana. Calling either one Anisha or Rashana failed to capture part of who they were or who they had been. So he decided that, in his head at least, he would refer to the sister who transitioned from Anisha to Rashana, who flew him to the island, funded the revolution, and now cowered on the floor, as Birla X, and the one who transitioned from Rashana to Anisha, who received the message from Hippo, crashed into the building, and now dominated them all, as Birla Y, to match the variables suffixed to their Onos, Geminis, and guards.

"Fertilex is gone, Rashana," the PhisherKing said to Birla Y. "The company you stole vanished with your identity signature. Forever. Your sister's lawsuit is no longer a threat. Just as your Ono said, there's nothing left for her to take back and no reason for you to pretend. Pursue the diamond dream again. Let me end bankdeath."

With the troubled eyes of the room upon her, Birla Y stood behind Ono Y and her other guard, facing the PhisherKing across the body of the Secretary of Blinding. Birla X stayed on the floor between her sister and the elevators. What remained of the gold-uniformed Birla X Guard taking cover nearby. The green cloaked Phishers cowering at the far end, where Hippo stood in the corner adjacent to Amon's vending machine, along the wall opposite the rupture. Their navy-suited Atupians spread out everywhere. The bodies—beautyed, epilepsied, dysphoriaed, deafblind, or dead—scattered on, under, and alongside heaps of chairs, rubble, and pixelfibers.

Under the fitful wind from the breach and the many holes, the warm air had long been blown away. The battle outside was far away, nearly fifty stories below, but Amon could hear the din blaring from the windows of Ono X and the Xenocyst crew. He was growing irritated with himself for lying behind the vending machine, observing in figment but taking no action while his friends inside the room and out risked their lives for what they believed.

"I knew you were Rashana," said Hippo. "Now act like her. Lead."

"Hurry," implored the PhisherKing. "We'll correct your identity under the new order."

"They're right. It's time," Ono Y urged her. "Be who you were meant to be all along."

With Birla Y's face armored, it was difficult to fathom her emotions. But her distress went on display when she let out a sharp hissing breath, her chest sinking, and stamped her proteanite boot. At this Amon felt inexplicably that he could relate to what she was going through, and an impulse seized him.

"Hey, Birla whoever—listen to me!" he shouted, rising from behind the vending machine, slowly so as not to draw nervous fire from Ono Y and her other guard, his gut butterflying with fear. Time dragged to a crawl as his thoughts rushed forth to make sense of what he was doing.

First was the significance of the heist. Perhaps it was Amon's experience of webloss— being flung into the naked world and facing the symptoms head on without any Er treatment—that helped him understand. The identity theft had not been the swap of mere data, leaving the so-called "true Rashana" and "true Anisha" intact, as Hippo, the PhisherKing, and even Ono Y seemed to imply. Amon knew better than anyone how dependent the bankliving were on recalling through LifeStream recordings and how vague their biological memories atrophied as a result. And he could see that such mnemonic deterioration would be especially severe for the sisters, who hadn't simply lost their recordings and ended up with nothing as crashnewbs did—their recordings had been replaced by someone else's. They'd have found it irresistible to view those eternally bright, colorful, accurate segs, and their own pale memories would have paled yet further each day by comparison.

Even worse, that someone was not just anyone but an identical twin with whom they were raised to be a single person, to whom all their recordings and memories had been bound since birth, and from whom they'd secretly fought for their entire adult lives to separate themselves. Only when their parents died and could no longer police their jumbled data were the sisters finally able to be individuals without deception. But as the PhisherKing had just demonstrated, that was the very day that their recordings were flipped. And to dodge the lawsuit over the identity heist or to seize Atupio—as the case may be—they had to imitate the other, speaking, moving, preferring everything just as the other would have, with teams of experts and specialized algorithms to assist them.

"Amon," marveled the standing sister, turning to him. She had identified his voice immediately. Thanks to an app, perhaps? What was he to Anisha but a pest who had obeyed orders to assassinate Barrow and grown suspicious of her plot? No. This wasn't simply Anisha. That was Hippo's mistake, believing that the twins had to be either one or the other always and forever. This was Birla Y. She had once been Rashana.

Less than a year had passed since the will meeting the previous summer, but given all the sisters had gone through, how could they not begin to question themselves, to look back at a certain moment and ask if it was a memory of an experience, or a memory of watching a recording of an experience? Where in this flux would there be space for a past self slipping into oblivion? Who in their shoes could have possibly sustained the line between pretending and being?

"Don't ever let anyone tell you who you are again," said Amon. "Not your parents, not the Fiscal Judiciary, not us. That's for you to decide and you alone. But you'll need to help us bring about universal access. Equality's not slavery. It's your chance to start over." *Just as I started over in bankdeath and again in banklife*, Amon thought.

Birla Y swayed from side to side as though stunned.

"No more stalling!" Amon cried, "Look!" raising his arm to toss the display windows of Ono X and the exiles into the center of the room. As the low-rez feeds of the exiles expanded, the shouts, screams, and patter of dust grew louder until it was as if the fighting were happening right there. Ty, Tamper, Vertical, and Little Book—alongside the rest of their cell—looked out through the glass doors of the lobby at the round platform from which they'd been forced to retreat. There, a stream of newly arrived Atupians crouched and knelt behind heaps of bodies as they showered the escalators and ramps with sleeping beauty dust and took nerve dust in turn, toppling one after the next. A ghastly choir of screams arose from every direction as grey suits finally abandoned protocol in this dire crisis and dusted bankdead, bankrupt, and bankliving alike, firing on the platform and any who approached it from different angles and depths throughout the encompassing cityscape—skyscraper windows, rooftops, doorways, the street.

A short distance away, Ono X peered sideways on his back from beneath a parked vehicle, shouting out orders remotely. The tarmac around him was covered in the unconscious bodies of the Atupians he had mustered, between which faux-leather shoes under grey pant legs crunched the accumulated infohail into advertainment slush.

Amon flicked these windows closed and planted the perspective of himself boomeranging out over the city for all to see. Liquidators poured along the streets from every direction, while PrivaPo and stundawgs closed the last gaps in their ring around GATA territory.

Tilting upward, Amon showed Birla Y and the other spectators the peacedrone tornadoes rising from the roofscape. Swollen larger now than even the largest skyscrapers, each was paired with a rival MegaGlom, forming six upwardly flaring double helixes that circled the perimeter of the financial no-fly zone. Mammoth dust cannons and rockets on the inside of each spiral segment remained fixed on their corresponding opponents through every revolution. In this way, the Philanthropy Syndicate and SpawnU Consortium squared off one-to-one, waiting on hair-trigger alert for some sign of who was at fault for whatever was happening at GATA, with enough nanobot firepower to melt the metropolis into a grey goo.

"PLEASE!" Amon beseeched her as he returned his perspective to his body. "Choose life. Choose the freedom to be yourself. Let us end bankdeath."

This finally spurred Birla Y to some kind of realization, because she looked to Ono Y as if for his blessing. When he nodded, she asked, "The Starters are going to Hahajima?"

"If we can get out of this," Amon replied.

"And your plan is to join them?"

"Right after we're done here."

"Then I'll go with you. I'll lead them. I'll be Rashana. I am Rashana." She puffed up her chest with a breath, as though she were trying to convince herself. Then to the PhisherKing, she said, "Finish your work."

Without a moment's hesitation, Monju crouched beside the Secretary of Blinding, appearing to Amon a glimmer from the jewel of hope they had lost. For in spite of the bedlam and peril around them, the end of bankdeath seemed near again.

Looking around the room from his own eyes now, Amon watched the PhisherKing place his hand on the Secretary of Blinding's chest for the second time that day. But no sooner had he initiated the flesh-hacking than Ono X voiced his Birla sister.

"Know that I'm watching over you," he said. "Gemini X roars in if anything happens. Just a little longer." Then his window vanished from Amon's visual field.

"He's gone off sharing mode," said Ono Y.

"What is he trying to hide?" Birla Y demanded.

"Ono X has acted independently," Amon assured her.

"He's not one of us," Hippo agreed. "He's a danger to us all."

"I've got him in my sights," said Ono Y.

"We mustn't overlook any of his movements," said Hippo. "That man has pieces of Fertilex and thousands under his command." Then he turned to the Atupians who had until seconds earlier been out for his blood. "I chose each of you because I thought you'd see through the lies when the time came. We need you to tell the others what the PhisherKing proved. Ono X and his master are imposters."

"No," said Birla Y. "Connect me to them directly."

"Of course," said Hippo, and a notification that he'd added her to sharing mode popped up. "Here's a line to our bankliving in the field."

Birla Y overlaid the giant digimake of a Birla sister atop her armored body, oddly proportionate to Amon's vision of the Emoticon Man subsuming her earlier, and she began to feedcast a video of herself taken from the air in front of her.

"Friends and visionaries, i-it is I R-Rashana," Birla Y stammered as though saying this took a force of will. But her voice quickly found confidence. "Hear the words of your leader. Hear of the deception perpetrated on you all . . ."

Curious to see how Birla X was taking the ousting from her identity, Amon glanced at her. She was lying on her side facing the elevators, arms crossed around her midriff. His gaze had just flicked away when he registered some subtle motions, looked back, and saw that they originated from her hands hidden beneath her armpits. Suspicion aroused, Amon opened her perspective over sharing mode and intercepted a text.

PhisherKing . . . it whispered in Birla X's voice at double playback speed. You shared data about us so your friends could act with clear eyes. Now consider the truth about Hakkotopia so that you can do the same.

The PhisherKing didn't reply, but—hunkered in his green cloak over the Secretary, one hand on the man's chest, and one gesturing wildly like a beached fish on fast-forward in tandem with his silently jittering lips—he tilted his ear towards Birla X to signal that he was listening.

Do you honestly believe that humans are the sort of animal that could have created such a community? the text whispered rapidly. Just think of desire. Our envy, greed, and covetousness. Our pride, lust, and sloth. Could anything be more contrary to coordinating action along a rational plan? . . .

Startled by this crisp challenge to the future they all sought, Amon swept the room for reactions and found that few had even noticed.

"My twin and her Ono are not who they seem," Birla Y proclaimed to all and sundry, standing proudly in her oversized digimake. "Fend off the Liquidators but beware the Ono. Capture him if you can . . ."

Hippo and the Atupians gathered closer, listening to her speech, while Ono Y and the other Y guard kept their armored feet planted amidst the mess, hands twitching, no doubt preoccupied with reconnoitering Ono X. But the Phishers—having each risen from the heaps to find a Blinder through which to access the House of Blinding system—imitated their mentor in tilting an ear to Birla X as they assisted his coding. Aside from Amon, only the remnants of the X guard had their eyes on her.

. . .For the sake of our egos, we make choices that benefit no one but ourselves, the whisper hurried on. For the sake of status and money, we fight amongst each other. For the sake of sex and procreation, we dominate those weaker and destroy our environments. . . .

Hippo suggested something to Amon about planning their exit strategy, but Amon barely heard him, held rapt by Birla X's deceptively quiet subversion. He only sent Hippo a harrowed glance, bringing Hippo's attention to where Amon was looking.

. . .Even if the majority were not like this, all it takes is an opportunistic handful to reap advantage from everyone else's restraint and the whole society is dragged into the mud with them. This is the petty creature that is supposed to pursue a shared vision in cooperation with millions, each in their own unique way, of their own free will? . . .

It baffled Amon to hear Birla X deriding the diamond dream when she had stepped into the room willingly disowned of her fortune for its sake, while Birla Y was rallying a crowd around that dream after deriding it in favor of Gyges Ring not minutes earlier. He had already glimpsed the fault line that the identity heist and lawsuit had opened in the grinding plates of their past and had urged one of them to decide who she was anew, but the reversal of the person values—Rashana and Anisha—for the identity variables—X and Y—was too sudden and extreme for his mind to keep up. Another glance at Hippo as he rewound his LifeStream and caught up on the whispertexts captured a grimace of even more profound vertigo.

"Clone is up to something," Ono Y reported. "Some of his detachments are hanging back from the battleground. Like he's . . ."

He stopped when he noticed Amon, Hippo, the X guards and now a few Atupians gaping at Birla X on the floor. But his shouts to draw his master's attention were drowned out as Birla X set her texts to play in the room and cranked the volume to music festival levels.

. . . Human desires are a cacophony, her sped-up voice punched through like some troglodytic preacher from the bowels of the earth. Our variant genetic natures play dissonant social chords. This contentiousness is what the anarchy of the Free Market seeks to harness. Competing actions and transactions propel economic growth. But the many wants of the Hakko-topians were a grand symphony. They happily submitted to the needs of the most fragile ecosystems. Why? Because of harmony pollen. . . .

This last phrase seemed to reverberate and stretch dementedly through the room, as Amon recalled the pulsating blossoms in Atupio. The PhisherKing seemed to stumble in his interfacing at the very same moment.

Birla Y initially reacted to her sister's blaring monologue by snorting in annoyance and raising her volume to match it. "Fear not, for I will pick up the torch," she continued. "Watch as bankdeath ends now under my—" Then she noticed Ono Y frantically waving to get her attention, cut her feedcast, and turned to her sister in alarm, while Ono Y took aim.

. . .It was not merely the actions of humans that were guided by political algorithms in Hakkotopia, the text boomed. So too were their genes, much like the bioautomatic organisms that comprised its infrastructure. Except only tweaks to their brains and nerves, their motivational arrays. Vibrant flowers redesigned the unconscious of the citizens that designed them. Factories for an airborne cellular editor to retune desire in step with data on present conditions. . . .

"Permission to shoot?" Ono Y shouted with just enough decibels to be heard. As Birla Y stomped towards her sister in a fury and her other guard raised her barrel, five of Birla X's guards leapt up to intervene. Three grabbed Ono Y and tried to wrestle the duster from him. Two pounced on the guard, but she extruded darts to drive them back and dusted both in turn, sending them shrinking with a whimper to the floor. Then she swiveled and dysphoriaed one grappling Ono Y's weapon, allowing him to epilepsy another, and launch a single twist of armor into a third guard's heart. The last two Birla X guards were further away on hands and knees, poised to spring up and attack, but they now slumped back down in a sign of capitulation.

. . . Invisible, scentless, tasteless pollen was just another background condition like water and education. It adjusted the desires of each citizen so subtly that they hardly noticed, even as their contribution to aggregate appetite raised the likelihood of total behavior tracking the adaptive goal state— maximum teeming and flourishing with enough production to satisfy human needs. A system of real-time ecogenics. . . .

Amon thought of painpress and wondered if his psychogenome had been fiddled with. Perhaps not because the trauma-deadening effects had worn off. But how could he be certain?

Amidst the ear-splitting racket, as everyone turned up their voices all at once, he could just hear Ty's unaugmented cries over radio but couldn't make out his words.

"Let me shoot!" bellowed Ono Y.

"No!" shouted Hippo. "Stop."

"Shut up now!" Birla Y screeched, as she grabbed up her sister by the collar and darts protruded from her raised palm.

Immediately, the shatter-tickle sulfur-echo bleated for one rotation around the building, and a clip of a miniature Gemini X colliding with GATA Tower played on repeat above Birla X's dangling head.

There could be no question about whether Ono X was bluffing. If his master died, there would be nothing to keep him from smashing the fractured floor. Amon glanced at the PhisherKing, wondering how many seconds remained in their procedures, hoping they might end bankdeath before they were all crushed or the Liquidators made it inside.

While Birla Y's spiky slap of death hung swaying in the air, her sister's fingers and lips texted heedlessly on.

. . . When vying for social position led to conflict, neural cells were edited to reduce envy. When lukewarm competition hindered productivity, new adjustments sent it back up. When predicted supply of materials for clothing rose, the vanity dial climbed. When denizens grew slovenly and unsociable, it dropped. . . .

With a stretched elastic hand, Ono Y swiped aside the looping seg of Gemini X's hypothetical collision and replaced it with a feed of its actual flightpath. Propelled by the cloud rotor positioned at the rear, the aircraft was receding at high velocity, blipping evasively in and out of view on an omnidirectional zigzag course as coils and ribbons of peacedrones riding a snaking nimbus of missiles gave chase over the skyscraper rooftops.

"The Twelve won't let it anywhere near here again," said Ono Y. "The threat is over."

Birla Y leered furiously at her sister but still her hand hung above her.

"Harming her would be unbecoming of you—Rashana," said Hippo, now using the name uncertainly. "Bring her for a fair trial among your people."

"No! Strike her now!"

Seizing this moment of indecision, Birla X tossed up a handful of segs.

"I am not Rashana." "Give me Gyges Ring." "The dark future of Hakko-topia 2.0." These and other video quotes of Birla Y bubbled and popped in the air. From this carbonated montage an arrow pointed to a group pic of Atupians and Starters below the banana yellow text "Friends and

Visionaries." Another arrow pointed at Birla X herself, over whom the bloody word 'Martyr" hung.

At this threat, Birla Y's enlarged face tensed with fear, as she looked around at the listening Atupians and seemed to finally realize that the PhisherKing wasn't her sister's only audience. Amon hovered his finger over the Atupians to preview their shared perspectives and saw that some were feedcasting the scene to bankliving in the field. He understood then what a grave strategic error Birla Y's hesitation was. And this was the second time at least that she was squandering a chance to eliminate or at least debilitate her sister and foreclose her and her Ono's opportunities to interfere, preferring instead to merely beat and humiliate her. Losing her Cognitive Handling Corps would have impeded her acuity and decisiveness, but not enough to explain this lapse of judgement. If Birla Y was truly prepared to kill everyone and herself as per the ultimatum she had delivered, why would she waver over the bane of her existence alone?

While her sister's attention was momentarily on the Atupians, Birla X shook her off, straightened to as dignified a posture as her sore side would allow, and finished mouthing the final lines of her text.

. . . Cooperation in pursuing the diamond dream was secured without stooping to coercion, propaganda, or forced conditioning. Everyone thought their own thoughts. They made their own decisions. They even voted on the algorithms. It's just that those algorithms determined what they desired.

By the time Birla Y reached a decision, it was futile. Lowering her gauntlet and retracting the darts, she had her guard and Ono Y sling their assault dusters on their backs so that the guard could twist her sister's hands behind her back, while Ono Y stuffed her mouth with a proteanite hand. But Birla X had stopped interfacing by then. As dense and piecemeal as it had been, her message was out.

"Friends and visionaries," Birla Y said, resuming her feedcast. "Do not be led astray by baseless fabrications. The records of Hakkotopia 1.0 reveal the true history."

It was indeed suspicious to Amon that Birla X made such elaborate claims without supporting evidence of any kind. But now her eyes painstakingly dialed a command and her body acquired a glassy sheen to signal that she had activated public glass mode, her data open for all to see and confirm for themselves.

Immediately, Amon noticed a shift in the PhisherKing's movements. When Amon flicked open his perspective, he found a wash of code, suggesting that he and his Phishers were programming universal access as planned. But he quickly realized that the complex commands didn't match the simplicity of Monju's gestures. On more careful inspection, a clip of his coding from before the crash seemed to have been set hastily to play on repeat; it was a decoy perspective, and Amon had to scour the man's desktop for a window into his present. Inside, he found the PhisherKing sifting at eye-wringing speed through the LifeStream Birla X had just revealed, shuffling segs into decks and flipping through them while toggling between the perspectives of his Phishers, who were analyzing other portions.

The Phishers had succumbed to the doubt that Birla X had sewn. They had stopped coding the end of bankdeath.

Presently, the Phishers drew entirely still. Then Ono Y asked, "Bankdeath is over?"

"No. We've finished our analysis of the 'Rashana' LifeStream," replied the PhisherKing. "It contains no evidence of ecogenics or harmony dust."

"Of course it doesn't," Birla Y snapped.

"You're wasting time we don't have," said Ono Y. "Finish!"

"First, give us the 'Anisha' LifeStream so we can examine that too," the PhisherKing told Birla Y.

"You don't actually believe her?" she scoffed.

"You're squandering universal access on the basis of mere allegations?" Hippo asked incredulously. "A Phisher? Without a shred of data to back any of it up?"

"Think," the PhisherKing hissed. "Once the financial barriers come down, the Ferment Culture Collective will fly the Starters to Hahajima and regrow the archipelago processor. They could seize control of human desire today. Then what would it matter if the glorious flow of information, the Great Treasure Matrix, is unleashed?"

"It would matter to millions of bankdead and Free Citizens enslaved by the AT Market," said Hippo. "Just end it please!"

The PhisherKing shook his head. "We would only replace a contingent kind of slavery for a permanent one."

As always, the PhisherKing was putting the pieces together faster than anyone, and Amon felt the his last drop of hope drain away, his faith in all versions of the revolution decimated. The Atupians looked on with maze-lost eyes, some holding their heads in their hands. Hippo too was stricken. Hunched agape, head akimbo, he clenched his suit jacket tightly at the waist, like a shame-lit candle that wants to melt faster into the floor.

"That threat would be decades away," he said feebly. "It took the original community years just to reach the mouth of Tokyo Bay."

Just then Birla X let out an inarticulate moan, struggled weakly against the hands that restrained and gagged her, and managed to launch an eye-dialed text. Harmony sleeperpuzzles, whispered a speech bubble extending from her head.

This brought to Amon a vision of microscopic specks blowing over the globe and interlocking with their waiting components in every region, desire adjustments spreading like wildfire across continents, burning freedom off the face of the earth. Was this the "dark future of Hakkotopia 2.0" that Birla Y as Anisha had claimed Gyges Circle was inaugurated to prevent?

"Another unsubstantiated lie," said Birla Y as Rashana, not minutes later.

"She *could* have been lying," said Amon uncertainly.

"I will not demolish our civilization to lay a foundation of could-have-beens for a new one," stated the PhisherKing, his tricolored eyes gleaming conviction. "Truth or nothing, come what may."

"Talk is death," Ono Y told his Birla. "What does it matter if they see your twin's past?"

"The truth about Anisha can never harm *you*, Rashana," Hippo agreed, though sounding uncomfortable again to call her by this name.

"Quickly!" Amon barked.

"Here," she snarled in frustration, as she took on a glassy sheen, and the Phishers launched into a flurry of interfacing. Reopening the PhisherKing's perspective, Amon watched them rapidly sift the subprofile Birla Y had revealed. Within seconds, he was convinced that the body of data inside deserved to be called the "Anisha" LifeStream, as the PhisherKing had put it. Not only was that the name listed inside, but the segs that comprised it recorded the life of someone called "Anisha." Initially that life had been led by Birla X, the original Anisha, until Birla Y, the original Rashana, stole it from her to seize Fertilex upon their parents' death.

Likewise, the body of data Birla X had revealed earlier deserved to be called the "Rashana" LifeStream. That was the name on the subprofile, and it recorded the life of "Rashana," whether led by Birla Y before she stole the inheritance or by Birla X after the identity was foisted on her. It was as though one sister had forced the other to exchange their batons so that they could take over running in different races, only to learn that the judges wouldn't let them trade back. With the legal battle between them raging, the transition had no doubt been tumultuous, full of interruptions and regressions. Nevertheless, the two LifeStreams seemed to be more or less continuous records of "Anisha" and "Rashana," respectively, even though the bodies and consciousnesses these appellations referred to had switched along the way.

But then which sister did I meet for the first time in Ginza, Birla X or Birla Y? Amon wondered, realizing that he was no longer sure who had been who in each of his interactions with either.

His doubts scattered at the sound of Vertical's voice. "Team, we need your guidance," she said. "Please."

Amon flicked away Monju's perspective and glanced at the low-rez display windows lining the bottom of his own. Through the lobby glass, all four looked outside, where stillness had fallen over the city. Each of their cameras gently panned and shook, the hail fell, and the peacedrones churned along the skyline, but from the body-heaped platform to the streets and towers beyond, nothing else stirred.

Perplexed by this unaccountable lull, Amon recalled the barely audible radio transmission from Ty and rewound his recording of the exiles' feeds. *All Liquidators are pulling back,* Ty had announced, at once triumphant and incredulous. *They're retreating!* A spate of similar reports, pleas, and taps from the others soon followed, all of them overpowered by the clamor or ignored amidst the violence of the past minute.

"Hello?" Ty said now. "Can anyone hear us? Hello?"

"Hold where you are," Hippo replied. "We're investigating."

Frantically, Amon toggled again through their windows in the present. The platform cleared of resistance, all Atupians and exiles nerved. Then he boomeranged through the hail and surveyed the streets below, where exiles, Atupians, and Liquidators alike lay fallen on the roads and sidewalks. Further from GATA Tower, he spotted clusters of Atupians gathered in plazas and intersections, and of exiles that had been driven away by the Liquidator horde. These latter cells now hunkered behind cars, on rooftops, and in alleys. Some pooled with citizens near the PrivaPo and stundawg cordon that formed a nearly complete circle around the base of the ad-less cylinder and cut off street level reinforcements, admitting only a slow trickle of returning Liquidators. As Amon flew across the border, he tilted his viewpoint up and merged with the dense air traffic, paired tornadoes of peacedrones spreading and unfurling around each other into the highest altitudes. Now looping and spiraling between them was a fleet of hydrogen planes digimade brown with baby blue and lavender stripes—aircraft newly arrived from GATA Osaka.

The implications of his momentary reconnaissance were clear. The grey suits had already smashed the agents of the Phoenix Revolution, their forces were amassing in the skies and on the ground, and many of the Atupians now bankrupt from *impeding justice* in GATA territory were calling to be cash crashed. And yet what Ty had said appeared to be true; on his return arc, Amon saw Liquidators flittering away from the vicinity of GATA Tower as though magnetically repelled, leaving their routed adversaries untouched. And rewinding the feeds of the exiles for a few seconds, he watched in stupefaction as dozens of grey suits who had even gained the platform returned down escalators to the street, others picking their way back up the bike pileup on the ramp. Meanwhile, the hydrogen planes held back, cruising harmlessly outside the no-fly zone despite having permits to enter.

"GATA has—retreated?" said Hippo, giving voice to Amon's astonishment perfectly.

"What?" said Birla Y. At some signal from her, Ono Y unspooled slobber from Birla X's mouth as he withdrew his armored fingers to begin interfacing with both hands. Then the Y guard thrust Birla X to her knees and began to assist him in his reconnaissance.

"They should be mopping up," Ono Y observed in confusion, as Birla X rubbed her wrists and moved her tender jaw on the floor beside him.

"We'd prefer they didn't," radioed Ty. "Tell us what to do!"

"This has to be human judgement," said Amon. "It's too crazy for an algorithm."

"Oh? I'd have thought the commanding Identity Executioner has *every reason* to follow through," said Hippo.

Amon knew Hippo would be right if—

"Comparative analysis of both LifeStreams complete," the PhisherKing announced. "No evidence of ecogenics or harmony dust in either 'Anisha' or 'Rashana.'"

"What have I been saying?" Birla Y replied. "Just hurry and—"

"BUT," the PhisherKing cut her short. "We've uncovered a hidden encrypted folder."

At this, the sisters both started, and looked at each other, one kneeling, one standing, eyes wide with alarm. Ono Y and the other guard, too, faltered in their interfacing. The guard took a protective step towards Birla Y, while Ono Y turned to the PhisherKing with his armored shoulders open, his bulky arms hanging wide, and his fingers spread at the level of his waist in a pose of fearsome readiness as though some taboo had been transgressed.

"Team, please," radioed Vertical. "Your guidance."

Returned to his train of thought about the situation outside, Amon arrived at a troubling possibility, and hurled his perspective through the ceiling. Past the cowering Judicial Brokers in the Fiscal Judiciary, the floors went by in a blur of exotic wallpaper, except for one that seemed to have the lights off. When his viewpoint came to rest at his destination floor, there too he found only darkness.

"The Executive Congress overlay is blacked out!" he shouted, back in the House of Blinding.

"The Liquidation Ministry too!" said Hippo, indicating the floor Amon had glimpsed on his way up.

"They've been cut from GATA's internal network," said a Phisher.

"Only those two floors?" Amon asked.

"No," another Phisher replied. "The basement—"

"To finish our analysis, we'll need the password for the hidden folder," the PhisherKing continued.

The sisters, both on their feet now, stared at each other for another moment as though dumbstruck. Then they blurted at once, "It's not mine," "It's hers," so that it was unclear which uttered what.

"Neither of you has access to a folder you share then?" the PhisherKing said sarcastically. "Data available in both your sub profiles and you can't touch it, is that it?"

"She put it there." "A plant." The sisters overlapped again.

From their scattered locations, the Atupians watched in a helpless daze this bizarre investigation of both the women that might have been their leader, made possible by the even more bizarre retreat of GATA forces. New oddities went on stacking up and yet the PhisherKing appeared indifferent.

"PhisherKing! We're being factholed!" Amon cried, flailing his arms near hysterics. "Someone is—"

"*They* were upstairs," Hippo spoke over him, pointing at Birla X and her two remaining guards. "Ono X cannot be—"

"The answer to all of this must be in the third folder," the PhisherKing replied coolly.

"Forget there ever was a third folder," Ono Y warned, as he lumbered towards him.

"And ignore the holes in their LifeStreams and readouts?" asked the PhisherKing. "We've compiled a list of missing segments that can only have been moved to an internal directory."

"All hers!" the sisters exclaimed together.

"They can't all be either of yours. They were clipped from both LifeStreams. The murder of your parents—"

"Begetters!" the sisters corrected in unison.

"—the execution of a Starter, cooperation with the Philanthropy Syndicate to adjust the bankdead population . . ."

Now the sisters gazed into each other's eyes as though asking the other silently what they were supposed to do, like little girls caught doing something naughty, their heads sunk below raised shoulders, their lips puckered, suddenly at a loss to explain anything.

"Leave her alone and GET on with it," Ono Y growled, now gripping the hood of the PhisherKing's cloak and winding up for a punch.

"Hurt him and security goes back on," said a Phisher.

"Bullshit," said Ono Y.

"The password. Give it," the PhisherKing demanded.

"One more time, PhakerKing."

"Ono, stop!" shouted Amon, moving without thinking to intervene.

The sisters just went on staring at each other, pouting, maturity draining from their faces.

"Come now, girls," Hippo cajoled, as though reverting to his grown-up attitude from when they were children. "Be cooperative."

"The password," repeated the PhisherKing. Ono Y yanked on his hood and socked him full force in the gut with an armored fist. The Phisher-King emptied his lungs in one wheeze and crumpled, his reaching hand thudding on the floor just shy of the Secretary of Blinding.

When Ono Y unslung his assault duster from his back, Amon picked up a heavy ergonomic chair, spun around with the chair held out at arms' length, and flung it at Ono Y. The chair hurtled towards Ono Y as he raised the butt of his duster over his head like a sledgehammer, glanced off his armored shoulder, and tumbled into the mess. Unfazed, Ono Y was preparing to bring his duster down on the PhisherKing when Birla X snapped, "Fine. You can have it."

"No!" shrieked Birla Y, growing spikes all over and charging at her sister.

"It's forty-nine—" Birla X stopped shouting out the password to sidestep her sister as Ono Y's duster came down with a *thwack* on the PhisherKing's side, and the Y guard lunged at Birla X.

But before the guard reached her, a Phisher bellowed at pumped up volume, "The doors! They're here!" and everyone looked to the elevators, as five snapped open a crack, revealing slivers of grey uniforms. While the revolutionairies jabbered in mindless disarray and squandered the precious seconds the GATA retreat had granted them, the Liquidators had arrived after all. That was all Amon had time to think before rivers of dust whirled confluent into the House of Blinding, and he dove again for cover, the sound of proteanite flower-drills, dust, howls, and nerve dust screams belting his ear drums.

2

By the time he took the impact of the floor behind the vending machine with his forearms, thighs and chest, and tossed his perspective into the air, the battle was already over.

From the slat between the doors of five elevators, gleaming barrels peeked—a knot of assault dusters from two, and a single dust cannon from three—slits of face above concrete grey fabric visible behind. Ono Y lay facedown unconscious atop the Secretary of Blinding, long hair spilling over the man's face, groins and chests almost aligned, their bodies surrounded by the twitching pixelthreads that had been his armor. The last Y guard, too, was sprawled out on the cluttered floor in front of the elevators. Without needing to rewind, Amon grasped what had happened to them: a barrage of haywyre dust from the cannons followed by spurts of nerve dust. But strangely, Birla Y had merely been shucked. The last remnants of Gemini Y fallen away, she stood trembling on the right side of the bank of elevators in a red and white track suit, fear twisting the features of her now life-sized digimake.

The Liquidators had left the others likewise unscathed. The PhisherKing took in gasping breaths and rolled slowly from side to side, hugging himself near Ono Y and the Secretary in their pathetic tangle. Hippo hunched by the far corner exactly as he had moments before the assault. The Phishers remained hesitantly beside Blinders or halfway scuttled to former hiding places. A pair of Atupians had dove for cover like Amon but the rest were in plain view. Most vulnerable of the phoenixes were Birla X—flat on her belly beside her upright sister with fingers interlaced behind her head—and her two kneeling guards, all mere steps from the gun-jutting elevators.

It would seem that the Liquidators were content to incapacitate the Birla Y Guard, heretofore the only able bankrupts. Amon was amazed that they would be such sticklers for protocol. Hadn't they already defied the rules in confronting the bankdead exiles?

The question was revealed to be misguided when several Atupians reached for their weapons and went down screaming under showers of dust.

"Stop and desist!" Ono X voiced from elsewhere.

The pair of Atupians who'd taken cover popped out, took shots that pattered harmlessly off doors, and fell in the same way.

"This is your final warning!"

At this the remaining Atupians froze. The Liquidators had withdrawn the three cannons and closed the doors of their five elevators to slats just wide enough to extrude the barrels of some dozen assault dusters. Although outnumbered more than two to one by the revolutionairies still on their feet, they had already taken aim at marksmanship software averaged points between target clusters from the protection of their pillboxes, whereas the phoenixes were caught in the open with weapons on the floor or still holstered. The sudden return of Ono X from messaging absentia also seemed to have spread confusion in the Atupian ranks. With the contradictions surrounding the sisters unresolved, Amon realized, Ono X's position in the chain of command was murky. Behind the vending machine, Amon was best situated to resist, but his hasty dive had left his head exposed, and he didn't want to risk any sudden moves. As if he stood a chance alone.

"Everyone hands on your heads," said Ono X. Most obeyed but Amon touched the grip of his duster at his hip and several Atupians kept their hands likewise at their sides.

The doors of a sixth elevator just to the right of the others opened a crack, admitting a single hand duster that began to pulsate with incandescent light to draw their attention.

"Hands on your heads or be paralyzed for life! Now!"

In disbelief, Amon clicked the muzzle to pop up the specs. It was indeed a total locked-in duster, or totalocker, bringing permanent brain damage that cut off all signals to voluntary muscles and locked consciousness in its unresponsive body.

"On your heads in three, two, one."

Amon and the last of the Atupians put their hands on their heads.

"Phishers, away from the Blinders."

Those green cloaks not already fled rose with hands on their heads and obediently stepped or crawled away from their access points.

Everything was unraveling too quickly for Amon. The alliance between Ono X and the Liquidators was inconceivable. Even so, it lent credence to a suspicion that had suggested itself to him not a minute earlier.

"You're safe now," Ono X messaged.

Birla X rose to her feet, and her guards retrieved blitz dusters from two of their fallen Y counterparts. When they took up positions beside Birla X, Amon was stricken with a sense of déjà vu. One male and one female guard flanked her in military posture with cradled assault dusters much as Birla Y's guards had done after her cataclysmic arrival.

The two scenes, remembered and perceived, did not match perfectly. Birla X and her guards in the present wore navy suits rather than proteanite shells, and standing in for Ono Y, instead of Ono X, was a male X guard whose name Amon didn't recall. The difference he found most conspicuous was that the sides the guards took were flipped, with the man on Birla X's right and the woman on her left, as if to symbolize the reversal of events. For he understood one thing at least: domination of the Phoenix Revolution had passed from one sister to the other.

And yet, when Birla X peered over her shoulder at the Liquidators behind their protruding guns, Amon was surprised to see a shadow of confusion pass over her expression of relief. It was as though she were taken aback by the coup Ono X had staged for her almost as much as Amon or anyone else.

"This is what you meant with your blubbering last night?" asked Birla X.

"Watch—you'll see," her Ono replied

Amon felt like an idiot. He'd taken the proposal as genuine, not even mentioning it to the others out of respect for the privacy of the supposed lovers. But coming on the eve of revolution, with so much Freedom set to rip loose from its harnesses for grabbling hands to seize, he should have been more circumspect.

Not missing a beat, Ono X group messaged, "Atupians, no more feedcasts. What happens here, stays here."

Then he voiced the sisters, "Turn off glass mode," and the sheen faded from both their bodies.

"Everyone out here," Ono X continued as a grid of translucent mannikin-like people lying facedown appeared a short distance from the elevators. Floating hands pointed at each ghostly dummy. "Move!"

"Not you, or you." Another hand pointed at the PhisherKing, then Birla Y. "You two stay where you are."

The PhisherKing had come to a rest on his back near the Secretary and Ono Y, while Birla Y had crept almost to the corner right of the elevators. The rest of the phoenixes began to clamber over chairs, comatose bodies, proteanite threads, and rubble towards the grid. Amon pulled his perspective back into his body and followed along, stopping on top of the dummy indicated by a finger that blinked for him and laying down prone to overlap with it.

His belly atop all manner of shapes, some warm, some not, Amon peered across the topography of mess towards the weaponized elevators and glanced at his overlaid clock. So much had happened so quickly that it felt to him like hours since the collision; in fact, less than ten minutes had elapsed.

"What's happened now?" asked Ty, his camera still capturing the city through the front entrance glass. "Tell us what to do already."

"Break out and reunite—run, find refuge," Hippo urged in a whisper, from his place on the floor a few spots to the right of Amon. "And tell the others I'm sorry. I swore I'd never let anyone make us their pawns again, whatever the sacrifice, and I failed. Our part in this is finished."

Amon was expecting Ono X to remonstrate with Hippo for communicating with the outside, but he didn't seem to notice or if he noticed to care. Evidently, Hippo's attempt to preempt the forces now perverting the revolution had been so thoroughly squashed as to hardly be worth paying attention to, and as much as Amon rued the idea of giving up, he had to accept Hippo's advice to the exiles. A quick toggle through their windows showed that no more than ten remained in the lobby. Faced with the better armed Liquidator horde unhampered now by the distinctions of protocol, the best the exiles might hope for was to save themselves.

As if to punctuate Amon's deepening despair, five elevators opened and out marched the Liquidators. They left behind several comrades, who sat or lay bleeding in each chamber, impaled by an automatic counter-volley of proteanite darts from Birla Y, Ono Y, and her guard.

When the grey suits formed two rows in front of the grid of captives, Amon was astonished to see a mohawk rearing high from a giant man taking his place in middle back. Of the thousands of Liquidators Ono X could have recruited to his merry band of turncoats, what were the chances one would be Amon's old squad mate Freg?

When the final elevator opened, he was half expecting to find Freg's inseparable partner Tororo. Then the lines of grey suits parted to allow the bearer of the totalocker to saunter out, and Amon saw who it was, confirming the suspicion he'd been nursing ever since he realized that the pullback was a human decision. With this, the blurry shape of the coup snapped into focus, and a slimy eruption of understanding chilled and sickened him. Although the man's nymphic bald digimake had switched to black eyes with olive skin, cratered cheeks, and suavely greased-back hair, the short stature and severe stoop were unmistakable.

It was the Minister of Liquidation, Yoshiyuki Sekido.

Clicking open the HeadKount app, Amon tallied seven Liquidators in each of their two rows and six skewered in the elevators. The total of exactly twenty indicated that this was not some random squad to the rescue. These were the ten pairs of reserves intentionally left behind to prevent algorithms from declaring an emergency. Amon had watched the Birla X Guard beauty them minutes earlier. They should have been comatose in the Liquidation Ministry for hours yet. But here they were on their feet. If anything they looked refreshed.

A Phisher lying to Amon's immediate left—the man who had earlier noted the disconnection of the two floors—nudged him in the ribs with an elbow and discreetly showed him his palm, on which rested an anchovy. Amon touched the tiny fish, thereby opening the feeds of the Birla X Guard recorded in the LifeStreams of everyone on sharing mode with them. The Phisher rewound the ten recordings and toggled quickly through each of the segs at a particular time. In the midst of the tense infiltration, when the other phoenixes had their attention on securing the House of Blinding, the guards had adjusted the settings on their dusters. On the descending elevator to the Liquidation Ministry, all had dialed them down to the lowest intensity. The Phisher then rewound a few seconds further, and showed Amon a single guard dialing hers up immediately after dusting Sekido in the Executive Congress. Thus while the Executive Council and Blinders had gone comatose, the Liquidator spares and their Minister had merely been put to sleep. Amon supposed that they had risen some minutes later and severed the overlay of their floors from the ImmaNet—perhaps using Sekido's local network privi-leges—to hide their absence.

Whatever they were supposed to have done then, Hippo's summoning of Birla Y seemed to have thrown it all off. The shock worn by the Liq-uidators as they gawped at the devastated room confirmed this. After Gemini Y crashed, Ono X must have improvised, first helping the exiles fend off the Liquidators while Sekido was asleep and hinting to Birla X that she should delay the PhisherKing, then dropping out of sharing mode in preparation to confer with Sekido when he awoke. While Birla X's subversive whispertexts stalled any irreversible reprogramming, Sekido had called off the encroaching host and taken the reserve pairs to the basement GATA armory—the third floor cut from the ImmaNet that the Phisher had earlier tried to mention. This was the only place, Amon knew, where they could acquire the haywyre cannons required to deshell Birla Y, her Ono, and the guard. The totalocker, on the other hand, was not in the GATA arsenal or even authorized for Liquidator use. It was banned by international credilaw, the severance of will and body deemed antithetical to Freedom itself, let alone a Free Market. Sekido could only have smuggled it in on his person, a credicrime Ono X would need to have paid with the remnants of Fertilex. So bringing the atrocious weapon had clearly been premeditated. But why had Sekido agreed to risk his personal safety and career to wield it? What was he doing working with Ono X rather than—

Amon's thoughts were overpowered by a yelp from Birla Y. The two Birla X guards—the only guards of either sister left standing—had tripped Birla Y and were dragging her from where Ono X had told her to wait, near the rightmost elevator. Gripping one ankle each, they marched over the clutter—her head bumping on limbs, conking off a brow, scraping over pixelfibers, up-flung hands flailing over everything. Then they dropped her heels unceremoniously to the floor and left her supine at the feet of her sister.

"What's my name?" demanded Birla X, her hand raised high across her chest, shaking with rage for the humiliations done to her.

"R-rashana," her sister stammered.

"Exactly *right!*" Birla X hissed through gritted teeth as she let her hand fall.

The impact with her sister's forehead seemed to split into triplicate, as Amon's memory of the Emoticon Man backhanding Mayuko last summer and Birla Y envisioned as the Emoticon Man backhanding Birla X earlier superimposed on the uncannily similar present as if viewed through drunk glasses. *Thwack thwack thwack.*

Ungloved with proteanite, Birla X's hand lacked the heft to topple her sister as she herself had been toppled. Seeing her still upright on the floor, she drew a frustrated nasal breath, eyes stretched wide, and wound up for a kick.

With a shriek, Birla X swung her heel into her sister's kidney. Intentionally or incidentally, this resembled a kick Birla X had sustained from her sister earlier. But again it was not hefty enough to slake her desire for vengeance, and she began to thrash at her sister's side with the same foot. Birla Y blocked this convulsion of kicks with her forearms and managed to get hold of her sister's pant hem. The two guards then snatched Birla Y's wrists and yanked her arms up, allowing Birla X two solid kicks to her side before Ono X intervened.

"Leave off for now," he said. "Your recompense will come. I promise."

Birla X waved away her guards, lording over her sister who was curled up in fetal position, the crotch of her track suit a shade darker than elsewhere, liquid pooling on the floor beneath. If not for the sisters' different attire and their shifted locations in the room, the similarity to Amon's memory of another moment earlier was so perfect he might have thought a sliver of his perception had been overwritten with video.

Amon felt a hand press on his back and his weapon was tugged out of its holster. He realized that the front line of Liquidators had dispersed during the altercation between the sisters. Levitating his perspective, he watched them disarm the revolutionaries. Grey suits moved between the rows of their prone bodies and bent down to confiscate their weapons one by one, or else gathered fallen weapons from the floor, before chucking them into the corner between the rupture and the elevators. Two collided in midair and spun into the floor-clutter. One went off target and skittered over the edge of the rupture into the city.

"PhisherKing," Ono X said. "Go back to the Secretary—connect."

"To what end?" the PhisherKing asked.

"You'll give Rashana Gyges Ring."

Here was the objective of Sekido and his Liquidators that had been interrupted. If not for Hippo's message to Birla Y, they would have woken and come down to the House of Blinding before the Phishers were finished their reprogramming. There they would have joined forces with the Birla X Guard, and as many Atupians as could be recruited on the fly, in commandeering executive access to the Blinding network through the Phishers.

"I don't have the Gyges program," the PhisherKing said.

"A half-truth," Ono X accused him. "We both know that you can adapt the program for universal access. Our cryptobreakers say you just have to change the range of the action-data distortion. You'll configure it for the set of signatures in Rashana's copy of the Phoenix Virus and no one else's. Then cure her while she's bankliving."

This was the possible future Ono Y had first revealed when he demanded it for Birla Y—the hijacking of universal access for a single individual, inviolable connection and action only for one. In other words, the endowment of absolute banklife. Birla and Ono Y been too hurried to realize how this future could be brought about. Only Ono X had the foresight to not only envision it long before anyone else but to devise its actualization. Even the PhisherKing was caught unprepared. Excuse outed, he did not reply.

"Move, PhisherKing," said Ono X.

"No." The forward momentum of history seemed to snag at this bald denial. Then the totalocker homed in on him.

"We'll find you a white room in the best hospital," Ono X threatened. "Make sure your eyes stay peeled."

"Not a taste of information to the long and bitter end," added Sekido, looking down the barrel of the duster he aimed.

Amon was stunned to hear his former boss speak with such concision and clarity.

"I've had enough life to fear it no more than death," the PhisherKing replied, waving his hand across his face to dispel his digimake and reveal the matrix of wrinkles beneath, his great age bespeaking an equanimous resignation. "I'd rather lose choice itself than choose what you're asking."

"But would you steal choice from the young?" asked Ono X as Sekido shifted his aim to a green cloak on the floor below Amon's feet. "You've already lost one of your disciples." Red glowing orbs hovered over the heap of piranha-picked bones in the far corner.

"Don't make us condemn the rest to a dull forever," said Sekido.

Amon could only think that someone was feeding him his lines. A gabkeeper perhaps?

"Even your Treasure Matrix will be lost to them," Ono X continued. "Can you really accept responsibility for that?"

Silently, the PhisherKing surveyed his facedown disciples in the rows, the spinning wheels of his eyes dragging to an uncertain crawl, the three colors of his eyes glimmering doubtful.

"Sekido, old friend!" Hippo shouted, raising his head from the floor five bodies to the right of Amon. "What are you doing?"

Sekido turned to take in Hippo's indignant scowl, still aiming at the PhisherKing, and his digimake changed—skin, hair, irises turning albino pale, his nose and ears shrinking to delicate ornaments.

"The Gyges Circle were my allies in overthrowing the kingpin of GATA corruption," the Liquidation Minister stated matter-of-factly. "But wise Ono X revealed their rotten underbelly. He proved that a new champion of Hakkotopia is here."

"Believe me when I say that this woman"—Hippo pointed at Birla X—"does not represent what you— "

Hippo was interrupted when Freg strode in and delivered a swift kick to the side of his face. As Hippo grunted and flipped onto the back of the

Atupian beside him, Sekido's expression remained flat and formal but his digimake switched six times in quick succession, a hyper slideshow of skin color and physiognomy, settling on a Hispanic man with bristly eyebrows.

"Kind Ono X will fly me from the heaven of government, to alight on the pinnacle of Fertilex lobbies," he said blandly. "There at last I will have the political influence to bring meaningful reform."

Why the face changes at this precise moment? Amon wondered. He'd never understood this fetish of his old boss. Even more puzzling now was his uncharacteristically stilted and to-the-point speech. He hardly seemed to have heard Hippo. Nevertheless, Sekido's words suggested an explanation for his odd refusal to work for Birla X as Rashana; he had been the source for much of Ono X's all-too detailed intelligence about the recent activities of the Gyges Circle. Birla X could not have been allowed to know about the relationship lest her sister, later Amon on glass mode, discover it through her LifeStream. Sekido might once have been an agent for Birla X, but he could only be a double agent for her Ono.

In this capacity, he would have been working surreptitiously after the exposé to break the Full and Absolute Choice coalition apart, only putting on a show of holding it together for the benefit of the Gyges Circle, not actually doing so as Birla X had believed. If so, his vote for the Secretary of Blinding appointment that morning had, likewise, not been in service of the cabal, but of Ono X's unfolding plan. Which in Sekido's mind furthered Hakkotopia 2.0. But how was the granting of Gyges Ring to Birla X—

The male guard swiveled his blitz duster towards Hippo, spread perpendicular across the backs of several Atupians with his jaw held in both hands.

"I wanted you to deal with him at your leisure," Ono X said. "But better to judge him now."

Birla X nodded sadly, and Ono X held up an origami video that unfolded in the air.

Rashana. I know that's your real name. Hurry to the House of Blinding alone and tell no one. No financial defenses will hinder you. I'll see to it that you have what is truly yours. We need your help to bring the future that we all deserve.

The audio message in Hippo's voice was being played by a perspective wearing a red and white tracksuit—Birla Y before the crash—seated amidst a blur of ghosting sky and city.

Amon supposed that Ono X had clipped the seg from her subprofile when it was on glass mode. Obviously, this was the moment he'd rewound Hippo's LifeStream for earlier. Upon reconnection of his BodyBank, Hippo must have dug up a contact listed as "Anisha Birla" from his data prior to identity euthanasia, believing her to be Rashana Birla, whoever that was.

The continuation of the video showed Birla Y trying to text Hippo back but only getting a notification that the recipient could not be found. Then she noticed a link he'd sent, providing access to his location, and opened a map, where a red dot representing Hippo approached GATA Tower.

"This man handpicked the Atupians to be his phoenixes under—" Ono stopped his inquest and barked, "Watch your sister."

"What is this?" Birla X demanded, her disdainful gaze dropping to her feet. Birla Y's arms were crossed around her midriff, hands hidden beneath armpits making subtle motions. Amon opened her feed and caught her sending a file at the end of a coaxing text thread with a Phisher.

"A leak from the encrypted folder," the PhisherKing announced, hurling a vidbomb.

Liquidators corralled a crowd of men, women, and children in moss and seashell clothes from the streets of a plantfoam city into a centicopter.

Where are they going? The perspective, who had Sekido's voice, asked a grey-suited man. Sekido's gaze turned to his activist girlfriend, her hair dyed black with red highlights, doe eyes meeting his with fear and longing as she was led up the ramp.

Cut to a slightly taller perspective observing her through a one-way mirror in a clinic. She was strapped to a bed above which a Fertilex logo glowed. In time lapse, a FillBot spidered up her fastened legs, gleaming cylinder inserted unwelcome between thighs, belly ballooning, a gaggle of doctors and nurses around her spread legs, belly flat . . . Strapped down, crawling machine, cylinder, pregnant, delivery, flat . . . The progression repeated as Sekido's girlfriend turned ever more haggard . . . When time lapse ended, the perspective sliced a still of the next cylinder insertion, searched through his contacts for a sender, and clicked "Rashana Birla," then "Anisha Birla."

"*We* were the recipients of that principal investigator's reports," Birla Y shouted to Sekido over the video. "Barrow was just our agent in the roundup. The islander women went to fine havens as surrogates for—"

Birla Y let out a sharp breath as one of the guards yanked her by the wrists to extend her arms and the other stepped on her ankles to pin her legs. Then the first guard stuffed the tip of her shoe in Birla Y's mouth, gagging her. Once again Amon was struck by the warped symmetry of events, as though the sisters were reflecting each other through a funhouse mirror that intersected time.

"Our lobbydeology brings supreme policy," said Sekido as he looked into Birla Y's feral, panicked eyes peeking past shoelaces. "The righteous cannot leave posterity to the wiles of your thinktank."

Sekido hadn't even taken a glance at the vidpolosion and spoke as though unaware of what Birla Y had said. His expression remained prim and officious, but his digimake had begun to shift at steady intervals like clockwork, the shape of his nose, contours of his brow, distance between and size of his eyes, hair type, skin tone, all ticking abruptly and disjointedly.

Amon was too disturbed to bare it any longer and swiped away the overlay. Here, for the first time, he saw his old boss' naked face, unveiled much like his old workplace not half an hour earlier. Amon was surprised to find no disfigurement, or even abnormalities of any kind. He was just your average middle-aged salaryman, brown eyes, clean-shaven, thinning short hair, a dollop of fat around the jowls from after work drinking. The only unusual thing about it was the motion of his lips, motoring along rapidly though no sound was coming out. Amon clicked open Lip2Text.

" . . . Soil of progress salted in unbroken code, assembly lines for justice blighted in communication glut, wrath of defect unforeseen in our buildings and blueprints upon the twice imagined earth. I am the end of connections come, you the undoing charge, they the last switch of a superconductor spirit to power our presentiments down. For we have reached the cessation of calculation, the beyond wherein number drops away into the uncounted hulls of our sunken arks, a covenant sealed with the zeros of maverick stigmata . . ."

A half-second skim through the transcript was more than enough, and Amon closed the app, noting how the tenor of the man's rambles had changed. Grown more archaic? Poetic?

The Phishers were all trying to lob something at Sekido and, turning the overlay back on, Amon saw that they were vidbombs, copies of the previous one. Black fuse-lit spheres kept glancing off the center of Sekido's gaze as though from an invisible force field and bursting around the edges of the room into the island roundup scene.

"Settle!" Ono X bellowed over the audio clash as Liquidators swung the aim of their dusters from Phisher to Phisher.

Where— Where— Where are they— go— go— going? multiple Sekido's playbacked slightly out of synch.

"Don't bother," the PhisherKing told his Phishers. "His perception is curated."

Looking at Sekido, oblivious to the deception at the heart of his sham of a life literally exploding around him, Amon wondered why he would alter his two-way connection with the world, filtering and translating all information in and out. Then he recalled Makesh Adani backspinning a turntable to silence Sekido's blathering in the jazz bar and wondered if Ono X might have infected Sekido with a curation virus, perhaps using a parasite like the one given to Amon. Ono X knew his master's preferences well after all.

When the Phishers gave up on hurling the vidbombs and the image-bursts stopped, the Liquidators turned their dusters away from the floored captives. One guard continued to restrain Birla Y, stretching her arms up while immobilizing her head with the gagging shoe. The other had unslung his blitz duster, and now reaimed it on Hippo. Whereupon Ono X resumed his judgment.

"This man handpicked the Atupians here to undermine us," he proclaimed. "He argued for the Birla Guard to trade blitz for beauty to weaken them. Then he called in Anisha. A coldblooded backstab if there ever was one."

The Liquidation Minister's face change had accelerated, now a deck of shuffling cards. He sustained his implacability until Ono X reached the verdict on his old friend; then five sad scowls ticked by like some forgotten sea beast breaching.

There was an audible click as Hippo finally relocated his jaw. "Sekido, we seek universal access," he slurred with tender joints.

"To demonstrate our will," Ono X explained to Birla X over Hippo's appeals. "You agree?"

Birla X shook her head in doleful acceptance and turned away as though disavowing what would follow.

"For the memory of your wise mother, who fought for anonymity," Hippo pleaded, "and Naomi, that sweet champion of a harmonious freedom, please—"

Hippo was interrupted when the guard fired.

"Out!" Hippo shouted, snapping abruptly to his feet. His gaze darted around the corners of the room as if searching for some elusive specter attempting to possess him. "Out I say!" he shouted again and hammered his temple once with a fist. "It was not I that sang. Another choir. Whatever you believe for me."

His gaze was turbid, head jittery, nose puckered, immersed in disturbing ruminations, until it suddenly occurred to him to look down at his chest and his eyes skittered over his navy suit as though reacquainting themselves with his body. He stood there, swaying strangely, apparently unsure which foot to put his weight on.

"I would have left that drafty room. On a November morning? No!" Amon gasped along with several others when Hippo's left hand reached up to tear his right ear off in one smooth motion, and he squealed in wonder as though surprised by the pain. "I don't even like chess. Where have you gone, going?"

"The fuck is that?" radioed Ty.

"Hippo?" said Vertical.

Hippo? Tamper glove-texted, while Little Book tapped alarm.

Blood sputtering down the side of his head, Hippo went with his right hand for his left eye but his left hand held it back by the wrist. "I would never long for a harbor that is yours by rights. You can't make me have hated that!"

The inclusion of this dust in the Birla Guard blitz must have been secret because Amon hadn't been aware, but he recognized what kind it was: autoalterity, redrawing the line between self and other.

While Hippo's arms wrestled in front of his face, his legs tripped each other, and he tumbled over the terrain of bodies, rubble, and chairs, arguing with himself as he went. "Yellow is your color . . . Do is . . . Do not . . . In childhood after."

"This is sick—stop it," the PhisherKing said.

"I don't like it any better than you do," Ono X told him. "It's all up to you."

"You can't pass off responsibility. I said no," the PhisherKing replied, but for all his acceptance of life and death, his voice wavered, his hands twitching out ineffective gestures.

Once Hippo had settled on his back in a hollow, he managed to bite off his left ring finger, allowing his right hand to slip free and unhesitatingly pluck out his eye.

Amon heard someone on the floor near him retch and caught the sour reek of vomit. Not believing what his friend was doing to himself, he lowered his perspective into his body and tried to get up and restrain him, but Freg immediately took aim and shook his head.

Hippo's mutilated hand then picked up a beautyed Blinder's hand and pressed the thumb into his nostril, while he shrieked disbelieving between snatches of his outer monolog.

"Away! Closer! Take those silk screens back where you came from! That is not my opinion. Off!"

Horrified beyond horror, Amon looked up at the appalled voyeuristic leers of the Liquidators lined up along the elevators, searching for someone, anyone, to do something. His gaze skipped over Birla X, with her eyes averted, and settled on Sekido. The area above his neck had gone blur, traversing a yearbook a second, impossible to follow. It was barely perceivable as a face at all, and yet, somehow, the man's expression appeared constant across all the variations, the one recognizable through-line in the torrent of features. A grimace, ten-thousand flickering rictuses of sorrow.

Sekido noticed Amon and turned to him. "Kenzaki," he said quietly, just for Amon. The whole of mankind that ever was or will be gazed its pathos into Amon's soul and his soul alone, while all others were engrossed in the spectacle of now. Down Sekido's strobe-stutter of misery, a lone tear trickled. At each stage of its journey—from rim of the eye to cheekbone, from cheekbone to jawline, along jawline to chin—he swapped through ten faces, the tear unable to dribble down the same face twice.

"Sekido-san," said Amon. "Are you listening? For Hippo . . ."

Desperate to reach the person beneath the preternatural masquerade, Amon opened naked view and found Sekido's lips caught on turbo, repeating the same motions again and again. Lip2Text decoded the mantra, and somehow Amon knew that it was meant for him.

"True freedom is faking it real to change the world. True freedom is faking it real to change the world. True freedom is faking it real to change the world. . . ."

Having imparted this tragic lesson to his former protégé, Sekido closed his mouth, wiped the tear dangling from his chin with fingertips, and turned back to Hippo. When his expression reverted to a politician's stern deadpan, Amon's faint expectation that he might stand up for his friend's mercy withered into nothing.

By the time Amon glanced over again, Hippo was writhing in a shallow pool of his own blood, holes bitten through his lower lip, front teeth missing, someone's hand plugged into his split nostril, a shard of wall adorning an eye socket, earless, a patch of his bald scalp peeled back, two and three-fingered hands groping crab-like over his body and the slopes of clutter beside him for intruding and lost parts, jibbers waning, cursing thoughts and feelings he would not own. Here had been a capable Identity Vitalator, a brilliant researcher, a fallen hero of the poor, a despairing waste, then an ally in revolution and finally a traitor. No—not a traitor. Tipped off by the Books about Birla X's unusual eye movements, Hippo had made an audacious and desperate choice with the only information he had, and his premonition had been right! Now he'd had the courage to challenge Sekido in the face of death and worse. He didn't deserve this. No one did.

"Monju," said Amon. "He still might pull through."

"And condemn humankind to the future Hippo was resisting?" interrupted the PhisherKing.

Amon hesitated, unsure. Was it right to trade for the life of a person the very reality they had risked that life to foreclose?

"We'll have our future either way," said Ono X. "My cryptobreakers are reverse engineering the procedures from your feed. They'll walk through your Phishers or one of Sekido's technicians if you won't help us. You're replaceable, PhisherKing. But save us time and save everyone the pain."

The PhisherKing's gaze flicked between Hippo's slowing self-mutilation, the guard's blitz duster, his prone disciples, and the totalocker pointed his way.

"If you cooperate, I'll grant Hippo a pardon now," Birla X assured him, "and unlimited access to information for all Phishers in your own autonomous kingdom under the new order."

Like Birla Y earlier, she could not cut a true Birla Deal. The benefit her offer promised was a far cry from superlative, but it was the closest she could devise on the spot. Another recycled scrap of past twisted in the present.

"I'll do it," spat out the PhisherKing.

Sekido signaled to Freg, who lifted his duster and fired, drawing from Hippo his loudest scream yet.

For a moment, the PhisherKing stared in blank horror at the man, still but for the trickle of blood from many small wounds. Then his nerves seemed to reach critical mass and his hands shuddered into motion. Amon watched through his perspective as, for the third time that morning, his fingertips touched down on the Secretary of Blinding and he connected to the network, agent of absolute banklife for another.

A rising wind misted the back of Amon's head and arms with faint cold droplets. Tossing his viewpoint to the ceiling, he saw that the hail had turned to rain. Beyond the breach, it fell with surprising gentleness, casting a strange calm over the cylinder of rooftops sealed in by the swirling peacedrones. The same calm pervaded the room, as Birla X picked her way to the other side of the prone revolutionaries and stopped beside the PhisherKing on his knees over Ono Y and the Secretary of Blinding, preparing to receive Gyges Ring.

"I'm beginning to understand," she said. "But before the PhisherKing is done, you must tell me everything."

"First, shut them out," Ono X replied.

A notification told the phoenixes that "Rashana Birla," in other words Birla X, had left sharing mode. Then the same Phisher nudged Amon again, and he zoomed in from the air on the narrow space between their bodies, honing in on the man's furtively revealed palm. Inside a display window shaped like a swordfish played two segs side by side, the AT readout of "Rashana Birla" and that of Ono X. Amon supposed that the PhisherKing had used his hacked executive clearance—beneath the notice of the cryptobreakers or whoever else was surveilling his glass-moded profile—to unblind their actions and transactions for the Phishers, This was a common Blinder procedure with bankrupts targeted by Liquidators, as Amon knew well (though with the added complication of reassembling data from each of Birla X's phoenix virus proliferating identity signatures into a coherent series). When Amon clicked the fish window to expand the readouts, he found that the file already included a plugin to relink each licensed word into the conversation it formed.

"The PhisherKing was supposed to be finalizing his code when Sekido got here," said Ono X. "All our technicians would have needed to do to give you the exemptions was tweak the universal access program. Hippo and your twin threw it all off. I'm sorry. But trust me—we can still make a recovery."

"All this to give me the Ring of Gyges?" Birla X texted.

"A diamond dream set in the Ring of Gyges."

"A diamond ring . . . Your token of our supposed engagement."

"And what's left of Fertilex my gift for the honeymoon."

Recalling Birla X as Rashana's account of her and her sister's hopes for the future, Amon saw Ono X's offerings for what they were, as though the gift wrapping were unfolding from each of them in turn. A key to unlock the fetters of fee and fine that hindered humankind, a pen to rewrite the palimpsest of its genetic identity across generations, a scepter to rule the community that it might aspire for, and perhaps, if harmony dust was real, a tuning lever for the strings of its dreams. In a word, he was endowing his master with both transcendence and control over the limits that defined human action, within the market and without. The freedom of all, present and future, would become the freedom of only one.

"I never asked for any of this."

"You agreed, you accepted my proposal."

"I trust you too much. You know I couldn't refuse."

"I thought about your wishes the way your begetters taught us."

"How could I have guessed you meant all this? The code was too difficult."

"It had to be or the others might have seen through."

It now added up better for Amon that Ono X would be so helpful in convincing his Birla to support Amon's nascent idea for the Phoenix Revolution, even going so far as to trade away his dirt on the Gyges Circle and abandon special protections for Hakkotopia 2.0 to obtain the cure for conception dust. For realizing the diamond dream would have pleased "Rashana" more than anything. But Ono X knew that Birla X had only been "Rashana" for mere months since the Anisha LifeStream was stolen from her, and that additionally attaining the Ring of Gyges she had until then sought was bound to satisfy the freshly buried yearnings of "Anisha."

This subterfuge was akin to the Onos' secret fundraising for the Birla sisters' cyber assault on their Cognitive Handling Corps in childhood and their construction of two Geminis at their coming of age. Like his Y counterpart, Ono X had independently pursued the object of his master's unspoken desires. Proposing as a coded message in case Amon was watching on glass mode—much as he had often evaded the surveilling Birla parents—was an act that fit with this clandestine servility. And Amon couldn't stop picturing Ono X's expression of raw love and fear as he knelt and looked into Birla X's eyes, astounded that it could have been a performance.

"Whadda you want us to do with these punks," said Ty. Three of the display windows heaved as part of an exile crowd rolling through the concourse of a mall, while Ty's window faced a pack of children on the streets outside. They wore armor like that of the Birla Guard and Charity Brigade except sky blue with the diamond painting from

Atupio emblazoned on the chest. All carried hand dusters and looked to Ty with puerile concern as if wanting his parental guidance. "Amon? Monju? Hippo?"

Hearing Hippo's name in Ty's troubled voice brought up Amon's momentarily forgotten horror and colored it with his imagined sadness of the exiles upon learning their leader's fate. But he resisted the urge to take a pitying glance at his waning friend and boomeranged outside. There he saw that all semblance of distinct MegaGlom spirals at the InfoFlux border had dissolved. Now, sparkling here and there with CareBots summoned from Delivery, the multifarious peacedrone armadas inter-leaved around the invisible tube of GATA airspace in ornate patterns of automated interception and evasion like convection currents of metal, glass, and plastic. Weaving perilously through at ultrasonic velocity were the streaking blurs of Atupio carbonjets. As they danced into the no-fly zone from all directions leaving twists and bows of contrail, thousands of Starters fastened to dropdrones could be seen ejecting from cockpits, leaping from hatches, rotoring towards the city, or landing on rooftops. Some like the ones with Ty, were already on street level. Amon couldn't begin to think what to do about them and didn't dare answer Ty with Freg, the other Liquidators, and the guard that ruined Hippo looming over him.

Birla X seemed to have noticed the fresh interlopers, perhaps hearing Ty through the PhisherKing's glass profile, because she said, "Is Hakkotopia still possible with my children here?"

Ono X sighed. "I ordered their guardians to stay put in Haneda. But those rascals wouldn't listen. They stuck up the guardians in their cockpits. Forced them into GATA airspace and drove them bankrupt. Seems they're worried about you."

"What if something happens to them?"

"My Atupians are working to round them up. Meantime, they can take care of themselves."

"How will we all get out of here?"

"Gemini X is hitched to a rocket for low orbit. On an intercept course for a mobile space station I just purchased. We'll load her onto a space-plane, currently undocking for reentry and touchdown on the rooftop. Once you have the exemptions, leash me and my Atupians downstairs so we can bring the Starters up to the landing pad."

"You must have forgotten those orbital 'field trips' our begetters forced us to take."

"We won't stay long out there. Tacticorps is calculating another reentry above Ogasawara as we speak. Drop you in the financial protection zone safely aboard Gemini X. The MegaGloms will never let us through the encirclement so we'll just have to hop over."

"Do we have the seating capacity for everyone?"

"We wouldn't want it."

"So I have to lose Amon for this."

"No, he'll join. I've made arrangements to be sure."

Like hell I will, thought Amon. But there was something ominous in the certainty with which Ono X spoke.

"What about their loyalty after the speech I gave?"

"Not to worry. Our gabkeepers are working on a story about what happened here. A founding myth for a new society, they call it."

"Not everyone will accept it."

"Enough will. If Hakkotopia 2.0 is going to succeed, we just have to make sure that no one who witnessed the originating moment is ever allowed to contradict us. Sekido and the Liquidators will stay behind to tell a different story to GATA and the Twelve. The Atupians up there with you will be *decontaminated* of bad ideas. The Phishers will get what you promised according to their merit. The Judicial Brokers only caught bits and pieces outside sharing made. We'll facthole them on our way out to be sure."

Amon glanced up, no longer spotted eyes peeping down through ceiling holes, and wondered when the Brokers had vacated the Fiscal Judiciary.

"Right now, there's only one person we need to deal with," said Ono X, and Sekido shifted the aim of his totalocker from the PhisherKing to Birla Y.

"First explain," Birla X said aloud, glancing at her sister, still laid out with arms drawn taut and a shoe in her mouth. Then returning to audio text, she typed: "You left out your plans for her."

Ono X did not immediately respond.

"What?"

"PhisherKing, almost there?"

"We're proofreading the code," the PhisherKing said, he and his Phishers gesturing and mouthing rapidly.

"Gyges Ring is moments away," Ono X told his master. "Now is time for the recompense I promised."

With dawning understanding, Birla X scratched her brow where Anisha's mole had once been.

"See, she was supposed to have Gyges Ring along with you, but dirt broke because she lost Fertilex. She'd have landed at Tokyo home office by then. Our forces could have snatched her up before she knew what happened. Worst case we'd have hunted her down. This situation now, unfortunate as it is in every other way, is perfect for handling her."

Birla Y let out a throaty sound, not quite grunt or gargle, and her eyes rolled up to her sister as though asking for the chance to speak. Then the guard pressed the shoe deeper and her voicebox relented, her body going limp. Evidently, someone had given Birla Y access to the conversation reconstructed from the unblinded readouts. Ono X either wasn't concerned or was too caught up in what he was saying.

"You must see it already," Ono X went on. "Death would deregister her genome from your ID signature. Cause an error with the Ministry of Access that GATA would have to correct. Might mean your liquidation. Ask our cryptobreakers—or the PhisherKing. They'll tell you the same thing."

Birla X turned to the PhisherKing and parted her lips as if to ask him aloud, then glanced around at her audience in the room and seemed to think better of it.

"But alive, she'll get the exemptions. Her freedom will rival yours."

Avoiding the sight of her sister, Birla X stared at her hands, ran her thumbs over her fingertips, then turned them over, studying both sides with a pained wistful frown, as though the past she recalled were the heat from a vibrant chemical fire too close

"Why don't we have the PhisherKing decouple our genomes?"

"That's a Ministry of Access procedure. The Secretary of Blinding permissions can't get the Phishers in. It's a separate network. You two will be bound to the end."

"'I'd prefer to nerve or epilepsy her. I might like her as a pet."

"Don't forget we have limited seating."

"I'm sure we can stuff her in somewhere. A baggage compartment perhaps?"

"You'd allow her in your presence? After she stole 'Anisha,' stole Fertilex? After she tried to steal 'Rashana' and Atupio? After she slapped and kicked and insulted you?"

"I want to devise her punishment in my own way—carefully. Your plan is too rushed, too restricting."

"She has evidence of what happened here. She can challenge our founding myth like no one else. There can be no question of true authority. Over Hakkotopia, over Fertilex, over—"

"We're ready," the PhisherKing interrupted.

Looking relieved to have an excuse to extricate from the disagreement, Birla X leaned towards Monju to accept Gyges Ring by touch.

"First give Sekido the sign," Ono X begged. "You can't let her have the exemptions for even a moment. See how eager the PhisherKing is to make that happen? We can't predict what she might do. Please."

With one hand on a part of the Secretary of Blinding's chest not covered by Ono Y, the PhisherKing reached to place his other hand on the shoulder of Birla X, as she took one last look at her sister.

"Do I have to say what I know you know?" Ono X pressed. "You've shared everything; you've even shared you. One of you can only become more if the other is less. So share nothing and take everything either of you has ever wanted. Your freedom to be yourself will be absolute only when hers is zero. Don't miss this chance to become you, one hundred percent you."

When the sisters' eyes finally met, the subdued one looked up with pleading terror, and the proud one looked down with anger but an unmistakable tenderness beneath. The scale of freedom between them, one pan empty and the other full, was hers to release.

While Amon listened to the argument, something in what both Ono X and Birla X were saying rung insincere. Every one of Ono X's moves had been crafty and calculated, but his reasoning now seemed shaky.

What difference did it make if Birla Y had Gyges Ring for half a second? It seemed more pragmatic to stand aside and let his master wreak her vengeance according to her whims. On the flipside, Amon wasn't convinced by her supposed desire for capricious malice. If Birla X was set on punishing her sister, why not do so in the way that minimized complications as Ono X advised?

By the time Birla X and Y locked eyes, Amon was struck again with the eerie symmetry of events. Just as Birla X was hesitating to take choice from her twin in life, Birla Y as Anisha had hesitated to take choice from Birla X through death, even though she'd been willing to kill everyone, including Birla X and herself. In other words, Birla Y had been ready to accept the annihilation of all that her twin was only if she too were gone. Did that mean, by the unfolding logic of flawed duplicity, that Birla X would accept her own total fulfillment only if her sister attained the same?

"Hey—listen to me!" Amon shouted at Birla X this time, as if hypnotized by the warped reflections of the past into fulfilling his part in their simulacral choreography. He had risen to his feet, all feelings—the horror, the frustration, the terror—falling away. His whole being grew light even as a line of gleaming weapons trained their scarcely-bridled violence on him.

"Hold," said Birla X, straightening up and away from the PhisherKing's touch

"No, shoot!" cried Ono X, voice wavering as though agonized by this act of disobedience, perhaps his first ever.

"You're willing to spare me but not your sister?" Amon asked Birla X, stepping over the phoenixes and the mess towards her, unperturbed by the manifold suffering ready to be unleashed upon him. For reasons he didn't fully understand, he was valuable to her. But even if she decided to cripple or destroy him, he was prepared to accept it. "When she's gone who will be left that can understand the pain your parents put you through? Who will you compete with? Against whose achievements will you find purpose?"

Amon's thinking became clear to him only after he spoke. What held Birla X back from nullifying her sister's will forever wasn't her desire to freely punish out of hate. That merely concealed a hidden wish: to be shackled out of love. Both sisters had hesitated for the same reason, their ingrained need for mutual enslavement.

"In the eyes of the world, your servant's advice is good. Sucking up all your sister's freedom might allow you to you do anything. But what would Fertilex, or the diamond dream, or the Ring of Gyges matter to you then?"

Amon still didn't know what he was saying but it felt true. And knowing that he was speaking the truth, he felt not a jot of fear, hardly hearing the threats and warnings hurled at him.

"You'd be the fly trapped in the expanding jar."

When Amon concluded thus, he had arrived at the space between Birla X and the PhisherKing. Looking down on her with all somber sincerity, he saw in her twitching eyes that she knew he was right.

"Out of the way," Ono X yelled, but Amon glanced over Birla X's head at Sekido's barrel impassively, knowing full well what he was doing. The PhisherKing's hands were a blur in his shadow. The two guards were almost upon him, and time seemed to slow down.

"Stop Phisher!" Ono X cried. "Dust the king! Dust Amon! Shoot!"

Amon grabbed Birla X and hugged her close to him as a shield. She thrashed wildly in his arms until he flung her at the feet of her incoming guard, just as the other came roaring in, and Amon grabbed his wrist, tossing him head over heels to the side. Then he dove the other way and barely dodged a *patter* of totalock from Sekido.

The moment Amon landed, his chin whacking into a chair leg, something strange began to happen to his sight and hearing. Digimakes were ripped off bodies, Sekido's changeling face strobing in midair like some spastic bird dying in midflight, while a granular screech of almost cosmic intensity tore through Amon's ears. His entire visual field was disintegrating into fragments of hue and perspective, each 4D shard bursting and bursting again, his soundscape crackling apart into runny tones and resonances, a watercolor firework clangor that cast up the elements of his world. Then light itself broke apart into its constitutive filaments, collapsing like crushed tinfoil into dimness, noise to effervescent static to crystal-bell whispers.

Amon was left in twilight gloom reminiscent of the District of Dreams. Arms-bearing forms reeled vertiginously on their feet, while the prone phoenixes clamped their heads or cried out, all under the same perceptual affliction. Multiple dusters went off, another shot from Sekido flying wide of Amon, several shots missing the PhisherKing, who was already scampering away as though he'd been expecting this. Amon was the second to recover his wits, having been severed from the ImmaNet before. But unlike after his cash crash, he remained conscious, neither blind nor deaf.

Not wasting an instant to consider why, he rolled away as Sekido let off more errant dust streams, eyes spinning in his head. The spectacle of this clumsy assault recalled to Amon when his infected hand had fired haphazardly at Freg in the jazz bar, which in turn connected to a memory seconds later of the last time he'd seen Sekido, cowering behind an upended table. Amon had had to flee, rather than deliver his reckoning, and before Sekido could return to his senses, Amon charged in through the mess, spurred on by a remembered scintilla of anger. Freg was the first Liquidator to whip his aim towards Amon, two others wheeling theirs close behind, but all three missed, deprived of their precious marksmanship apps.

"Get up and fight!" bellowed Amon. "They're shooting wild."

Sekido went trigger-happy *chrinkle chrinkle chrinkle* while Amon zigzagged ever closer in leaps and bounds, from Blinder hip to chair to rubble-heap to leg, shots flying just wide. Other dustfire and screams sounded as Atupians and Phishers launched past him for the grey suits like scrambling torpedoes.

When Amon was only steps away from Sekido and the man's aim centered in synch with his pupils, Amon ducked under the line of fire, sprang upward, and plowed his shoulder into Sekido's stomach, sending him stumbling back. Before Sekido could regain his balance, Amon straightened up, slammed his left forearm crosswise into the wrist of Sekido's gun arm, and twined his other arm beneath Sekido's bicep to try for an elbow lock. But Sekido began to oink and writhe, his arm too slippery for Amon to get leverage. Then the painful crack of someone's fist into Amon's shoulder blade knocked them both spinning in a confused knot of limbs, and Sekido's bucking head bashed Amon's brow. The room whirled as Amon went cross-eyed, barely staying on his feet.

With his hold on Sekido's elbow loosened, Sekido begin twisting the muzzle around to the back of Amon's head, when two bodies slammed into him, ripping him loose from Amon entirely and leaving Amon to fall flat onto his butt.

It was the Birla sisters, now rolling on an inert Blinder, wrestling over the totalocker just beyond where Sekido was splayed on his back. Amon leapfrogged onto the seat of an upright chair and sprang towards the brawling sisters, hoping to seize the weapon, but the moment his feet touched down on the floor, the leg of a guard stuck out and tripped him. He flew headlong into the sisters, a shot of dust flying just over him. His shoulder bumped the hip of one sister, sending them tumbling into an open elevator, the totalocker landing on the threshold between him and them. On his side, Amon watched the twins alternate in scrabbling towards the weapon and dragging the other back, and reached out to pluck it away from their grasps.

Rising, he turned and felt someone tug his right wrist outwards before slugging him in the opposite jaw. As he spun out hard, Amon glimpsed that it was Freg, before he tumbled down a hillock of clutter. Winded, dizzy, spots swirling in his vision, he forced himself to his feet, and realized that he'd dropped the duster. It had found a resting place in the brown-suited crotch of a Blinder, and Amon watched Sekido bend over to retrieve it, noticing too late that Freg, disarmed, lip bloody, was closing his grip on Amon's collar and sleeve.

As Sekido raised the gun, a brawl was unfolding behind him. Navy suits and green cloaks lunged and tangled fiercely with grey opponents, but many lay already dusted in the debris, the revolutionaries overwhelmed, unarmed from the start. Amon struggled to get loose but Freg held him fast in his gargantuan clutches and Sekido stepped closer. Disconnected from aim assistance or not, there was no missing a stationary target at point blank range. Only a single expression of sadness this time on his salaryman face, as he swiveled the weapon to deprive his protege of action forever.

Crunch. Freg hollered out in pain, his body tilted to Amon's left, and his grip loosened. Amon shook himself loose and dropped to the floor, where he watched Freg's leg crumple as a woman in black withdrew her foot from a kick to the side of his kneecap. While Sekido was reorienting his aim down, a grappling trio bumped him, bowling him over onto his side, and Amon crawled woozily over the wastes towards him, grabbing the barrel and trying to pull it away. But Sekido had a solid grip on the handle, and despite Amon's size and the advantage of being on top, they fought for control with Amon kneeling over Sekido and the duster pointed obliquely over his shoulder. Under the opposing force of their muscles, the barrel shook and wavered.

"You're not all that ugly—on the outside," said Amon looking down into his brown eyes.

"Nuh," Sekido whimpered with a grimace, realizing that his face was exposed, and shut his eyes, as if by seeing no one, no one could see him. It was for no more than a split second that his sight was off the weapon, and he immediately opened his eyes, but that was long enough for Amon to let the muzzle drift off the mark and push it too low for Sekido to ever regain leverage. Infuriated by his mistake, Sekido spat in Amon's face, a glob dripping back onto his own nose, and scrunched up into fetal position, cradling the duster with his whole body.

No sooner had Amon curled around to dig inside for a better grip than he heard the grunts and thuds of impact above. Three men had locked shoulder over them, and a fourth soon arrived. More and more men and women rushed in and slammed into each other, the locus of the fight gathering around the most dreaded weapon. Someone stepped on his buttock, another fell on his back, and the weight of bodies began to press down. There was no way to wrest the duster from Sekido now that Amon could hardly move, so he held on tight, too panicked and battered to think of any other course.

Pinned facedown on the floor, he saw through a perforated patch another room below. The vague outline of stacked chairs and boxes. Hot, nauseous, barely able to breath, it took all the strength of his arms and legs to nudge the squashing mass enough that his lungs could expand, until another body flopped on top somewhere and emptied him like a bellows. A random fist pummeled his hamstring and teeth dug into his left shoulder, but he lacked even the breath to cry out. The frail remnants of the floor creaked as cracks opened up, and he could hear muffled roars, dust patter, thuds, and screams. When these sounds around him, the feeling of pressure on top of him, and the sight of the floor beneath him all grew hazy and distant, Amon fought to hold onto consciousness, to maintain his hold on the hard thing in his hand, though he could no longer recall what it was or why he needed it . . .

The sting of rugburn brought Amon to. Someone gripping his ankles was yanking and yanking and yanking, loosening his grip on the important object in his hand. Just when Amon remembered what he held, he was dragged away from it onto a lump of debris and turned over onto his back, gasping for breath, ready to fight to the last.

The man holding his ankles was Tamper. Beside him, Ty fired the assault duster mounted on the backrest of his shielded wheelchair at the few Liquidators that still wriggled on the ground. Amon recalled the woman in black who had kicked Freg amidst the fray and recognized now that it had been Vertical. He was too lightheaded to be relieved or surprised by the presence of the exiles.

"Get that man under the pile!" he wheezed, pointing to Sekido's ankle sticking out. "Get his weapon."

There were only three inert bodies on top of Sekido now, and Tamper and one of the Atupians began to pull them off while Vertical waited to the side with duster ready. But when the last body was tugged away, Sekido's arms flopped open as he rolled onto his back, the duster clacking to the floor beside him. His head lolled, open eyes unmoving, paralyzed.

3

"Here," Amon said to Vertical, reaching for the totalocker. She handed it to him, and sprang back as a guard crawled out of the pile. When the guard lunged for Amon's ankle, he staggered away, with no intention of ever using the atrocious weapon in his hand. Then Tamper beautyed the man, his head dropping to the floor.

More grunts and scuffling followed as Vertical pulled Atupians and Phishers from the heap, while Ty poked barrels into gaps between bodies to disable the rest. Still catching his breath, Amon lurched back and put the duster into the inner pocket of his jacket, for safekeeping until he could dispose of it.

Soon only two Liquidators remained upright, one grappling with a pair of Atupians beside the breach, the other straddling and choking a supine green cloak near the far wall. Vertical sprinted at the first and dusted him in the side at close range, sending the Atupian pair falling on top of him. The other took dust in the back from Ty and flopped limp on top of the Phisher, who rolled him off with a frantic thrust. No, not just a Phisher; it was the PhisherKing, rasping in air and rubbing his throat.

After that all was still, but Amon remained on his toes, searching for danger, disbelieving.

Under the pale light was an undulating junkyard of ergonomic chairs, vending machines, rubble, pixelthreads, pools of blood, dusters of all sizes, bones, and inert, groaning, dead or trembling bodies. As far as Amon could tell, only seven Atupians, four Phishers including Monju, and the three exiles were still mobile. With the collar of his jacket, he wiped away the sweat dripping down his face. Were all threats really finished . . .? A glance outside the breach told him no. Mongrel armadas rotated in layer after layer, eclipsing the city and sky beyond, blocking all light but for discoball glimmers. It was as though GATA Tower were at the bottom of a swirling well built of every conceivable destruction. Financial barriers held the MegaGloms at bay. But for how long? In all this tumult, Amon questioned the dependability even of the market.

"Atupians, Phishers," he said, his voice frail despite his best efforts to project it. "I want three of you to crew the cannons in front of that gaping hole over there. The rest watch the elevators."

The remnants of the phoenixes nodded and began to retrieve scattered weapons. Amon went to pick up the nearest assault duster, but feeling lightheaded, he let the barrel swing back to the floor.

"Are you okay?" asked Vertical.

Unsure of the answer, Amon leaned on the weapon and hung his heavy head as his vision heaved. Aching all over, there was a sharp pain in his shoulder blade, his temples throbbing.

"Vertical," he said, recalling Freg's crumpled leg. "How did you three get in here?"

"Elevator hacks," said Ty.

Tamper reached into a pocket and displayed a handful of what looked like black buttons. Now it seemed obvious. The exiles would have needed similar devices to break into the lobby and take cover beforehand.

"You came back," said Amon.

"We had to," said Ty. "The bankliving on the streets were freaking out. Looking around all confused and scared, like strangers in a strange land. Some of 'em screaming. The Books were the first to guess that the ImmaNet had cut out and Vertical agreed."

"I know what it's like," she said.

"That's when she asked Tamper for one of his gizmos and bolted for the tower. Danced through the Liquidator circle while they were still in confusion. The Atupian circle too I bet."

Vertical nodded.

"The rest of us charged in after, rolled over the 'dators, cut through the 'tupians. The others covered us while Tamper wheeled me down to the garage, under shelter"—Ty patted the transparent shield curving around the front of his wheelchair—"We took the elevator to ground floor, then up from there. You've got to understand. We *had to* go against Hippo's order. Who could sit on their hands when he was shrieking like that?"

"No one with any heart," said Amon. "You did the right thing."

"Where is he? Is he okay?"

Amon shook his hanging head, raised it halfway, and took a pained glance at the spot where Hippo lay. Vertical and Tamper pattered over while Ty wheeled through the mess as close as he could. Vertical gasped and put her fingertips to her lips. Cringing, Tamper crouched over the pocket of blood to feel Hippo's pulse.

Amon averted his eyes to his armpit, sad and repulsed beyond thought or word. Then he turned to watch the three phoenixes he'd assigned each haul one of the blackout cannons closer to the breach. When he glanced at the other eight arranging themselves in front of the elevators with dusters raised, he remembered something.

"Does anyone see the sisters?" Amon asked, scanning the mess. No one had an answer, and the phoenixes joined him in looking about. There was the colossal body of Freg strung out face down over a standing chair; Sekido strewn paralyzed, staring at the ceiling with an awful blank gaze; other Atupians and Phishers in manifold poses of harm among the spread of Blinders. But the sisters were nowhere to be found. Last Amon recalled, they were tussling in an elevator. In retrospect, it had probably been the one Vertical had come up on, but he couldn't remember which it was and the doors seemed to have automatically closed, making them indistinguishable from the rest. Could the sisters have fled to a different floor? Amon went to cast his perspective into the shafts to check where the elevator might have stopped, hoping to then boomerang and survey outside. When the gesture had no effect, he remembered that he had lost the ImmaNet again. Unlike the first time, he hadn't passed out, nor had anyone else. Why?

"Alive," Tamper declared and withdrew his fingers from Hippo's mangled nose. "Barely."

"Quickly," said Ty, "we've got to staunch the bleeding."

Vertical had already removed the jacket of a nearby Blinder and was tearing it into strips. Tamper withdrew a boxcutter from his pocket, handed it to Ty, and headed towards a still-standing vending machine along the wall opposite the breach.

"Fucker," grumbled Ty, as he began to cut up another jacket with the boxcutter. "Who did this to him?"

Amon thought for a moment and said, "He did it to himself in more ways than one—and he did it for us."

Before Ty could inquire any further, the PhisherKing croaked, "I wouldn't worry about the entrances." He had just risen tentatively and stooped with palms on thighs. "No one will be coming for us any time soon."

"You," Amon said, pointing an accusing finger. "Hiding the identity theft from us."

"I had no intention of hiding anything."

"Then I guess you deceived us by accident, did you? You knew about the encrypted folder."

"The propertied class are each an ocean of secrets, and the Birlas the deepest and darkest. Of all the facts we trawled up about them, we simply didn't know which to share."

"No? A coverup around the inheritance lawsuit and Ono X asks you for evidence of the other sister not being herself. I mean, Birla X altered her face and genes. She changed herself inside and out. If that isn't important enough to tell us, what is?"

"Easy to say in hindsight, now that I've connected the facts for you. The adjustments she made were minor—basically negligible. Until Hippo said that both sisters resembled 'Rashana,' who could have guessed that a so-called identical twin would try to become truly identical to her twin . . . ?"

Amon was admittedly perplexed about this very development. But that was largely due to the PhisherKing's hurried presentation of the identity heist. There had been little time to think through the evidence given.

"Us maybe," Amon replied, "if you'd given us the pieces to put our heads together."

"So you'd have preferred I dump a hodgepodge of data on you? With you and the Birla sister on glass mode? With you and Hippo on a leash? With all of us living in Atupio HQ under biosurveillance?"

Amon glanced at Hippo, who'd been forced for similar reasons to keep his doubts about Birla X to himself until the decisive moment that day. Tamper was pouring water from a vending machine bottle onto the stump of Hippo's severed finger and Vertical began to wrap it while Ty continued to cut strips of fabric. Amon still couldn't believe what Hippo had done or what had been done to him.

"We're not getting into this now," he told the PhisherKing. "Whatever you did to the system, fix it. Let's get this done and get out of here."

Amon pointed at the Secretary. He was still on his back in the center of the room where he'd lain since the crash, though Ono Y had been rolled off him. The PhisherKing made no move to approach the Secretary, hobbling instead towards Amon.

"I'm sorry, Amon," he said. "The wasteland can never be rejuvenated in the way we imagined."

"What are you talking about? We're here. Let's end bankdeath. Or have you had other ideas all along?"

"I wish we *could* end bankdeath. There was nothing we wanted more. But that's no longer possible—I've lost her . . ."

"Who?"

"The Great Treasure Matrix . . ."

"What did you do?"

"I had to shut myself out to save us."

"Explain yourself!"

"The program we Phishers designed for the Phoenix Revolution was supposed to distort the action-data of all Free Citizens before they were routed from the House of Blinding to the Ministry of Monitoring so that no movements ever matched an action-property. But when you stood in front of me and gave me cover to code for our sakes, I rewrote it. Instead of distorting everyone's action-data like it should have, the program distorts our identity signatures. Now when our signatures are routed to the Ministry of Access, they never match the ID of any registered citizen."

"What does that mean?"

"All identity signatures transmitted are now invalid. When they reach the Ministry of Access, they bounce. So GATA no longer recognizes anyone as a citizen. It rejects our requests to connect to the ImmaNet."

"Then how come we're still conscious like this? I've been through a cash crash before. There should be all kinds of symptoms."

The terror Amon had experienced waking up blind and deaf in the alley came back to him.

"Think about the liquidation process. Usually when someone cash crashes, their identity signature is erased. This shuts down their BodyBank entirely. All operations run by the implanted devices are interrupted. One of these is processing of auditory and visual input. Without this intermediary filter, our nervous systems take a shock. But our signatures were never erased. Our BodyBanks are still running. They keep on transmitting our signatures. The Ministry of Access just isn't recognizing them. So our devices continue to process our sensory input as before, but nothing is overlaid on top because we're not connected to the ImmaNet. Simply put, we're seeing and hearing the naked world via technology. Since our brains are adapted to this mode of perception, there's no disruption."

"If my BodyBank is still running, how come I can't access my inner profile?" Amon did some command-gestures and scowled at Monju.

"Because the apps you would use all require Ministry of Access permission to function. In the Year of Acquisition, we designed the standard

BodyBank to be useless when it's kicked offline for any length of time. This has kept users from bypassing the AT market."

"Ok. I get it. You disconnected everyone to give us the chance to resist. And we've beaten them. So what are you doing just standing there? Turn the ImmaNet back on so we can end bankdeath." Amon pointed again at the Secretary of Blinding.

"I would if I could, believe me."

"Why can't you?"

"I didn't have time to make any exceptions to the range of applicability of the program. It was designed to apply to action-data. I rewrote it to apply to identity signatures. It was all or nothing. So I made all identity signatures invalid . . . even mine."

"So what? You're disconnected along with the rest of us?"

Monju nodded.

"That's why you said we don't need to worry about anyone coming in here. The elevators won't budge even for bankliving. And no one can sic drones on us."

Monju nodded again.

Amon glanced at the bank of elevators. He realized that the sisters would have been disconnected inside, unable to press the floor icons. Since no one had mentioned anything, Amon wondered if he was the only one who had seen them tumble in during the melee, but some as yet unarticulated instinct urged him not to mention it. Looking back instead at the PhisherKing, he frowned, grappling with the implications of his choice.

"But what does this even . . . What you did isn't just going to cut us off the ImmaNet, is it?"

"No. Since no one has a valid ID, none of the action-data flowing into GATA belongs to anyone."

"Which means we're cut off from the AT Market as well."

"For all intents and purposes, yes. Millions of action-transactions are occurring each second but they're being performed by zero citizens."

"Fuck. Come on. We came here to give everyone universal banklife, forever, irreversibly . . . and you're telling me that we gave them universal bankdeath instead?"

"Technically speaking, it's not bankdeath because our BodyBanks are still active."

"Don't quibble with me, Phisher."

"Practically speaking, we're as good as bankdead."

"Then . . . maybe it's not all bad. We achieved half of what we came here for. We liberated everyone from the AT Market . . . But no . . ." Amon shook his head when he saw the consequences more clearly. "No. We've gone too far. This is a disaster! People won't be able to use vending machines. They'll starve. They'll be locked in their rooms. With no way to communicate. No way to call for help. No culture. Medical equipment will reject patients. The terminal ones are probably dead already. It'll be madness in the streets. And the bankdead, I mean the ones without BodyBanks . . . at least they can access feeders. But how long will the meal-replacement ink keep flowing without anyone to tend the supply line? This is awful. We haven't seen anything like this since . . . ever?"

"Since the Great Cyber War, at least."

"You Phishers really can't do anything about this?"

"We're just coders. Without a link to the Treasure Matrix, our talents are useless."

"Someone must be coming to fix this. They can't just let chaos reign."

"I wouldn't count on it."

"But the Blinders"—Amon gestured to the spread and pile of bodies in their GATA uniforms—"When they wake from their comas, they'll do something. And other GATA technicians will help them."

"They might try to reconnect somehow once the panic of naked oblivion subsides. But they'd have to run a diagnostic to even figure out what we've done. And they'd need walk-throughs and how-tos for the byzantine procedures to undo it. In other words, they'll need the ImmaNet just to get started. It's a catch-22. GATA Tower was built to withstand a shindo 11.0 earthquake or a nuclear blast and remain online. There are no contingency plans for complete denial of service."

As the PhisherKing spoke, Amon noticed him doing interface gestures and took this for a lingering habit. "Then technicians from other GATA regions will come," he said.

"And lose their identities the moment they arrive in GATA Tokyo's jurisdiction. Or if they find a way to maintain connection to another GATA region, they'll be unable to access the network here. Whether inside or out, there's no way to log in. Not even we Phishers can do anything though we stand in the heart of the House of Blinding and know exactly how the program works."

"Then it'll have to be the MegaGloms." Amon pointed out the breach at the peacecraft encirclement.

"What MegaGloms?"

This question seemed to still even the breathing in the room. There were no MegaGloms? Amon supposed there couldn't be, at least not within GATA Tokyo's region of authority, the territory of Japan. Without actions and transactions, action properties had no value, which meant corporations had no assets . . . he thought of their plan to turn Fertilex into a provider of access overnight. If an organization could transform in an instant, it could also dissolve in an instant.

"The MegaGloms still exist in the rest of the world," he said. "You don't think they'll resolve this somehow?"

"Maybe, maybe not. Imagine they reverse my changes to the House of Blinding. Imagine they figure out which person matches which ID signature, and the AT market is back running again. That would be no small technical achievement already, but the even more difficult problem of valuing and allocating their assets would still remain. GATA would need some mechanism for dealing with the astronomical backlog of unmonitored actions for every citizen. Who did what owned by whom when, and how much was each property worth as a result? Will they transport everyone back to the moment the system broke down and treat all the interceding actions as freebies? Will they somehow collect the action-data recorded in the BodyBanks of the whole citizenry and transfer funds accordingly? Answering these questions is only the first step. Think of all the currencies and derivatives whose value hangs on what they ultimately decide. And think of all the transnational assets that are bundled together with those. This is not a domestic problem. A chunk of the global economy has vanished in a wink. I have no doubt that the impact is already being felt everywhere. There will be endless discussions, conferences, lawsuits. And who will be the final arbiter when so many losses and gains hang on every decision? GATA will be in shambles and the MegaGlom blocs are already at loggerheads over a whole range of issues like they haven't been in decades. It's hard to see the lobbies of the Twelve cooperating in the way the Tokyo Roundtable did, but that is the sort of feat that would be required."

There was another pause as everyone took in this dire assessment.

"So all those people who will suffer . . . and you have no idea how to help them?"

"I built the system myself. If I could find a hole in the code, I'd already be wriggling my way in."

Rippling from head to toe with rage and disappointment as he accepted this, Amon dropped the weapon he'd been leaning on, clenched his fists, and stepped towards the PhisherKing. He wanted to slug him as Ono Y had done, to punish him for the pain and death of untold billions that his decision seemed to have wrought. But Monju wouldn't be cowed and stood his ground, chin raised with gallant resignation to what might come. And when Amon met his contrite but unflinching gaze, all strength drained from his arms, his fists unravelling. For he was seeing the PhisherKing unshrouded up close for the first time. Amon had never been so rude as to expose his naked face during the preparations for the revolution. Now he was in awe at the spectacle.

Through skin so weathered the wrinkles had branching wrinkles of their own ran threadlike black wires and silver filaments from the long obsolete silicon BodyBank, bent and twisted by the many pleats and folds. He looked to be over a hundred years old, though his back was straight, his chest upraised, the spryest centenarian you could imagine, dark hazel eyes alert and sparkling even in the pale light. His huge pores practically dripped with wisdom. Unable to harm such a delicate aged specimen, Amon channeled his emotions to his tongue.

"You fucking idiot! I gave you the idea that started all this. Rebirth. We would change the world through rebirth. And I got in front of you. Was ready to give up all my freedom . . . even to move. Not so you could— Why? Why the hell would you do something so . . . *Why?*" Amon's voice cracked. He was on the verge of crying with frustration.

"I had to think quickly. I was inside the blinding system, with executive access. We needed some way to get out from under their heels. Reactivating the security system crossed my mind. But it wouldn't have touched the Liquidators. Perhaps with half an hour and all my disciples assisting, I could have spoofed its target recognition criteria. Not in seconds. The only tool I had to work with was the program to distort action-data."

The PhisherKing gazed off wide-eyed into his own private distance, seeming to marvel and fret simultaneously, as though troubled by some tainted wonder.

"I must confess that the possibility of modifying the program to distort identities instead didn't occur to me only in that moment. Ever since I received the antidote for conception dust, my imagination has been fertile with new ideas and this one was the very first that came to me. You had just explained your idea for the Phoenix Virus. We would use your Death Codes and Hippo's Birth Codes to infiltrate GATA and bring about universal banklife. The powers of financial life and death could be harnessed to give that life to all. And I thought to myself, what if that same cycle of rebirth could be put in reverse? What if those powers could be used to realize universal bankdeath instead? It was as though you'd shown me the light of the sun and I couldn't help but see the shadows it cast. So as I prepared the code to complete the revolution, I could see permutations and branches at every step, the algorithm for a sort of dark reality running in parallel to the one we were supposed to create."

"You were *planning* to do this then, to let all those people die."

"No. I planned to run the banklife program. But my desires are another matter . . . The truth is that the alternate version lurked in the back of my mind ever after like a black spell, forbidden but seductive."

"You *wanted* to do this."

"Don't misunderstand me. I was ready to plunge with you into the deep unknown, Amon, for the chance to jailbreak truth. It's not as though we Phishers were in the business of hacking and blackmail just so we could live in that hole in the ground. All our profit went into the acquisition of more data. We stole and dealt in information only so that we could afford to breach the biased algorithms and financial gates that distort and dam its flow. I knew from the moment I met you that you had the potential to knock these barriers down. Universal access. What need is there for money when knowledge is available to everyone?

"And yet . . . and yet . . . A part of me couldn't forget that my reward for conceiving the House of Blinding architecture was the impairment of my power to conceive. A part of me has watched bitterly as this child of my mind built to protect anonymity in keeping with Lara Sekido's theories was exploited to bolster the property rights of a corporate regime. A part of me always believed that no institutional modification or revision would suffice to yield justice, that rejuvenating the wasteland was only possible through its total decimation. I was hardly aware of these thoughts and feelings these five decades.

"Then everything went wrong today and you gave me an opening and I remembered the spell and I started to write it from memory. I've never coded so quickly in my life. It was like a revelation pouring through my body into the void. And I did the unthinkable. I silenced the ImmaNet, the ether by which the Treasure Matrix speaks . . ."

The PhisherKing cringed and performed a series of hand motions as if praying to a deaf deity.

"But you could have used that opening to do what we came here for," said Amon. "If you'd activated the program you already made, we'd all have access."

"I had time to install one of the programs, but not to also complete the procedure to lock us out. If I'd chosen banklife, Ono X could have had Sekido dust me, and reversed the changes with the help of their cryptobreakers. But universal bankdeath will stick because it denies us access inherently. It was the only means I had to stop Ono X from giving his Birla freedom entire, and having his way with you all. Whether this was a mistake, I leave to your consciences.

"What I regret is refusing banklife for all before Sekido arrived. If only I'd known that the result would be accepting their bankdeath . . . Then again, if the sister's whispertexts about Hakkotopia were true, the future we enabled may have been even worse. I simply don't know. She did not grant me the vision. I'm truly sorry"—The PhisherKing's eyes did their waking dream flicker as he bowed to no one and everyone—"The ways of the Treasure Matrix are strange."

At these words of reverence, Amon's chest glowed with a certain dreadful wonderment, humbled by the mysterious inevitability they expressed.

"Alright, PhisherKing," he said. "I for one believe that you did what you had to. Let the future you've unlocked be your judge and sentence both."

All present had been listening intently to the exchange between Amon and the PhisherKing. Amon could tell because, whether they guarded the elevator and breach like the Atupians and Phishers, or worked to save Hippo's life like the exiles, they would glance over at crucial junctures. Each word shaped the meaning of the most momentous endeavor they would ever take part in. Now that it was clear they were agents of a botched revolution, Amon swept their eyes for comment or disagreement on his verdict about the PhisherKing but found only a tableau of perplexity, disappointment, and exhaustion. The past hour might have been a decade for the toll it had taken on all of them. None could ever be the same.

"You heard. We've done all we can here," said Amon. "No need to watch the elevators or the breach. Let's gather the dead and injured. Ty, I want to know what's happening outside."

Amon felt uncertain of his authority now that the chain of command had collapsed, but the Atupians and Phishers didn't question him, giving a nod and holstering or putting down their weapons. While they spread out in search of their dusted comrades, Amon righted one of the ergonomic chairs, dragged it to a patch of uncluttered and unperforated floor, and sat, letting the weight of ache and strain sink him into the pliant seat. The wind had stopped, the air neither hot nor cold, the temperature a variable waiting for a value. Much like the world.

While the PhisherKing pulled up another chair, Ty rolled over from Hippo's side, where he'd left a pile of fabric strips for Vertical and Tamper, and pressed a button on his wheelchair armrest.

"Little Book, Jiku, Yané what's going on out there?" he asked.

One of the Phishers approached with an armful of beverages and snacks from the vending machine Tamper had hacked. She handed each of the three seated men a drink and unloaded the rest in a hollow.

Ty took a sip of the bright purple liquid in his clear unlabeled bottle and muttered, "Ahh, so good," while listening on his one earbud. He nodded vigorously as though his interlocuters were in the room, still not at home with remote communication. With the smell of death hanging in the still air, Amon didn't expect to have an appetite, until he took a sip of what had to be Cloud9 Nectar. Then his thirst and hunger flared, and he found himself leaning eagerly towards the cache of goodies to pluck out a rice ball. Others swooped by between tasks to scoop up bottles and packets. Soon everyone was crinkling, chugging, and munching away, refueling after the depleting calamity they had endured.

The exceptions were Tamper and Vertical who remained on their knees beside Hippo. Now, only his mouth and nose showed from the fabric wrapping his face in lieu of gauze. The hand with the severed finger was propped on the leg of a sideways chair to elevate it above his heart, a makeshift tourniquet on the forearm. The two of them now worked quickly and methodically to undress and clean his chest. It occurred to Amon that nerve dust may have helped someone for once. It seemed to be working like an anesthetic. He hoped their ministrations hadn't come too late.

"Jiku has a group of our people beyond the drone curtain," Ty reported. "Waiting for us but keeping their distance."

"Tell her to look for gaps in the PrivaPo lines," said Amon. "We need to find a way out."

"She should find medical equipment as well," said Vertical. "For Hippo."

"Jiku, you have scouts?" Ty said into his radio. " . . . Yeah . . . Any hospitals around there? . . .For supplies . . . Hippo . . ."

"What about the others?" Amon asked.

"Hold up. I'm waiting for Book to come interpret LB . . . There he is. Yup."—Ty nodded with such conviction Amon thought Little Book might manifest in the room—"Yeah. Uh-huh. Sounds like the Books and Yané are inside the circle but in different corners?"

"What's the situation like on the ground?"

"They say it's total mayhem—bands of Starters, Ferment Culture operatives, and Liquidators roving wild. None of them can get organized."

"Do we have any information on Ono X and his detachment downstairs?"

"We rammed through those suckers on the way in. By now they'll have bounced back and then some."

"Have the Books head near the drone well, help Jiku find a crossing from the inside. But tell Yané to wait, somewhere out of the way but not too far from here. We're going to need him to get out of here."

While Ty conveyed these instructions, Amon studied the Atupians. They worked in pairs to carry groaning, twitching, and limp bodies towards the elevators. Amon was grateful to Hippo for personally selecting them, rather than allowing Ono X to vet them for his schemes. Now that Ono X had put them in grave danger, it seemed certain that their loyalty to him was spent. But Amon wasn't sure how many had received a link from the Phishers and been privy to his conversation with Birla X. And he wondered what might happen when they reunited with their brethren on the streets, who had not borne witness to all that had befallen the revolution.

Two dusted phoenixes had now been laid out in the corner between the elevators and the breach among the many confiscated weapons hurled there earlier. Before the grimy buzz of waning adrenaline beneath his skin could give way to the drab stiffness creeping up, Amon pushed on his armrests to rise and help gather the rest. He skirted mounds to a heap near the breach where a woman who had served under Hippo crouched over a nerved Phisher. While she gripped his ankles, Amon hooked the man under his armpits from behind, and together they lifted him off the floor. Backwards through the clutter he plodded carefully, sending glances behind his feet and over his shoulder to check for hazards. Part-way, the load lightened as another Phisher supported the man's buttocks, and soon the three of them were setting him down alongside six others.

Amon was turning from the elevators when he heard a faint thump and muffled voices. The Phisher beside him perked up, until he found Amon looking around impassively as if in search of someone to assist, and headed back across the room, apparently convinced it had been a trick of the ears.

Down the length of the room, Amon could see everyone working in tandem. Tamper and Vertical stripping off Hippo's bloodied pants and wiping him down. The PhisherKing and an Atupian rolling a Liquidator off a navy-suited woman. A Phisher hugging around the chest a man whose legs rested on the back of Ty's wheelchair. Others either carrying a body or getting set to lift. With each sweep of his gaze, Amon's focus kept snagging on the giant protrusion of Freg on his chair, face down with thighs on the edge of the seat, his belly propped on the backrest, head lolling, arms hanging, butt angling into the air, bent leg painful even to look at. It seemed odd somehow that Tororo wasn't arranged in similar contortions on a neighboring chair, as if to complete a grotesque art installation. Although the two men had been Amon's colleagues and almost friends until their failed attempt to liquidate him, he felt neither remorse nor satisfaction at the sight of Freg so defeated. Perhaps Amon was numbed by shock. Or perhaps he'd been cleansed of the enmities and amities of who he was in their last meeting by the many ordeals that followed.

Nowhere could Amon find anyone short on hands, and he decided that now was the time to confront someone about whom his feelings were more complicated. So, taking a deep breath to brace himself, he stepped over to his resting place. Here was his old boss, the man who had groomed him to defend the Free Market, used him to corrupt it, and then tried to cheat him of its financial graces the moment he began to think for himself. Still but for his breathing, Sekido lay on his right side in a dark politician's suit among pixelthreads and rubble, right arm pointing straight out above his head, left hand in his closed crotch, head leaning onto a patch of punctured floor between a woman's feet.

Sealed inside that body was a fully aware mind that could think and feel as ever but never again act. Although Amon had no love for the man, he didn't wish such a fate upon anyone. He wanted to believe that it was an accident, that the pressure on Sekido's hand in the pile-on had forced him to pull the trigger. But Amon had to accept the awful possibility that he had pushed it by mistake while trying to pry the weapon loose. Or even more disturbing that Sekido had pulled the trigger on purpose, though it was hard to imagine Sekido depriving himself intentionally of the power to hide his original face, even just with his hands or clothes. The loss of his erstwhile will to move had left him with one countenance, a single aspect exposed forever.

Or had it?

As Amon stared down at his paralyzed eyes, brown bloodshot eyes pointed blankly towards the ear of a man beside him, he recalled Birla X's stories about Sekido and thought he could see layers to that face, a composite shroud that bespoke the history of a man. The idealistic youth who had fallen for a supporter of Hakkotopia 1.0 and ID euthanized Hippo to make Xenocyst possible. The tormented technocrat who had been tricked into destroying all that mattered to him and whose misdirected desire for revenge had allowed those same tricksters to use him again and again. The avenged mole who hoped to make up for the wrongs he had done in the service of Gyges by bringing back Hakkotopia. Was there yet another face, a deeper face, that explained why he invariably donned the mask of guilt?

Amon considered whether Ono X had indeed infected Sekido with a virus to regulate the contact between his perception and that of others. He could think of no better explanation for Sekido's concise speech today. But the many credicrimes required would have been an enormous ongoing expense, so it seemed likely that Sekido would have noticed the compensation and sought out a cure sooner or later. Could the curation of his reality have been at least in part voluntary then? After all, its outward expression, in the form of shifting digimakes, was a habit that went back decades. And the faceovers seemed to overlap with the moments in which he compromised his principles, beginning with his early bureaucratic ascent after the island crackdown, accelerating with his ID murder of Rick, his tricking Amon into crashing Barrow, and his infecting Amon's hand with the virus, and peaking earlier when his old friend Hippo was tearing himself apart. *True freedom is faking it real to change the world.* The sifting of incoming signals may have been an attempt to filter his own view of the world just as the transformation of his face was an attempt to filter the world's view of him. How else could he have squared the trauma of being forced to ruin his love and his ideal society with the lies he had to tell and accept to navigate the different lobbydeologies in service of his vendetta?

If any of this was accurate, then might Sekido have decided, after the ImmaNet fell away and he was thrust unprotected into the version of life where his choices had never stopped advancing the ends of his enemies, that it was better to free himself from the burden of choice altogether . . .? Whatever the answer, Amon knew he ought to hate him, if for no other reason than that he had stood idly by while Hippo destroyed himself. And yet, he found that he could not. Even his remembered anger was gone. For search as he might in the deadened eyes of the figure at his feet for a familiar person to whom such ill-will might be directed, he came up empty. His only emotion was pity, not for the unique tragedies that had shaped him as an individual—everyone present had their fair share of those—but for the irreversible damage he had been subjected to. It was as if the power of anonymity Sekido's mother contrived had finally effaced his identifying features in its collapse.

"May you come to terms with yourself in there," said Amon. Crouching down, he closed his eyelids, peeled a jacket off one of the unconscious Liquidators, and lay the gray fabric over his face. Even though Sekido could not react to the gesture, Amon was certain that that was what he would have wanted to do.

When Amon looked up, his fellows seemed to have just finished gathering the fallen. In the corner to the left of the elevators, two Atupian men leaned over and tallied the collected bodies. Some twenty were laid out, eyes closed or open, visibly battered or unscathed. Most were motionless on their backs, though one sat rocking and drooling; three curled up on their sides quivered fitfully, jolted by the tail end of seizures.

On the other side of the elevators, Ty sat bolt upright watching everyone charily and nodding or muttering the odd remark to his radio. Beside him, the PhisherKing was installed in his ergonomic chair, staring off into space and occasionally flicking his fingers. The three Phishers huddled around him were all but still, and it occurred to Amon that he had yet to see them succumb to gesturing like their mentor. If the PhisherKing was beholden to a habit born of their profession, why didn't they feel the same compulsion?

An Atupian man led a trembling deafblind woman by the hand across the room. Two women left and right of center snaked towards the far end, scouring section after section of the clutter. The lines of their worry and disbelief seemed to deepen with each failed glance. It was obvious who they were looking for, but Amon decided not to tell them how futile their efforts were. Of even more concern were two men dragging Ono Y from a heap. Amon couldn't imagine what for. To execute him? Certainly not to bring him along?

Stricken with a new sense of foreboding, he turned to the men in the corner and called out, "Have you finished your tally?"

"We count eleven incapacitated and five dead," replied a stocky Atupian with a wispy moustache.

"Six of us injured," said the only able Phisher woman. "Three dead."

"There are seven of you standing." Amon addressed the Atupians. "That leaves one unaccounted for."

"Takigi fell through the hole," said an Atupian woman solemnly, halting her search to turn toward them.

"That's everyone then," Amon concluded, as the stocky man pointed one by one at the fallen and silently double-checked his count.

One of the two men lugging Ono Y swiveled his head and said, "What about Rashana?"

"What about her?" asked Amon, disturbed that he would still cling to that name.

"Has anyone seen her since the ImmaNet went down?"

Heads shook. Some lowered their eyes ruefully. Amon maintained his silence.

"Then we've got to send off a search party," said the man.

"For a wild goose chase through a hundred floors when we need all hands just to break out of here?" said Ty.

"We don't have time," Vertical agreed. "Tamper and I have done what we can but Hippo needs real medical attention—right away."

They had moved Hippo to a patch of open floor closer to the elevators. Many strips of navy, brown, lavender, and baby blue fabric wrapped his upper body like some vibrant slapdash mummy. Already blood was beginning to soak through in places, though the pants they had changed him into remained as yet unstained.

The Atupian man and his companion were taken up with the exertion of laying Ono Y down by the other fallen and could not reply. His fellows exchanged doubtful glances, saying nothing. Amon sensed disagreement and wasn't about to wait for them to sort it out.

"Alright everyone," he said as he approached the fallen. "We've got to figure out how to transport them. I hate to say this, but we may not have enough hands to carry the dead."

Those nearby gathered around him to plan their exit. It was thus, with nearly everyone in earshot of the elevators, that there was another thump and the high-pitched staccato of muffled voices.

"What was that?" said a Phisher.

"Right here," said Vertical, dropping to one knee and taking aim at a pair of doors near the middle.

Alarmed, others retrieved or drew their weapons, and the pair of women who'd been searching the room dashed over. Tamper waddled into the line of fire and put his ear up against the metal surface.

"Mutters and whispers," he reported.

"Someone's hiding in there," said Ty.

"We've found her!" exclaimed the stocky man.

"Open the elevator," said the taller of the two Atupian women who had just arrived.

Tamper gave his slight nod and rummaged in a pocket.

"Don't!" said Amon, more imperiously than he intended. Tamper froze with the black button of a door hack in his outstretched hand, as his and all other eyes in the gathered semi-circle turned to Amon.

"Hold on," he said, more calmly. "We need to decide what to do with the sisters."

"What makes you so sure they're both in there? Or did you know that all along?"

Glowering at him was the man who'd proposed the search party while carrying Ono Y. Tall and sinewy with a bent once-broken nose and rugged sun-mottled cheeks, he held his shoulders back but leaned his weight to one side, sending his puffed chest askew. His name was Kaneki, Amon knew, because the man was under his authority. Had been under his authority.

"I wouldn't have thought one of them would be talking to herself," said Amon, neither affirming nor denying the accusation. "Now let's think carefully about this. Is it safe to let them out?"

"You're willing to bring the corpse of that devil, Hippo," said Kaneki, "but you'd leave Rashana alive in a box?"

The man had no compunctions about hurling pejoratives at their dying friend, and Amon did not like it at all. He could see Ty's jaw muscle bulge, anger held in check. Then he turned to Amon with a look of tortured confusion and asked, "Was Hippo really a traitor?"

"No. He was the bravest and most perceptive of us all," Amon replied without hesitation. "He risked everything to do what he thought was best for us and for everyone."

"Oh? Giving away the revolution to Anisha was *best for us*?" Kaneki scoffed.

"It could have been a lot worse. Any semblance of success we have today is thanks to his guesswork. The Books will know his reasons. Hippo said they opened his eyes about our patron."

"You never wanted us to find her, did you?"

"The Birla sisters don't matter anymore," said Amon, astonished by the import of his own words. "They're penniless, powerless."

"Don't matter? Without Rashana, who will be the face that unites us?"

No wonder the man had been trying to rescue Ono Y. Could he and the other Atupians be expected to simply drop their shared enterprise after dedicating much of their lives to the preparations? *Yes,* thought Amon, if holding out hope left sanity to slip away. There were so many cracks in what Kaneki had said that Amon needed a moment to decide where to wedge his retort.

"You don't actually *believe* that we can settle those islands now, do you?"

"No, I don't believe it. I'm certain of it."

"But we're all bankdead, disconnected."

"The Starters have the activation protocol for our organic algorithms memorized. Once the island network begins self-assembling, Ferment Culture technicians can work out the rest."

"And you expect we'll make it there, out in the middle of the Pacific with no jets, no rotorcraft?"

"Can't he"—Kaneki nodded towards Tamper—"hack boats?"

"You do realize we've lost our navis."

"We'll find our way by the sun and the stars if we have to."

"Then I guess you'd have us defend the shores with bamboo sticks? Without the market, we've lost our financial protections. Without the backing of Fertilex, we've lost our military."

"If there's a will, we can find solutions. Hakkotopia 2.0 is the only safety we'll have in this madness. We need Rashana more than ever."

The region of focus between the locked eyes of Amon and Kaneki was a pin cushion for the gazes of everyone else. A strange weightless energy seemed to fissure the space as though the laws of physics were crumbling.

"We're not going to sort this out here," said Ty. "Let's go, talk later."

"We have to get moving," Vertical urged them. "Hippo is dying!"

"And put that traitor's life above Rashana's?" said Kaneki.

"Who could you possibly mean by Rashana?" Amon demanded.

"The one who was Rashana to begin with of course," Kaneki replied, "who was forced to play Anisha after her identity was stolen. There's no question about her loyalty. She chose to join us today when we gave her the chance."

"Then you mean to bring along the sister complicit with genocide," said the PhisherKing, "the population adjustment that destroyed Xenocyst and killed millions in the District of Dreams? The sister who's been working with the Gyges Circle since not long after their parents' death? Who was expecting the action exemptions today and threatened to kill us all unless I gave them to her?"

There was a moment of silence as they took in these chilling implications. Despite his lingering confusion about the identity heist, Amon recognized that they were discussing the woman he'd labeled Birla Y, and it amazed him that anyone could want her anywhere near them, let alone as a leader.

"Rashana would never let innocent people die," said the stocky man. "She dedicated her life to humanitarian work"—he turned to the exiles—"She was one of the main investitarians when Hippo was getting started."

"But she's not the Rashana you knew anymore," said Amon. "Not since she had to live and act on her sister's memories."

"They're right," interjected the taller Atupian woman. "It's the sister who *became* Rashana that we have to take with us, the one who led us here today."

"Yes," agreed her partner. "She helped Xenocyst in crisis with the exposé. She stopped the full horror of the genocide. She took you in"—the woman looked towards the exiles—"when you were almost starving. She gave us a chance for universal access and a new home for humanity."

"Then you mean to serve the sister who spent decades guiding the Gyges Circle until she was forced out after their parents' death?" said the PhisherKing. "Who murdered an innocent Starter to spite her sister for stealing her inheritance? Who led us into Ono X's trap today and let him ruin Hippo to monopolize freedom?"

"Ono X put her up to it," said the taller woman.

"He must have," said her partner. "None of this is Rashana's fault."

"The sisters can think for themselves, can't they?" Kaneki told them. "It's the original Rashana who has integrity like I said."

Kaneki looked to the three Atupian men who had not spoken to weigh in, but they just shifted from foot to foot and continued to watch in consternation. Amon respected them more than their outspoken comrades. Believing you could untangle the knot of the sisters with the scarce clues they had took a certain kind of arrogance and faith—or perhaps desperation.

"This is stupid, I'm taking him now," said Vertical, and began to rise from her knee but Tamper stopped her with a hand on her shoulder.

"Pointless waste," he cautioned.

"You won't make it past the lobby, not even the three of us would," said Ty. "I can't stand this yammering either, but we need all the help we can get—for Hippo's sake too."

Vertical gritted her teeth, eyes glittering, then returned her aim to the doors and shrieked, "Then let's just *go*, all of us!"

The outburst startled everyone coming from Vertical. A second passed before Kaneki said, "Nothing is resolved."

"Nothing at all," the stocky man agreed, his eyes on the PhisherKing. "Why should we believe what you claim about them?"

"I'm only stating the evidence."

"Memories of evidence, you mean."

"No. The Phishers and I each downloaded portions of their LifeStreams when they were on glass mode. I'm viewing the compilation at this very moment." His eyelids flickered half open and closed as he said this.

"You said that was impossible."

"For you, yes. But the original BodyBank operates with limited functionality offline. I can still use some native apps and access the data in my hard drive."

Amon traced again the fine device woven through Monju's intricately wrinkled skin and recalled his story about being conception dusted after a medical checkup in preparation for installation of the now ubiquitous biological BodyBank. If the adverhistory Amon had learned was correct, the old silicon version had been scrapped due to problems with the body rejecting invasive components. But it worked while disconnected? Such features might reduce the costs of phishing operations, by allowing the user to evade certain fines. Clearly, the PhisherKing had seen the supposed upgrade as anything but.

"You expect us to believe that?" said Kaneki.

"Takahiro Kaneki. Date of birth: November 2nd, 13 FE. BMI: 23.6. Favorite flooring material: heated tile. Least favorite sushi topping: eel. Mother's name—shall I do this for all of you?"

"Just let it go," Amon told the Atupians. "You want to believe that there's one good sister called Rashana and one evil sister called Anisha, but they just can't be divided cleanly that way. Whoever Rashana is, she's not fit to rule. If you truly care about Hakkotopia, you'll take neither."

This logic seemed to go too far for the Atupians, and they scowled to a person. But they were combat operatives, not intellectuals or rhetoricians, and their responses were simple.

"He shows his true colors," said Kaneki.

"Coward," said the stocky man.

"Open the elevator," repeated the taller woman.

"Please," said her partner.

"No," said Amon.

Kaneki grunted and snatched the black button from Tamper's hand. Before Amon could grab his wrist to stop him, he had snapped it onto the metal surface.

In the instant the doors slid apart, they glimpsed in the center of the floor a skein of bare brown skin, limbs, and hair. But this unraveled and split in twain with such panicked hurry that it was hard to believe it had ever been, and the two sisters were crouching with backs nestled into opposite corners, nude from head to toe. Their clothes—underwear, bras, socks, shoes, navy jacket and pants, red and white track suit—were strewn haphazardly, garments torn and soiled, the stagnant sweetness of urine spiced with fear wafting out.

A pall of stasis fell, the swell and sink of the panting twins' bosoms the only reminder of time's passage. They shivered enthralled at the armed intruders to their chance lair, the pulsing egg of the Fertilex logo cracked. The intruders, for their part, were in awe at this primal diorama, queens of finance as bedraggled and vulnerable and vulgar in their nudity as some neglected chattel; nipples, birthmarks, and mounds exposed for all to see.

It was an uncanny interval of mutual stall. The sisters waited in terror for the motley crowd to reveal their intentions, but none could settle what those were. For here were identical twins, one of whom had altered her genes and visage to match the other, a pair as indistinguishable as two humans could be. Even their postures, their positions, and the bruises on their foreheads from the backhand of the other were similar. Amon couldn't help scrutinizing their bodies for differences and did indeed find subtle variations: in the spotting of their areolas, in pubic hair coverage, in the protrusion of their bellybuttons, in the size of each breast relative to its neighbor. They also had unique patterns of scratches and scrapes. But none present had presumably ever seen the sisters naked—let alone naked in the naked world—and so lacked a model for comparison.

Any reasonable reaction would have hinged on their being able to tell the sisters apart. The duplicitous spectacle rendered moot the whole preceding argument. Only when the sisters began to wilt under so many unwavering, probing eyes—hanging their heads and crossing their arms to cover their breasts—did the spell break. The barrels of the Phishers and Atupians gradually dropped and drifted from their helpless targets.

Before the seconds could stretch too thin and fraught, Kaneki said, "Don't be afraid, Rashana. We're breaking you out of here to ferment the ultimate freedom like we planned."

An awkward pause followed. Then the sisters slowly tilted their hung heads to exchange harrowed looks, before rolling them back to center.

"W-which one of you is coming with us?" stammered the taller woman.

"Who will be the champion of the diamond dream?" the stocky man asked.

The sisters exchanged looks again, lips drawn down in mutual disgust, cheeks drooping with resignation. Heartbeats pulsed by with no response forthcoming, and Amon thought he understood why. Disconnection had cut the sisters off from their digital memories and their utter nakedness from any other clues to their past, leaving them equal in their undifferentiated blankness, two zeros bereft of time, with no means to offer unique signs of who they were. It was a stalemate, and neither would go out on a limb by making the first move.

"If you have nothing to say on your own behalves," said the Phisher-King, "we'll need the password for the third folder."

At this, their shivering stopped as all their muscles tensed, and they swung their heads towards each other, abruptly this time, puckering with distress. It was the same children-caught-red-handed expression they'd displayed when Monju questioned them before.

"The password," the PhisherKing repeated sternly. "Then we can compare the holes in your memories and establish who is who."

The twins' eyes remained locked, their shame seeming to transcend humiliation into a kind of shared terror, bottom lips folding outward and upper lips sinking inside their mouths to stretch their faces into a pouting mask of infancy. The day had wrought an eerie metamorphosis upon the Birla sisters, their present form clashing with Amon's memories of their regal bearing. He wondered what it was about the folder that had triggered this final deterioration. It was like a toy or property neither wanted. Or like an identity left to—

"It's the Makesh Adani profile," said Amon. He recalled the wistful look Birla X wore when describing her teenage clash with Birla Y over their fused past. This had followed the divvying of their names, the very inception of a separate Anisha and Rashana. The virtual folder wasn't just a place for them to talk in private. All those segs for which ownership negotiations had failed needed to be stored somewhere. And these became the kindling memories of a character they would both play when dissociating themselves from their actions. An ever already lost brother avatar built of pieces of denial? "The segs in that folder are of your appearances as Makesh. That's where evidence of ecogenics is, of Mayuko, isn't it?"

When Birla X talked about Makesh, hadn't she touched her eyebrow, the spot where "Anisha's" mole should have been? The bizarre risk of using a shared alias. They couldn't help themselves.

"It's not mine," muttered the sister on the left, almost too quiet to hear.

"Not mine either," echoed the sister on the right.

Then both rolled their heads back to center and stared at the floor again, shivers occasionally erupting through their clenched bodies. The spooked Atupians hardly seemed to breathe. They and the Phishers held their weapons loosely as if no longer sure what they were for. Only the three exiles remained stiff on target, Vertical on one knee inside the semi-circle, Tamper standing to the right, Ty seated left with his duster resting in a notch of his shield.

"Try testing their memories without the password," said Kaneki.

"Pointless with the mess their LifeStreams are in," the PhisherKing replied.

"It doesn't even matter!" cried Vertical. "We have to go."

"We can't leave without one of them," Kaneki insisted.

"Alright, here's a proposition for you, sisters," said Ty. "Give us the password now or we dust both of you. How about that?"

"The Mother will not be threatened," warned the stocky man.

"No, they will not," Kaneki agreed. Then to the sisters, he said, "Rest assured that no harm will come to either of you, that's a promise. But we need you to tell us the password. We must know which of you will lead."

The sisters lifted their heads, pointed at each other and opened their mouths as if to speak, until their eyes met and they froze. Despite these generous assurances, they were still reluctant to be open. Amon could only think that the deeds recorded in the hidden folder had to be truly abominable. The one sample they had viewed—reproductive torture inflicted on Sekido's love—supported that. Perhaps divulging the password would reveal atrocities committed in their roles as propertied oligarchs that were so inhuman that anyone with a conscience might be inclined to renege on merciful commitments.

As the sisters continued to lock eyes, their gazes seemed rich with wordless understanding of the kind only possible between deeply intimate minds. What had they talked about in the confines of the elevator, together in private with no surveilling handlers or rules or even distractions for the first time in their lives? How did they end up naked? Could it have been a ploy of one sister to make them indiscernible? Of both sisters? In the instant the doors opened, had they been wrestling or embracing? Almost simultaneously, they turned their heads to face the crowd.

"The folder is not ours," said the sister on the right.

"Not ours," said the sister on the left with a firm nod.

"We've been over this," said the PhisherKing impatiently. "The folder is shared between—"

"No! We are Rashana and Anisha,"

"Yes! Anisha and Rashana!"

They exchanged one more glance, as though excited and relieved to have arrived at this conclusion.

"This is fucking deranged," said Ty. "If they're not going to give us the password, we—"

"—need to bring both of them," interrupted Kaneki.

"But we can't tell—"

"We'll decide later. This is our last chance to free humankind. Our saving grace after everything else has failed."

The more vocal Atupians nodded in agreement. The Phishers and their mentor looked on impassively. Encouraged, the sisters began to rise, their backs sliding up the corners.

"Not another move," said Tamper, aiming at the sister on the left.

"No one has agreed anything," Vertical hissed, aiming at the one on the right.

"*What* did I say about threatening the Mother?" the stocky man barked.

The other Atupians shifted uncertainly, watching, poised, the sisters sliding back down in fright.

"Relax, it's not a threat," said Amon, "We just haven't finished discussing what to do with them."

"We know what you think," said Kaneki. "They're coming with us." He put one foot over the threshold of the elevator and told the sisters, "You can get dressed now."

But Amon grabbed Kaneki by the top of the sleeve. "No" he said. "Listen first."

Kaneki turned on Amon and glared, chin to chin, hot breath close on his face.

"Let, me, speak," said Amon.

One of the men who'd been silent put a placating hand on Kaneki's shoulder. "We can hear them out one last time, right?"

After a tense moment, Kaneki nodded and stepped back into the semi-circle, his pugnacious gaze on Amon, who was gathering his thoughts.

"We need to be careful," he said to everyone. "Because it isn't just the two sisters that are mixed up. Their dreams are too."

Saying this, Amon realized that he had given up on Hakkotopia. He had agreed to settle it as a condition on gaining Birla X's help with the Phoenix Revolution. He had taken pleasure in imagining the alternative society they were working to create. He had looked forward to setting foot in the forest. But somewhere in the pandemonium, his belief in that vision had faded, like an echo of a mirage.

"The Ring of Gyges and the diamond dream?" said the stocky man. "They're nothing alike!"

"See," said Kaneki, "a waste of breath."

"Think," Amon persisted, "Hakkotopia was supposed to create the conditions for the best of all kinds of freedom. Citizens unfolding in step with nature while following our own dreams and designing the algorithms that guided how we pursued the dream of the community. It's a beautiful and inspiring ideal. But it doesn't take seriously the diversity of human desire."

"It does—"

"No! Our dreams are as numerous as . . . as the ashes scattered to the winds after fire has scorched the earth."

Amon recalled his dream upon waking up in the sensory deprivation orchard, the blaze that melted time and space, the phoenix rising.

"Spare us your poetry." Kaneki spat at Amon's feet, but he was too caught up in what he was saying to care. He could almost see the countless holes in the wall as ashes in a storm that flurried into the sky.

"To make the hard crystal of a shared ambition, ten-thousand personal ambitions have to be pounded together through force and violence and domination. Unless our motivations are tweaked until we're something all too cooperative to be human. And whatever freedom is, when others determine what we want, our choices may be voluntary but they can never be free."

Amon glanced at the sisters and thought of how their parents had raised them.

"There's no evidence for ecogenics or harmony dust," said Kaneki.

"There could be in the Makesh Adani folder," said the PhisherKing.

"There can't be," Kaneki replied. "The diamond dream was realized once without that technology. History proves that we can do it again."

"We'll never know unless we try," said the taller woman.

"But we have tried," said Amon. "Just look at what happened today. The Birlas, the Onos, me, you, the exiles, Hippo, the PhisherKing. Our desires all coincided around the revolution. And what was the end result? A small group like ours couldn't even stay coordinated for a day, forget a nation or the world over decades and centuries."

From the looks of dismay around him, he could tell that he had shaken the scaffolding of meaning and purpose each had built around their existence. He opened his mouth to urge them once more to leave, sensing that the moderate Atupians might agree and compel Kaneki to follow along this time, when a sister cleared her throat.

"How can you disparage the diamond dream when it is your dream like no one else's," she said.

"You were order-grown on Hahajima like the others, engineered to accord with its ecosystems perfectly across time," said the other.

"That's why I, Rashana, tracked you, the sole survivor of Hakkotopia 1.0."

"Y-you said my mother was Iwabuchi," Amon stammered, unsure which sister he was addressing.

"In a sense she was."

"She was one of your designers."

"Some of her defining gene sequences are inside you."

"You're saying I'm not human, like one of the Starters?"

"Where did you think your frugality and self-control came from?"

"That's just p-part of my personality, I—"

"And the forest?

"Your very cells cried out to be there."

"You dreamt of it, like a migrating sea turtle following magnetic currents."

"It's too bad for her, for us, that our begetters wouldn't let her near the DNA holdings of their BioPens, or we would have cloned you a thousand times over."

"She had to wait until you reached adulthood."

"Until we could intercept your SpillBot sperm collector."

"Analysis of your blood from her SampleQuito will help me and us improve future generations."

It disturbed Amon how they seemed to meld the first, second, and third person between them.

"You are the only adult with the right neurological makeup to guide the Starters."

"A paragon of willpower, restraint, and loyalty, ready to sacrifice momentary gain for long term goals, with a dash of gullibility to follow the directives of the algorithms."

"You truly are a bit of yogurt from the old batch."

Amon felt like he was going to faint, the persuasiveness of her, their, story about him rising up into his head like giddying thermals, buoying painful doubts about his past. His betrayal of Mayuko for his job, his scrimping and saving, his dedication to Liquidation above even his friendship with Rick, his endurance of privation in the camps. When he thought he'd been sacrificing his fleeting desires for the deepest yearnings of his soul was he merely tugged along by the twisted, vestigial instinct to fulfill the goals of a long dead society? Was his service to GATA, then Xenocyst, then Atupio just a programmed urge to dissolve himself into whatever organization subsumed him, whether governmental, human-itarian, or private? And what about his desires from now on? What was driving him? Who was he?

"It is your genetic destiny to be on the island, to lead."

"With your help, the diamond dream will shine like never before."

"Rashana" was speaking to him without RaconTeur. It was coming from her, them, all of it. There was no way she, they could fabri-cate something so plausible so quickly on her own, without even a LifeStream. Could they? Or was his ready belief in everything and everyone—the InfoFlux, Sekido, Book, Hippo, Barrow, Rashana—just an inbuilt tendency to align his mind with others? Could he be suc-cumbing to it right now? Could—

"See, Amon," said Kaneki, patting him on the back. "You're one of us."

"We'll all bring it about together," said the stocky man. "The diamond dream."

"*The diamond dream!*" intoned the Atupians in unison.

"Come twin Mother," said the taller woman, beckoning the sisters.

"Mother of freedom," her partner cried rapturously.

The sisters rose, traded a smile, clasped each other's hand, looked ahead, and took a step together towards the world beyond the box that contained them.

Whir chrinkle chrinkle chrinkle chrinkle chrinkle chrinkle chrinkle.

Amon dropped and rolled, reaching for the weapon in his jacket, and whipping it out before he remembered what awful kind of dust it fired. There were thuds as bodies fell. Already the skirmish was over.

The Phishers stood there dumbfounded, Vertical and Tamper were aiming at each corner of the elevator, and Ty sighted along his duster from where he'd wheeled himself behind them all. The seven Atupians and the two sisters lay comatose on the floor.

"Shit," said Ty.

"What happened?" Amon cried.

"I had enough of those wackos—spouting religious bullshit," Ty growled, flashing his teeth between one side of his lips. "We couldn't let them take over like that. But I didn't mean for the sisters to go down—not yet."

"I heard the shots," said Vertical in disbelief. "I thought they were attacking."

"Just pulled the trigger," said Tamper.

Speechless, Amon looked between Ty and the newly fallen bodies around and inside the elevator. Could he be blamed for his snap decision? A cult, the Opportunity Scientists, had murdered his family and kin. Perhaps he was right. The soft finger of reason could never have penetrated the unyielding shell of fanaticism or smoothed out the distortions of a hagiographic faith. But was silencing them with violence the only option? Vertical and Tamper stared in shock at the naked bodies of the sisters. So many secrets locked away in that hidden folder, never to be—

A horrid realization came to Amon, and he put his face in his hands. He had made too many mistakes to count. Innumerable souls would suffer as a result. But that was too big and complicated to chew on now. Instead, his awareness fixated on an issue that was miniscule in the grand scheme of cataclysm, a single ripple on a typhoon.

"Okay," said Ty with a slap of his hands. "We flew off the leash bit. But let's not get hung up about it. Come on."

This seemed to snap Vertical and Tamper out of their stupor; Amon could hear them sliding their weapons into their holsters and stepping in the direction of Hippo.

"Can we put the injured in chairs?" Ty suggested. "Stack them somehow?"

The exiles and Phishers must have noticed Amon because only silence followed. Fighting the weight of anguish, he lifted his head, ignored their worried gazes, and turned to the PhisherKing.

"Are there any clues in their LifeStreams?" he asked.

Knowing immediately what Amon meant, the PhisherKing shook his head.

"So we definitely need the password?"

The PhisherKing nodded solemnly.

"Of course it would be in there," Amon muttered to himself. "Where else?"

This concerned him most of all because the Makesh Adani folder was where the sisters hid the unspeakable. The Emoticon Man's abuse would no doubt be recorded there. But what other horrors had been wreaked upon her? Dread frothed up slowly and steadily from the pit of his stomach.

"Oh no, Amon," said Vertical, realizing. "I'm so sorry."

"Sorry," said Tamper.

"It's not their fault," said Ty. "I'm the one who should be sorry, Amon. It was me that set them off."

Too upset to reply, Amon forced back the tears as he looked to the PhisherKing. He needed to ask the question even though he was sure that he already knew the answer. "Is there any way to break in somehow?"

"Not with the encryption we designed. Certainly not without the ImmaNet. I'm cut off from all the apps that might have helped."

"Forty-nine didn't work?"

The PhisherKing cringed sympathetically.

"Can't we figure out the rest?"

"I tried other combinations. But we don't even know the total number of digits. That leaves infinite possibilities. Each time I fail the folder locks me out for twice as long. Already, I have to wait ten minutes. At this rate, the probability we'll get in during our lifetimes is vanishingly small . . ."

"Maybe we can take the sisters along," said Vertical, as she and Tamper bent down to lift Hippo into a chair. "We could try questioning them when they wake up tomorrow."

"They'd be in no position to refuse," said Ty. "I'll work them personally."

The Phishers sent over glances of concern as they wheeled chairs to where their brethren were laid out with the others in the corner. Suddenly Amon couldn't bear to face them anymore and a shudder of distress jolted him into motion. He set off across the mess, stopping in front of the breach.

Beyond the jagged frame, the swirling well of aircraft was seamless as high as he could see. It receded to a point of grey cloud, no longer raining, from which an insipid glow fell on the blighted circle of skyscrapers within, a pallid reef of monuments to something that never was. Further below curved highways and byways snarled in off-kilter traffic, the vital commerce of movement ground to an indefinite halt. Erratic winds blew in the rupture, now brushing one cheek, now the other, now settling, now blasting cold through his suit, and Amon tuned in to an accompanying noise he'd been too distracted to notice before: the beat and whir of thousands upon thousands of rotors enclosing this lone tract of city to the skies, stirring up wayward currents.

Behind him, he could hear the exiles arranging their escape over radio. Locations of hostile forces, rendezvous points, retreat vectors. Amon knew he should be contributing but sadness manacled what depleted focus he had left.

Crowds of streetwalkers and rooftop unsalarymen crept and milled without direction or purpose, lives flung helter-skelter from information-guided habits like children from a broken theme park ride. As though searching the heavens for signs to reveal the meaning of this unheralded curse upon the metropolis, many tilted their heads skyward. Their faces were too distant to make out but Amon didn't doubt that some were looking towards him, a lone figure perched high above in a hole in the world. Once they learned the full extent of what they had lost, how would they feel? How would they act? How would she . . .

"Amon," Tamper said from close behind him. "Report came in from the Books."

"Seems there's infighting among the Atupians, and between the Atupians and the Starters," said Ty. "Some side with Ono X, some not."

Amon continued to face the city, no longer seeing it, sensation murky with the pain.

"It should be easier to bring along the sisters," said Vertical. "We can slip through in the confusion."

Even without turning around, Amon could hear in their sunken intonations the carven lines of guilt his friends wore. Their plan was tempting indeed. He could picture it now. They would wheel the sisters out on chairs alongside Hippo and the incapacitated Phishers. Perhaps with cowls so none would be the wiser, distracted by internecine squabbles.

Recalling the debates over universal banklife at the planning sessions, Amon realized that the Atupians had been divided from the very beginning. Some in the Ferment Culture Collective had argued that transforming the AT Market was the perfect complement to rebooting Hakkotopia, others that it was foolish to give up their financial defenses. Now that Ono X's gambit had come to light, jeopardizing everything for his master's absolute liberation, the rifts would have only deepened. If they exploited the conflict and disarray, they just might squeeze through unnoticed. Then they could bring the sisters to a quiet place. Interrogate them. Learn many truths. And Amon would uncover the fate of Mayuko at last. Find her. Already he could see her face—

But when this wish-fulfilling apparition of his beloved gazed back from the city before him, her incisive eyes cut him to the quick, unearthing the blackboard in his soul reserved for sketches of abstract premonition. There Amon saw the nexus where tributary futures poured into the river of now. Inchoate currents of uncertainty awaited the molding hands of choice. Their form would be bestowed by what they all decided to do next. And he knew that Mayuko would never approve of the gamble they were contemplating, even for her own sake.

A warmer breeze reached him, sieved through the encirclement. The smell of death was swept away when it arose and returned more pungent when it waned. Auguries telling them to depart.

Amon turned from the breach and wound back towards the elevators, the exiles in toe. The fallen now rested on a line of four chairs. Three chairs bore the six Phishers, each with one seated and another straddling, while one bore Hippo, red blots growing in his multicolored wrapping, all waiting to be wheeled out. Amon stopped before the elevator kept open by Tamper's device, framing a floor littered with the sisters and their rags.

"Tamper," said Amon. "Would they suffocate in there?"

"What are you suggesting?" asked Vertical.

"Would they suffocate?" Amon repeated.

"Nope," said Tamper. "Earthquake design ventilates well."

From the cache of drinks and snacks on the floor, Amon scooped up an armful and dumped it into the elevator at the sisters' feet.

"Close the doors," he said.

Tamper didn't move.

"Are you sure, Amon?" asked Vertical.

"We've got four chairs and there are eight of us," Amon said. "One person to push and one to provide cover. If we add an extra chair, two will be undefended."

"Then we'll just have to fight harder," said Vertical.

"We're game to try if you are," said Ty.

"This is not a joke," Amon snapped. "You saw how the Atupians behaved in here. Everyone outside heard the contradictory speeches of the sisters from the feedcasts. They'll behave just the same. Some will support one sister, some will support the other, some will be angry with Ono, the moderates will be confused. The Starters too. Those kids will be just as desperate for someone to follow as someone to blame. The quarrels will be endless. They have no records to sort it all out, no networks through which to talk it out either. But the moment they see the sisters—one of them, both of them, they won't care—they'll set it aside. They'll rally. They'll slaughter each and every one of us—capture us if we're lucky. They'll join together. Then their plans might still be possible."

When Amon blinked, a vision came to him. The sisters crouching at the center of the green clearing from his dream. From beneath their dark green dresses, they laid dozens of eggs out of which feathered humans hatched, each with the adult face of Amon. The runic third eye of these wet doppelganger fledglings each shone a beam of light through the diamond rings their mothers wore.

"I won't allow that to happen just for a shot in the dark. The sisters might not know where she is. She might not be alive. Chances are we'll deliver up the keys to a sick future and lose our lives for nothing. But if we leave them, it's only a matter of time before the disagreements become intractable. Eventually their followers will break up and disperse. This is the most volatile moment. Now is when we decide which direction to tip the world."

The exiles and Phishers watched Amon silently with apologetic pity and acceptance.

"Close it," he said, certain even as the leaden ballast of sorrow dragged his spirits into the abyss. "This is the first choice we have to make."

7
OTEMACHI, UNDERGROUND, THE KINDOMINIUM

Once Amon, Vertical, Ty, Tamper, the PhisherKing and the three Phishers had lined up the ergonomic chairs bearing their incapacitated fellows along the right side of the lobby, Tamper crept along the front wall to the rightmost door. There he crouched down to cautiously peer outside through the glass, and Amon went over to join him.

"Why is there no one here?" he wondered aloud, leaning his head out just above Tamper's.

When the elevator doors opened, they had not been overly surprised to find the hallway and then the lobby empty: credilaw had kept out unauthorized bankliving, and the doors would remain shut to everyone now that bankdeath reigned. But nothing, financial or material, impeded the approach to GATA Tower, and yet the only people Amon saw on the platform were unconscious in piles. One Atupian lay bloodied near the middle, head pointing to the sole broken pane as though he'd been used as a battering ram.

"They must have been driven off," said Vertical.

"The Atupians, okay—Where are the Liquidators?" said Amon. "There should be a sea of them surrounding us."

"Sekido's orders to stay back would have remained in effect," said the PhisherKing. "We gave him no chance to reverse them."

"Yeah, but you'd think they'd at least come to see what happened," said Amon. "I mean, the whole city is disconnected."

"It's weird," said Ty, "So what do we do?"

Amon leaned out further to better scope the scene beyond the heaping platform. Some three stories up in a skyscraper to the left, a band of Starters peeked from a line of broken windows, barrels propped on the sills. Several stories higher straight ahead, Atupians hunkered behind balcony fences and the overturned tables of a rooftop patio. To survey the right side, Amon stuck his head out all the way and spotted Liquidators two stories below the platform, kneeling behind bikes at the top of the fallen-bike-and-rider-cluttered ramp leading down into GATA parking. The three bands traded dustfire sporadically while keeping a watchful eye on the entrance.

Amon withdrew his head and turned to his fellows, who stood with hands resting on chair backs, itching to leave.

"Locked down," he concluded.

"Won't make it two steps," Tamper agreed.

"*If* they can aim naked at that distance," said Ty.

"That's not an issue for the Starters," said Vertical. "I've trained with those little sharpshooters."

"Can Yané's people run interference?" Amon asked.

Ty shook his head. "They're about as close by as they can get without running into trouble."

"Please decide *something*," Vertical urged, holding two fingers against Hippo's wrist with a scowl of distress.

They all sent Amon bleak stares, seeking his judgement. He was considering strategies, when Tamper said, "Hear that?"

Amon frowned with puzzlement as he tuned in to a faint rumbling. The sound seemed to enter the lobby through the hole in the middle door and, looking outside again, he noticed that the city was tinged with a reddish light. If the InfoFlux had been on, he wouldn't have thought twice about it, but his perception was supposed to be naked. A heartbeat later, he realized what it was.

"We go now!" he barked, bolting over to the chair he'd been wheeling.

"What is—"

"No time!" he interrupted Ty. "Now!"

Tamper hurried across the room to slap one device each onto the two leftmost doors, the locks opening with a soft click, while Vertical rushed over with Hippo's chair. Tamper took his spot beside her and together they used the chair to push open the far door, wheeling Hippo out. Then two Phishers wheeled one of their brethren through the other door, followed by the PhisherKing and Ty with a third occupied chair, as Amon helped another Phisher roll out the last chair behind Vertical and Tamper, his whole body prickling with fear.

The moment he stepped onto the platform, the rumble swelled to a roar and the fiery glow began to flicker more brightly. The groups of Atupians, Liquidators, and Starters all gaped up towards GATA Tower in awe.

"Don't look, hurry," Amon said, just loud enough for his friends to hear over the noise. He and his partner followed the others left across the platform, weaving and walking the chair legs around splayed limbs and heads. Only when he reached the escalator did he glance up over his shoulder.

The zenith was a grey dot of cloud, the only area of sky not blocked by the cylinder of peacedrones that squirmed into the higher reaches. Plummeting from the center straight for GATA Tower was a bolt of flame like the blazing pupil of some cosmic eye—the spaceplane Ono X had prepared to evacuate his Birla. A fleet of divebombing GATA hydrogen planes on autopilot spiraled threateningly around the intrusion. Following the automated landing procedure Ono X had initiated, the craft had completed reentry and was engaging propulsion to slow for a vertical landing on the rooftop.

Turning from the spectacle, Amon helped his partner balance their chair on the escalator step, and glanced up to his right just as the embattled watchers pried their eyes away too. But by then, his motion downward was putting the buildings and platform between them, and he let out a long sigh of relief.

The bodies that had earlier clogged the bottom of the escalator had thankfully been plowed like snow drifts into piles on either side, allowing easy passage for their office chairs and Ty's wheelchair.

Once Amon stepped onto the sidewalk, he found the boulevard along which he had always commuted transformed yet again. Lining each side of the long concrete island that split the road were two lanes of stalled cars. These invariably had at least one smashed window, some of them bloodied, and were empty of drivers or passengers. The island and the sidewalks on both sides were littered with the bodies of Liquidators, Starters, Atupians, and a few ex-citizens. Most lay still under the influence of beauty or nerve dust, but many revealed the handiwork of the Starters, who chose dusters according to their preference and had no compunctions about using even the most mischievous or sinister variety. Wriggling or vomiting uncontrollably, farting from blimped-up bellies, hiccupping spasmodically, lowing and ululating beast-like, somersaulting, non-stop hand-licking, patting back in futility handfuls of epidermis flaked to the pink and tender, masturbating to injurious excess, soaking mushy in a deluge of sweat and lymph. Such were the multifarious victims that Amon and crew observed on the boulevard as they wheeled their chairs along the righthand sidewalk with horrified trepidation, skirting a man who slithered soft-boned here, a woman babbling newborn inanity there.

Nowhere was there an upright soul in sight, until they had proceeded for half a block and Vertical whispered gruffly, "Over there." She pointed across the street to the front entrances of two neighboring towers, where some thirty Atupians lurked. Vertical, Amon and the others ducked down, rolled their chairs over to the curb, and crouched in the gutter behind a pair of sedans. Through the passenger compartment glass, he watched the Atupians rush across the opposite sidewalk to take cover behind curbside vehicles in the same way.

"Stay where you are!" he bellowed. "We're in this together."

Ignoring his desperate overtures, the Atupians crept onto the road between the bumpers of the first lane of cars, then crouched behind the bodies of the second. Outnumbered fourfold and unable to run with the injured to transport, Amon gripped his weapon so hard it shook, bracing to be overwhelmed.

But when the first handful of Atupians stepped onto the concrete island, patters sounded from further along the street, and two fell into comas. A different band of Atupians at the next intersection had their barrels propped on the hoods of cars stopped perpendicular to the street. Then Amon heard glass shattering above. He craned his neck to peer over his shoulder as glittering fragments showered onto the sidewalk and saw ten children steadying their submachine dusters at broken windows several stories up. It was the Starters who'd been guarding the platform, now come through the building.

"The traitors of the revolution are here!" Amon heard Ono X shout and glanced back across the street as he and a dozen more Atupians leapt from the safety of a building entrance, assault dusters blazing. "For what they did to the Mother! For the diamond dream!"

This stirred his Atupians into a frenzy, and they raised a wild yell, those on the road mounting the concrete island and firing on all sides while Ono X charged in behind. As alarming as their approach was, the Starters were the more imminent threat and Amon looked back again. For an instant, his eyes met those of a girl of around eight. In her bright focused gaze, he read her surety that he had no hope of turning around and raising his weapon fast enough. None of his friends did. All she and the other Starters had to do was tilt their muzzles down ever so slightly. In this mutual acceptance of his helplessness, they shared a moment of understanding, and Amon felt a peculiar equipoise come over him, like a cornered prey offering itself as a gift to the predator.

Then the girl looked beyond him to the street, and the first action of her and the Starters was to shower dust instead on Ono X and his charge. Trained offline since birth, none missed, sending the front line of Atupians collapsing onto the island, the near road, or the hoods of cars, where they writhed strangely and tripped those that followed.

Then a war cry rose from further along the opposite sidewalk, and Amon looked to find a contingent of exiles led by Yané just emerged from an alley. Six dozen strong, they began to open up in unison on the Atupians hunkered at the intersection, Ono X's band stranded on the street, and the sniping Starters, toppling many into comas and driving the rest to cower where they could.

"Go!" Vertical cried as she and Tamper pushed and dragged Hippo's chair bouncing over bodies along the sidewalk. Amon and his Phisher followed with their doubly laden chair, doing the same. The exile rescue team poured across and lifted Hippo, Ty, and the pairs of injured Phishers from their seats, hauling them in fireman's carry. Suddenly unburdened, Amon hurtled and hurtled again the near lanes of cars, did a diving roll over the island, crawled like mad past more cars to the other sidewalk, and stumbled down the alley where he was absorbed into the crowd of exiles, running alongside his fellows from inside the tower.

The alley opened into a two-lane street of more abandoned traffic, everything held up by the vehicles set for manual control when universal bankdeath struck. Here and there between dusted bodies, Atupians and Liquidators boxed and wrestled. Many of these high level combatants lay entangled on the wet sidewalks or between cars, scraped and bruised, resorting to the oafish grind of hand-to-hand after their marksmanship apps failed. This pathetic travesty seemed to Amon like a symbol of what was to come, talents rendered useless without the software that completed them, cooperation disintegrating without the glue of networked communication and command, civilization collapsing in a flash.

The exiles split in half and marched along both sidewalks in loose triple file, kicking anyone who got in their way into the gutters. Yané was at the head on the right side, and Amon took a place in the center, feeling safer with allies on every side. Once a handful of Atupians launched a clumsy assault from an alley to his right, but a quick volley of return fire quelled it, and the entourage had moved onward before he even saw what happened.

When they had put more than two blocks between them and the warzone near GATA Tower, he began to spot cars with their windows intact. In these, the occupants had remained. Some were no doubt waiting with impatient bewilderment for tech support. Others were beating on the glass and calling for help. Unable to activate even the doors but not frightened enough to smash their way out, they allowed themselves to be prisoners to their devices.

There were no passersby anywhere, but Amon saw scattered Liquidators wandering the streets near and far in a daze. When he noticed one grey-suited woman squinting at the skyline in perplexity, he recalled his naked viewing of GATA Tower earlier that day and guessed the reason for their absence from its vicinity. With the building's digimade design and immensity gone, and only the section of its shaft above the breach rising from behind a few diminutive subsidiary skyscrapers, none of the

Liquidators could even recognize it. They were lost! And Amon could picture thousands more roaming mapless over the metropolis, in search of their castle, perhaps never to find it. Odd to think that in some not so distant reality, he might have ended up one of them.

The sound of dust patter ripped him out of his reflections. He glanced back across the street as half a dozen Starters attacked the rear from a catwalk, dropping two exiles onto the concrete. Nearly ten exiles on each sidewalk knelt at roughly the same moment, took aim, and let off a return barrage, sending a small boy flopping to the metal grating and pushing the remaining Starters onto adjacent rooftops within seconds. Then the entourage continued to trudge ahead with the new casualties hoisted—one humming tunelessly, the other flapping his arms as though trying to take flight.

Whether deprived of their customary apps like the Atupians or fully adjusted to the naked world like the Starters, the scattered bands that remained seemed to lack the coordination to pose a worrisome threat. But the scrutinizing gaze of street brawlers and rooftop or window lookouts Amon occasionally noticed along their march suggested that the situation could have been otherwise. For they reminded him how the Starter girl's sharp eyes had passed him over, reckoning Ono X a more pressing danger, and he became convinced that their transit would not have been so easy if any of the bodies the entourage lugged on their shoulders had even remotely resembled one of the sisters. Then cries like the one Ono X had raised would have almost certainly gone up and a truce would have been called, as the thousands within earshot, Atupian and Starter alike, thronged to the banner of hope "Rashana" represented. In other words, all signs told him that he had chosen prudently in sealing the sisters away, a reassurance that did nothing to lighten his remorse.

Within ten minutes of leaving GATA Tower, the thunder of myriad rotors and engines grew nearly deafening, the fitful winds blasted with greater force and frequency, and the curve of whirling peacedrones began to loom over the rooftops. As Amon and the entourage approached the perimeter of the no-fly zone, their ranks swelled with new exiles converging from every direction. All wore black windbreakers with the girl in popping bubble emblem, and some had a flag bearing the same fluttering wildly on their backs. Ex-citizens were amassing as well, enormous crowds bottlenecked at intersections in their attempted exodus, and Amon felt like he was on a supply pilgrimage to Delivery, though they were in the heart of Free Tokyo.

By the time he and his fellows numbered in the hundreds, they were proceeding along a street parallel to a wide thronging thoroughfare that edged the border. To his right down one intersecting street, beyond the milling hordes, he glimpsed a PrivaPo checkpoint. Ranks of polymer exoskeletons twice the height of a man, flanked by stundawgs snapping grotesque silver maws for show, were statuary in individual alcoves of the churning drone wall. Sleek black aircraft cycled above, behind, and beside them, warning off passage as much with their jutting cannons as with their shearing rotors and swinging armored bodies. Mere steps separated the front of the crowd from these menacing machines, and Amon thought they were wise not to test them. There was no guessing the semi-autonomous reactions of the exoskeletons now that the PrivaPo operators they encased had been disconnected, nor of how heavily the stundawg and peacedrone algorithms were weighted towards violence absent human command.

When the lines of exiles ahead reached the next crossing, they turned right and headed for the border. Amon followed their lead, rounding the corner and trotting straight for the multitude that fronted the PrivaPo cordon and curve of swirling aircraft. He couldn't imagine how they would ever get through, until Yané at the head of the entourage approached the crammed intersection and the sea of people began to part, as hundreds more exiles stretching leftward within the crowd began to push in two prongs, prying open a narrow and tenuous pathway that ran diagonally across the street. This ended at a stairwell leading beneath the far sidewalk—the way under that Jiku and the Books had scouted out. Ex-citizens trickled steadily down in search of passage. As the entourage poured into the rift and began to fill it, they crowdsurfed the incapacitated towards the stairwell, with Hippo at the front of the wave. It was for him more than anyone, Amon knew, that so many were putting themselves in danger by lingering or returning to Otemachi, and he wondered what the exiles would think when word of Hippo's leak to Birla Y spread.

Hippo soon disappeared down the stairs along with Yané and the others at the front, and Amon had just jogged into the rift himself when many heads around him snapped to the border in alarm. Hundreds of men and women wearing military uniforms drab without digimake had stepped through the deadly roiling curtain into GATA territory. The crowd at the center of the intersection wilted from the upraised dusters of the PrivaPo as they began to troop towards the exiles. Amon had assumed them trapped in their exoskeletons but now supposed there had to be an offline emergency release, illustrating the superior preparedness for such eventualities of the Twelve over GATA. Whether the MegaGloms had pre-authorized the expense of their infantry trespassing or the ground commanders had made an independent crisis decision, Amon had no idea. Whatever the procedure, it seemed that the PrivaPo had pinned blame on the exiles and were out for retribution.

With an armed platoon tramping ominously through the press, stirring up panicked currents, the right side of the path ahead of Amon began to shrink and warp despite the exiles straining with all their might to shore it up. Ty was shouting into his radio as he rolled along beside him, and everyone around them readied their weapons, the ever more frantic stretch of crowd between the PrivaPo and the exiles thinning rapidly.

A few shots of dust had already been exchanged when savage hollers broke out from the direction of the border. Over the heads of the throng, Amon watched Jiku's forces spill between the stalled exoskeletons. Many were knocked flying by the unpredictable swipes of their giant robotic arms, or fell in electric convulsions as stundawgs leapt up and headbutted them. But enough penetrated the cordon to fire on the backs of the PrivaPo.

"After me!" Ty cried as his transparent wheelchair shield slid up in front of him and he flicked on the microbiome motor Tamper had installed. This launched him towards the PrivaPo, knocking aside the last of the fleeing ex-citizens, as he held down the trigger of his beauty duster. Vertical sprinted into the lane that had opened in his wake at the head of an exile charge. Amon tried to join them but he was buffeted hither and thither by the hysterical scrum around him and could hardly move.

It was while he pointed his duster above the mad crush and tried to steady his aim on a PrivaPo target that he witnessed the catastrophic moment. The rear PrivaPo line had peeled back to confront Jiku's flanking host. They were firing on them, killing some with heartstop or stroke, others with flechettes or bullets, when a spray of dust hit an exoskeleton mounted on a flatbed truck. This was repelled by the nanobot-wicking armor and ricocheted up to strike a peacedrone. The peacedrone had to be the property of a MegaGlom rival to the employer of the PrivaPo whose shot went stray because its dustcannon swiveled and unloaded on a second peacedrone, which began to froth and spatter liquified globules of its armor as it fired in turn on a third. From that moment, Amon lost track of what happened. All he perceived was a spreading chain reaction of attack and counterattack. Within seconds, an intricate web of crossfire had broken out around the no-fly zone, transforming the encompassing well of crewed and uncrewed aircraft revolving to the stratosphere into a single vortex of scrambled dogfight blur.

A tumult of whooshes, whines, and sonic booms sounded as dustbombs burst on the rooftops and the streets and dustrockets sang in the skies. Plumes of nano-particulate began to rain every conceivable horror onto the border-side edge of the crowd. Some catalytic medley thereof caused rooftops and walls to erupt, spewing chunks of concrete, glass, plastic, and insulation up and across Otemachi.

The battle between the PrivaPo and exiles dissolved as everyone began to flee for their lives, screaming or collapsing into some awful symptom or lying still. While Amon shoved and yanked his way through the flailing mob, peacecraft in various states of unravelling, fizzing, melting, spinning out, plummeted on radial trajectories around the no-fly cylinder like a shower of deranged meteors. Then a shockwave knocked him onto his back atop others.

In the second Amon was down, he was held transfixed by the mayhem in the skies, a swarming spiral of war reaching beyond the breaking clouds. Bolts and donuts of luminous energy angling up from subsidiary towers outside GATA space pelted the aerial fray, flinging electronically stunned rotorcraft on inertial collision courses, and streams of soap-bubble black holes accordioned regions of space-time with every imploding pop, compacting entire jet formations into slow-flowing tumbles of debris, as corporate doomsday weaponry long-nurtured in clandestine facilities was finally unleashed.

Then Amon shook off the grabbling hands as he sat up, and his vision went white. Crawling like mad over concrete, asphalt, and softer struggling things, the next thing he knew, his head was poking into a stretch of open street, and he sprang to his feet, running in blind desperation, dodging or bumping anyone in his path.

When at last Amon fought his way to the stairwell entrance, the crowd almost pushed him past it, but he managed to fling himself with a scrabbling leap on top of those descending ahead and, after much inconsiderate wriggling, to find purchase on a stair, first with one foot, then the other. Squeezed almost falling down the diagonal tunnel beneath the street, he was twisted around and caught a glimpse of GATA Tower. Against cracking slabs of grey cloud ascatter with aircraft tangling into the distance, the tip was just visible. That morning, it had already been a shrunken facsimile of the graphic-decorated monolith he had revered. Now that they had defused its inner impetus, it seemed a gutted symbol, an architectural husk bled dry of meaning. When Amon was jostled further down the stairwell and the crowd blocked the tower from view, something told him that he would never see it or the sisters again, the secrets that might have brought him solace or closure locked away forever.

While Amon was inching his way along the narrow shop-lined corridor of an underground mall, members of the entourage recognized his face amidst the crowd and escorted him to the rendezvous point arranged by Jiku—the basement of a parking tower. There, he was relieved to find that Ty, Tamper, Vertical, the PhisherKing, the Books, and all nine Phishers, incapacitated and able, had survived the havoc in one way or another. From what Jiku told them, the exile losses were nowhere near as severe as anyone had been expecting. Many of the injured had already been collected from the warzone and plans were underway to retrieve those left behind once the InterGlom skirmish had subsided.

Still, despite these fortunate turns, Amon and the others were in a somber mood. For not only had the revolution come to disaster, but despite their best efforts to save him, Hippo had died.

In the gloom of the underground parking floor, lit only by a camping lantern propped against a wall, he lay on a stretcher, still wrapped in the now blood-soaked bandages, arms crossed, palms resting on shoulders. On the tarmac around the cart were several open crates containing cubes, cylinders, tubing, and other vague shapes—the components for a life support system Jiku's scouts had ripped from a nearby hospital. If they'd had time, Tamper might have rigged up a power source and hacked the device. But he didn't bother to assemble the parts. Even in perfect working order, the machinery could do nothing for a body gone cold.

Once an exile mortician had checked Hippo's vitals, confirmed the diagnosis, and left the parking floor with her condolences, Vertical, Tamper, Ty, the Books, Monju, and the Phishers gathered at the foot of the stretcher, like a mourning party before a casket. Standing at the center of the group with Hippo straight in front of him, Amon was grateful for the shadows that draped his ravaged face, not yet believing even after witnessing his demise and the ebbing away of his life that he was actually gone. He knew one of them had to say something to inaugurate the informal ceremony and felt that it ought to be him, but there was a lump in his throat too big for words to pass. Amon looked around at his friends and found each gazing down into the shadows of their own private pain. All remained still, except for Tamper, whose hands shifted restlessly over the front of his bulging windbreaker as though in search of the many pockets in his usual outfit. Ty was the first to break the silence.

"You never told us how this happened," he said to no one in particular.

Amon and the PhisherKing exchanged sad grimaces, asking each other who would have the duty of explaining.

"One of the Birla Guard dusted him," said the PhisherKing. "It made him harm himself."

"Under Rashana's orders?" asked Ty.

"Call her Birla X," said Amon. "Saying 'Rashana' makes it even more confusing."

"Under Birla X's orders?"

"Ono X's," the PhisherKing replied. "But she went along with it."

Ty clucked his tongue in disgust.

More silence followed. This time it was broken by Vertical.

"You were the one who gave me the news, Amon. Rick died after I ran from Delivery," she said, her voice tremulous. "I told myself that I would be there for the people I cared about this time, whatever the dangers. But I couldn't make it . . ."

Vertical rested her chin on her sternum, shoulders hunched, and wrung her hands, directing her desolate stare under the stretcher. Amon traced her doleful profile and well-honed physique, understanding now what had spurred her fierce training for the revolution and admiring her even more.

"Vertical, Hippo's choices led him to this," said Amon. He pictured her running alone to GATA Tower after the ImmaNet went down and dancing her way through a legion of adversaries to reach them. Then, remembering Freg's broken leg, he added, "It's thanks to your courage that I'm here to tell you that."

This drew Vertical out of herself, and Amon gazed into her glistening eyes, urging her to accept his gratitude, to forget what she could not control, to forgive herself.

"You told us he's not a traitor," said Ty, his voice unusually soft and tender. "How can that be?"

"These two can explain I think. Can't you?" Amon turned to the Books.

Little Book was perched on Ty's old tricycle, sliding his stylus over the tablet attached to the handlebars as he recorded the conversation, his expression as inscrutable as ever. Beside him Book slouched, absentmindedly pressing the inside of his fists against his front teeth while stretching the skin of his cheeks with either thumb, brow drawn, slitted eyes tight.

"If he was indeed a traitor, then I must take full responsibility," he said, removing his hands from his mouth to address them.

"To state the central issue frankly, since the time that Lawrence Barrow's deceptions became apparent, I have not been confident of my capacity for lie detection. It was on the basis of my erroneous assessment of his story that the Xenocyst council admitted former CEM Barrow into our membership, and I subsequently failed to detect his conspiratorial murmurings, which ultimately precipitated the destruction of our city. Consequently, when I noticed after taking up residence at Atupio a certain peculiarity involving Rashana—or Birla X I should say—my initial reaction was to doubt myself.

"From the time of our initial acquaintance, Rashana's eyes seemed to issue the motions that I would have usually associated with misleading speech. However, in all prior cases, subjects who displayed these distinctive patterns did so occasionally and only when discussing topics of personal significance. Birla X, by contrast, displayed them frequently, and always in conjunction with exceedingly banal conversation.

"This discrepancy between present and past observation appeared to confirm my belief that I could no longer accurately identify verbal mendacity. I judged it inconceivable that she would be insincere when saying good morning or commenting on the weather, while all of her contributions to an endeavor that promised to change the course of history—her proposals at the planning sessions, for example—were entirely genuine. Moreover, even under the assumption that I was interpreting her correctly, she was demonstrating her dedication to the most crucial matters: i.e., universal access, Hakkotopia, etcetera. Therefore, I concluded that, whatever the status of my competence, we had sufficient rationale for ongoing cooperation with her.

"Nevertheless, as a precaution, I persisted in analyzing the motions of her eyes at every inconspicuous opportunity over the weeks of our preparations in the Atupio underground, and I discovered that I could not plausibly discount the recurrence of highly suspicious combinations. Consequently, I began to worry about the invisible repercussions such a quotidianly disingenuous leader might affect upon her organization. The problem was reminiscent of my experiences in Xenocyst after the Philanthropy Syndicate forced us to remove plutogenics from our curriculum. As an educator at that time, I witnessed firsthand how bias and omission in higher institutional strata can percolate downward to pollute an entire community in the long term. My fear was that such pernicious influence might have already infected Atupio. Thus I felt it incumbent upon me to offer my opinion of Birla X for the consideration of all our compatriots.

"Unfortunately, the likely ubiquity of biosurveillance throughout the compound presented a prohibitive obstacle. Even the most promising channels for confidential reporting—namely, tapping to Little Book or drafting a coded letter to Tamper—were foreclosed because I had no doubt that Ono X's cryptobreakers could crack either—our cryptographic pig latin notwithstanding. However, Little Book proved a keen observer of my mannerisms and, within days of his return, he had successfully inferred my thoughts. At the time, I perceived this development as fortuitous. In hindsight, I . . ."

Book's deep, nasally voice choked up, and he cast a woebegone glance at Hippo's corpse. When he removed his glasses (brand new with two intact lenses courtesy of Birla X) and dabbed at his cheeks with a handkerchief, Little Book paused his writing and reached over to give his hand a single momentary squeeze. Tamper patted Book on the back, and Amon and the other mourners soaked in their own sadness while they waited for him to gather himself.

"You may recall that, during our planning sessions, Little Book and I sat to the right and left of Hippo, respectively, in imitation of our former placement at the Xenocyst council. I studied Birla X's eyes intently when she spoke, and Little Book would initiate the scrawling of his pen over his tablet at the beginning of her statements and pause for several seconds at the end of her statements. We had employed an identical procedure at hearings in the Cyst. Our objective was to indicate to Hippo that we were operating in our roles of recording testimony and evaluating its truth value only vis-à-vis Birla X.

"Under usual council circumstances, Hippo would have inquired about the veracity of her statements. Thereupon LB would have tapped once to indicate true, twice for false, and I would have nodded in confirmation. Hippo's explicit questions were precluded by our company, both imme-diate and remote. Little Book nevertheless performed occasional double taps. We considered the level of risk for discovery acceptable because we had only deployed this usage in the digital quarantine, ensuring that the cryptobreakers had no prior data from which to glean its, admittedly straightforward, semantic function.

"The instance I believe when Hippo finally understood was on our visit one afternoon to the gymnasium. While Birla X and Hippo were praising

Vertical's performance on a self-reassembling obstacle course, I turned my back to Birla X in order to view her reflection in the wraparound mirrors rather than examine her eyes directly as per usual. I distinctly remember Hippo's inquisitive frown in the hallway afterward."

Book wiped his cheeks again and sniffled.

"I regret that I could not explain my meaning with any precision. I merely wished to bring his and your attention to a behavioral outlier for which there was no satisfactory explanation. Hippo demonstratively interpreted our message in the most extreme manner—as a warning not to trust Birla X whatsoever. If not for our being so ambiguous, the revolution might have succeeded and . . ." Book glanced again at Hippo as tears slipped down his cheeks. "My remorse is beyond measure."

When Book got onto his knees and pressed his head to the floor in apology, Amon bent down to tug on his collar and said, "Get up. There's no need for that."

"Yes, there is," Book sobbed. "I'm sorry, Hippo, I'm sorry to you all."

"No. You're misunderstanding the result of what you and Little Book did."

"I do not believe so."

"I know so."

"Amon is right," said the PhisherKing. "Hippo's message to Birla Y didn't cause the revolution to fail. It disrupted Ono X's plan to take it over. Your honest attempts to inform us of an urgent insight under difficult circumstances prevented the worst possible outcome."

"But Hippo is gone because of it. Just look at him . . ."

"I doubt that Hippo or many of us here would have survived Ono X's purges," said Amon. "If anything you should be proud of your one small success." He wanted to add, *I wish I had as much,* as a scathing sea of despair swelled within him, but he thought better of drowning his friends in it.

"As for Hippo himself," Amon continued, glancing at Ty, "it turned out that he was right to doubt Birla X, even if it wasn't for entirely the right reasons. If you believe as I do that he would have warned us earlier if he could and that he acted for what he thought was the greater good, then don't ever let anyone dare to call him a traitor again. I say he should have a proper sky burial at least. Will you all join me in a moment of silence?"

Once Amon and the PhisherKing had helped Book to his feet, they joined their fellow mourners in facing Hippo with heads slightly bowed and their palms together at their chests. Then Amon began to reflect on Hippo's life and to consider what had led him to the realization that Birla X had not originally been Rashana.

Although Hippo had once claimed that he could tell the twins apart, he didn't appear to have had any doubts that Birla X had ever been anyone else on the two occasions that they met at the Cyst during Amon's sojourn in the camps, nor at the conference to seek her assistance with the Phoenix Revolution, nor in the early weeks at Atupio that followed. This oversight was understandable, considered now in light of the PhisherKing's revelations, as these meetings would have occurred after Birla Y's theft of the Anisha profile had forced Birla X to adopt the Rashana identity as her own. Birla X would have already tweaked her face and genome to become all but indistinguishable from her sister, and been smoothly imitating her behavior with the help of gabkeepers referring to the Rashana LifeStream, a stable of myriad conmen whispering hoodwinks in her ear. Once Hippo donned his training bank, her appearance would have been just as persuasive whether he viewed her digimade or without the overlay. And the resemblance wasn't reserved for mere surfaces or genetics, but cut to the core of the sisters' desires and aspirations, with Birla X pursuing the diamond dream while Birla Y led the Gyges Circle. Birla X's elaborate performance—if performance it was—had been believable enough to convince the Starters, who had been raised in part by Rashana and who were much more familiar with her naked visage than Hippo ever could have been. It was perceptive of him to see through her at all, and this only thanks to the seed of suspicion Book had planted after Little Book returned.

What had ultimately convinced Hippo that Birla X was not entirely the person she seemed to be? Amon could only speculate. After the incident in the gymnasium, perhaps he had begun to pore over the minutiae of his interactions with her. Perhaps he had noticed unaccountable pauses, when Birla X looked up the content of Rashana, a micro-lag before her gabkeepers supplied the right memory, so brief as to be nearly imperceptible to others. Amon only realized now that he had overlooked these signs of her dissembling in his own conversations with Birla X. At odd moments, she had often watched her thumb sliding over her fingertips, or scratched the eyebrow where Anisha's beauty mark had been removed. If he could only consult his LifeStream, something told him there would be other, less obvious cues that he was missing.

For Hippo, who had known the sisters for decades, the timing of these quirks might have seemed unusual, always occurring when he reminisced about events at which only Rashana was present or of which only Rashana could have been aware—humanitarian matters from the days of her Xenocyst patronage, perhaps, or private conversations long after in the digital quarantine. Could there have been a little twitch of the finger or lip, a flutter of those razor eyelashes? Or was there just something off about her vibe, an incongruity too subtle to describe?

Whatever it was, Hippo had come to his disturbing epiphany under the same surveillance lockdown as the Books—worse because he was on a leash with Birla X herself, every action tallied on her readout. He couldn't say a word without stopping short the revolution, an endeavor that filled the emptiness left by the collapse of Xenocyst and kept him on his feet, rather than staring indifferent into a dark corner. But he believed that inaction would allow Birla X, the woman he now thought of as Anisha, to get away with perverting their joint efforts to some unknown but surely heinous end, not fully grasping that it was Ono X he was contending with. Allowing a just enterprise to be compromised was something every particle of his being rejected, whatever small victory might be gained in exchange. For to secure Xenocyst's continued existence, he had once let the Philanthropy Syndicate squash their education program, reducing the city to a literal breeding ground for uncritical human resource producers juiced up on multiply-thy-seed, only to watch the Syndicate turn around and dismember the community when it suited the bottom line. Never again would he cut such a pragmatic bargain or capitulate to the distortion of his ideals, especially when the nature of that distortion remained unclear. So he worked quietly to negotiate advantages for his people that would come to fruition on the day of their mission: urging Tamper to build cameras and radios as a back communication channel, arranging to have capable exiles posted with Ono X in case of mischief, picking the Atupians who would accompany him and Amon into GATA Tower, and arguing that everyone carry non-lethal weaponry to deprive the Birla Guard of their more powerful blitz.

These sly maneuvers paved the way for him to invite the sister he trusted, who he needed if the revolution were to stay true to its intentions of realizing universal access and Hakkotopia 2.0, a home for his exiled people. Because if he was going to gain the cooperation of the Atupians in overcoming the Birla X Guard and deposing the false Rashana, he needed the real Rashana to rally them. It never occurred to him that if one sister was not fully and wholly Rashana that the other sister might not be either, a critical blindspot that, for all his foresight, would be his undoing. Hence his confusion when he saw Birla Y deny that she was Rashana, refuse the reins of Atupio, and demand Gyges Ring . . .

Amon believed that Hippo must have run through some such thought process. His legacy would no doubt be tainted by his failure to keep Xenocyst together, his ensuing torpor, and this last desperate gambit. But Amon felt certain that he would have given them further reason to redeem him if only they could have had a chance to ask.

Hippo the Identity Vitalator, Amon the Identity Executioner, one bestowing banklife, the other taking it away, one choosing bankdeath at the hands of another, the other at his own hands, to at last share the codes for birth and death and join in a brief financial resurrection . . . Now the giver of banklife had died an actual death, while the dealer in bankdeath remained actually alive. Something in the final, irreversible symmetry of their stories bore the air of inevitability, and it grieved Amon to think that it could not have been otherwise, that there was no true version of today in which they greeted the future together.

When the mortician returned with three helpers and began to wheel Hippo's body up the ramp to the roof of the parking tower for a Xenocyst-style funeral—leaving him to the crows—a messenger came to report that Ono X had been captured.

The woman led them down a ramp to a deeper parking floor, where Yané and a heavyset man with an assault duster stood guard in a corner. When they drew closer, Tamper switched on his penlight and illuminated Ono X's face. Even under the glare, Ono X didn't flinch or even blink, remaining on his side with his legs splayed into the corner, his gaze skimming the concrete floor towards the shadows at their feet.

"My scout spotted an Atupian gang hauling him to the border," said Yané. "So I sent a crew in to get 'im."

Once the new arrivals had gathered around, Amon said, "Ono."

"Amon?" The moment Ono X spoke, his body parts began to move in a strange uncoordinated spasm—legs sliding in different directions, arms smacking into each other, hands and feet spiraling on their joints, fingers wriggling as though each had a separate mind. Within seconds, it had subsided, but his head kept turning in jerky arcs, as if searching for Amon.

"What kind of dust is that?" Ty asked.

"Crisscross," Amon replied, recalling videos of similarly disabled victims from Liquidator training.

Tap-tappa-tap . . . "The effect is to rearrange connections between motor neurons so that commands are routed randomly," Book interpreted, as Little Book tap-scrawled on his handlebar tablet. "Whenever he wills an action, his body responds with a motion other than that he is accustomed to."

"Was it the Starters that got him?" asked Amon.

"It would have to be," said Vertical. "No one else had weapons like that."

While they talked about Ono X as if he weren't there, his neck continued to tick erratically, eyes swirling on different orbits. Amon decided to do him a favor by stepping where he was facing. His head then came to a stop and his gaze settled on a spot around Amon's collar. Amon bent and leaned until their eyes met.

"Is Rashana with you?" Ono X asked. Control of his voice was unaffected. Amon had heard that the PrivaPo and Charity Brigade often used crisscross in interrogations.

"There rarely was any such person," said Amon.

"You know who I mean. Is she there?"

Amon exchanged knowing glances with his huddled friends to see if anyone would volunteer an explanation.

"Where is she? Have you done something to her?"

"Listen, Ono," said Amon. "Don't fool yourself that you're in a position to ask questions. None of the others here know what you did, but once they find out, they're going to want blood. So I'm not even going to offer you a Birla Deal. You answer all my questions honestly and *maybe* I'll protect you. You keep anything from me, fudge even one tiny detail, and I let them have their way with you for sure. Sound fair?"

"Yes. F-fine." Ono X's body remained still, showing no signs of fear, but he sounded terrified. Who wouldn't be terrified? He was the very definition of helpless, reeking of his own waste.

Amon decided to start with the question that weighed most heavily on his mind. "Where is Mayuko?"

"M-mayuko?"

"Yeah, Mayuko Takamatsu, my childhood friend, from one of *your* BioPens. I asked you to help me find her."

"I told you—"

"I know what you told me! What do you know?"

"I gathered all the intelligence I could."

"But you told Birla X, the one you call Rashana, that I would agree to lead Hakkotopia even after what you did. You were going to use Mayuko as leverage, weren't you? You know where she is!"

"N-no. I-I had to sound confident t-that Rashana could still have you. I needed her to agree. I was going to dump you on Hahajima. Thought you'd grow to like it."

"Because of harmony dust."

"I don't know anything about that. I only heard about it today when—"

"Come on!"

"No, r-really. I thought you'd settle in to the forest because of all the years you saved up to go there. You'd accept paradise because you'd have nowhere else to go."

"If you can't be honest, you're on your own with these people."

"But I can't tell you what I don't know," Ono X pleaded.

Amon looked to Book who'd been staring into Ono X's eyes. They were just as still as if Ono X were meeting the gaze of his own reflection in a mirror.

"His abnormal state is confounding," said Book. "However, as far as I can determine under these conditions, he seems to be telling the truth."

"There were some things that the twins never told us, or the gabkeepers, or anybody," said Ono X. "They kept them in that hidden folder. If you help me find Rashana, I know she'll have the answers you're looking for."

Amon's heart seemed to fall into the pit of his stomach. It was his worst fear given voice. He'd thrown away his last chance to find Mayuko.

"Where is she?" Ono X repeated. "She can help you. I know it."

"What did 'e say about asking questions?" Yané snarled, kicking Ono X in the buttocks. This triggered another disjointed limb spasm, and Amon had to hop back to avoid a swinging leg. When it was over, Ono X was twisted up with his face pointing towards the ceiling.

"I-I-I'm sorry," Ono X quavered. "I-I'm just worried about her."

Amon stepped into his eyeline, looming as he peered down over the tip of his nose. He thought that what Yané had done was cruel but seized upon the awe it afforded anyway.

"Always thinking about Birla X before anyone else—even yourself, huh?" said Amon. "You didn't even blink when she became a different person after the identity heist. Just kept serving her like it didn't matter who she was or what she was after. You became a different person yourself. Started soaking up the memories of your clone as if they were yours. Is there anything you wouldn't do for her? Are you insane?"

"I-I'm not the only one. The Birla Guard and the gabkeepers and the Cognitive Handling Corps and the tutors. We were custom grown and reared to observe the sisters closely, guess their desires however dark or well-hidden. Promotions and demotions and rewards and punishments. Our happiness rose and fell with how well we gave them what they wanted before they knew it themselves. Their begetters made sure that the will of their heirs was always carried out on our initiative. S-service is all we know."

Amon recalled again Birla X's tale about the Onos' secret fundraising for the sisters' childhood cyberattack and their secret construction of two Geminis. It was this covert service, Amon realized, that he may very well have owed his life to, as Ono X had supposedly been the one who shifted him to Green Ladybug instead of abandoning him in the District of Dreams with the rest of the Hakkotopian children. And yet, now it had ruined the idea that was the culmination of that life, stealing all that the Phoenix Virus might have achieved to offer the ultimate gift—absolute freedom. What else could the Onos have done to satisfy the unconscious urges they perceived in their masters? Suddenly another puzzle fell together in Amon's mind.

"It was you who gave the Charity Brigade an early warning about the Delivery sabotage," he said. "You wanted them to crack down on us to get more compelling footage. Semi-lethal crowdcare weaponry doesn't look brutal enough on camera so you made sure there was a stampede. You probably had career volunteer agents spurring it on from the rear. The Atupio journalists got cleared out too quickly to capture it. But you were expecting that, weren't you? That's why you had drones outside to record everything, like the SampleQuito you smuggled in to track me. Birla X said she didn't know anything about this. And I bet she didn't. It was you. You did it all yourself. You knew how much she wanted to influence the election."

"I-I admit it," said Ono X. "It's true. I did it for her."

"Rick is gone because of that," said Vertical. "How many innocent lives have you put at risk for her sake?"

"I-I'm sorry."

Overhearing the interrogation, several exiles crowded around the huddle to watch. Their approach caused Ono X's head to roll and yaw, his decoupled eyes rotating in wayward spirals, searching in fear for whoever had arrived. When these motions had settled, he was facing Tamper's shoes.

"Hold still," said Amon. Cupping Ono X's chin in both hands, he gently turned his head upward again. Although Ono X's right eye pointed straight ahead, his left eye had rolled up into the upper corner, so Amon closed his left eyelid and glowered into his one open eye. "Now tell me. Why did you call Sekido?"

"Y-you would have been Anisha's hostages if not for him."

"That was just a coincidence. That was just because of Hippo. You didn't even know Birla Y would be there. Why did you arrange that trick with Sekido in the first place?"

"Because of our training. All of their handlers were raised to—"

"We heard what you said. But you can think for yourself, can't you? You were taught to give your master what she doesn't even know she wants herself, but you're not stupid. You can guess the consequences of your choices as well as anybody. You knew what we were trying to achieve, how many people universal banklife might have helped. You knew how much we all sacrificed for this. All the sweat and blood! She would have been satisfied with what we achieved, for fuck's sake. But you took it upon yourself to steal from the world and all of future history just to give her that little bit more. You betrayed us of your own free will. Why? You must believe in something more than just duty to go to all that work, to put together that elaborate scheme that undermined everything we—Why?!"

Under the harsh beam of the penlight, Ono X's face muscles undulated into a bizarre caricature of an expression, his lips smiling even though his jaw had drifted far to one side, a single eyebrow frowning, the opposite nostril flaring, both cheeks puffing, his eyes slingshotting left to right. Amon was sure it signified an emotion but no one could have hoped to read it.

"I wanted to tell her that she has family," Ono X whimpered, his cracking voice conveying what his face could not. "It was the only way I could think how."

At this Amon understood, and felt the bittersweet ache of sympathy, recalling the story Birla X had told him of the sisters' upbringing. Raised according to a cold, efficient plan by begetters who saw them merely as tools to perpetuate their corporate empire. The cloned Birla Guard playing with them, brought up with discipline but receiving more care from their SubMoms than the sisters were ever allowed. And the two favorites, the Onos, looking upon this isolated pair, these beautiful, capable, intelligent, powerful, proud, but tortured women, and wanting to give them the warmth they needed to grow apart, while painfully aware that they could never step out of their position.

What a fitting token of affection the conjunction of their two dreams in the diamond ring must have seemed to Ono X when he conceived of it. A way to finally express his feelings, if only encoded as an act of service. That was why he had looked so sincere in the recording of his proposal. He loved her as a sister even if he knew she couldn't understand what that meant.

Amon supposed that loving one of the twins through her change in identity must have been something like loving both of them. But Ono X could never expect for either to reciprocate and treat him as a brother so long as their entanglement with each other choked off the space in their hearts for family. Hence his dangerous fixation with having Birla X consent to paralyzing Birla Y on the verge of the former's apotheosis. Only by taking from one sister everything that either might have been and bestowing on the other all that either had ever wanted to be could Ono X pry apart two poorly fitted selves and remold the pieces into a whole person that might learn how to love.

Ono X's pathetic breakdown seemed to temporarily deflate the outrage that had been brewing in the crowd, for when Amon looked around he saw heads shaking and eyes averted. Then someone muttered, "Despicable," and an indignant stir spread.

"Whadda you mean 'tell her she has family'?" Yané sneered. "Doesn't make any sense." He wound up for another kick, but Amon put a hand on his shoulder.

"No more of that, Yané," Amon told him. Then he turned to a group of exiles he trusted and said, "Please carry him to ground level—dump him on the sidewalk."

And he began to walk away.

"Where are you going?" Ono X croaked, his voice full of the tears he could not shed, and Amon heard the soft thudding and rustling of another spasm behind him. "Can't you just tell me if she's alright?"

This last desperate entreaty wrung Amon's heart and he came to a halt, as it made him think of Mayuko. By choice and necessity, he had left behind the only two people that might have led him to the woman he loved. Now he could lead to those two people someone that loved one or both of them. But he refused to aid anyone involved with Atupio in tracking down the Mother, while the slimmest chance remained that the fractious bands might reunite. So not turning around, he said, "They're both safe, Ono. Your brother too. For now."

It was unlikely that Ono X would survive the week in his condition. Nevertheless, as Amon stepped out of the parking floor, he imagined the Onos reuniting with the sisters in the filthy shadow of some bridge or trash heap, fallen from the pedestal of finance and freedom that had kept them beyond reach.

When Amon put his foot onto the ramp, he felt a hand grip his bicep. Turning, he found himself face-to-face with Yané, tailed by Tamper, the PhisherKing, Ty, Vertical, and the Books.

"The fuck was that?"

"If you want to talk, come somewhere private," said Amon, glancing through the doorway at the crowd of gawkers. Then he started up the ramp.

The few thousand exiles that had gathered so far occupied basement floors five through twelve, so the Books led them to B3, empty but for a handful of teenagers lounging on the trunks and hoods of parked cars. The eight of them formed a circle in one of the lanes. There Tamper placed his penlight on a small stand on the floor to light them from below.

"Why are you letting that snitch go?" Yané demanded.

"You like that word, don't you?" said Amon. "I thought I was the snitch."

Amon glared at Yané until he looked away. While the exiles' esteem for Amon and the other organizers of the revolution would be tenuous after the debacle that morning, Yané's authority had become irredeemable since he misjudged Amon, who had at least saved them from starvation.

"Ono X isn't going anywhere," said Amon. "Those symptoms are permanent. The best he can hope for is someone dropping him off at a hospital once everything is back online."

"If *anything* goes back online," corrected the PhisherKing.

"I heard it was 'cause of him that everything went wrong," said Yané.

"And that's why you kicked him," said Amon, "a man who can't do anything but talk and shit and piss?"

"Didn't he kill Hippo?"

This gave Amon pause. He had intentionally left out any mention of Hippo's forced suicide from his accusations against Ono X and was glad now he had done so. Yané, who appeared to have heard something over radio, might have incited a mob.

"Someone needs to be punished for what was done. Right?" Yané looked around for support, unable to meet Amon's fierce gaze. Ty gritted his teeth and squeezed the rims of his wheels, but not answering Yané, he looked to Amon, giving him the benefit of the doubt.

"If we keep him with us, they'll tear him limb from limb," said Amon. "That's not punishment. Just barbarism."

"We don't have to allow that," said Ty. "He could be useful to us in one piece."

"That man is a wealth of intelligence," said the PhisherKing.

"With the ImmaNet gone, his memory is priceless," said Book.

"And make him our information gimp?" Amon asked them all. "Is that how we kick off a new era, with slavery? No!"

Before Yané could reply Vertical said, "I agree with Amon."

"That bastard killed your boyfriend!" Yané cried.

"Not true."

"What?"

"I'll never be able to accept his apology. But whatever was responsible for Rick's death was much bigger than just one person—Barrow, Ono X, or anyone else. And now that thing is gone. We destroyed it, for better or for worse. So I think the time has come to start fresh."

Amon was impressed with her clarity. She was expressing something he had already decided for himself in coming to terms with his own grief.

"We must leave the debts and deeds of the age that passed at the door to this one."

Amon wasn't sure what possessed him to say this. But somehow it felt right.

After Yané sullenly conceded, he told them that Jiku had asked him to oversee a search team, ringing the signal bells on street level to attract lost stragglers. Once Yané was gone, Ty raised the issue of where they would go next.

"We're hidden down here for now," he said, "but we've got no clue what will happen at ground zero. Better get a jump on the MegaGloms and get a move on."

"As food and shelter are paramount, we ought to select a location where their provision will be simple and easy," said Book.

"With plenty of vendors to crack," added Tamper.

"Like the District of Dreams?" suggested Vertical. "Not that I want to go back."

"How long you figure the meal ink and Fleet keep flowing?" said Ty.

"Whatever the duration, a location in Free Tokyo would be preferable," said Book. "CareBots are more sensitive to vending machine burglary than the security drones here."

"Better not tempt fate," Tamper cautioned.

"I guess Atupio is out, huh?" said Ty, with a wince of his cheek. "That is the most comfortable place I have ever been in my whole life. Too bad about the company."

Amon knew that Ty was thinking of his rehabilitation at Atupio. It was supposed to have continued on Hahajima. Now that he could go to neither, he might never walk again.

"I would invite you to our abode," said the PhisherKing, "but it would be too small for everyone. And it's only a matter of time before the MegaGloms come knocking."

"Perhaps our Ferment Culture Collective scientists and engineers could assist us in *growing* food and shelter," said Book.

"Ferment Culture?" Amon asked perplexed.

"The Books bumped into some of them on the streets," Ty explained. "Talked them into going rogue after they learned about Ono's tricks."

"So they're here—in this parking tower?"

"Yup. A few floors down last I checked."

"That is encouraging news," said the PhisherKing. "We had already begun to discuss collaboration in the Atupio underground. It excites me to think of the new technologies Ferment Culture and Phishers might conceive together in the future . . . But their work requires a well-equipped biolab—plenty of computing power as well. We can't expect to benefit from their talents today."

"Not to praise my own painting or anything, but I can put my talents to work for you right now if you get me some tools and parts, " said Ty. "Nothing like bicycles to get around with all the roads blocked, you know. Tamper could build us more devices with a workshop of his own."

Tamper gave the slightest nod.

"You're talking about a place with anadeto," said Vertical.

This gave Amon an idea. "How about Jinbocho?"

"That decadent old book town?" the PhisherKing scoffed.

"Not just books, but analog treasures of all kinds. Tools, materials, collectibles. And some of the buildings, like the Tezuka where I used to live, have coin-operated vending machines. They should be a cinch to crack without any worry about drones. Plus lots of empty rooms. It's never exactly been a popular place to live, what with all the nosties."

"Isn't it kind of close to Otemachi?" said Ty. "I thought we'd want some space between us and those peacecraft."

"You won't want to stay forever," said Amon. "But it should be a good place to rest and refuel."

"The word 'books' was sufficient to persuade us," said Book, and Little Book gave a tap. "What is the consensus?"

"We'll join you," said the PhisherKing.

"Fine with me too," said Ty.

But Tamper shook his head. "You go ahead. Got to pick up my son."

Before the revolution, Tamper had asked Ono X to deliver his son a radio and leave him a message to secretly pack his most important belongings. Tamper's plan had been to beckon him down a ladder from the veranda of his foster home and motorbike him to a riverside helipad from which they would have flown straight to Hahajima. (He'd made sure that the rotorcraft was stocked with plenty of Cloud9 Nectar.) But now the shutdown would have sent the foster parents into a panic. If they found the radio, confiscated it, and rushed off somewhere, or did something drastic, Tamper might lose touch with his son forever.

"I won't be coming along either," said Vertical. "I . . ." she faltered, pressing her eyes closed with downturned lips as though ashamed to explain herself, and it only took Amon a moment to guess why.

During the preparations, she had never mentioned her husband. A successful workaday lawyer couldn't be expected to sever his links to the AT Market for some incomprehensible ideal. Perhaps she would have reached out once banklife was universal. But now that bankdeath reigned instead, he would be one of the helpless masses, no longer tied to the career that had kept them apart.

"Go to him," Amon told her. "Run there as fast as you can and make sure he's ok. That's what Rick would have wanted for you."

There was no reason anyone, living or dead, should stop them from being together, if that was what they desired in spite of the years of distance that had surely changed them both.

Vertical looked at Amon with teary eyes and nodded. "Thank you for understanding. I'm so sorry about everything."

"Sorry," echoed Tamper, his hands beginning to roam over his belly again.

Ty shook his head with a pained scowl and waved his hand side-to-side in denial of their responsibility. The PhisherKing watched with lips pressed in sympathy, Book with an uncomprehending frown, and Little Book with his usual blank attentiveness.

"Don't waste another moment fretting about it," said Amon. "Better two of us than none."

At these words, the shadows of their circle seemed to lengthen and wilt on the ceiling.

Once Tamper and Vertical had said their goodbyes and departed, Ty, the Books, and the PhisherKing began to discuss the logistics of transporting the injured to Jinbocho and what route might be safest. But the conversation petered out when Amon shuffled away from the ring of glow and hung his head, facing his shadow cast on a concrete wall, so faint it was barely distinguishable from the surrounding gloom.

In a flash, he saw everyone impacted by the crisis they had triggered. The Gyges Circle caught in Tokyo's financial blackout, their metamorphosis into beings beyond rules supplanted by an equalizing disconnection that left them among the rabble. MegaGlom executives elsewhere scrambling for an interim equilibrium between the Philanthropy Syndicate and SpawnU Consortium after the dissolution of Fertilex. Citizens around the world watching in disbelief the adfonews about GATA Tokyo in whatever self-serving form each MegaGlom decided to deliver it, reeling from the economic shockwaves of a whole national market vanishing. Bankdead hordes flowing through Delivery to trade babies for supplies, wondering at the initial career volunteer and Charity Brigade disarray, later their absence, until the day the automated system broke down without human maintenance and the lineups exploded into riots. Liquidators scattered throughout the metropolis and GATA technocrats locked in the tower or off work somewhere else, not just out of a job but out of the reality they had upheld. Nosties in Jinbocho and elsewhere clinging to their precious anadeto, only to find rapacious eyes on it from all quarters as the value of everything else plummeted by comparison. BioPen youth breaking away from their panicked SubMoms and stepping out into the world orphans. Xenocyst exiles, OpScis, Atupians, Starters, PrivaPo. Amon even thought of the only woman he'd ever been with, now stripped of the images that allowed her to become either Akane or Aoi, as if she were still working as a prostitute seven years later.

He was genuinely happy that Vertical and Tamper had a chance to find those they cared about, like so many other families, lovers, and friends no longer divided by financial walls. At the same time, he lamented his decision, as prudent and unavoidable as it had been, to leave the sisters behind. He missed Mayuko more than ever.

Presently, he felt a firm hand on his shoulder.

"I tried a few more but they didn't work," said the PhisherKing. "We'll just have to keep our eyes out for her."

Amon imagined Mayuko alone in the unfolding troubles. She was a strong and resourceful woman, but even those with the support of a community like the exiles might not make it through. Though he didn't want to believe that she was already dead, even just knowing that would have given him some hope of moving on. Instead, the uncertainty and his memories of her, both joyful and tragic, were set to haunt him to the grave. Amon wished that Birla X had never tried to divulge the password. It made the possibility of finding Mayuko seem so tantalizingly close.

"Forty-nine," he muttered bitterly. Then something occurred to him and he turned to the PhisherKing: "That's the number of years between each jubilee."

"It certainly is," said Monju.

"The sisters were involved in charging me for jubilee."

"Perhaps. No definitive evidence can be trawled from their LifeStreams."

"But couldn't the connection be some kind of cypher?" he said.

"Well, the present year is 50 FE, forty-nine years since this age began. Did you notice that the House of Blinding was on the 49th floor? Some fiction trilogies I've heard of have forty-nine chapters. Until Vertical and Tamper left there were seven of us—the square root of forty-nine. My mind has been full of such patterns all morning. Once you attend to them, the world seems to brim with hidden mathematical meaning. Sad to say, these manifold enigmas have yet to yield a useful answer."

Amon stared into the PhisherKing's shadowed eyes in silence, wracking his brain while Ty and the Books looked on, but his budding excitement quickly shriveled into doubt. What hubris to think that Amon could guess the password when the great cryptobreaker, Kai Monju, was at a loss. He hung his head again and held it, pressing his palms into his temples with fingertips meeting at the back.

Tap, tapataptap . . . Little Book's steady scrivening on his handlebar tablet suddenly became audible.

"Unlikely," Monju replied. "If I make a mistake now, I'll have to wait hours before I can try again."

"What did he say?" Amon asked.

"He suggested I try the amount of the jubilee charge. But I don't recommend it. It doesn't begin with forty-nine."

Little Book had questioned the PhisherKing in the Atupio mess hall about the amount that Amon had been charged and that the Emoticon Man had offered Mayuko. Amon had overheard the part of the exchange where Little Book made the PhisherKing recite the 83 digit number a second time to check for errors.

Tap, tap-ataptap, tap, tap . . .

"No. How did you arrive at—" The PhisherKing stopped, his eyes going wide.

"What?"

"Wwowww!" the PhisherKing marveled so loudly that the heads of the teenagers turned. "Of all the infinite multiples . . . I was stuck on the digits four and nine, in a mental cage of my own making . . ."

"Stuck how?"

"The charge for jubilee is equivalent to 49^{49}! You're a genius!" The PhisherKing's eyes set in wizened skin sparkled with child-like wonder above Tamper's penlight as he shook Little Book by the collar. "You did all that in your head?"

Little Book gave a single tap and without anyone having to interpret, Amon knew what it meant from his smile. It was still an awkward smile, but the warmth it expressed became ever more convincing by the day. A child who invented his own tap language and mastered the changing codes for Xenocyst's official letters had to be mathematically gifted, but this . . . Even Book gaped at his protégé in astonishment.

"So that's the password that got interrupted?" Amon asked, in the timbre of a desperate prayer. "Forty-nine to the power of forty-nine?"

"I'm inside the folder!"

"Then what about Mayuko?"

"Can I have a second or two to check?"

Less than a minute after gaining access to the Makesh Adani folder, the PhisherKing found a seg that seemed to concern Mayuko. It was from the perspective of Makesh, presumably digiguising a Birla sister, and showed a bespoke journalist relaying a report from an OpSci about a woman who was visiting Opportunity Peaks. Makesh instructed the journalist to have the woman picked up and transported to somewhere called "the residence." Monju knew from other sources that this referred to the Birlas' main Kindominium in Tokyo.

As the PhisherKing went on to explain, Kindominiums were special facilities where the Birlas housed the families of their Cognitive Handling Corps and other essential servants. The arrangement guaranteed loyalty, as any betrayal was met with punishment to the betrayer's kin. Apartments were lavish, and the residents were generally allowed to come and go at will, but they were basically pampered hostages. They either lived in cushy comfort or simply disappeared. Servants signed contracts that granted them high pay and subsidized the great luxury of naturally born babies only to discover the unwritten threat that tacitly accompanied these advantages. It was like having a Birla Deal hanging over your head at all times. This finally clarified for Amon how the Birla sisters could allow their thousands of gabkeepers, cognitive butlers, and other remote handlers to access sensitive portions of their LifeStreams without fear of leaks.

The PhisherKing surmised that the woman might be Mayuko for several reasons: both the journalist and the Birla sister as Makesh avoided using the woman's name; the seg had been relegated to the folder for shameful memories; and the woman was presumably bankliving, since Kindominiums were not equipped to house the bankdead. Given that the last place Amon thought Mayuko might have been was the gates of Xenocyst, based on a rumor from Vertical of a woman asking around about him, her later appearance at not-so-distant Opportunity Peaks seemed plausible enough, if worrisome . . .. What this all amounted to was a bankliving woman searching for Amon in the District of Dreams who a Birla sister thought worth the expense of holding hostage and was ashamed of doing so. Not a conclusive identification, but it was difficult to think who else might fit the description.

The Kindominium was in Ayase, near the northeastern border of Tokyo, to which Monju said he would guide Amon with a map saved in his BodyBank. Unfortunately, he lacked the ImmaNet to indicate their position, limiting the map's usefulness, and neither of them were familiar with that area of the naked metropolis. Since the woman might leave if they got lost on what already promised to be a walk of several hours at least, this presented a dilemma until Little Book offered to navigate. It seemed that Tamper had installed a GPS device into his tablet that piggybacked on ambient transmitters to connect to antique satellites. Between this and the map, they had the tools to trace a fairly direct route.

Because the seg's date had been removed, there was no telling when the woman might have been brought to the Kindominium, whether she was still there, or what might have happened to her. All they could do was go there and hope.

With the trains stalled, cars blocking the roads, and crowds overrunning the streets, they decided to make their way underground, along subway lines and their branching service passages.

Once they were on their way, trekking through a long tunnel, Amon and Little Book adjusted their pace to the PhisherKing. Although he was incredibly supple for his age and by no means slow, it was more than ten kilometers to their destination and he needed to pace himself, leaving them time to talk.

"So which one of the sisters threw Mayuko—or this woman—in the Kindominium?" Amon asked.

Little Book's tricycle squeaked faintly as he peddled beside the two men, his handlebar light gouging a cone from the narrow darkness ahead.

"That is a complicated question," said the PhisherKing. His hands jittered constantly in the shadows, sifting through his newly unlocked treasure.

"Even with both their LifeStreams and access to the Makesh folder?"

"Especially."

"Hey. You made a living finding patterns in the biggest collection of information humankind has ever produced. Three folders are tripping you up?"

"Not just any folders. The sub-profiles have been switched, hacked, and edited. The segs they dumped in the Makesh folder are a jumble, with date stamping and user signing deactivated. Imagine trying to sort a heap of broken glass into panes. Without the ImmaNet there's no way to corroborate anything. I can't use any of my usual apps. And those are the easy problems."

"What are the hard ones?"

"I've detected an encrypted folder inside Makesh."

"A sub-sub-sub profile?"

"Perhaps. Whatever it is, the missing segs tucked away there confound all my attempts to impose continuity on the ones I can access."

"Just give me what you have. We can work it out together."

"We can certainly try. I'd better start with the identity of the sisters. The puzzle of puzzles."

While they walked, the PhisherKing began to stitch together his account. He began with the year FE 26, when, among other things, the sisters turned twenty and Hippo presided over their identity birth. The negligible genetic difference between them allowed him to assign their two genomes to a single ID signature. At this point, the sisters had already chosen who would be Rashana and who Anisha, and had begun to divide their assets and data in secret, so the fusion of their profiles flouted their efforts to grow apart. In the same year, they were ordered to destroy Hakkotopia, an experience that inspired their respective life's work—the Gyges Circle for Anisha and Atupio for Rashana.

Then, two decades later, the PhisherKing peddled the Onos a leak of several passages from the Birla parents' will, and the sisters learned that Anisha would take majority share of Fertilex. But it wasn't until several years later, just the previous summer, over the three days prior to Amon's cash crash, that the sisters finally put this knowledge to use. On the morning that Amon practiced blink reduction at home, saw Rick and Mayuko embracing while on his way to work, and listened to Sekido's enticements about a mysterious promotion, Amon and Rick cash crashed Minister Kitao. That very afternoon the Birla parents died; that evening, while Amon and Rick argued over drinks, the executers of the Birla estate met to review the will; and that night Rick was dispatched by Sekido and the Gyges Circle to liquidate Barrow.

"Do you think the parents were murdered?" Amon asked.

"Personally, I don't put any credence in InfoFlux reports—I doubt it was an accident. As you and others have noted, the political timing was a little too convenient."

"One of the sisters told me that the other was to blame."

"I'm sure she did. They both had the motives and access to the ship that sank."

"But which one actually went through with it?"

"Whoever it was, they were careful not to leave records—or not enough for us to draw any conclusions."

"What if we were betting?"

"I'd wager it was one of the Onos—or both of them working together."

"A parricide service tag-team."

"You could call it that. If only we had the evidence to be certain whether it's true."

On the morning of the second day, Amon was assigned to liquidate Barrow in Rick's place, after he was ID murdered for asking too many questions the night before. That afternoon, the sisters were called upon to receive their inheritance in Tokyo. The will stipulated that they had to be together in person, presumably as a move by the late parents to nudge them out of their estrangement.

Here, Amon recalled the PhisherKing's vidbomb of the Birla Guard shaking hands in the boardroom. A cryptocorps had exploited this brief skin-to-skin contact to flesh-hack via the Y guards into their X counterparts' BodyBanks, while simultaneously exploiting the security holes in the sister's sub-profiles to remotely hack via Birla Y into Birla X. Within seconds, every pair of Y and X profiles had been switched, the data inside cleansed of any related recordings. Amon could only imagine Birla Y's triumphant smirk when she accessed her sister's LifeStream on her own hardware and knew that she had succeeded at the most profitable heist the world had ever known. The PhisherKing had found another seg showing her slipping out of the boardroom with her guards ahead of Birla X and boarding an elevator for the rooftop. In satellite video a minute later, Birla X arrived in her box of guards at the landing pad, found Gemini X gone, the other Gemini waiting instead, and realized at last that something was wrong.

"This is the place where things get messy," said Amon.

"It certainly is," said the PhisherKing.

"I mean, up until now, there are just two sisters, Anisha and Rashana. Anisha works with the Gyges Circle, and Rashana runs Atupio. Then there was the identity heist, and look what had become of them this morning, less than a year later . . ."

"We'll never understand all the ins and outs. The best we can do is unpack the stages each of them went through in adopting their new identities. The key point to keep in mind is that the sisters transitioned in different ways depending on their legal situation."

Once Birla Y, originally Rashana, had stolen the Anisha LifeStream from Birla X, she preempted her sister by launching a lawsuit to regain Atupio, which both sisters had been surprised to learn was awarded to Rashana. After Birla X realized that the Rashana LifeStream had been foisted on her, she countersued to win back the Anisha LifeStream and her rightful inheritance of Fertilex.

Birla Y began the court case on stronger footing because she went in well-prepared. She had assembled a highly capable litigaticorps, attached Judicial Brokers to her purse strings, and erased all evidence from both LifeStreams in advance. Nevertheless, she had to behave outwardly like Anisha, and her Y Birla Guard like their X counterparts. Otherwise, her sister might hack LifeStream segs to establish that they had ever been anyone else. Playing Anisha meant distancing herself from Atupio until she could take it back, whether by legal ruling, a buy-out with her newly pilfered fortune, or some other maneuver yet to be determined.

Birla X, on the other hand, would have only weakened her case by behaving like Rashana. For any such segs hacked by her sister could provide false evidence that Rashana was who she had been all along. So Birla X did her best to pick up her projects undertaken as Anisha. Despite having been robbed of all data associated with that person, including her contacts, she managed to get in touch with Gyges Circle members through other means and continued to work with them as though nothing had happened.

"So the sister that approached me that evening, right after the identity heist—I mean the activist in Ginza—who was that?"

"Birla Y—I'm certain. She had asked Ono Y to purchase your digiguise from me the previous day. He had someone follow you home from work. That's how she found you."

"But you said that Birla Y was behaving like Anisha for the sake of her case."

"For the most part. She seems to have deemed you worth the exception, but only in her guise as Makesh."

"Right . . . Birla X told me, after I woke up in Atupio, that she introduced herself as Makesh, not Rashana, because she didn't want me to take the job just for the money. She wanted to make sure my dedication to the cause was sincere. But I always found that hard to believe. And I was right. That was bullshit. Birla X wasn't even there in Ginza. It was Birla Y and she had to be Makesh to maintain plausible deniability for the court case."

"Remember also that Birla Y didn't have Rashana's LifeStream or Atupio then, so she wasn't in a position to be forthright. All she could do was put out feelers to you and hope that she would get back Atupio before her sister recruited you for a plot she didn't yet understand."

"Including Barrow's ID assassination that night. Birla Y didn't know about that?"

"Not with any clarity. The sisters kept sensitive information encoded and spread between their servants, including the Onos, to hide it from their surveilling parents. So Birla Y was still working on decoding Gyges Circle operations in the Anisha profile."

"Then it was Birla X who oversaw the assassination. Atupio paid for all my credicrimes because the organization was under her legal control, not because her sister temporarily seized it as she told me."

"Correct. Birla X did not then understand Atupio's significance. Birla Y had erased all information about Hakkotopia and the Starter BioPen from the Rashana LifeStream before foisting it on her. So the only value Birla X saw in the subsidiary was as a source of funding for Gyges Circle activities."

Amon thought this over as they walked.

"Okay . . . I understand all that. But if it wasn't Birla X who talked to me as Makesh, how did she know so much about that meeting? The scene wasn't in her LifeStream when she put me on glass mode, which of course it couldn't be—she was never there—but she seemed to remember it so clearly."

"Because Ono X hacked you while you were unconscious with the infection and fed your LifeStream to her gabkeepers."

This surprised Amon so much that he stopped abruptly in the tunnel, bringing the others to a halt with him, Little Book's tires swishing on the concrete.

"Fuck. You have evidence of that?"

"Some but isn't it obvious? It's the first thing I would have done in Ono's place."

Amon clicked his tongue at himself. "Shit . . . When you say it like that, it does seem obvious. Ono X reenacted some of the things I said in that meeting. But Birla X never played any of those segs on the Gemini, I guess because I'd have seen they were from my perspective, not hers . . . Ono X even helped me hack into my own BodyBank to get Mayuko's contact details . . ."

Amon thought back on his conversations with Birla X and felt certain that there had been other moments where she had used his LifeStream to deceive him. Could these have coincided with one of the awkward pauses that poor Hippo must have noticed?

Before Amon realized it, darkness filled the tunnel around him. The PhisherKing had resumed walking, and Little Book was cranking along beside him. Amon hurried after them, rejoining the travelling light.

The morning of the third day was when the sisters began to uncover the dreams they had hidden for decades from each other.

Birla Y's cryptocorps succeeded in decoding many sections of the Anisha LifeStream that involved the Gyges Circle. The PhisherKing had found a seg of her consulting with Ono Y, torn about what to do with this discovery. If Birla Y was to play her role as Anisha impeccably and mount an unbeatable defense of her claim to Fertilex, it would be wise for her to become involved with the group in place of her sister. If she was to pick up where she left off as Rashana, it would be wise to expose or undermine them. But Ono Y warned her that if she did either, she would deprive her sister of her most cherished aspiration. Then there was no telling what drastic retaliation she might wreak upon Atupio while it was in her possession—already she was draining its funds. So Birla Y continued to pursue neither Gyges Ring nor Hakkotopia, maintaining her forking stance as Anisha in public, sometimes Makesh in private, and Rashana in her heart until the court verdict could be reached, hoping that her sister would never discover the chthonic BioPen.

Birla X's parallel efforts to understand the secret life Rashana had led proceeded more slowly since all related sections of the LifeStream had been systematically expunged prior to handoff. Her sole clue was the subsidiary she had unexpectedly inherited, and that morning marked her first visit to Atupio Home Office. Another seg the PhisherKing found in the Makesh folder had her stepping out of Gemini X into the steel-tiled hangar with her fully armed guards and then warily prowling the upper floors of the compound. There she discovered that Rick was in Er for the Giftless, and that afternoon, had Barrow admitted into a different zone, initially to cover up his ID assassination.

"When I was on glass mode with Birla X," said Amon, "I viewed a seg from the Rashana LifeStream that showed her accepting Rick into Atupio. But that couldn't have been Birla X, could it?"

"No, his intake was in the morning, before the identity heist. Birla Y, then still Rashana, authorized it."

"That means I thanked Birla X for saving Rick from Welcome Chasm when she never did!" Amon cried. "And she actually pretended she deserved it!" He shook his head in disgust.

"Don't forget that Birla X could have turned him over to the Gyges Circle."

"Right . . . So why didn't she?"

"We can assume that she considered the threat posed by his limited information about the ID assassination neutralized while he was under her control. That may have been her reason for setting him aside at first. But I think she saw the value of his intimate knowledge about you after she discovered the BioPen downstairs and later uncovered your role in its objectives."

It wasn't until early evening, after Birla X had apprised herself of the various humanitarian wings of Atupio, that Ono X stumbled upon a genelocked elevator that none of the above ground staff could explain. Overseeing her guards, while they sawed through the elevator doors and floor and dronedropped into the shaft, kept Birla X busy into the night. Thus she could only remotely attend the interview with Amon in the jazz bar, appearing as a figment of Makesh, the alias Sekido knew her as, and authorizing Amon's infection with the virus when his contact with her sister proved him a liability.

At 11 p.m. that night, while Amon dashed through the city on the verge of bankruptcy, a final verdict was reached on the legal dispute. The PhisherKing couldn't piece together the details of the case because the sisters had factholed it. But from the few available segs in the Makesh folder, he had gleaned that Birla Y had been suing for Atupio by quibbling over the wording of the will, which granted her *all* subsidiaries of Fertilex even as it granted her sister *one* of them. Birla X, meanwhile, had assembled a variety of digital forensic, genetic, contextual, and psychological evidence to prove that the Anisha profile had been stolen from her.

After both had exhausted every appeal, delay, lie, bribe, threat, hack, and blackmail in their repertoire, the highest court of the Fiscal Judiciary ruled in favor of the defendant for both suit and countersuit. In other words, it upheld the provisions of the will as is. Birla Y was certified as Anisha, owner of Fertilex, and Birla X as Rashana, owner of Atupio forevermore.

"In terms of wealth gained and lost, the identity heist and ensuing legal battle were a massive success for Birla Y," the PhisherKing said. "The Judicial Brokers in her pocket gave her a whole MegaGlom in exchange for a measly subsidiary. But in terms of deepest desire, it was the ultimate failure."

"Why didn't Birla Y just forfeit the suit to her sister?" Amon asked. "Then she could have reverted to 'Rashana' and made Atupio hers again."

"Because Birla X's lawyers would have had a heyday. The credicrime fines from the Fiscal Judiciary and penalties from the executers of the will for stealing the inheritance would have been enough to ruin her. In the worst case, she might have had to relinquish or sell off Atupio anyway. Birla Y had to go on playing Anisha like her life depended on it—and perhaps it did, or at least her banklife."

The three of them had by now turned several bends, clattered across a long bridge of metal grating above a black pit, and descended a curving passage that cut a sloping C through a bare concrete wall. When Little Book tapped to tell them he was getting a signal on his GPS, the PhisherKing stopped to shine a penlight on the handlebar tablet and check their coordinates on his map. Then they proceeded along the tunnel, and the PhisherKing resumed his account.

Midnight of the third day, early morning of the fourth, he claimed, was the beginning of the end of the sister's interim identity period. The PhisherKing seemed reluctant to describe the seg he was viewing and looked almost nauseous in the half-light; the first sign of the shift that the sister's underwent was a video message in Makesh of a young boy running around shrieking without skin.

The court ruling had left Birla X worse off than her sister, with no Anisha LifeStream, no Fertilex control, and no justice for the theft of either. When none of the residents in the BioPen would cooperate with her questioning, it sank in that even Atupio, her sole legal win, was of little use to her. So, apoplectic with rage and groping for some way to strike back, Birla X invested in having Ono X flay dust a Starter and send the recording to her sister along with a demand: unless Birla Y gave her Fertilex, she would savage everyone in the underground floors, whether Ferment Culture Collective or Starter, and demolish Atupio Home Office.

Birla Y didn't see this message until she woke up hours later, and, shocked, called on Ono Y for advice. There was no record of their conversation, but the PhisherKing had a fragmented seg from a lawyer's husband showing an Ono seeking legal advice at that time and could guess at Birla Y's conundrum. On the one hand, trading back Fertilex would be a reversal of her carefully orchestrated success in court. Even worse, it would demonstrate Atupio's importance to her—evidence that Birla Y had once been Rashana. Then Birla X would have grounds to reopen her suit over the identity theft and might even win. On the other hand, not capitulating would mean the slaughter and annihilation of who and what she most cared about. Under the pressure of her sister's brinksmanship, Birla Y didn't know which choice to make; there was no reply to Birla X's ultimatum in the message thread.

This silent treatment seems to have only infuriated Birla X more, because the hours that followed had been clipped from the Rashana LifeStream and were not in the Makesh folder. Presumably, her reaction was too shameful or incriminating even for there, and the PhisherKing could only fill in the blanks with inference.

"This is the morning when the virus in the hand of your BodyBank disclosed your location to the Gyges Circle. Birla X must have insisted on hunting you down personally. To her associates, your LifeStream was a threat to the coup. But to her, you yourself were another valuable trinket to hold hostage or brutalize in revenge."

"What you're telling me is that Birla X was the Emoticon Man. She was the one who hacked and abused Mayuko."

"There's a seg of a Birla sister in a horrible mood contacting Anisha's preferred digimaker to order a new digiguise. I think we can conclude it was Birla X—by process of elimination. Birla Y had turned off all communications in her despair over the ultimatum. Her LifeStream, as discontinuous as it is, shows her hardly getting out of bed for the entire day."

Amon's gait slowed, forcing Monju and Little Book to match his speed, as he frowned into the gloom ahead.

"I once came close to accusing Birla X of being the Emoticon Man. But I was dumb enough to accept her denial without any proven alibi."

"You're being too hard on yourself, Amon."

"What do you mean?"

"Do you remember Birla X's speech right after you implied her guilt?"

"Vaguely."

"At one point, she said, 'Data has nothing to guarantee its truth other than itself.' Then a few seconds later, 'Whoever I claim to be, at some stage you'll just have to take my word for it.' Those are direct quotes from me."

"From you? Why?"

"Her gabkeepers knew that I'd earned your trust when I used those precise phrases the first time you visited my kingdom. Their psychalytic algorithms calculated that months later you were unlikely to recall me verbatim but that repeating those words would elicit a placating effect by association with your subconscious memory. Advertising often works on the same principle."

Amon was speechless and could only shake his head while gazing at the toes of his shoes tramping through the shadows, ashamed that he had fallen for such deviousness.

"This is the evidence I alluded to earlier, by the way, that Ono X hacked your LifeStream," the PhisherKing said. "There's nowhere else Birla X could have borrowed my lines."

Soon they turned left through a portal into a subway tunnel, where the hysterical uproar of a crowd reverberated towards them from the nearest station. Little Book had signal again so Monju checked their coordinates, before using one of Tamper's hackbuttons to raise a massive garage-type door on the left wall. The opening led up a long ramp of bumpy plate metal wide enough to accommodate construction vehicles.

Once they were alone with their clanking footsteps, the tricycle squeak, and the guiding cone of light, the PhisherKing reached the point in his account where Amon committed identity suicide and collapsed into naked oblivion. This, he claimed, was roughly when the sisters began to let go of who they had been before the heist and accept who they had to be. Because it wasn't long after that Birla Y rose from her state of torpor and finally reached a decision.

Contacting the Gyges Circle, she provided all manner of proof that Birla X was an imposter, including that the name in Birla Y's profile was Anisha Birla. If giving up Fertilex would ruin her, it seemed she was determined to keep it. And since keeping Fertilex entailed allowing her sister to have her way with her dream, with Atupio, Birla Y would have her way with her sister's dream.

Now ousted from the Gyges Circle, it was Birla X's turn to slip into despair. And within days, she had reached a conclusion that mirrored her sisters'. She would begin to run Atupio responsibly, rather than draining its assets for other purposes, and would find some way to ingratiate herself into the BioPen. For she had seen the incredible bioautomated technologies, much like those of the community she and her sister had destroyed in their youth, and she wanted them to wield for herself.

This was easier said than done; the genelocks rejected her and the strange children reviled her for the abduction of their brethren, recognizing her as Anisha by her naked face. But in familiarizing herself with the District of Dreams as manager of Atupio's humanitarian divisions, she learned of both geneshine and don juan dust, and hacked into Birla Y's sub-profile to copy the biometric data needed to program the mimicry. Then Birla X purged her LifeStream of any signs of the profile switch, 'Anisha" disappeared from Atupio for several days, and 'Rashana' made her homecoming, staging a liberation of the BioPen with her Birla Guard charging in at her side and claiming that she had won a lawsuit to restore her rightful control of the subsidiary. With this, Birla X was on the road to becoming Rashana just as Birla Y was already becoming Anisha.

"I tried calling Makesh Adani just before I committed identity suicide," Amon said. "Birla X told me she got the message. But from what you said, it sounds like that would have been Birla Y. She gave me her card in Ginza, and she was the one who was in mourning over the Starter."

"Mourning or at least wallowing in failure."

"Then how did Birla X even know about the call?"

"Think about it."

Amon did until it hit him, and his next step clonked awkwardly on the metallic floor. "Shit. My LifeStream . . . But Rick told me that Birla X brought up my message when she talked to him in the Delivery lineup, months before Ono X could have hacked me."

"That wasn't Birla X in Delivery either."

"You're kidding me."

"Not at all. Birla Y started searching for you in the District of Dreams not long after she listened to your message. Whether to give you up to the Gyges Circle, bargain with her sister, or please vestigial remnants of Rashana, I cannot say. Birla X only thought to look for you in the camps when she caught wind of a manhunt conducted there by Philanthropy Syndicate and Fertilex freekeepers. That was why she questioned Rick about you in Er for the Giftless."

"That fits well, actually. If I recall, the sister at Er never mentioned my message to Rick. You'd think she would at least bring it up if she'd got it."

"One would also think that she would detain Rick at Atupio. The Gyges Circle had likewise lost interest in Rick; by the time they were notified of his release thanks to his licensed-out genome, they no longer considered him a threat. But Birla Y used his genetic data to track him to his first supply pickup, hoping he might tell her your whereabouts."

"So it was Birla Y I saw in line . . ." said Amon. "That was another seg missing from Birla X's LifeStream."

Amon realized that his initial instinct to be wary of the sister at Delivery had been correct, in spite of Hippo' and Barrow's insistence that he could trust Rashana. Birla Y as Anisha would never have lifted them from poverty or saved Rick from his eventual end. She might have crushed them both. Then it occurred to Amon that approaching Birla X as Rashana would have been its own kind of pitfall. His instinct would have been correct on some level either way.

"What about Hippo's meetings with so called 'Rashana' in the Cyst?" Amon asked. "I mean, the seg of her visiting him to ask about me wasn't in Birla X's LifeStream either. Was that Birla Y, too?"

"It was. The confusion around your identity suicide and the SpawnU decoys I set up had already convinced the Philanthropy Syndicate it was too costly to keep their freekeepers on the search. This left Birla Y with a much diminished team. She flew to the Cyst because she knew Rick was there. From his use of feeders inside the compound. She and Ono Y had nothing else to go on."

"Okay. And the sister who came to the Cyst when we summoned her to help with the exposé. That was in the Rashana LifeStream I saw, so that had to be Birla X, right?"

"Yes. By then, Birla X was running the Atupio BioPen and the Gyges Circle was in her sights."

The PhisherKing went silent to let Amon chew on this. Only now did Amon hear the faint swish of Little Book's scrawling on his tablet, over the rhythmic tricycle squeaks and their footfalls. The boy went on noting everything that he saw and heard, even now that the council for which he had been charged with keeping records was long gone.

After they had turned off the metal ramp into a high cylindrical chamber walled in obscure gutted machinery, navigated a maze of densely interlocked piping, and began to pass through a series of branching concrete tubes just wide enough for the three of them side by side, Amon asked, "Can I return to my original question about who we're going to meet? The woman you think might be Mayuko. Who kidnapped her?"

"My guess, after thinking it through, is Birla Y."

"Are we headed for Birla Y's Kindominium?"

"The sisters share."

"The family of their Cognitive Handling Corps live together?"

"Only in the same compound. Their quarters are separate. This is a relic of the way their parents set up the hostage loyalty system. They wanted their heirs to share in everything. So the woman being there says nothing about who brought her. More telling is that she was picked up around Opportunity Peaks."

"Because of Birla Y's relationship with the Gyges Circle? They have links to the Quantitative Priesthood through their Philanthropy Syndicate members."

"Exactly. I wasn't sure if this mattered because the bespoke journalist in the seg could have worked for Atupio. But while we were walking, I found other segs in my database that show he was a freelance pitypromoter. This all suggests that he was employed by Birla Y—though directly by Ono Y."

"So Ono X was telling the truth earlier? He really didn't know where Mayuko was."

"No, but I think he knew who had her."

"What makes you say that?"

"For one thing, Ono X hacked Mayuko's BodyBank when the Birla X Guard attacked her. She'd deleted all info about you from her LifeStream but it still would have been a wealth of behaviorlytics. Licensing this out to spies is standard operating procedure for the likes of Ono X, and I wouldn't put it past him to include his clone—with a contract that included favorable conditions in case she was found of course. The Onos were known to cooperate when it suited them."

"You're saying Ono Y would have been unlikely to find her without the behaviorlytics? That's a bit thin, don't you think?"

"True, so consider this. Don't you find it strange that when Birla X offered to let you fly down to the island she didn't threaten you? Going to the forest would have been heaven for you, the ultimate reward, so where was hell? Where was the punishment, the other half of the Birla Deal?"

"You think Ono X had to know he could get his hands on Mayuko? He would have cut a deal with his clone so that they could blackmail me?"

"If you hadn't told Birla X your idea for the Phoenix Virus, I think it's possible. Trading their intel about the Gyges Circle might have been enough. But I'll stop speculating now. I'm not even certain that this woman is Mayuko."

"I hope she's okay," said Amon, his heart fluttering with anxiety.

Monju realized eventually that he was lost. It took some minutes traipsing through tunnels and peeking into alcoves before they found a short stairwell. Little Book dismounted his tricycle, and Amon carried it to the top, where there was GPS reception. Once they had checked their location, they backtracked to the junction where they had made a wrong turn and were soon on course again.

When they reached a door that led to a much longer stairwell, they at last began to climb out of the grimy warren, landing by landing. The PhisherKing carried the tricycle this time, and Little Book left the tablet attached to the handlebars, forgoing his scrawling to keep pace with the adults on his small legs. But Amon could feel the boy's watchful gaze, committing everything to memory for later noting.

"When do you suppose the sisters completed their transitions?"

"The moment that pretending became being?"

"Yeah. I mean, they started off taking up the mantle of the other's dream out of necessity. But when we saw them today, they actually seemed to *believe* in those dreams."

"I'm sure the change was incremental."

"But there must have been a point along the way where you could say for sure that there was no going back."

The PhisherKing thought about this until they reached the next landing. Then he paused, gripping the banister with the hand not cradling the tricycle, and said, "For Birla X as Rashana, wouldn't it have been her agreement to help with the exposé? That went beyond any practical advantage or even revenge. It was the active destruction of Anisha's life's work."

"Makes sense. . ." said Amon, mulling the issue over beside Monju as they proceeded up the following flight. "If so, then I think the moment for Birla Y as Anisha was cooperating with the population adjustment in the camps—and maybe offering Barrow the Birla Deal to fracture Xenocyst. Committing these atrocities seems to me like a moral point of no return."

"The shift was never entirely complete, though, was it?" the PhisherKing contended. "Consider Book's story today. Birla X showed physiological signs of lying when she talked about the weather and said hello."

"But Book found her honest about anything related to Hakkotopia," said Amon. "When it came to the core of who she was, only Rashana was left even if on some mundane level she was still someone else. I bet the same was true of her sister. Birla X told me how they became different people with the dreams they discovered in response to the myth of Gyges.

Reversing those dreams, even just in make-believe, was reversing exactly what made them distinct."

"But they never abandoned their original dreams," said the PhisherKing. "We saw that today when Birla Y gave up demanding Gyges Ring and agreed to lead Atupio, and when Birla X sent me her whispertexts against Hakkotopia and was ready to accept the Ring of Gyges. You could argue they had no choice under the circumstances I suppose."

Although Amon knew right away what he wanted to say, it took him two whole flights of stairs to find the words.

"I think for them it was more important to be different from each other than to worry about what those differences were, more important to be on opposite poles than to fret over which one they were on at any given time . . . That was why the sisters couldn't bear to annihilate each other. Without the contrast that defined them, they would be nothing, no one, a stream of thoughts and sensations lacking any desire or dream to unite them across time . . . They are either the ideal or its shadow, depending on how you look at them. Just like their dreams . . . A diamond dream to give meaningful striving without freedom for all, and the Ring of Gyges to give an empty sort of freedom without a dream for the few . . . two tangled balls of yarn spun from threads of both light and darkness . . .

"Just like that painting of the diamond in the Atupio conference room," Amon mused.

"In what way?" the PhisherKing asked.

"The first time I saw it, the day I woke up from the fever, I wondered which side it was meant to be viewed from, the hallway or the room. The same question came to me again when we had our meeting there. The answer is neither. For all the many facets it seems to display, it's one painting whichever way you look at it."

"That is quite the analysis, Amon. You should have gone into psychiatry—or horoscopes."

They reached a large underground storage room, the walls lined with shelves bearing shut down maintenance drones, cleaning carts, and folded up work uniforms. The PhisherKing set down the tricycle, whereupon

Little Book mounted and began to peddle diagonally across the room to a doorway in the corner. Amon followed him alongside the PhisherKing and stepped over the threshold into a cracked tile hallway, where a draft of fresh air greeted them, clearing away the dank smell of the tunnels.

"You never said anything about jubilee," Amon observed as they walked along the hallway. "How come?"

"I thought you would have realized," the PhisherKing said.

"So you think it was Birla X. Because she was the Emoticon Man. Because she tried to bribe Mayuko the same amount as jubilee."

"No, no, no. It had to be Birla Y."

"But she didn't own Atupio then. Birla X did. So she wasn't in a position to offer that Blinder incentives for taking the bankdeath penalty. Just like the lures this morning. If any of them had gone bankrupt for the cause, they'd have been accepted by Er for the Giftless or rescued from the Gifted Triangle. Assured an honored position in Hakkotopia 2.0. I can't think of any other worthwhile tradeoff. No amount of money can make up for giving up even the possibility of money. Only Birla X could have promised a comfortable bank afterlife in exchange for the Blinder's sacrifice."

"Only the owner of Atupio could have—think of the timing," said the PhisherKing. "You were charged for jubilee a full day before the lawsuit between the sisters was resolved. Birla Y would have been expecting to win Atupio back with the Fiscal Judiciary in her pocket. So she could have had the Blinder agent go bankrupt, on the assumption she'd pick him up when the verdict was reached."

"That's just speculation."

"Educated speculation. Remember, Birla Y had executive control of Fertilex too. Her sister lacked the authority to fabricate a property called jubilee, include it in the MegaGlom's assets, and have their customer service blacklist you. Birla Y, still holding on to Rashana then, also had the motive. Consider her speech as Makesh about financial equalization. Don't you think it has affinity with the idea of jubilee as the cancellation of debts? In the same conversation, she expressed her frustration with your faith in the AT Market. The jubilee fits with that. You can't have failed to notice that the large unjust charge it represented precipitated the end of that faith."

For dozens of steps and a turn down another corridor, Amon had no idea what to say. If the PhisherKing was right, then his awakening had begun with the sisters, and perhaps now had ended with them.

"So both sisters were interested in jubilee?"

"We already knew that, didn't we? Forty nine to the power of forty nine is the password for the folder they share. And they sought to bring their plans to fruition in the 49th year of the Free Era."

"Then the word must have had some deep importance for both of them, something related to their tangled dreams."

"Perhaps."

"So what does it mean?"

"There's not one mention of the word jubilee anywhere in either of their lives until you brought it up with Birla X's figment in the jazz bar."

"What about the number forty nine?"

"Nothing."

"Nothing?"

"It appears incidentally in some math problems they solve in school, the value of many of their properties, and so on. Nothing relevant."

"Not in all three folders?"

"I'm afraid not."

"Then there has to be something in that deeper folder."

"There could be. But we will probably never know."

Amon found this conclusion profoundly unsatisfying but tried not to dwell on it. Jubilee had already taken on a new meaning for him, as something that had to be brought about. Or so he had convinced himself. Now that they had failed and so much of what he believed had proven false again, could he have been wrong about its significance? Could he have been wrong about everything?

Perhaps sensing Amon's disappointment, the PhisherKing said, "Can I offer another thought?"

"Please."

"This is only a hunch. There is no information of any kind to support it. But something tells me that, whatever jubilee is, the sisters themselves never truly understood it."

In a capacious dome—perhaps a lobby of some kind—they halted so that Monju could hunch over the handlebar tablet and reorient. Sunlight glowed through high encircling windows, a sure sign that they were almost back to street level.

"Let me ask you about ecogenics," Amon said when they had set off again. "You told us earlier that there was no evidence in the sisters' LifeStreams."

"None. One might expect to find it in the Rashana LifeStream. But Birla Y erased everything to do with Hakkotopia and the underground BioPen before she handed it off to her sister, as I said."

"What about in the Makesh folder?"

"Not one related seg."

"There must have been all kinds of documentation. Research, protocols, discussions."

"I cannot find a single instance of the word 'ecogenics' in any of the data I possess until the moment Birla X used it in that filibuster this morning."

"How about harmony dust?"

"Likewise absent."

"I guess . . . what I really want to know is, what about me? Birla X told me months ago that I was the son of Iwabuchi, the founder of Hakkotopia 1.0. Then the sisters said in the elevator this morning that Iwabuchi designed me to mesh with the political habitat. But I wouldn't put it past them to make that up to protect themselves . . . though I guess it would have been harder without gabkeepers. Do you have any evidence that goes either way?"

"I'm afraid not. There are segs in Makesh of Iwabuchi as a fertility slave after Hakkotopia was destroyed. But no segs that prove she gave birth before then."

Amon felt great pity for all the women, like Sekido's girlfriend, who had been forced to give birth in captivity. Yet the thought of Iwabuchi undergoing this torment added little to it. He had no recollection of her and had never even seen her image; the MegaGloms involved in the crackdown had tried to wipe her from history.

"The sisters claimed earlier that the Starters were designed on the basis of my, um, samples. That would prove that my genes were of special interest. I guess there's nothing about them accessing my SpillBot?"

"That would have been nearly eight years ago, when you started using the device. The age of at least some of the Starters appears to roughly match. But there should be a record of it in your AT readout because you would have been compensated for violation of your genome rights . . .unless you accidentally consented to gene harvesting in the fine print of the terms of use for some app."

"I doubt that. And my privacy settings for the SpillBot were strict. The samples should have gone to Fertilex anonymously."

"Then they would have needed some other way to link them to you. But consider that neither sister had records of your DNA after you cash crashed. Otherwise they would have detected you instantly in the District of Dreams."

"Good point . . . though their parents could have denied them access to my samples once they found out I guess . . . Anything else?"

"That is as far out as I can wade into this particular enigma with the information I have. We'll have to stay in the surf of inconsistencies unless you have memories that might guide you deeper."

Taking Monju's cue, Amon began to reflect on himself. Willpower, restraint, loyalty. Frugality, naivety, credulity. Time and again he had demonstrated these qualities. Some he had been proud of. Others had got him into trouble. But were they calibrated for a society that pursues a delicate interrelationship with fragile ecosystems? Had he been designed to harmonize his desires with the ideal of the community? Was he a different sort of creature than everyone else, his ambitions fine-tuned by others, his very being sapped of freedom worthy of the name?

There was no overlooking the lacuna of his early childhood. Before Green Ladybug, he had no memories of who he was, and his SubMom had provided few clues.

Without hard proof, the idea that the motivations of a citizenry could be statistically regulated through tweaks to their neurobiology was hard to believe. Harmony dust? Did such technology really exist? Had it truly been perfected in the way Birla X had claimed? She had given the speech to delay them and gain the upper hand. The sisters' collaborative story about Amon's genesis had also been timed to sway the situation to their advantage. They had strung him along with so many fictions . . . And yet, it fit with his feeling about the forest dream. The island had called to him in just the primal way they described.

After another turn, the hallway brightened. At the end was a stairwell that led up to a landing with a large window. Another flight of stairs, and they would be on the ground in Ayase, the Kindominium only a short walk away. The three of them would soon part ways, and Amon realized that this might be his last chance to seek answers from the PhisherKing.

"Well, what do you think?" Amon asked. "Am I . . . different?"

The PhisherKing looked up from Little Book's tablet to meet Amon's gaze with his dark hazel eyes.

"From the moment I met you, I thought you'd find wisdom to carry us all to our rejuvenation. That was my intuition—and I told you so. And your ideas *have* brought change, for better or for worse. You're unique, Amon. There's no doubt about that. But you would have been a dud in any other time and place, without all of us here to help you. Each one of us is unique as well, and isn't that the whole point? Isn't that diversity exactly why the diamond dream was doomed from the start?"

"Yes! It always seems obvious after the fact, doesn't it? I've been fooled so many times. By Sekido, Barrow, and now the Birlas, even as they all fooled themselves. I feel like such a gullible idiot! Maybe I *was* designed to follow along just like the sisters said."

"Your sincerity has certainly allowed others to take advantage of you. You open your heart to those you meet. But that quality is what has earned you the respect of people like me and Hippo, bless his soul. It has also saved you more than once. So you are deeply flawed, Amon. And that is exactly why you are loved."

Flawed, yes. He was flawed. Like the time he had cut himself on Barrow's sword and hesitated to liquidate him. Or the time he had lashed out at Barrow in the Cyst and Yané in the alcove. Didn't those incidents demonstrate recklessness? Although the instances where his willpower, loyalty, and self-control had broken down were rare, he was sure that he could find others if he thought more carefully. Didn't this fallibility prove that he had been human all along and that the sisters were either lying or mistaken? Perhaps there never was ecogenics, and a diamond dream could be realized without it after all. Or perhaps Amon had found freedom in spite of his instilled genetic purpose.

"Thank you, Monju," he said. "I wish I could chalk it all up to my weakness the way you're willing to. But I can't help feeling that I'd be letting myself off too easy. Like if I'd paid more attention to the signs of all the lies, things could have turned out better. I was too caught up in where I wanted to take us all that I lost sight of where we were actually going."

"As were we all."

"But so many people will suffer and die in the crisis we've made."

"Would you reverse everything you've done to be a Liquidator still serving the action-transaction market, or a settler living in the forest?"

"No," said Amon, without hesitation.

"Then be glad that you made honest choices when you could and tried to do what's right when you couldn't and come out the other side of your mistakes with open eyes. I made you promise to seek answers to your questions and you've honored that promise far more than I ever could have expected."

"But what have I learned for sure? After Birla X told me her story, I thought I had answers. Now other perspectives have come to light, and there are so many contradictions, so many gaps."

"Stories are houses for who we are built of bricks that change with the eye of the beholder. The only complete and absolute story is the totality of information, but that is just noise. This is the Treasure Matrix's most important lesson."

"What if we find out something new, like in that sub-sub-sub-profile, and it's all overturned again?"

"Inquiry entangles us in questions while certainty traps us in answers. Wisdom comes from embracing doubt and accepting what little truth stays in our arms."

"Come on. My ignorance has dragged me from one disaster to the next. The coup at GATA, Mayuko, Rick, Xenocyst, the District of Dreams, Hippo. And now Tokyo, the world, everyone."

In this regard, Amon realized, he was much like Sekido, self-deception warping his will to justice at every turn.

"History is what happens when we're busy reaching for a future that will never be," said the PhisherKing. "Unwittingly, our many visions of what ought crashed together, and we bumped our tottering reality in a direction that no one expected. I will bear a heavy heart for my part in this calamity. But the disaster we have wrought is where we must search for hope. The bright side of chaos is that there are no barriers to creating something new."

By the time they had made their way out a small exit into an alley, it was twilight, and the air was warm with a crisp, pleasant breeze.

They paused at the mouth of the alley, looking along a four lane street. In the leftmost lane was a neat line of more cars left shattered and abandoned. The other three lanes and the sidewalks were loosely filled with pedestrians, wandering, standing, sitting, no longer panicked, simply dazed and perplexed.

From the confusion of the streets, the drab and blighted buildings rose in their usual disarray, stripped of all images and text and meaning. Above them, the clouds had dissipated, but for scattered blots now departing. In the eastern sky, bands of navy shaded into indigo at the zenith. Only in the west did a splatter of azure linger on the rim of the cityscape as the sun threw up its last hint of dazzle.

"Over there," Monju said, pointing to the skyline, and Amon bent low to follow the direction of his arm. "The building that's mostly windows. Do you see it?"

"It's hard to miss," said Amon. It was the largest skyscraper in sight, an immense glittering rectangle with rounded edges that dwarfed all other structures. The thickening darkness of the sky seeped onto its reflective shell, a mirror for what was coming.

"What's the floor?" Monju asked.

"Twenty-seven," Amon replied.

"And her room number?"

"Twenty-seven oh three."

"There's an emergency stairwell to the left of the main entrance. Can you get inside?"

"Tamper's door openers haven't failed me yet." Amon patted his left pant pocket.

"What's that room number again?"

"Twenty-seven oh three."

"Are you sure you don't need our help?"

"I'm used to getting around without navis. It'll be quicker this way."

"Do you want us to stay here? We can guide you back to Jinbocho. We don't mind waiting a few minutes, do we LB?"

Tap tap.

"I appreciate that, but . . . if she's not there, or if . . . if something has happened to her, I may need some time . . . alone."

The PhisherKing looked Amon up and down as though imprinting him in memory. "You really should come back," he said.

"Who said . . ." Amon stopped himself short. It was futile to be evasive now that Monju had guessed his intentions. "I think a lot of people would prefer I didn't."

"Some may blame you for today. But in the uncertainty ahead, we need someone with the courage to take risks and fall hard more than ever. No one can deny your talent for finding seams in the inevitable and unravelling our fate."

"Why won't people stop trying to recruit me? Sekido, Rashana, Anisha, Barrow, Hippo, Kitao, and now you. I'm sick of working for people."

"Then lead."

"Lead? Me? After all this?"

"That's what you've been doing since the world fell to pieces today, isn't it?"

"You don't want me in charge. I'm a wandering catastrophe." Amon couldn't keep the bitterness from his voice.

"With Hippo gone, the exiles will be lost," the PhisherKing said. "If we're going to survive, we need to pool our skills."

"Let them all decide as a group what to do. They can vote."

"Someone's voice is always heard loudest. You know that."

"I don't have the vision to lead. And frankly, I don't want to."

"That's exactly what makes you the right person. Anyone who wants to lead is power hungry or deluded and should be disqualified from the start."

"Spare me your paradoxes. If you want someone who isn't interested, ask Tamper to lead. Or why don't you?"

"Look at me," said Monju, raising his palms towards his face. The bark-like pattern of lines radiating from his mouth was an etching of something more like resignation than bygone smiles. Whatever longevity treatments he had been receiving would likely be unavailable now. Not so far off, Amon could imagine him a hobbled toothless wisecracker. "I do my best to catch the wisdom of the present but soon reality will outstrip me. We need a flexible mind from the next generation, someone who still has the power to adapt."

Amon glanced over at the glass tower, growing antsy.

"I'm going, Monju. Thank you for bringing me here and for teaching me so much."

Amon looked down at Little Book, sitting on his tricycle and scrawling on his tablet.

"Thank you most of all," he said. "You saved my life and now you've given me this chance to find her." Then to both of them he added, "I hope we meet again. Someday."

Tapapa-tap-tapapaptap . . . "Even if you won't lead, I need you to come back for a visit," the PhisherKing interpreted.

"Why?" Amon asked.

Tap-ta-tap-taptapatap . . . "I have so many records, heaps of information. I want to code them into a form that will be easier to absorb. Yours especially."

"What do you mean code records?"

Tap-tataptap . . . "I'm telling your story, Amon, but I can't finish it unless I know what happens to you next."

"A story? You mean a book? You're writing a book about me?"

Tap, taptaptap . . . "About all of us. All the threads tied around you. If I have ever have the opportunity, I hope to publish it, either on a network or in concrete form."

"What will you call it?" the PhisherKing asked.

"*The Jubilee Chronicles*," said Little Book in a strange wheezy voice. He stopped writing for a moment to lock eyes with Amon and smile.

After saying his goodbyes to Little Book and the PhisherKing, Amon headed along the street towards the glass tower.

Immediately, its tip sunk beneath the looming swathe of buildings in front, the pool of shadows they cast thickening as twilight shifted to evening. He wanted so desperately to run. Stepping into that room was the event horizon for who he would be from now on, his unknown future self hanging in suspense. But he stifled the impulse, worried he might lose his way if he rushed, the exhaustion and shock of the day ready to envelope his awareness at any moment. Instead he walked quickly with a tense focus, counting the intersections as Monju had advised.

The streets were packed now, and Amon had to be careful not to bump or trip on anyone. Streetwalkers roamed erratically without destination or purpose, the guiding spectacle gone, nothing to do or buy and no money to pay for it. Some darted harrowed eyes about as if they might see hanging in the naked metropolis a rewind button for existence, or a clickable arrow leading to yesterday. Others stood with bowed heads, or sat with backs against walls and storefronts, or crouched on the damp sidewalks, jibbering or face-palming or sobbing. One man lay spread-eagled in the middle of the road, jittering his heels against the tarmac. All were distressed, mystified, terrified, each eye movement and fidget and mumbled word a prayer for this nightmare glitch to be fixed.

How many millions will die because of what we've done? Amon wondered. *How many already have?* Hospitals defunct, life-support crashed, transportation stalled, sustenance weaponized, shelters locked, commerce crippled, citizens and non-citizens hurled indiscriminately into desolate anarchy. The revolution had utterly failed to bring jubilee . . . or had it?

Turning a bend, Amon spotted a mob of BioPen escapee children gathered in a semicircle around a vending machine. One boy charged in with a yell and drop kicked the thick plastic shell, adding very slightly to a dent already made. He received a puff of revulsion dust in the face and turned away, too disgusted to look. Another boy followed up with a running punch and was driven off in the same way. This reminded Amon of his own attempt to break into a vending machine barehanded after his cash crash, except these kids were not alone or suffering cognitive impairments. They were together and well, and he could sense their inchoate comradery, born of fear and a shared ordeal.

Pushing into the semicircle, Amon put his hand on the shoulder of a girl winding up with a golf club and clicked one of Tamper's devices onto the side of the machine. When it began to spew food and drinks into the bin, Amon bent down to pluck out four rice balls and two drinks, which he pocketed. The rest he left behind, and the kids raised a cheer before swarming in.

As he jogged away, Amon thought of all the people locked in their apartments and offices who needed to be released, and glanced at the skyscrapers around him, as good as cages. Once the denizens recovered from the initial shock, perhaps kids like these would serve as instigators, rousing them from their consumer isolation to help each other out.

Turning down an alley, Amon found the voices that sounded along the streets seeping into his tired awareness with unexpected clarity. The dominant note was terror, many crying and screaming and wailing. But it was complemented now and then by the unmistakable tinkle of laughter and conversation, and he could detect a new cadence of something like fevered anticipation or excitement.

Wondering what this might signal, he crossed a small plaza and noticed a woman craning skyward to gaze at the darkening blue above. Most likely she was expecting some adverpromo seg to stoke her desire or impel an action. But Amon pictured her and others like her taking such compulsive glances at the cosmos and realizing one day that they were searching for answers, as he had done unconsciously in the camps, addiction to information transmuting gradually and imperceptibly into a quest for something that transcended the day to day.

That was when he knew beyond a doubt that their old way of being would never return however much they might wish otherwise, the entrance to the cave closed off forever. Even if the breakdown were only local and temporary, even if the network were repaired and everyone tried to go back to business as usual, the people would never be able to forget this intermission from finance and phantasm. It would stand out in their memories as an alternative, a pin in the balloon of false inevitability that had buoyed everyone into intoxicating clouds. Soon a new set of requirements would arise to define their existence, and Amon could see eras following each other one after the next like the notches of history's inexorable clock.

When the glass tower of the Kindominium reemerged in the crack between skyscrapers, Amon began to run. Suddenly he perceived his breathing in vivid detail, his diaphragm rising and falling, the warm air going out of his nostrils and the cool air coming in. *I have found the space between breaths, the gap between blinks*, he thought, neither in nor out, neither up nor down, but that gap of tense stillness, at once settling into calm and charging itself up.

Maybe that was all freedom was. The space between determinations, emancipation in the moment of destruction, a chance to pick which firefly to reach for in the night, an opportunity to dance through the strobe-light flicker of being. The thought made Amon feel weightless, as though he were floating unfettered in the liminal vacuum that spanned transformations, floating in the sky.

No, not floating. Falling. Drifting down towards himself. Always something intervened to keep him from the other Amon waiting on the ground and this time it was a hard crystalline shell. In the sky, he was encased in a diamond. And from his perspective both inside and below the diamond, he could see light leaping into it from all across the metropolis, trickles combining into tributaries merging into rivers that rippled towards a single point in the sky, all the glowing dreams of the people converging in a timeless instant.

As more and more light poured into the diamond, it quivered like a plucked string or a xylophone key and began to crack. Each dream made the diamond more fragile, until every facet was a matrix of crisscrossing fissures, a thin rupturing frost ready to shatter at the lightest flick of a finger. As though defying fate, the diamond remained whole in this infinitely precarious transition for what seemed an eternity. Then somehow, without ever breaking, it came apart, Amon's desires and the desires of billions fragmenting and dispersing in the air, grey and devoid of magic, raining down on the metropolis like ash, yet sprouting color where they struck, painting the cityscape speck by speck into a familiar landscape. The forest.

As Amon sprinted through the streets, he fell towards himself again, in the same forest he'd seen in his dream. And in Tokyo too. Whether he opened his eyes or closed them, he was in the same place. The metropolis was the forest after all.

Without fear, Amon let the impending collision flow upon him, the earth/tarmac rushing closer as he reached down/up his hands and touched fingertips with himself, waking and dreaming in synch at long last.

There was no joy in this moment. He still worried for Mayuko's safety, and for all those who would suffer. But he felt release, sloughed off a heavy lifetime of memories and regrets. The world was starting again. He decided that he would too.

His dream had returned for the first time since he was charged for jubilee, the first link in a chain of events that had brought him here. What had it been? A course-correcting message emergent from the complexity of the system? A stroke of luck? A sign from some god or buddha?

Whatever its origin or purpose, the meaning of jubilee had come to pass, for all debts had been erased, all slaves freed, all sins forgiven. With many troubles looming it was hardly a time for celebration, but Amon thought he heard another laugh amidst the panic and bewilderment of the crowd he passed through, as fear and a dawning sense of liberation mingled in this transient respite, the eye of the storm of history.

What was this forest metropolis around him, this concrete dream? Could it be the future? Everything everywhere was alive, the walls gardens, the rooftops a canopy of vines and crops, the skyscrapers many trees intertwined, waterfalls spilling from windows, mills turning in rivers that flowed between sidewalks, people walking and cycling and breathing the fresh air, industrious but at peace. A true political habitat against all odds.

And living within it were his friends. Book taking students on a tour of his library, a new trove of analog lore to sate their information hunger and guide their conscience. The Phishers coding systems of security and privacy with display gloves linked to an organic network grown by Ferment Culture engineers. Tamper in a workshop with his son as apprentice, surrounded by shelves of bioelectronic components and racks displaying new inventions. Ty leaning forward in his wheelchair to adjust the spokes of a wheel on a truing stand, while eager children gathered round with tools in hand. Yané, Jiku, and a work crew in straw hats laying compost on tarmac for a parking lot farm. Vertical leading men and women in tracksuits on a run around the algae greened waters of a filtration garden, her husband nearly out of breath at the rear. Little Book perched on his tricycle with stylus sliding over tablet, recording the annals of them all, even Hippo and Rick in memory. Each one resilient, with something to give.

And what about Mayuko? Staggering to a halt at the front doors of the glass tower, Amon wasted no time before dashing up the emergency stairwell.

On the 27th floor, Amon stepped from the doorway into the intersection of a hallway T. Through the windows at the end of each of the three hallways, a pale light from the just fallen sun struggled to reach him. The white painted walls and ceiling were a murky grey in the dim, the floor nearly black with a carpet of unrecognizable color. It was warmer than outside, the air conditioning still operating despite the absence of valid users.

Panting, Amon staggered down the longer line of the T, his footsteps deadened by the fluffy hairs of the carpet. Weary almost beyond enduring, he appreciated the cushioning on his sore feet. 2727, 2730, 2729. Doors with alternating odd and even numbers passed by on the left and right. The clotted napalm of hope and dread seared the pit of his stomach, and he almost tripped over himself as he began to run again.

What will I say to her? What if she's not here? What if something has happened to her?

When at last he stood before the door to 2703, Amon froze, sick with anticipation so fierce it verged on terror. Half of him wanted to flee, half wanted to barge in that second. Sweat beaded his forehead, and he swallowed, hand trembling as he reached into his pocket for the hackbutton and clicked it on.

The door slid open, revealing a living room. It was dimmer even than the hallways, with frilly white drapes covering the floor-to-ceiling window on the opposite side. A few steps from the doorway was a shadowy mass that looked like an armchair, behind that a small dinner table, and behind that, in silhouette against the drapes, a woman beside some other vague piece of furniture.

"Ma-mayuko?"

"Who's there?" the woman asked with a start, turning his way.

"I-It's . . . it's . . ." Amon crossed the threshold. The woman faced him in hunch-shouldered alarm. After two more steps, the glow from outside illuminated her face and he was certain. It was that unmistakable comet hair.

"Mayuko!" he cried as he rushed towards her, banging his shin on the side of the armchair and hardly feeling it.

"Stop!" she commanded, retreating a step and raising her palm. "Stay away!"

Amon stopped, looking for answers in her furious eyes. "Mayuko . . ." he said softly, tentatively.

Mayuko let out a frustrated sigh. "I'm so sick of this," she said.

"Of what?"

"Don't act like you don't know."

"About what?"

"You think I'm magically going to be fooled this time?"

"Could you tell me what—"

"I'm not stupid."

"Seriously, Mayuko. Are you mad at me? Because if you are I—"

"I don't know who you are. Go away!"

"Have you forgotten?"

"You don't even look like him."

"But I am—"

"Couldn't you at least come up with a better imitation?"

"Oh," said Amon, beginning to understand. "Mayuko, can't you see—"

"No! I—"

"JUST LISTEN!" he shouted. "The ImmaNet is down. We shut it all down. I've searched so long and hard for you. Thought about you so many nights. I know I must look different. I'm not who I was back then. But it's still me. I'm here. *Please*," Amon stretched out a supplicating hand, yearning desperately to approach but not wanting to frighten her.

Mayuko shook her head slowly in disdain. "This is the best that you can do? As if turning off the lights is going to make me believe your lies."

"But I'm not lying. I would never—"

"And I would never trust you. Not after—"

"Mayuko!" Amon staggered towards her, unable to hold back any longer.

"No!" she shrieked and raised her fists in front of her face.

Amon stumbled to a stop.

"Stay away!" she commanded again.

Shoulders sagging with disappointment, Amon gave her a pleading look as the tears began to fall. Here she was, finally, safe and sound, and she was treating him like an enemy. After the strains of the day, he just couldn't take it. Their reunion wasn't supposed to be like this. Never in all his renditions of this moment. "How can I convince you? It's me, Amon. Is there anything I can say that will make you believe?"

"I've heard it all already," she said. "I know you've done your research. Your actors play Amon better than he can."

"What can I . . . you have to believe . . . I've . . ." The time and energy he had spent, the endless fretting, the many nights he had climbed to the disposcraper peaks in Xenocyst and— Then it came to him.

"Do you remember the rooftop of the BioPen?" he said, sniffling.

"No, go away."

"Yes, you do—you must" Amon wiped the loose tears from beneath his eyes with the back of his hand. "We were children. Barely more than toddlers."

"Whatever you say."

"The sky was beautiful that day, full of so much color. And there was a glitter in the blue. Could it have been Venus? I don't know. It was still light out, afternoon. We saw it together. A star. No training banks. No ImmaNet. Just you and me, hanging on the fence at the edge of the rooftop . . . It's my oldest memory for fuck's sake. It's where we first met. How could they know that? With what record? Whoever's been messing with you. How could they . . ."

Amon could almost feel the end of summer breeze on his skin and recalled his burning wish to stay there until night fell, watching the sky change with her warmth leaning into his. Mayuko stared back in silence, studying him, suspicious. Then her fists loosened.

"Mon-chan?" she said, voice rising in pitch, eyes glittering.

Amon nodded, begging with his eyes for her to believe, too exhausted to say anything more.

She took a tentative step closer, then another, and another. Then her incisive eyes seeing him for who he was, "Mon-chan," she whimpered and fell into his arms.

Amon felt the spasms of her sobs against his chest as he curled over her, letting his tears drip on the back of her sweater. He couldn't believe it. Mayuko was there, right there in his arms, after all his waiting and hoping and dreaming, she was there. They hugged each other tight, hearts sharing reverberations, her body quivering, her cool tears soaking through his jacket and shirt.

"Amon," said Mayuko, pulling away suddenly to look up at him. The dim room was a grey cloud on the dark surface of her wet puffy eyes, Amon's face floating before its colorless billows. "How long before they take you away?"

"Never."

"What do you mean?"

"I don't know who's been keeping you here, but they're gone."

"Gone? Where?"

"Nowhere. But they're not the same people they were before. Everything and everyone is different now. The AT Market is dead."

"Dead? How?"

"We destroyed it."

"What? Who? Why?"

"It wasn't what we wanted. It was an accident. It . . . I don't have the energy to explain it all now. This has been the most tiring day of my entire life. But just know that what we've done is permanent. You're free now."

Amon pressed the sides of her shoulders reassuringly. Sighing and breathing deeply, they shared a moment of silence as they looked each other over, reacquainting themselves. She wasn't overly skinny like the last time he'd seen her, the curves of her figure and face fuller and healthier. The worry lines in her forehead, though, had deepened. Less than a year had passed and yet already she had aged. They had both aged, as though the physics of time hastened the further they were apart.

Mayuko withdrew a handkerchief from her pocket to wipe her cheeks, and Amon did the same with his sleeve.

"How on earth did you find me?" she asked.

"It was no easy task, believe me . . . So many people helped me. Some time I'll tell you everything. I searched every way that I could."

At this, Mayuko's throat tensed and her lower lip trembled. "I'm so sorry, Amon," she said.

"For what?"

"You told me to go into hiding. I could have lived anonymously for decades. I won all the lawsuits. The compensation was more than enough. But I wanted to find you. I couldn't go on forever without trying. You have to understand . . . I . . ."

"I know," said Amon. "I would have done the same. You came to the camps?"

"Only after I tried everything else. I did platinum research. Paid career volunteers and Er therapists for tips. Bought surveillance data. I couldn't think of any other way. I had to go to the District of Dreams myself. First on a slum tour, but they never went far from the resorts. So I hired a nostie treasure seeker and some mercenaries from an investitarian startup that the MegaGloms hadn't acquired yet. I paid them well and made them click strict non-disclosure agreements. We went from enclave to enclave asking about you. Even as far as the southern tumbles. You wouldn't believe everything that happened on that journey. All the things I saw . . ."

Mayuko gazed disconsolately at the high corner of the room, disturbing thoughts playing over her eyes. Worried for all that she went through, Amon reached down and took her hands. She looked at him and smiled with wistful gratitude.

"Come, let's sit down," he said, guiding her to the oblong dinner table. He slid a chair around from the other side so they could sit across a corner from each other and hold hands.

"It was in Opportunity Peaks that they finally caught me," she said. "That politician you liquidated. For some reason he was there."

"Minister Kitao," he said, squeezing her hands in concern.

"Yes. He was all over the political feeds last fall. They made him out to be a pervert. When we started asking around about you, the Quantitative Priesthood invited us to a banquet inside the mountain. We didn't touch the food of course. But Kitao was there. He was some kind of priest. He said that he knew you. I was really surprised."

"He must have learned my name from his ex-wife. She was sort of taking care of him."

"He kept saying something about making me a flower girl. It was really creepy."

Amon recalled his nightmare—or was it a memory?—of Kitao and his flowerpots. "Did they try to hurt you?"

"I thought they wouldn't dare touch us. The ones in the lower castes seemed to really believe that Free Citizens are sacred. They literally kowtowed whenever we entered a room. The Quantitative Priesthood knew better but they seemed so friendly. Then men in leather cowls crawled from a hole beneath the table. They dragged down our guide and . . . They must have thought we wouldn't have the funds to fight back, but I authorized my mercenaries to dust our way out."

"Kitao too?"

"No, but one of my men kicked him down when he tried to run."

Amon remembered Kitao's hunchback in the Delivery lineup.

"No one got in our way after that but a few of them tailed us to the foothills. Then a peacecopter came down and dropped off some PrivaPo. My mercenaries threw down their weapons right away, the cowards."

Amon supposed that the Philanthropy Syndicate had made them an offer she couldn't match. "Did they hurt you here?" he asked

"If you mean physically, then no. The food isn't bad. The drones keep the place clean. There's a little room where I can exercise. It's comfortable. Only . . ." Mayuko deepened the new lines in her face and squeezed his hands hard. "Once I was settled in this room, they dragged in a man in chains, so heavy he could only lie twisted on the floor. He looked just like you. His voice, the way he spoke—almost a perfect copy. And he knew all sorts of things that only you could know. Even the calls and messages that came from him every day had your imprint on them."

Amon thought of his many messages to her and understood why they had gone unread.

"It was all fake," he told her. "Your captors were renting out my likeness by then. I bet they were using a whole mimicorps."

"I knew it had to be fake. But he begged me not to do what they told me to. It was exactly what you would have done. And some days he looked terrible, with bruises and scrapes like they'd been beating him. They said that if I ever left, they'd kill you. . ."

"The door was unlocked all these months and you never went out?"

"I opened the door sometimes and looked out into the halls. I was worried about you."

Amon felt a puckery, sour flush of gratitude and guilt for her dedication, and sent her a smile of sympathy, giving her hands another squeeze. It was a devious cost saving scheme, blackmailing her into staying of her own volition instead of racking up the larger fines for physically restraining her, and he wondered how many others in the Kindominium remained in the same predicament.

"Now you're finally here," she said. "I'm sorry I didn't trust it was you just now."

"Anyone would be suspicious."

"I should have known the difference. And I think I would have, except . . . After I erased everything about you, all I had left were memories. I lived in those memories—day in day out. But I could never be sure I recalled you correctly. Not entirely. And you've changed so much. You're like someone else. Do you understand?"

"Completely," he said, thinking of all the times he had remembered her atop the disposcrapers in the night and felt somehow that she must be remembering him. Now he knew that he'd been right. "Did the Birlas ever visit you?"

"The Birlas?"

"Yes."

"As in Anisha and Rashana Birla?"

"They're the ones who own this facility."

"I was told it's the family holding center for the SpawnU Consortium."

"Oh . . . Well I heard something different . . ." What Mayuko had learned could very well have been a lie, but Amon wasn't confident enough in the PhisherKing's guesswork to immediately discount her. Already his understanding of what happened was changing. Perhaps it would go on changing forever. Perhaps that was part of what it meant to know. "Anyway, it doesn't matter right now. You've—" Amon heard a sound. "What's that?"

Mayuko let go of his hands and rose. Amon stood up to follow her and heard it again. A voice.

"I didn't know how to tell you," she said, as she stepped over to the small piece of furniture by the window. Night had fallen and through the translucent drapes, he caught a vague glimpse of twinkles between cracks in the roofscape, the sky clear, as he went to her. Stopping by her side, Amon studied the object she was standing over, lit by a panel of starglow from the edge of the drapes. He saw what it was.

A crib and in it a baby.

"Is this . . ."

The baby was so tiny and delicate, with downy brown hair on its soft head and tiny eyes barely open.

"Yes."

The baby looked at Amon with a startled intensity, fascinated by this mysterious being come out of nowhere. Amon was at least as astonished. Seeing this baby atop the tiny mattress edged by low bars, he thought of the infant receptacles in Delivery and the nursery in the Cyst. But here was something different, a new life under the loving gaze of his mother, no financial strings attached. Here was a fresh beginning.

"Is he . . . she . . ."

Amon looked to Mayuko for answers. Now he saw why her figure was fuller, her aura more mature and authoritative.

"A boy."

"What's his name?"

"Rick."

"Rick," he whispered, remembering something his best friend had said as the last of his life drained from his eyes. *If I'm lucky maybe one of my seeds will bear fruit.* "Rick," Amon whispered again, as more tears warmed his cheeks, his chest aching bittersweet, joyful that Rick's dream had come true, sorrowful that he was not here to see it.

"The night you and I stayed in the weekly mansion," he said, recalling. "Before I fell asleep, you were drinking . . . but you must have already been . . ."

"I felt awful about it for a long time."

"So you knew?"

"My period was all over the place from work stress. But MyMedic kept prodding me to get tested. The day Rick disappeared, I finally did."

"And you decided to drink anyway?"

"I know this is terrible to say, but I never thought I'd go through with it. I didn't think it would matter if I drank. But Rick was dead and then you disappeared . . . and the compensation from all the credicrimes had left me with enough money to give birth . . . and I decided that this is what he would have wanted . . . I felt guilty about drinking that night for a long time. I drank a lot. Even more than usual . . . but Rick is fine. All the tests show that he's a perfectly healthy boy. Isn't he handsome?"

"Yes, he is." Then Amon thought, *And he looks like his father already . . .*

Amon realized that she'd been pregnant when the men attacked her and was glad that he never knew or the memory would have haunted him with even more diabolical force, wondering if she'd miscarried. He imagined her wandering around the District of Dreams with her belly already swelling and was amazed by her courage—or was it reckless-ness?—in seeking him out. To think that if she had found him, Amon could have brought her to the father. What a shock that would have been for both of them—and for Vertical. Even now Mayuko seemed to believe that he'd jumped in front of a train. Should Amon burden her with the sad knowledge that he'd come back only to die again? Another time. Another time. If they made it through the crisis in one piece, there would be countless other occasions for sharing memories, whether happy or infinitely tragic.

Mayuko picked up the boy—Rick!—and began to rock him. Rick stared up at Amon. Unlike his father's eyes, little Rick's contained no brooding sadness—and they never would. Not if Amon could help it. He remembered something else Rick had related before the end: his fond recollection of the time, soon after his parents abandoned him in the BioPen, when the kids were bullying the newcomer and Amon and Mayuko had taken him to their viewing point on the roof. Just seconds later, Rick had said, *I wanted to raise someone beautiful and wise and good* . . .

"Come on," said Amon, putting his arm around Mayuko's waist, looking into her quizzical eyes, her comet hair radiant and her face enchanting under the glow from the window. "Wrap one of those blankets around the little one. We can finish our conversation somewhere else."

"Where are we going?"

"To the rooftop. There's something I want Rick to see."

"What's that?"

"The stars."

ACKNOWLEDGEMENTS

This novel took much longer to finish than it should have. If the cards had fallen right, it could have been in stores at least two years earlier. Alas, a global pandemic and other factors not worth enunciating intervened.

During those two plus years, while my work as a translator of Japanese literature picked up steam—with the release of my first novel translation, *A Man*, and several short stories and essays—my writing career was effectively frozen. I experimented with writing a book of political theory, a book of short stories, and two linked novellas, without managing to complete anything.

I conceived of the idea that would become *The Jubilee Cycle* when I was 19 years old, half my life ago, and turning that idea into story has absorbed the bulk of my creative energy for the past decade. With an unfinished project of this scale and personal significance hanging over me, I struggled to commit to anything new.

It is ironic, perhaps, that I allowed myself to be trapped by a work about the meaning of freedom. I cannot adequately express my relief at finally having it done and knowing that my imagination is free to travel where it will.

Many thanks to Dr. Wei Ge for his advice on genetics, particularly the genetics of twins. Chris Molloy for surviving an atrocious early draft and even finding things to like about it. Jack Alexander for his hardnosed edits and honest gripes. Robert Priest for his stylistic ministrations and pinpoint exasperation. Perry Ge for his succinct and articulate plot impressions. James Cotellesse for his deep investment in the world and characters. Wendy Uchimura for her careful reflections and kind compliments.

A shout out to Ron Eckel for pushing to get this book from publication purgatory to press.

Finally, a special thanks to all the readers I have never met who stuck it out to the end. You have convinced an obscure novelist that this is his calling.

SELECTED GLOSSARY OF FREE ERA TERMS

Absolute Choice Party, the: One of two dominant political parties, including the Moderate Choice Party, that compete for seats on the Executive Council. Policies tend to favor privatization of borderline volitional actions such as blinking, breathing, urinating, defecating, swallowing, and heartbeating in order to increase fiscal resources for credicrime fine reductions. Traditionally funded by the Philanthropy Syndicate. See *Moderate Choice Party, Executive Council, Philanthropy Syndicate.*

action-property: Digital assets specifying the movements that define particular actions. Though managed by the Ministry of Access, most are owned by The Twelve and One. See *Ministry of Access, The Twelve and One.*

action-transaction market/economy, the: Global economic system since the dawn of the Free Era. Citizens pay a transaction fee or fine for their actions. See *Free Era.*

action-transaction readout: Record of individual action-transactions accessible by every Free Citizen. Includes name of action-property, amount of fee or fine, time of transaction, and licensor name. Readout, AT readout. See *Free Citizen, action-property.*

action-data: Data from BodyBank sensors that record each Free Citizen's every movement. Transmitted to the House of Blinding where it is decrypted for processing by the Ministry of Monitoring. See *Body-Bank, Free Citizen, GATA, House of Blinding, Ministry of Monitoring.*

Akane/Aoi: Prostitute that Amon met in Eroyuki. See *Eroyuki.*

akrasiapocalypse: An existential risk scenario. Sleeperpuzzles that assemble indulgence dust are activated in regions across the planet, causing a global loss of self-control and economic collapse. See *sleeperpuzzles, dust, indulgence dust.*

Amon Kenzaki (剣崎亜文): Former Liquidator and Identity Executioner. Central figure in the *Jubilee Chronicles*. See *Liquidator, Identity Executioner, Jubilee Chronicles.*

anadeto: see *analog detritus.*

analog detritus: Pejorative term for collectible items and antiques. Anadeto.

Anisha Birla: Heir to Fertilex. Youngest daughter of Shiv and Chandru Birla. Identical twin sister of Rashana Birla. Member of the Gyges Circle. See *Fertilex, Shiv Birla, Chandru Birla, Rashana Birla, Gyges Circle.*

Archives, the: Ministry of Records database for storage of the action-transaction readouts of Free Citizens and the LifeStreams of crashdead. See *Ministry of Records, LifeStream, crashdead, Free Citizen, action-transaction readout.*

Atupio: Subsidiary of Fertilex. Founded and managed by Rashana Birla. Operations include Er for the Giftless and humanitarian reporting outfits. See *Fertilex, Rashana Birla, Er for the Giftless.*

Atupians: Dedicated Atupio personnel and supporters. See *Atupio.*

Atupio Home Office: Headquarters of Atupio. Located on the Tokyo Canal. See *Atupio, Tokyo Canal.*

AT readout: See *action-transaction readout.*

autoalterity dust: Semi-lethal cognitive weapon that causes a mis-identification of parts of the self for the other. See *dust.*

AutoBarter: Automatic currency trading app.

baby laundering: Practice of hiding the crashborn origin of extracted infants and selling their profiles as order-grown for a higher price. Fertilex plutogenic algorithms and brandclans specialize in this business, which is unique to the MegaGlom due to its monopoly on the order-grown resource market. See *crashborn, order-grown, Fertilex, plutogenic algorithm, brandclan, MegaGlom.*

bankdead: People not connected to the action-transaction market or ImmaNet. The state of being such a person. Most live in bankdeath camps. See *action-transaction market, ImmaNet, bankdeath camp, bankliving, Free Citizen.*

bankdeath camp: Regions densely populated by bankdead. Supplied by the Philanthropy Syndicate. Pecuniary retreat. See *bankdead, Philanthropy Syndicate.*

bankdeath penalty: Largest fine issued by the Fiscal Judiciary for violation of credilaw. Amount is always higher than the value of the global economy, ensuring instant bankruptcy of any culprit. See *Fiscal Judiciary, credilaw.*

bankliving: People connected to the action-transaction market and ImmaNet. The state of being such a person. Free Citizen. See *action-transaction market, ImmaNet, Free Citizen, bankdead.*

bankrupt: Free Citizen who has lost the right to possess a BodyBank and remain connected to the action-transaction market or ImmaNet due to an excess of debt. Must be cash crashed by Liquidator according to GATA protocol. See *Free Citizen, BodyBank, action-transaction market, ImmaNet, cash crash, Liquidator, GATA.*

Barrow: See *Lawrence Barrow.*

BioPen: Rearing facilities for minors whose genomes are registered with GATA and who are in preparation to become Free Citizens. Profits derived from sale of human resource profiles. See *genome registration, GATA, Free Citizen.*

Birla Guard, the: Elite guards that protect the Birlas. Anisha and Rashana Birla share ten pairs of clones.

Birlas, the: See *Anisha Birla, Rashana Birla, Shiv Birla, Chandru Birla.*

Birth Codes, the: Codes used to grant identity signature and activate the BodyBank of a person whose genome is registered with GATA, usually a minor. Memorized and employed by Identity Vitalators. See *identity signature, BodyBank, genome registration, GATA, Identity Vitalator, Death Codes.*

blitz dust: Combination of at least five varieties of dust fired by the standard weapon of the Birla Guard: droneburn, epilepsy, piranha, dysphoria, and autoalterity. See *dust, Birla Guard.*

BodyBank: Biological computer integrated with the body of all Free Citizens. Enables connection to the action-transaction market and ImmaNet and transmits action-data to the House of Blinding. See *Free Citizens, action-transaction market, ImmaNet, action-data, House of Blinding.*

Book: Crashborn man who facilitated and advised the Xenocyst council. Can detect lies by observing the eyes of a speaker who meets their own gaze in a mirror. Mentor of Little Book. Has a penchant for book collection and study. See *crashborn, Xenocyst, Little Book, nostie.*

brandclan: Groups of bankdead selected by the same plutogenic algorithm. Encouraged to form into communities through provision of supplies with matching brand design and logos. See *bankdead, plutogenics.*

Bridge of Compassion, the: Bridge in rear of Delivery. Connects the District of Dreams to Tokyo proper and serves as a dam between the Tokyo Canal and Sanzu River. See *Delivery, District of Dreams, Tokyo Canal, Sanzu River.*

carbonjets: Jets powered by hydrocarbon fuel.

CareBots: Drones deploying non- and semi-lethal weaponry for crowdcare. RiotDrones. See *crowdcare.*

career volunteer: Salaried staff of venture charities, usually employed at Delivery. Not involved in crowdcare, as opposed to freekeepers. See *Delivery, crowdcare, freekeepers.*

cash crash: Erasure of a Free Citizen's identity signature resulting in disconnection of BodyBank from AT market and ImmaNet. The state of being so disconnected. Cash crashing is conducted by Identity Executioners using the Death Codes. It is the first stage in the liquidation process. Used as noun and both transitively and intransitively as a verb. See *Free Citizen, identity signature, action-transaction market, ImmaNet, Identity Executioner, Death Codes, liquidation, Ministry of Records, Collection Agent, LifeStream, AT readout. Archivist.*

centicopter: A Type of rotorcraft with numerous rotors, typically one hundred.

Chandru Birla: Late co-founder of Fertilex. Husband of Shiv Birla. Father of Anisha and Rashana Birla. See *Fertilex, Shiv Birla, Anisha Birla, Rashana Birla.*

Charity Brigade, the: One of two varieties of Delivery staff. Unlike career volunteers, they are armed and are charged with crowdcare. Freekeepers. See *Delivery, career volunteer, crowdcare.*

Charity Gift Economy, the: Grey market nested within the AT market. Bankdead receive charity in the form of meal replacement ink and

Fleet supplies, and provide babies ostensibly as voluntary gifts, which are marketed as human resources in BioPens. Processes are automated via plutogenic algorithms that mark bankdead as either gifted or giftless and divide them into brandclans. Primary source of human resources for the Philanthropy Syndicate. See *action-transaction market, Fleet, BioPen, plutogenic algorithms, gifted, giftless, brandclan, human resources, Philanthropy Syndicate.*

chicken little dust: Non-lethal weapon eliciting hallucination that the sky is falling. *See dust.*

Chief Executive Minister (CEM): Presides over Executive Council and oversees cabinet. Formerly Lawrence Barrow until identity assassinated by Amon. See *Executive Council, Lawrence Barrow, identity assassination, Amon Kenzaki.*

cinderworkers: Xenocyst artists who fan the glowing flakes of dissolving embyrbrycks and embyrsculptures into ephemeral images. See *Xenocyst, embyrbrycks, embyrsculptures.*

Cloud9 Nectar: Popular carbonated beverage owned by MegaGlom TTY. Favorite drink of Tamper's son. See *MegaGlom, Tamper.*

Cognitive Handling Corps: A variety of specialized human teams utilizing AI to provide assistance with particular cognitive tasks. These include strategizing, forecasting, calculating, communicating etc. Only affordable for MegaGlom executives and the propertied class. Handling corps, corps. See *MegaGlom, ~corps.*

Collection Agent: Employees of the Ministry of Records charged with the second stage of liquidation: transporting cash crashed bankrupts to the Archives for BodyBank data upload. See *Ministry of Records, cash crash, bankrupt, Archives, BodyBank.*

conception dust: Dust that damages brain systems that allow for the conception of new ideas in language, especially computer language.

Used on the PhisherKing after he constructed the House of Blinding. See *dust, PhisherKing, House of Blinding*.

crashborn: A person who is born bankdead. As opposed to crashdead. See *bankdead, crashdead*.

crashdead: A person who is bankdead due to being cash crashed. As opposed to crashborn. See *bankdead, cash crash, crashborn*.

crashnewb: Crashdead who has recently cash crashed. See *crashdead, cash crash*.

credicrime: Violation of credilaw, illegal action. Legal actions incur fees which are paid to action-property owners (i.e. MegaGloms) while credicrimes incur fines paid to the Fiscal Judiciary. Fines are one of GATA's primary sources of funding, alongside bankrupt asset auctioning and LifeStream licensing. See *credilaw, action-property, MegaGlom, GATA, bankrupt, LifeStream*.

credilaw: Laws upheld by GATA whose only penalty is the payment of a fine. Legislated by the Executive Council and judged by the Fiscal Judiciary. See *GATA, Executive Council, Fiscal Judiciary*.

creditability: A person's value judged by reference to their financial assets, spending, earning, and habits. The term "discreditable" is considered a slur in the Free World. See *Free World*.

crowdcare: Management of bankdead through non- or semi-lethal violence. Facilitated by CareBots and the Charity Brigade. See *Care-Bots, Charity Brigade*.

~corps: A coordinated group of specialized human and AI that assist MegaGlom executives with a specific cognitive task. Examples include prognosticorps, tacticorps, litigaticorps, and cryptocorps. See *Cognitive Handling Corps*.

Cyst, the: Condo at the center of Xenocyst used for various purposes. Meeting place of the Xenocyst council, hospital, daycare, armory, rooftop helipad. See *Xenocyst*.

Death Codes, the: Codes used to erase identity signature of Free Citizens in a cash crash. Memorized and deployed by Identity Executioners. See *identity signature, Free Citizen, cash crash, Identity Executioner*.

decision network: Group of users that offer crowdsourced advice via apps such as Career Calibration. All-purpose, budget decision assistance as opposed to personalized and specialized Cognitive Handling Corps. See *Cognitive Handling Corps,*

Delivery: Philanthropy Syndicate facility in the District of Dreams where bankdead receive Fleet supplies and gift babies. Headquarters for the Charity Brigade, career volunteers, and many venture charities. See *Philanthropy Syndicate, District of Dreams, bankdead, Fleet, Charity Brigade, career volunteers, venture charity*.

demolition dust: Nano-device that dissolves disposcrapers and other Fleet structures. Commonly deployed by the Charity Brigade in slum clearance. See *dust, disposcraper, Fleet, Charity Brigade*.

digiguise: Type of digimake intended to hide user's regular digimade appearance. See *digimake*.

digimake: Software that allows users to modify their appearance on the ImmaNet. A user's appearance so modified or the act of modification. See *ImmaNet*.

disposable room: Fleet shelter provided to bankdead at Delivery. Self-assembles from roombud. Dissolves after expiration time. See *Fleet, bankdead, Delivery, roombud*.

disposable skyscraper: See *disposcraper*.

disposcraper: Skyscraper or architectural mound built by stacking disposable rooms. Disposable skyscraper. See *disposable room.*

Distinction: Fashion assistant app.

District of Dreams, the: Largest bankdeath camp on earth. Located on an artificial island occupying most of what was once Tokyo Bay. See *bankdeath camp.*

don juan dust: Nano-cosmetic treatment to alter facial features. Commonly used by slum tourists. *See dust.*

dust: Clouds of aerodynamic nanobot formations programmed to bring about precisely targeted effects. Well known varieties include nerve dust, tear dust, sleeping beauty dust, and revulsion dust. Often launched by a gun called a duster. See *nerve dust, tear dust, sleeping beauty dust, revulsion dust, duster.*

duster: Gun that fires dust. Categorized by size and technical specifications. Varieties include: hand dusters, submachine dusters, assault dusters, and duster cannons. The most infamous is the nerve duster, standard issue for all Liquidators. See *Liquidator.*

Elsewhere Gaze: Eyes of bankliving when viewed by bankdead or other person not perceiving the ImmaNet. See *bankliving, bankdead, ImmaNet.*

embyrbrycks: Brick-shaped supplies provided by Delivery in winter that produce heat. Composed of a Fleet composite. See *Delivery, Fleet.*

embyrsculpters: Embyrsculpture artists associated with Xenocyst. See *embyrsculptures.*

embyrsculptures: Sculptures made of melting embyrbrycks as they approach their expiration time. See *embyrbrycks.*

Er: Rehabilitation facilities for crashnewbs suffering from webloss. Most admit only crashnewbs chosen as gifted by plutogenic algorithms. The sole exception in the District of Dreams is Er for the Giftless. See *crashnewbs, webloss, plutogenic algorithms, District of Dreams.*

Er for the Giftless: Er facility run by Atupio that admits giftless crashnewbs. See *Er, Atupio, giftless, crashnewb.*

Eroyuki: Club (kurabu) in Ginza.

Executive Council, the: Elected GATA parliamentary body with legislative authority. Presided over by the Chief Executive Minister (CEM), who selects the cabinet. Balance of powers realized through blinding, monitoring, and judicial oversight by the House of Blinding, Ministry of Monitoring, and Fiscal Judiciary, respectively. See *GATA, Chief Executive Minister, House of Blinding, Ministry of Monitoring, Fiscal Judiciary.*

facephone: Video chat app.

FE: See *Free Era.*

feeder: Vending machines in the bankdeath camps that print food from meal replacement ink. See *bankdeath camps, meal replacement ink.*

Ferment Culture Collective, the: Organization of radicals, mostly researchers and engineers, who founded Hakkotopia 1.0. See *Hakkotopia.*

Fertilex: MegaGlom with more assets than any other due to monopoly over fertility-related actions and technologies. Founded by Shiv and Chandru Birla. Inherited by daughters Anisha and Rashana Birla. Traditionally provides order-grown human resources to the SpawnU Consortium. See *Shiv Birla, Chandru Birla, Anisha Birla, Rashana Birla, order-grown resources, SpawnU Consortium.*

fight'R'flight dust: Causes either the fight or flight response depending on whether the target is ready to fight (flee), flee (fight), or neither (either/or). See *dust.*

FillBot: Variation on SpillBot for women. See *SpillBot*.

firefLyte: Portable lantern made of Fleet. See *Fleet*.

Fiscal Judiciary, the: One of the seven institutional organs of GATA. Judicial Brokers assisted by AI receive commission for detecting actions that do not comply with credilaw. Fines issued to those in violation. Also serves as court of appeal for credicrime. Contributes to balance of powers and oversight within GATA. See *GATA, Judicial Broker, credilaw, credicrime*

Fleet: Nanomaterial used to build a wide variety of items, including bankdead clothes and shelters. Gradually flakes away and dissolves after a pre-programmed expiration time. Sometimes sold under brand name Hakanite. See *bankdead, disposcraper*.

FlexiPedia: Online encyclopedia any Free Citizen can edit for a fee. Content usually managed by MegaGlom PR teams. See *Free Citizen, MegaGlom*.

Free Citizen: Person with a BodyBank who is connected to the action-transaction market and ImmaNet. Bankliving. See *BodyBank, action-transaction market, ImmaNet, bankdead*.

Free Era (FE), the: Era inaugurated by the establishment of the AT market and GATA after conclusion of the Tokyo Roundtable. See *action-transaction market, Tokyo Roundtable*.

Free Tokyo: All regions of Tokyo excluding the District of Dreams. See *District of Dreams*.

Free World, the: General term for the world inhabited by Free Citizens. Contrasted with bankdeath camps. See *Free Citizens, bankdeath camps*.

freekeeper: Member of the Charity Brigade. See *Charity Brigade*.

Freg Bear: A Liquidator formerly on Rick Ferro's and Amon Kenzaki's squad. Enormous in size. Similar in appearance to his liquidation partner, Tororo Xiong. Known for laughing at Tororo's bad jokes. See *Liquidator, Rick Ferro, Amon Kenzaki, Liquidation Ministry, Tororo Xiong.*

Full Choice Party, the: Splinter political party. Originally a fiscally conservative faction of Moderate Choice that opposed credicrime fine increases. Core member is Yoshiyuki Sekido. See *Moderate Choice, Yoshiyuki Sekido.*

gabkeepers: Cognitive Handling Corps team specialized in storytelling and speech assistance. See *Cognitive Handling Corps.*

GATA: Global Action Transaction Authority. The sole public organization. Charged with maintaining global action-transaction market. Branches can be found around the world and govern their respective regions. Consists of seven institutional organs. See *Executive Council, Ministry of Monitoring, Ministry of Access, Ministry of Records (including the Archives), Ministry of Liquidation, Fiscal Judiciary, and House of Blinding.*

GATA Tower: Location of each local branch of GATA. Found in urban centers around the world, including Tokyo. See *GATA.*

Geminis, the: Two highly sophisticated rotorcraft, Gemini X and Gemini Y, each designed for one of the Birla sisters. See *Anisha Birla, Rashana Birla.*

Gemini X: See *Geminis.*

Gemini Y: See *Geminis.*

geneshine dust: Nano-treatment for slight edits to genomes of somatic cells without (or with negligible) phenotypic change. Commonly used by friends and relatives of crashnewbs to facilitate acceptance into a brandclan by plutogenic algorithms. *See dust, crashnewb, brandclan.*

genome registration: To be eligible for BioPen intake and eventual endowment of identity signature, all infants must have genomes registered with the Ministry of Access by age one. Minors so registered are human resources. Registration conducted by Identity Vitalator. See *BioPen, identity signature, Ministry of Access, human resources, Identity Vitalator.*

Gifted Triangle, the: Triangular region of the District of Dreams immediately south of Delivery where many gifted brandclans live. See *District of Dreams, Delivery, gifted, brandclan.*

gift: The act of a bankdead parent providing their baby to the Philanthropy Syndicate (or in rare cases to Fertilex for baby laundering). See *bankdead, Philanthropy Syndicate, Fertilex, baby laundering.*

gifter: A parent who gifts.

gifted: A bankdead whose genome has been deemed likely to produce marketable human resources by the plutogenic algorithm of some MegaGlom. See *human resources, plutogenic algorithms, MegaGlom, Philanthropy Syndicate.*

giftless: A bankdead who is not gifted. See *gifted.*

gift receptacle: Devices in Delivery that automatically receive marketable babies from gifting mothers. See *Delivery.*

Global Action Transaction Authority, the: See *GATA.*

Great Cyberwar, the: Historical crisis said to have precipitated the Tokyo Roundtable and the inception of the AT Market. Interpretations vary. See *Tokyo Roundtable, AT market.*

Green Ladybug: Fertilex-owned BioPen in Tokyo where Rick Ferro, Amon Kenzaki, and Mayuko Takamatsu were raised. See *Fertilex, BioPen, Rick Ferro, Amon Kenzaki, Mayuko Takamatsu.*

Gyges Circle, the: Alliance of Philanthropy Syndicate executives and Anisha Birla. See *Philanthropy Syndicate, Anisha Birla.*

Hakkotopia: Community founded by the Ferment Culture Collective on Hahajima. Name means "place of fermentation." See *Ferment Culture Collective.*

Hinkongo: Pidgin dialect of Japanese. Includes words from such languages as English, Russian, Chinese, and Korean.

Hippo: Founder of Xenocyst. Former Identity Vitalator and Fertilex fertility researcher. Sought identity euthanasia at the hands of Yoshi-yuki Sekido. See *Xenocyst, Identity Vitalator, Fertilex, identity euthanasia, Yoshiyuki Sekido.*

House of Blinding, the: One of the seven institutional organs of GATA but semi-independent. Charged with maintaining the individual anonymity of all Free Citizens. Encrypts action-data for processing by the Ministry of Monitoring and identity signatures for ImmaNet access eligibility verification conducted by the Ministry of Access. Contributes to balance of powers and oversight within GATA. See *GATA, Free Citizen, action-data, Ministry of Monitoring, identity signature, ImmaNet, Ministry of Access.*

human resources: Potential MegaGlom employees whose genomes have been registered with GATA. Extracted resources are those gifted by bankdead to the Philanthropy Syndicate. Order-grown resources are those genetically designed by Fertilex to staff its own subsidiaries, SpawnU Consortium MegaGloms, and elite positions at Philanthropy Syndicate organizations. All resources are raised in BioPens. Profiles are auctioned upon approaching their identity birth day (at the age of 20). See *MegaGlom, gift, bankdead, Philanthropy Syndicate, order-grown, SpawnU Consortium, BioPen, genome registration.*

Identity Vitalator: GATA staff employed by the Ministry of Access. Charged with bestowing identity signatures on eligible human resources using the Birth Codes. ID Vitalator. See *GATA, Ministry of Access, identity signature, identity birth, Birth Codes.*

identity assassination: See *identity murder.*

identity birth: When a human resource is assigned an identity signature and their BodyBank is activated with the Birth Codes. BioPen minors reach their identity birth day at the age of 20. See *human resource, BodyBank, Birth Codes, BioPen, genome registration.*

identity euthanasia: An identity execution (cash crash) conducted on someone who voluntarily requests it. See *identity execution, cash crash.*

identity execution: Erasure of a Free Citizen's identity signature. Cash crash. Conducted by Identity Executioner using the Death Codes. Only legal when conducted on a bankrupt. See *Free Citizen, cash crash, Identity Executioner, Death Codes, bankrupt.*

Identity Executioner: Higher-ranking Liquidator who has been taught the Death Codes and authorized to execute the identity of Free Citizens. See *Liquidator, Death Codes, identity execution, cash crash, Free Citizen.*

identity martyr: Person who goes bankrupt and cash crashes willingly for a particular cause. See *bankrupt, cash crash.*

identity murder: To execute the identity of a Free Citizen illegally, i.e. when they are not bankrupt. Includes identity assassination. See *identity execution, Free Citizen, bankrupt.*

identity signature: Code that uniquely identifies each Free Citizen. Transmitted by BodyBank to House of Blinding. ID signature, ID sig, sig. See *Free Citizen, House of Blinding.*

identity suicide: When an Identity Executioner uses their Death Codes to execute their own identity. See *Identity Executioner, Death Codes.*

ImmaGame: Games played on the ImmaNet. See *ImmaNet*.

ImmaNet: Network of information and images overlaid on the naked world. Free Citizens connect through BodyBanks. Access is managed by the Ministry of Access. See *Free Citizen, BodyBank, Ministry of Access*.

indulgence dust: Dust that destroys areas of the brain involved in delayed gratification. See *dust*.

Inflation Singularity: The result of a nuclear price war. Lies beyond an economic horizon of self-inflating prices, where value cannot be calculated or predicted. See *nuclear price war, price nuke*.

InfoNature: A sub-genre of the InfoFlux that covers non-manmade processes. Includes: InfoCloud, InfoSun, InfoWind, InfoSky, InfoStars, InfoRain, InfoMoon, InfoRainbow, InfoRiver, InfoTyphoon, InfoGhosts, InfoMist. See *InfoFlux*.

InfoFlux, the: A flux of promotional information that permeates the ImmaNet. A wide variety of phrases are used to describe its many nuanced categories including: ad, adfoshow, adstory, advermercial, advertainment, advertinfo, advertisement, commercenticement, commercitainment, communitainment, communixchange, datatainment, eduinfo, edumercial, edupromo, edushow, edutainment, edutisement, eduinfo, edumercial, entermotion, entertainment, entertisement, image, immaGame©, immaMercial©, ImmaTainment©, ImmaTisement©, incultainment, info, infoenticement, infomercial, infopromo, information, infoshow, infostory, infotainment, infotisement, marketainment, narramarketing, poetainment, poetisement, promo, promoglow, promomercial, promonticement, promoshow, promostory, promotainment, and promotale.

infohum, the: Ambient sound of the InfoFlux. See *InfoFlux*.

inner profile: Protected personal data of each Free Citizen. Includes LifeStream, name, biometrics, etc. See *Free Citizen, LifeStream*.

Instant Get: Dating app.

InterGlom War: War between MegaGloms. See *MegaGloms.*

InterrPet: Budget app that assists with interpreting between languages.

investitarian: Free Citizen who invests in the Charity Gift Economy, plutogenic derivatives, and/or related assets and industries. See *Free Citizen, Charity Gift Economy, plutogenic algorithms, philanthropaneur.*

Jiku: Former Xenocyst councilor. See *Xenocyst council.*

Jubilee Chronicles, the: Narrative account of key historical events in 49 FE and 50 FE. See *Free Era.*

Judicial Broker: Official employed by the Fiscal Judiciary. Charged with detecting credicrimes. See *Fiscal Judiciary, credicrime.*

Kai Monju (文殊海). See *PhisherKing.*

kansha hotel: Hotel where bankdead are able to express gratitude to investitarians and philanthropaneurs by spontaneously falling in love and accompanying them to their rooms. See *investitarian, philanthropaneur.*

Kitao: Shota Kitao (北尾翔太). Former Minister of Records. Extremely tall and lanky. Fetish for association between women and flowers. Quantitative Priest. See *Ministry of Records, Quantitative Priesthood.*

KonTour: App that searches for hidden weapons.

Lawrence Barrow: Former Chief Executive Minister of GATA. Half New Zealander and half-Japanese. Famously eloquent. Dandy nostie. See *Chief Executive Minister, GATA, nostie.*

leash: Consensual link between the accounts of two Free Citizens whereby one pays for all the action-transactions of another. Automatically grants the payer access to the other's AT readout during period of leash. See *Free Citizen, AT readout.*

LifeStream: Audiovisual recording of a Free Citizen's life saved in their inner profile. See *Free Citizen, inner profile.*

LimboQuarium: Tanks used for the storage and treatment of crash-newbs suffering from webloss. See *webloss.*

liquidation (to liquidate): Multistage procedure conducted by GATA on bankrupt Free Citizens. Liquidators apprehend bankrupts, an Identity Executioner executes their ID (cash crash), Collection Agents transport the crashee to the Ministry of Records, where Archivists upload their BodyBank data, including LifeStream, to the Archives. The Ministry of Access subsequently deregisters their genome, removes their BodyBank, and ships them to the nearest bankdeath camp. See *GATA, bankrupt, Free Citizen, Liquidator, Identity Executioner, cash crash, Collection Agent, Ministry of Records, Archivist, BodyBank, Archives, Ministry of Access, bankdeath camp.*

Liquidation Ministry, the: One of GATA's seven institutional organs. Charged with the apprehension and identity execution of bankrupts. Overseen by the Liquidation Minister. *See GATA, identity execution, bankrupt.*

Liquidator: Employees of the Liquidation Ministry. Duty is to apprehend bankrupts. Armed with nerve dusters. See *bankrupt, duster.*

Little Book: Crashborn boy. Scribe for the Xenocyst council. Protégé of Book. Prodigious memory and mathematical talent. Mute, perhaps due to early childhood head trauma. Communicates using tap language he invented. LB, puchiboo. See *crashborn, Book, Xenocyst council.*

manga mansion: Condominium filled with comics and inhabited by nosties. See *nosties.*

Mayuko Takamatsu (鷹松真由子): Childhood friend and former girlfriend of both Amon Kenzaki and Rick Ferro. Raised with them in Green Ladybug. Worked as a designer. See *Amon Kenzaki, Rick Ferro, Green Ladybug.*

meal replacement ink: Liquid said to provide all necessary nutrients that is 3D-printed inside feeders into various foods and edible wrappings. Most commonly fed to bankdead in bankdeath camps. See *feeder, bankdeath camp, bankdead.*

MegaGlom: Large conglomeration of conglomerates. Megaconglomerate.

Mindfulator: Attention prompting app that utilizes mild electrical currents and warnings.

Minister Kitao: See Kitao.

Ministry of Access, the: One of GATA's seven institutional organs. Oversees access to the ImmaNet network and identity registration. See *GATA, ImmaNet, genome registration.*

Ministry of Monitoring, the: One of GATA's seven institutional organs. Checks whether action-data forwarded anonymously by the House of Blinding matches any action-property and authorizes the owner to withdraw the appropriate licensing fee from the actor's account. See *GATA, House of Blinding, action-property, action-data.*

Ministry of Records, the: One of GATA's seven institutional organs. Safekeeps the Archives, where the LifeStreams and AT readouts of crashdead are stored. See *GATA, Archives, LifeStream, AT readout.*

Moderate Choice Party, the: One of the two main political parties that compete for seats on the Executive Council. Tends to favor legislation increasing credicrime fines to fund nationalization of borderline actions such as blinking, breathing, urinating, defecating, swallowing, and heartbeating. Traditionally funded by Fertilex and the SpawnU Consortium. See *Executive Council, credicrime, SpawnU Consortium, Fertilex.*

Monju: See *PhisherKing.*

Moratorium on Catastrophic Pricing: Twelve and One agreement and set of algorithms to regulate action prices through simulation of tangible assets. Cooperative measure to reduce the risk of a nuclear price war. See *Twelve and One, nuclear price war.*

MyMedic: Medical self-diagnostic app.

nerve dust: Dust that stimulates pain receptors and thereby knocks targets unconscious. Nerve dusters are standard issue Liquidator weapons. See *dust, duster, Liquidator.*

nostie: Enthusiastic collectors of analog detritus. Varieties differ depending on preferred analog detritus. For example, dandy nosties collect high class anadeto while grime nosties prefer kitsch. See *analog detritus.*

nuclear price war: Escalating retaliations of price nukes by competing pricing algorithms. See *price nuke.*

Oneiro Express: Express train that runs to Yume Station. See *Yume Station.*

Ono X: See *Onos.*

Ono Y: See *Onos.*

Onos, the: Refers to Ono X and Ono Y, a pair of clones order-grown to be the playmates of Anisha and Rashana Birla. Each serves as captain of half the Birla Guard and head of intelligence for one of the sisters. Skilled ventriloquists, actors, and spies. See *Anisha Birla, Rashana Birla, Birla Guard.*

Open Source Zone, the: Area of Tokyo temporarily in the public domain. Common refuge for near bankrupts.

Opportunity Peaks: Twin-peaked mountain built of disposable rooms. Holiest site of Opportunity Science. Located west of the Gifted Triangle. See *disposable room, Opportunity Science, Gifted Triangle.*

Opportunity Science: Religion popular in the District of Dreams. Doctrines include rebirth in the Free Market and purification of DNA through gifting. Presided over by the Quantitative Priesthood. See *District of Dreams, Quantitative Priesthood, gift.*

Opportunity Scientist: Believer in Opportunity Science. OpSci. See *Opportunity Science.*

OpSci: See *Opportunity Scientist.*

order-grown resource: Human resources engineered for future jobs in accordance with plutogenic algorithms. Fertilex holds a monopoly on production, has a distribution deal with the SpawnU Consortium, and sells high quality resources to the Philanthropy Syndicate. See *plutogenic algorithms, Fertilex, SpawnU Consortium, Philanthropy Syndicate.*

OtaPlay: Area of Akihabara where otaku play ImmaGames. Otaku Playground. See *ImmaGames.*

PanoptiRoach: Cockroach shaped drones with human eyes that lay ImmaNet sensors in the bankdeath camps and may or may not have surveillance capabilities. See *ImmaNet, bankdeath camps.*

parasite: Device placed on the skin that can hack into a BodyBank. See *BodyBank.*

pecuniary retreat: See *bankdeath camp.*

PeelKlean: Disposable item for cleaning the body without water. A common supply in the bankdeath camps. See *bankdeath camp.*

PennyPinch: Accounting consultant app.

PhantoCopters: See *Geminis.*

philanthropaneur: Free Citizens who invest in or manage Charity Gift Economy initiatives such as venture charities. See *Free Citizen, Charity Gift Economy, venture charity, investitarian.*

Philanthropy Syndicate, the: A MegaGlom bloc that comprises half the Twelve. Acquires the majority of its human resources via the Charity Gift Economy and funds the Absolute Choice Party. Traditional rival with the SpawnU Consortium and Fertilex. Consists of six members: No Logo Inc (most active member), R-Lite, LYS Dynamics, Latoni Sedo, LVR, Kavipal. See *MegaGlom, Twelve and One, Charity Gift Economy, Absolute Choice Party, SpawnU Consortium, Fertilex.*

PhisherKing, the: Leader of the Phishers. Architect of the House of Blinding. Conception dusted so that he could never build a system to rival or disrupt it. Kai Monju. See *Phishers, conception dust, House of Blinding.*

Phishers: Information thieves and dealers. Twelve disciples follow the PhisherKing. They share a mystical reverence for the ImmaNet, which they call the Great Treasure Matrix or the DataGod.

piranha dust: Gradually dissolves target's body tissue, leaving only bones. See *dust.*

pitypromo: A type of promotainment that promotes pity for the bankdead and thereby encourages Free Citizens to donate to venture charities. See *Free Citizen, bankdead, venture charity.*

plutogenics: Adjustment of a populations' genetics in accordance with the predicted demands of the market. In contrast to eugenics and dysgenics, adjustments of a population's genetics in accordance with an independent notion of "good" or "bad," plutogenics is ostensibly value neutral.

plutogenic algorithms: Algorithms that control automated vending machines and gift receptacles in the bankdeath camps according to plutogenic principles. Bankdead are administered different qualities of supplies and food depending on how likely they are to gift babies with genomes that will become marketable human resources as adults. See *gift receptacle, bankdeath camps, plutogenics, bankdead, gift, human resources.*

price nuke: A sudden, arbitrary increase in the price of an essential action to economically catastrophic levels. See *nuclear price war, Inflation Singularity, Moratorium on Catastrophic Pricing.*

Quantitative Priesthood, the: Organization of priests that preach Opportunity Science. Based in Opportunity Peaks. See *Opportunity Science, Opportunity Peaks.*

raConTeur: High quality speech assistance app supported by gabkeepers. See *gabkeepers.*

Rashana Birla: Eldest daughter of Shiv and Chandru Birla. Twin sister of Anisha Birla. Heir to nearly half of Fertilex. Founder and owner of Atupio. Past supporter of Xenocyst. See *Shiv Birla, Chandru Birla, Anisha Birla, Fertilex, Atupio, Xenocyst.*

revulsion dust: Nonlethal weapon that causes target to be unbearably revolted by the last object they saw. A typical component of Free Tokyo vending machine security systems. See *dust.*

RiotDrone: See *CareBot.*

Rick Ferro: Amon's best friend and former Liquidator partner. Childhood friend and former lover of Mayuko. See *Amon Kenzaki, Liquidator, Mayuko Takamatsu.*

roombud: 3D printed devices that self-assemble into the disposable rooms that compose disposcrapers. See *disposable room, disposcraper.*

Sahar Iwabuchi: Woman who led the Ferment Culture Collective to found Hakkotopia. See *Ferment Culture Collective, Hakkotopia.*

SampleQuito: Mosquito-shaped drones that take nonconsensual blood samples for genetic analysis.

Sanzu River, the: River separating the eastern shore of the District of Dreams from Tonan Ward and the rest of Free Tokyo. Divided from the Tokyo Canal by the Bridge of Compassion. See *District of Dreams, Tonan Ward, Free Tokyo, Tokyo Canal, Bridge of Compassion.*

Secretary of Blinding, the: Official in charge of the House of Blinding. See *House of Blinding.*

ScrimpNavi: App that teaches Free Citizens the cheapest route to any destination. See *Free Citizen.*

seg: See *LifeStream.*

Self Serve: Restaurant in Shinbashi serviced exclusively by vending machines.

Shiv Birla: Late co-founder of Fertilex. Wife of Chandru Birla. Mother of Anisha and Rashana Birla. See *Fertilex, Chandru Birla, Anisha Birla, Rashana Birla.*

Shuffle Boom: Jazz bar in Kabukicho.

sift team: Groups of remote workers employed in the service of budget apps such as SiftAssist that provide low quality assistance with the rapid sifting of information.

sleeping beauty dust: Weapon that causes the target to fall into a coma at most levels of intensity. See *dust.*

sleeperpuzzles: A Weapon of Undetectable Disruption (WUD). Molecules in the atmosphere indistinguishable from environmental waste that are in fact dormant components for different varieties of dust. Activated when recombined with missing component. See *dust*.

slum resort: Leisure facilities inside the Gifted Triangle where slum tourists can view a curated scene of poverty in comfort and safety. See *Gifted Triangle*.

SpawnU Consortium, the: MegaGlom bloc that comprises half the Twelve. Acquires order-grown human resources via Fertilex. A rival of the Philanthropy Syndicate. Traditionally funds the Moderate Choice Party. Six members are UT Ltd., Yomoko Holdings, H&H Kenko, XXX Trust, Xian Te, and TTY Group. See *Twelve and One, MegaGlom, order-grown resources, Fertilex, Philanthropy Syndicate, Moderate Choice Party*.

SpillBot: Autoerotic robot that extracts and collects sperm for Fertilex. See *Fertilex*.

Starters: Youth raised to initiate Hakkotopia 2.0. *See Hakkotopia*.

SubMom: BioPen employee. Duties include managing human resources and serving as surrogate for clones and order-grown resources. See *human resource, BioPen, order-grown resource*.

Sushi Migration: Restaurant in Tsukiji.

Tamper: Former vending machine designer, former Xenocyst resident, skilled electronics engineer. Overweight, wears a jumpsuit made of pockets, and has extremely restless hands when upset. Lost his son due to pachinko addiction.

tear dust: Semi-lethal crowdcare weapon that stimulates the production of tears. See *dust, crowdcare*.

teleport surprise: App that allows a user to manifest their digimake in a separate location from their body. See *digimake*.

Tezuka, the: Manga mansion in Jinbocho where Amon once lived. See *manga mansion*.

Tokyo Roundtable, the: Historical meeting at which the action-transaction economy was putatively devised, inaugurating the Free Era. Interpretations vary. See *action-transaction economy, Free Era*.

Tonan Ward: Southeastern area of Free Tokyo. Island separated from the District of Dreams to the west by the Sanzu River. See *Free Tokyo, District of Dreams, Sanzu River*.

Tokyo Canal, the: Saltwater canal that runs between the western shore of the District of Dreams and the mainland. Separated from the freshwater Sanzu River by the Bridge of Compassion. See *District of Dreams, Sanzu River, Bridge of Compassion*.

Tororo Xiong: A Liquidator formerly on Amon's squad. Enormous in size. Similar in appearance to his liquidation partner, Freg Bear. Known for telling bad jokes that only Freg laughs at. See *Liquidator, Amon Kenzaki, Freg Bear*.

Tumbles, the: Vast area occupying the southern half of the District of Dreams. Residents are the most malnourished and worst supplied due to distance from Delivery. See *District of Dreams, Delivery*.

Twelve and One, the: 13 MegaGloms that together own nearly all of human action. Half of the Twelve are the six MegaGloms of the Philanthropy Syndicate. The other half are the SpawnU Consortium. The One is the largest MegaGlom, Fertilex. See *MegaGlom, Philanthropy Syndicate, SpawnU Consortium, Fertilex*.

Ty: Crashborn man who helped defend and maintain Xenocyst. Raised by bicycle nosties. Fierce and mouthy. Carried a children's tricycle on his back at all times until the Xenocyst diaspora. See *Xenocyst, nostie.*

VentriloQuick: Low quality speech assistance app. Contrasted with high quality app raCouTeur, which employs gabkeepers. See *raConTeur, gabkeepers.*

Vertical: Crashdead woman who served Xenocyst primarily as a scout. Former Olympic runner. Separated from her husband by bankdeath. See *crashdead, Xenocyst, bankdeath.*

vitalate: Act of an Identity Vitalator using the Birth Codes to bestow a human resource with an identity signature. See *Identity Vitalator, Birth Codes, human resource, identity signature.*

Wakuwaku City: Area of eastern Tonan Ward. Mixed theme park residential.

webloss: Cognitive and affective condition resulting from the info withdrawal that attends disconnection from the ImmaNet, usually after a cash crash. Symptoms include crowdcrave, focusburn, naked oblivion, marketitch, spilllust, cogwither, promohunger, infoyearn, and perceptual fracture. See *ImmaNet, cash crash.*

Welcome Chasm: Disposcraper chasm in District of Dreams where many giftless crashnewbs are dumped. See *District of Dreams, giftless, crashnewbs.*

Xenocyst: Democratically organized community in the District of Dreams that once aspired to help bankdead become independent. Founded by Hippo. Funded early on by Rashana Birla. Rival of Opportunity Science. See *District of Dreams, Hippo, Rashana Birla, Opportunity Science.*

Xenocyst council, the: Democratically elected council that governed Xenocyst.

Yané: Former Xenocyst councilor. Beard streaked with grey despite youth.

Yoshiyuki Sekido (関土由順): Liquidation Minister under three separate governments: Lawrence Barrow's Moderate Choice cabinet, the Full/Absolute Choice coalition, and the Full Choice majority. Former boss of Amon, Rick, Freg, and Tororo. Infamous for abstruse circumlocutions and habit of changing digimakes regularly. See *Liquidation Ministry, Lawrence Barrow, Moderate Choice, Full Choice, Absolute Choice, Amon Kenzaki, Rick Ferro, Freg Bear, Tororo Xiong.*

Yume Station: Train station on the far southwestern edge of Tonan Ward. Close to the Sanzu River. See *Tonan Ward, Sanzu River.*